COLLECTED STORIES

LIST OF WORKS BY OSBERT SITWELL

Published by Macmillan & Co.

PENNY FOOLISH. A Book of Tirades and Panegyrics
MRS. KIMBER. A Poem
THOSE WERE THE DAYS. Panorama with Figures
ESCAPE WITH ME! An Oriental Sketch-Book
TWO GENERATIONS. A Double Biography
OPEN THE DOOR! Short Stories
A PLACE OF ONE'S OWN. A Ghost Story
SING HIGH! SING LOW! A Book of Essays
LEFT HAND, RIGHT HAND! An Autobiography
  Volume I. LEFT HAND, RIGHT HAND!
  Volume II. THE SCARLET TREE
  Volume III. GREAT MORNING
  Volume IV. LAUGHTER IN THE NEXT ROOM
  Volume V. NOBLE ESSENCES OR COURTEOUS REVELATIONS
DEMOS THE EMPEROR. A Secular Oratorio
WRACK AT TIDESEND
DEATH OF A GOD. Short Stories

Edited by Osbert Sitwell

A FREE HOUSE! Or, The Artist as Craftsman.
By Walter Richard Sickert

With Edith and Sacheverell Sitwell

TRIO. Dissertations on Some Aspects of National Genius

With R. J. Minney

GENTLE CAESAR. A Play in Three Acts

Published by Gerald Duckworth & Co.

ARGONAUT AND JUGGERNAUT. Poems
TRIPLE FUGUE. Short Stories
OUT OF THE FLAME. Poems
BEFORE THE BOMBARDMENT. A Satirical Novel
WHO KILLED COCK ROBIN? Reflections upon Modern Poetry
DISCURSIONS. An Illustrated Book of Travel
THE MAN WHO LOST HIMSELF. A Novel
MIRACLE ON SINAI. A Novel
WINTERS OF CONTENT. An Illustrated Book of Travel
COLLECTED POEMS. (Ordinary Edition, and Limited Edition signed and numbered)
DUMB-ANIMAL. Short Stories
SELECTED POEMS, OLD AND NEW

With Sacheverell Sitwell

ALL AT SEA. A Social Tragedy in 3 Acts

With Margaret Barton

SOBER TRUTH. An Anthology of Strange Occurrences in the Victorian Era
VICTORIANA. An Anthology of Strange Sayings in the Victorian Era

With Nina Hamnett

THE PEOPLE'S ALBUM OF LONDON STATUES

COLLECTED STORIES

*

OSBERT SITWELL

LONDON · 1953
GERALD DUCKWORTH & CO. LTD
MACMILLAN & CO. LTD

PRINTED IN GREAT BRITAIN

CONTENTS

PREFACE

HERE, at the beginning of my collected short stories, I propose for a little while to discuss with the reader how and why they were written — if I know how and why —, and then, ascending from the particular to the general, to proceed to survey the contemporary development of the short story and of the novel (for though very different in essence, one can never be divorced from the other), and so relieve my mind of various ideas I have formed. . . . To approach, then, the first theme: writers are accustomed, I think, to being asked silly questions, real conundrums which have in their own right no answer, but to which we are forced by politeness to invent glib replies; nevertheless, when, the other day, a woman fixed me with a glazed drawing-room stare, and demanded 'How do you write short stories? My son wants to know. He thinks of going in for it', I was really floored. I floundered. . . . How did I, I wondered, and why, and, in the first place, before approaching the short story, why does a man write at all, what impulse drives him to it?

One can only speak for oneself; I wrote, I think, rather as a child begins to build a sand castle, in an attempt to preserve certain things I had seen and felt from the encroaching tides of oblivion, racing in, one after another, or else to give an objective existence to some idea that had hitherto existed only in my mind. I wrote also, perhaps, out of vanity and ambition, and further because I retain a Victorian esteem for the triumphs of the human spirit and regard achievement in the arts as the highest form of human endeavour and reward, assessing Shakespeare — as I have written elsewhere — as a much greater victory for the English people than ever was Blenheim or Waterloo: (just as today the appearance of a great new English poet would, more than all its cups of tea and biscuits consumed in offices, prejudice me in favour of that political and economic deep-freeze, the Welfare State). That, I think, is why I began to write

— why I began to write short stories is another matter.

Thirty years ago I started to write short stories, for these several reasons that follow: firstly because novels and short stories had always been my favourite reading; secondly, because I wanted to escape for a while from the orbit and range — I nearly wrote *rage* — of the poetry reviewers who had been the only critics concerned with my work so far; and thirdly, because I designed to save my stories for my own pen, since a friend of mine, a well-known author, a charming man, and a truly appreciative listener, had taken to writing the tales I could not resist relating to him, and to producing them either as his own short stories, or as episodes in the witty, rather bumpy novels he wrote. In this way I had seen — it was, of course, my own fault — several good things go out of my keeping, until finally, after I had told to an American friend, who knew the circumstances, the story that afterwards became *The Machine Breaks Down*, she said to me, 'Either you write that story tomorrow — or else I write it for you!' And so I began, sketching it out the next day in London, and elaborating it further at Renishaw. . . . The attributes I brought to my self-imposed task were mostly negative: no preconceived notions, no education (I can never recall having had a lesson in English grammar during the whole of my school career), and a hatred for dullness. Always, too, I set myself down before a blank page with a longing to write, and to tilt my pen at the appropriate angle. The epoch I began to write in was a fragmentary age, but still contained such masters of the short story as Rudyard Kipling, Somerset Maugham and D. H. Lawrence, as well as numerous experimentalists — perhaps more numerous than in any preceding period in England: and I was fortunate in coming of the last generation of writers — others, I hope, will emerge later — who belonged to a world, as opposed to a region. We did not seek in particular to be left-wing or right-wing, to be woldish with Yorkshire or wealdish with Kent, to be north-country, south-down or Welsh, but just to be writers, great writers if we could. And though the age *was* fragmentary, the ceiling had not yet come down (at first it seemed to be the ceiling, but it soon proved to be the sky): the world had not yet split in half, nor with it the human heart. No curtains of iron on one side, or of cotton-wool on the other, cut off East from

West. It was as easy to journey to China as to Paris, it only took longer and was more expensive.

In this last respect, we certainly possessed advantages of which the younger generation has been deprived — though to counterbalance this loss, they have enjoyed, many of them, the advantage of being taught professionally, and professorially, how to use words. . . . But can, or does, even the most inspired and inspiring of professors ever impart it successfully to the young, or that most necessary secret of the craft — how to tell a story? Other abilities may derive from early reading, from the snubs and rewards of childhood, from the impressions of countless busy or lazy days: but this last is a gift that a man is either born with, or without; it can be found in the possession of minor writers, as much as in the works of Tolstoy or Balzac or Dickens. Cakes, moreover, are still cakes, a short story is a short story, and the same old rules apply. If you made a cake in King Alfred's time, Queen Victoria's or today, it burns as easily if untended. You should bring to the task of baking it instinct as well as experience or education; how far one can replace the other, I do not know — nor does anyone else as yet. In short, no recipe exists for writing short stories and each practitioner must find his own way.

To my self-appointed task as a short-story writer, I brought, I believe, two positive gifts, as opposed to negative: a love and understanding of human beings — a writer must from his earliest years have been an observer of people, interested as a painter must be in their physical aspect and their nervous tricks, no less than in the working of their minds and in the impulses of their hearts —, and that certain useful vanity I have mentioned.

It has sometimes been objected to one or two of my short stories, such as *Low Tide* and *Staggered Holiday*, that I have shown no sense of pity. This emotion is for the reader to feel and for the writer to make him feel; and the very complaint shows that the reader has felt it. As to the writer, it is difficult to write between sobs.

Never did it strike me that I might not be able to write a short story, for all art was one, and success, of however minor an order, in one field, portended, even ensured, success in at least a similar degree in another. Of three things I was certain: that I was going to become a writer of short stories and novels; that, as Somerset Maugham has succinctly stated, every story must have a beginning, a middle and an end; and that, in an age of rather misty half-statements and half-feelings, everything I wrote should be clearly visualised and strongly coloured. I did not want to write a Russian short story or one in the French mode: (when I began to write fiction, the Russians were in fashion in London intellectual circles, just as the French had been in the nineties: shades of feeling under fruit trees in bloom — see Katherine Mansfield — and faint Liberal regrets and aspirations lost in a cloud of ineffectuality and indecision set the pattern; to state anything outright was vulgar). Though I greatly admired the living masters in this medium, Kipling and Maugham and de la Mare, and several others, I proposed to myself no model, but held that each story should be conceived as a poem and fashioned in the style, couched in the language, that itself and its theme imposed — in fact, in the American slang phrase of today, that it should be 'dreamed-up'. Thus I sought to be eclectic, and was always surprised after reading a story of mine over, to find on it so clearly my own signature.

For the writer the short story — very short story — possesses its own most vivid technical interest. It is fascinating to be occupied with a medium that so stringently dictates its own terms and rules. In everything it must be the opposite of what a long book would be: every phrase must stand on its own, rather than be a modulation of, a reference to, another. Except in the long short story, the use of the long sentence — a device so often strangely neglected of latter years — must be avoided entirely. (Incidentally, I hope the publication of this collected volume may explode the popular critical fallacy that I write only in sentences of three or four pages, and at the same time employ these long sentences by mistake.) Even after it is apparently finished, a short story should be read by its author and re-read until its words smoulder in his mind, and in consequence every unnecessary word or action is able to be expelled.

It may be, indeed, that some happy writers begin their work with this condition fulfilled; but I belong, for better or worse, to that other category of those who cannot compose in the head, but only with the hand — with pen or dictaphone. I bring to my desk nothing but the essential plan or idea. . . .

On re-reading, however, I always want to rewrite; a temptation that today I fortunately find easy to withstand, since to attempt to reshape the hundred and fifty thousand words odd that this book contains would constitute no light task. The very reading of them takes the writer back to the beginnings at a stage when he might still be going forward, and since I keep — as Samuel Butler used to say — a cold larder of ideas in a notebook, equally with the desire to rewrite comes the urge to create something new. The germ of a short story and the plan for its execution may arise out of the sudden collision and explosion of two ideas in the mind, or through remembering some old experience, perhaps recalled to the writer by reading some passage in another author's book — the book need not be good, but the writer who has thus been enabled to recapture an event or a mood will always be grateful to the author of it. Some stories, again, may be born of a feeling for the times we live in — such is *Defeat*, a story that follows.

My first short story — which was, as I have mentioned, *The Machine Breaks Down* — I elaborated with some difficulty, because my father had somehow discovered — or surmised — on what I was working, and would repeatedly, and all in one movement, knock at the door, enter the room, and rush through it with his very rapid walk (which he claimed as an indication of the similar rapid action of his brain), saying with a note of injury and even of restrained agony in his voice, 'Two brains are better than one. . . . Such a mistake *not* to consult *me*!' The light, pattering footsteps would then depart, until another identical interruption would ensue in twenty minutes or so. (My father, though he mistrusted, and even hated, fiction, would always favour those staying at Renishaw with criticism of my work in this medium, and confided in Constant Lambert one day, when I was writing *Before the Bombardment*, that 'Osbert is writing a novel: it will be an odd sort of book, with no hero or heroine, and no love interest!') . . . My second story, written at Amalfi, where I pen this preface, was of a very different kind, on a different level; *Low Tide* (which the typist in New York who recently copied out my List of Contents, renamed *Low Tick*, so that it nearly made its appearance here under this new guise) had been travelling round the inside of my head for a number of years — ever since, in fact, I had begun to observe people and things, and to comprehend to what a spiritual extent material objects and habits could be an expression of men and women, as well as noting for myself the tricks played by the implacable Fates, the sequences of riches and poverty, and the stern revenges of nature, and — such as the plagues of the Middle Ages — of the poor upon the rich: beliefs which I have always in my writings tried to emphasise. It was full, this story, so far as I could make it, of little things I had seen for myself, no less than of the huge unpredictability of mankind, its fears and fevers and loves and hatreds and superstitions, all liable to sudden and treacherous changes, because such emotions are founded solely on the personality of him who feels them — emotions that rack the elderly, rich and respectable, no less than the young and inexperienced; full, too (again, as far as I could make it), of the ape-like excesses, shallow or outrageous, and the angelic heights and diabolic depths to which Man, 'that paragon of animals', will stride or sink.

When the story appeared in print, I was successful in eluding the reviewers of poetry, and was more fortunate with the new band of critics I encountered — though I remember the late James Agate, who liked my books, pronounced of *Low Tide* that its first page contained every mistake it was possible for a writer to make. . . . With these two, and the stories that followed, I tried, then, to force the reader to see and realise utterly the persons, places or objects as I had seen them; for the achievement of this purpose I had to materialise them very vividly, and it happened, sometimes, for example, that in working at a description of a flower, I so successfully re-created it, at least for myself, that it would seem to scent the whole room, and, forgetting, I would turn round to see where the fragrance came from, and whether there were not a rose, or whatever the blossom might be, near me. . . . What I hope is that in some of my stories I may have been able to communicate to the reader a comparably vibrant sense of this world, and that in others I may have been similarly able for a moment to transmit 'overtones from worlds unknown', intimate, slight, to be heard like music in the mind. The short story is, in addition, perhaps the form to which local colour, the ruin of so many books, is the most appropriate. It should be, too — though I doubt whether it is — as perfect and brilliant a vehicle for the national genius as the water-colour, that English invention, has proved to be in the realm of art: since a power of conciseness and an eye for essentials (as well as for quirks, customs and eccentricities) have always distinguished the masters in our tongue. The writer of short stories must also know how to translate into his own medium and approach Blake's dictum that the senses are the gateways to the soul. Thus only is it possible for him to surmount the barriers of age, race, sex and class, and to recognise mankind as one and indivisible.

If, as I have suggested, short stories can be very near in their conception to poems, they may also be akin to them in the way in which they rise in the mind of the writer — rise in the mind, I have written, for that seems to me precisely to describe the process — sometimes singly, sometimes in batches. For instance, I made full notes for six or seven while in bed one afternoon with an attack of gout — a disease which is said at first to sharpen the mind, and then at times to cloud it, as with a drug. This occurrence of stories in groups affords to a writer of any versatility a great chance in their treatment, as well as exhibiting its own peculiar fascination in that it enables him to identify and trace the veins of ore that he possesses running through the mass of his mind. If they are many, he may only reach the same vein once in the space of twenty years. For example, I tapped one in 1922 when I wrote *Triple Fugue*, but I did not again find it until 1945, for it cannot be reached at will or deliberately. On the other hand he may discover it more often, and *Before the Bombardment*, part of *Those Were the Days*, and in this volume *Low Tide* and *Staggered Holiday*, all manifest a similar run of feeling and expression: just as clearly as *Death of a God* belongs in essence to the vein which underlies the five volumes of my autobiography, *Left Hand, Right Hand!*

The majority of the later stories were written at Renishaw during the last war, but the earlier volumes were composed wherever I happened to be, so that to me reading through them brings back many far and strange lands — for as I have declared earlier, we were not, the writers of my generation, fettered by regionalism — Guatemala and China, Italy, Spain, Greece, Portugal and Morocco, islands in the Mediterranean and the Atlantic, France and Switzerland. I was compelled to write almost anywhere I found myself, for financial stringency, due to natural extravagance, forced me to work, even if I did not want to, and thus widened the natural aptitude. I had to make money and — contrary to the lament of publishers — I found short stories easy to sell, as well as interesting to write. Moreover, in the sort of life I led, where I was obliged — or, by the stupidity of my conduct, obliged myself — to write articles on every sort of subject several times a week, short stories were less difficult to write on the days off than were novels; which require an immense stretch of time without worry, to start them, let alone bring them to completion. To write at all with any continuity, I had to go abroad where my father could not contrive by any parental claim to kidnap me and perpetually to divert my attention. So I wrote the earlier of these stories in bitter cold or in great heat, in a disused kitchen in Antigua, Guatemala, where a vulture had been placed on guard outside the window by his aerial unit to signal if necessary the latest news of my health to his circling brothers in the blue dome above, or in a room of a house in the Tartar city in Peking, where the wind would often deliver on my desk a sample of dust from the Gobi Desert, or in a square box of a room, its outside walls covered with the waxen orange trumpets of *Bignonia grandiflora*, on the roof of a small villa in Madeira, in my whitewashed monk's cell at Amalfi, or on a terrace at Marrakesh, and in many ordinary hotel bedrooms, cabins on boats, and in the special ivory towers I can temporarily but most successfully erect for myself in railway carriages. Much as I love the anonymous conversation in trains, I like still more than to talk, to write in them. Thus, *The Man Who Drove Strindberg Mad*, the first draft of it, was written in the train going down to Brighton on a Sunday in the notorious frozen February of 1940. Certainly I was given more hours in which to work than I had bargained for: because the train which started on its normal run at eleven, and should have arrived at noon, was delayed by the intense cold freezing the damp on the electrified line and therefore did not put in its expected appearance at Brighton Station until nearly four o'clock — at which hour it was time to return, without luncheon, to London. After hours of dragon's breath on the air, red noses and half-tipsy community singing, I eventually reached Victoria at ten at night, too late to get dinner. The downward journey had been quiet, if slow, however, and time had passed as quickly for me as I wanted it to pass for the reader. At any rate, I returned cold but safe, and clutching a note-book that contained a story thus chiselled out of chaos.

I do not know when the first short story came into being, or how; I do not know when the last will be read, or what direction it is taking at present. But I recall, and must in turn remind the reader that during the whole of my lifetime the Decay of Fiction has been almost continuously announced in the literary journals. Yet looking back through the years fiction can now be seen to have remained almost the one solid fact in a dissolving universe. Those who have perpetually foretold its approaching demise have slid downhill with a bump, but, while fact ceases to be fact, and matter itself ceases to be matter, fiction remains fiction. Kings and kingdoms have come and gone, great empires have ceased to exist, but still the output of the novel and short story, though it may be uninspiring for the most part except in its sheer torrential spate, floods the countries of the world. Scientific barbarism encroaches on every side, the living — as opposed to dead — arts have become unpopular: only the novel and the short story flourish on the dunghill that men have made of the world. So that, after all, fiction may have a future (the Future of Fiction is another well-known theme in the newspapers): though the future of fiction must depend on the future of those who write and read it; and the prospect for them both seems rather dubious at present. If a third, and in every sense final, War to End Wars, descends upon us within the space of a few years, let us say seven, then a very limited period of development lies before it — and us. Or, again, we may be about to pass under the portcullis of Antland, and ants do not make good heroes or heroines. Moreover they have no time to write novels — or to read them: (they are only permitted to read instructive treatises on how one ant may learn to do the work of seven — or, better still, of seventy). But for the purpose of our diagnosis and prognostication, it is necessary to postulate a long period of time in which works of art and commerce can be born and prosper, as well as decay and die. If such a stretch should lie before us, it is possible to foresee an enormous enriching and widening and deepening of fiction, and its progress along many new lines, scientific or psycho-analytical, in a world of leisure, a society freed from the cramping effects of class, though shorn equally of its fascinating shibboleths. In such an atmosphere, fiction should flower again, or continue to flower. The truth is that novelists die, but not the novel. And the reason, I suspect, is because the novel is not an art form.

Of course it can be made into an art form by anyone who happens to be an artist — and I for one am biased, because I am an author who, for better or worse, cannot write without making of what he is writing a work of art. . . . No, fiction is not by its very essence (unless it is written by an artist) an art form, as, for example, must be any poem. It is merely a convenience. Thus, in reality, to talk about the Future of Fiction is comparable to talking about the Future of the Suit-case or Grip (ex-portmanteau). It depends on who packs it, what it contains, and on where the traveller is going and whether his journey is necessary — albeit the journey can be in any direction. And protean as the novel continually proves to be, in this respect the short story surpasses it. In the course even of the past two decades an immense advance in the scope and technique of the short story has been effected, and in the splintering of life which it represents.

It is necessary always to bear in mind that fiction has, withal, obtained a great hold upon the affections of the public. This, I apprehend, is due to Man's conceit, and in its quiddity resembles the compelling attraction that a piece of looking-glass exercises upon an ape. Man dominates fiction. It is entirely concerned with him — and therefore to him fiction is good. But alas! — and this militates against future development —, the ape has of late years grown hysterical; to the point that he is now more hysterical than inquisitive. The reality of his own reflection is no longer what he is after. Now he must be shown himself as he *wishes* to see himself: a noble, but not an intelligent, ape — nobility consisting in the form in which he likes to see it — a patriotic ape to the patriotic ape, or let us say, a socialist, fair-shares-for-all ape to the socialist, fair-shares-for-all ape. But the general tendency in fiction, though each community of readers is catered for by writers of like mind, has been for the tramp, the down-and-out, in the course of a century to usurp completely the place of the old Byronic hero, just as the hobo's feminine counterpart has ousted from her throne the exquisitely civilised hostess of Henry James's novels, and has come to be regarded as the ideal after which mankind should strive. Mademoiselle de Maupin, the heroine of the romantics, to a new generation now yields in interest to the really awfully plucky charwoman who stood her ground in the air-raids and is known to everyone as 'Ma'. During the war, and the few years immediately following it, the public, drunk with its own heroism, demanded only stories of war fortitude, revelled in tales of bombs, well or ill directed, of the happy community life of bomb-shelters, of overcrowded trains, running late, of queues and the noble, tenpenny hardships of rationing. (Even painting came to be occupied with the same themes.) Yet the artist — in the widest sense — must, even to deal with such incongruities, be allowed to get his nose off reality for a little: he must be permitted to remain for a while aloof, and for a few moments, but only for a few, to pop into an ivory tower, even if it is only a railway carriage. . . . But after the war ends — an eventuality no one ever expects, because to think of an end to it during the course of a modern, democratic war, which is by its nature so terrible that, in order to endure it, the feelings of the public have continually to be whipped up to the pitch of hysteria by those in charge, constitutes treason — after the war ends, I was saying, and when its foggy aftermath of feeling has dispersed, no one will read any more of bombs and bomb-shelters, and even the idolised down-and-out may too have to be shifted back to the rubbish-dump, a most unfair and unfriendly proceeding.

Fortunately, the reporters of events — those Mercuries whose names I forget, but whose works, *Muscling in on the Fal of Paris*, or *Tiddlywinks in Berlin*, are to be seen on every railway bookstall — have rescued fiction from the tyranny of unwanted contemporary fact, in the same way that the invention of the camera rescued painting. Fiction must now find its own educated public, and then its future will lie in all directions. . . . I wrote just now that much depended on who packed the suitcase, where the traveller was going, and whether his journey was necessary; Wells, for example, was always on his way to a Socialist rally or a Scientific Study Group, Arnold Bennett to a directors' meeting at the Grand Babylon Hotel; Henry James, armed prominently with a first-class ticket, *en route* to spend Saturday to Monday with a cosy but scintillating company in a famous country-house; Aldous Huxley on a journey with many changes, starting from Garsington, via the villas of Florence, to a cœnobitic enclave in Hollywood; D. H. Lawrence from the Sunday suits and prosaic smoke-stacks of Nottinghamshire to the dark and hidden gods of Mexico and Etruria; myself from — but no, my own journey can be traced through the stories that follow, and the reader who has accompanied me thus far is now at liberty to turn to them, and epitomise for himself my voyage. He will find, no doubt, that in each story I have contradicted in practice several of the theories I have promulgated in the foregoing pages.

OSBERT SITWELL

AMALFI
March 16, 1952

DEFEAT

BATTLE alters the face of the world, but defeat and collapse may at first leave it intact, just as a gutted house often shows no change, except for its dead, blank windows. . . . So it was with the little town of Château-Vignal, formerly so prosperous. Ruin and chaos were implicit in it, but, at first sight, did not show themselves. Its structure was bony and enduring, and its grey-white streets ran from either side of the Loire like ribs from the backbone of a carcase. The trams still creaked down narrow alleys under the overhanging sculpture of gothic churches; in the one broad boulevard the shops still boasted displays of goods at high prices; fruits and vegetables lay heaped up in baskets, level with the knees of the old peasant women who sold them, under the hot and radiant sunshine of the open market, and, though meat, sugar, spices were unprocurable, other, younger peasant women carried hens under their arms and cackled to each other across the struggling, feathered bodies. Beneath the tall, glossy-leaved trees on which magnolias, large and white as the soup-bowls of the almshouses near by, were flowering sweetly, the local idiot still sat slobbering in the empty public garden. The only change noticeable was that the tramps, who usually slept here at night, were now seeking this escape during the day-time and formed those almost inconjecturable mounds of rags — lifeless save for a slight, nearly imperceptible, heaving — which could be seen lying in several directions upon the yellowing grass. The fishermen still lined the banks of the river, with its high and, as it seemed at this season, unnecessary stone walls, and one or two, more intrepid, stood in the water up to their knees. (Indeed, owing to the scarcity of provisions, there were, perhaps, more of them, and they were even more patient.) The cafés were still open, too, though the regular clients were ruffled at being unable to obtain their favourite drinks, and in the chief café the band of four ancient men in dinner-jackets still played 'Selections from *Carmen*', the 'Barcarolle', and various waltzes, and a woman singer, in a pink evening dress, and carrying with her the invisible prestige attaching to many diplomas from many provincial *conservatoires*, still sang the Jewel Song from *Faust* and various well-known airs from the operas of Puccini.

Little change manifested itself: nevertheless the poison of defeat ran through the corpus of the people in the same manner in which a poison circulates through the body with its blood, by the aid of its own blood. And the outward form that the poison took during this stage, which resembled the unconsciousness of a patient, broken by fits of delirium, was a chaotic, meaningless placidity, relief at the coming of a peace that did not exist, varied by sudden spasms of virulently anti-foreign, and especially anti-British, sentiment. But this xenophobia did not extend towards the conquerors. The German officers, the German soldiers were even regarded momentarily with a certain admiration, a certain wonder at their hard, mechanical bearing and efficiency, and the women of the town looked at them more curiously, and longer, than at their own men, yet covered, many of them, with dust, slouching past impassively in twos and threes, unshaven, silent, vacant-eyed, puffing at cigarettes that never left their lips even when they exchanged a few words.

It was a Sunday afternoon. On the terrace of the public gardens, under the delicate fluttering of acacia leaves, the usual Sunday family groups, the usual Sunday combinations — like a family tree in reverse — of grandfathers, grandmothers, uncles, aunts, parents, all in dark clothes, with, as their culmination, a single, small, pale child, wandered and stared without purpose, and from the interior of the Café de l'Univers came the familiar dull crack of billiard balls and shuttered laughter. Vanished were the Algerian, Moroccan and Tunisian troops who usually lent colour to the scene, but at a few tables some French soldiers were playing cards, and at another sat a Captain in the French army, the young girl to whom he was engaged, and her mother. . . . Not far away, near the entrance to the public gardens and divided from it by the usual line of green boxes containing nameless evergreen shrubs, a German officer, with a creased neck, ox-eyes, a monocle and a tunic that appeared to contain a wooden body, was consuming a *bock*.

The Captain did not look at him. He had only returned home yesterday. His eyes were entirely reserved for his younger companion, the daughter of Doctor Dorien; in a way she was pretty, but her essential correctness — the result in conjunction of a convent upbringing and the inherited burgess virtues of her home —, her clothes, with the typical dowdy *chic* of the French provincial town, and her carefully coiffured hair, all combined to impart to her an air of insipidity, of primly decorated nullity, as though she had long been prepared, and was still waiting, for the vital forces to descend and give her life. Her smile, on the other hand, was quick and alert, and her eyes soon warmed, soon lost their emptiness and gained fire.

The face of the Captain, sensitive and, in spite of the several ribbons he was wearing, almost feminine in fineness of cut and expression, was drawn and exhausted, for he had only stopped fighting three days before, and within him his soul was dead. Notwithstanding, the bond that united him to Estelle, that mutual but indefinable flow of sympathy which seemed to pour into every cell of each body from the other, comforted him. They had been friends from childhood, and their marriage had been arranged since their earliest infancy. . . . Perhaps theirs was not love in the romantic sense, but, from the Latin approach, it constituted love. On his side composed of tenderness, affection and physical desire, on hers it rose out of her respect for his qualities of command and valour, and from a need for mental and physical subservience. He fully appreciated the nature of it, that Estelle looked up to him, and he was relieved to find that this feeling of hers still persisted after what had happened. . . . But he knew it was deserved, because he was no coward and, where many brave men had been routed, he had stood his ground.

He realised — and she had been able to make him realise — that this respect for his valour, like his valour itself, had suffered no diminution from defeat — 'defeat'. . . . He supposed it must be because he was so tired, but through the tinkling phrases of the Delibes ballet music now being played, the words 'defeat', 'defeat', 'defeat' drummed in his ears, and with his inner eye he still watched — and, he thought, would watch eternally — the armoured columns advancing, those immense and senseless machines, trundling and thundering along at a rate no Frenchman could have anticipated, could still see them, hear them, crushing the heads of men like nuts ground under the heel, could still see the cowering, surging waves of humanity upon the roads, the household goods, upon barrows and carts, the clocks and trunks and vases, for better protection covered beneath the best mattress, could still see the old women and the ill left behind, fallen in the ditches beneath the grey and suffocating hedges, could still hear the nearing remorseless thunder, and rattling machine-gun fire from the dive-bombers, swarming above the civilian crowds, scattering them and rounding them up as they ran hither and thither, all wearing, as though in self-protection, the sheep-coloured, shameful livery of the dust. Such sights and sounds were as yet more real to him than the silvery perspective of tall, shivering poplars and flowing river, its cool islands of willow and tamarisk lying like full baskets of feathers upon the water, upon which his glance now rested, and were not far from him even when he gazed into the calm and limpid brown depths of Estelle's eyes.

He must pretend to be the same or it might shock her. . . . But he knew that he had changed, and the world with him, and he wished the band would not continually play the old gay melodies of a dead life; it was like seeing the ghost of someone you had loved. . . . '*Defeat.*' . . . And yet there were in it certain pleasant prospects, though tinged with the year's shame. The war, a bad war, badly begun, had stopped. His men would no longer be slaughtered. Above all, his marriage, hitherto delayed first by the previous economic collapse and then by the war, could take place almost immediately, their parents agreed. And their old affection remained steadfast. . . . But sometimes he almost wished that the kind of affection he read in her eyes, that respect for a man who was brave and could command, had ceased to exist, replaced by some other kindred but more reasonable sentiment; for of what use was courage, individual courage, now, against this armoured mass; how could flesh pit itself against iron?

Meanwhile their conversation, albeit desultory, was, on the surface, gay enough. They avoided all mention of the war, but teased one another and preened themselves like any other young couple in ordinary times. They discussed how they would live after their marriage, and seemed to forget for a while the presence of her mother, and then, all at once, to remember it and try to make amends. All three of them made their cakes and *tisane* — for there was no coffee — last as long a time as possible.

'Remember, I shall have to find a trade now,' the Captain said, 'I shall no longer be in the army. I shall have to get up every morning to go to the office, and probably my temper will be very bad, for I am not used to it. . . . And you will have to prepare for my home-coming, and walk back with me so that I get air, or otherwise I shall take the tram to be with you the sooner, and so shall soon grow old and fat.' (Her face fell, he noticed, when he told her that he would leave the army; evidently she had not fully grasped that the French army was in dissolution.) 'And I shall dine every night with you and Maman,' he continued, taking the older woman into the conversation, 'but I shall be very cross unless you both give me the food I like.' (But inside his head, the words 'defeat', 'defeat', sounded like advancing columns.)

'And what about *me*?' Estelle answered; 'you will have to study me now, and come home early so as to be with me. If you leave the regiment, there will be no talk of being "on duty", or of "having to dine in the Officers' Mess". . . . No excuses will exist any more.'

But all this talk, he felt, meant so little. Like the scene itself, it was curiously on the surface, with no shades or undertones. The sun glowed down now through the acacia leaves, seeming to consume them, and rested full on the faces round them. The woman in the pink evening dress had, amid much applause, stopped singing, and conversation and laughter swelled up from the tables.

Then the band struck up again, a waltz, the 'Wiener Wald' by Johann Strauss. . . . Hardly a place empty. . . . A party of four or five gaping soldiers came in, near the entrance by which the German officer was sitting. They passed him, and came towards the Captain; they dragged their feet, were dishevelled and untidy, talked loudly and smoked cigarettes. He recognised them; they were men who for long had served under him, but they stared at him idly, without saluting, and slouched past him to a table beyond. They were noisy, but possessed the very look of men who have lost all spirit, except a new will to insolence. ('*Defeat*': this was defeat.) He looked away and did not glance at Estelle, fixing his eyes upon the distance, where the water rippled by the edge of rushes and flowering clumps of yellow iris. . . . But suddenly a guttural sound obtruded and made him take notice. (The conversation stopped at the neighbouring tables, though the aproned waiters continued to perform their clever acts of equilibrium, with arms poised and trays uplifted above the heads of their customers, in the manner of jugglers.) It was the German officer, summoning and beckoning to the men; the Captain's men. Now they pulled themselves together. Their false aggressiveness ebbed away and they filed back solemnly and saluted the foreigner, as he bade them.

'Now go back and salute your Captain,' the enemy continued in his thick, distorted French.

The men sheepishly did as they were told. . . . The Captain acknowledged their salute in the customary manner, nonchalantly and as though at his ease, and his soldiers returned to their table. . . . *Defeat.* Defeat. This was Defeat. And the world lay broken round him. He felt, perceived immediately, that nothing in his own life would ever be the same again. This incident had transformed Estelle's view of him, and her new attitude towards him was defined and without the possibility of retrieval: it was final; he knew it, deep in his bones. The bond had snapped. Never now would they be married. It was as though for her the virtue had gone out of him. His manhood lay shattered for both of them, wrecked by the clumsy courtesy, or (who could tell?) the cruel courtesy of a victor. . . . But he was tired, so tired that he scarcely suffered. It was over.

THAT FLESH IS HEIR TO . . .

OR

THE HISTORY OF A BACILLUS

'. . . Disease, then, represents this struggle for life, and it is in this sense an advantage : for without " diseases " man would quickly fall victim to the injurious agents which surround him. Man is essentially a potential invalid, since he is a potential battleground in his struggle for existence. Disease is the chance of victory.'—ALAN MONCRIEFF, in an article entitled ' The Nature of Disease ', in the *Nation and Athenæum*, March 16, 1929.

'. . . Man may be a potential invalid, but he is not an invalid by choice.'—*Ibid.*

I

WHEREAS a man can only die and be born once, the race of microbes suffers a thousand grievous deaths in each human recovery and is born anew, a million times triumphing, in each corpse for which it has hungered, and as I hope to show, planned. But this very wealth, this plethora of energy, makes it hard to compress the birth, the upbringing, the career of a germ within the space of a short story : more difficult, indeed, than to force into the same compass the span and achievements of a human life. There are other reasons, too, that force me to regard the task as a piece of work not lightly to be undertaken. This story is essentially one of adventure, and it is not easy, for example, even with the aid of a map, to concentrate so much picturesque geography, so much tragic social-history as it demands, into a few pages. Nevertheless it seemed, in spite of all obstacles, that the experiment was worth attempting, if only because I would fain place my little offering of personal observation as a tribute upon the altar of science.

Yet, being no professor, I am not compelled to take up with this subject a whole volume, however well it might be filled. All that duty imposes on me is to state the story, and to indicate, for the benefit of those who specialise in such things — but who, not having the imaginative writer's outfit, cannot detect for themselves the connection between these footprints in the sand — its subsequent and certain developments. If one were to write a life of that Count of the Empire under Charlemagne who was the founder of the Este family, it would be well, as throwing light upon his destiny, to indicate that he was the common ancestor of the royal houses of England, Saxony and Ferrara: but it would be obligatory on one neither to prove their descent, nor to write the history of every later member of the family. So, too, I shall not essay to correlate the microbe, which is the invisible but most potent hero of my story, with his obvious descendants, interesting as such a digression would be, nor to dwell upon the more crucial and public stages of that career of conquest which found its culmination in the dengue-fever epidemic that devastated Greece in the autumn of 1928 and in the influenza outbreak of the winter of 1928–9: a wave which swept across the whole world. That is the business of those who come after, and whose calling lies in such research.

A microbe, I have said, is the hero of the tale which follows: and this necessitates that, when it so suits the author, the hero should be regarded as both singular and plural, as an individual and a tribe, as a great general and a mighty army in one: nor is this all that one is forced to demand of the gentle reader, for, since microbes neither marry nor are given in marriage, the hero is also heroine, is masculine and feminine as well as singular and plural: for such licence I must crave the reader's indulgence, asking him to consider and weigh the difficulties of my task.

So enormous, then, is the subject to be imprisoned within these limits, that one is forced to be ruthless, to prune the Mediterranean cities of their tingling life, their hoarse shouts and shuddering glamour, the desert of its beauty born of solitude, the blue, transparent sea of its dolphins leaping up and down through the waters in segments of circles as though they were swift wheels, revolving partly above and partly below the surface, and of its strange fish that at night carry their own illuminations through the glassy depths. Moreover, apart from the protagonists, who will, whether one wishes it or not, most surely demonstrate their characters, the minor figures — our companions on this odyssey, or the royal victims, the attendant train of diplomats and consuls, the crews of ships and staffs of hotels, who are the dramatis personae — should as far as possible be puppets, ninepins to be knocked over at very rhythmic but ever shorter intervals by the overwhelmingly simple, yet accurate and terrible, machinery invented by our super-germ.

To the working of this engine I now hold the secret. And as, with, it must be confessed, no little pride, I reflect upon this discovery of mine, my mind goes back once more to that dark winter night of two years ago, and to how little then I expected the curious developments that were so near me.

II

I hurried away from the paraphernalia of polite leave-taking, from the clustered top-hats and walking-sticks, down the steps gilded by the light of the open door, into the dead November square. Each lamp-post bore aloft a wavering halo of golden drizzle, and the tall, contorted red-brick houses had assumed a tone of purple, until, beneath the uncertain and swinging illumination of this windy month, they seemed but a faint discoloration, an opaque deepening of the night itself. What a charming, rather mysterious woman Mrs. Chitty was, with that indefinable and enigmatic smile and the glowing intensity of her brown eyes! (Fitful and anonymous farewells still pursued me from the gaping mouth of her mansion: cars began to purr, and keen patches of light sped over the muddy wastes of the road.) I hurried, hurried on, for I was not feeling well — rather shivery — and hoped the walk would warm me. . . . Charming woman, but a little mysterious . . . unusual. How peculiar, for instance, was the composition of her dinner-parties: the human ingredients never varied. Why should a woman, whose interests in life were mainly musical, artistic and literary, thus live almost entirely in the company of diplomats, Foreign Office officials and scientists? Even though it might be that this choice imparted to her house an atmosphere distinctive and rather cosmopolitan, what was there in her mind to make her thus yoke the scientist with the diplomat? Yet I enjoyed these gatherings, for the diplomats lisped to one another in undertones or babbled in foreign languages, and thus I was left to listen to the scientists, whose theories one needs must love for their wealth of fantasy, intense but serious.

That night, for some reason, the conversation had mainly turned upon the influenza epidemic of 1918: a scourge that, it will be remembered, helped to enwrap the final phases of the 'Great' War in a blaze of glory — for glory is ever strictly in proportion to the number of dead bodies upon which it is fed, and this particular wave of illness had made the war-casualties appear almost minute. Seven million people, it was roughly calculated, had perished of it in six months. By christening it *Spanish Influenza*, however, instead of bestowing upon it some picturesque, gothic title such as the *Black Death*, the doctors reduced for us both its terror and romance, even if it cannot be pretended that this castanetted euphemism in any way diminished the death-rate or revealed the cause of the pestilence. And, though nine years had now passed since the outbreak, little more light could be thrown upon its origin. Climatic conditions could not much enter into the matter, for in India, glowing under the tropical heat like an ember, entire communities had been wiped out in a few hours. Mrs. Chitty, who was fond of travelling, had been there when it started, and told us that often by the time the nearest medical aid could be rushed up to some distant village, the cruel, dusty red sunlight glared down on houses in which there was no human movement, no sound, not even a cry.

I had, at the time of this plague, formed about it my own opinion: which was that Nature — who often must be regarded as the Goddess of Reason, a divinity, that is to say, indulging in anthropopathic flights of logic, and only differing in kind from man because of her greater power — had, as she watched the war, very justifiably concluded that since men were so plainly bent on their own extermination, herself had better have her fling and join in the fun. After all, killing people had always been her divine monopoly as well as her chief hobby (thorough good sportsman, Nature!). In England, before a cygnet is killed and eaten, the Royal sanction must be obtained: so, too, Nature expected that before any human being died, before even a doctor was allowed to slaughter a patient, her aid and permission should be invoked. It might only be a formality nowadays; but why, she asked herself, should she sit there quietly — especially considering all the new, untried microbes in her possession — and see her prerogative usurped by man, an animal she had never much cared for ? Of the many beasts she had created, he was the only one that had become discontented, then mutinous ; had attacked her rights and privileges, attempting to curb her supreme power and to degrade her rank from that of Goddess-Autocrat down to a mere constitutional monarch. Indeed in every direction this pitiable creature had challenged her authority. She had given him a skin of his own for his covering, and he had chosen to wear that of others (often murdering a fellow-beast to get it) : she had provided him with plain, simple food to eat, and he had chosen to warm it and burn out of it its virtue ; with caves in which to live, and he had built huts and houses ; she had given him rain to wash him, and he had collected the water, cooked it and taken unto himself soap ! But her little influenza-germ would soon put things to rights, for this latest-evolved pet was house-trained, most flourished exactly in those circumstances man had rebelliously contrived for himself.

Thus, I imagined, had Nature argued and plotted in her own mind. But, since 1918, influenza had periodically returned, and one had been forced to abandon such a theory. Now, in the winter of 1927, a season singularly exempt from this particular evil, as I walked home — feeling rather odd and cold — I was just as much in the dark about its origin as any of our scientists could be. (How icy it was, and my eyes were beginning to ache ; a curious sensation as though the eyeballs did not belong to their sockets, square eyeballs in round holes. However, one should never encourage pains by thinking of them, and resolutely I focused my thoughts back again on to the conversation at dinner.) We had been informed that, ever since the close of the great epidemic, the medical and scientific authorities had kept constant watch for this criminal bacillus, who even now might be moving unidentified among us : for influenza was peculiarly difficult to cope with, in that, upon each new and considerable outbreak, it assumed a fresh disguise. Like Charley Peace, it was able after every crime entirely to alter its outward appearance, while leaving invariably some novel and obscure disease in its wake. Thus the name 'influenza' was merely a courtesy-title conferred by popular consent upon an anonymous and dangerous microbe (here Mrs. Chitty had smiled her curious, enigmatic smile), just as the author of the terrible Whitechapel murders had been known far and wide as 'Jack the Ripper'. Attempts had been made to fix the responsibility for these recent outrages in many quarters, but so far without success. A million germs had been caught and kept under observation for long periods, only, in the end, to demonstrate unmistakably their innocence.

The stories that Professor Chilcott and Dr. Bidham had told us only served to confirm my impression that science had lately grown a little wild, somewhat apt to overlook and overleap the obvious. They admitted that, in their nervous eagerness to solve the problems of this illness, they had kidnapped an enormous quantity of the free field-mice of Great Britain, and were keeping them captive all the winter in order to observe the various infections which they might breed. This, I had thought, was surely going too far (the dark, furry and whiskered tribe, thus, to its surprise, comfortably installed in winter-quarters, had, as a matter of fact, never since ailed, but had thrived and increased like the seed of Abraham) . . . and, even if it has now been established that bubonic plague is engendered by starving squirrels in Central Asia, which, in dying of famine, pass on the fleas that live upon them to the black rat; and that, when the black rat, travelling all over the world, dies of the pestilence, the flea then attacks human beings and infects them, yet why attempt to lay the blame for influenza upon the poor little English mouse, a harmless and quite different creature? I had thought myself bound, in fair play, to protest. A suspect tribe, the rodents: and for a little I had tried to arouse pity and interest on their behalf among these icy, calculating hearts by drawing attention to the extraordinary and romantic vicissitudes of fortune which had lately been their lot. Think on the piebald and downy guinea-pig, I had urged, hailing originally from the suffocating forests of South America, brought across all those leagues of ocean to become a pampered pet. I had seen its image lolling or frolicking among roses or exotic flowers, set over the elaborately carved doors of Prince Eugène's winter palace in Vienna. Then subsequently it had become the playmate of wealthy children, its ears flopping freely upon the honest English breeze. But, suddenly sinking into poverty and obscurity once more, it now only exists here as a subject for medical experi-

persuasive, it was less of Sarah Bernhardt than of Savonarola that one was reminded, although mimicry was the last, and most genial, vice which one would have imputed to that cavernous-eyed and dreary burn-book. It seemed as though in everything she did there was concealed a religious, if unfathomable, intention. Yet not for a moment was she priggish, redeemed from it by many unexpectedly human frailties. She was, for instance, feminine in an almost extinct, Victorian way. Passionately devoted to all other animals, she hated mice and cried if she saw one. Then she had developed a special technique of dropping and forgetting things, so that they must be picked up or fetched for her by her men friends thus enslaved — for this mechanism was calculated, I apprehend, to deal out either reward or punishment according to the manner in which the request for help was made — and was always a little late for everything. These superficially clinging characteristics, however, cloaked a will that was Napoleonic in strength and purpose: indeed the dropping and forgetting of things was, perhaps, but one of the means she had devised for getting her own way. It showed her men friends how helpless, how dependent on them she was, and that, in consequence, it was cruel to oppose her. Yet all her failings, all her devices, quite genuinely and without her being aware of it, only helped to throw into relief her essential mystery and attraction.

She was, one understood, a rare, very sensitive, and in many ways delightful character. And much there was about her that charmed while it eluded one. Even her worship of diplomats was intriguing — not, of course, that I am suggesting that there is anything peculiarly bizarre in choosing them as companions, but that she seemed to bear toward them a devotion that was almost fanatical. A party at the Foreign Office, to be received at the top of those marble stairs under the allegorical, monster-patriotic paintings of Mr. Goetze, would be her translation into a temporary, but none the less heavenly, heaven. She was aware of the exact position of every member of His Majesty's Diplomatic Service abroad at any given moment of any day, for her life's supreme interest was in the news of the latest swops, the promotions or occasional degradations. These she followed with the same passionate attention that a schoolboy devotes to the cricket averages of the paladins of his chosen county, or with which a retired official of the

Indian Civil Service, now living in England, regards the vagaries of the barometer in his draughty hall. Yes, she was a remarkable and curious woman, I decided. Under her manner, which displayed the identical combination of flaring pride and meek submission that in the animal world distinguishes the camel from other beasts, there was something really interesting, something that matched her obscure and haunting beauty. Further, there was nothing that she did not — or rather could not — comprehend, and, when it pleased her, she was both witty and subtle.

· · · · ·

It was with definite pleasure, therefore, that in the spring of 1928 I heard that Mrs. Chitty was to be of the same party as ourselves. Seven of us had already decided to travel together and visit various Mediterranean towns. We were to start on a liner which was setting out for a pleasure cruise: and it had been arranged that where we wished to stay longer than the other passengers, we could wait behind and catch the next boat. The tour we had planned was rather an extensive one and would occupy some two to three months. Our proposed itinerary was Genoa, Palermo, Athens, Constantinople, Rhodes, Cyprus and Beirut. There we were to disembark and visit Damascus and Jerusalem: after which, returning to Beirut, we hoped to catch a boat for Alexandria. We were determined to spend some time in Egypt, seeing everything that it was possible to see. We were to ride on camels out into the desert, and to sail up the Nile on a dahabiya. From Egypt we were to go by car to Libya, that enormous and fascinating country which has only so recently been opened up, thence return to Italy, visiting the various places of interest that lay on our road back to England. (See map.)

The party in all was to consist of Mrs. Rammond, Frank Lancing, Mrs. Jocelyn, Ruth Marlow, Julian Thackwray, Mrs. Chitty, my brother and myself. This, as it afterwards turned out, was to be the human material for Mrs. Chitty's experiments: but in our innocence at the time it was about Muriel Chitty, rather than the others, that we felt anxious, for though we all knew that she was an expert traveller, she was rather delicate, and we feared that so strenuous and prolonged a tour might fatigue her.

A letter from her that reached me a few days before we

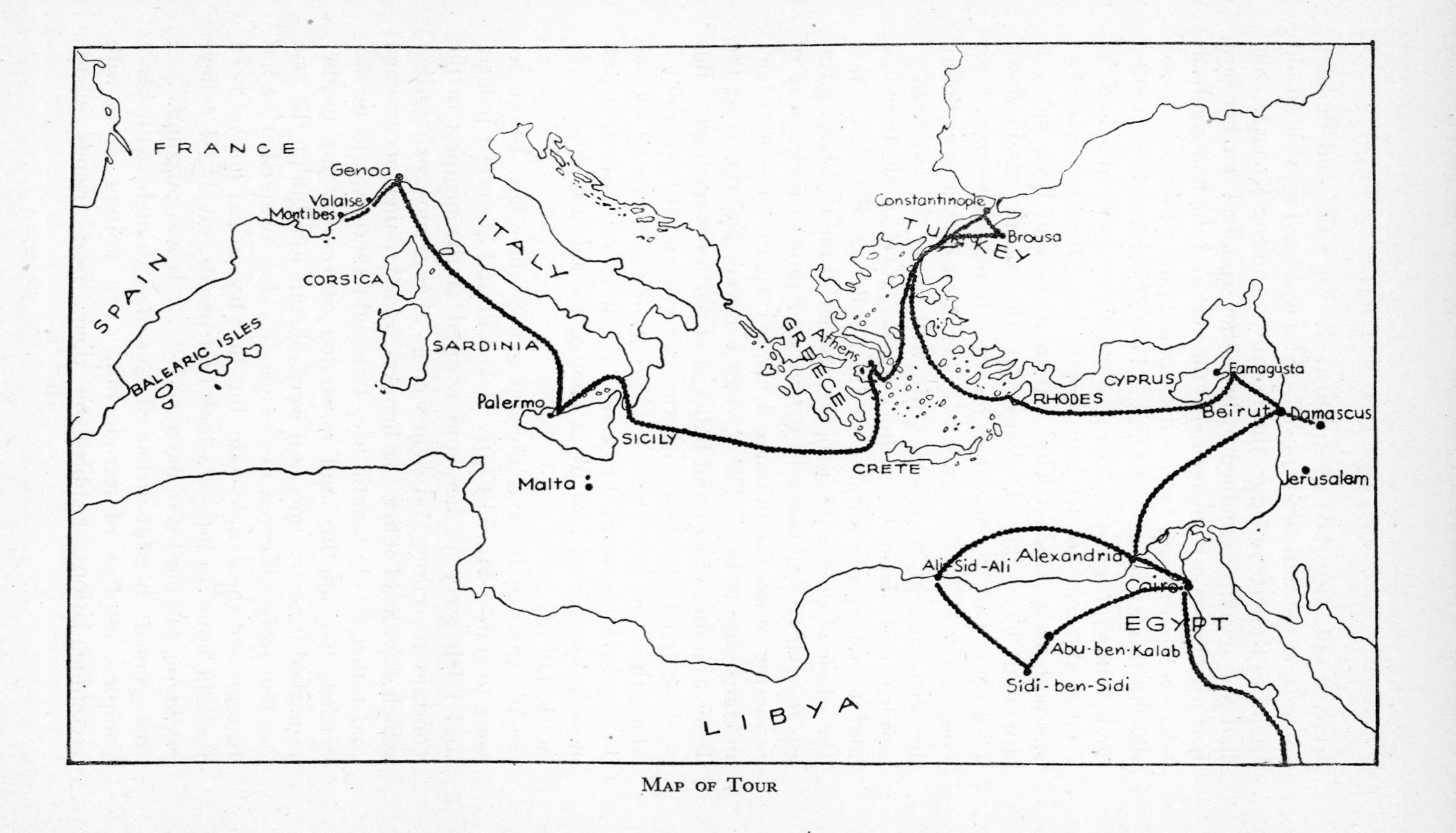
FRANCE
SPAIN
Genoa
Valaise
Montibes
CORSICA
SARDINIA
BALEARIC ISLES
ITALY
Palermo
SICILY
Malta
GREECE
Athens
CRETE
Constantinople
TURKEY
Brousa
RHODES
CYPRUS
Famagusta
Beirut
Damascus
Jerusalem
Alexandria
Ali-Sid-Ali
Cairo
EGYPT
Abu-ben-Kalab
Sidi-ben-Sidi
LIBYA

Map of Tour

were to sail, disturbed us still further. In it she said that for some time she had been unwell. She was staying with an old friend — Robert Sutledge, the novelist — on the Riviera. She had not actually remained in bed, she explained, for her host had made so many engagements for her, and she had resolved, whatever happened, not to disappoint him. Fortunately she did not think that he had realised how ill she had been, with a high temperature, and feeling altogether wretched; and, of course, she had not let him observe it. Dreadful headaches she had been afflicted with, but then she had been sad and grieving, for — had I noticed? — the death of Professor Chilcott. Did I remember meeting him? An *extraordinary* coincidence — he had dined with her alone only a week before he died, and he had been quite well then. It had been so sudden, and, naturally, a shock for her, such an old friend — and it seemed so ironical — to die of influenza like that, when the whole of the last years of his wonderful life had been given up to trying to discover its origin, and thus to find a way of rendering humanity immune from its ravages. Yes, that had, of course, upset her. The Riviera was very gay this year, the letter went on, Opera and Ballet, and parties every night. But she wondered, she wrote, whether there would be much illness along the coast this year? (It was an odd question to ask me, I thought, for how was I to know?) But, in any case, ill or well herself, she would join us at Genoa, for she was determined not to fail us.

We met safely, and dined together the night before we were to start. Muriel Chitty looked ill and austere, I judged, and I felt sorry for her, and worried at the prospect of the constant travelling and sight-seeing (always most exhausting) which was ahead of her. In her eyes, added to their accustomed and rather lovely fanatic fire, I thought there was to be discerned, too, another and unwonted expression (my brother remarked it also): one, as it were, of conscious guilt; the look so often to be observed in the eye of a dog aware that he has transgressed the canine code, but that his sin has not yet been brought home to him — a look that pleads, saying, 'I believe *you* know, but *don't* give me away'. . . . It was puzzling. . . . She seemed cheerful in herself, and had brought with her a countless number of introductions, and visiting cards with recommendations scribbled on them, from friends in the

Foreign Office. Indeed it seemed as though there were at least one or two letters apiece for every Ambassador, Minister, Consul-General and Consul in the Near East, Syria and North Africa; not altogether, the rest of our group secretly agreed, a blessing, for our days were limited in number considering how much there was for us to do in them, and the mere personal delivery of this script must occupy, one would hazard, a solid month of time.

The whole journey, despite its adventures, seems in retrospect to have passed very quickly and in a succession of cinema-like flashes. The next morning we embarked. Genoa, frost-bitten in the early February wind, piled itself up dustily behind us on its terraces, amid the clanking of trams and hooting of trains and liners, and we were soon heading for the undulating serpents of the sea, that here and there lifted a white-crested, venomous head. Notwithstanding how rough it was, and that the remainder of our party stayed below until we reached Sicily, Mrs. Chitty sat on deck and talked to me. She made of her deck-chair a little nest of her own and everybody else's fur coats, and in this remained snug and warm — like one of those mice, I thought, for whom the scientists had prepared such comfortable winter-quarters. But our conversation was not in the least monotonous, for she would banish any chance of this by indulging in occasional frantic pantomime. Here all her latent powers of acting found an outlet. She carried with her — and they must always be near her — a great number of large, brightly coloured, leather hand-trunks, each filled with a different species of railway-ticket and foreign money, for she never believed, she said, in putting all her eggs into one basket. Thus, if by any mischance she lost the miniature portmanteau which contained her ticket to Damascus, she might still have that which held her ticket to Cairo, or if she lost her Greek money, she would still have Syrian or Egyptian.

First, and as prelude to the play, she would strike an attitude which at once and most expressively conveyed to all in her neighbourhood the idea that she thought she had lost one of these 'little bags'. There would be a moment's dramatic, tragic pause: and then a wild scene would ensue. Rugs and rainbow-lined fur coats would execute mad furlanas and jotas in the air as they were feverishly searched in turn. All the men on deck would soon be bent double or would be crawling on all fours to examine obscure crannies between the wet and slippery boards, until it looked as if a game of 'animal-dumb-crambo' was in progress, or again, taking Mrs. Chitty and one of these figures as a separate group, the detached spectator, if mortal so hardened could exist, was reminded of that moment in the bull-fight when the matador, drawing himself up tautly, waves a flaming scarlet banner, behind which he shelters long, agonising darts, or his sword ready for the blow, in the very face of the charging bull. But now, it might be, there would be a triumphant gesture of discovery, and the miming would cease, for, as suddenly as it had vanished, the 'little bag' had materialised once more. She had been sitting on it, it appeared, or it had perhaps been in her hand the whole time, or even inside another 'little bag'. But this was by no means all her repertory, albeit it was the piece in which she most frequently presented herself. Sometimes, for instance, when in really high spirits, Mrs. Chitty would explode, as though it were a gigantic bomb, a special 'little bag', full of letters of introduction and visiting-cards. A miniature snow-storm of whirling white envelopes and oblongs of cardboard would zigzag up above us on an eddy of salt wind, and for several minutes the whole ship's company, and all the passengers well enough to be out, led by Mrs. Chitty herself, would be running along the deck together, with a frequent rhythmic halting and leaping high up into the air, until, in example of her art, this time they resembled a well-drilled corps-de-ballet under the guidance of its prima ballerina.

Indeed, so practised did all on board become at both these games, that the deck appeared to have become the sports-ground on which a number of celebrated athletes were rehearsing for some great occasion. Mrs. Chitty would make the initiatory gesture, equivalent to the revolver-shot that opens such mysteries. Before that, and quite automatically, all the men had crouched down, their bodies thrown forward, ready to start. One . . . Two . . . Three . . . Go! and now they were off! There would be a sound of rushing, a tremendous scuffling and scrambling, as they sped past. But soon the referee would make another familiar gesture and we would await the next event. Whenever, during the course of this story, we are on board ship, the reader must conjure up for himself these constantly recurring pantomimes. They were a feature of our tour.

In the interval of such games as these, Mrs. Chitty would talk to me . . . talk with her face rather close to mine, otherwise, no doubt, the words would have been lost on the disinfectant wind. She dwelt much on her illness at the Villa Sutledge (I wondered, for her eyes glowed as she spoke of it, whether she might not still boast a slight fever ?). She had, she said, in spite of that queer attack, enjoyed the visit enormously, though the Riviera did not usually appeal to her. But the garden was delightful, and Robert Sutledge was such a wonderful host. Her chief difficulty, really, had been that he was so kind, far *too* kind. She had not taken many frocks with her, for she knew that we would not want her to bring too much luggage on her travels, and, besides, dressmakers were so expensive now, and one had to be careful in these days about money. (At this point a 'little bag' broke open with the tinkling sound of a musical box, and a torrent of Greek drachmas, Turkish piastres or Syrian silver coins bounced, rolled and spun about the deck. Eventually, and by the united efforts of all in the vicinity, this particular currency was stabilised again, and Mrs. Chitty was able to continue.) About money, careful about money — Oh, yes ! she remembered now. She had been going to say — but Robert would insist on carrying her off to royal dinner-parties : and it was so awkward having to attend them without the proper clothes. She was surprised that a genius like Robert cared for that sort of entertainment. Personally, she would much have preferred to sit quietly in the garden — though, of course, it became cold at night — talking to him, or playing the piano — a little Beethoven. . . . Now she *had* enjoyed seeing the Russian dancers at Montibes — but, after all, it was not as though it amused her to meet the Grand Duke Gabriel, the ex-King of Milesia (who couldn't talk in any language, but instead barked like a dog), or the old Duchess of Chester, that guttural Guelph Amazon, however wonderful she might be for her age. . . .

Yet, as she mentioned these royal names, her whole face was illumined . . . and this, again, what could this mean, I wondered. For assuredly she was no snob. What, then, did this light of pleasure signify ? I tried to trace it, by analogy. It might, it seemed to me, have glowed in the face of a burglar after some unprecedentedly large haul, or have played round the stern, ascetic features of a missionary, who one day to his overwhelming surprise discovers that he has converted an entire tribe of natives, led by the Princes of the Blood — a tribe of which for many years now he had despaired.

We arrived at Palermo in the lime-green early morning. Then the sun came up, first gilding the two horns of the Conca d'Oro. Trucks of oranges and lemons stood near the docks, and the gaudily painted carts, drawn by straining mules, were jingling over the cobbles. We dawdled about; and after luncheon, Mrs. Chitty elaborately organised herself for a call on the Consul, while the remainder of us went up to Monreale. On the way I bought a continental edition of the *Daily Tribune*, and opened it as the tram slowly screamed up a sharp hill through a tunnel of giant red geraniums. At once my eye was caught by a heading:

SERIOUS ILLNESS OF WORLD-FAMED NOVELIST!

CRITICAL CONDITION OF ROBERT SUTLEDGE IN RIVIERA HOME

As, an hour or so later, we were still staring up at the vast gold mosaics, subtle and mysterious as Mrs. Chitty, and not unlike her in their personal style, we heard a dramatic, hollow voice, and turned round to find that she had driven up to join us. I broke to her the sad news about her friend, but she showed less surprise and dismay than I had feared. He had looked ill for some time, she said: and she imagined that his constitution was a very strong one. He did not catch things easily, she knew . . . yes, she was sure of that. Incidentally, she added, the Consul was charming. She wished we had come with her: we should have liked him. . . . He was rather a delicate-looking man (she had taken quite a fancy to him), but he had told her that Palermo was a very healthy place — practically no illness there ever.

For the next few mornings I neglected to buy a paper, and did not indeed see one for several days, since we soon set out on that wonderful journey to the Piraeus. The sun set and rose in Homeric splendour, and the purple shadows of the Greek islands fell down upon us. Mrs. Chitty was very cheerful, appeared to be enjoying herself, I thought. From the Piraeus we drove straight to our hotel in Athens. The city lay white and dusty beneath its primrose-coloured sunshine, even the bare bones up on the hill almost glittered, so strong and pulsing was the light. I tried to persuade her to come with us to the Acropolis, but she declined. She *must* call both on the British Minister and the Consul-General, she said, or Gerry Flitmouse, who had given her the letters, might be offended. He was always rather easily hurt, and snuffled terribly for months if one annoyed him. A dear boy, but delicate.

We walked up the steps that lead to the Acropolis, hot and dazed with the beauty of the light that seemed actually to glow through the tawny marble, and lingered among the huge, broken drums of the overthrown columns that litter the ground about the Parthenon. But, as we approached the great temple, our attention was drawn away from it by the sound of scampering feet, and we looked round to find a strange procession, a ribald frieze from a Greek vase come to life. It was, in fact, merely the arrival of the 'Friends of Greece' off their steamer, the *Dionysus*.

Twice a year these tours are arranged, at very high prices. The boat sets out from London, with a select list of passengers, and its own staff of attendant lecturers on board, for a course of intensive culture. They anchor for a day or two at all the places of Hellenic interest, Sicily, Corfu, the islands, on their way to Athens, and then on to Constantinople and Asia Minor. Never a morning, afternoon or evening passes without at least one instructive lecture. Most of the passengers are rich and ignorant, while others are enthusiasts who have saved up toward this trip for half a lifetime.

As they drew nearer us, the noise increased. First came a running battery of cameras, held by eager, whistling schoolboys under wide grey felt hats; then followed a succession of hatless schoolmasters — some of whom I remembered from Eton — tripping swiftly across the boulders with a curious lurching, lumbering gait as though still dribbling across the football fields: then a famous dean, with two sprained ankles, supported on the arms of numberless admirers; then an esthetic duchess caught in a cloud of gauze; now again, several deaf clergymen, a rather dingy lecturer, and finally a bevy of rich ladies, while two men wearing sun-helmets, in unspoken opposition to the schoolmasters, wound up the whole thing with an exotic flourish. To my surprise, Mrs. Chitty, looking very beautiful, with, as it seemed, an expression of religious ecstasy, only softened by her charming smile, stepped out suddenly from the middle of them. It was unlike her, for she detested crowds. . . . But she explained that she could not resist it — there were old friends of hers among them, and soon they would be leaving Athens, moving off toward numberless islands. No doubt the ship was comfortable. But it must be a rough life. . . . There was no doctor on the *Dionysus*, she was told, and not a medical man, not a single one in all those lonely isles which they were about to visit. . . .

Then she took me up to introduce me to Lady Richborough, who exuded a pale, esthetic, clipped muddle-headedness. 'Love Athens,' she was saying, 'delightful place. Like it even more than what's-the-name, you know, Muriel, that place we stopped at — but of course you weren't with us — with the large old buildings on it. And then there was that lovely island too. . . . I shall never forget it — and the Greek exchange is so good — I never can remember quite how much you get — but such a lot for a pound — better than the French exchange. . . . Do you suppose our own exchange will *ever* be so good?' After which, still pondering the possibilities disclosed by this question, we turned away.

As we left what is perhaps the most venerated skeleton in the world, I heard a delightfully modern sound. A Greek child of about seven, but with, already, an enormous scimitar of a nose, and black eyes that sparkled like new boot-buttons, was shouting, '*Dily Mile* an *Dily Tribeune* on sile — *Dily Mile* an *Dily Tribeune*'. I bought a paper. On the first page was the photograph of a familiar royal face, an iconic and dignified countenance.

SERIOUS ILLNESS OF GRAND DUKE

I read; and again:

The Grand Duke Gabriel's countless friends in England, and indeed all over the globe, will hear with full measure of sorrow that he is the victim of a new and obscure disease, which is causing the doctors grave anxiety. In its simpler aspects, it somewhat resembles influenza. Several people in the neighbourhood have recently been attacked by it, but so far there have been few fatal cases, though the illness is not one to be treated lightly.

The Grand Duchess, four nurses and His Imperial Highness's

six physicians-in-ordinary are in constant attendance, day and night. Letters and telegrams of inquiry, many of them from Great Britain, and requests for the latest bulletin on the distinguished patient, arrive without intermission at the door of Nishkynashdom, his palatial Riviera residence. The Grand Duchess, who has been a tower of strength in the sick-room, has helped the doctors in countless ways, though it is not as yet generally known that Her Royal Highness has adopted the uniform of a nurse and has abandoned her proposed exhibition of water-colours.

His Imperial Highness, who has been a well-known and popular figure on the Côte d'Azur for half a century, is seventy-eight years of age, and married in 1871 a Princess of Mannheim-Düsseldorf. He is also President of the Mont-Ferrat Golf Club and the Société Anonyme des Agronomes de Nice, the corporation responsible for running the New Casino outside the town.

Further down, in a chat-column, I read:

Hopes are still entertained, Delilah writes me from the Riviera, that Robert Sutledge, England's most famous novelist, will be well enough to come home in two or three weeks' time. It would be little less than a tragedy for his friends were he obliged to abandon his famous annual visit, for which an immense amount of entertaining takes place: but it is, alas, no secret to them that, for the past ten days, he has been very seriously ill.

I drew Mrs. Chitty's attention to the illness of the Grand Duke Gabriel.

'How very odd,' she said to me, with a bayonet-like glint in her usually warm eye. 'So soon after poor Robert, too. It looks almost as if they must have caught the same germ, doesn't it? Perhaps I had it also. I felt very ill at the time, but wouldn't give up. I've always said, "If you want people to be ill, go with them to the Riviera." By the way, I think I must have had a slight temperature again last night.'

The next few days in Athens passed very swiftly and without event, except that Muriel Chitty, who insisted, apparently, on sleeping without a mosquito-net, was, in consequence, very badly bitten. It was curious, for usually she was so careful, even fussy about herself; and we had advised her to be on her guard . . . yet she was the only one of us to suffer in this way.

The passage to Constantinople was ideal. We arrived safely, and were duly astonished at the number of bowler-hats:

but even that could not destroy our excitement, or the beauty of the setting: the water on every side, and the silhouette of numberless, grey, spider-like domes, very squat under their needle-shaped minarets, that crept over every hill, and crowned the lower ones.

Mrs. Chitty decided that she felt too tired to visit Santa Sofia, and that, instead, she would rest a little and then leave letters for, and call on, the British Representatives. She might, perhaps, meet us afterwards — somewhere in the town — perhaps near the Delphic Serpent. . . . And indeed as, later, we looked at it, lost in wonder at its long and marvellous history, a hollow, oracular voice, with all the ecstasy of divination in its tones, woke us from our reveries by exclaiming just behind us:

'Well, here I am. . . . But you none of you look very well . . . I hope you're all right?'

It was Mrs. Chitty, fresh from consular triumphs.

While I was waiting in the hotel before dinner I saw, lying on a table, a new copy of the *Daily Tribune*, just arrived. I opened it.

SUDDEN ILLNESS OF EX-KING BORIS OF MILESIA

was the caption that met my eye.

ALL ENGAGEMENTS CANCELLED

His Ex-Majesty was suddenly seized with illness after attending, as is his wont, the Friday 'Dîner Fleuri' at the Hôtel de Bordeaux. His companion, Mlle Donescu, immediately summoned a doctor.

On the next page I read:

SEVERANCE OF LAST LINK WITH GEORGE III

DEATH OF H.R.H. THE DUCHESS OF CHESTER

We regret to announce the death of H.R.H. the Duchess of Chester, who passed away peacefully in the presence of her family during the early hours of this morning. The sad event took place at her marine residence, the Villa Britannique. Her Royal Highness, who was in her 92nd year, was the last surviving granddaughter of George III, and with her passing a notable link with the past is for ever severed. The Duchess, always one of the most beloved of English princesses, was a wonderful specimen of English grit of the

Old School. During the war, though then in her 81st year, she spent several days in the trenches, distributing chocolates to the men, and even in the tightest corners contrived to keep a stiff upper lip. Deservedly popular with all classes, it was Her Royal Highness who popularised the word 'Schweinhunds' for the German troops during the war.

It is worth recording, as an instance of this wonderful old lady's undiminished activity and interest in all that pertained to literature up to the last, that only three weeks ago she attended a dinner-party in her honour given by Mr. Robert Sutledge, the novelist (now, unfortunately, himself an invalid). During the evening, Her Royal Highness, who loved everything modern, gave an exhibition of her skill on the saxophone. Accompanied, on the piano, by her Lady-in-Waiting, she played Liszt's 'Liebestraum', Mendelssohn's 'Spring Song', and ended up, amid great applause, with 'You're the Whitest White I know', and her own rendering of the 'Black Bottom'. Two days later Her Royal Highness was suddenly taken ill, and the doctors, seeing that the end could not long be delayed, summoned the family.

I showed these three paragraphs to Mrs. Chitty when she came down.

'Quite a coincidence,' she observed bitterly. . . .

And these words, it seemed to me, were addressed to myself rather than to my companions; were spoken, moreover, as though she thought they might convey to me an inner significance hidden from others.

'No wonder you were ill, Muriel darling,' I heard Mrs. Rammond say to her. 'I've always maintained that the Riviera was unhealthy: a perfect death-trap. Think of the microbes there must be hanging about those hotels and villas, not to mention casinos! It's extraordinary, though, this year. Absolutely everybody there seems to be ill.'

But at this, though it did not very much differ from the sentiment herself had expressed at Athens only a few days before, Mrs. Chitty suddenly became cross. (Perhaps, one thought, the mosquito-bites were still irritating her, making her sleepless.) She dropped two bags, half an earring and a diamond pendant, and so, for a time, her conversation was lost to me. As, however, we emerged from under our various tables, she was saying very decisively, and in a tone of voice which suggested that she considered herself slighted: 'Well, all I can tell you is, there was no one ill there before I arrived: no one. I was the first — and probably most of them aren't ill even now. They are a regular pack of old *malades imaginaires*: that's what *they* are. If they were to become really ill, goodness knows what would happen to them!'

Our time at Constantinople fled past us, with little personal to record except that it seemed to me that every day, as she was further removed in hours and miles from home, Mrs. Chitty became ever more feminine — but in a distinctly Victorian, rather than modern, way. It was there, too, and more specially in Brousa, that she first began to parade her ardent love for animals. There were several vociferous and vituperative differences between herself and the drivers of donkeys. The Turkish language won, for its throaty sounds suggested, even to those who could not understand them, a wealth of obloquy not to be attempted in English or French. But Mrs. Chitty was left with that comforting, unimpeachable serenity which comes to all those who defend dumb brutes.

Borne on by blue phanariot breezes, that yet hardly ruffled the surface, we visited in turn Rhodes and Cyprus. Here, again, there was little to record. At Rhodes, an island that rises from a sea paved with medieval stone cannon-balls, we found great activity among the restorers and strippers of ancient buildings, while huge white peonies, like water-lilies, were in bloom under the darkest shade of cedars. Furthermore, as we approached this much-conquered island, we heard an American lady summing up the confusion of our epoch by inquiring of her companion in a plaintive voice, 'Tell me, dear, where *used* this to be?'

At Cyprus, on the contrary, we discovered a British island, full of discontented, undersized Levantines, gorged on honest British beef and suet. No building had been restored, but there were hill-stations and topees, and the ponderous red shadow of India brooded over the western hills and streams.

But the journey seemed to suit our health. We all felt peculiarly well — generally a bad omen — and even Mrs. Chitty's mosquito-bites were healing. She liked the place, and while calling on various officials, had met the Anglican Bishop and made great friends with him, she said.

Sailing from Famagusta to Beirut, however, the sea suddenly began to grow rough again: and soon Mrs. Chitty, my brother and myself were once more the only members of our party to venture on deck. But on this occasion she was not so communicative; seemed lost in her own thoughts. Yet we could not help being impressed, and rather intimidated, by a new and singular manner of looking at one which at this time she developed. It was a steady, unfaltering brown gaze that united the watchfulness of a doctor expectant of symptoms with the frigid, measuring, detached glance of an undertaker: a gaze that one could never afterwards forget.

When, though rarely, she talked, she would tell us of the south of France. Perpetually she reverted to it: to the kindness and subsequent illness of Mr. Sutledge, to the dinner-parties she had attended, the Royal Personages she had met. It was unlike her. César Franck or changes in the Foreign Office would have been more usual, more in style. . . . But no! Back we would go to the Riviera. Really, I said to myself, it was as though she had committed some murder there, among the planted-out and varnished palm-trees, the carefully manicured carnations (each one was stated to be given its own hot-water bottle at night), and must ever return in spirit to haunt the scene of it. She resembled those poisoners who, though their guilt has passed quite unsuspected at the time, inevitably attract attention and are in the end caught because they insist on revisiting of their own free will the spot where their evil deed was perpetrated, to inquire, too innocently, of the police whether anyone had died in the neighbourhood? Or again, one said, she behaved as if, with some atrocious crime on her conscience, she thought that I had guessed her share in it: and so, partly out of bravado, partly because it was a subject that quite genuinely she could never banish from her mind for an instant, and partly moreover to test how much I knew, and to try to trap me into some speech, look or action which would betray that knowledge, she would, and with a show of indifference, continually persist in talking of the lonely village where it had taken place, boasting how often she had been there and how well she knew it.

At Beirut we had intended only to spend an hour or two, just long enough for Mrs. Chitty to call on the Consul (how *could* it amuse her, I wondered, for she was very tired?) and then to drive on at once to Damascus. Nevertheless, we were delayed a little, for since she was determined to see him personally, in the end we were all invited to tea. The conversation was rather formal: but I heard her ask him in anxious tones whether there was much illness in Syria at this season? None at all, he replied.

In Damascus, on arrival, I bought a copy of the *Daily Tribune*, despatched by air from Paris. There was nothing very new in it. The body of H.R.H. the Duchess of Chester had been carried on board an English battleship, with the customary honours, and was to be conveyed to a final resting-place in her native land. Another column informed us that ex-King Boris of Milesia was making a plucky fight against an insidious and treacherous foe. He had now been ill for many days. His pulse was feeble, his temperature high. Robert Sutledge was, it appeared, still in bed: in fact, had experienced a slight relapse, and his friends continued to suffer much anxiety for him. About the condition of H.I.H. the Grand Duke Gabriel there was an ominous silence.

Mrs. Chitty had been somewhat dejected, and had complained of feeling ill in Damascus (though I think she enjoyed seeing the ruins which mark the French occupation of that city): so I did not show her the paper until we were on board the steamer bound for Alexandria. I had feared the news in it would depress her still further, but she took it well, and became quite cheerful.

One morning, while we were on the boat, she turned to me, and with an intensity of emphatic meaning in her voice, asked, 'Do you know Valaise?' I replied, no, I didn't. 'Well, that's a pity, a great pity,' she rejoined. 'It's such a lovely little place, on the hills just above Beaulieu. I drove there several times with Robert Sutledge. An old Saracen village; just a cluster of white houses with flattened domes. You'd adore it. . . . But I shouldn't say it was healthy . . . a lot of illness there, I'm sure.' And suddenly she laughed, looking at me as though she expected me to join in her cryptic mirth.

It was this significant confidence, as a matter of fact, which finally gave me the clue. We disembarked at Alexandria and, as soon as Mrs. Chitty had left her letters of introduction, proceeded to Cairo. The next morning I remembered to buy a copy of the *Daily Tribune*. I opened it and read — right across the top of the paper:

RIVIERA VILLAGE DECIMATED

OUTBREAK OF MYSTERY DISEASE AT VALAISE

For a moment all the things that in bad novels are said to happen at such a crisis happened to me together. I was struck speechless; the print danced before my eyes; my teeth chattered; my hair stood on end; I felt I had an iron band round my forehead; there were icy shivers down my spine; and the very blood in my veins ran cold — for at last I understood. Everything explained itself; I understood only too well. Mrs. Chitty was no longer a woman, but merely the living vessel that contained a microbe, a versatile master-microbe who never repeated himself. She was the fully disciplined, loyal slave of this ferocious and tyrannical germ; the medium for a single-purposed and evil control. She was a person possessed, not, as in the old sense, by a demon, but instead by a bacillus — albeit one of very phenomenal power and completeness. It was thus a physical, not a spiritual possession. The only aim of the governing organism within, and of its innumerable progeny, was to procreate and spread still further. Toward this one purpose, every cough, every movement, every decision that Mrs. Chitty made was calculated: but though to every act she imparted the appearance of free-will, all she did depended, in reality, on the secret wishes and plans of this inner and invisible dictator. Why, her very resolve to join us on this journey, what was that but another scheme for propagation? For this tour was no ordinary one, but the brave missionary voyage of a militant and proselytising microbe; a journey equivalent to the first Mediterranean mission of St. Paul.

And of course . . . I realised it now: she was, from this point of view, at once the ideal means of transit, the best possible laboratory for experiment, and a model breeding-ground and nursery for young germs. Delicate enough always to harbour them, she was yet too weak, too thin and nervous, her blood too impoverished, to afford continual sustenance for so mighty and immeasurable a tribe. An imperialist bacillus, ambitious for the future of his race, could find no land that would offer so perfect an upbringing and training-place for the young as did Mrs. Chitty. Just as the sparse diet, hard work and meagre earnings which Nature enforces there, compel the

Japanese nation, heaped up on its rocky, barren and picturesque isles, to seek fresh lands for its surplus but very hardy population, so Mrs. Chitty's spare and bony frame, though unable to support the countless progeny of microbes it had raised so frugally, taught them to be all the more self-reliant and courageous. They were forced to find a new outlet for their energy, and became adventurous, crusading, piratical as our forefathers of Queen Elizabeth's reign, would execute with gusto the most daring raids on stronger and more active people, would seize colonies, found an empire. But here all parallels stop short, and the microbes clearly have the advantage of men. For Mrs. Chitty was their magic carpet as well as Motherland. While the English and the Japanese are forced to emigrate from their emerald isles set in the sapphire sea, are forced to go long journeys by boat, the microbes are conveyed to the very portals of each promised land, not by a ship, but by their own country itself. Think of what that must mean. How little compared with us will they feel the severance of home-ties! Imagine the interest and change implied for the entire population, if England could travel each year to Canada and India! Mrs. Chitty was truly the land in which to raise a breed of heroes, an imperial race.

Nor need this moving, living Motherland ever fear revolution, be afraid lest her children should turn against or seek to harm her. Even if they attempted it, they could not kill her, for she was not full-blooded enough to kill. Moreover, brought up within her, they cherished a true sentiment of loyalty toward their home and must be aware, withal, that her every thought was for the furtherance of their cause since she still placed herself at the entire disposal of the governing germ.

And how every idiosyncrasy in her character, every action of hers, notwithstanding that it may have seemed erratic and without purpose at the moment — became clear and rational under this sudden apocalyptic illumination, declared itself beyond doubt as part of the wily and Machiavellian scheming from which the hidden control never ceased, for it worked remorselessly day and night. In the same way that the painted ceilings of certain Italian eighteenth-century churches — such as San Pantaleone in Venice or Sant' Ignacio in Rome — at first appear to the stranger as a meaningless muddle of distorted architecture, puffy clouds and inflated goddesses, until he is led to one small circle in the centre of the marble floor, and looking up, is now able to behold the roof opening up like a flower, blossoming into a strange, miraculous, but yet quite logical and lovely world of its own, so, once one had gained the clue to its perspective, the planning and arrangement of Mrs. Chitty's life became quite simple and easily comprehended. For example, if you were a modern-minded, rather hustling germ (a real 'go-getter' as the American phrase is) who wanted to get about the world a bit, and quicker than Mrs. Chitty could take you, what better instrument could you find for this constant voyaging than a member of His Majesty's Diplomatic or Consular Services? No wonder that Mrs. Chitty loved those that dwell in Foreign Offices and took so lively an interest in every swop and promotion: no wonder that she called on every Minister and every Consul in each town abroad she visited, and, in addition, left on them letters, the envelopes of which she had fastened, sticking down the flap, and thus personally infecting them, with her own tongue! Then, too, I recalled the talk at her dinner-parties — conversations that so often turned on the newest mode of combating, and, if possible, extirpating, the influenza and kindred microbes. And all the time, these methods, and the experiments that led up to them, things on which science had concentrated so much toil and hope, were being explained to one who was not only Mother, home and country to these actual microbes, but, as well, an immense and living testing-ground for their researches, a laboratory in which they were continually engaged in the most lively counter-experiments.

III

The position was in all truth serious enough. For several days two members of our party had been ill, though their symptoms differed. Ruth Marlow had a temperature that raced up and down continually, and was forced to live entirely on orange juice. Julian Thackwray complained that he had a headache that nearly blinded him, that he could only see half of the palm-trees and pyramids, that his right arm was quite numb and that he had lost the use of the index finger of his left hand. Obviously, then, the germs were in active and experimental mood, and who could tell what novel and acute diseases they would not leave in their wake after the first alarm had subsided? The doctor, called in, pronounced it to be 'only influenza'. 'Only', indeed!

I took precautions, bought cinnamon, bottles and bottles of it, eucalyptus oil, gargles of every description, quinine and a thousand disinfectants. And thenceforth it seemed to me that Mrs. Chitty's Theotocopulos-like and lachrymose eye reflected very clearly the new consciousness of her protean master-microbe within that myself was his chief enemy, and that, in so far as I was concerned, he was in for the battle of a lifetime, a fight to a finish. I cannot think that this was conceit, or that I was in any way exaggerating my own importance. No, he was a good sportsman, and recognised that by nature, as much as now of intention, I was going to be a particularly rare and difficult bag . . . indeed, he had foreseen it long before I had discovered Mrs. Chitty's mission . . . and that was, no doubt, why she had so often sat on deck with me and talked: for to be heard above the winds that, born from its speed, leap and play like dolphins round any ship, it is necessary for those who converse to bring their heads near together; a splendid opportunity for infection.

Meanwhile one must not despair. The news in the paper the day after my revelation a little allayed concern. The account of the progress of the Grand Duke Gabriel was reassuring. I read:

H.I.H. THE GRAND DUKE GABRIEL

His Imperial Highness's many friends will be relieved to hear that his medical advisers are confident that, should no new complications arise (and, of course, it must be remembered that even now it is impossible to rule out such possibilities; that to estimate the likelihood of such developments, the length of time during which the Royal patient has been ill must always be borne in mind), His Imperial Highness should be out of danger in another two months' time. A week ago he recognised the Grand Duchess for the first time (she was in nurse's uniform), and though still suffering from shock, he was well enough yesterday to be propped up in bed, and to enjoy the broadcasting of his favourite song, Tosti's 'Good-bye'. He also received the latest shipping-signals from Rio de Janeiro and Vladivostok. His Imperial Highness is now encouraged to take proper nourishment, and was yesterday ordered half a glass of hot milk with a dash of the national beverage, vodka, in it.

One was glad to see, too, that Robert Sutledge had survived his relapse and was now really 'making headway'. It was hoped that in another week or two, if he continued to recuperate with the same speed as heretofore, and if the present fine weather held, he might be allowed to sit out in the garden for half an hour.

On the other hand the mystery epidemic at Valaise showed no sign of abating, and the Rockefeller Institute had despatched scientists to study the outbreak on the spot and draw up a report upon it. The remains of H.R.H. the Duchess of Chester, borne on a battleship, escorted by four cruisers, had arrived at Southampton, and there was a description of the Municipal Brass Band playing the 'Last Post' as the Death Ship drew in to the harbour of a city hung with funebrial purple.

What was to be done? There was no time to be lost. . . . I determined to confide in Mrs. Rammond and my brother. They were the ones I most wished to save from the holocaust. At first they did not take my discovery very seriously, terming it 'ridiculous' and 'fantastic'. Ruth and Julian were soon able to move about again, and it was now supposed that they had caught a 'mere chill'. But both of them protested that they were still desperately ill, and almost paralysed. Mrs. Chitty herself had not been idle. She, too, had achieved a racing temperature but, though she owned that she felt desperate, was determined to see everything, and not to '*give in*': quite a new development on her part, for hitherto she had absented herself from any sight-seeing expeditions and had harboured all her strength for calling on Consuls. But now she tramped tirelessly through the heat, while, in addition, continuing to visit every possible British Representative, diplomatic, consular, military, or naval.

Ruth and Julian seemed well enough to accompany us, and we were just about to start our trip up the Nile on the dahabiya, when Mrs. Jocelyn and Frank Lancing collapsed, and were taken to the British Hospital. But as soon as we had seen the new invalids comfortably established there and had been assured that they were at present in no actual danger, we thought it best to proceed with our original plan. However, the fate of our two friends depressed the party considerably, and Mrs. Rammond and my brother began to treat more seriously the theory I had advanced to them.

On the dahabiya the situation became acute. Since Mrs. Chitty now fully recognised in me her microbe's chief antagonist, she sat by me whenever possible . . . and still there were no signs of my ailing. Obviously the new offensive, to the preparation of which her germ had devoted so many anxious months of careful experiment and audacious imagination, was failing, was breaking down. (So it must have seemed to her.) The microbe was not, after all, invincible: and a bitter sense of disappointment must have swept down on her. Certain it is that under the charm, of which she could not divest herself, fear and hatred could be seen mingling in her poignant glance, and that the prolonged and cheerful sound of gargling which ostentatiously issued from my cabin constituted to her ears a most melancholy and distressing music. Perhaps the best thing she could do, she must have thought, was to turn her attention to my brother. But, here again, she was checked and, apparently, crushed. There we sat, under brown awnings that never stirred, and watched each sunset unroll its panorama of coloured-picture-postcard tints; palm-trees, springing lithely, several stalks from one root, camels silhouetting themselves vulgarly against an oily red-yellow sunset — a sunset that had never progressed since the oriental paintings popular during the Second Empire — or else narrow-waisted figures moving through a fertile field in short white tunics and with long, shaven heads, performing against it their second-rate hieroglyphs and bas-reliefs, while the alligators thawed to movement in the sticky yellow water beneath us. . . . But as each sunset died away in cheap flames, and then remained for an instant a stain upon the luminous canopy, faded away, as it were, with the last self-conscious if well-practised bow, of a famous prima donna acknowledging her applause, Mrs. Chitty, though not yet giving up hope, became sadder and ever more sad. . . . But, since fortune is so fickle, one who does not admit defeat is never defeated. Now a change occurred, and Fate unmistakably declared itself for her. The crew suddenly fell ill, and, because they were natives, unused to any such northern infection, with them it took a much more severe form.

At one moment it looked as if we might have to work the ship back to Cairo ourselves. The invalid members of the crew now lay on the deck, under canopies, with Mrs. Chitty looking after them, while we sweated in the miniature engine-room and were instructed by a survivor or two in their hot and oily trade. We began to grow nervous. Cut off from the outside world as we were, and overwhelmed by the microbe's unexpected and very decisive victory, we could not help wondering what new developments might not be taking place, might not greet us on our somewhat problematic return? But, in sweet content, Mrs. Chitty sat on deck, gently tending the sick, and smiling. It was, indeed, a smile altogether beautiful to behold, a smile of pure, kindly joy, of a spirit uplifted, such, one would have said, as might have lighted up the austere features of Florence Nightingale when, rustling through the wards at night, shading the lamp with her hand, she looked down on all those whom she had saved. And near the surface of the thick yellow water, the alligators, too, bared their sharp teeth in a subtle but appreciative grin, and played and tumbled quite lustily.

The crew behaved, as it turned out, very well, and contrived to get us back to Cairo. There we found the two patients out of hospital. It was true that they were so weak they could scarcely drag themselves along, so tired that they could see and understand nothing, so poisoned after their illness that even cigarettes were no solace to them, but they were alive: that was the important thing. And as — for it was, naturally enough, at that moment the only thing that interested them — they discussed how possibly, and where, they could have contracted this infection and, without any suspicion of the identity of the link that connected the two things, happened to observe that they had read in the newspapers at the hospital that there was a good deal of this same sort of odd illness on the Riviera, once again I saw a smile, but of a different kind from that we have just described, play quietly round Mrs. Chitty's ascetic and thoughtful countenance. It was the smile that had so often perplexed me in the past; an enigmatic and beautiful curling of the mouth, which seemed as though, after the manner of the Gioconda's, it had been summoned up by the sound of hidden and distant flutes.

For many days I had seen no newspaper, and it was evident,

we die', was the motto engraved on our, as on their, hearts. There, then, we sat on, recklessly quaffing the flowing bowl of quinine, and wantonly sprinkling our cubes of sugar with camphor and eucalyptus, until the early hours of the morning — notwithstanding that the feathers of the palm-trees which lay motionless on the air above us were the only plumes, and the sound of the heavy and inexorable snoring that issued from Mrs. Chitty's tent was the sole and rather menacing music afforded us for our feasting. Indeed this rhythmic rising and falling announced all too plainly that the germ was still on the march; almost amounted to a solemn declaration of new hostilities.

The days passed and still we held on. Mrs. Chitty perhaps now felt genuinely ill, for she was again becoming desperate. As we advanced further into the desert, her Victorian helplessness was manifested more and more often. It was no easy matter to find the English or Libyan coins that she scattered in such thoughtless profusion among the golden grains which lay spread round us for hundreds of miles: and many an hour we passed, hot and tired, scratching and grubbing in the sand like so many animals burrowing, until a miniature sandstorm was raised about us, while Muriel Chitty sat a little way off, continually repining. . . .

The weather, she said, was cold. She had always expected the desert to be hot. She wished she had brought another fur coat with her (just a little one, like the one I was holding): except that she thought the desert must be full of moths, for, she added with a slightly malicious smile, she continually smelt camphor — she supposed it must be against moths, for it was entirely useless against anything else. . . . The palm-trees were ugly, the sunsets monotonous, the camels lazy — they were always lying down — and greedy; though she had always felt sorry for them hitherto, because they looked so long-legged, round-backed and awkward; and she was sure they were badly treated. She didn't like the faces of the camel-drivers, wouldn't trust them, wouldn't trust them an inch, herself. Perhaps it was as well that one did not understand what they were talking about. For what did all the natives eat? One couldn't eat dates for ever. And then the water — she was sure that the drinking water in the oases was not *reliable*: but she could not drink mineral water because it contained no camphor and quinine, began to fail for a day or two — and then fell victim. Like a hero he stuck to his post. Even when finally overwhelmed, he refused to acknowledge defeat. Mrs. Chitty was, naturally, the first of us to notice the symptoms. To her it was like watching a race with the prospect of an exciting finish. Her colours were ahead now. Daily she became more worked up. It was certain, too, she must have supposed, that Mrs. Rammond and I would catch it. . . . The desert: the *wonderful, wonderful* desert. There was, she reflected, something incredibly beautiful and romantic about it — what glamour! Doughty, and all those slow, eternal camels, and the Arabs, such dignity, and palm-trees and Colonel Lawrence and all that. . . . Wonderful. . . . But Mrs. Rammond and I were without hope and drank cinnamon without end.

In the few, recurrent, lucid moments which his illness granted him every day, my brother explained to us the precise nature of the microbe's ravages. The sensation, he told us, was comparable to being knocked on the head and drowned simultaneously. Only for about five minutes a day, just long enough to realise how sweet life could have been, was he permitted to come up to the surface, take a few breaths, and then, once more, he was sent spinning down again into the depths. He could walk, even talk a little — but automatically, as though he were in a trance. For the rest, there was an intense aching in the roots of his hair, shooting pains in the eyes, slight deafness, acute anguish between the vertebrae, pains in the toes, a perfect agony in the lobe of each ear and a sense of partial paralysis in the left hand. This journey was something to which for a whole decade he had eagerly looked forward, as to something transcendent and unattainable, and here he was being whirled through the desert (for at Sidi-ben-Sidi we had met our car) in a state of unconsciousness, or, at best, of semi-consciousness.

Her horse, Mrs. Chitty must have thought, was just rounding Tattenham Corner; but on the contrary, the invalid came to, suddenly after a week, to find himself in the large native city of Abu-ben-Kalab. We were staying in a little white hotel, owned by a Greek. It was very clean, and had a quite pretty garden which, by an extraordinary stroke of luck, was planted with such trees and shrubs as eucalyptus, camphor and castor-oil. Moreover, in one corner of it there even flourished a cinnamon-bush. Out of this shady and restful grey-greenness, aromatic and health-giving breaths were wafted on every slightest fluttering breeze. From the first moment Mrs. Chitty evinced a particular aversion to this spot, declaring that when she was in a garden, she liked to *feel* she was in one, and not in a chemist's shop.

The town itself was fascinating, I thought. For hours you could wander round the *souks* — the light falling through the branches that roofed them to dapple and splash the bearded, bartering figures beside the stalls — without feeling a moment's fatigue, so new and alive was the scene. In the public places one could listen to poetry being declaimed, with an accompaniment of gourds and gongs, to an entranced circle of yellow-faced, squatting figures. And sometimes, too, one could hear tall, lank Senegalese minstrels, the colour of black-lead and wearing necklaces of cowrie shells, singing their high-pitched songs, see dancers, belonging to the unknown tribes that inhabit the interior of the continent, whirling round feverishly in a cloud of white dust, or watch the dark mountebanks from distant Marrakesh performing their grotesque and epicene antics. Such was the fascination of the city, strange and varied. But Mrs. Chitty liked it no better than the garden. There was not a Minister in the place — not even a consul; no European shops, no papers (so that it was impossible, she said, to tell what was going on. Everyone in England might have the plague itself, and one would not know about it.)

It was a complete transformation. This subtle lady, who at home was intensely cosmopolitan, eschewing English phrases wherever possible, and substituting for them Foreign Office *clichés* in French, German and Italian, was each day becoming more English, more Victorian. As though in an effort to sum up her own tendencies, she asked me one day to go into the town and find her a bottle of Rowlands' Macassar Oil — the very sound of which conjured up in my imagination ottomans, crinolines, double-jointed little parasols edged with black lace, beaded flowers, plush chairs, draped table-legs, soft, sentimental whiskers and curling, pomaded locks. . . . Assuredly this was not the place to choose for such a whimsy. Nor, perhaps, ought one to have encouraged a caprice so exotic in this place and century, unless one was certain (and this was improbable) that it was comparable to the longing for a 'dish of apricocks' entertained by Webster's Duchess of Malfi. However, Mrs. Chitty's eagerness was so pathetic that, though fully aware of the futility of my errand, I tramped up and down the *souks* for hours, searching for this strange and ancient elixir. And hereafter at every village, however small, and even if entirely composed of wattle-huts, I was asked to get out and look for it.

At Abu-ben-Kalab, it was, withal, that the ever-increasing feeling of fondness for animals that she paraded reached a point that was unpleasant and even dangerous in its consequences, as much for them as for ourselves.

It cannot, I am afraid, be disputed that the natives of these regions ill-treat their animals, though I do know to what extent this neglect or brutality can be palliated by the fact that there live, not so far away, great numbers of dangerous and disagreeable beasts — lions, leopards, apes and crocodiles — and that the men themselves, or their not-far-distant ancestors, have suffered cruelly at their paws and teeth. Meanwhile, in the interior of the continent the dusky brothers of these men — and the brothers of these animals — still wage against one another a grim and endless warfare. This must, if one comes to think of it, alter the human attitude toward other creatures. In England, it is the animal which has to be afraid: all the ferocious creatures of our country, fox, stag and otter, hares, pheasants, rabbits, ordinary field-mice and guinea-pigs, must by now have learnt their lesson. But to ignorant Africans an animal, even a domestic animal living among them, is regarded much as an interned German was regarded in England during the war. Not a word it says is understood, and its every action ought to be regarded with suspicion, as part of a plot: nor would it seem fair, they might urge in conversation with us, to be too kind, too generous with food to these brutes, whose brothers and cousins are killing our relatives and co-religionists the other side of the Atlas.

Mrs. Chitty naturally did not share or indeed comprehend these feelings, so different from our own. Apart from mice, she had no enemies or rivals in the animal world, and was horrified at the African outlook on brute beasts. She therefore secretly resolved to buy a few of the worst-treated animals, and undertook a self-appointed pilgrimage of pity round the town, guided and advised by a black and evil interpreter. Unfortunately, as we learnt afterward, whereas she never made an offer for a whole, unmaimed, unscarred and well-fed animal, she was willing to offer comparatively fabulous sums for any halt, maimed, starved, wounded, scarred or diseased mule or donkey. This was disastrous. Even those Arabs who had hitherto been kind to their animals, had been governed in this rather by financial than moral principles. A healthy, well-fed brute had been, up till Mrs. Chitty's advent, a paying proposition. But now it was so no longer. Her motives eluded them, and they very logically concluded that here was a mad-millionaire-white-woman with an unhealthy passion for seeing animals suffer. And since their faith taught them that, while both women and animals have no souls, Allah inspires the insane, and because life had taught them that gold was necessary to men, it seemed only right — and certainly good business — to gratify her curious desires. Thus, it appears, all night they would sit up, ill-treating their unfortunate beasts, kicking and beating them, inflicting hellish and ingenious tortures upon them, in order to be able in the morning to extort a good price from her. A suffering mule was now worth ten, twenty times even, a healthy, happy one. Acute speculation in sick animals set in: there were, of course, fluctuations, but, on the whole, it was a steady, rising market. The results were lamentable and heart-rending.

Ignorant of that which had been in progress, we returned to the hotel one day, after an expedition, to find it besieged by a mob of eager, shouting natives, determined to sell Mrs. Chitty their tortured beasts; for it had somehow become known that we were leaving the next morning. Flocks and flocks of suffering and ill-tempered creatures, including a number of gigantic, knock-kneed and macerated camels, and crowds of jostling, bargaining, jabbering, quarrelling natives, all wrapped in a suffocating cloud of thick, white dust, surrounded the building. The proprietor was at the same time both furious and in a panic. He protested that all the guests were leaving, his business was ruined, and the authorities accused him of attempting to stir up sedition among the natives. Mrs. Chitty began, in her turn, to grow equally angry. (That Rowlands' Macassar Oil was unattainable only made matters worse.) Moreover we were forced to speak to her, however gently, about the suffering to dumb animals that her kindness was causing. And personally, though I did not permit myself to tell her so, when I considered how little she allowed the ills of human beings to count with her as against the welfare of her microbe, when I reflected on her indiscriminate massacres in the south of France, her attitude genuinely shocked me.

Nothing we could say would melt that heart. She only grew more resolute, more obstinate. And even if, on this occasion, the very abundance of the sick beasts defeated her, she never subsequently lost a chance of repeating her conduct. Only their price limited her opportunities of well-doing: for each day their cost increased. It is surprising how swiftly news travels in these dark, intuitive lands, and all round Africa spread the legend, ever more exaggerated, of the immensely rich, mad, white woman, with her strange *penchant*: until in Guinea and the Gold Coast, Dahomey, Ashanti, Benin and the Congo it was rumoured that she was on her way, and the naked, grinning figures dancing round the fire spared the last missionary, abandoned their cannibal feasts, in order that they might rush to their kraals and prepare their animals for her coming. It might be, even, that she would give them a string of glass beads, a bottle of whisky or a pocket-knife in exchange! And they set to work with a will. Thus, perhaps, some may consider that in the end she did good: for in the excitement many human beings were saved, though the animals suffered.

As my brother grew stronger, and Mrs. Rammond and myself remained immune, Mrs. Chitty began visibly to pine. Her respect for us had, I think, increased. She would now take the greatest trouble to prevent one from discovering what plans she was maturing, what manœuvres she had already carried out. Her craving for Macassar continued unabated, but she found out how to make a use of it. Let us assume that, without my knowledge, she had effected some tremendous bargain — a donkey, perhaps, so ill that it had died in the night — and that, in her anxiety to dispose of the body, she had reached the conclusion that the best thing for her to do was to have it tied on with the luggage at the back of the car. Before we started, then, she would lament the Macassar famine, and would be so charming (and her charm was ever irresistible), would allow such a wealth of pathos to creep into the hollow but musical tones of her voice, and such a deep well of tears unshed to shine in her eyes, that of my own accord, and without the slightest suspicion of what was on hand, I would volunteer to search the village for the magic Macassar. Tired, hot and footsore, I would limp back to find the car ready, Mrs. Chitty, swathed in veils and rugs, comfortably enshrined there, and behind it, neatly rolled and folded up on the top of the luggage, a grey and furry carcase.

'I thought we might leave it somewhere on the way', she would urge. 'Perhaps, if we could find a pretty spot, you wouldn't mind digging a grave for it? Nothing elaborate, just a plain grave. It's very good exercise, and you don't look too well. They have no proper animal cemeteries here. It's a disgrace!'

We passed a night or two on the way and then arrived — truly it was one of the chief attractions of the whole of our long journey — at Ali-Sid-Ali, that great native city only recently opened up to tourists. Capital, shrine and trading centre in one, it is a place of pilgrimage for all Mohammedan Africa, yet this sanctity is not allowed to interfere with the ever-growing volume of business transacted with Europe. The hotel, too, is a fine and new one, and after so much rough travelling it was most agreeable to be in such comfortable quarters. But, alas, worry returned with civilisation, for we found a telegram waiting for us to announce that our four friends in Cairo were back in hospital, seriously ill.

Though she had brought with her a letter of introduction to the British Consul-General, Mrs. Chitty, to our surprise, for once failed to deliver it in person. She, or rather her microbe, was evidently engaged in devising a different system of tactics. . . . Mrs. Rammond and myself were still in good health, my brother was fully recovered. Such a state of things could not be allowed to go on. Something *must* be done. Accordingly, she went to bed, immediately evolved one of her racing temperatures, and during several days made brave endeavours to consume our whole stock of medicines. This, doubtless she felt, would put her in a better position for developing her new offensive. But I had a hidden reserve of cinnamon and quinine, and thus she found herself unable to exhaust our supplies. Indeed, I think that so great was the quantity of these drugs which her new scheme of tactics forced her to swallow, that in all truth she began to feel ill. Certainly her temperature touched unprecedented heights. Meanwhile, she had posted her letter of introduction to the Consul-General and had explained in a letter of her own, enclosing it, that she was unwell, most unwell.

The atmosphere of Ali-Sid-Ali at this season was most fanatic. It was the fast of Ramadan, and the Mussulmans could be heard, in every direction, knocking their muffled heads against the marble floors of the mosques, while the holy dancers gyrated wildly round the street corners. The muezzin singers were in most formidable, if beautiful, voice: and at night, all night, a sonorous music, a deep bass chanting that was ominous and extremely impressive, conveyed continually the glory of Allah to every nook of the city, and floated above the flat roofs up in a stream towards his sacred garden.

Mrs. Chitty seemed to gather unto herself some of this surrounding fanaticism. As she sat in her large, airy room, decorated with Saracenic icicles, painted bright red and blue, it was easy to detect in her eye the kindling of a new religious fire. More than ever did she resemble Savonarola, but there was, too, now more than a touch of the dancing dervish, a suggestion, even, of the Mad Mullah himself. Her voice sounded a note of doom that was menacing and unmistakable.

Her bedroom faced a Mussulman cemetery, and tethered in this was a little white kid which frisked and gambolled so prettily that the children used to come and play with it. But Mrs. Chitty, seeing them hugging it, maintained that they were ill-treating the poor creature, and after much bargaining, succeeded, behind our backs, in buying it.

There was an uproar in the hotel. Every manager and director came and shouted at us, until eventually we understood one of them, who said that only yesterday he had been obliged to ask an English lady to send away her pet Pekinese, and that, therefore, he was very sorry, but he must quite definitely refuse to have a goat brought to live in the hotel. No doubt it was usual in Europe, but here people did not understand that sort of thing, he added.

Mrs. Chitty, securely established in bed, refused to give way, and the kid was tethered in the corridor outside. The authorities became yet more frantic. They had heard about the lady before: a guide from Abu-ben-Kalab had told them about her behaviour there. The hotel proprietor in that town, they understood, was in consequence of it a ruined man. Well, she could not repeat that sort of thing in Ali-Sid-Ali. It wouldn't do here, and they weren't going to stand it. . . . Perhaps the police could arrange matters. . . .

It was an *impasse*, a deadlock. We began to fear race-riots, so intense was the feeling. But, by the greatest good fortune, at this very moment a note was brought round to Mrs. Chitty from Lady McAlister, the wife of the Consul-General. In it she invited the invalid to stay at her house, saying that she and her husband would be only too pleased to nurse and look after any friend of Gerry Flitmouse. Mrs. Chitty at once accepted, scenting new victims for her germ. And then, too, there would be Foreign Office talks and every sort of delight.

When she went to pay her bill, she took the kid down to the desk with her, and, still accompanied by it, walked through the hall with great dignity. She then bore it off in triumph to the McAlisters. Lady McAlister, we heard afterward, was sympathetic: but Sir William, an old gentleman with white corkscrew moustaches, a Vandyke beard and an eye-glass, drew the line at such a guest, and made his wife explain that it would be difficult to find suitable food for it. Mrs. Chitty now (I thought rather brutally) abandoned the little thing, and sent it back to the cemetery whence it had come. And there, since it was now ownerless, it would quickly have starved to death had we not been informed by the vindictive hotel-manager of its plight and decided to make it a small allowance in perpetuity.

Mrs. Chitty remained in bed for several days, 'having a rest', and being waited on and made much of. Soon, however, her interest was aroused by the news that Forling, the explorer, was coming to stay, and she decided to get up to meet him. Lady McAlister kindly asked us to luncheon the same day, and I thought I had never seen Mrs. Chitty look more beautiful, nor ever had her charm impressed me more.

One of Forling's chief assets, the thing which had perhaps aided this great man in his wonderful career more than anything else, was his remarkable constitution. Moreover, he was, like so many persons of immense achievement, extremely modest: and his only boast was that, though now seventy-three years of age, he could walk as far and do as much as a boy of twenty, and, above all, that he had never spent a single day of his life in bed. Very foolishly (but then, how was he to know?) he mentioned this at luncheon . . . and once more I saw Mrs.

Chitty smile her dark, enigmatic smile. At tea-time she had a relapse, and was forced to go to bed again.

Mrs. Rammond, my brother and myself felt that we must return to Cairo in order to look after our four invalids there. We went to Muriel Chitty's bedroom to talk with her. She did not feel well enough to travel, she said, and decided to stay on with the McAlisters. They were very kind, so hospitable, and, besides, she would like to see more of Forling: an exceptional man, that. . . .

We said good-bye to Muriel, but with real regret. It was impossible not to admire, not to be fascinated by her; indeed her faults only accentuated her strange charm and beauty, and the subtle wit and understanding that, though they were not always with her, often came to surprise and please one. . . .

But forty-eight hours afterwards the explorer began to feel unwell. The following morning, just as we were leaving Ali-Sid-Ali, we were told that he was very seriously ill, and the Consul-General had felt himself compelled to wire to Cairo for a specialist. He was expected to arrive that night by air. Alas, the rest of the story is known. The specialist arrived, but it was too late. Forling had spent his first, and last, day in bed, and the microbe had won a notable victory. . . .

In Cairo, a few days later, I bought a copy of the *Daily Tribune.*

Mr. Robert Sutledge, I read, had been ordered a sea-voyage for three months. One of the Russian dancers was dead. His Imperial Highness the Grand Duke Gabriel had been allowed out in the garden of Nishkynashdom for the first time since his illness. He was said to be looking very frail, and was supported on each side by a hospital nurse. A memorial plaque had been erected to the memory of ex-King Boris of Milesia in the foyer of the Folies Bergère at Monte Carlo, and a bronze statue, life-size, of H.R.H. the Duchess of Chester had been unveiled on the sea-front at Montibes. . . . The summer was coming on, and the epidemic at Valaise was dying down. . . . That was all. . . . But was it? . . . I read on.

There was, I noticed, a curious outbreak of illness at Palermo and Constantinople. . . . The French General in Command at Damascus had retired, pleading ill-health. The Governor of Rhodes was indisposed. The Anglican Bishop of Cyprus was on his way home after several weeks of illness. At

Alexandria our Representative had been granted sick-leave: the Sultan of Libya had abandoned his first levee . . . Stop press: 'Liner *Dionysus* with Friends of Greece on board in quarantine Gibraltar, owing to mystery outbreak. Notable invalids on board include Lady Richborough and Dean Squirrel.'

The future, too, held its sequels. In Greece, dengue fever, which had doubtless been gathering strength for months, broke out as an epidemic in August. It was stated, at the end of September, that there had been 300,000 cases in Athens alone—Athens, where, it will be remembered, Mrs. Chitty had been so badly bitten by mosquitoes. During the winter months of the year a great wave of influenza spread over Europe. But Mrs. Chitty had gone again to the East . . . the unknown East, which is the cradle of the human race, the birthplace of every religion, every mystery, every disease. . . . Who knows what may not again come out of the East, the unchanging East, or what the year may bring? . . .

· · · ·

And even as I have sat writing this story, a ghostly influenza, conjured up out of its pages, has attended me, and I have not the strength to pick up my pen. *Absit omen*: let me pray that the reader of it will not be similarly afflicted.

STAGGERED HOLIDAY

MISS LUMSFORD always put her aunt away upstairs before she came down to dinner, even in the summer. It was so draughty in the lounge. Usually she played patience by herself afterwards until bedtime, or sometimes bridge with three other ladies of her own age, who were also looking after relatives. But tonight she must begin her packing, for they were going down to the country on Monday — the first time since the war began — with dear old Miss Flittock and her companion, Miss Brimbleby, and it would not do to leave everything till the last. Country air for a month would do them all good — you could see Aunt Fanny needed it. Aunt Fanny was not rich, and so, in addition, it would be a comfort to be able to share the expense, as well as have someone to talk to. All the same, Miss Brimbleby was . . . well, rather worldly and mercenary in her outlook: but then a paid companion was *never* like a niece, could not give the same affection: how could she? It was different.

It seemed quite like old times having a holiday — though later in the year, September; perhaps that was what was meant by 'staggered holidays', of which she had read in the papers (the papers were so puzzling now, and difficult to follow, not like what they used to be). They were taking two Daimler hire cars, and Miss Flittock's Bedlington — dear dog — and her maid would go down with them. It was quite a short run, and the motors were big enough to put a bed in. . . . And when they came back, they were going to move into the Fairlawne Hotel so as to be *together*. It would make a lot of difference to the old ladies — much *nicer*, that way. Of course it was really too expensive, but as Miss Flittock was rich and took a lot of extras, and was a valuable client, and because Miss Brimbleby had told them how *quiet* Aunt Fanny was, and that she ate so little and gave so little trouble, the management had agreed to make special terms for her.

It was really wonderful the way — with all her disabilities — Aunt Fanny made friends. People would often come up to look at her and say, 'Well, I hope when I'm her age, I shall be like that'. . . . Not that she was really old, only seventy-six — whereas Miss Pandlecross, who lived in the room next door and still did her own hair, was ninety-two, but with all her faculties about her — except for those silly fits of hers, when she thought she was somebody else. . . . Somebody more important ; who was it ? . . . Miss Lumsford couldn't remember.

'You're very *distrait* to-night, aren't you ?' her bridge partner inquired towards the end of the rubber, and after Miss Lumsford had lost, and had gone upstairs to bed, this acquaintance had confided in the porter that she thought Miss Lumsford was 'getting queer'.

. . . .

A broad road and several sets of railings still divided Hyde Park from Kensington Gardens, the statue of Peter Pan, Watts's Horse and the groups of shouting, playing children. By the Round Pond their cries filled the air under the elm trees. But below, towards Kensington Gore, there is a corner, running from the Albert Memorial to the beginning of Gloucester Road, that seems devoted to old people. Deeply sheltered on each side by banks loaded with flowers and flowering shrubs, is an asphalt path, in fine weather lined with seats and chairs. From here you see nothing of the town, only the golden dagoba that forms the top of Albert the Good's mosaic shrine. The rich, closely cropped grass, with the undulating line of its herbaceous border, the beds that fitted so cleverly into its shape ; all this is varied with semi-exotic trees and shrubs, each bearing its own zinc identity disc. And the flower-beds themselves are full of new varieties of old favourites, or of flowers that have been trained to come out at the wrong time and are now all ablaze in their perverted season. . . . Nature is tame and easy here, and the roses smell particularly delicious as their freshness mingles with the acrid scent of tar from somewhere hidden but near by.

The sun usually seems to be out in this corner, even when it is late autumn, and it is here that the inhabitants of those yellow-stuccoed hotels of South Kensington, whose tribes form a city, almost a nation, by themselves, gather together to sit and talk and knit. It was always crowded and everybody appeared to know everybody else — or, at least, certain sets to know certain other sets — and this inspired an air of seeming gaiety, of perpetual, superannuated garden party. Passing by, you would hear women say, while they gave a violent dig with a long stiletto-like needle at a piece of knitting as in other ages they would have lunged at a lover's glowing heart, 'Really, you would never think you were in London!' so that, obviously, it was the resort of those who would rather be in the country or at a spa. You never — or hardly ever — saw children here, but dogs, lots of dogs. A border of steel hoops, and leashes and cries of peremptory affection, kept these off the flowers.

If a child strayed hither with a nurse, he would feel uncomfortable, and his supplanters and substitutes would set up an intolerable barking. There were fox-terriers, fussy and inquisitive, and rough-haired terriers, with square-cut noses, Pomeranians, one or two Dalmatians, dogs shaggy and dogs smooth-coated; some dogs were clipped and some wore jackets; there were Airedales and Scotties and Sealyhams and pugs, and one or two proud but slinky Bedlingtons, with mauve fringes, curled like Parma violets. . . . These last looked out of place here, where Queen Victoria and her son still ruled. They seemed too modern among these quilted forms and trailing draperies, grey waistcoats and grey bowler hats, as well as every variety of soft hat.

Nevertheless, fashion occupied only the middle of the path, and formed a self-provided pageant for the watchers, the knitters, solitary or clustered. Sometimes, it was plain, those who loved trees and nature resented the display; they would fix their gaze on the leaves, green or golden, and pretend not to see the procession of presumptive colonels and their wives, though hardly able to resist giving a smile and a pat to the accompanying dogs. They would say nothing, but keep their lips as straight as parallel straight lines — though, after they had passed, they would bestow a glance of shrewd estimation upon their backs, or, if grouped, would whisper together. An unwilling backward flicker of the eye on the part of the victims who had run the gauntlet would show that they were conscious of their ordeal: but this awareness never prevented them from walking past again in the opposite direction.

But I have kept the chief feature of this walk until the last. If you stood at either end and looked up and down the gay and flowery aisle, umbrageous yet dappled with hot sun, looked at the silks and laces still here extant, and the hats that were like the good things you used to see exposed for sale in peace-time in the windows of the Maison Lyons, the impression was of a series of courts being held, round thrones on which the kings and queens reclined rather than sat: for the place was so *nice* and countrified, yet never dull, and so the elder daughter, or the niece or the companion, or sometimes the two daughters, would wheel hither their mothers or aunts or protectors in their various chairs or on their various trays. . . . It meant just a quick bolt across Kensington High Street at the broad part. The policeman by the island was always kind and held up the traffic for them to pass, and even the bus drivers, though brought to so abrupt a halt, would be kind too, and try to look bored and yawn and so not rivet their gaze upon the phenomena being shot past underneath them; creations by Breughel and Bosch, but adapted to a mechanical age subject to wheels and levers and a hundred ingenious devices to enliven and give speed. It was *extraordinary* how kind people were. No trouble seemed too much. And when they had crossed over, the attendants at the new brick public lavatories just outside the garden by the railings would be sure to be there in the doorway, and would come out with a smile and a nice word for the invalid. Miss Lumsford often said you felt that they would go through fire and water for Aunt Fanny.

'And how is Mrs. Hampton-Ditchcote this morning, Miss?'

'Well . . . don't you think she *looks* better today, Mrs. Dingle, now that she's got that nice new hat? . . . We're quite smart today, aren't we, dear? . . . All right, you old dear, don't try to answer if it's difficult. You mustn't worry yourself. We know you like it. Yes, *like* it. Do you hear her, Mrs. Dingle, she's telling you she likes it. Yes, li' it. Isn't she *splendid*? And Dr. Mactavish was so pleased with her yesterday. . . . We're going for a holiday, too, on Monday — the day after tomorrow.'

'That will bring the roses back to her cheeks, won't it, Miss? I don't wonder you're proud of her!'

They always had a little talk like that, and then they would turn up a path and soon be in the strip of paradise that I have described. . . . The ritual was the same every week-day; but on Sundays it was different. Then the crocodiles that joined together from the various hotels came out later that day, for, before leaving their rooms, the daughters, nieces or companions read prayers to their captives, bound hand and foot by infirmity, and decked out in special Sunday finery, with ribbons and bows. When at last they issued forth, there was less traffic and in consequence it was easier to cross the road; and the lavatory attendants were wearing their best clothes too. And Mrs. Dingle would be sure to say, 'And have we been to church today? . . . You look as if you had, Miss. I always love the way you dress Mrs. Hampton-Ditchcote on Sundays — so many of the ladies are just alike. It's not easy to be original.'

'I thought it better not to take her *today*,' Miss Lumsford would reply. . . . 'Perhaps next Sunday. But it is dreadfully hot in church, and my aunt was always so keen on fresh air, and it is not easy to get out.'

That was life on Sunday; but today is Saturday, and now we can view with a full knowledge the whole scene as it was on a summer day in early September. The trees, the sunlight mixing with the leaves, the gay, feathery shadows, the flowers, in broad bands and splashes, all preparing a sort of *fête-champêtre* atmosphere, and then the little animated knots of people, each surrounding a chair or a tray that jutted out into the path, and, in the middle, the promenade of red-faced men with jutting chins and arthritic hips, whom we have classified as colonels and civil servants, hobbling along with their wives, pale from too long a sojourn in southern climes, and dressed in flowery fantasies that are the ghosts of garden-parties given a quarter of a century ago, while, over all, there spread the noble anthem of free, English dogs, barking like drawn string, on and on and on, to their hearts' content. Dear Little Dogs.

Dear Little Dogs! . . . On their ledges and various supports, the invalids watched them fondly: there were old ladies who sat up with an effort and talked; there were old ladies who reclined at full length, so that all you could see was the front of a baby-cap and two gleaming eyes; there were old ladies, red and rotund, who seemed to be roasting before an eternal fire, and old ladies who trembled and shivered as if fixed and remote in an arctic world of their own creation. Some faces were mottled, some purple, some jaundiced, some bore on their surface large brown patches, and one, well known, was of a pale and silvery blue. The worse the condition of the invalids, the more cheerful their attendants had to appear; their faces wreathed in smiles, it seemed as though an insane gaiety inspired them. There was constant movement, flow and chatter, from one court to another, though those that reigned were static. And it was to be noticed that the gallant old gentlemen who passed from time to time and stopped to talk to invalids, never addressed them in the conventional second-person plural, but all of them adopting the same jocose formula, asked, 'And how are *we* this morning?' or 'Did we have a good night?' But it was not easy to hear the replies, for those dear little square-cut Scotties or Airedales were bouncing up and down on their straight, squat legs, barking as though they contained rattles within them.

Very strong was the scent of roses this morning, for the gardeners seemed to take a special pride in this walk and spent endless hours cherishing each blossom and sprinkling it with water, and seeing that the zinc labels were clean and could be easily read. The war had made no difference to this yet, nor much to the general tone of the place. If men in uniform passed through, they hurried. This was no haunt for them. One or two soldiers from far away, Canada or Australia, sometimes strayed here and sat for half an hour or so, musing and mute. Miss Lumsford had been surprised, only the other day, at the bold manner in which Miss Necker, that horrid old Mrs. Lamberton-Jenkins's niece, had accosted them, going up to talk to them and offer them cigarettes! But that was exceptional, as a rule people behaved beautifully. The old ladies seemed scarcely to see them. Most of those on trays moved their heads with difficulty, so they were obliged to take a special interest in the groups opposite them.

And here, in friendship, as so often in love, the law of natural selection, which ever favours the average, manifested itself. Just as people not seldom select mates because of the opposite qualities they possess, so here, an old lady, rubicund and with weak eyes, would prefer the shade, while the old lady opposite, with mauve or yellow skin and a terrible internal shiver, would prefer the sun to warm her bones. Since their favourite stands were immediately recognised as theirs by the laws prevailing here, no one would dream of usurping another's pitch. In consequence these two would be opposite each other every fine day for years; for death comes to this sort of invalid by instalments, and there was only one more lot to pay. Thus confined to staring at each other across the path, warm friendships would grow up, often without speaking, and each old lady would from time to time flutter a finger or even the end of a mittened hand — or perhaps her companion might have to take it and wave it for her — at her opposite number.

It had been in this precise fashion that Mrs. Hampton-Ditchcote and Miss Flittock had met — if met it can be called. Mrs. Hampton-Ditchcote spent the morning under a weeping acacia that looked as if it had been created to shelter a nymph, while Miss Flittock lived in the brave sunshine.

'Look, Aunt Fanny!' Miss Lumsford would say, 'there's Miss Flittock! Wave at her, she's smiling at you. Shall I run over and tell her how much you're looking forward to going to stay with her at Horsham on Monday? (How happy you two will be, seeing such a lot of each other!) Look, again: Miss Brimbleby's helping her to wave!'

Certainly, Miss Lumsford reflected, as she sat down to talk to Miss Brimbleby, it was a pretty place and convenient. It seemed so safe and nice. People were so kind. That dear Mrs. Dingle — they had made friends the day Aunt Fanny had fainted. The doctor had told Miss Lumsford that she could expect this symptom, and to look out for it — but it wasn't always easy to *tell* when the old lady had fainted; for she wasn't very mobile or animated. Suddenly, sitting here just as they were this morning, she realised it had happened and had run to Mrs. Dingle in the lavatory. Kind soul, she had at once brought out lavender-water and eau-de-cologne, and even a thimbleful of brandy, and these cross-Channel restoratives had soon pulled the old lady round. It was a relief to feel there was someone like that *near*; for Miss Brimbleby, though no doubt a charming woman — lots of people found her charming — was not so practical, not so quick or resourceful in a tight corner.

Tranquil times, you would have thought, lay ahead for these old ladies on whom so much care was lavished. But suddenly, that very day, things altered. They had gone back there again at four in the afternoon, it was so warm and sunny, and, just as the last invalids were being wheeled away, a battle took place high above London. The sirens sounded but no one took much notice. Nothing had happened up till now. And the noise only made people feel pleasantly that they were '*in* things'.

Miss Lumsford stopped wheeling Aunt Fanny, and *made* her take an interest. It was good for her.

'Look there, darling,' she cried, 'more aeroplanes. Look, you can hardly see them. Up there! and the pretty white puffs. They're chasing one another, do you see, over there? Puff! Puff! Puff!'

Aunt Fanny stirred uneasily on her tray.

A fire began that evening, and the first real bombing of London occurred. Once or twice, the enormous noises of the night approached very close to the city of yellow hotels that seemed always to exist within their own protecting fog; very near. It seemed, indeed, at one moment as though some vast extinct beast or reptile had been woken from millennium-old sleep in the Natural History Museum near by and had begun to bray at the strange orange glow that suffused the eastern sky. Yet that first night was not so bad. People were alert and amiable and talkative — and there was something to talk about — and dinner was nearly over before the noise became overwhelming. Miss Lumsford went upstairs then and sat with her aunt, and tried to explain about what was going on.

'It's *fireworks*, darling,' she insisted kindly, 'only fireworks. You used to love them, do you remember, at Cheltenham? Listen, there's another — such a fine one!'

It was difficult to know how much Aunt Fanny took in, Miss Lumsford thought. What a blessing it was that, though high up, they were so near the lift. But it would be difficult to dress her aunt and take her down to the air-raid shelter. It had looked so damp and draughty, and the old lady would be sure to catch cold, so, as they were going away so soon, it was wise to get on with the packing. The noise could not continue like this for long. As she wrapped things up in tissue-paper, she tried not to hear it. But she wished Aunt Fanny had got a dog. What a comfort an Airedale would be now! The noise seemed to be getting worse instead of better! All the same, she managed to go to sleep.

The next morning, Sunday, everything was calm and fine

and quiet, and at half-past eleven they set out as usual. Nothing between the hotel and the gardens seemed to have been destroyed.

After they had crossed the road, Mrs. Dingle came out to talk. She looked pale and untidy this morning, quite unlike herself. But she did not complain, but said:

'And did Mrs. Hampton-Ditchcote, dear old lady, mind that dreadful bombing?'

She oughtn't to speak like that: Aunt Fanny didn't know! But the Lumsfords had always prided themselves on showing nothing, so Miss Lumsford restrained her anger, and merely replied:

'Not at all!' and then added, 'It's the sirens my aunt does not like. They make her so nervous; I thought she was going to speak when she heard them. But she doesn't mind the bombing; not a bit.' ('We don't mind the bombing, do we, dear?' she asked the old lady, tidying her hair, and tugging at a muslin collar.) 'You see, she's used to that sort of thing. Why, my mother told me that Aunt Fanny, before her illness, often used to go out shooting with the men.'

When they reached the path, embowered in blossom, it was peculiarly empty, except for a few invalids, whose incomes were so close cut to the *pension* terms in their hotels that they could make no preparations for going away. Hardly any courts were being held, and the usual promenade of Anglo-Indians did not take place. Some women still sat knitting, but even they were talking in a lower voice than usual, as if afraid that some German aeroplane might overhear them. . . . Still, it was quite pleasant there, in the sun — except that Aunt Fanny lay there in the fronded shade, with no complement opposite. One could not help missing dear old Miss Flittock, and Miss Brimbleby. No doubt they had decided to stay at home at Fairlawne today and do the packing: Miss Brimbleby was rather the kind of person who liked to leave things till the last. Never mind, the two old ladies would see a lot of one another in the next month, so it did not matter. There was a new catalpa in bloom today, she noticed; creamy blossom, yellow and pink-tongued, clustered among broad leaves that, unlike other green trees at this season, seemed always to hold the green of the spring within them. She pointed it out to Aunt Fanny.

'Look there, darling,' she said. 'Even the Huns can't keep the catalpa from flowering.'

She spoke in a rather loud and ostentatious voice, and the knitters lowered their tones still further in contradiction. Or were they talking about her? she wondered. But they couldn't be. 'Odd,' she heard one of them say, 'odd in her manner.'

About 12.30, just as they were starting home for luncheon, the alert sounded again. If it had not been for kind Mrs. Dingle, they would *never* have got home in time. But Mrs. Dingle had hurriedly put on her hat and coat, locked the lavatory door, and helped push Mrs. Hampton-Ditchcote home on her wheeled tray.

'Well, we must say good-bye nicely to Mrs. Dingle, mustn't we?' Miss Lumsford had said to her aunt, as they reached the hotel. 'We're going away tomorrow for a month, for a lovely holiday with Miss Flittock and Miss Brimbleby — you know, Mrs. Dingle, the two ladies opposite — an hotel in Horsham. Oh, we're looking forward to it *so* much. It's a lovely country place, they say, with two converted oast-houses in the garden. Say good-bye, dear! Good-bye! Do you see, she's saying good-bye! Thank you, thank you!'

It was really extremely kind of her — especially as she was worrying the whole time in case she might have locked someone in. Still no message from Miss Brimbleby about the motor. It was strange — still, she was always a bit unpunctual, casual as it were. She was sure to telephone tonight. Not until after dinner about half-past eight did she receive the explanation, when the other guests came up to talk to her and told her that Fairlawne had been blown up last night, with everyone in it. The bodies were still being looked for.

She didn't know *what* to do — and it would be a great shock to Aunt Fanny: what *could* she tell her? For Aunt Fanny knew all about the holiday, she was sure about that. And they couldn't go by themselves, it would be much too expensive for two people alone: on the other hand, if she started unpacking, Aunt Fanny would notice that at once — she was so sharp — and begin that funny noise, like someone humming, that she made sometimes. . . . She decided to say that Miss Flittock had got a slight cold, and the holiday was 'put off'. But just as she was telling the old lady this, the bombing began again — and without the sirens sounding first.

Really one could hardly hear oneself speak! Suddenly she felt annoyed, overwrought. Something in the way her aunt lay there and said nothing annoyed her. Miss Lumsford began to shout.

'They're bombs you hear! *Bombs*! The same things that killed Miss Flittock and Miss Brimbleby. Can't you hear, can't you answer? Do speak; I'm tired of always doing the talking' — and she gave her aunt a slight shake. 'There it is again! Bang! It's a *bomb*!'

Afterwards she regretted having spoken like that: but the old lady naturally hadn't taken it in. She said nothing more about the holiday, and decided to leave the unpacking until the next day.

. . . .

All that night her aunt had been very restless. It had been impossible to sleep. And then, about six, she had seemed to be quieter. Miss Lumsford woke at nine (how late they were!) and opened up. At first she hardly remembered — and then it came back to her. But really now she didn't bother much about the night and its happenings; had forgotten the way she had spoken to her aunt, could not worry over Miss Flittock and Miss Brimbleby — that was past. What could you do about it? She ordered her aunt's breakfast and took in the tray herself. She propped up a pillow or two and began to feed the old lady. But Aunt Fanny was still in one of her difficult moods, and would not co-operate, but kept her mouth open. Well, you can't *make* people eat. If they won't, they won't. And one meal more or less, the doctors say, makes no difference. But it was trying of her, when everyone was tired.

Miss Lumsford had difficulty too, later, in dressing the old lady. She began to feel angry with her again. Of course, partly it was her illness, but all the same she made no effort, none at all. Indeed, today she seemed, if anything, to be resisting the clothes that her niece was putting on her. (It reminded Miss Lumsford of how she used to dress her doll, oh, so long ago now!) No, she ought to *try* more. If she didn't make more effort soon, Miss Lumsford decided she would give her another shaking. But no, she mustn't: after all, her aunt depended on her.

Eventually she finished dressing her. It was a hot day again, by the look of it, so she put a nice wide, lacy hat on the old lady's head, with a transparent brim that shaded the eyes. And then she got her somehow into her chair without having to call Elsie, the housemaid, to help. (Somehow or other, she wanted to do things by herself this morning, didn't feel inclined to have a lot of people running in and out of the room.) She went into the passage, rang for the lift, wheeled her aunt into it, took it down, and wheeled her out of it, through the hall, into the open air. Yes, it was a lovely morning again.

After they had reached Kensington Gore and crossed the road in the usual manner, Mrs. Dingle came out again to speak to her.

'Oh, Miss Lumsford,' she said, 'what a *dreadful* night! . . . I don't think you should have brought the poor old lady out again this morning. You said you were going away. It would be much better for her. There'll be another attack soon, I expect.'

Miss Lumsford kept her temper and did not explain, though she would have liked to argue. (She felt like that this morning.) She merely said to the figure on the tray-chair:

'We can't wait in all day, can we, Aunt Fanny?'

The particular immobility which the invalid showed this morning attracted Mrs. Dingle's attention.

'I know Mr. Fowler, next door, wants to say good-morning, Miss,' she said, and fetched him to have a look. They both gazed curiously at the old lady, who was staring in a fixed way beneath her lace hat.

As Miss Lumsford passed on, wheeling her charge in front of her, the two attendants looked at each other.

'Well, whatever do you think of that, Alfred?' Mrs. Dingle asked.

'Scarecrow's a bit potty, I should say,' he replied. 'There's something wrong there! Better tell the constable.'

Miss Lumsford settled herself and her aunt in the usual place, under the acacia. Everything seemed so quiet. Even the day seemed depressed. The little paradise was empty except for the few invalids who were so poor they still could not manage to go away. Down the broad road on to which the street of hotels converged could be seen the strangest procession, all the morning long, of huge old-fashioned motors pounding away to the country, carrying their precious freight. Some had beds in them, with figures lying at full length; others contained sitting figures, but shaking, quaking, so that they had to be strapped into place, shivering over their reins like a baby strapped into his chair; others, again, bore figures stiff, yellow and richly dressed as the images held high at religious festivals.

Miss Lumsford sat with her back to them as they passed, and between was the barrier of shrubs and flowers, a wide stretch of grass, and the line of railings, like spears. But she could hear the sound of the traffic, and no doubt it brought back to her the idea of their lost holiday. She talked a little to her aunt.

'Look, dear! The catalpa has come on wonderfully,' she said.

But it was no use. Her aunt seemed to take no notice of anything today. She could not help feeling annoyed again; it was better to employ herself somehow, good for the nerves. So she was just settling down to knit when a sergeant of police and a constable passed by. . . . They looked at the old lady rather intently, she thought.

Then they turned and came back to her.

'She oughtn't to be 'ere, Miss,' the sergeant said to her. 'She's *dead*. Look at her eyes, poor old lady!'

Miss Lumsford began to argue.

'Is it likely I should wheel about a corpse?' she asked haughtily — and then suddenly began to laugh. Peals of laughter sounded in the green shade under the acacia, until the pounding of the huge motors along the road obliterated this other sound. But she was still laughing.

THE LOVE-BIRD

'. . . The paragon of animals! And yet, to me, what is this quintessence of dust?'

It was impossible not to wonder what Robert Mainwroth would be like as an old man, or even as a middle-aged one, for elusive, witty and individual as he was, one yet could not fail to assign him to these especial years of which I write. And it is, actually, so much more difficult to be purposely amusing at seventy-five years of age than at thirty-five, so much easier to be so without the intention. His little eccentricities might by that time have sunk into absurdities. But old age was to be spared him. We shall never know now what manner of development or deterioration would have ensued, for he died, a few years ago, in his early forties.

He left me his journals and writings, but these served to reveal little of his character. One simple entry, however, I thought was an exception: though this may have interested me so much more than his ambitious pieces of writing only because I had witnessed the beginnings of, or at any rate the prelude to, the episode described. Yet it certainly seemed to me that this slight, obviously true, story contained more poignance than all his efforts at literature. It implied, one felt, a curious and sad allegory, which, though he may have been unconscious of this, summed up a side of his life, and filled him, even if he did not interpret it, with a deep sense of melancholy. I know, from the diary, that a sense of dejection out of all proportion to the trivial event itself did actually attend it in his mind.

The facts, then, slight as they are, were jotted down quite plainly, with no attempt to throw them into any form. I had always intended to sort them out, but time passed, my memory betrayed me and I might never have done so if I had not happened, a week or two ago, to look in at the window of a large antique-dealer's shop in King Street, St. James's. There in front of me, behind its sheet of ice, stood a very magnificent bird-cage, containing a stuffed or made-up bird that would doubtless chirrup when a spring was pressed. This rich and artificial prison seemed about to waken in my mind a very definite string of associations, for I was sure I had seen it before, though at first I could not remember where. I wasted a little time, therefore, in staring at it, and suddenly the scene of our first acquaintance materialised for me, summoning up round it a number of varied and scintillating objects. Convinced that it was the identical cage itself, and recalling very vividly the part it had once played in the life of my friend, the minute drama it had once housed, I went back to the forgotten diaries, determined to try to draw together the fine threads of which this story is composed.

. . . . .

To those who did not care for him, Robert Mainwroth gave an impression of being a scoffer, one who was rather eccentric and outside life. To those, on the other hand, who liked him — and, as his sensitiveness gradually evolved round itself the defensive armour of a perfect but laughing worldliness, they formed a steadily increasing band — he was a pivot of very modern, if mocking, activity. He was so intensely aware of all that was going on in the many different worlds round him, albeit so much of this action and effort appeared to him in itself to be ridiculous. In any case his character, under its outward suavity, whether assumed or innate, was definite enough to drive even those who met him for the first time into either one or the other pen, and matched the strongly drawn, rather Habsburg cast of his features, his natural air of quiet, ugly distinction.

His chief interests had always lain in art, music and literature. But as a young man he had passed a year or two in the Civil Service, and had, during that time, quickly obtained a reputation, deserved if not difficult of achievement, as a wit. Indeed, in the decorous deserts of our public offices, amid the glue, the ink, the roll-top desks, he must have seemed an oasis of pure fun. In those days he had been penniless except for his salary, but a sudden heritage both removed him from his office and provided a much wider circle of appreciation for his wit.

Most people take the extreme strokes of Fortune, whether good or bad, in much the same manner: there is little variety in their reception of them. But Robert, it must be admitted by enemy as much as friend, regarded his good luck from a personal angle and treated it in his own particular fashion. Finding himself encumbered with houses and estates that lay scattered over half England, the new Sir Robert Mainwroth, in spite of a certain family pride which stiffened him at moments, proceeded at once, and with characteristic energy and enjoyment, to divest himself of everything that did not appeal to him personally, either esthetically or through his humour — and his senses of esthetics and humour were perilously akin. By so doing, he defeated in many different parts of the land rustic proverbs, such as

> Come may, come what, much ill will fall
> When Mainwroth parts with Mainwroth Hall,

and, I apprehend, was rather pleased at the storm of tumbling superstitions he had provoked, thereby sharing that particular modern sensation originated by the famous lady who first carried a pig up in an aeroplane, and thus killed a proverb stone-dead. It was so simple, he said, to build up for one short generation your own part of an antiquated family machine, but so hard to smash it deliberately and inaugurate in its stead a new instrument tuned to the times.

Consequently, estates, which had belonged to the Mainwroths since first they had begun to bully their male and marry their female neighbours, were sold, without apparently causing their vendor a pang of any sort — but then they were very well sold. This was not all. The portraits of his ancestors in armour, as much as the armour itself, the pictures of later Mainwroths in long coats and periwigs, in tie-wigs, in powdered wigs of short, natural hair, the loose-lipped ugly beauties of Charles II's court, caressing the most innocent and beribboned of white sheep, then the family beauties, eighteenth-century sisters as a rule, swaying outward from, as it appeared, one slender-waisted stem, miniatures of Elizabethan and Jacobean members of the family, in ruffs and with their coats spattered with the spring flowers of English history, miniatures again, of the later epoch, mincing, rose-coloured but wistful — all, all were disposed of in dusty auction rooms, together with two vast libraries, one of which had been formed for an ancestor by Gibbon, and a whole corps de ballet of Meissen and Chelsea figures, pirouetting with their fragile, too pink-and-white legs over the greenest of green grass, sprinkled with the little blossoms of innocence, or blowing their minute, soundless pipes under the shade of never-fading trees. He also caused to move in the direction of the sale-room a jingling mountain of plate, Charles II and Queen Anne silver, the second of which, especially, by its utter simplicity and want of imagination, sent a thrill of excitement through every silver-bore in London (and the silver-bore, to be seen top-hatted and at work each Sunday afternoon in the marble halls of the Victoria and Albert Museum, constitutes a sub-species sans-pareil of his tribe). Still the work of breaking up the centuries continued. Now oak settees of elaborate and embossing design, tall, gilded chairs and tortoise-shell cabinets, ivory dressing-tables from Mogul India, painted chests from Italy, leather screens from Spain and lacquer ones from China, French clocks of green enamel, tapestries that re-created the tents of the Middle Ages, were all torn apart, snatched out of the entity they had helped to form, and went to find a living death in the petrified perfection of some millionaire period-room.

Such smaller, in the sense of less valuable, objects as the moth-eaten heads of stag and buffalo, eagles with fly-blown plumage, rare albino rabbits, the varnished masks of ferocious fish, their glass eyes glaring wildly, and fossils that resembled small Catherine-wheels, which must, at some time or other, have caught Medusa's eye, Robert divided among his numerous relatives. More especially did he distribute among them the multitudinous triumphs of the chase, furry or feathered mementoes. And a very long chase it had been: for, ever since the dawn of English history, the Mainwroth family had carried on a ceaseless but victorious feud against stags, otters, hares, badgers, rabbits and any bigger non-domestic animal of which they were able to get within reach, every kind of fish, and pheasants, grouse, snipe, woodcock, partridges and a quantity of other birds, and thus, during the passing of the centuries, had collected innumerable, but rather frayed, bits of them. All these Robert now, as we have said, presented to the Mainwroths, and felt a great joy both in the giving of them and in their reception. But of the large, valuable things he kept practically none and certainly gave none away. And the disposing of all this accumulated matter was no light business, occupied him for many months : nor do I regard it as inspired by selfish motives, though there is little doubt in my mind that he was pleased at having created this false impression of brutal lack of sentiment.

Actually and in fact, he had been thoughtful and practical, had adapted his situation to his time. It was pointless and hopeless, he felt, in these days to own vast, draughty, machicolated mansions, ugly in their conglomerated selves, even if full of beautiful objects, all over one small land. The modern world dictated its terms to the rich, and the moneyed nomad, with a few tents pitched ready for his use in various parts of the world, in, let us say, Paris, London, New York, Seville and Budapest, and with very easy means both of reaching them and leaving them, was the fortunate man of today. His heirs, as much as himself, ought to be gratified at the firmness and foresight he had evinced, for many a man would have been intimidated by the mere weight of such possessions into keeping them. Now they, too, would be equipped as modern men out of the increased income into which all these belongings had been transmuted, and would have no desire, and certainly no room in their small houses and large motor-cars, either for monumental pictures and pieces of furniture or for loads of clustering, clattering little things. No! Housemaids, those cross, shrill and superannuated vacuum-cleaners, were the only ones who must incur an inevitable loss. (Moreover, he used to add, he had been forced to these actions by the horde of indigent uncles and cousins inherited with the estates.)

Far from the ruthlessness of this prodigious sale being founded on a want of proper feeling, he maintained, on the contrary, that it had been to a great extent inspired by sentiment. Consider, for example, the family pictures. To display a preference for one ancestor over another constituted a species of favouritism : he hated favouritism — and in any case, what principle was to guide you in it ? If you decided to retain one picture, because it was a fine one, excellently painted, you both made a considerable financial sacrifice and slighted the other dead members of your family, who were doubtless just as estimable in life : probably more so, for, alas, the wicked man, no one will ever know why, is inevitably recorded by a better artist than the righteous man. Perhaps, Robert suggested, this might be because the profligate never considers expense or his heirs, and therefore pays the best artist of his time to paint his portrait: whereas the good man, ever mindful of future generations, at the time saves money on their behalf by commissioning a fifth-rate artist, recommended by a country neighbour, instead of a first-rate one, to execute his likeness, and through this act of thrift fines them an enormous fortune in subsequent years. It could not be too much stressed that in buying or ordering contemporary works there is nothing that pays in the end like 'wanton extravagance'.

Similarly, how could you be guided in your selection by the interest attaching to the persons represented? For the rake and wastrel notoriously absorb more of the attention of later generations than the prudent, diligent or prudish — Rochester and Pepys are remembered where so many more worthy are nameless and forgotten — and, indeed, the excesses of an ancestor tend in time, he thought, to become a source of real pride to his descendants.

Out of the very substantial wreckage of his inheritance, then, all that Sir Robert Mainwroth elected to keep was such light flotsam as a musical-box, on the top of which, when you turned a handle, a few white-wigged figures in minute, ever so dusty, brocaded dresses danced a very staccato minuet; a French *singerie* panel of playful indecency, which was rescued from a gutted panelled room; a photograph, in a red plush frame, of two of his great-aunts, now very much of the old régime, and proving it by their constant abuse of Robert and his behaviour, but here depicted riding on a tandem bicycle, dressed in bloomers and straw hats; some humming-birds in a glass case; some birds of paradise mounted in the same way; a silver snuff-box which played a tune by Mozart; an illustrated contemporary edition of Mrs. Hemans's poems; an 1820 razor, with a carved ivory handle and a hunting scene engraved on the blade; a tablecloth in blue and pink sateen, with a lace fringe, bought at the 1851 Exhibition; a signed photograph of Lord Tennyson, wearing a Scotch cape; a group (1848) of the Royal Family in Derby Biscuit; some water-colours representing the arrival of King Louis Philippe in England, on a state visit, with all the details of the decoration of the dining-car and saloon of his train, and culminating in a meeting, bright with uniforms, of the English and French Royal Houses;

a French eighteenth-century watch of ingenious mechanism and impropriety; a copy of the first of Bradshaw's Railway Guides; a water-colour by one of his aunts of a lonely lighthouse and a sunset; and two rare Victorian ornaments, again under glass covers, wrought in pinchbeck that comprised three shades of gold. Since these require a more elaborate description than the items catalogued above, but are most difficult to sum up in words, it may be best to state plainly that they represent little dolphins, holding bunches of grapes in their mouths, and climbing or wriggling up rose bushes, of which the actual blossoms are fashioned in pink-and-white and blue-and-white porcelain, and to ask the reader to construct them boldly for himself in his own imagination. These last, airy if substantial, mixed metaphors were a source of keen pleasure to their new owner, as was one other object we have not mentioned in the list: a really magnificent bird-cage made of tortoise-shell and nacre, in which a bird, feathered but inanimate, sang very sweetly when a spring was pressed. If one were to seek the derivation of this lovely toy, one would evoke Turkey, the eighteenth-century turbaned Turkey of Bluebeard's Palace and a thousand irrigated gardens of rose and myrtle, as its natural home. The materials of which it was made were much esteemed, though in quite ordinary use, there. It might well have been the solace in long, idle hours of some Sultana in a harem; for the secluded life, the lack of education and outside interest, induced in its victims a great passion for all mechanical toys, and, more especially, for such other artificial beings, singing in their ornate and costly prisons. Robert, however, used to say that he liked it because the sham bird sang just as well as any real one, needed much the same care and affection and differed only from the living creature in that it was cleaner, never sang save when you wished it, and did not impose upon its proprietor the necessity of ever peering about in fields and gardens for a tuft of groundsel.

Robert, now that he had successfully disengaged himself from his inherited effects, bought a small house in London, a flat in Paris, an apartment in Venice, a cottage in Bavaria, a little wooden palace on the shores of the Bosphorus, and two motor-cars, all of which resembled one another in their comfort and gaiety. Thus fitted out, he turned away from any profession toward his own enjoyment.

He was, in fact, a dilettante, but one in the best sense: for he aspired to be nothing but what he was. He talked well and amusingly; painted and wrote fluently, even with talent of an order. He often asked me to read what he had written, and occasionally, very occasionally, I thought I could distinguish another quality ruffling the surface of it, something sad and understanding that, it might be, he was at great pains to hide. So it seemed to me. Yet when others averred that he was artificial, cynical and heartless, these were accusations difficult to rebut, for such sayings and tastes of his as we have detailed lent some colour to them. People wondered if he had ever loved, loved anybody or anything, had ever really cared? And what could one say, for as he sat in his drawing-room, smoking a cigarette, laughing — his usual mood — and surrounded by his, it must be admitted delightful, toys and musical-boxes, it could but appear to the casual onlooker rather as though he was engaged in keeping life at arm's-length.

Yet if this was so, there must — and this his enemies could not comprehend — be some very good reason for it. It is easy, of course, to credit people with too much feeling, but had not something, I wondered, wounded him very deeply in early life? Might it not be that this Puck at the end of a long line, who mocked us all with his practical modernity, hid far down, but very far down, an unusual sensitiveness; that perhaps, he had so much felt the fear, love, excitement, terror and beauty of existence, had been so early singed by these things, that he would rather avoid life if he could, while yet, in attempting this, he had understood that by so doing he was forfeiting many things of inestimable value, and ran the risk of losing among them the very thing which might have tamed and humanised life for him? Or again, had these emotions existed formerly, and were they now, under the mask of fun and witty observance with which he had overlaid them, atrophied through long disuse? Creative talent might have cured him, I thought, but he had, and by so little, missed it. As it was, the refuge of the romantic lay, as ever, in illusion. Just as Pirandello's Enrico Quarto found his happiness and his reality in a false and distant epoch from which he refused to emerge, so perhaps did Robert Mainwroth discover his reality and his happiness, which in this case signified calm, among all the paraphernalia of his carefully planned months, full of little, beautiful surprises, birds that jumped out of boxes and sang, or photograph-albums that played the Wedding March.

However, whether he loved or did not love, whether he felt so deeply or did not feel at all, there was no doubt that he was a delightful companion and a very good friend. Numberless people genuinely liked him. His nature was interesting, too: because in spite of its mocking quietude, there were obscure lapses of hot temper, and one was able to obtain out of him suddenly, when it was least expected, some angry response. At the time of which I am writing he was in his early or middle thirties, yet in some ways, in manner for example, gave an impression of being older. Underneath his calmness, moreover, he could fret about small things after the fashion of the elderly: and, though he knew many people and entertained many, when he was alone he seemed more alone than anybody I knew. Not that he was often bored, for he was in his own way energetic, and made a continual use of his continual leisure: in addition to writing and painting, he read an enormous amount. Or again he was perfectly happy engaged for hours in some entirely futile and pointless occupation, such as himself inventing a small, silly toy or executing drawings and caricatures from old photographs. At such things, he evinced considerable skill: and the more futile they were the better he was amused. Yet it looked as though every year there would be less room, less use, for singing birds, real or artificial: even less for artificial than for real ones. (Perhaps this was why he loved his toys; some predilection for lost causes?) And he was, I believed, too wise behind his frivolous mask not to be aware of this.

· · · ·

Though, as we have suggested, Robert was usually too busy, too much engaged in weaving his silken web of life, to be bored, he was nevertheless occasionally liable to moods of apparently reasonless depression: but are any moods of depression in fact unjustified? In his case, the origin of them may have been that he was conscious of possessing everything that, according to his own theory of life, was necessary to his happiness . . . and therefore, if temporarily he knew himself to be unhappy, his misery was by that much further aggravated.

In the full dead heat of one chattering July in London he

was virulently attacked by such a feeling of heaviness at heart. It was, perhaps, because he was tired; so he comforted himself, but for some days it had seemed to him that nothing he did was worth doing, nothing he said worth saying, nothing he bought worth buying. He had, in fact, bought a model of a small piano, in ivory, which played Chopin waltzes when wound up: for he had attempted to use money in this way as a drug, to make him forget. And the antique-shops were so many caves of oblivion and hallucination. But it was not a success: the melancholy, nostalgic, minute tinkling that ensued served merely to emphasise his state of mind. Naturally his gloom deepened as Saturday night set in, with its misleading, noisy promise of incipient Sunday. And he had made no plans for warding it off.

On Sunday morning, he thought of a thousand pleasant things to combat the calendar — motor down to Bath for the day, visit some friends in the country, spend the afternoon at Millbank examining the modern pictures, or go to sea or river to bathe — but no sooner did one of these ideas occur to him than it at once lost its attraction.

Outside it was brilliantly warm and fine. The Boy Scouts, or some kindred black-hand association, were making a great noise of marching milk-cans and mad motor-horns not far away. Further, there was a group of sweating Salvationists not far off, howling in joyous unison to the tinny accompaniment of their tambourines, while two maimed soldiers in the distance were playing 'The Rosary' on a clarinet and phonofiddle. (And then, Robert reflected, people insist that we are a musical nation: as though any other people in the world would tolerate such musical dementia in public places!) For the rest, top-hats and prayer-books and feather boas could be seen returning from church, and the smell of warm tar came in heavy gusts of acrid scent through the open windows. It was, in fact, a typical Sunday noon, and he felt that he did not want to go out. Yet he could settle to nothing. He sat down at the piano, and played for a few minutes, then shut it, and got up. He turned on every musical-box in his rooms in rotation, pressed all the buttons on his various trick clocks, so that little figures shot out at him unexpectedly, while an eighteenth-century tune lifted its sweet but feeble rings of sound into the air. He tried the wireless, but found himself listening to the sermon which was rounding off a children's service in Edinburgh. The clergyman was just explaining to 'his little ones', as he called them, that every flower was a love-letter from God (Robert decided not to go to Kew that afternoon, after all, and switched it off). He went back to the piano: then looked through some caricatures he had done, and an old album of valentines. Now he rapped out a newly invented spelling-game on the dial of his automatic telephone. Then he played for a little with those strange Victorian pictures, in cut-paper frames, of sailing-ships which, when a tag at the bottom is pulled, turn into mid-Victorian beauties, with ringlets, holding a bouquet, next into a cornfield sprinkled with red poppies, and in the end into a bleeding heart bordered with pansies and forget-me-nots. Alas! nothing really amused him. He could not read, but began to examine each sentence critically. Now everything outside was quiet: but suddenly a hymn-tune, called up by the Sunday quality of the day outside, and borne to him on a wave of ennui issuing from the countless dead hours spent in school-chapel, buzzed round inside his head like a sleepy bluebottle. For a moment, its inevitable, wheezy circlings amused him. But there was no means of ridding himself of it. Finally, he went to the piano and played a few bars of 'God Save the King', hoping in this manner to impress mechanically upon the stranger within, who was responsible for the melancholy outburst, that he had endured enough of it. Even this did not suffice. He now, therefore, deliberately summoned up in his memory the most vapid refrains to combat it. Eventually the tune left him, but still he could settle to nothing, was more than ever depressed. It was ridiculous, a confession of failure, he felt, to be surrounded here by everything one wanted and yet to suffer this vague discomfort, this sense of something lacking or amiss. . . .

At last, just before luncheon, an excellent meal to which he sat down alone, a new plan entered his head. He knew what he must do. It was best to struggle no longer, but instead submit, yield utterly to Sunday. (Why had he not gone to church? It would for him have been an experience.) Was there anything, he asked himself, that was more typical of a London Sunday afternoon than a visit to the Zoological Gardens? Alas, he was not a member of the Society and so would not be able to obtain the necessary ticket of admission

— and then remembering that I was in London, he rang me up and asked if I could take him there. It was arranged: and he would send his car round for me first.

I came into the house for a few minutes before we started. When I entered, he was finishing luncheon, and on the sideboard were little mounds of fruit, peaches and grapes. Real this time, not artificial, and I recall asking him whether he fed his clockwork birds on them? Then he took me up to the drawing-room. I decided that the house was charming. There was about it an enchanted absurdity, of which beauty was born. And how refreshing, I thought to myself, to see a rich man in possession of a house which he has made for himself, that has not been foisted on him by some firm of exotic but willowy decorators, or taken out of cold-storage on his behalf by immensely learned period-mongers. How happy he ought to be here, in his own world! The sunlight struck glittering reflections out of countless glass-cases, each one of which held in its convexity the dissolving mirage of another until the entire room seemed full of variously shaped, transparent bubbles, and played within them upon the lyre-shaped tail of a bird of paradise, crystal flowers or a miniature ship, of which the hull, sails and rigging were all wrought of glass, or drew flights of colour from the flashing throats and wings of humming-birds as you walked. Each footstep made little jewelled nightingales, in their glass cages, quiver among their enamelled, blossoming trees, of which the branches were made of watch-springs, so that bird and flower ever moved as though upon an invisible breeze, and the room was soon filled with trills of bell-like music that resembled the smallest jets of fountains. Everything — flowers, carpets, chair-covers, the modern pictures which hung on the walls — praised life, as it were, against the living death that every period-room hymns. Many of the objects were beautiful in themselves, and all seemed so here, linked together as they were by the elusive personality of their owner. I remember particularly admiring the magnificent cage that has been already described, and the very tuneful singing of its mechanical prisoner, as, at a touch of the spring he fluttered into life, opening and shutting his beak and wings. Once more I thought, as I looked round, how happy Robert ought to be here, in his own world. But today I could see he was restless, unsettled, and longing to escape out of his artificial paradise: and we hurried down into the car and off to the Zoo.

Samuel Butler has said somewhere, I suppose in his Note Books, that there is no cure for nerves or unhappiness so complete and effective as to watch the quiet antics of the larger animals; it is possible to lose oneself entirely in observing these moving hills of natural energy. Certainly the healing effect of it upon Robert was remarkable. His mood was changed abruptly. First we went to see the elephants, plodding heavily, swinging their trunks lithely from side to side, and regarding the world of men with an infinite wisdom, a great experience of good and evil, from those narrow little eyes set in the enormous, grey, wrinkled bulk of their heads. Then there were the polar-bears, with their little heads set upon cruel, thick necks and clumsy shoulders, beckoning with abrupt and coaxing gestures to their keepers for more, many more, still-living fish. The terrible, beautiful whiteness of these animals imparted a spectral quality to their movements, and made one think of the men done to death by these quietly padding, shuffling ghosts in the frozen silence of a Polar night. Nothing, one knew, could stand up against the machinery of their strong and stealthy muscles. Meanwhile, near by, little brown bears were rattling at the bars of their dens, screaming with rage like spoiled children, at the sight of jars of honey or golden syrup being carried past them to other animals. Then there were lions and tigers, panthers and black pumas, all of them executing within their dens, for they expected to be fed soon and were restless in consequence, the superb *chassés* of their lithe and ferocious tangos; and hippopotamuses and rhinoceroses, deep in their armoured dreams of Africa and its hot and turbid rivers, or, it may be, lost in some far more ancestral, prehistoric vision of a quilted world dominance, when the steaming swamps of the world were their playground, and they could wallow in the conquered mud of the five continents. Well, those days were over; and here they were, limited to small cement baths within a den, and, temper to be deduced in each gouty, swollen limb, they grunted loudly, after the fashion of old men in clubs. Other dreamers, too, we visited: giraffes lost in their high-minded visions of the young green shoots of palm-trees — palm-trees that were ever trying to starve them, for the higher up grew these tender morsels and the barer grew their long and plaited trunks, so much the farther up had their necks to stretch through the generations. We watched, too, the tribes of deer and antelope, leaping, spitting and butting on their terraces; the supercilious, self-indulgent camel, carrying the burden of its seven stomachs; and that paragon of virtuous motherhood, the kangaroo. We ignored the turtles, peering cautiously out of their armoured umbrellas, the crocodiles smiling within their heated, stinking pools, and the monkeys leaping and chattering on their hill, swinging and hanging head-downwards from the branches of their trees. The seals and sea-lions, combining all the charm and cleverness of both land and water animals, engaged our interest for a little by their evident enjoyment of their own obviously highly perfected technique in games and tricks. But now we passed on to lesser things, to the blue-crested pigeons of Australia, and, from them, to a venomous little rock-garden sprinkled with delicate flowers. Indeed, this small plot of ground offered a rational explanation for the horror of rock-gardens which every person possessed of an esthetic sense must feel. It had always seemed a strange phobia, without foundation: but here, under every demure Alpine or sub-arctic blossom was coiled a very malignant little serpent, or stretched in pretended death like a dead twig, lay a virulent lizard. At first you did not notice them. Only a running movement along the coil, a glimmer down the scales, would give warning of the viper, only a wicked occasional flickering of the tongue would betray the presence of all these dwarf dragons. New ones quivered into squamous life each instant, as one gazed at rocks and flowers. Robert, I remember, pointed out to me the similarity between this sensation and the one which seizes on him who looks for a minute or two at 'The Convent Garden', that masterpiece of pre-Raphaelite art, in the Ashmolean at Oxford. The Nun, in her grey clothes, stands in a garden. The grass at her feet is powdered with the innocent faces of spring flowers; in the foreground lies a pool, with a tadpole floating through it . . . apparently a solitary tadpole. But if you regard the painted water with sufficient care, tadpole after tadpole wriggles itself into your consciousness, and where before you saw only this one, now you see half a hundred. Counting them, seeing who could spot the greatest number, was at one time a recognised sport. So it was here, in this garden, where gradually, if you watched long enough, every pansy and rock-pink revealed a minute, spotted and poisonous monster. All the same, I reflected, this little flowery enclosure displayed rather the same brightness, the same counterfeit innocence and cheerfulness as Robert's home. But then, as for that, so did the parrot-house — into which he insisted on going, for he was very much attached to the conjunction of their brilliant colours and inconsequent chatter — albeit the squawking and screaming there was very different from the clear but stifled music that issued out of his every room.

We spent a considerable time in watching the birds ; blush-coral, stately cockatoos like palest-pink dowagers, that mumbled gently for a few minutes and then suddenly emitted an ear-splitting screech, their crests rising on their heads as though we had pressed the spring of one of Robert's toys ; the macaws, like lackeys in their gorgeous liveries of blue and scarlet, chained to their perches, and pecking at the world with cruel, sneering beaks ; and then the little love-birds, nestling close to each other in couples — all, that is to say, except a solitary, green-feathered one who sat quietly on a perch of its own. It could not have mated yet, we surmised, for they say that when a love-bird dies its mate dies too.

Sometimes an animal or bird shows an immediate response to a human being, and this little bird showed signs of approval as we approached him, coquetting with head on one side, and advancing along the perch to meet us. Perhaps he thought we brought him food ; he remained extremely amiable, but on closer acquaintance evinced a quite unmistakable preference for Robert Mainwroth. This was a love, too, that was returned, for Robert could not tear himself away, stayed there for nearly half an hour, stroking its green, downy head and talking to it. Moreover, as he turned away, he confessed how much he wished that he was the owner of this fascinating little creature — or one resembling it. But probably, even if he could contrive to get possession of it, there would be no room for it in his house, he added.

He drove me home. We parted, and the rest of the episode, or shall one say the sequel to this episode, is extracted from his diary. No sooner had he returned to a solitary, very solitary tea, in his drawing-room, when in at the wide-open window, from this typical Sunday afternoon of chirping sparrows and distant, rasping-voiced dogs, there flew a green love-bird — to all appearances the same one he had so recently left. It fluttered round the pink-painted ceiling, but without any of the bumping of fear or surprise: nor did it for an instant, as might so easily have happened, knock into any of his clustered fragilities.

Robert was startled at the coincidence, for though it could scarcely be the actual bird from the Zoological Gardens, this, too, was an Indian love-bird, identical to look at, so that only another love-bird could have presumed to tell the difference. He had expressed a wish. Here, and in so short a time, it had been answered. That, in itself, constituted an occurrence of such rarity that it was sufficient both to please enormously and rather to frighten one. And, after all, the love-bird was not a common feature of the English landscape or townscape. No, it was a surprising, extraordinary event, which one would never forget. And, as the bird fluttered round about him, there seemed to him something symbolic and incomprehensible in its flight, in its arrival. It must have escaped from somewhere, he supposed. He had heard it said by the superstitious that it brought bad luck to the owner of a house if a bird flew into it; but that, he comforted himself, applied more to choleric, red bullfinches and homely starlings than to a jade-green parakeet from distant Asia. Meanwhile the bird was shortening the circles of its flight. Suddenly it settled near him, showing no terror, but remaining there quite contentedly. He grasped it firmly, and placed it on his other hand. It balanced itself on an outstretched finger, and allowed him to promenade with it round the room. He rang for the footman, and told him to bring some fruit for it up from the dining-room. It was brought, and the bird accepted a freckled strawberry from his fingers with grace and promptitude.

And now a quite irrational joy seized on Sir Robert Mainwroth for his good fortune. He was more pleased, excited, than he had ever been at his large and unexpected inheritance. A deep, inner joy welled up in him and he was in a different world from that of the morning, when the gloom of this particular Sunday had for him summed up and crowned the depression of a hot and tiring week; a tiring, pointless week that had seemed the epitome of a lifetime. A different world — and yet the same, save that his whole house looked as he had wished it to look, and that every object, every toy was fresh in its appeal. But now a fear swept down on his heart, a new fear — lest he should lose this lovely, living green toy, which appeared to know that it belonged to him: a terror that it might fly away again, be caught by cats, or singed by the lights in the room even. It was necessary to be practical. But there was no bird-cage in the house. It was Sunday, and impossible to buy one.

And then he remembered his cage. The only thing to be done was to place the newcomer in the grand mother-of-pearl and tortoise-shell affair that contained the stuffed bird. The living thing could not injure the dead one. But the parakeet would not enter, and Robert was afraid of hurting it. They resorted to stratagem. The small gate in the vast cage was left open, and grapes, strawberries, and bits of peaches were pressed enticingly between the precious bars of the further side, opposite the door. At last the love-bird responded, entered the trap, consented to be shut into this transparent, harem-like magnificence and solitude. Alone again, perhaps it thought. Alas, not so alone, after all; for now, of a sudden, its round, twinkling eyes espied the brightly coloured, though somewhat moulting, bird-effigy that, with a certain stiff pride, occupied the centre of the golden perch. Its staring, unquivering beads of glass mocked the whole parrot-tribe. The love-bird was first struck motionless, and then made a high, shrill sound of anger. For a moment it hovered, a green flame in the air, round this stuffed image in a minute but quite comprehensible dance of rage; after which it fluttered at it with sharp claws and tearing little beak in full battle-array of ruffled plumage. In the beginning it must have thought the creature alive, but this hard, inanimate dummy of an enemy that it proved to be was even more unendurable: and it pecked at it long and viciously, loosening one or two feathers. The scene was in its way so comic that Robert was almost tempted to wind up the machine and make the effigy pipe out its song. But this would be unkind, he felt. Already the little bird was disheartened, spurned the cornucopia of honeyed, jewel-like fruits with which it had been provided, and that matched so well the richness of its prison. Retreating now to the far end of the perch, it swivelled its green head right round behind, after the manner of all parakeets, and burying it in the green, soft feathers under the back of its neck, appeared to sleep. In any case it remained completely irresponsive to the coaxing of its new master, paid no heed at all to him. But after about an hour's rest, it roused itself again, sidled gently toward its hated rival, and proceeded to peck it once more, but this time slowly, deliberately and with no sign of anger, as though to discover to what lengths one could go, to what extent attack it without provoking an onslaught in return from this larger and most unusual bird. Then, having carried out this scouting expedition, it retired again to the farther end of its golden perch, and slept, or pretended to sleep. So it remained that evening, until a cloth was put over the cage for the night.

But none of these happenings altered Robert's new mood. They only made him love this toy the more. At any rate, it was safe in the cage for the night: nothing could attack it. And he went to bed in this new happiness and easiness of spirit, his only fear that in the morning the owners might trace and attempt to reclaim it.

The next morning Robert found his love-bird still cross and sulky. The fruit was untouched. But this did not worry him, for soon it would have a cage to itself; and he left the house at once to buy it one.

When, within half an hour, he returned with his new purchase, the drama was over. The artificial bird had been torn feather from feather, its remains spread all over the splendid cage; even the glue, with which the plumage had been stuck on, was revealed upon this now hideous, bare mockery. But the little love-bird lay dead, too, in a corner.

There seemed to have been no reason for its death: though it might, the housekeeper suggested, have died, poisoned by some preservative in the feathers of the sham bird it had fought, or perhaps the sparrows had chased it and pecked it the evening before. But it had seemed well enough on its arrival in the house. . . . So the real bird, then, had been killed by the artificial one it had fought, had died from jealousy of it.

. . . . .

An intense sadness, it appears from Robert's journal, fell down upon him: a sadness quite out of all proportion, sensible people would have said, to the actual loss. Here he possessed everything he wanted, could possibly want, and yet was moping over a bird — and one he had only known for a few hours. If he had not minded selling all the furniture and pictures of his own family, why should he mind a small thing like this, they would have asked? Perhaps it was only because a perfect and beautiful little incident had ended so pitifully. Or was it that some meaning he could not fathom was concealed in it?

He never found out to whom the bird belonged or where it had come from. The cage he had bought for it was hidden and put away: but he could not bear to see the other, beautiful cage either. The effigy was never repaired, nor a new one constructed. And now Robert, too, is dead — has been dead three or four years. The bric-à-brac he loved, the mechanical nightingales, the clocks and musical-boxes, are broken or in dusty shops for sale, since nobody wants them. Little is left of him save this story — and this itself was dependent on the chance which led me to look in at the window of the antique-shop in King Street. But certainly I recognised the large bird-cage of tortoise-shell and nacre: and I thought that the renovated, stuffed bird within looked younger and more modern than when I last heard him sing in Sir Robert Mainwroth's house.

PRIMAVERA

By his entire nature the Italian is both simple and subtle. Vincenzo, though he came from Sicily, was no exception to this generalisation. His remarkable good looks, his delightful, tumbling English, spoken with an Italian lisp, accompanied by a smiling and innocent character (innocent in the sense that a young animal is innocent), but with, in contradiction, a certain almost Chinese wiliness over matters of buying and selling, had served him well. In the space of twenty years he had risen from being a waiter, with no friends, no money and little education, to owning two fine businesses—he dealt in antiques—which necessitated knowledge and judgment, numerous clients and a fair amount of capital.

He had spent his first year as a waiter in London, and had then taken a job in an hotel in Oxford. During his spare time there he had attended lectures in order to educate himself, in a cap and gown given him as a tip by an undergraduate who was leaving. Then in about 1908, in that brief glory of Edwardian days, he had returned to work in London, and had lived somewhere near the Crystal Palace (*Il Palazzo di Cristallo*: that figure of speech so compelling to all of Italian race who know the rock-crystal cups and jewelled crystal dragons of Benvenuto Cellini and his followers, and who see in the phrase some towering, overwhelming, superlative creation of the same kind).

He had lodged with Miss Miranda Starbottle, the granddaughter of a Sicilian refugee from oppression. Her grandfather had served Garibaldi and had been obliged, with his daughter, to seek sanctuary in England during the forties of the last century (his wife had died on the journey). In those days refugees had glamour, were not the broken, pitiful creatures that they are today, and this girl, who was beautiful, had soon married an Englishman, a merchant, who had fallen passionately in love with her. Materially, it was a better match than she could have hoped for at home. But Miss Starbottle certainly proved a queer offspring of so romantic a marriage. Her mother had died when she was three, and she had never been to Italy, could speak no Italian, and, except in her dark hair and now faded yellow complexion, showed little sign of southern descent. Indeed, she had always appeared somewhat ashamed of even this element of nonconformity to English Victorian standards.

When Vincenzo first met her, her father, too, had long been dead and she must have been about sixty years old, or perhaps more; equally, she might have been seventy. She seemed never to alter, a typical late-Victorian spinster, frozen into whalebone stays and layers of thick clothes covered with meaningless, fussy ornament, with lace and embroidery and filigree, and with a fringe that crept in black, Medusa-like curls over her forehead; a style which she made no attempt to modify or soften. If she went out — which was seldom — she carried on her head a large black creation, crowned with purple and white ostrich feathers, and in her gloved hands a mauve-silk sunshade with a filigree silver handle. Over her left temple and the upper part of the cheek spread a large birth-mark: but her face, apart from this livid continent, was sallow and lined, for she possessed the Victorian horror of face cream and rouge, of lipstick and 'enamel'. She still occupied her father's substantial house in Penge, but she had come down in the world, money was scarce, and she now took in a few lodgers — a few, I say, but no doubt as many as the house would hold. Under her vague superintendence and direction two or three servants attended to their wants. She, as a rule, did little herself for them.

All Sicilians, whether nobles, bureaucrats or officials, are related, and Vincenzo, being in some manner a connection of hers, had been recommended to her care. At first her frigid manner of living — to an Italian so empty and desolate — her severe abstainer's outlook, her horror of wine and good food, of comfort and of warmth, had repelled him: but gradually he had grown to like her and respect her admirable characteristics, her hidden kindness, her shrewdness — except in business matters — and, above all, her reliability. And perhaps the Italian sun, so strong in his blood and skin and bones, called out some response in her. . . . At any rate she thawed, became his chief confidante and adviser, a very kind and devoted friend, willing to forgive in him various trifling and impulsive faults which in others she would with severity have condemned.

Thus his occasional excesses of various kinds were overlooked. Perhaps she reflected, in a heart now hidden away, that he was a foreigner and knew no better, or perhaps, even, some similar but repressed strain in her own nature made her exult secretly in his southern conduct. While Vincenzo lived in her house, his parents died in Sicily, and the sense of his loneliness gave her a new and motherly affection for him. 'Poor boy', she used to repeat to herself, 'poor boy!' And, though formerly she had, because of the same taint in herself, despised foreigners, she now encouraged him to bring his Italian friends to see her. Moreover, Vincenzo dramatised and presented her, until, to a whole circle of Italians living in England, 'Miss Miranda', as they called her — for their tongues could not form the alien, syllabic music of Miss Starbottle —, became for them, like the Crystal Palace, a symbol of England. And though, indeed, they laughed at her, they respected her, revelled, even, in her thoughts and sayings, as being those of an unfailing representative of her nation and period. And no doubt their coming and going made her blossom a little, softened the hard edges of that drying heart.

Meanwhile, Vincenzo had started his antique shop in Oxford Street, and was making money.

. . . .

When he returned to London in 1919, after the war, Vincenzo decided to open a branch establishment in Naples, and to have a flat there as well, for he was longing for Italian life once more. But, though his shop had prospered, owing to the boom in old furniture during the war years, Miss Miranda and her affairs had, on the other hand, gone very much further downhill. All her small investments had collapsed, and she could no longer afford to keep on her old servants: yet without them she was lost. She could not do the housework herself and her general inefficiency aggravated the situation. . . . She must, by now, have been seventy or over (some people said seventy-six), but outwardly she remained just the same, with no diminishing of the settled richness of curled fringe or lace or jewellery. Her large hat still sported the ostrich feathers; no paint or powder disfigured her face and only the birth-mark seemed to have become emphasised in its wrinkled pallor.

Just the same; except that she cried a little when she saw Vincenzo, and that he had never seen her cry before.

Directly he observed the state of the house, he realised what had occurred. Something must be done to help her, and his warm, impetuous nature decided him at once what to do. With her permission an English friend of his, a lawyer, examined her affairs. It transpired that if she sold her house, she would be left with about eighty or ninety pounds a year upon which to live. In those days the pound was beginning to buy many lire and so that income would suffice her in Italy.

Vincenzo arranged, therefore, that Miss Miranda should dispose of her belongings and come to live with him in his flat in Naples. In order to overcome her possible objection he told her that it would aid him financially if she were to pay him a small sum every week and 'look after the flat' (though, since it was plain that she could not look after her own house, and could speak no Italian, this aid was problematic). . . . Indeed, she must have been lonely while he was away, have craved his company and that of his friends, because though her character always led her to oppose any plan, even when she secretly wished for it, she soon acquiesced, after a few protestations that she would 'only be in the way', and that before long he would want to marry and be rid of her. . . . Previously she had shown little enthusiasm for Italy, but now, at the age of over seventy, she faced the total change of climate and living that awaited her with complete equanimity.

. . . .

By the spring of 1920 they were settled in Naples. Their flat, the top storey of an eighteenth-century palace, faced the Castel dell' Ovo (the fortress that grew, so the Neapolitans say, out of a magic egg placed there by the sorcerer Virgil), against the classic Neapolitan view of sea, island and mountain. Furnished with part of the stock from the shop, the magnificence of its big and lofty rooms, its gilded beds and chairs and painted hangings and later Empire furniture, might have proved somewhat overpowering to one fresh from Penge. Further, though Miss Miranda's self-respect was propped up on a small weekly contribution to Vincenzo for food and rent, she exercised from the beginning only the empty shell of house-keeping prerogatives. A woman, Maria, came in to cook and do the work, and Pancrazio — a relation of Vincenzo, a boy of sixteen who aided him in the shop — slept in the other spare bedroom and occasionally condescended to help with odd jobs in the house.

Pancrazio was lazy, everyone saw that at once. He was also untrustworthy and a liar: but the sleepy warmth that broods on the ruined Greek temples of Sicily, where flowers grow from stones and snakes lie baking under them, glowed in his eyes, in his smile, in the movements of his limbs, and this birthright brought him with ease many friends, persuading them to condone the execrable qualities of his nature. His voice, his hands even, had this warm, animal glow that pleaded so eloquently for him. Moreover, in the shop, he was quite useful, a born salesman (people liked to buy things from him), and in the house he was quiet. . . . Something of the old apprentice attitude to life still lingered in Italy, and so Pancrazio — or Pancras, as Miss Miranda uncompromisingly called him — being, as it were, both friend and servant, would always accompany Vincenzo and Miss Miranda on their excursions and picnics.

His duty it was to unpack and arrange the luncheon and pour out — and help to drink — the wine. . . . Yes, *wine*; for Naples was helping to thaw Miss Miranda's disposition still further, and already she drank a little wine. And perhaps — for it could not surely be the beginning of vanity? — perhaps the heat of this spring, when summer had for once started in April, was responsible for other changes. Certainly she had modified her clothes. Her hats had ceased being architectural, were now flimsy, quite gay affairs, suited at any rate to the climate, and she must have steeled herself to throw away several petticoats and tight stomachers, with the result that she had become — though no younger — by several degrees more human and less like an African idol in the process. Even her fringe she had discarded, and Vincenzo had persuaded her to consult a former London friend, a hairdresser, now chief of his trade in Naples, who was enchanted to advise her concerning the best fashion for her to assume. In fact, Vincenzo was obliged to confess to himself that she had come out of her shell nicely, and reflected credit, and not ridicule, as subconsciously he may have feared, on her rescuer, her Perseus.

Nor did she appear to feel homesick or ill at ease in this strange city, though there was nothing for her to do but to sit on the little arboured terrace, dawdle round the flower-pots, fetch the London papers or occasionally call at the English Tea-rooms for a chat. . . . No, she was not bored: for her, she was cheerful and jaunty. She loved particularly their excursions: for once or twice a week he would run them out to lunch at Sorrento, La Cava, Castellamare or Pompeii in his little motor.

How much they had all three enjoyed Pompeii! How often and how long they had laughed during the meal! They continued frequently to refer to this with pride (because simple minds seem to consider laughter as a virtue in itself): how much they had laughed! . . . They had not been able to have a picnic within the walls, but had been obliged instead to go to a Swiss restaurant, just outside them. This place, created for tourists, might almost have been built by Bulwer Lytton himself, so full of ancient Roman colour was it: but the food proved to be good. They had eaten *lasagne*, had drunk *gragnano* — that purple, sparkling wine of the district, with its faint, sweet taste of sulphur and strong, deep taste of iron — had listened to an over-ripe warbling of 'Sole Mio' by a fat Neapolitan determined to resemble Caruso, had heard blind men clawing at mandolins and singing with a horrible false gaiety 'Funiculì, Funiculà!' and had, further, watched the antics and grimaces of an old man and woman, dressed in exaggerated peasant costumes of a hundred years before, who had danced the tarantella with a scrawny exaggeration of youth and grace — all for the price of a rather expensive luncheon. They had drunk a lot of wine which had flushed their faces and given fire to their laughter, and Pancrazio had sprung to life: his words, usually few, had now torrented over one another. He was transformed. All his sleepy grace became active and vigorous. But Miss Miranda, though she looked at him often, could not, of course, comprehend what he said, though she must have understood his mood. . . . They stayed there, drinking coffee and *strega*, until long after the other luncheon guests had departed on their earnest task of sightseeing.

When at last they entered the dead city, the heat of the sun, beating down upon them and reverberating up from the tufa pavements, seemed to bring with it a life of its own, so that instead of the individual existence of man or beast, brick and stone formed an entity, lived and quivered. The droves of visitors had passed on, and the three of them were able to laugh and joke by themselves, alone, except for the custodians of the ruins. The animation, derived equally from sea, sky, air and landscape, of which formerly this extinct pleasure-town had been the scene, seemed to inspire them, so that they laughed on through the streets of broken houses, feeling no fatigue.

It had been, in fact, an unforgettable day; one of those few occasions that happen to come flawlessly right, so Vincenzo thought; a day with a memorable quality of both satire and perfection. Even the phalluses carved on pavements and walls, and always so carefully indicated by the guides, albeit explained vaguely away as 'fecundity symbols', appeared in no way to shock Miss Miranda. (Notwithstanding, Vincenzo, with the curiosity of all Italians in these matters, could not help wondering what the old lady made of them and of their frequency in this buried past.) She had seemed positively anxious to enter certain houses, forbidden to her sex by the authorities, in order to examine the erotic paintings therein. But the custodian obliged her to sulk impatiently in the atrium, while he showed her instead articles of feminine vanity, scent-bottles from which the perfume had evaporated two millenniums ago, and pots of rouge cracked and riven by two thousand years of cinders. . . . But soon the others joined her, and they were outside again, laughing and talking, or sat on a roof watching the faintly glowing plume of smoke that blew just above the baked, purple cone of the volcano.

Naples and the long, viridian spring appeared altogether to soften and humanise Miss Miranda. . . . But in the month of May the atmosphere began to change. At that season the country invades this great city with a magic unknown elsewhere. It turns stones and pilasters, pedestals and broken columns to life. Flowering weeds flamed down in festoons from every cornice and every roof. Age-old and fecund, every scrap of ground, even in the centre of the city, is covered with innumerable and diverse flowers; purple and blue and pink and yellow, they grow from the feet and shoulders of statues and under the trampling hooves of bronze horses. The air itself blossoms with an indefinable life and scent, and a peculiar excitement and heightening of human senses pervades the square and street and room — a sense of expectancy. A subtle uneasiness seems to spread circumambient to every object and every person, and as thus day followed day, Miss Miranda appeared, equally, to become increasingly different, increasingly more human ; a touch of coquetry, even, started to manifest itself now in the style of her dresses and her hats.

Presently, indeed, Vincenzo thought that he had noticed that she had begun to use a little rouge and powder. But the idea was untenable. It just could not be, knowing her prejudices. . . . Certainly, though, it looked as if the birth-mark had begun to fade out beneath a coat of some thick paint. That was different : probably the consciousness of it had long haunted her, and now, in her new independence, she wanted to be rid of it. Then, too, her hair surely had become fairer ? . . . He would try and allude to it some time, in a non-committal, inoffensive way. . . . But before long, there could be no doubt that she *was* using scent — and a good, French scent. Vincenzo was pleased : he felt it a tribute to his powers of civilisation.

The whole time that these gradual yet comparatively sudden changes were in progress, the full Neapolitan spring was entering into the darkened rooms. The sun, reflected from a thousand walls painted pink and scarlet and tawny red, crept through the shutters and played quiveringly upon the objects within. On the terrace outside, the massive foliage of orange and lemon was sprinkled with white stars, gold-dusted, and the heavy, obsessing fragrance swept through the apartments on every puff of warm air. The vine of the arbour, too, had released tight golden coils, like the hair of the Parian statues of Antinous and Ganymede which still littered the bed of the sea that now, day after day, exhibited a hundred different suffusions of blue and lilac and green and silver. The Greek frieze of mountain and island that lay above the water on the horizon, every moment adopted in this golden month new aspects, legendary and fantastic in their beauty. Sometimes Capri opposite looked hazy and remote as the Hesperides, sometimes so near that those who gazed at it felt they could clasp its white houses in their hands.

Within the apartment, shuttered in order to obtain cool air, the atmosphere became darkly oppressive. It was often too hot to talk, and things unformulated in speech, and almost in thought, lay behind the lips of these three people, as they sat staring at the sea, waiting for its cool evening breath, or moved with a sullen dream-like quality through the ponderously ornate rooms. Their silence, masked with an unreasoning irritability, held in it no contentment of mind or body.

Even Vincenzo, in spite of his happy and easy-going disposition, must have shown his feelings. He often longed to be alone, and wished with fervour that Miss Miranda would not smother herself in scent and — there could be no secret about it now — thus daub herself with rouge. She looked, he admitted to himself at this moment, grotesque, with her hair turning golden (alleged to be its natural colour revived by camomile shampoos), and with her old, wrinkled face smeared so badly with paint that the spot of high colour on each cheek flared up in contrast against the dead white powder of the rest. Her birth-mark, shaped like South America, showed, too, through its camouflage. Why, she was like a Goya; exactly like! All she needed was a bridal veil and a wreath of orange blossom to make her into one of his *Caprichos*. She was old enough in all conscience, and, as every Italian knows, dignity and reserve belong to old age. This fantastic mask, and these short dresses and short sleeves, accorded but ill with the corrugated, tortoise-like neck! It would cause any man a passing shudder.

By June, everyone agreed that it must be an unusually hot year. . . . Yet Miss Miranda, who had never hitherto set foot abroad, remained unaffected, scarcely seemed to feel it, except that the dark substance she spread in the hollows under and over her eyes began to run, tingeing the pink and white. But she was never ill for a day, was always there. And Pancrazio, too; silent, furtive, brooding no doubt over some unpleasant secret of adolescence. . . . Well, by the look of him, Vincenzo thought, he would have adventures. But there it was; the boy was probably bad, he admitted, yet, in spite of his lies, he liked him for his young and sulky grace.

Toward the end of June sleep became impossible. All night long the crowds from the slums of the old city sought cool air on the promenade below, laughing, talking, singing. Odd fragments of unconnected song — silly Neapolitan songs — floated in at the wide-open windows until four or five o'clock in the morning. (What could these revellers be doing, Vincenzo wondered.) During the long nights, as he lay there, he began to question whether the flat was not perhaps haunted. Or was it merely that he was so exhausted by the heat and by trying to sleep? . . . Certainly on several occasions he had imagined that he heard sounds and movements and whisperings in the darkness. Stealthy steps crept along the passage, boards creaked, or there was a secretive shutting of a door; *shutting* was scarcely the right word, it was too muffled and padded and gentle a sound for that. The hushed sibilance of voices, the suppressed and distant echo of a laugh, seemed to lie under the noise from outside, and to come from within the large old flat itself. Yet, it may be because he was tired, he did not wish to investigate. Something, though he had little belief in ghosts, held him back. The sounds must be, he told himself, of his own imagining. But he did not mention them to the others, did not wish to give his companions any information, or they might start a scare, and begin talking and talking and talking about it in the heat of the day.

Then one night — it was just before three — he heard something. . . . Unable to bear the mystery any longer, he sprang out of bed and flashed on the light in the passage outside. . . . There, dazzled and blinking, creeping and sidling along from the direction of Miss Miranda's room, was Pancrazio. He wore an old pair of trousers, but was naked above the waist. Even in these strange circumstances, a certain grace and beauty surrounded him, Vincenzo saw, but something was wrong — he could see that too — and shouting 'What are you doing there?' Vincenzo seized him, dragged him into his room, shook him until his bones rattled. A silly smile stretched over the boy's face, but he made no effort to struggle or escape. In his hand, Vincenzo found a hundred-lire note. '*Ladro!*' he shouted, striking him, 'Thief!' But Pancrazio, though he cowered, seemed stupefied. 'She gave it to me, Vincenzo,' he said. 'I am not trying to deceive you. She gave it me. I have spent the night with her — many nights, *la vecchia putana!* You never told me I was not to. . . . But it was no pleasure to me, so why should she not give me money? . . . But it *is* true, I'll prove it. You can tell for yourself. You know English. She taught me to say these words, though I don't know what they mean.' And then out of his mouth issued, pronounced with extreme care, a repetition of words and phrases of the most obscene and erotic significance. He articulated syllable after syllable, but without emphasis, like a child who has learned a lesson. Word after word blossomed lewdly, evilly from his lips in the surrounding and culminating silence — for at the moment there came no other sound.

SHADOW PLAY

You must imagine three young girls, each an only child, all beautiful and all rich, immensely rich. They were not related, but among their parents prevailed that particular sentimental feeling, stronger than friendship, composed of intimacy, good-fellowship and complete interdependence, that exists only among the cosmopolitan-millionaire class. . . . Well, these three children had been brought up together, had played together, had spent each Christmas together, shared the same governesses, the same instructors in riding and dancing. Together they had learnt French, Italian and German (which, unlike the members of their mothers' generation, they could speak with fluency and correctness). They had been trained, too, to be 'simple' and 'unspoilt' and slightly infantile, as the super-rich like their children to be, but they had been taught nothing about how to manage their fortunes, how these had been amassed or why they would one day inherit them. Finally, they had been sent to the same fashionable finishing-off schools in Florence and Paris. Now they were eighteen, and the waiting earth lay at their feet.

With the hard, brilliant prettiness of a diamond, Zoë carried prettiness to an extreme. Her hands and feet were exquisite, and her voice, though in no way ugly, was so distinct it would have cut glass. Pauline was like crystal, a little larger in her loveliness, so clear but by no means soft, with the body and carriage of a young goddess walking over hills in the dawn, and a deep, throaty laugh. Her hands, too, were small and beautiful. Both of them looked outwards on the world: but they fastened their bright gaze upon it with such eagerness that they saw nothing.

The third friend, Lorinda, was different. Slim and tall and dark and restless, she had large mournful eyes that looked inwards on herself, and so sometimes saw the world. Perhaps because of a latent softness of heart in that long, slender body, others, not of her sort, and living in the wild places beyond the gold bars, interested her: her blood beat in common with the blood of all human beings. In consequence, she seemed to herself among her own friends always a little unpopular, a little upon the edge of life. Being very young, moreover, though occasionally she made her own observations, she had not found out how to deduce from them.

Zoë, Pauline and Lorinda, in that dawn of the world as it was for them, spent much time together. It was as though this had been ordained. No one had ever suggested to them that they would be happier apart, and so they met continually, went expeditions, visited shops and art-galleries together. Their mothers, as they played bridge of an afternoon in their drawing-rooms, so full of light, among the French furniture — signed pieces, and formal photographs of plumed and helmeted personages — signed pieces, and Ritz and Fabergé *bibelots*, said to each of them, in their tired voices, 'All right, darling, you can go, so long as the other two girls are going. Don't stay out too late. And you'd better take your fur coat, and arrange not to be called too early. . . . And don't forget to come and say good-night to Mummy before you leave the house.'

That kind of life was only just starting. It was in the twenties, and the young and rich, if they would promise to remain content with the gold bars behind which they were fastened, would find their pleasures in plenty and brimming over. They would have, as their mothers said, 'a glorious time'. In the spring, of this, their first year, the families of Zoë, Pauline and Lorinda went to stay in Paris; they took up their quarters, two in their own houses, one in the Ritz. In May, they would return to London; after that, in the autumn, they would go to New York.

During this visit to Paris, then, there was to be one afternoon a sale of stuffs, silks and velvets and brocades, and the three girls decided to attend it. They had been there for about ten minutes, in an enormous, crowded, hot room, and Lorinda had been looking inside herself, not paying much attention to the frenetic yet dawdling tumult around her, when suddenly she saw Zoë and Pauline as though for the first time. Schooled in the arts of elegance though they were, they had for the moment shed these accomplishments. Their hands, always so cool and pretty, had become claws, like those of an Egyptian Hawk-God, and all the possessiveness and greed of those ancestors, generation after generation, robber barons, Dutch from New York, railway kings and market-riggers, and New England farmers squeezing the last ear of wheat out of the soil, who had built up these vast fortunes now tottering under their own weight, manifested themselves in their furious, grabbing fingers, swollen by the excitement of possible bargains. Their eyes remained fresh and glittering as usual, their features cameo-clear, but their hands grasped and wrenched and plucked and clutched and tugged at the stuffs on the counters.

And this appeared to be the point, too, at which the touching *camaraderie* of the super-rich broke down, for neither of the girls seemed, during this delirium of shopping, to be conscious of the other's presence — let alone of that of a third, and non-possessive, party. When they saw her, they elbowed her out of the way; she was nothing, thistledown. They, Pauline and Zoë, were worthy to fight between themselves for a prize, or bid in competition at an auction, where the race and reward is to the richest, but, for all her wealth, Lorinda, so their grappling, despoiling hands and knife-sharp elbows told her, must just keep herself out of the way!

Directly they left the shop, they were themselves again, with a well-defined sweetness and steely distinction, their hands pretty as flowers. But for Lorinda, the scene she had witnessed retained an extraordinary, almost apocalyptic quality. These two other young creatures had become amazons, beings to be feared. Sometimes in nightmares she saw their hands once more turning the stuffs on the counters, pulling and grabbing them, feeling their web and the texture. The hands then held some fulfilment in them, a hint of menace that eluded her when she awoke, became vast raven-hued clouds overshadowing her whole future.

Lorinda was young, and the lines of her life were as yet vague, unset. When she gazed within herself the vista was indistinct; while outside herself things seemed almost as she had been told they were; *almost*, for she was one of those who develop late, and already she noticed that they did not tally absolutely. How was it that she saw in some directions differently from her mother and her mother's friends? Why did the idea of staying in nearly every afternoon to play cards so much appal her? And what was the world, for example, to which the work of the great musicians carried her; a world wherein her closest friends, Pauline and Zoë, appeared to have no part, nor her family, neither her father nor her mother?

But she only attained to the kingdom of art long afterwards. . . . Now she was eighteen. Every night she attended dances, so as to meet the young men with one of whom it was supposed that, after a few months, or even a year or two, in which to decide her preference, she must spend the rest of her life. A semblance of gaiety masked the seriousness which underlay these occasions. Huge awnings flowered in red and white outside the great yellow-stucco houses, and the rhythm of dance music, a beating and tattooing without tune, drifted out from them into the squares and gardens, and down to the hot pavements where always stood a few lonely watchers, silent, hungry, curious, their ragged poverty consuming with straining eyes these riches. On the balconies the young couples would look at them and say, 'What a funny old man down there!' and from top to bottom, rooms, staircases and halls were full of happy, meaningless chatter.

This kind of life seemed to continue for a long time, she could hardly tell, so confused did the delicious, long slumber of late hours render her, how long. . . . And gradually she found that she had fallen in love — or thought that she had fallen in love — with Ivor Harley, a young man who was shortly sailing for India with his regiment. It was understood between them that they should marry. He was young and gay and good-looking, and his eyes were full of truth.

He was leaving England in August, and so, some time soon, she must tell her mother, and then, next year, she would join him in Delhi, and they would be married. . . . She did not think that her mother would welcome the idea, for though he was rich, he did not belong to the super-rich; in whom alone virtue resided. It would be, she expected to be told, throwing her fortune away, — two fortunes, for one was to come to her from her father and one from her mother. She foresaw difficulties, but she knew she could obtain her parents' consent in the end, since it was a match to which no reasonable person of their world could object, and, in her own way, Lorinda could assert her dark, mute will, if her mind was made up. Besides, her mother, she knew, would like Ivor, for his good looks, his manners, his quickness. . . . She would tell them in August, before he left for India, but at present she did not want any awkward discussions to mar the happiness of their meetings.

However, in the early part of July a dreadful thing happened. Her mother died suddenly from heart-failure. The event convulsed Lorinda's whole life and outlook. To the young, death is so remote as not to exist at all and, in spite of the difference between their temperaments, she had always been very close to her mother. In the days that followed she had gone down to their country place with her father. She felt so sorry for him that she almost forgot about Ivor, though they exchanged letters; at first, every two or three days. As if the yawning of the grave had for the time chilled his emotions, the warmth in them had a little died down. She could understand that. No doubt he did not wish to intrude his own sentiments, did not quite know what to say, except to offer sympathy and continue to offer sympathy. She could hardly ask him here at present, so she would be compelled to go up to London to see him, and arrange matters before he left. It would be quite easy, because the house was near London.

Under the grey and sulphurous skies that herald thunder the early August heat brooded, lying heavy upon the gardens and the old trees, and in the large, hot, dark rooms, padded with brocade and full of expensive objects, china, bronze, furniture, pictures, the loneliness of their lives became more apparent to Lorinda and her father. . . . The only thing that comforted her was the splendid way in which Zoë and Pauline behaved; kindness itself. She had written to Zoë, soon after leaving London, confiding in her about Ivor, and asking her to look after him, in case, without her presence there, his last few weeks in London should prove dull. And Zoë — it was evident from Ivor's letters — could not have taken more trouble to be helpful. While Pauline, in order to cheer her friend up, came to live with them for the summer and, with her practical nature, took off Lorinda's shoulders the domestic burdens of seeing the servants and ordering the food. (How much she hated these things! And her life would be full of them now, for, by her mother's will, she was already a rich woman.) In consequence, Lorinda was able more fully to give way to her grief.

It was silly in a way, she knew, to grieve continually as she was doing. Everyone told her it would do no good and could not bring her mother back to life; but she could not help it. (Pauline was sensible and left her a great deal to herself: she appreciated that.) Her days were poisoned by the shock and by the sense of her loss, although they possessed a trance-like quality, unreal in the extreme. And she could not sleep. Uneasy slumber came to her for a few hours, but even then, full of dreams, sinister dreams, with grasping, dominating hands. . . . But perhaps they would stop when she went up to London to see Ivor. Her father, now that Pauline was here, could surely spare her for two or three nights! And she could stay with Zoë. She could not at present face her own home, after what had happened there. It really was kind of Zoë to stay on in London, right into August, when all the gaieties were over, in order to look after poor Ivor. . . . Lorinda thought of Ivor, and it calmed her. In her mind, she looked into the candid depths of those blue eyes, in which all truth and frankness dwelt, and presently she fell asleep.

The next morning she wrote to Zoë, explaining that she was obliged to come up to London for a few days the following week to see Ivor, and asking if she might stay with her. The reply came by telegram, 'Certainly darling and may I motor to lunch with you to-morrow Zoë'. Lorinda was enchanted. She longed to see her old friend again, and they could talk of Ivor. (He had not written, she remembered, for some days.) . . . It was curious, though, Pauline did not seem to be at all pleased when she heard that Zoë was coming down, and said something about how reluctant she herself would have been to push her way in like that! . . . Rather silly of her, Lorinda thought, as she was there already. But that was only Pauline; she got into these moods sometimes. They meant nothing, so Lorinda let it pass.

When Zoë arrived, driving her own motor and looking enchantingly pretty and competent, they kissed, and then Lorinda took her into the garden. . . . The leaves lay flat as cardboard on the air in the curious hush of full summer, no sound to be heard except the heavy droning of insects, which seemed, from the surrounding silence, to obtain a new and menacing tone. The enormous trees towered up, leaf upon leaf above them, towards the sullen, dove-coloured sky. It was very beautiful; a sort of peace descended on her at last, and as she walked between the huge green masts of the avenue, she felt a presentiment that all her life she would remember walking here with Zoë. . . . At first they did not talk much. How silent it was! Lorinda, looking at the leaves of the horse-chestnuts which composed the avenue, noticed how they extended towards her, motionless; (like swollen, stretching hands, she thought to herself). They made their way to a pillared temple by Kent at the end of the avenue, so that they could sit and talk undisturbed.

Zoë looked lovely today, prettier than she had ever seen her, Lorinda decided. Zoë took off her gloves and placed them beside her on the old carved and painted garden seat. And Lorinda, who seemed to find herself nearer the surface, as it were, today, perhaps from the pleasure and surprise of her friend's visit, thought to herself, as she examined Zoë's hands, how silly — and jealous, too, she supposed — she had been before to imagine that, even for a moment, they had not been pretty. They were beautifully formed, slender, with almond-shaped nails. . . . Zoë was holding up her left hand at arm's length, staring at it in an absent-minded manner. What a lovely ring she was wearing! It must be new. Lorinda had never seen it before. It was not the *sort* of stone she liked but it *was* a beautiful stone: her mother would have admired it, she thought with a pang; the pang of one who had forgotten for a moment the newly dead. . . . And so for a while she pursued her own sorrow, her own thoughts, not attending to what Zoë was saying. Zoë had put on her gloves again, and was laughing and talking almost too much. . . . Lorinda began to listen.

'So I shall sail for Bombay on the 7th of next month,' she was saying.

'I had no idea you were going there,' Lorinda interrupted, 'but isn't it rather early? Won't it still be frightfully hot? . . . I wish you'd stay here. I shall miss you dreadfully, darling.'

'But I've got to go. I can't help myself. . . . I was telling you: Ivor and I are to be married in October.'

. . .

Pauline was horrified when Lorinda told her of it after Zoë had left. Lorinda had related it quietly, without comment. She was becoming trained to life.

'I should have thought her family would have stopped Zoë from making such a fool of herself,' the other said; 'after all, they're both very young. And he isn't such a rich man as all that. . . . I think you are well out of it, Lindy, if you ask me,' Pauline continued, 'but then young men bore me. *I* like people of experience,' and she flourished a hand, a pretty hand.

At the time, Lorinda thought she was merely trying to be kind. But, some considerable time afterwards, she saw her friend had meant what she said. For it was not until a full year after her mother's death that Pauline and her father announced their engagement.

THE MACHINE BREAKS DOWN

HUGH DEARBORN was already middle-aged when I first remember him some ten years ago, but middle-aged with an unparalleled elegance, an unimpeachable style. His greying hair, his mask-like face, through which peered those witty, rather wicked eyes, his hands of carved ivory, were all made with an exquisite but rather snuff-box-like finish. This well-groomed and tailored figure, this Voltairean mask, rather too developed for the slender frame and covered with small, delicately chiselled wrinkles, formed but the very gentlemanly shell for an intense vitality out of all proportion to it — formed, in fact, the beautifully finished cabinet-gramophone case, from which sounded a wonderful but intolerable music. Not that his voice was musical, in the sense that our grandmothers used that term. It was not. His laugh never resembled a peal of church bells sounding at eventide, or a rather carelessly played xylophone, as did the elegant tremolos of various old Victorian ladies. On the contrary, his voice, touching every emotion for the necessary moment, never sank into cloying sweetness, having, rather, that enchanting trick of putting a note in the wrong, unexpected place, and then recovering, which you find in the best modern music — find originally in Rossini's *Can-Can*, that first clear gem of modern music, and then in Debussy, Ravel and Stravinsky.

The actual manner of his conversation was perhaps less modern than its content. Artists of the spoken word vary in their methods. One, whose manner I admire most of all, talks, argues, sinks beneath the logical waters, is on the point of drowning, but as he touches the ocean bottom, finds some new pearl, and swiftly brings it to the surface: his is an absolute reliance on his own brain and tongue, never afraid to risk all on an absurd argument, never fearing to sink, knowing always that he will find a new treasure. But Hugh's system is different, formal; it is as the Garden of Versailles compared with that of Hampton Court — stiff, mathematic, well ordered; his voice a terrible instrument, his art one that dies but never surrenders.

From the first Hugh Dearborn possessed a peculiar interest for me — an interest aroused by some apparent contradictions in his character. Here was this exquisite shell, the fruit of fifty or sixty years of toil, but an instrument for an hour's conversation — conversation that like a flower blossoms and then dies — a mule-like art without hope of progeny. Usually the artist is led on by a desire for immortality or perhaps fired by a craving for money, but here was a real case of 'Art for Art's sake'. The best Hugh could hope for was an invitation to dinner, but the very perfection of his conversational technique, the very insistence and monopoly of his great art, often tended to prevent his humble end.

And this art itself, unpremeditated and yet such a technical achievement, surely could not flower on the barren air without any but purely physical preparation? Then again, after Hugh's performance of the new Symphony at the luncheon table, I once heard a rather unkind friend say to him: 'Really, Hugh, you ought to put it in a book!' And this made me wonder why he had never employed these gifts in some other, more permanent, form. And how much longer, in any case, could this delicate, ageing instrument stand the ceaseless wear and tear of such a vitality?

Thus, from the first, Dearborn interested me and I collected information about him. It was certainly a mysterious life. A friend of mine, I found out, had met him originally in the garden of Walter Pater. I pictured the scene. To us children of sadder and wiser days the eighties of the last century seem a halcyon but ever-so-distant age; Alfred Lord Tennyson ever so much more distant than King Alfred burning the cakes; the young manhood of Mr. Arthur Balfour ever so much more remote, more legendary, than the youth of King Arthur or the Quest of the Holy Grail. A halcyon time indeed, with spring always in the warm crystal-clear air; with the laburnums, the lilacs, the lobelias and copper beeches in a perpetual riot of unsubdued and unbridled colour. There was a continual movement and sparkle in the lives of the well-to-do. Poet Laureates still wrote quite successful odes to members of the reigning family, who were then of greater interest to their subjects than professional cricketers or the doped death of Miss Flossie Highfly. The county families were yet safely out of the way, secure in their distant tea-bound mansions, busy killing the beasts of the field, the birds of the air. Riches were still respectable, the rise of a millionaire was yet a romance. On the other hand, you could be poor without being thought insane, and the silver epergne was gradually retiring into the lodging-houses of Bloomsbury. Shepheard's Hotel would soon be open in Cairo (or was it already?), and we were on the verge of an optimistic young Imperialism that would grow to a climax with Kipling and Lady Butler. And, to those who liked it, there was a pleasant stir in the world of art. Painting and prose were both stretching themselves after a long sleep that had been broken only by the short Pre-Raphaelite nightmare. This was the time of the neo-Greek: white marble mantelpieces, Alma Tadema, the prose of John Addington Symonds, the drawings of Du Maurier and Frank Miles — all were supposed, rather vaguely, to recall, to equal even, the art of Phidias. Bustles, bonnets, straight profiles and diamond myrtle-leaves were the order of the day. For the more precious there were water-lilies, almond-blossom and flowing draperies; for the very knowing, chatter about Whistler and Walter Pater.

Thus, in the garden of that old-world city, through Parnassian groves, over smooth classical lawns that glowed, as they would have said, like sad green velvet, under weeping willows which wept more gracefully than they do now, and through which there always rattled a slight fresh wind from the East, suggestive of the clattering of willow-pattern plates, wandered our young hero, in ever so clean white-flannel trousers, talented and exquisite. The old esthete, who seldom committed himself to prophecy, leant over to my friend and said: 'That young man will go far!' . . .

From those days, alas, until the early nineteen-tens I know little of Dearborn's career. He went everywhere, knew everyone — poets, painters, the first lady who wore 'bloomers', boxers, philosophers, and Channel swimmers, wasting the perfect blossom of his art on the worthy and unworthy alike. His art developed continually. His talk became something outside himself, a disembodied spirit. From a fine art it became a devouring growth, that in the end swallowed up the author of its being. He was Frankenstein, his conversation the monster . . . but a monster with charm.

To meet him was always a pleasure, to part with him the subtle torture of a thousand farewells. Perhaps Hugh himself wished to leave you, but his art forbade him. It made him linger, led you to the longed-for terminus with a hundred little anecdotes that crucified your spirit; though regarded objectively they were round, full, delicate and smooth as a ripe peach. But his conversation, monstrous ectoplasm that he materialised, wound round you like a serpent, bound you with a thousand octopus-like tentacles, released you for a moment, like a cat with a mouse, and then grabbed you again, draining your blood like a vampire.

Dull people used to think it funny to say: 'I wonder what he does when he is alone'. Others suggested (and this was to me an interesting hypothesis) that he only existed in relation to his friends and acquaintances — his conversation but the magic rope up which clambered this fabulous spinner of words, like an Indian juggler, till, ceasing to climb it, he dissolved into the void. This perhaps might account for that lingering farewell; for when it was said, Hugh too would cease to exist for a while. But he was too personal, too positive for that; and, like all people of talent, as opposed to genius, he was too dated. He had little tricks, and these tricks belied his mask and proved him to be real. That manner, for instance, of wiping his eye, on entering a room, with the corner of a beautifully-folded, slightly scented pocket-handkerchief, as one who was still laughing at some witty conversation that he had just left, did not that betray him? Was not that conversation one that he had held with Whistler, Pater or some other already legendary figure? — was it not perhaps only a forty-year-old memory? On the other hand, it may have been a signal, like a bugle call, for focusing the attention; for Hugh, a true artist, liked to have the attention of his audience, and, if slighted, if interrupted, a strange fury gleamed from those wicked little eyes.

Like all beautiful objects, Hugh never aged, only becoming a little more worn — worn with the thin wrinkled elegance of a Chinese grotesque; but his talk became always fuller and richer. He was never silly, never dull; and again, like all *objets d'art*, though mannered, he was never really affected. Yet there was about him a quality that was sometimes a little sinister, sometimes a little sad; a mystery, certainly. But from the first, being an artist myself, I guessed that his art was a hard mistress. I have said that Hugh Dearborn knew everyone —

the world, the flesh, the devil, the ass and the artist. Among his greatest friends (for his art was bilingual and surmounted all obstacles) was Henri Schmidt, the famous Parisian portrait-painter, himself a master of conversation, in an age of which he and Hugh were perhaps the only two high exponents of that art. Schmidt painted his portrait, and it is a masterpiece. Dearborn is presented to us sitting in an armchair with his beautifully crinkled grey hair, his mask wrinkled and wicked, and rather over life-size, looking straight out of the picture. All his attributes are here — ring, cigarette-case, tie-pin, cane and, so to speak, the rest of the artist's equipment. This, then, was Mr. Dearborn when silence took him . . . when he was — alone! On the exquisite mask was a smile, like that Leonardo portrayed on the face of the Gioconda, the smile which, we are told, was caused and maintained by the music of hidden flutes — and this wonderful smile of Hugh is as surely caused by hidden music, by the dead music of his own young voice, by remembered passages from talks with Whistler, Pater, and Oscar Wilde. This picture ranks high as a work of art, but its sadness is unbearable.

Hugh was, however, grateful to the painter for it, and many of his preambles ran: 'As I was saying to an old friend of mine, who I know would interest you, especially with your real interest in, and love of, modern Art (but I expect you know him already?) — a man who really is, I think, one of the most interesting and (though perhaps I ought not to say it, for he is one of my greatest friends) amusing, but I mean really one of the most (*crescendo*) brilliant men, the painter, Henri Schmidt.' . . .

The war came and went, rolling me over, submerging me as it did most of the younger generation, filling our souls with anger, rancour and hatred, with pity and love. Mr. Dearborn, unsubmerged, began to work at other things than talk for the first time in his life. He worked hard and usefully translating various papers for the Government, being a master of languages as well as of language. The war did not break his indomitable spirit; he never grumbled, nor did he envy the younger men in the trenches, as did so many of our over-age patriots. He behaved, in fact, like what he was — a gentleman. Though there may have been little cracks in the foundation of his spirit, he appeared more elegant and gay than ever, and even took to dancing once more. After working ten arduous hours, with very little actual conversation, in a horribly improvised office, he would dine and then dance till five o'clock in the morning. His vitality was more amazing than ever. High above the coon-born music, above the vulgar, savage and sentimental strains, one could hear the floating 'dying fall' of his voice. Never was anyone so gay, so young, for his age as Hugh Dearborn, but it must have been a strain even on that giant energy. He would go to bed at three o'clock, at four o'clock, at five o'clock each morning, in the highest spirits; but who can bear to think of him, as he slept alone and old, in his charming flat? But the next day at ten o'clock he would walk to his office, gay and beautifully dressed as ever, and alas (as journalists write about royal visits), with a word for everyone.

Soon after the war I paid a visit, in search of health, to the plaster shores of the French Riviera; and at Monte Carlo we met. Every morning at twelve o'clock, to the droning snort of a brass band, Mr. Dearborn, in white flannel trousers (oh, how long ago was that day in the garden of Walter Pater! . . .), would descend the steps on to the pink-sugar terrace. The war had altered him, and although looking no older, he was beginning to show signs of eternal youth. But under the blue skies, in this hard, trembling light, enhanced by cacti and tropic flowers, and by this sugar-icing world, his appearance took on a new quality, his voice a new tone. He became more real, his warning voice took wing, soared out to sea like the albatross in the *Ancient Mariner*, borne in, as it were, on the crest of a returning toy wave. His essentially aristocratic finish, and even the rather tired rasp, felt more than heard, of his voice, put the population of international profiteers to shame. It would be many years before these beaked harpies could produce an article with such a finish. . . . I saw and heard a good deal of Mr. Dearborn that spring, and grew to love his conversation. My mind would wander in it, as in a forest; I would lose my path, led away by strains of unfamiliar music, and then be pulled up suddenly by some well-known landmark — the name of Henri Schmidt, or of Durant the boxer — and in that forest I found many homely things that I little expected, and, though on the whole exotic, it was decidedly less so than the war, which at the time we conspired to consider a natural life — and much more restful.

In May I left Monte Carlo, and for nearly two years lost sight and sound of Mr. Dearborn.

Two years afterward I was wandering about Italy with young William Erasmus, the writer. It was his first visit to the peninsula, and he was very much on the look-out for copy, though his calm, languid air, as of one dwelling on Olympian heights, was calculated to disguise the fact. But he was always watching, listening, and peering. He had, I suspect, written several Italian travel-sketches before leaving England. He was, however, a charming companion — a companion only too appreciative and receptive, his appreciation of anything amusing or interesting that was said being made even more obvious later, and in print, than at the time. Truly we must have livened up the landscape with the necessary grotesque touch, I with my fleshy Hanoverian face and big body, William, tall and thin as a young giraffe, with the small head of some extinct animal, some kind vegetarian creature that subsisted on the nibbled tops of young palm-trees in the oases — the Giant Sloth, for example! And how often, when I saw silly little jokes of mine appearing under the guise of musical or scientific articles in the weekly papers, did I wish that his character had been true to his appearance, that he had indeed resembled more nearly the Giant Sloth instead of possessing that vast and terrible assimilative and possessive energy.

After leaving South Italy we visited Rome and Florence, from there exploring some of the smaller Tuscan towns. The country was in the full efflorescence of early May, only the vines were a little backward, the leaves and tendrils still looking like golden coils about to spring out and release their stored-up energy. Little hills vibrated into the distance like rings of smoke, and the foreground was full of blossom — not the impressionist drifts of colour that you find in northern Europe, but flowers of every colour, each one separate, stiff and geometrical in design, as those in an Italian primitive, or in one of the landscapes of the Douanier Rousseau. The days grew even hotter, and any sudden little blue wind that rose among the distant hills, and played for a moment in the flowering fields, bore an unimaginable load of scent.

One morning we reached the delightful small town of Lucca, finding our rooms in the chief hotel, which had been the palace of one of the noble families in the eighteenth century, when Lucca had been a rich and independent State. The hotel was full of large, lofty rooms with golden curls and network, the prevailing tones of the old paint being light blue or pink, the whole effect being more that of the French than the Italian eighteenth century. The rickety bedstead, shabby German tablecloth and dingy modern furniture looked very remote in these chambers built as a background for gilded beds, rich brocades and powdered wigs. The sounds of the street — shouting, snarling song and shrilling bird-chatter of the market-place — were very faint at these patrician windows, lapping at them softly like small waves. Everything in the room was bright and quiet as in a coloured glass slide. In fact, the whole hotel had an indefinable atmosphere.

The town itself is a lovely one, with gardens and avenues of chestnuts, whose heavy leaves support their glowing, torch-like flowers on the thick battlemented walls that girdle it. We examined the churches, mostly Romanesque buildings of black and white marble, exotic as zebras, of a fabulous sculptural beauty, but seemingly less connected with the present town or its inhabitants than any pagoda whose blossom-like bells drip down their honey on the Chinese gardens. Yet none of the inhabitants seemed to feel the contradiction between their lives and their back-cloth. There the cathedral stood, like a zebra in the market-place, or like an elephant supporting a howdah — they paid no attention to it. In England these things are different. Any stranger stranded under the wide arches of York station for five minutes would guess instinctively the nature of the Minster, the Bishop's Palace, and even of the Archbishop himself. There is no need to explore. Anything queer will soon be tidied up, and, as they say, 'put to rights'. But in Italy civilisations crowd together: marble churches of the twelfth century, brick-built Gothic palaces, gilded rooms with bellying balconies, and finally the iron bedstead and newspaper, universal symbols of modern culture, cling to each other, each the concrete form of a different view of life.

Thus we explored the town, talking. Then followed an early luncheon, after which Erasmus, who during his four and a half weeks in Italy had already become more Italian than the Italians, even talking the language with such an exquisite *bocca Romana* that the Romans were unable to grasp his meaning, retired for that siesta which was to him the crowning proof of belonging to a cosmopolitan *intelligentsia*. He had, however, already peered into the visitors' book for copy, but found none — not even a resident or casual Englishman in the hotel, which was, as he remarked, none the worse for that; and no doubt comforting himself with thoughts of how unspoilt was this really very sophisticated small town, he retired to rest.

The afternoon passed quickly, and the day dwindled into the dinner-hour.

For a time we walked about the brightly lit town, but the cinemas were full, and we had seen *Lucia di Lammermoor* the previous evening, so that we returned through the humming streets to our hotel. William went to bed at ten o'clock. Half an hour afterwards he called me excitedly into his room, high, gilded and full of dead air that magnified each sound. His lanky pyjama-clad figure and receptive ear were pressed ecstatically against a door — one which led into the next bedroom. 'Who can it be? Who is it? Who is it?' he whispered. And then, quite clearly, each word taking on a greater significance in this room that seemed like a gilded tomb, I heard . . . 'As I was saying only a few days ago to a man, a great friend of mine, who has, I think, really one of the most amusing and interesting personalities — a man who, I know, would delight you, with your knowledge and genuine appreciation of modern Art — a really witty, but, I mean to say, brilliant and delightful man, Henri Schmidt.' . . .

Thus the poor tired voice dragged on, trailing away into the huge silence of the palace. Hour after hour the monologue continued; sometimes the voice stumbled and there was a weak repetition. Often the stories belonged to an earlier date, the references to those long in their coffins, and through the weak tones of an old man you could catch the fresher notes of an art whose technique had not then been perfected to such a metallic pitch. His smiling, trembling voice conjured up the applauding laughter of other days, when he had possessed a more appreciative audience than latterly. This, then, was how Hugh had talked to Whistler, to Pater; this was how . . . But now at three o'clock in the morning the voice sank down to a slight moan. It haunted me, the stillness of the room. What was the mystery of that beautifully finished being, lying in that vast apartment that belonged to another age of perfected technique? Whose voices answered him in his mind? Whose laughter?

Morning came to find Erasmus charmed and inquisitive, myself uneasy, not daring to break into the darkened silence of that room. No name was in the visitors' book; no one was to be seen, no voice sounded. Luncheon came, and we watched with mute inquiry.

But at about two-thirty Mr. Dearborn came downstairs, elegant and gay; his mask was rather heavy, tired and ill at ease, though the detail of his appearance was as fresh as ever. But there was a curious thick dragging of his speech, an occasional twitching in the muscles of his mouth. He gave me a hearty but uncertain welcome, avoiding my name. He told me he had been rather ill, and had come here to be alone until he was better able to face the world — his world.

Then it was that I understood — realised the full tragedy of that vocal practice in the small hours. He had been pleading with his art, his Muse, his cruel mistress, to return to him, but the string was broken; she had spread her wings and left the tired old mask: the shell, though still perfect, was empty. The cabinet-gramophone case was complete and beautifully finished; but it was made for only one purpose, and there came no sound of the old music. Art is a hard mistress, mysterious in her intentions. As I left him, never, alas, to see him again, there was a slight return of his powers, and, looking at me, he said: 'One spring afternoon I was in the garden of Walter Pater, walking over the lawn.' . . . And then I remembered the Parnassian groves, the weeping willow-pattern trees, the exquisite and talented youth in white-flannel trousers, and the words of the old esthete: 'That young man will go far!' . . .

DUMB-ANIMAL

(For Francis)

RAILWAY carriages provide a perfect, neutral ground for conversation. There is enough grinding and rumbling to enforce the voice being a little uplifted, and this in itself gives confidence, sureness of aim. If, for example, a public speaker begins his exordium in too quiet and diffident a key, his speech will hold no ear, brings no conviction; is doomed to failure. A competitive noise, however, will remedy such a weakness. As a rule, too, the Englishman only talks of impersonal things that neither interest him nor the person to whom he is speaking: for we are a shy, silent and especially a polite race, wherefore it is our convention that the talk must be adapted to the intelligence of the stupidest person present, and, if we are unaware of the mental calibre of anyone in the room, we must, out of good manners, presume that he is fatuous. But the anonymity of the railway carriage, once conversation is started, gives us release, makes confession, personal confession, quite easy. It is the under-the-rose intercourse of disembodied, nameless spirits floating swiftly through the air, inspired by the same ear-behind-the-grating anonymity that makes the confessing of their sins possible to Catholics. And subjects which require both thought and feeling are there approached as continental nations approach them, without embarrassment.

From York onwards the train was certainly a slow one, and the afternoon dark, for all the shimmering reflections into which the planes of the countryside had been transmuted. There had been a heavy fall of snow, and trees and telegraph-poles were hung with festoons and cobwebs in white and silver. But the windows were frosted with our breathing, and if you wiped them to look out, left a track of dribbling dirt on glove or newspaper: and all this, combined with such details as the heavy tin foot-warmers, resembling milk-cans that angry porters had hammered flat, the cigarette-smoke, the faint but nauseating smell of tunnels that never quite cleared away, the rattling of windows and doors, tended to focus the attention on the human elements rather than their surroundings. Up in the roof a star of yellow gaslight blossomed like a cherished plant beneath an inverted and sweating bell-glass. To this star our eyes now and again rolled upwards in despair. In every station the red-nosed porters shouted to keep themselves warm, threw their loads heavily, and then, still cold, threshed their arms together.

After a time, however, a pleasant conversation sprang up. The cheerful young doctor at my elbow took off his pince-nez, rattled a paper by his side, lit a cigarette and began to talk. Soon we were all of us exchanging intimate memories of childhood. The direction veered from time to time towards a semi-scientific discussion of the dawn of memory or the difference between the animal-mind and the child-mind. The glum, yellow-faced man, with the trembling red fingers, opposite me, turned out to be a famous, now fever-stricken big-game hunter, though I have by this time forgotten his name. He told us of the pygmy-race he had discovered, and of its primitive beliefs. Perhaps the need to worship differentiated man from the other animals. Once, he told us, he had lived for several years in Central Africa, inhabiting a two-storeyed house of whitened mud, built round a large central courtyard. All the little iron-barred windows, high up in the walls, gave on to this enclosure, for it was not safe to have them facing outward. One evening a huge and ferocious man-ape was captured and brought in from the great forest many miles away. The span of its hideous, hairy arms was something that even he had not been prepared for, accustomed as he was to these forest-giants. It was, I do not remember why, impracticable to kill the creature that night, and accordingly it was let loose in the courtyard, for there it could do no harm. At first it grimaced horribly, and drummed in a martial way upon its chest; vain summons to its distant wives — though when darkness fell it became quiet. But in the middle of the night the hunter was woken up. He did not know what had wakened him, but he experienced a sensation that something was happening, something curious and a little disturbing. He had been dreaming of an enormous cathedral, where people were praying for salvation under vast arches, sprinkled over with little lights, and had woken suddenly. He looked round his room. Green, tropical moonlight was splashing the floor, lay on it in pools, like water. He crept to the window, for an odd, low monotonous sound — did it remind him of chanting, he wondered? — was wafted therefrom.

He looked through the thick bars. The moon was round and high in the heavens, and just under him, in the brilliant, jade-green arena of the moonlit courtyard, was the gigantic, shaggy, heavy-shouldered form of the ape, engaged in a sad, most moving ritual, bowing low to the moon, walking backward before it, prostrating himself on hands and feet, and making the deep but quiet, never-ending rhythmic mumble that had woken him. . . . And so this dull, shaking little man opposite, one realised, had witnessed a unique spectacle, the very dawn of religion.

. . . . .

Skating lightly over that quicksand for conversation, the wisdom and long-memoried gratitude of elephants, once more we reverted to children. At what age, we wondered, does the child begin to surround the central fact of being, of existing, with little clusters of things felt and seen, pleasant and unpleasant? At what age does the memory, once a temporary affair of days and weeks, apply itself to years, and remain unimpaired through decades? The nose, of course, rather than eye or ear, is guide to the past. Memories of each long summer and winter come back borne on a stream of smell, of flowers in a garden, warm scents of box and rosemary, stocks, carnations or wallflowers, of bread being baked or jams being made, of bonfires blazing in the dull late autumn air, of paint and varnish and a thousand other things. My first memory, I thought, was of my nurse and sister under a tree covered with golden apricots — but where it was has always baffled me. But at what age do emotions first remain within our consciousness, somebody inquired? I certainly remember, I said, the inability to express my thoughts in words, a very early memory that must be: yet there are those who maintain that no thought is possible without the appropriate words to clothe it, that no colour is seen by us for which we have not a name! There had been some paltry, infantile crime of which I had been accused falsely, and could not, for want of words, make clear my innocence. Only the blind faith of children in their elders made me feel secure. Of course they would understand: and their failure to do so overturned my whole childish world, shook my being to its foundation. God had tumbled out of the star-spangled heaven in which I had placed him.

The young doctor snapped his pince-nez into a case, and said he would tell us a very youthful experience of his own. He was getting on now, he was thankful to say, quite well, had a satisfactory practice ('This kind of weather,' he added, laughing, 'helps us a lot, you know'), but in the past his dislike — no, his horror — of animals, especially dogs, had hindered him. There were a great many old ladies, bath-chair and armchair old ladies, in the seaside town from which he was travelling (indeed, they were the chief source of local medical income there), and they all owned two or more dogs. Naturally, if they saw him wince at the advances of their pets, they classified him at once as an 'odd sort of man'. It did not matter so much with cats, but every man should love dogs. Well, latterly he had contrived to simulate a liking for them, and he hoped his lapses had been forgotten. But the horror, actually, still remained. It had been during his whole life a source of pain and injury to him, and was founded on a particular incident that had occurred in childhood.

It was impossible to be sure at what age it had taken place — three or four, though, he supposed: between the ages of three and four. He knew that he looked strong enough now, but we must imagine a delicate little boy, left in charge of a nurse in a small seaside village, a collection of a few square, red-brick houses with blue-slate roofs, on the East Coast. His parents had bought a cottage there, in which to spend the summer months; had bought it, probably, for his sake, since he was weakly and an only child, and they were nervous about his health. Yet this, of course, he was too young at the time to understand. During the winter, then, he was left alone: quite alone there with his Nurse, who, though of rustic origin, was a very reliable, highly trained young woman. She cooked all his food herself, so frightened was she of its possible contamination, and had a real hospital horror — quite rightly — of dirt and germs. In consequence she would never allow him to play with the other children of the village, who were rather squalid and unkempt. He supposed really that his Nurse had been very fond of him, but she was a thoroughly sensible woman, and believed in her modern, educated way that it was wrong to show sentiment, dangerous to show affection, to children. Moreover, his parents, in their kindness and concern for him, exercised a similar control. It is likely that it pained them very much to leave him, and not to be able to see him more often. But this again was beyond his comprehension. To beings as young as he was then, life appears in its most simplified form: if people wanted you to be with them, you were with them. And they never allowed themselves to show any sorrow at parting from him, for the Nurse said that one ought to be very careful not to upset children, and as a child he had been very easily upset.

His first impression, thus, was one of loneliness, and, much worse, of being unwanted; a feeling that undermines existence, and, with the feeble, in the very old or very young, can make for death. The background against which these sensations were to be placed was eroded, grey, high, gloomy cliffs and a winter sea. The cliffs were not high enough to be imposing, but only to be forbidding, and their erosion was a matter of feeling. You knew instinctively that they were stricken and retiring bulwarks. The sea, on the other hand, imparted an overwhelming and savage sense of power, as the long grey battering-rams rolled on towards you, breaking on the nearer rocks into explosions of white, dying wings.

We must picture, too, a stretch of tawny sand, along which two figures promenade: the pale, nervous little boy; the Nurse, straight, tall and unsentimental as a young tree. And, to finish off the scene, we must conjure up the image of a few stray dogs, their barks and howlings lost in the muffled thunder of the sea, and the feel of an intensely cold wind that tears the flesh of face and neck with its numbing iron beak. Sea air was good for him.

Here was the dawning of his memory, the first certain thing he could draw out of the universal darkness that had preceded him. He could not be absolutely certain of his age . . . but he could see the dogs now. They seemed an Ishmael race, ownerless and outcast. And among them, especially, he remembered his first friend. He had loved it; but, regarded from an unprejudiced angle, doubtless it would have appeared a horrible, cringing, mangy little cur of a dog, very dirty and uncared-for. He could see it now though, spinning round after its tail like a whiting, curled up. Searching its tail, he imagined now, for fleas. A toffee-coloured dog, with long, sharp ears and deep yellow-brown eyes. Its stomach was fawn-coloured, and it rather resembled an ill-bred fox-hound. In spite of its ugliness, however, it had the alluring grace of all young animals.

Actually, he had not taken to this dog in the first place. But it had been so patient in its show of affection for him, had so obviously adopted him, that he had grown to love it. It waited for him every morning on the sands, jumped up and kissed his face, played with him, and, in fact, was a companion. Indeed this daily meeting with the mongrel became, secretly, the event of his day, and if by any chance it was too wet for him to be taken out, he was most unhappy, as he thought of the dog, soaked through, waiting by the seashore. But this he kept to himself, for grown-up people, he had already discovered, were intent on killing every pleasure.

This state of affairs lasted some time, and the Nurse paid little attention. But one day, quite suddenly, she realised how dirty, how filthily dirty, the dog was. Perhaps she had not noticed it attentively before, for she would often stand gazing at the sea, while her ward ran and played near at hand behind her on the beach. Of what use, she must have demanded of herself, were all her care and cleanliness, her sterilisings and boilings and washings, if the child behaved in this way behind her back? A strange, mangy cur of course harboured innumerable germs, was no fit companion for a delicate child. Having driven the dog off with the threat of a stick, she seized the boy by the hand, shook him, and dragged him home.

'Master Humphrey,' she cried, 'you ought to be ashamed of yourself in your nice clean suit, playing with that little wretch, so dirty and unhealthy-like. If you lets him jump up at you like that tomorrow, I'll kill the little beast, I will.'

He wondered how his Nurse, whom he knew to be fond of animals, could be so suddenly cruel. And yet he knew that she was direct, a woman of her word. He believed her. What was he to do? . . . If the dog came near him, she would kill it, then.

A deep sense of gloom and tragedy enveloped the small boy. If only it would rain tomorrow, so that he might put off his decision. . . . For at any cost he must save his friend from this fate, steel himself to be brutal if necessary. All night long in his dreams, the dreadful situation presented itself: and his courage failed him.

The next morning dawned, a clear winter morning, with a thin, false blue canopy spread over all this bareness. In the clean, very ordinary light, he was confident that so terrible a thing could not be true; this vast cloud of sorrow which had blown up over him. He dreaded the beach, cried a little as he approached it. The Nurse wondered to herself whether he was not well — he had seemed restless all night — and promised aloud to give him a dose that evening.

There, sure enough, was the dog, waiting for him, very alert and joyful, for it was sufficiently inured to rebuffs not to have taken the Nurse's threat with her stick very seriously the previous morning. Now, the boy realised, before his Nurse saw him, was his chance to save his loved comrade: and taking up pebble after pebble, he threw it with all his strength at the dog.

At first the mongrel thought this was only in play, and skipped and leapt gaily to one side: at the third or fourth stone, it stopped, cringed away, making itself small. Then it gave a howl of pain, and was sure: slunk away into pariahdom, its tail between its legs, ever and again looking round, the orange-brown eyes full of a mute but immeasurable reproach, at this friend who had encouraged and then denied it. The pebbles still followed the cur, as it crept and cringed away, pleading: for the boy stood there, intent on saving this only friend, throwing stone after stone, while tears streamed down his face.

The Nurse, who had been watching the fierce play of the waves, had completely forgotten about the dog of yesterday. All at once, she looked round and saw what was happening. 'Oh, you horrid little boy, you,' she exclaimed, smacking his hand very hard. 'Oh, you horrid little cruel monkey, torturing dumb animals,' and took him home.

He had been afraid of animals ever since. He was sure that was what it was.

. . . . .

The train roared through a tunnel, gave a bump. We collected our coats and papers, called for porters and were lost, disembodied again under the vast arches of foggy darkness, lit up, as it seemed, by the tinsel splinters of huge circus lamps.

THE GLOW-WORM

(For L. D.)

WHEN the war broke out in 1939, Sebastian Corble — *of course* you know the name — was nearly forty. At first sight he still kept a look of youth, almost of being boyish; except that he seemed too large, just as a child-impersonator on the stage often succeeds in giving an impression of being childish, but in an over-life-size manner. His hair, though a little thinner than in Oxford days, still retained a thick golden gloss as, in rather tattered array, aureole-like, it encircled his round cranium. Each individual hair, each tooth, each pore, seemed to claim more value in the whole presentation of his appearance than formerly; that was all. He was pale, and this lack of colour imparted to him, if the light came strong enough and from the right direction, a certain aspect of nobility, an air almost of that holy illumination to be found in the transparent countenances of the boyish saints depicted in late nineteenth-century church windows: but from this lack of humanity, his charm — his all-pervading, rather rancid charm — rescued him.

In every succeeding generation, a journalist makes a substantial fortune out of certain subjects: gardens, fashionable chit-chat, spiritualism; but who would ever have imagined that in a wicked age — for, to the good people of today, it seems as though any age in which the world was not dedicated to the high mission of destruction and massacre must have been a wicked age, lacking in democratic ideals — a fortune could have been made by the skilful exploitation of mere goodness and domesticity? This, then, had been Sebastian's discovery. To him it had been left to find out and explain that religion could be 'fun', and eternity, 'cosy'. He could make his million readers feel at home in Heaven. A more masculine Mrs. Beeton, he would sometimes begin an article by describing the 'divine' new curtains in his bedroom, and end with an account of his child, Little Tessa, talking to him of God. But he did not belong to the Mrs. Winniver School, he could be strong as well as good. Strength, rather than sour whimsy, tempered so much sweetness, and he was adept at scenting-out and denouncing moral dangers. Such authors as D. H. Lawrence and James Joyce he had flogged through his daily, and flayed in his weekly, columns. The peroration of his famous Sunday article denouncing Joyce's *Ulysses* is still remembered by many who have never read the book: 'And after that I had climbed a little hill to gaze into the eyes of God's Primroses, I rested, but still the foul miasma of that book pursued me, until I cried aloud, "Pshah! Who will sweeten my nostrils with an ounce of civet?" . . . And a small sweet voice behind me said, "I will, Daddy!" . . . And there behind me, in the sunshine of that spring day, stood Little Tessa. Rather would I that she quaffed the hemlock cup than that one day she should read another such book if another such book there should be!'

Yet sweetness always followed such outbursts of strength, and, on Sundays especially, a great army of admirers turned to him for comfort; and oh, the comfort, pressed down and of full measure, which they received! Round them he distilled the sweetness of his own home. Of difficult domestic material, even, — of his wife's telling him not to be silly or of Tessa having German measles — he was able to make some of his most appealing articles. He was never ashamed of sentimentality, and when a reader read one word, he knew what the next would be. To give a single instance, in no way remarkable, I recall a 'splash' headline of 'Wot's Wong? by Sebastian Corble'; a description of how Little Tessa tottered up to him on her 'baby feet', and, 'gazing up into his eyes', 'hissed out' — no, I am not giving you the right counter, I mean 'lisped pleadingly' — '"Daddy, wot's wong?"', while a linnet flew in at the window, and trilled its way backwards and forwards over their heads as if in an effort to comfort them.

And something *was* wrong: for, good in the main as Sebastian found both this world and the next, a sense of discouragement, an inevitable feeling of disappointment, would sometimes assail him. For example, his fellow-writers were often unappreciative, seemed to perceive the beauty of his writing no more than the peculiar virtue of his life. Again, Margaret, his wife, whom he really adored, was too retiring, even threatened to leave him if he brought her into an article.

She would not play any of the parts he would have liked to assign to her, while Little Tessa — to be frank — trod the boards too heavily. . . . But then Tessa, everybody said, was 'just like her father'.

Thus both father and daughter lived, you might almost say battled, for publicity. She had become nearly as popular as he was, yet he dared not stop it, for in a sense they were complementary and, also, there were the funds she brought in to be considered. Her vogue was, all the same, fantastic. Every autumn, a calendar, specially illustrated, was on sale for the New Year; reluctantly, no doubt, edited and selected by her father, it contained a gem, in the form of a question, for every day in the week: Jan. 1: '*Why is the snow white, Daddy?*' Jan. 2: '*Why did God choose white, Daddy?*' Jan. 3: '*Is it because white is good, Daddy?*', and so on, seasonally, until the end of the year. . . . Admiration grew, sales mounted. Her adherents founded 'The Tiny Tessa Tub' (she could not say 'Club', her father had written) and thousands of children who modelled themselves on her wore a special button, with a photograph of her enamelled upon it, in the buttonholes of their coats.

Soon she would be six. . . . 'Nasty little publicity-hound!' her father reflected to himself in an access of irritation. It really was time for her to give up all that baby-business, and be content to merge decorously into his background. But such, plainly, was not her intention. . . . And she was as clever as she was good. Often she sent for representatives of the Press on her own initiative (already she could use the telephone as well as if she were twenty!); and if he were to become too repressive, she was quite capable of summoning interviewers, and with those great, welling eyes of hers of blurting out to them, 'You don't think my Daddy's jealous! It's a wicked "fought".' (That would be a nice sentiment to have to record on the calendar for 1939.) . . . Of course, he was devoted to the little thing (he must be, he knew): but sometimes he wondered in his heart whether he really cared much for children. His wife would say, 'Don't be irritable with her, Basty; she's too much *like you*, that's all it is.' And then, in her turn, she would warn the little girl, 'Now, Tessa! I've told you. Don't irritate Daddy on purpose. . . . And I've said before, you're too young to be photographed for the *Daily Mirror*! And don't whine!'

He knew that, for all his goodness, he *was* irritable. The strain of writing, the strain of money-making, the strain of always being good, had in time caused him to be afflicted with insomnia. His own goodness, as it were, kept him awake at night. He found it difficult to endure the ridicule of the music-halls, as well as that of the comic papers — for, in addition to being a very popular writer, his renowned virtue had made him a very popular joke (a combination that could only exist in this country). But he did not allow such mockery to deflect him from the straight and narrow path. Virtue still offered him a very glittering reward. Think of those articles, those great articles that rolled away into infinity! The very titles of some of them come back to me: 'I Believe in the Old Stories', 'Saints Have Haloes', 'Don't Insure Your Life, Insure Your After-Life!', 'Cleanse the Stables!', 'Who's Who in Heaven?' Politicians praised him and sought his advice: but somehow, his popularity survived their fleeting shadows. The immense esteem in which he was held extended its bounds to the United States, the citizens of which adopted with fury the new cult. Tessa, too, remained more than a good second. . . . It was gratifying. . . . Yet, as he would have phrased it, the maggot bitterness still dwelt in the heart of the rose. For some people — some poor, lost, unregenerate and ungenerous souls — laughed at him in a disagreeable way: he knew it. In a news-film, for example, he had been shown making a speech at the opening of 'The Tiny Tessa Garden of Friendship' on the roof of one of the great London stores, and the public had laughed till the words were inaudible.

Then war came — and with it that great advance of moral values everywhere in Great Britain that war is always said to bring us. The values of peace-time were precisely reversed. The Common Man, recognised as arbiter, now in his generosity did not denounce the political leaders and incompetent club-room soldiers who had betrayed the men and women of two generations, but instead turned fiercely on the artists and writers of the last twenty years who had given that period its chief claim to distinction. Anything that helped us to kill was good, and Sebastian's goodness helped the killing, and so was better. His former popularity became an all-devouring rage. And many writers in the Press openly gave expression to an opinion that countless readers echoed: 'If only we could have Sebastian

Corble or Our Gracie as Prime Minister, the War would soon be over!'

He worked day and night. The Government, observing his vast influence with public opinion, allowed him special facilities for directing it. . . . Scarcely ever was he at home in Hampstead now. One night he would spend in the Maginot Line ('impregnable as the front line of Heaven', he wrote), the second flying over the lines, the third on board a submarine, the fourth in a tank, the fifth on a destroyer in the North Sea, the sixth in the 'Clipper' *en route* for a week's lecturing in the United States. He was sent on picnics with soldiers and sailors and airmen and munition workers, he was allowed to attend Divine Service in the Desert during the Libyan War, he flew to Malta and back to collect money for Spitfires. He and War Publicity illumined each other equally. But though the aid he rendered was invaluable, he wore himself to a shadow, spent himself utterly in the cause. Fortunately, the good, the real good, he was doing gave him new strength (and think of the money he was earning, even if half of it went to the making of the war which was making him!). 'You're a Saint', people used to say to him, and he was able to feel that there was a grain of truth in their praise.

There *was* something saintly about him now, and the look of a saint, which he had always a little possessed, had greatly developed. And he was much less irritable and nervous, though he missed dreadfully his home. . . . At last, tired out but happy, in September 1940 — just a few days before the first intensive bombing of London began —, he went home for a week of rest, a week of utter peace.

. . . . .

Tessa looked forward to his home-coming even more than did Margaret, for, with the outbreak of war, she had swung a little into the background. She was nearly eight now, and had been very excited ever since she had heard the news. She smelt publicity again, her mother thought. It was so bad for her — and she prevented the child from telephoning to editors, to tell them that 'Daddy was on his way home', or, as she put it to her mother, 'to give the Boss the low-down'. . . . She was allowed to stay up for dinner, an unusual treat, the night he arrived.

Everyone had always noticed how very observant Tessa

was. 'So wonderful of a little thing like that to see everything', her parents' friends used to remark, with a secret sense of unease, and would then add, with a conscious and shameful lack of frankness, 'But for all that, she's a thorough child; dear Little Tessa!' . . . After being fairly quiet throughout the meal until she had finally consumed the sweet, an ice-cream of which she was over-fond, she then proceeded to bounce up and down on her chair, on a new method she had discovered, until the room shook. Sebastian expelled all feelings of irritation and radiated love towards her; also on a new method he had discovered. He comforted himself, moreover, with the reflection that, if *he* were to dance about like that immediately after dinner, he would feel sick, very sick — but that was being uncharitable, he must be ever on the watch. 'T*es*-sa, d*ar*-ling!' he called lovingly to her, dwelling on each syllable. . . . For a few moments she sat in silence, motionless, watching him — with suspicion, you might have thought, as if she imagined he was trying to gain some advantage over her —, and then her restraint broke down, and suddenly, angrily, she burst out with:

'Daddy, what's that funny light round your forehead?'

For a moment her father's mood changed. 'Silly little beast!' he reflected uncharitably, in a spasm of annoyance, 'indulging in stupid fancies!' He said nothing, however: but, as the words passed through his mind, Tessa added, in a voice that showed traces of relief:

'It's gone now, Daddy!'

Margaret regarded her daughter with curiosity. It was evident to her that she *had* seen something, which herself had missed.

'I didn't see anything, Tessa,' she said. 'What do you mean?'

But Tessa jumped down from her chair and ran up to the nursery without answering. When her mother later went to say good-night, she found the child looking earnestly at her own head in the mirror.

. . . . .

The next day, Sebastian was busy. It was a Thursday, and he had to work on an article for the *Sunday Debacle*. It was one of the best, literally the *best*, he had ever written. But all the time, even while he was composing it, Tessa's strange remark had hovered in his consciousness, behind every word and every thought. Probably the child had meant nothing; but it was odd. . . . And an unusual sense of contentment, of being at one with Nature and the Universe, seized upon him; a feeling of inner peace and satisfaction, as though he had been engaged in utter fulfilment, physical as well as spiritual, not so much after the manner of a great painter executing a great picture, as of a peacock expanding its scintillant and jewelled tail, or a swan exchanging the ruffled beige of cygnetcy for its adult and undying white.

After tea, Tessa continued to eye him at intervals with a singular persistence: until her mother, misinterpreting the effect upon Sebastian (for this evening her intent gaze in no way troubled him), sent her to bed. She protested, but it was long past bed-time already, and she had only been allowed down to dinner last night on her solemn promise not to expect such a treat again. So she was led upstairs, moaning, 'But I want to see Daddy when it's dark'.

Margaret and Sebastian went to bed early too that night, and in his prayers he made a special recommendation for notice and mercy on behalf of his 'darling child, Little Tessa'.

. . . .

When they were called the following morning, the sunshine seemed to fall with peculiar strength upon the pillows. Before long, Margaret had to ask Sebastian to pull the blind down, so that the light did not catch her full in the eyes. Then they had breakfast in bed, and though himself did not so much notice the brightness of which she several times complained, somehow he could not succeed in arranging the blind to suit her. As soon as he had jumped out of bed, she would — almost before he had reached the window — cry, 'That's better!' but the moment he got back into bed she would declare that the light was dazzling her again. . . . A year ago, all this jumping in and out of bed at a woman's caprice would have irritated him: but not so now. He was master of himself. . . . He opened a letter. It proved to be from an admirer, and began, 'You're a Saint, a *real* Saint!' . . . At this moment a suspicion, bordering upon a certainty, of the immense and impossible truth entered his brain.

It grew dark about eight o'clock that evening and, before dinner, he had a bath and changed. And it was while he was brushing his hair, in the dusk, in front of a looking-glass, that he first noticed the faint, bluish-white radiance spreading after the fashion of a diadem or crown about his forehead. . . . He recognised it at once: a halo, it *was* a halo, plain, without the red bars to it one sometimes sees in church windows. (He was glad of that, he did not wish to be ostentatious.) His spontaneous feelings were those of gratification rather than of surprise, together — and this was odd — with a wish to hide his new spiritual distinction from his wife. . . . No, he had to admit it, he did *not* want her to see it — at any rate, not yet! So he had better avoid Tessa, who would be sure to spot it at once. . . . Otherwise, he was pleased. After all, it constituted an award from the highest authority. And it would aid his popularity and circulation. (In his mind's eye, he could see the enormous placards round the tops of the buses, 'Corble, The Man With Halo, Writes For The Daily Dustbin Only'.)

At dinner he turned up all the lights in the room so that his new nimbus should not be observed. Tessa was upstairs — he felt too tired, he said, to climb to say good-night to her — and Margaret noticed nothing unusual about him. The evening passed quietly and pleasantly enough, and they went to bed early. . . . Almost before Margaret's head touched the pillow she fell asleep. But Sebastian, on the other hand, found it unusually difficult to relax. The light from his head kept getting into his eyes. Even if he shut them, he could still perceive the glow. Really, it was blinding now! . . . And the more patient he grew, the more careful not to become flustered or angry at this unnecessary waste of candle-power, and of the time he so urgently needed for repose, the stronger grew his aureole in intensity, a positive dazzle. . . . What a blessing, he reflected, that Margaret could not see it — and then, all at once, as he experienced a contradictory spasm of annoyance because she had not beheld, or *would not* behold, it (a wilful manifestation of a sort of spiritual blindness that afflicted her), the light faded a little of itself, and slumber, in consequence, engulfed him.

. . . .

Though he was on holiday he devoted the next morning, Saturday, to seeing his editor and to good works. He lunched at his club, and then visited old friends in the East End, insisting on reading to them his favourite extracts from *The*

Stones of Venice, and from a new book by the head of the Foreign Office, entitled *The Trail of the Hun*. He wound up with 'a few little things of my own'. He did not return home until after dark (they were going to have supper late that night). And as he walked back from the Tube station, once or twice he heard an angry, brusque voice calling from the darkness, 'Keep that light down, man, can't you?' or 'Don't flash it about like that, or you'll find yourself somewhere you don't expect. Didn't you hear the sirens?'

Tessa was already in bed, and her father again alleged that he was too tired to go upstairs and say good-night to her. She was anxious to see him, it appeared. And Margaret pleaded for her:

'After all, Basty,' she said, 'the child is devoted to you. You know she is, and you oughtn't to neglect her.'

But he would not give way. The doctors had told him not to exert himself or do anything that was against his inclinations.

Still Margaret noticed no change in him, and they enjoyed a quiet evening until they had just finished supper, when the bombs of the first great night attack began to rain down on London. He must write about it at once for the New York paper. ('Hot News from Sebastian Corble', he could already picture the caption, splashed across the page.) What did danger matter, after all, he asked himself, and slipped into the garden, alone, for Margaret preferred to stop indoors. He repressed his annoyance as he tumbled over a stone toadstool with a tin gnome sitting on it, and had soon reached the little terrace at the end. Once there, he forgot everything else in the interest and horror of the scene below.

About a quarter of an hour later, the telephone bell rang in the house. Margaret answered it. A voice said:

'Is that you, Mrs. Corble? This is North Hampstead Police Station. We are informed that someone is signalling from your garden, but we know you too well to suppose that you would permit any foreigners about the place. You don't think, perhaps, as Miss Tessa 'as got hout and is being mischievous with a light?'

Margaret promised to make inquiries, and then to speak to them again in a few minutes' time. But no sooner had she put the receiver down than she heard an urgent knocking at the door. She opened it, and a very angry and officious air-raid warden informed her that he had seen lights floating in the garden.

'There's too much of that sort of thing going on,' he added. 'Shooting's too good for 'em.'

She contrived to calm the new-comer by telling him that she had already promised to investigate the matter for the police, and that her husband, Sebastian Corble, was there, and together they would search the place thoroughly.

'Oh, I didn't know it was Mrs. *Sebastian* Corble to whom I have the honour of speaking,' the warden answered. 'I'm a great admirer of your husband's. There's real *goodness* for you, and *guts* too': and he left, mollified.

Sebastian's virtue had its uses, his wife thought, as she shut the door, but, all the same, life was growing insupportable with all these silly scares. Was it likely that anyone could get into the garden and signal? . . . But she had better tell Sebastian, so she went out to join him. . . . It was certainly mysterious that *two* complaints should have been received. What *could* be the explanation; just hysteria, she wondered? . . . Then, as her eyes grew accustomed to the darkness, she understood! Sebastian's halo was visible, its pale yet scintillant radiation coming and going like that of a firefly.

But the effect of it upon her was indeed unexpected. Perhaps the noise of the bombing had unnerved her tonight, though she had not been aware of it, for she laughed out loud, and could not stop, laughed all the more as, when this ribald sound asserted itself beneath all the banging from earth and sky, she watched the aureole of her husband's sainthood and suffering glow yet more brightly.

Weakly, nearly crying, she said to him, 'Basty, *please* go inside, or you'll be fined!' . . . With a gentle air of reproach and dignity, he asked her why she laughed, and she told him that the police and the A.R.P. authorities thought they had caught a foreign spy signalling from the garden. 'And now,' she added, 'I must go into the house too, and tell them what I've found. "It's only my husband's new halo, Inspector."'

. . . . .

Neither of them slept well that night. In the morning he said to her apologetically:

'Darling, I'm afraid all that dreadful bombing kept you awake last night?'

'No, Sebastian,' she answered, 'I didn't mind the noise, but your halo kept getting in my eyes. I can't share my bed with a Saint; that's all there is to it!'

They had a quarrel about this — both of them were feeling rather on edge no doubt — and his radiance temporarily faded.

He looked in the glass before leaving the house, and decided that in the day-time it only slightly accentuated his usual pallor, and a certain air of distinction which he hoped he had always possessed. Of course, if he put his head back on a cushion, for instance, the light played upon it, but that merely resembled the 'shaft of sunlight' which, in a romantic novel, always falls upon the hero's face as he is saying good-bye. . . . No, it was in the evenings that it was a nuisance.

He did not talk much to Margaret, for he wrote all day in his room, and only saw her at luncheon, when she was engaged in keeping Tessa's mind occupied. At seven he had to address a meeting of the Golders Green Branch of the Tiny Tessa Tub. . . . Usually he walked about bare-headed, but tonight, without Margaret seeing him do it — for he did not wish to provoke another of those very trying hysterical scenes, they must be so bad for her — he encircled his head with the two regulation thicknesses of tissue-paper. That should prevent his being stopped, or threatened with a summons: people would just imagine that his cap was too big for him and he was trying to make it fit. . . . In the brightly lighted hall nothing would show. . . . So he could take the whole thing off in the cloak-room and leave it there until after the meeting.

Alas, on the return journey, after the meeting, he found that his attempts to comply with the regulations had been of no avail. Men could not understand. For them, a halo was merely a reprehensible light, to be treated with hard words and fury. The old complaints sounded from the darkness. 'Switch it out, man, can't you?' 'I'll summon yer for this, young feller, if yer don't alter yer wise. I'll tike yer nime and address.' 'Wot yer think yer doing? A blarsted light'ouse, are yer?' . . . And, which made the scene the more distressing, at each undeserved rebuke, the light of its own accord grew stronger.

No peace anywhere! But one must be good and meek and gentle. He took off his coat in the darkness and covered his head with it. Thus he managed to reach home without being arrested.

He could not, when he arrived, avoid going to say good-night to Tessa, for, as well as its being Sunday, they were sending her away tomorrow to avoid the bombing. . . . She had been unusually reserved the whole day, but now she threw her arms round her father and said simply, sleepily:

'Good-night, Daddy, I'm a glow-worm too!'

Her father looked at her, but she must have fancied herself into the statement. It would be most unfair if the daughter — even of such a father — were to receive the same award. He could see no sign of it, not a ray.

. . . . .

That night, alone in the spare bedroom, he thought things out. . . . A Saint has no place for earthly ties, he decided. Like Saints of Old — was it St. Andrew, in the hymn? — he must leave home and kindred. He made no charges, no allegations of want of faith, never even reproached Margaret, but the next morning he left to join the Fleet and gather material for a new and stirring article. He arrived just in time for the famous Battle of the Bombs, as the Press called it — the only journalist present. It was the first scoop of a Saint. But the Admiral never discovered that it was the trail of a halo that, by indicating the position of the ships, was responsible for so much damage. In whatever direction Sebastian moved, he was sure to be followed by an explosion and a cry, 'By Jove, that was a narrow squeak!'

Always, he was in the thick of things. Even if he went on a lecture tour, every town at which he stopped the night would be raided, and this, in turn, would provide him with the material for a splendid and heartening article the next day. (To protect himself against the police, he had now adopted a steel helmet with a special lining of cotton-wool. It appeared to be impervious. But often, when he was sure of being alone, its weight would induce him to take it off for a moment.) His rhetoric was unmatched, and he became the highest-paid journalist in the country. Little Tessa was hopelessly out-classed.

'He can't always escape like that,' people used to say as they read of his adventures. 'One day the enemy will bag him!' But they never did. For, in the end, peace came, and with it the great deterioration of moral values which is always said to manifest itself in a period when killing again becomes a sin. In time — in a very, very short time — the public changed its allegiance and went whoring after new gods. The Common Man — still, of course, arbiter of taste — no longer read Sebastian Corble's strong stuff on the evils of peace, but threw him, together with Shakespeare, on the scrap-heap, and turned with relief to the life-stories of the new Hollywood favourites. Before long, a bitter note crept into Sebastian's denunciations: they grew still more strong, and, in these degenerate days of which I write, as they grew stronger the readers became fewer. And, as the note of bitterness deepened, so did the radiance fade, until Sebastian Corble was mere man again.

HIS SHIP COMES HOME

Arthur Bertram, or not to deprive his personality of its full efflorescence we should perhaps record in their entirety the names Arthur Otho Augustus, had for many years enjoyed that distinction implied in being what is sometimes referred to in the obituary notices of fashionable journals as 'a familiar figure about London'; and, for his proper appreciation, it is necessary to consider what this to him so particularly appropriate journalistic phrase is intended to convey. Surely not merely that he spent his life wandering through the various streets, metropolitan or suburban, of our island-capital? Nor, to the initiate, would it suggest for a moment that his demeanour was marked by any peculiarity that would make him the centre of a vulgar attention, prompting children to cry out or point a finger, as, to give an instance, was noticeable in the behaviour of that retired General whose wont it was for many years to stroll down Piccadilly neighing like a horse. Idiosyncrasies of this kind are apt to make their owners too conspicuous, and the rather unconventional conduct of this latter gentleman did focus a part of the public attention upon him — so much, in fact, that when finally he attacked a hay-cart passing down the street in front of his military club, in order, as he said, to find forage for himself, he was, as we think, erroneously deprived of his personal liberty. Injustice is sometimes more visible to children than to those better able to express their feelings, and, even at that early age, it seemed to us that the poor General, as a soldier, a cavalryman even, who had mixed more with horses than with men, and indeed always made a point of neighing himself rather than speaking, had in reality some claim to that distinction which he boasted; while, for the rest, there can be no doubt that he set a fine example to his fellow-clubmen, on whose part a gradual awakening to the fact that they, too, had practically become horses, could but add to the amenities of our social life. But no obsession, such as this, separated Arthur Bertram from his kind. He was much more human than horse-like. His behaviour, on the contrary, was noticeable for its extreme correctness; so that the phrase we are discussing must be taken not to mean that he paraded any of the many streets in the town, but as indicative of the fact that he knew in what streets to walk, there to be observed by fellow-readers of the fashionable journals. Summed up, then, it implies the possession of enough leisure to display in the correctly chosen place characteristics sufficiently, but not too, personal to be noticed by others of equal leisure but less individuality. Thus a seemingly hollow little phrase can, like a cipher, convey an exterior, an outlook, a way of life almost, to those for whom it is intended.

Yet it was only as a middle-aged man that Bertram's ugliness, enhanced by a highly stylised manner of dressing, became so intense as to shed upon him a certain lustre. When he was young, it was his companion whose smile crowned him with a reflected glory, like the Aurora Borealis that plays round the Northern skies, giving him more interest even than that possessed by the original. From the beginning of his life as a man of fashion, he made it his rule always to be seen in the company of the Woman-of-the-Moment, and, if possible, to be in love with her. He had one remarkable gift in that he could foretell the advent of fame six months before it blazed up. This gave him time to make friends. His instinct in this matter was really unusual. He was seen, first with the leading professional beauty of Marlborough House days, then with the wife of the rising playwright, the most famous actress of the year, or the sister of an artist whose renown had at this moment reached its zenith. The discrimination he showed in, so to speak, 'spotting the winner', gave a flattering quality to his attentions, which no doubt helped him to other conquests. His affection became the equivalent of a bestowal of a public laurel-wreath upon the lady, or upon her brother, or husband — a halo of which Arthur kept just a chip, sufficient to illumine himself, as commission. It helped him, too, with other women to be seen in the company of some famous person: to those who did not know him he seemed a distinguished, almost a brilliant, figure.

But the world hinted that Bertram occasionally reaped other, baser, more material rewards than the acquisition of fame, or requited love, from those connections — or should one write transactions? — that the laurels turned to gold within the hands of this alchemist; that he was not above writing to the 'Woman-of-the-Moment', informing her, rather needlessly, of his poverty, in letters which she would be unwilling for her relatives to read, hinting, as they did, at some association between them which had, in fact, never really existed; and if his hints, his demands, were not satisfied, would always refer to her in public with a tender leer of implication. Combined with these tastes and recreations Arthur was a fervent Catholic, and an arbiter of good form, though, as the public suspicion of him gained ground, he cleverly cultivated the style and manner of a successful brigand.

Scandalous rumours, such as these we have mentioned, are often the fruit of the imagination, the invention of enemies; yet if, as was apparently the case, Mr. Bertram had no fortune of his own, it must be admitted that he enjoyed an unexampled run for other people's money. A younger son of a younger son, his natural advantages were limited to a magnificent air, an amount of self-possession, certain aristocratic relatives, and an ugliness that in its ultimate blossoming was to attain a real significance. To these was added a talent for dress, into which he threw all the energy usually absorbed in, and the imaginative qualities often killed by, the practice of cricket or golf. Also he was generous, undoubtedly generous. The bouquets which he was in the habit of presenting to his favourites would have filled the Crystal Palace, the fruit would have won first-prize at any show; however poor he was, however short of money the recipient of these soft tributes, he never failed in their offering. But, afterwards, would come a day of reckoning.

Arthur must have first assumed his rôle as a very young man in the early 'seventies of the last century, a period that offered to any adventurer of aristocratic connection an unrivalled opportunity for polite plunder. 'Society'—the word was one of bounded application never then used to indicate any community including brain or manual worker—was undergoing those changes that would, in the space of another thirty years, put an end to it in this sense. It was, though seemingly stagnant, already in a state of corruption that would make it a perfect Golconda for any adventurer with the right attributes. For, being a world much talked of, but unknown except to a few who never spoke of it, it possessed a certain glamour, like that appertaining to some superlatively secret form of freemasonry — a glamour which, with its gradual expansion, it was to lose for ever. As in those days large hotels and restaurants were nearly unknown, it follows that the habit of eating in public was not much indulged in by any class. It was not even easy, therefore, to see the world unless you were of it. This cloak of invisibility was very valuable, giving to it the attraction of the unseen, as well as of the unknown: here was some influence in the midst of us, some veiled mysterious power, the respect for which was like that felt for the Dalai Lama — a feeling which, were he to show himself, would swiftly diminish. Yet the process of visibility had already begun, so that at this particular stage 'society' was like a partially materialised spirit at a séance, something that might appear in your own house if you encouraged it sufficiently with baked meats or human sacrifice, employed the right medium, had enough superstitious belief in its existence, and would swear not to turn the light on suddenly or ask an unexpected question. Mr. Bertram might, if suitably rewarded, attempt to materialise it for you in your own rooms, though possibly he promised more than he could achieve.

Arthur Bertram was related to more than one peer; and all through the first three-quarters of the nineteenth century members of the English nobility were regarded with the reverence due to an almost supernatural order of beings. Illustrative of this is the following quotation from the second volume of a trilogy which we found recently:

'"Oh, Lady Arvon," said Hester, in a scared kind of voice, "will Mr. Brown, I mean Martin, ever become a peer? I did not think of that." . . .

'"Certainly he will, little Hester, if IN THE NATURAL COURSE of things HE should outlive HIS FATHER," answered Lady Arvon, as she lovingly kissed the flushed cheeks.' . . .

One would diagnose the years 1860 to 1870 from the descriptive passages in the book; for in its sentimental pages the ladies recline on circular settees — ottomans, as they were called — from which their skirts billow out in front at the angle of falling water, while the gentlemen, with dark whiskers still clinging to their cheeks, lean over them in positions of polite but easy elegance. But, actually, this book, perhaps the last of a long tradition, was written in the year 1888 and dedicated to William Ewart Gladstone!

This respect, this reverence, for the invisible world of which the peerage formed a sacred inner core, deepened with the wealth of the person who felt it. To bathe in this radiance, to share this true light, was the ambition of many. Thus, though 'society' was still dominated by the great territorial magnates, and yet enjoyed a certain political power which was the legacy of the eighteenth century, the great outcrop of rich people created automatically by the diversion of trade to this country from France and Germany during the war of 1870 was already knocking at the door with a golden nugget. Their method was at the same time to propitiate and outbid the world, by the magnificence of their entertainment; and Arthur Bertram, trading on his advantages, was often a guest at the intensely respectable but otherwise rather Trimalchio-like banquets of Sir Gorgious Midas.

Though his ugliness was yet in its raw stage, Arthur had already shown the sureness of his instinct, not by any attempt to improve those qualities of heart or head in which he may have been slightly deficient, but, on the other hand, by a resolute insistence on his bad ones. This gave him what was taken by many for an easy, aristocratic air. Through these gilded saloons, full of tall palm-trees, that soared up into the hard gas-light of mid-Victorian nights like so many giraffes, their glazed and withered leaves spreading out bone-like structures till they seemed like the skeletons of some extinct monster, through smaller rooms full of roses, orchids and carnations, the exquisite colours of which threw into a more hideous contrast the suffocating draperies of that dusty age, through corridors full of huge plants, their leaves blotched with corrupt colours like those of decaying flesh, he would strut to the bobbing tune of some now obsolete polka, talking in a loud insolent voice about the rarity in these places of 'really well-bred people'. He would stare long and impertinently at those not fulfilling his standard in this respect; nor would he spare his host or hostess, for, whereas others laughed at them fitfully and behind doors, Bertram had the courage to do it constantly and in the open. His calculated drawl, a dry creaking sound as of some box with rusty hinges slowly opening, alternated with slow important clearings of the throat, and was accompanied by a complete set of facial grimaces, regular as Swedish exercises. There would be that fascinating twitch of the mouth, or that lifting of the skin from the forehead; an enchanting shutting of one eye, opening of the other, such as were introduced as the symbols of Upper and Lower Egypt into the ceremonial mummification of dead Pharaohs. All these little touches were added to his appearance in order to combine a quality of dignity with natural fascination. The open eye, however, was alert and twinkling, the skin, sallow and rather lined, had about it something of the texture of crocodile-skin. If any woman, particularly one of his famous companions, was mentioned, he would smile in, as he thought, a pleasing way; the rusty hinges would creak open and eject some phrase such as 'poor little woman', or 'divine little creature', by which you were intended to assume that the lady referred to had loved and lost; for he based his policy as a professional on the axiom that nothing succeeds like success; and it was his arrangement with the world, an understood thing, that in his rôle of Don Juan he was irresistible.

Thus, past those same circular settees that we have mentioned, now burdened with no crinolines, where men, moustached and not whiskered, talked, with perhaps less easy elegance, to ladies with bunchy little skirts, sitting demurely upright under palms mangy as tropical beasts in an English climate, by plants that seemed to harbour cruel insects of the burning forests, Arthur Bertram would lounge, strut and swagger. While, from the near distance, the sound of a string band, like the humming drone that comes up from jungles, would reach you with warm gusts of air. Against this background his dry voice would be heard, alternately insulting the rich and deploring his own poverty; but always he hinted, in his own phraseology, that one day his Ship would Come Home. But in what that frail barque consisted, — Corsair, Indian treasure ship or the floating barge of Elaine — was never to be discovered.

Thus his life passed easily enough, except for periodic financial crises, which always seemed to be the worst of troubles. He lived in two small rooms, dark as Caliban's cave, in Ebury Street. But one could not think of him in that setting; for out of his dingy retreat, dirty and uncomfortable, he would appear resplendent, bearing his daily tribute of flowers, a gardenia in his own buttonhole, glorious as any peacock leaving its nest, and mouthing such phrases as 'well-bred', 'distinguished-looking', 'Soi-disant, of Our Class'.

For a brief interval of three years the regular course of his life was interrupted by marriage. It soon resumed its normal trend when, true to his reputation as a gallant man, he allowed himself to be divorced. Much sympathy was felt for Arthur. On the one side was to be considered a certain financial gain, on the other his reputation as a man of the world, a modern censor of morals (for such he had now become), his profession of the true faith, which does not allow of divorce, and his rôle of gentleman. It was a struggle for him; but in the end Arthur was relieved of his religious scruples, and Mrs. Bertram of a share of her small fortune and her husband's bullying manner. Let it be understood, however, that his wife regarded it as a bargain.

She had, in any case, been too poor for her husband. A pretty, rather silly woman of provincial upbringing, she had been caught by his amazing manner, by the reflected glory of his friends, the distinction of his relatives. He was so well-bred too. While Arthur, for his part, imagining her to be richer than she was, felt a longing for a quieter, less transient way of living. Perhaps, too, owing to difficulties, he had been forced to realise his assets rather suddenly. Then, though Ina was of bourgeois origin on her father's side, her mother came of Russian princely stock. This gave Arthur a new opening. He would meet you in the street, and roar like an angry lion about those pretenders to Russian princely rank whose names were not even mentioned in the *Almanach de Gotha* . . . 'while my wife's mother tells me' . . .

Poor Mrs. Bertram sank back into a welcome obscurity, and Arthur resumed a life based on the broad foundations of his small, though slightly augmented, capital and his renown as a Don Juan. In this third phase, which was but a continuation of the first, Arthur wore a double tiara: the aureole of success in affairs of the heart, of failure in those of the world; the latter, by its interest and appeal, helped him to fresh conquests. And his appearance, too, was more developed. By now he possessed a really magnificent ugliness, and one of which he made every use. It may have been due either to some form of esthetic perception, or to quite unconscious artistry, but having always had a slim, rather elegant figure, he appeared early in life to have realised the great artistic truth that elegance of form and distinction of dress enhance the quality, whatever it may be, of the face above; that a slim figure and well-made, well-thought out clothes can make an ugly face more hideous a thousandfold. How much more effective would Caliban be in what is known as 'faultless evening-dress', than in those conventional clothes of the cave-man which he usually affects! Thus Arthur used his figure, his dress, his manner even, to enhance the awfulness of the face that crowned them, set like a grotesque jewel. And, indeed, in contrasts such as these, lies the whole art of the grotesque. The gargoyle aids the leaping spiritual beauty of flying buttress, Gothic arch and spire, while the cathedral in return lends its loveliness to display each individual gargoyle. A dragon makes plain the ideal and peaceful beauty of a Chinese landscape. The sad ugliness, the useless effort of a dwarf, enhance the richness of seventeenth-century costume. Thus, Arthur pressed his youthful slim figure and stylised clothes into the service of the sallow muzzle-like face that surmounted them. No woman could pay a greater attention to her toilet than did Bertram. He achieved distinctly the personal note. In London he wore an idealised version of the usual dress that belongs to the familiar figure about London: striped or check trousers, beautifully creased, a black tail-coat — what used to be known as a 'fancy waistcoat' — a stock-tie with a pearl pin, the gift of his unfortunate wife, and, finally, balanced above that head as by a conjuring trick, a grey top-hat. A Malacca cane of unusual height completed the effect, while his walk was so calculated as best to display each elegance.

The background of the early 'nineties against which Arthur now found himself, after the rapine and triumphs of nigh twenty years, had a certain amount of character. Our hero would explain 'that things change so fast nowadays' — for the Opopanax and White Rose of his early youth had now given way to the odours of 'Chypre' and 'New Mown Hay'; odours which were actually allowed to mingle in the drawing-rooms with the fragrant smoke of Egyptian cigarettes! What is more, certain young men did not hesitate to wear in public, in London even, shoes of brown leather, a recent discovery.

But the London background of this period had more character than the present one, was more essentially different from that of other cities; and Arthur, in his small way, had become one feature of a familiar prospect, since sadly altered. The narrow streets, full of shops engaged in a more dignified competition to attract the senses, were fresher, brighter than they are now. There was then about Bond Street and Piccadilly an almost patent-leather finish. Everything shone with paint and sparkled with varnish. Through the large sheets of glass, shelves and rows of bottles gleamed like coloured crystal. The frayed edges of Northern sunlight rehabilitated themselves in the depth of these green, silver and crimson waters, even recovering and giving out a little warmth, bringing the perfume out of the bottles as they would draw the secret breath out of country flowers, or press it out of tropical blossoms that live but a day, until a surge of scent, stronger than that of any garden or forest, poured in overwhelming torrent from the shop into the street that lay cold and hard as a canal outside. Passing on farther, behind yet more glass, we see sparkling silver, crystal and scaly leather mirror-like with varnish — those ugly useless ornaments for which the English are still justly famous. Everything is neat and well ordered, everything is well made. Here the smells of leather, of lion and crocodile skin, of sweating African jungle and slimy Indian river bed, were strong enough to frighten the horses — arranged in pairs like those animals you see advancing into a diminutive ark in early tapestries — were they aware of anything but attentive grooms in comfortable stables, or, perhaps, of being given apples and carrots on Sunday mornings after church. Flowers, arranged skilfully yet with an unbelievable want of art, pressed their hot faces against the crystal walls that imprisoned them — the open pleasant faces of roses, orchids like battle-scarred generals, flowers of fever and blood, and carnations, looking as if they were cut from stiff, frilly paper, while little india-rubber bands held up their chins from an elderly sagging, giving a forced, fresh look of youth. Among this well-organised, rather tired, riot, a love-bird pecks at steel bars with hard metallic clatter. Then there were windows full of baskets of fruit, of the full, healthy scent of mould and autumn orchards, though in the same place were queer toys, fruit scaled like reptiles, so that no man would willingly eat of them, and oranges, round and warm as the sun. Then follow open marble shelves of cold, shiny fish that look as if they came from the Dead Sea, displaying damply white tones or circles of rainbow colour, while near by hangs a whole world of birds, hams and meat, that would please equally a housekeeper or the denizen of a jungle.

In the centre of this narrow street stands, like a granite rock, a broad figure in a large square blue coat, with boots like ships and a hat that is a blue dome. This is the guardian of 'lor-an'-awder', straight out of the last Drury Lane pantomime harlequinade, a gruff, burly, blue figure with one white-gloved paw held up in warning. This uplifted hand holds in check, as if by magic, a line of vehicles more frail, more fantastic, than any in the world. Stranger and more unreal than any gondola that cuts the Venetian waters with knife-like prow are these angular, black scallop-shells on high, round wheels, scallop-shells like those from which Botticelli lets his golden Venus be borne in upon the foaming tides. High up above the shell, so that his weight must surely overbalance his frail equipage, sits, like a monkey, a red-faced figure with shiny top-hat, whip and red buttonhole. Fabulous, indeed, is the speed of them, as they roll along, jolting slightly in the fashion of a man walking a tight-rope. And, straight out of this queer, narrow perspective of houses, shops and carriages, two figures impinge on our sight. A tall good-looking lady, in leg-of-mutton sleeves and a little hat, and — with her — a well-dressed, elegant figure, mouthing and twisting its great muzzle like some Red Indian chief in war paint. It is Arthur Bertram with the Woman-of-the-Moment; and how this background displays our hero! About him is the same ugly element, the same hideous smartness. The shape of his top-hat fits in with the perspective of the chimneys, the glaze of it echoes the paint and varnish of the shops. His patent-leather boots reflect, as in a black mirror, the huge slabs of glass in the windows, the trivial objects behind them, while they in their turn send back a watery reflection of Arthur and those glittering ornaments that distinguish him. Even the well-marked brick of the houses helps to show off the texture of his face.

But, alas! this townscape dissolves as we look at it: the strange vehicles have been dashed up like shells by the raging tides, shattered on the beach of time. Here and there are survivors, in the museums, beside a family coach. Perhaps one may lurk in the back alleys of those streets of which for so long it was the ornament, sought out and made much of, but now an outcast. The Woman-of-the-Moment is thirty years older, and Arthur — well, Arthur is just his own dear self!

In the country, or still more at foreign watering-places, Arthur could give freer rein to his personal taste. There, quite frankly, and, we think, from his point of view, wisely, he based the harmony of his clothes upon the brigand-theme: flowing blue cloak, romantic hat, long gauntlet-gloves and a cane, higher than his London one, persuaded the inhabitants that here was someone of immense renown. Used as they were to the ways of the English, yet here was something odder still. No one, surely, but a Personage Incognito would dare to attract to himself so much attention; surely that face, too, was the property of one of the European Royal Houses, a Prince in Exile, the King of . . .?

The years went by, ever more swiftly, as is their way, but Our Familiar Figure would still be seen walking down the customary streets at the correct hour, though he was more often alone than formerly. His nimbus was now his own. With head erect, balancing that grey top-hat apparently without an effort, he would straddle down the street, snuffling like a bull-dog, grimacing horribly to himself and making wry faces. The innumerable little leathery lines in his countenance were led up to by the single immaculate crease in each trouser, or thrown into bold relief by the sober patterning of his cravat. A friendly but rather unprepossessing leer would greet his friends. There would be a roar, the angry roar of an old man, rather inarticulate but ending in the well-known phrase, 'Soi-disant, of Our Class'. Then he would remain silent for a moment, and, drawing a folded handkerchief out of his pocket by its angle, would brush away invisible specks of dust from his sleeve. The friend would now be treated to a fixed stare of some duration, followed by a writhing of the facial muscles, and then, swivelling one bright-gleaming eye round the corner, he would remark with the usual drawl, the usual loud, dry-throated rasp in his voice: 'Ah! there goes that divine creature; such a well-bred woman, too, which is none too common in these days. We used to be great friends.' Or, 'Do you know who that is? If you'd known her, my boy, as I did (poor little woman) twenty years ago.' . . . Then would come variations based on the same theme, and the climax would be a short sermon on the morals of the day, followed by the customary dissertation upon his own poverty, which was indeed becoming a problem for him.

By now between the ages of sixty and seventy years, Arthur may fairly be said to have reached the Awkward Age. Women with famous husbands or brothers now preferred the company of these relatives to the tiresome attentions of, as they put it all too frankly, this old bore. No more loans of fifty pounds from ladies, following upon a written account of Arthur's romantic dramatisation of their friendship, came his way. But he never lost faith, firm in the belief that one day his ship would come home — a supposition that had sustained him through many difficulties and for many years. Though the impoverishment of the whole world, as a result of the war, made existence more difficult for him, though he was now forced to spend a great part of the year in being looked up to by the English colony in cheap foreign watering-places, yet he was still always to be seen in London at the correct time, in the correct place. His manner, his air, were more in the Grand Style than ever. He let it be seen and understood that he was a relic of a past epoch, a grand old English gentleman, damn it, such as could not flourish in this degenerate age! Still there were, undoubtedly, moments in the night when Arthur asked himself what the future held for him. It might not be a long one, but it might be extremely unpleasant. His bills became to him a maze, which he walked blindfold, and with no hope, while through the thick hedges peered the evil gleaming eyes of his enemies. And when he woke again to the still blackness of the middle night, it must have seemed as if the banquets of Sir Gorgious Midas were, too, but delightful, fantastic dreams. He would sigh, reflecting how his world had changed out of all recognition, but unaware of the minute part himself had played in this dissolution of the old order, as is the ant of the overthrow of a garden-bed, or the coral insect unconscious of his destructive yet creative mission.

The Midas family, though they, too, had changed with the times, were still on very good terms with Bertram, whose insolence in the house of the old merchant was transformed into obsequious praise in the grandson's ancestral hall. No one could play the old family-friend better than he could, and a long-standing connection like this was felt to be part of the Midas feudal make-up. Bertram used to tell his friends that it made him blush, absolutely blush, to think how the country had treated Lord de Normanville, old Sir Gorgious's grandson. No one had been more 'keen-on-the-war', no one had lent more motor-cars, believed more spy-stories or given more vegetables to the wounded than had this peer! No one had so swiftly observed — immediately before the Armistice, indeed — the danger of our falling into the enemy's trap by accepting their complete submission — by, in fact, allowing a premature end to the war; no one had denounced this folly of unheeding statesmen more energetically than had Lord de Normanville from his seat as hereditary legislator; and, finally, no one was more surprised when asked to contribute towards the cost of our glorious battles!

The family of old Sir Gorgious were now fast selling the great bulk of their inherited acres, and were content with two motor-cars, where formerly they had been forced to employ seven. In fact Lord de Normanville could cry poverty with the richest in the land. But though the stately homes were going one by one, there were consolations; and on the top of all his other sacrifices he still managed to entertain a few friends from time to time, though, of course, in a very simple manner. It was at one of these pleasant gatherings that Arthur met his second destiny, whose rôle was filled by the ample fortune and generous figure of Mrs. Fullard: this lady, a fascinating widow, was possessed of much wealth and sprightliness.

These parties always had something very original about them, quite different from other people's. Lady de Normanville always liked to *mix* her guests; that was the secret of it, she confessed — though at first sight the personnel appeared to be much the same as at other 'simple gatherings' of the kind. In a curious way the talk always showed a tendency to return to finance, by which was meant the iniquities of taxation — though, of course, other subjects would be touched on. Dinner, on the first night, was most amusing. Arthur sat next to Mrs. Fullard, while the eruptions of green and purple brocade and the numerous ancestral portraits on the wall threw into rich relief every detail of their appearance. Old Sir Hankey Twadham, the former Minister at Sofia, was there, too, with a new — or at any rate new to him — rather *risqué* story, the worst of which was that, as he confided to all the guests in turn, you had to be careful to whom you told it. His eye wandered round the table mournfully, in search of a possible victim. Then that round disc of glass behind which his eye was displayed like some precious object in a crystal *vitrine* would twinkle gleefully, and he would say: 'I shall try it on Mrs. Fullard. She's all right! It will make her roar. It makes me laugh every time I think of it.' Dear old General McKinnan was also one of the party, and could be seen heavily crunching his red, swollen mandibles, or moving a hand like a lobster's claw in occasional explanatory gesture of some killing anecdote in connection with the Irish Rebellion. 'The curious part of it, too, was that the leaders were all clever men. But they don't go far, do they?' he asked with a first suggestion of passion. 'Look at Curzon! I remember him at Eton. Could anyone call *him* a *clever* man? and look where he is now!' This peroration of the General's made an immediate appeal to the audience, who took it up and worried it in couples, carefully, in their various corners. Again he focused attention by another of his *killing* stories about the rebellion. 'What an extraordinary thing!' everybody screamed. But the conversation did not remain long at this frivolous level. The Prince of Wales's tour of the Empire was discussed. It was marvellous how the Boy had Smiled. The General expressed it as his opinion that once he had got over those blackguardly hurdles, or hurtals, or whatever they are called, the Royal Tour would do more good than a thousand machine-guns. Meanwhile, at the other end, Lord de Normanville held the field with some interesting reminiscences of his more recent disputes with the Inland Revenue and Super-Tax Authorities. He felt it his duty, though always unwilling to make himself conspicuous, and, indeed, always trying to pass as an ordinary citizen, to write to them pointing out that after deducting Income Tax, Super-Tax and his annual expenditure, he was left with an income of six hundred a year. An answer had been returned to him, couched in the most insolent terms, suggesting that he should cut down his expenditure. He had replied, with dignity but without loss of temper, making it clear that any curtailment of his expenditure would increase unemployment, already sufficiently prevalent, and that he was unwilling at this juncture to do anything that might in any way injure the Commonwealth. Followed a short but very interesting discussion on Bolshevism; Sir Hankey, who plunged into this discussion off the deep end, forgot the point of his story in the middle, and, instead, gave minute details of what he had heard in Sofia before the war. If, he added, he told them only half what he *knew* now . . . and the pearls encircling billowing necks became a shade paler in their radiance. Several people, indeed, felt positively faint. Lady de Normanville rallied the talk by appealing to General McKinnan. 'General, if you had to have your portrait painted, whom would you choose?' The gallant old soldier, who considered portrait-painting as quite a different thing from any other form of painting, and always attended the opening days of the exhibitions in Bond Street, was immensely flattered by this question — much more so than if his opinion had been asked on tactics or horses. 'Why not Oswald Birley? There was a man who could paint what *he* saw, what *you* saw!' Mrs. Fullard, who was very artistic, suggested McEvoy, but Arthur thought McEvoy's work was rather *too* weird, wasn't it? Lady de Normanville pointed out that he never seemed to finish his portraits; besides he made everyone look alike. Whereas Glyn Philpot finished them all, absolutely, and made everyone look different. 'A clever man, that!' said the General suspiciously.

Conversation split up again, drifting into sets of twos and threes, and it was now that Evelyn Fullard completely captivated Arthur Bertram by confessing, with that pretty trilling little laugh of hers, that if she had her way she would *make* the miners go down the mines and work. While people with fifteen thousand a year were paying nearly half their income in taxation, the colliers — who had nothing to keep up — were earning five pounds a week and paying no taxes at all. As for herself, she had been obliged to borrow money from the bank this year to pay her Super-Tax! It was this adorable mixture of wit, charm and common-sense, that fascinated Arthur. He proposed after three days; and they were married within three weeks of their first meeting. It was a real romance!

The honeymoon was spent on the shores of Lake Maggiore, in the Pucciniesque setting of soft air, palm-trees and lapping waters; a neighbouring casino added interest to the natural beauty of the landscape. While there Arthur managed quite quickly to solve that Super-Tax trouble. Wherever they went, the romantic couple attracted great interest. They were an interesting pair. Arthur was triumphant; he appeared, bathed in that tender, rosy glory in which the later Venetian painters depict, on wall and ceiling of patrician palaces, the apotheosis of Procurator or Doge. And, on his return to London, he became a more familiar figure than ever. He had entered the third phase; he had conquered the Awkward Age.

It looked, in fact, as if his ship had come home at last. Alas! it was merely the Hundred Days over again, the ship but that *Bellerophon* which was to make him an exile in a foreign land. For now Mrs. Bertram made manifest the devil within her; her pretty little golden laugh showed itself to be the key to a temper infinite and terrible in its variety. The plebeian origin of his wife, to which Arthur had willingly and, as he now said, foolishly blinded himself, peeped out from behind the enamel. She made it clear that she had no intention of allowing Arthur to relieve her of the necessity for borrowing from the bank to pay her Super-Tax; she even refused him a small allowance. She irritated his susceptible nerves at every turn with vulgar little tricks, and displayed a revengeful, unforgiving spirit. How, he asked himself aloud, could he introduce such a woman to his friends? It was impossible . . . Mrs. Bertram, in a fury, the varnish cracking in every direction, shouted out that he had no friends now, if he'd ever had any! Finally, in an almost apoplectic temper, the fair one had him turned out of the house. An intense domestic warfare of manœuvre and counter-manœuvre, attack and counter-attack ensued. Arthur fled to Atterly, her 'place' in the country, and succeeded in enlisting the sympathy of the agent, who particularly disliked Mrs. Bertram. But the agent received orders — which he could not disobey — to cut off the water and the electric light, and was thus prevented from following the dictates of his heart. Then Mrs. Bertram came down in person to superintend the siege. Arthur was ejected — but with great skill commandeered his wife's motor-car, and before she could arrive back in London by train had already seized her house there. Finally, both of them felt that the position was an undignified one. The lawyers now swooped down, and by their various proposals netted in a good haul. Arthur's old religious scruples returned to him with redoubled force. His fervour was extraordinary. He became a Savonarola. Would he consider ten thousand pounds down for the selling of his soul? Certainly not! Twenty thousand? But even this did not tempt him. He became too obstinate in his desire to outwit his wife; and Mrs. Bertram became thoroughly out of temper again. She made up her mind to be rid of him without any payment at all, and — being a woman used to getting her own way — by sheer brutality, ill-temper and insult succeeded eventually in dislodging him from her home. Arthur was goaded into such a fury that he left of his own accord, to spend the remainder of a broken life declaiming against the former object of his affections, or, as he now called her, 'that scheming old woman'.

His clothes remained glorious as ever, his manner as magnificent; he still talked of his ship coming home; but gradually poverty forced him into a bitter exile. One heard of him taking his aristocratic relatives out from their camphored chests, and airing them, before old ladies, in those *pensions* of France, Germany and Italy that had become for him a series of more comfortable but even more desolate St. Helenas. The tale of his wrongs, one heard, was ever fresh in his memory. Bravely as ever, no doubt, he pursued his allotted path; but silence sank down on him, and the London that had known Arthur Bertram for so long, knew him no more.

· · · ·

The sea was smooth as a watered-silk banner, and no wind lifted the white edges. Hot and calm was the water on that summer day. The growing detail of the harbour approached us swiftly, veering in its position from time to time. Lighthouses, piers, quays, trolleys and cranes, dividing up the horizon with angular but rhythmic precision, were imprisoned in the tawdry blue, in the transparent ball, of sky and sea, as in crystal. Every sound seemed struggling to escape from the hard, material globe that contained it. Porters cried nasally, old women hawked oranges and chocolates, while small boys cried ecstatically the French versions of the names of English newspapers. All round us was the usual disorderly bustle that masks the deadly efficiency of the French people. We were discharged over small bridges into this throng and out of it —

and beyond, almost automatically, into a motor-car. The streets were dull, the coast-line flat; nothing to do in all this weary waste except, we supposed, to watch the ship come home each morning from England.

And just then our attention was suddenly riveted by a familiar figure bearing toward us. Magnificent in flowing blue cloak, his long gauntlet-glove made a majestic movement with a very high walking-stick, as this straddling, snorting personage, grimacing and making wry faces, went on his way towards his ship that had already come home. He was rather late that day, and in his hurry did not notice us.

CHARLES AND CHARLEMAGNE

'What has not fired her bosom or her brain?
Caesar and Tall-boy, Charles and Charlemagne?'

About a month ago it must be now, I was sitting in the glassed-in cage at the top of a motor omnibus which had settled down amid an inanimate fleet of similar conveyances. It had sidled itself along and was anchored, apparently for all eternity, against the pavement in Park Lane. Only the gentle purring that pervaded the whole vast machine communicated any hope, announced to the passengers a mechanic conviction that sooner or later this stagnation would thaw, and it would be able again to roar its way along the streets like a red, armoured lion. The present passive state in which we found ourselves was rendered the more irritating because the other side of the road, by the Park railings, was completely unencumbered, and large, gondola-like cars were gliding, vans and omnibuses thundering, along its smooth water-coloured surface. Beyond, over the railings that divided up the green grass into rectangular, coffin-like compartments, I watched the listless afternoon life of the Park. The trees looked metallic as the green tin trees of a toyshop, and under them a few weary individuals rested on green tin seats. One or two crouching, whiskered horsemen, crowned with grey bowler-hats, and conscious enough of their obsoleteness to assume an air of defiant importance, trotted slowly along: and I reflected that in all probability the whole of this traffic block, in which we found ourselves thus frozen, was due to one solitary horse with a van, happily lumbering its way along somewhere in the heart of the City. Now there was a slight jolt: we moved on for a few yards, and then, tantalisingly enough, stopped again. My eye turned from the Park to the buildings which overshadowed it. Huge edifices were being improvised . . . buildings that resembled impregnable cliffs, full of luxurious caves in which the rich middle classes were encouraged to hide themselves before the coming of that Day of Judgment, so often invoked by communist orators near by at Hyde Park Corner, when with a loud-mouthed bellow of trumpets and running of blood the virtue of the workers would be recognised and rewarded. Sprinkled among these rocks, however, are still a few old-fashioned, bow-fronted houses: and suddenly I found myself looking down into one . . . staring down into the familiar, but now derelict, dining-room of Lady de Montfort's house. Above the window, standing on a gibbet-like framework, two large black-and-white placards, that resembled in their angles the jutting-out prow of a ship, announced the sale of a 999-years' lease.

The room was, as I had last seen it, decorated as a grotto; but now that it was empty of furniture, now that dust had formed the thickest possible carpet and the windows were already dim from Time's hands, it was more realistic, seemed a cavern, crumbling and forgotten, from which the sea had receded and withdrawn its life. And I wondered whether her impersonal, lacquered but vivacious ghost — a ghost that would never, one felt certain, be clad in any of the multitudinous styles that had pertained to its lifetime, but would always be robed in the latest creation of the moment in which it materialised — did not sometimes roam among these artificial ruins of her earthly past? And then I thought of a cage built of steel and crystal, borne on the deep currents of a tropic sea, bumping and turning over and over, with a rattling of dry bones midway between air and ocean-bottom, an anonymous yet unique end from an anonymous beginning . . . and meditated how strange it was that a life which belonged essentially to its own day, which was responsible for some of the stir and gaiety, and much of the gossip of those hours, should, soonest of all, sink into oblivion: for that which is the most typical is often the most transitory. Herself, I felt, albeit she had cared little enough for public interest, would have been surprised at so evident a lack of it in so short a space. How strange, again I reflected. The travellers on each omnibus will look down into this empty room, and will consider it a grotesque and useless piece of decoration, nothing more; will entirely miss its significance, its very actual foundation in life. And I recalled the time, not so many months ago, when one glance from a passing omnibus at the decoration of Lady de Montfort's dining-room (the easiest room in the house to overlook) would reveal to the initiated a whole section of her life and the progress of a passionate and inquiring physical love.

. . . . .

Almost the first thing I can remember is one of my parents remarking to the other how astonishingly young Lady de Montfort looked. And if it was astonishing in 1896, it must have been very much more so in 1930. For though the art of looking young has in the meantime become a vocation like conjuring, and by that degree less rare, nevertheless when I saw her for the last time, it was clear that she remained at the top of a difficult, and even upon occasion dangerous, profession. In a sense, however, it still remains in the hands of the amateur, for though every suburb now has its beauty-parlour, yet only the rich can afford to indulge in the very real physical torture that beauty-worship imposes on its devotees.

Lady de Montfort, then, had been one of the pioneers of the Peter Pan movement; for that play, I fancy, popularised the notion that there was something glorious in never growing up. Peter Pan in fact was the child-father of face-lifting. The ethical side of the wish to remain young out of season is not easy to grasp, any more than is the practical. Alas, life must end in the same way for all. The full stop closes every sentence whatever the joy or agony of its meaning. The anonymous death, the death of the rich, well-preserved nomad in a richly appointed hotel, for example, has the same pathos as that of a wrinkled old woman of the same age in some pauper institution, and more, it seems to me, than the death of an old, rheumatic crone in a cottage. Much better is it to pass through the seven allotted stages, much better even to be cut off, as the phrase is, 'in the flower of her youth' than in the artificial flower of a deceptive youth. Yet the sums of money spent on this pitiful aim are prodigious, while hints on the subject (combined with details of free-insurance schemes and lists of the sums paid out, which point to a very regrettable mortality among the registered readers of daily newspapers; a mortality, indeed, so remarkable that it seems almost perilous to subscribe to these journals) compose much of the Press today, so there must be an appeal in it to our natures.

But if Beauty is Truth (which, incidentally, it is not), certainly the results of beauty culture are a lie, and should therefore be recognised as ugly. To all those who can afford the best advice, false youth, when attained, imparts an identical appearance: the same corn-gold hair, the same angular, fashion-plate eyes, raised upward at the corner, the same straight nose and lips carved into a double curve, the same strained mouth — slightly open like the mouth of a Roman Mask of Tragedy — that the knife of the plastic surgeon dictates. They have the same figures, the same hands and finger-nails, more or less the same dresses, and the same impersonal, cosmopolitan accent, with, rising and falling smoothly within it, the concealed sound of an American elevator. They do not look young, except by convention, but, instead, they all look the same age: almost, indeed, the same person. And of these Adèle de Montfort was not the least.

But let not the reader conclude that Lady de Montfort's character was after a similar standardised pattern. It was not. For notwithstanding that most of the Regiment who adopt the uniform and faith we have described, do so from a quite genuine desire to resemble one another, Lady de Montfort elected it as a deliberate disguise for a very natural, if rather varied, character. We must, then, lift up the mask, and peer for a little underneath, if only to understand the mask's significance.

. . . . .

Originally, it must be assumed, she had been small and pretty and golden-haired, with a fair, almost pallid skin, behind which roses blushed from time to time, and the tiny hands and feet that are the birthright of every American woman. 'Fresh' was the epithet often used to describe her, for in those days a naïve lack of artifice was much admired, and she was without any of the elegance which she ultimately evolved round herself. Somewhere in the early 'eighties this girl had materialised herself out of what was then the misty void of the great American Republic. She did not belong to any of the few families who at that time floated garishly on this dull, nebulous surface: but she was distantly related to various American women, well married in England, and her fortune, which was adequate to the game she meant to play, was all the more respectable for not being unwieldy. But of her parentage and upbringing, people in England knew nothing, while she speedily contrived to forget more about herself than others had ever known. Outwardly she bore no labels except a slight accent, which only manifested itself in moments of anger or excitement, when suddenly, too, she would fall back into the use of transatlantic idiom; inwardly none except a secret, and, in those days, most rare, lack of them, combined with an adventurous spirit. Indeed her own mind was so free of conventional prejudices that in others they positively attracted her. Thus she set out, like a female Dick Whittington, to seek her destiny: thus, like Venus fair and pale, she had risen from the billows. In fact, if it had not been for the anchor of her independent fortune, she might have passed as that free spirit of the air, an adventuress: and so by nature, and at heart, she was. For all adventuresses are not bold-looking and hard-mouthed. And a quiet adventuress is the one whom the world should fear.

Arrived in London, she sought the protection of her American relatives (who were then much older than she was, though forty years later all of them looked more or less the same age), and under their tutelage made an appearance in the world. They formed at once the guarantee of her character and the guardians of her secret: the almost sordid respectability of her origin. For, though each of these ladies allowed it to be known that in the land of her birth her own 'social standing' had been exceptional, there was yet between them all a tacit, undefined agreement that no home secrets should be revealed. Adèle served her apprenticeship to this guild and learnt much that was of use to her: that, for example, although before marriage it was wise to dress as simply as possible, and look exactly like an English girl, after marriage she could reap the advantage of being an American. For while English women, with a singular obstinacy, persisted in buying their clothes in London, or even in the provinces, she, being of a less insular outlook, could obtain them from any of the great dressmaking houses in Paris: nor would she look *odd* in them. Paris clothes were in the American blood. At the worst, people would say she looked 'rather foreign'. And the men liked it.

Adèle proved clever and adaptable. She was presented at Court, danced, hunted, played tennis, did all the right things and triumphantly concealed her possession of a sensuous intelligence, modern and acute, if rather apt to swing at random. This was a secret, too, which her preceptors respected. Apart, however, from a quiet but continual attendance at concerts, and a constant but hidden reading of poetry and novels — habits which, in her native country, she would have been forced to parade — her general behaviour undoubtedly entitled her to an honorary place among the English ruling class of that epoch. Yet she did not marry for several years: and when she did, though it was a sound marriage, it was scarcely as brilliant a one as her chaperons had hoped. Like her fortune, it was nevertheless all the more respectable for not being of a sensational order. A title was a title, even if it were only a baronetcy: and it attracted her by its strangeness, would add to life the zest and romance (until she became used to it) of a perpetual masquerade.

The name of Sir Simon de Montfort sounds almost too good to be true, and, in fact, was so. Old Solomon Mondfeldt, grandfather of the present baronet, had crept out of a German ghetto about ten years before the Battle of Waterloo, and, looking round, had very wisely decided to settle in the city of London. There he had established himself as a merchant and banker: more, he helped to found the whole edifice of international finance. For he, and a few friends in other countries, maintained at their own expense a reliable news-service, and whenever they heard of a victory for any country in which they were operating, they first announced a defeat, and then bought up all the shares that would be affected. Subsequently the news of the victory would be made public, the shares would rise, and they would sell out. Peace consolidated their efforts, and now he adhered to the more strictly legitimate side of his business, in which, as his obituary notice proclaimed many years later, 'his native shrewdness and foresight swiftly won him recognition'. (It was, perhaps, easier to have foresight then, when there were no possible dangers to foresee.) He was, in fact, a clever, vulgar, grasping, kindly old ruffian, very religious withal; a pillar of the Synagogue, always willing to help his co-religionists — even with large sums of money.

Despite a certain pride in his race — or, at any rate, a loud insistence on it — it was not long before the rough Saxon syllables of Solomon Mondfeldt had melted into the chivalric enchantment of Simon de Montfort. Moreover, his eldest son, another Simon, was smuggled somehow or other into Eton without protest; though at that time it was a difficult school for a boy to enter if he did not conform to the nationality or religion of his comrades. Once installed at Eton, he was popular, for, since he was the only little Jew there, his schoolfellows did not recognise the genus, but appreciated that in the understanding of life in some aspects he was their superior. He bought more and better strawberries than they did, and paid less for them: and on them he forcibly fed his friends. How intelligent in reality he was, who can tell? But it is certain that he very quickly seized on the principles of English public-school education, for he openly refused to learn anything, became maniac about cricket, exulted in the correct shibboleths of dress, speech and deportment and adopted ostentatiously the public-schoolboy-code-of-honour; which, summed up, encourages bullying, but forbids 'sneaking'—thereby assuring the bully of an absolute impunity. And a jolly good code it is, too, if you mean to be a bully.

By this time the family were in possession of a castle in Scotland, and a fine old 'place' in the 'Shires', with all its furniture, portraits, silver and tapestries intact, and its own chapel. A baronetcy followed. He had married at an advanced age, but even before the old man died the Christmas parties, when the house abounded with bounding young de Montforts, solidly eating their way through the week, were models of what such gatherings should be. And after his death the young baronet quietly slipped into the Christian faith. He put up several new armorial windows in the chapel, and it made one almost cry to hear him read the lessons every Sunday. Soon he married into an impoverished aristocratic family, so that his children were well-connected. And, indeed, by the third generation, the conventional, unquestioning stupidity of the children was as genuine as formerly it had been assumed: one symptom of which was that themselves were entirely taken in by their own faked pedigree, and were even apt, when they talked about a cousin, to say of him, 'Oh, of course he has the de Montfort eyes', or, worse, 'he has the de Montfort nose'. Entire books, connecting them with the ancient de Montforts, were written under the supervision of the elder members of the family, by specialist authors who found in it their living. Innocent outsiders, withal, were beginning to believe. Thus in two generations was built up a feudal house.

When the third Sir Simon, Adèle's husband, succeeded, the

elder branch of the family had become, like so many great families, convincingly impoverished. The business had been allowed to pass into the hands of cadets, because they were more interested in it, and so that the Sir Simon of the day should always be free for country pursuits, engaged as he was, would and should be, in shootin', huntin' and fishin'. Our Sir Simon, therefore, spent the greater part of his young bachelordom either in these sports or in sitting, as befitted an English sportsman, in the smallest, ugliest room of a large, rather beautiful but very cold house, surrounded by stags' heads, an imported bison or two, fish in glass cases, fossils, pipes and cigar-boxes: and, in order to keep warm, even in this den, he had to drink a great quantity of port, which gradually undermined his constitution.

Brought into this, for her exotic, environment, Adèle was an undoubted success. Her husband was devoted to her, while her fortune, too, was most welcome: since the prize-pigs and potatoes, the model dairies and cattle-breeding that were incumbent on the head of a historic family, combined with an iniquitous income-tax of a shilling or so in the pound, had made dreadful inroads into the estate. For Sir Simon, Lady de Montfort completed life: and for her, brought up as she had been, it must have been an experience that transcended reality. Nor was it, in any case at first, monotonous: for there were two sides to it. One was a miniature Royal-Family existence, spent in opening bazaars, sales of work and jumble-sales, mouthing at unknown and indistinguishable babies, and in giving or receiving prizes (it seemed to her afterwards that a large part of her early married life had been spent in giving or receiving prizes) for fruit, flowers, potatoes, onions, shorthorns and agriculture generally: while the other unfolded the whole pageant of a barbarous society. There were family parties and shooting parties; there were the 'bloodings' and the 'rattings' ('No fun like rattin'', Sir Simon used to say), and innumerable other forms of well-meant cruelty to animals, which must have satisfied some primordial female instinct in her; and, best of all, there were the hunt-balls. Even now, reading over the lists of 'those present', in some newspaper of the day, one can comprehend a little the ecstasy into which these festivities threw her. For far more than the Roll of Domesday do they sum up, by the very sound and rhythm of the names, the life of that time, and, even, the queer results of the Norman Conquest: moreover, apart from the odd juxtaposition of names essentially matter-of-fact with others so unusual as to be romantic, the lilt and rhythm is in itself fascinating, there are unexpected trills, and the vagaries of fortune are reflected in the inexplicable runs on names beginning with the same letter, the long and the short runs, comparable to those unexpected runs on one number or colour that are encountered on the gaming-tables. For example, on January 18th, 1888, we read in one of the leading London papers:

About 350 guests attended the Hunminster Hunt ball, held at the Queen's Hotel, Hunminster, last night. Godefroy's Pink Hungarian Band, of Hunminster, supplied the music.

In addition to the Master and Lady de Montfort, those present included the Earl and Countess of Hunminster, Viscount Humble, Miss Mowker, Miss Marcia Mowker, F.M. Lord Cummerbund and the Honble. Cycely Cuddle, Miss Moocombe, Miss Malcolm, Miss Mink, Miss Denyse Malpigian, Miss Myrtle Malpigian, Major McCorquodale, Lady Cundle, Miss Coote, Mr. Hartopp Hayter, Miss Hunt, Miss Handle, Mr. Handcock, Mrs. Haviour and Miss B. Haviour, Mrs. Bullamy, Miss Heather Hellebore, Major Colin Coldharbour and Lady Isabel Hamilton-Hootar.

The Earl of Dunbobbin, the Honble. Doughty Dullwater, Miss Daphne Diddle, Colonel Haggas, Lady Hootman, Dr. Prettygole, Mr. Palmer, Mr. Plummer, Miss Plummer, Mr. Plymsoll, Captain Pymm, Miss Penelope Pitt-Pitts, Mr. Percy Pitman, Miss Frolick, Mr. Fumble, Miss Rowena Rowbotham, Miss Donkyn, Miss Dunderhead, Mr. Roger Randcock, Major Minney, Miss Dingle, Mr. Malcolm de Montmorency, Mrs. Slinkworthy, Captain Hercules Slowcoach, Lady Slaunder, Miss Slowcombe, Mr. Sleek, Miss Eager, Mrs. Stanley Stobart, Miss Serpent, Colonel Cooper-Copeland, Sir Joseph Slump, Miss Eileen Shrivel, Major Spiridion and Lady Muriel Portal-Pooter.

And then the rollicking aspect of the festivities captivated Adèle. She loved to watch the huge, thumping dowagers romping round in their bustles, covered from head to foot with jewels like Hindu idols and whirling round in the figures of the Lancers until they seemed to have as many vast, red arms as those deities. She liked to talk, or be silent, with these long-legged and languid men, with their drawling yet clipped talk and military moustaches. Certainly, then, she enjoyed herself at first. And all these people liked her, though, of course, to begin with they had thought the Parisian clothes, which she had now adopted, 'quaint'. But soon they became accustomed to her, and would remark enthusiastically, 'Nobody would ever take her for an American'.

So the first years passed . . . and then there were her children, three of them, born within the first seven years of their marriage. In her later period, one was astonished that anything as elemental as child-bearing should ever have formed part of Lady de Montfort's life: but so it was. And there were short visits to London. She had never renounced her Guild, and corresponded regularly with her early preceptors, though seldom asking them to visit her. But she saw them in London, and this made the atmosphere different for her. She seemed contented enough, they thought: but she never really talked to them, never said anything except what the world expected of her. But in about 1890 a change came.

As she was clever as well as pretty, her ascendancy over her husband became complete. Now, suddenly, she insisted on spending half the year in London. He was in no position to object: she had taken an infinity of trouble with his friends and relatives, while much of the money was her own. But for him the reality was to be worse than the anticipation. His wife for the first time revealed an intense, American interest in the arts notwithstanding that Sir Simon had a wholly British prejudice against artists. The species positively invaded his London house at this period; but it never actually descended to blows. As he said about the matter to his friends, 'After all, one must live and let live . . .' and so, when it became too much for him, he would instinctively go back to the country and kill a fish or a bird instead. . . . Alas, there was worse to come. He could not be away from her always. And now there were — musicians in the house! She had always been musical; he had been forced in secret to recognize this — musical in a passive sense. But this was different, this was monstrous; amounted almost, he said, to deception, so little had he suspected it. . . . For all at once she produced a certain, if limited, executant ability; that is to say she installed two pianos, side by side, in the drawing-room, and upon them she loved to play duets with eminent musicians. This she did well and gracefully. On one piano, however, and, as it were, by herself, she floundered hopelessly and was lost; a dangerous symptom — if her husband had identified it — the symptom of a temperament that, in spite of its native American independence, demanded, and relied on, continual masculine assistance. Notwithstanding, at present her behaviour grew no less conventional, her conversation not a whit more individual.

Sir Simon's troubles, if he had known it, were but beginning. Now was the first time she indulged a repressed desire for house-decoration; one which later, as we shall see, became unconsciously entangled with sex-expression, and almost developed into a mania. And innocent as it seems from this distance, her initial attempt annoyed Sir Simon quite as much as any of her subsequent ones. The Louis Quinze *salons* of the de Montfort mansion in Park Lane were scrapped from top to bottom; and, instead, oak beams squared white ceilings, Morris chintzes enwrapped the chairs and sofas, and a gothic wallpaper supplied a background of dim, golden nebulosity. The two pianos were draped in faded Japanese kimonos, but this could not muffle the thousand minute, clear-throated songs called out from countless blue-and-white china bowls and plates when any note was struck: for the whole room was a-clatter with willow-pattern porcelain. On the top of the wainscoting, even, fragile objects were perilously balanced. Then there were drawings by Simeon Solomon, and, in the place of honour, two large portraits of the master and mistress of the house, by Godwyn. (Poor de Montfort had particularly objected to sitting for his portrait, but had been forced into it by Adèle.) Lacquer was there too, of the Oriental, not the European variety, and many Oriental screens crept like angular, gigantic caterpillars across the floors. Oscar Wilde sometimes attended the musical parties which Lady de Montfort had now inaugurated, and these screens were the subject of a famous telegram. She had written to him, saying that she had received from the East a consignment of lacquer screens, and hoped he would give her the benefit of his advice as to their arrangement. In answer, she received a telegram: 'Do not arrange them. Let them occur.—Oscar.'*

* Great letter-writers have been plentiful, but, as far as one can judge, Wilde was the only great telegram-writer that the world has seen as yet. A volume of his collected telegrams would make very good reading. And who, one may wonder, is the master of the long-distance spoken-word, the telephone — short, concise, witty?

Yet, though her parties became celebrated, the character of the hostess still seemed vague and diaphanous. At what precise age her appearance of youth first called for comment, I am unaware; but at these entertainments, I apprehend, guests were already saying to one another, 'How wonderfully young our hostess looks tonight'. After a few years, however, these gatherings came to an abrupt end. Sir Simon did not enjoy them, though he talked loudly, and without a moment's pause for breath, throughout every evening of music. But even when there was no music, he felt out of it, and as if they did not want to listen to him. The Wilde scandal occurred, and Sir Simon, who, furthermore, was aware of having sat, as it were, for one of that author's most applauded jokes,* insisted on having the decorations torn down. The house, as he said, must be 'decently furnished again'.

The change that took place was just as startling in its way as any of those subsequently organised by Adèle. The Godwyn portraits were removed, but preserved in a lumber-room in case they might some day become valuable, and hastily improvised likenesses by Herkomer were substituted. Armchairs in flowery chintzes, little gilded chairs, eighteenth-century footstools which tripped up every visitor who walked into the room, and Dutch brass chandeliers soon restored the house to its accustomed worthiness; while to add a special touch of incontrovertible respectability, Sir Simon transported from the country several stags' heads and pike and salmon in long, glass-fronted cases, and personally superintended the sprinkling of these about the house. In all this, he was successful. Yet it was the cause of the first quarrel between Lady de Montfort and himself, and it is to be doubted whether she ever forgave him.

At the time, though, he scored a point. Visits to London were few, and Adèle relapsed from a metropolitan into a provincial life. In England, of course, this last is more exclusive, more difficult to enter, more the 'right thing': but now it had lost for her its fascination. It must be remembered that by type she was an adventuress. And, having established one method

* One day Sir Simon had led the esthete up to his portrait by Godwyn, and had said to him, 'I don't like that: my wife made me sit for it. But you're supposed to know about that sort of thing. What do you think of it?' — And the author had replied, 'Sir Simon, it is a speaking likeness . . . but there are occasions when silence is more welcome'.

of life so thoroughly and completely, the adventure was over, should be disposed of.

In the few years that were to pass before she was free, something happened to Lady de Montfort. Books no longer lent her their support, and though music retained its purely sensual attraction for her, she lost now the magic key which had enabled her in a moment to enter other worlds. Novels and poetry no longer disclosed enchanted avenues along which she might wander, and, instead, she welcomed romance on a more material plane. Presently, and for the first time in their married life of nearly fifteen years, Sir Simon had cause for jealousy. She was always to be seen in the company of a neighbouring, notoriously unfaithful peer. Sir Simon, with a touching ancestral belief in the word of a Gentile, made his wife sign a paper in which she undertook never to see Lord Dunbobbin again. Why she signed it, I do not know: but she did. Alas, she broke her promise.

Bicycling was now the rage, and strange as it may seem, though there were no motor-cars, people contrived to have serious accidents. Clad, therefore, in those peculiar clothes immortalised by the painter Seurat, those clothes which seem specially designed to bring out the miracle of the bicycle's spider-like feats of balance, for, regarded from the back, the whole line, from shoulder to wheel, forms an inverted pyramid, Lady de Montfort and her lover would speed down lanes that have never since been so leafy; propel themselves down the centre of these green tunnels at such a prodigious rate, as it seemed that the little nuzzling winds of the spring would attack the mesh of her green pointillist veil, and even push her round straw hat to the back of her formalised fringed head. Such happiness could not endure. A governess-car was the machine planned by the gods for its destruction. The physical damage was not severe, but a lawsuit was threatened. The case would be reported, and Sir Simon must be told. He lost his temper, created a scene: tactics which, for the last year or two, had ever crowned him with success. But this time Lady de Montfort joined battle. At every point, he was defeated. He shouted 'Divorce' at her. She replied that he had no evidence, but should her own action, based on his prolonged cruelty, fail, she would be delighted to supply it. But neither of them wished it in reality, for divorce was then, even so short a time ago, a step down into obscurity rather than up into fame. 'For the sake of the children,' they decided, 'it must not be.' So, for a year or two longer, the children were forced to know them together and quarrelsome rather than amiable and apart. During these months, though she lived in his house, Adèle behaved as she wished.

With King Edward on the throne the whole atmosphere had changed, and now the relaxation began to be felt even in these fastnesses of an almost palaeolithic Society. In about 1906 a separation was arranged, and she took over the Park Lane mansion, while he continued to live in the country. From time to time, after this, they would meet pleasantly and without reproach, each delighted to be independent: nor did either strive to prevent the children from seeing the other parent, but, with good sense, encouraged it. And here, having mentioned the children, we can dispose of them. They grew up, as they should, into rich but deserving men and women. When with their mother in London, they spent as much time as they could out of it, on golf-course or tennis-court — in the evenings attended the right sort of musical comedy or revue, and could soon whistle every tune out of every 'show', as they called it, with the ease and accuracy of an errand-boy. Moreover they could banter one another with a thousand memorable clichés culled from the repertory of their favourite comedians, enjoyed 'fizz' and 'bubbly', and believed, generally, in 'having a good time'.

Meanwhile their mother's life was assuming a new texture. This was a second, but transitional, period for her. The last adventure was over and complete. The next one must be to smash it and conquer a new world. Her pioneer blood was still in the ascendant. Edwardian days were in full, overfull, bloom: now she could avow her artistic proclivities, consort with people of her own type. Many of them, like herself, were American. She became a mote in new sunshine, whirled in a gilded, pointless activity, organised balls or tableaux in aid of any charity that asked her help, displayed real ability in selling the tickets. Her appearance in one of these enterprises, as Penelope spinning, will long be remembered. She dressed now in the exuberance of fashion, and created a stir — unrivalled by any horse — in the Royal Enclosure at Ascot. Sheathed in a mauve Directoire dress, with a large silver bangle on one ankle, where the split in the dress revealed it, and balancing a vast picture-hat on her head, she attracted the Royal attention, as much by her clothes as by the well-enamelled spring of her complexion.

She prospered, achieved a reputation for beauty as much as for youth, and became sufficiently friendly with King Edward to ask for that signed photograph which afterwards remained the one fixed star in an ever-changing sky: for, whatever the wild revolutions of her house which I shall describe later, this royal, bearded geniality continued to authorise her indiscretions. She gave musical parties, played duets with all the leading pianists. From having been unlabelled, a person, indeed, to whom it was impossible to attach a label, she now manufactured for herself a very recognisable one: so that it was easy for her many new friends to foretell exactly what she would say in any given circumstances. Thus they were enabled to mimic and, by so doing, to advertise her. She became, and remained for many years, a familiar, and therefore popular, landmark of London life. And the fox-hunting squires, as they looked at the weekly illustrated papers, would gulp their port, gape and roar with surprise as they gazed upon the likeness of this very young-looking, elegant spectre of the world of fashion, who, even then celebrated for her youth, had once moved so unostentatiously through their midst.

But her triumph was so quick, so easy in the more cosmopolitan life of the city, that for Lady de Montfort it lost its savour. Her next adventure must be to break this too; break it, if she could. But her popularity was almost too strong.

King Edward died, and there were many who would have liked, many more than one would have imagined, to move back the hands of the clock. People began to look forward with pleasure to a renewal of the Victorian era. But Adèle was not among them. Her heart had never accepted the Victorian fog of morality. Indeed had she been able to diagnose her misfortune, she would have known that she had been born thirty or forty years too early. She was a post-European-War type. Moreover, the predilection for monogamy, so strong a trait of many characters, was lacking in hers. To be true to one man was against her nature: but this very deprivation, which for so long she had undergone in order to play her part, full of the lure of the unknown, in the primitive society of the Shires, had, in fact, communicated to her for a time a rather perverse sensual enjoyment. But those days were finished.

Perhaps her attitude to love was rooted in her blood. The Americans run to extremes, oscillate violently, for instance, between Total Prohibition and Total Inebriation (and each makes the other an inevitable reaction). The Pilgrim Fathers, when they left England, were most surely essaying to run away from themselves, to elude the strength of their own passions, that, pent up, had distilled them into so gloomily bitter and cantankerous a minority, quite as much as to escape a problematic religious persecution. As well attempt to avoid your own shadow.

And when they reached the Land of Promise and had set up their rigid little gods, planted the altars firmly in this alien soil, perhaps they found it already possessed. It was almost as though the native gods of this continent, hidden far away under vast, dreary plains and huge, rocky mountains, had laid on this race that was to come a peculiar curse, had decreed that the descendants of these seekers after an iron-bound truth, these people who sought so hardly the things of the spirit, and despised the flesh and the fleshpots, should be endowed with every material blessing, every comfort that wealth and prosperity could give, and yet should always be restless, unable to achieve a spiritual consolation or any balance between the body and the spirit. The fruits have been twofold; one exemplified by Purity Leagues and book-bannings, the other by the enormous quantity of divorces in America, and the very free codes of behaviour that characterise life in the American (Bohemian) quarter of Paris. And it may be that Adèle was now unconsciously bent on exacting in one lifetime — rather late in it, too — an adequate compensation for all the repressions of her ancestors.

She began then — at first, quietly — to indulge in affairs of the heart. But, however discreet, she always loved with fervour. Meanwhile her mind, small, free, erratic and original within the compass of its power, roamed at ease in the upper air, released from those dungeons of despair guarded by the twin Freudian ogres of Inhibition and Complex.

Soon she paraded her lovers a little more openly: and it

was now that a second passion, to become inextricably entangled with the first, definitely manifested itself.

In the days of her tableaux, her home had been comfortable, exotic, full of incense, cushions, orchids and tuberoses. One room alone in all the house had been permeated by a gentle, phthisic pre-Raphaelitism: monochrome cartoons by Burne-Jones and a large painted cupboard by the same wistful hand figured in it. But the rest of the house had been conceived purely as an impersonal background, adjunct of scents, dresses, flowers. Little tables swarmed with the precious inutilities of Fabergé: miniature trees in gold and silver; flowers made of the wings of butterflies with emerald calyxes; jade toads, with ruby eyes, holding a lapis ash-tray; pink quartz rabbits, nibbling green blades of chrysoprase, that proved to be bells; crystal owls that were inkpots.

But now decoration obsessed her, though at first she exhibited no symptom of the virtuosity — for virtuosity, however ludicrous, it was — that she later displayed. Perhaps she did not personally supervise, left it to others in this first instance. Indeed it lacked the charm, even, of the house as she had dramatised it twenty years previously; seemed a pitiful example of that period-furnishing which was already laying waste her native land. A Mermaid Tavern ensued. There was much expensive German-oak panelling, while upon every ceiling, very obviously put up in squares, mermaids played their lutes, and the plaster roses of secrecy bloomed in the least expected places. Old oak settees, cupboards, dressers filled every room with a creaking, numskull woodenness, and there were oak armchairs, built up entirely of a sequence of hard, wooden protuberances, electric, unflickering candles, iron bolts of a truly lockjaw rustiness upon oak doors, wooden latches with strings attached and many other of the cruel, catch-finger devices of the Tudors: last, but not least, there was an Elizabethan lover. He was a pioneer of the waste places (or is it spaces?), a man as much given to climbing mountains as any schoolmaster during his summer vacation, an explorer, a poet; but, like all his type, alas, his exploring was better than his poetry. The Elizabethan phase lasted for a year or so. But one day the lover left — or was dismissed; the house was dismantled, refurnished, and a Roman Prince reigned in his stead.

Far from wishing to drop her because of this indiscretion, people now gave her an instance of how staunch friends can be (for there is only one unforgivable sin in the eyes of such loyal, worldly friends, and that is loss of money). They flocked round her, eager to see every detail of the palace that had been born within this bellying, yellow-fronted Regency house. And they admired the Ispahan carpets and Genoese velvets, the tall, gilded chairs, the Venetian brocades, the hooded mantel-pieces and *torcieri*, the bronzes on tables of Italian walnut, painted balustrades from churches, and fine pictures. It was effectively scenic. From a decorative, as probably from an amorous point of view, this was a successful moment in her life. The house looked well, had developed airy vistas, seemed bigger: the Prince was large, handsome, cultivated and attentive. Then, after many months, there was a sudden reversal. The Prince went back to Rome, and, as if by magic, an over-elegant young German, like a too-willowy, canary-coloured bulldog, was found in his place. Within a week or two, the de Montfort house had turned München, 1914. Its shiny black walls were now splashed with rich orange and pale yellow, there were divans of red and purple, black-glass bath-rooms with sunk baths of malachite, and the whole place was filled with very excitable Munich glass and groups of Nymphenburg china; for the Germans are a patriotic race, and German trade followed German love. Her friends had noticed, too, that the food varied with each régime, in accordance with style and lover. Plain Elizabethan fare of an overwhelming abundance, pies and puddings and oyster-and-lark patties, had given way to more elaborate and Machiavellian dishes, to ducks, for example, that were assassinated, torn limb from limb before your eyes, then pounded and boiled in brandy, and now yielded again to over-rich, German dishes. It seemed as if everything was stuffed with lobster and truffles, and served up with cream.

The young German stayed, month after month. But now the two processes, which were starting to work together, though not yet at an excessive rate, were arrested by the 'Great' War. Upon the outbreak of it, Lady de Montfort was, I think, glad to intern her lover. At any rate, she 'did up' her house as a hospital at great personal expense. She had forgotten, however, to consult the War Office before putting the work in hand, and when, now that it was completed, she offered it to them, coupled with an intimation that she did not desire rent for the premises, technical difficulties ensued. Various War Office departments played battledore and shuttlecock with the question for several years, but since the war ended before they were ready for its beginning, nothing was ever decided. And so Lady de Montfort had to be content with living there herself (as she said, it brought the war home to one) and with doing her own modest bit, by 'giving the boys on leave a good time': though for this she was unrewarded, and received no recognition from an ungrateful country. The war stopped at last — and the next time I saw the house, the white paint, the white enamel furniture, the iron-rations laid by the place of each guest, as graceful, picturesque adjunct to a rationed diet, and, as remembrancer of mortality, the smell of chloroform with which during those years she had so modishly invested it, were gone, gone for ever: and the sober Park Lane shell now contained a Petit Trianon.

. . . .

It was with this Petit Trianon period, I consider, that Lady de Montfort entered on her grand period of beauty, youth and fame, and that the processes, which we have watched at work, grew together like two trees and culminated in monstrous blossom after monstrous blossom. From now onwards, until she disappears out of this story — and it ends — the mask is the same, even though the clothes vary: the manifestations are, to all purposes, identical, and the flowering is mechanical. We have lifted up the mask a little, in order to understand how human features have grown into it. Just as in Soviet Russia it has recently been discovered that under the varnished ikons, which are so alike as to be indistinguishable, an original art and form lie hidden; and that to see them the restorer is forced, so thick and deep are the later coatings of paint with which the personal delineation of a true artist has been covered up year after year, to attack the outer surface with a chisel, so here we have attempted some such rather rough operation. But now it is finished. We must accept the appearance — and replace the mask.

Let the reader at this very moment picture Adèle for himself, but do not let him place this lacquered apparition in the dress of any one period: rather let him, instead, animate for himself a fashion-plate, the most fashionable fashion-plate he can find, from the illustrated papers of whatever week in whatever month of whatever year it may be in which he reads this story. Thus will he see for himself our heroine, as she looked, wished to look, would look — if she were alive. For, however different, the heights of fashion in a way resemble one another. It is the intensity of it that matters. We realise that this is the 'latest thing'. Even though she be dead, we must take her embalmed corpse and clothe it in the dress of the actual moment. In this manner she will most assuredly come to life . . . only the reader, for his part, must always remember to make her look 'astonishingly young'.

. . . . .

Whether I was the first, the only one at the moment, to watch the development of these strange traits, to comprehend the unfolding of these curious and perverse flowers, I do not know. Certainly myself discovered, quite by chance, how it was possible by riding past the front of Lady de Montfort's house on the top of a motor-omnibus to deduce the main outlines of the drama that was taking place within it. Just a glance from above through the dining-room window, as one was whirled along, and I could divine with tolerable precision, if not the name, at least the nature, of the favourite of the minute: notwithstanding, of course, there were moments of bewilderment, as the kaleidoscope revolved with ever-increasing swiftness. Still, as a rule, a single glance would be enough. 'Hullo,' one would exclaim, 'the Spanish attaché has been dismissed, and by the look of the walls, it must be a Russian refugee now.' Or, again, 'So the Austrian dramatist has gone — I thought so. I imagine that macaw in the cage must mean a South American of some sort.' And I found, even in these most transient attempts at decoration, a quality that was a little touching; the revolving of a primitive machinery, very unexpected in one so modern and removed from nature, which love alone can set into action . . . the instinct of a bird to build a nest. And this perpetual building and rebuilding of a nest that served no purpose was to me rather pitiful.

And now, lest it should be thought that this was the interfering, salacious curiosity of a stranger, let me try to explain the peculiar nature of the link that subsisted between Lady de Montfort and myself. It must be clearly understood that, while never familiar with her in the sense of an intimate exchange of sentiments, I was yet a certain amount in her company: that albeit rather seldom bidden to her house, except for large parties to which all the world was asked, yet from time to time I was, though not one of her very definite 'set', so invited. Perhaps she felt obliged thus silently to enable me to watch her, thus tacitly to let me into her secrets, since doubtless she was aware, as I was, of an indissoluble tie.— Everybody is somebody's bore. (Nor need this for an instant be taken as a reflection on anybody's particular bore, for the boredom is contained, not in him, but in the relationship between him and the person he bores. In fact, with very few exceptions, it takes two to make a bore.) Moreover this relationship is a thing preordained by an inscrutable Providence. I, then, was Lady de Montfort's bore; recognised it, made the most of it — nay! gloried in it. To be, after this manner, a specially appointed bore by divine warrant, carries with it its duties as much as its privileges. In this story we are not dealing with her voyages. They pertain to one that is yet to be written. But she belonged to the floating pleasure-seekers of Europe. I travelled too. So that, whether I saw her in a London ballroom, in a Berlin concert-hall, at the Opera in Vienna, at the 'Ritz' in Paris, bathing at Antibes or whatever the fashionable beach of the moment might be, sitting at a table in the Piazza at Venice, at a dance in New York, or in Fez, Cairo, Leningrad or Seville, I made a point of talking to her . . . or, if not talking, of remaining a little by her side. For what God hath joined together, let no man tear asunder: and we were, as it seemed through all eternity, bound helplessly together in the coils of an intolerable, though on my part interested and admiring, ennui.

I observed Lady de Montfort with care, but there was no longer any actual need for it. The world now knew everything about her, except her age and the means by which she kept it secret. At first her friends, again, were startled by the quite brazen parade of her lovers which she affected, for she would never lunch or dine with them unless she were allowed to bring with her the man of the moment. (She always had a delightfully inappropriate phrase to explain the appeal he made to her.) And sometimes, as though by a feat of prestidigitation, a new man would appear without warning in place of the one who had been expected, and a new phrase would surely be found ready to describe him. For, since her war experiences, another strongly racial quality had grown to inspire her passions: an insatiable demand for novelty. But she loved with an equal ferocity, with her body and her soul, whether it was for a year or a night. And her love affairs were very defined: the next began where, and when, the last had ended.

Yet, notwithstanding their infinite variety, there was at the same time now visible in her lovers — with one or two notable exceptions to which we shall revert — a quite evident line of descent. Heretofore they had not resembled one another; but now, of whatever shade, colour, creed or disposition, it was possible to reduce the majority of them to a common denominator, so that they ought perhaps to be considered, either as manifold expressions of some ideal lover, or as the persistent, identical expression which she called out from any miscellaneous sequence of men. Her lovers must amuse, as well as love her: they must learn to laugh, act and 'do stunts' in much the same manner, they must be able to mimic her friends. Above all, they must take as much interest in decoration as herself, and, finally, must play the piano sufficiently well for them to form a rock to which the delicate tendrils of her duets could cling: for now she had discarded the eminent musicians, and only desired to play duets with her lovers. But however much approximation to type there was in these men, yet, as one succeeded another, the spiritual differences remained so marked that her friends never lost their curiosity about them.

As for herself, Lady de Montfort had become a more amusing character than one would, twenty years before, have deemed possible. It would, perhaps, be incorrect to describe her mind as being fashioned on unconventional lines, since this would impute to it too much importance. But if on the whole conventional, there were yet ominous gaps that could never be filled, depths that it was impossible to plumb, unexpected corners of knowledge, and hidden trap-doors from which the most personal, puck-like of harlequins would leap out on a sudden and rap you with his baton.

She had, of course, long ago given up reading novels or poetry, things which had once supplied an element of beauty in her life: consequently, her thoughts were more original, in the sense that they were less borrowed, while at the same time the discovery that many years ago she had read this or that book, and that it had left this or that impress on her memory, brought into her conversation all the elements of surprise, pleasant surprise. And just as she had speeded up the tempo of her life, so had she allowed the engine of her mind to race. She had, in fact, torn off her label. Far from being able to predict, as in her middle period, exactly what she would say, now her friends never knew what she would say next: or, again, it would be more accurate to state that they knew now that they never knew what she would say next, so that after all, and despite herself, this very absence of labels amounted to a new one. She had wanted to smash her former mode of life, but all these things meant that her friends remained as much her friends as ever. She could not shock, she could only amuse them.

And then she was so energetic that, however much she had longed to destroy her creation, she did not want to give up her activities, being content to outrage the conventions without forgoing the pleasures they sheltered. She lived always in a whirl of activity. Even the ease, one suspected, with which she looked 'astonishingly young' must have consumed an ever-increasing portion of those years left to her. For she who wishes to remain young out of season must now submit her body to an iron discipline, must be ready when least disposed for it — when, for example, still sleeping after the ball of a few hours before — to contort herself into the most unusual and ungraceful of postures, to be flung round and round her trainer's head like a lasso, to roll, undulate and writhe on the floor, to forfeit for ever the solace of good food and good drink, to go for days with nothing but half a cup of *consommé* to support the flesh, to sit through long and exquisite meals, eat nothing, and show no symptom of torture, to stand up for hours against a wall daily, while an attendant turns on her naked body a hose of battering, pommelling water, alternately ice-cold and boiling-hot, and finally at intervals to be carved about like a fowl, and without complaint or any reception of sympathy: because she must never admit how her days are engrossed, and least of all may she confess to the brutal knife of the 'plastic surgeon'. Suttee would teach these ladies nothing. But then women are more single-minded than men, and, though uncontrolled and uncontrollable, it was extraordinary to observe how serenely Adèle had disciplined herself in some directions, how, furthermore, she was willing to subordinate everything to one purpose, use everything she possessed toward an intensification of love.

And in addition to love, there was the rival passion, decoration; which, as we have said, now even extended to the food. She was at heart eclectic, I fancy, with no particular sympathy in her own mind for any one period. Out of each one she adopted, she brought very easily, very cleverly, its particular characteristics, and also added to it, perhaps, something of her own. And with the full flowering of this talent, however absurd, it was as though she furnished a house with such skilful understanding that it actually materialised for her some ghost of the time she aimed at, or conjured up for her some daemon of the element or machine, or whatever it might be, that at the moment she was attempting to paraphrase. For now she was no longer content with period-furnishing, but essayed things more difficult, elusive. And, incidentally, she showed real genius in the continual, recurrent disposal of the furniture. Expensive as the habit sounds, she often made, rather than lost, considerable sums of money over each unfurnishing. But then, she attended to it personally, bought the things herself. And often I would meet her in auction-rooms, bidding feverishly for her fetish of the hour, or would see her returning home, her smart, lacquered car loaded very inappropriately with all this new fuel for a new fire.

It is, indeed, impossible to say where love began and decoration ended. Did the man dictate the style, or the style the man? For ever could this point be argued, since it is comparable to the old question, not nearly so silly as it sounds, as to whether the hen lays the egg, or the egg the hen. Did the man keep pace with the house, or the house with the man: or did they keep pace together? It is a sequel impossible to drag apart. Sometimes there would be a lull of a few months, and then change would succeed change with an inconceivable, a stupefying, rapidity. Some of the men and houses, it may be, promised well, but were, in one way or another, in practice disappointing: or, again, it might be merely that she was in a fickle, uncertain mood. Then the Park Lane mansion would break into short, syncopated fits of decoration, that would serve to put anyone save a great detective on the wrong track.

One day it would begin to assume a grand, *settecento* Italian air, on the second a prudent Biedemeyer, the third an elegant Chippendale, the fourth a fiery Magyar, the fifth a frigid Norwegian, full of painted furniture and Viking designs, the sixth it would be School of Fontainebleau, the seventh a solid Queen Anne. The alteration wrought within each of the earth's short transits would seem almost a miracle in its abrupt completeness.

During those frenetic hours of preparing, in which the work gathered momentum like a boulder rolling down a hill, Lady de Montfort would be present, in order personally to cheer the workmen on, or would occasionally herself mount a ladder and join in with a paint-brush: for the house must be finished before she wearied of the man . . . was that it? And I wondered if the honest British workmen to whom she gave such constant and diversified employment had formed any just idea as to the nature of the intrigues which they were thus called upon to assist? But Adèle herself had developed such a truly amazing technique of arranging her house, that it was quite possible that soon she would be able to dispense with their services altogether. One touch from her long fingers enabled even the most cumbrous objects to move as though affected by some occult process of levitation. Huge pianos, enormous cupboards, vast tables, all slid, ran or leapt upstairs with scarcely any assistance.

. . . .

It is, of course, impossible to remember all the changes. The Petit-Trianon period endured for some little time. The cause of it was a young French diplomat of good but boring family, who was a skilful, rather skittish writer upon the gallantries of the period. He told amusing little stories, and played the piano well. Panels of old *toile-de-Jouy* lined the walls, the chairs and sofas were exquisite with their slight, gilded frames and *petit-point*, while tall specially designed *vitrines* exhibited arrangements of pastoral skirts, shoes, shepherds' crooks and flat, ribboned hats of straw, and in smaller glass cases stood painted fans and snuff-boxes. The food was delicious, simple French food. But now there intervened a rather bad, late-Léon-Bakst fortnight of Oriental lampshades, cushions covered with tassels, poppy-heads treated with gold paint, and arranged in wide glass bowls, luxurious divans, incense of an Oriental, unecclesiastical variety, while kebabs, yaghourt and Turkish Delight were the only refreshments supplied. Sherbet was served with the coffee after dinner. This proved to be the necessary dramatisation for a young Jewish musician. Then, suddenly, all such trumpery was swept away by a breeze from the great open spaces of Empire. A rough lover from New Zealand (though he, too, adhered to type, played the piano and sang a little) succeeded, during which the high plaster ceilings were hidden by wattle roofs, supported on carved totem-poles, and guests at luncheon and dinner openly complained that their salmon was tinned, their mutton frozen: but this fortunately for them proved as mutable an affair as the decoration indicated. A relapse into a Queen Anne style followed. This was occasioned by a young literary critic who enjoyed excavating that period. Together Adèle and he played the composers of the time, and she offered to her guests good, plain, substantial English fare. But a surprise was in store. Without any warning the house in Park Lane broke out into the most complete and fantastic *chinoiserie*; old Chinese papers, lacquer furniture, dragon tables and gold temple flowers. Adèle's old friends were really alarmed, for a rich young Chinese Prince had just arrived in London to be educated. Nevertheless, their fears proved groundless, and (did they feel rather disappointed?) the man who had inspired the decoration turned out to be a young German writer on art, a specialist in this style: but the chop-suey, the pickled sharks' fins, bamboo shoots, lily-of-the-valley and narcissus bulbs soaked in white wine, the hundred-year-old eggs, so beautiful to look at when cut in slices, with their malachite-green yolks and polished, deep black, outer rings, and with their curious taste of all things buried in the earth, of truffles, mushrooms and their like, did not tend to make him popular with those who frequented the de Montfort house. This lover lapsed, and a young Frenchman succeeded to the position: a Frenchman whose family had sprung up under the shielding wings of the Imperial eagles. An airy Empire style, therefore, with plenty of gilded caryatids supporting branched candelabras, ensued. The walls were painted in bright colours and the beautifully made furniture of simple line suited the proportions of the rooms. A French chef was encouraged to do his best, and was not restricted by any fantastic rules. But there followed a reversion to Charles II, though on this occasion without any Italian influence: a dignified, gilded Charles II.

The daemon of this transformation was a writer, again: a writer, moreover, upon gallantries, but of course upon those of the Stuart period. Nevertheless, he used for his work the same 'devil' formerly employed by the Petit-Trianon lover; a poor, half-starved, religious, mild, grey-haired, Church-of-England, spectacled little woman, named Miss Teresa Tibbits, who was the last surviving descendant of a thousand curates, and who now, rigged out with a green shade over her eyes, like a pirate with a bandaged forehead, was forced by her poverty thus for ever to grub away among the most intimate possible details of the love-affairs of dead duchesses in the Reading Room of the British Museum. And since she must be acquainted with the most scabrous minutiae, she was continually forced to blush for herself by having to ask the attendants for the most daring and unexpected books; the most lurid of which, she was informed by them, with a look of intense disapprobation, could only be seen by someone duly armed with a certificate, which guaranteed moral rectitude and the fact that the bearer was a responsible person, autographed by the Archbishop of Canterbury and witnessed by all the Trustees of the Museum. Miss Tibbits occasionally visited the house in Park Lane on business, and I wondered whether her trained eye observed the living material that waited for some unborn Miss Tibbits of the future.

The luxury, the gilding, the soft carpets of this Charles II epoch suddenly went — as the hair of someone struck with an appalling sorrow is said to turn — white in one night. Everything was painted white. The furniture was stripped; beautiful old gilding and old paint were torn remorselessly from the objects to which they belonged; and ash-colour and mouse-colour were the only tints, however faint; grilled bones and peeled oranges the only food, however monotonous, that were permitted. This, again, was mysterious; seemed to her friends to indicate some fresh aberration. Lady de Montfort's phrase, to explain this favourite, too, was embarrassing. She would say, 'Why, he's wonderful. One glance from him strips you bare.' But, in the end, it was discovered that this denudation portended nothing more exciting than the fact that the new favourite was a psycho-analyst, who boasted that he could unravel and strip the soul.

Life never stops still, and soon colour came back to the house — rich, abundant colour. It was transformed into a Spanish palace. The 18th Duque de Bobadilla, 10th Grandee of the First Class, the 17th Duque de Miraflores y Mirador, the 15th Duque de Salamandar, the 12th Duque de los Nuevos Mundos, the 10th Duque de Alcama Alcarbareo, the 20th Marques de Carabas Viejo, the 19th Marques de Guadalajara, the 18th Marques de Rosina Media, the 28th Visconde de Nuestro Salvador and 42nd Conde de la Estramadura Este, reigned over it in perfect unity, for they were one person. There were Sevillian, white-flashing *patios* with white flower-pots and the inevitable jasmine and orange-blossom, and out of them led the saloons furnished with Spanish rugs and tapestries, Mudejar plates of a strange, gold bronze and cream intricacy, lovely cabinets of tortoise-shell, ivory and gilded wood, and deep sombre velvets. Pictures by Goya and Velasquez hung on the walls. And the food was tinged, too, with the prevailing fashion: there were such stuffed and pungent dishes as Huevos à la Flamenco, Arroz Valenciano, Olla Podrida, Tortillas, Pollo Cubano, such soft melting sweets as Turron and Membrilla. And it was in this period that there took place an unfortunate incident which occasioned a lot of talk at the time, and even found its way into the Press: for example, 'Dragoman' of the *Daily Express* reported it in full.

It is, of course, impossible for us to be certain whether the face-lifting operation of that summer — it would be about August 1924 — was the first that she had undergone, but, at any rate, if not the first, it was the most noticeable, tightening, as it did, all the lines of the face, and imparting to the mouth a strained pursing of the lips that prevented her from closing her mouth. The healing occupied some weeks, and she was ordered to go abroad in order to recuperate. Filled with enthusiasm for all things Spanish, she set out in September to visit Spain with Lady Robert Chickmuster, daughter of Mr. Silas Minkin, Third. This fascinating woman had recently suffered the same treatment at the hands of her plastic-surgeon. Conversation cannot have been easy, for the actual muscular movement of the lips, which talking induces, still occasioned both of them great anguish, and, in addition, each was aware of, but must not mention, the fact of this identical agony. They motored to many places, including Seville, where they stayed with the Duque de Bobadilla. One morning the two ladies wanted to see the Cathedral, and while standing in the Capella Mayor, a verger approached them. This unfortunate man was afflicted with deafness and, looking at their faces, very naturally concluded from the shape of the sewn-up mouths that they were whistling. Explanation was impossible, and they were turned out of the Cathedral for sacrilege. . . . A most painful scene ensued. Tension mounted for weeks. The British Embassy made representations to the Spanish Government and the Vatican: but the deaf verger stuck to his guns, and no apology to the two ladies was ever forthcoming.

Nor was this all the harm that so small an unpleasantness engendered. The Andalusian peace of the Casa de Bobadilla was shattered by a most bitter quarrel which broke out between Lady de Montfort and Lady Robert; a quarrel which rent London for more than six months. It must be remembered that both of them were doubtless much tired after several weeks of arduous sight-seeing, a very fruitful begetter of trouble, and that Lady Robert had in the near past been exacerbated by various matrimonial difficulties which had culminated in an annulment.

But such sudden tempests always arise out of a trifle. Lady de Montfort had said, 'I think, dear, you should be more careful. Of course, knowing you as I do, the old man's suggestion is absurd. But since that last little illness of yours, before you came abroad, you do shape your mouth in a peculiar way, as though you were whistling.'

'Is it *likely* I should whistle, Adèle? *I* can get all the attention I need without that sort of thing, thank you. *I* don't have to whistle, I assure you. I'm not as old as all that.'

'I don't quite see, dear, what "being old" has got to do with it? We're all as old as we look, they say.'

'Well, I don't think what *you* did made *you* look any younger. You mustn't mind. Of course everybody knows you look "astonishingly young", Adèle. The papers are always telling us so.'

'Well, I thought by the way you were talking to me you must be older than me. I don't know, I'm sure.'

'But I wasn't whistling, and I saw no one.'

'And if you had been whistling, nobody would have looked. . . . But I wish you'd stop lecturing.'

'Well, dear, then that's all right, but . . . How do you mean, "looked"?'

'Anyhow, Boo-boo, if you didn't whistle *then*, you needn't shout at me *now*.'

'Shouting at you would be no use. It would be like shouting at an *image*. I don't know what's the matter with you. Your expression never changes.'

'Well, yours is quite different, Boo-boo, to what it used to be. You used to look so smiling and good-tempered. All I meant was that it seemed kind of silly to whistle at that foolish verger.'

'Verger yourself, Adèle. What d'you mean, "verger"? I'd like to know. And if I am, is there anything wrong in it?'

'No, my dear, I didn't say that — you know I didn't. It's a misunderstanding. I said "verger" — you know . . . the man in the Cathedral.'

'Oh, then there *was* a man in the Cathedral, was there? I didn't see him, but I'm not a bit surprised. . . . I suppose now you'll have that house of yours done up as a Cathedral, won't you? . . . I can just see the gargoyles.'

'Well, if I do, dear, I shall ask you to come and whistle in it.'

At this moment, fortunately, the Duque de Bobadilla, his attention attracted by the noise, entered, and the ladies melted into tears.

Possibly this unpleasantness embittered Lady de Montfort against all things Spanish. In any case, on her return to England the Spanish background was swept away, and there ensued, for a time, a quick, rattling succession of styles, culminating in an African house of little wooden stools and rice-bowls. 'Queer . . .', people said, and personally I received a shock, for one day I visited an auction-room, and was much perturbed to see Lady de Montfort, obviously in high spirits, herself openly bidding for negro fetishes, for ivory masks from Nigeria and wooden ones from Dahomey, for tusks of carved ivory and bronzes from Benin: while the fact which lent colour, if one may use the expression, to these black innuendoes was that the man of the moment now never appeared at luncheon or dinner, though everyone knew that a man there must be and was, and even as they wondered, the sound of a gurgling, jungle-like song would be heard from an upper storey.

Relief, therefore, was general when before six weeks had elapsed Lady de Montfort fell in love with a hunting-man. This was a break-away from her usual type, for, unlike even the last invisible and anonymous ghost, he was unmusical: no jungle-song rolled deeply from under the roof-tops, and only very occasionally a fragment of 'D'ye ken John Peel' would break what seemed almost the dumb silence of the animal world. But the foundations of this new affection must have been well and truly laid, for it endured six months. And though he seldom spoke, he had side-whiskers and a handsome face, and was quite happy for hours sucking a straw. Moreover, if he was not altogether at home in the world of men and women, Adèle found the means whereby he might feel less strange. Promptly she had her bedroom done up as a stable. All the chairs, even the bed itself, were re-stuffed — with horsehair. The curtains, too, were of box-cloth. The dining-room became an ostler's room, with bits and harness, and such other things, hanging from wooden pegs. Roast mutton, toasted cheese and ale were the order of the day for guests.

Next, as far as I can remember, came a famous Russian singer. Now she reverted to type. But, nevertheless, Lady de Montfort suffered a great shock. There is no doubt, I think, that they loved with passion. Moreover, each of these two, who in spite of certain tastes in common appeared to be so different, idealised the other. In Lady de Montfort he saw the perfect English liberty-loving aristocrat: when she looked into his eyes, it seemed to her as though she were gazing down into the dark depths of the Slav soul. He was, for her, the Slav soul personified. And when by chance they found that in reality they both hailed from the same home-town in the Middle West, on each side the disillusionment was utter, the upbraiding acrimonious. Each felt as though caught in the revolving, circular movement of maelstrom or whirlwind. However far we travel, we come back to our starting-point, whether we wish it or not.

Next morning the blood-red domes of the Kremlin faded out from every wall, and Park Lane went Mexican. High plumes, jade masks, crystal skulls, silver ornaments of a later period, and a young Mexican oil magnate of musical and artistic tastes, completed the effect. Followed soon a Charles X period; romantic, redolent of Balzac and Chopin. Fans once more littered the tables, and there were small walnuts, with white kid gloves folded up in them, to show how tiny the dead hand had been. Miss Tibbits reappeared from her lair in the British Museum, for, again, it was a young French writer who had evoked this change.

So the days passed. Take, for example, the chart for just a month or two from one of the later years. Where facts are uncertain, the space is left blank: where one must deduce one's own conclusions, a question mark is substituted.

STYLE OF DECORATION AT PARK LANE
(and, where details are remembered, of food offered to guests)

1928		*Description of Man*
Jan. 1–22	German Baroque—silvered tables and chairs. Wiener Schnitzel and Moselle.	German Baroque Baron with grey hair.
Jan. 22–25	Rumanian. Painted boxes and painted clothes. Caviare and Rumanian sweets with every meal.	Rumanian Pianist.
Jan. 25 to March 3	Ceilings painted light blue or dark blue, with appropriate sun or stars. Furniture made of broken propellers, curtains of grey balloon silk.	Musical young Airman.
March 3–13	Moghul. Curries served with 'Bombay duck'.	?
March 13–26	Portuguese 18th-century.	Dwarf Diplomat.
March 26 to April 28	Cinquecento Italian.	Italian Count.
April 28–30	Gipsy Caravan. Hedgehogs baked in clay.	?
May 1–10	Czechoslovak.	
May 10 to June 2	Toucan and parrots' feathers.	Peruvian Diplomat.
June 2–18	Dutch pictures and furniture. Tulips in bowls.	Dutch Novelist.
June 18–19	Norwegian painted furniture installed. Smoked salmon.	?
June 19–23	Mid-Victorian. Very long meals. 'Roasts' of every description.	Young Photographer, English.
June 23–29	Persian 18th century. Tiles, carpets and silks. Two cypress trees in tubs outside the front door. Lamb, served with almonds and roots of lily-of-the-valley.	Young Persian Prince.

It was in 1932 that Adèle branched off very sensationally from the type she generally cultivated. She fell in love, desperately in love, with Thomas Cruikshank McFlecker, the famous deep-sea fisher; a man who for his own pleasure moved through the dangerous, undulating vegetation of tropic waters. Sometimes he would descend just for a few hours, in the outfit of a diver — that rare, armoured robot of the seas, attached by so slender an umbilical cord to his mother, Earth; or, perhaps, he would instead be lowered down into the depths in a device of his own invention, a large steel and glass cradle, and would there remain for days or weeks, dangling in front of the tantalised but ogling sharks and giant cuttle-fish, until they gradually lost their appetites and wilted. Actually McFlecker had come to England on business, for he had placed the contract for one of these new and improved cradles (this one was to be as big as a small room) with a firm of ship-builders, and was waiting until it was finished, and he could return to his work. Meanwhile he needed recreation.

Adèle let herself go thoroughly in every direction. She bought eight new ropes of pearls (for now, since the war, she was a very rich woman), and filled the house with dolphins, mermaids and seaweed; that is to say, chair and table assumed marine shapes, being supported by silver dolphins or mermaids, or a bearded Italian Neptune, with a rakish crown and a trident like a gigantic toasting-fork. The armchairs were all of them restuffed for the second time — on this occasion with seaweed, which, she said, was much more healthy, she was certain, than feathers, wool or horsehair. The mattress of her bed, of course, was filled with seaweed and enclosed in a gigantic shell — a real, not artificial one, from the South Seas. In all these rooms there were flat glass bowls in which were arranged shells, pearls and sharks' teeth under shallow, flickering surfaces of water. Chinese goldfish, with three tails, goggled and performed their crinolined tangos up and down the length of their narrow, oblong tanks. The dining-room was now a grotto, a beautiful imaginative grotto, in which the chairs were modelled after open scallop-shells, and the table itself was made of nacre, while above it, over the heads of the guests, was suspended a vast sunfish which concealed a light. Here, during the whole of the season, she gave a series of fish-lunches and fish-dinners, which she would preface, when she sat down, with one of her explanatory phrases. Pointing at the deep-sea fisher, she would say in her voice with its slightly rising inflection: 'That is a very remarkable man. He teaches one all that there is to know about the ocean bed.' In the drawing-room she had installed a sizzling machine that shot out sparks at unwary guests and filled the house with ozone, until, in consequence, it smelt like a night-club or Tube station (the only places in which ozone is ever consciously encountered). Furthermore, her face had again been lifted that spring, and the fresh tightening of the mouth had made it assume a very piscine expression.

. . . . .

The end was drawing near. . . . He must return to the islands. New and interesting studies awaited him there. The steel and crystal cradle was ready. She determined, which was unlike her, to accompany him. So, early in October, they set out, sailing first to the West Indies.

I met her the day before she left England, and never had she looked younger or more radiant. She was now a famous beauty, whose photograph, taken upside down from an airplane or from below by the photographer — who must lie flat on the floor while she was suspended head downwards, like the sunfish, from the ceiling — appeared in every week's illustrated papers; a renowned forcible-feeder whose food no one was enduring enough to refuse; a figure in the land, in spite of every mitigating circumstance; and one felt that her absence, even for a time, would make a gap, would sadden, not only her friends, but every gossip-writer in this country — of which gossip, gramophones and biscuits at the time seemed the only flourishing industries.

My readers know the rest. Arrived at the ocean-gardens of the Southern Seas, the cradle, which, like a submarine, manufactured its own air, was let down by steel cables. A terrible storm, unexpected by the Weather Bureau, and of an unequalled severity, blew up without warning. Something, we know not what, occurred to break the metal ropes. And so, deep-down, turning over and over, bumping on every current, the steel and crystal cage, devoid of any decoration, essentially stark in outline, now floats along with its two skeletons. She is still dressed in the fashions of 1932, and wears eight rows of pearls; a grotesque exhibit for the fishes that peer and point their cruel sneering or sworded beaks at it, or lash at it in fury with their tails. Or, again, as though in mockery of an idyll that is over and yet is thus forced for ever to parade its continuance, the cradle settles for a while in some leafy, spring-like glade of the ocean bed, some watery glade that resembles a grove in England, with little flowers blowing from the rocks, and small highly coloured fishes moving through the foliage, as birds move through the branches of the trees on land, and over all the refracted light plays in an illusional splendour of sunrise, patches falling here and there: and sometimes the light hits the glass of the cabin, and reveals within it the terrible white-fingered figures, knocked together by the rolling, until, as it were embracing, their mouths meet in a double, lipless grin. Then the swell comes, and the figures fall apart: and so for countless ages, these figures, in their barnacled hut, moving and tumbling on every tide, will dwell in a semi-eternity of endless green water, alone, and now forgotten. For though, at the time of their deaths, people could, as the phrase goes, talk of nothing else; though the memorial service was very largely attended, and letters and telegrams of condolence reached Sir Simon from all quarters and from every class, yet now, and after so long, there has come a generation that knew her not. The gossip-writers have passed to other and newer topics, and the house in Park Lane — that seems with its grottoes, though emptied of its painted fish and oceanic effects, to mock her end — is dusty. And even at this very moment the vans may be calling to remove the furniture from the piled-up lumber-rooms . . . as they called so often in her lifetime.

PLAGUE-CART BEFORE HORSE

Now the flights of pigeons that executed their strange symphonies far above us — for each bird had tied to its body a wooden whistle — had stopped their music. The sky had become an immense blue dome, deepening in colour, and no wings seemed to be beating in it, or against it. . . . The evening belonged to the first spring heats, and the air was scented with the lilac, which in this climate had sprung to blossom in a day. We sat out in the courtyard, five of us, talking and drinking cool drinks, and to us, through the immediate and outlying silence, reached the cries and sounds of a great Chinese city: cries and sounds which were to continue without ceasing, drums and gongs and bells and wooden clappers (no one who has not visited China can imagine the variety of sounds that wood striking wood can produce), each one denoting a trade — peddler or juggler or mountebank or fortune-teller — until the morning, when the terrible anthem of the pigs being killed, thousands of them having their throats cut at the same moment, would complete the concert.

The talk, like one of the kites that could, in the day-time, be seen zigzagging up into the sky, veered hither and thither — first touching on people in general, thence to criminals, to crime, and then on to what part, as it were, the scenery might play in a drama. . . . I had seen, I said, in a far, dead island in the western Mediterranean, a house which had the reputation of being cursed: in every generation some terrible, irremediable event occurred within its precincts. This miniature palace lay nestling only a little way above the tideless blue waters that lapped the very foot of the garden; a beautiful, pink marble, eighteenth-century house, surrounded by giant olive trees and by palms. On its scented terraces, broken and crumbling, brooded the doomed Latin decadence of D'Annunzio's novels; here mother killed son in one generation, and brother killed brother in the next. And the criminals whom this little sea-palace bred were handsome and noble, terrible in their crimes. Through the hot days and nights the house smouldered in that dark wood by the sea. There was nothing gloomy about it, only something infinitely passionate and beautiful, but indefinably wicked, so that it was impossible not to wonder whether, at least in this instance, the house had not in reality influenced its inhabitants towards their various cruel deeds and inexorable fates, rather than that the inhabitants had influenced their shell. . . . This delicate, pale rose-coloured dwelling, so elegant, so lovely in proportion and design, was yet an expression of the dark and ancient soil out of which it had grown; its strength — one had almost written 'virtue' — rested in the earth in which it was rooted — and what strange histories haunt that luxuriant, desolate shore! . . . Thus it may be that, if a modern palace were built at Mycenae, on that tremendous and terrible hill, the Furies would come to life again and rush full tilt through the ravine below, till the air would sweep shuddering up to its halls for a moment, as now the tops of the trees, after the aeroplanes have passed, cower down and tremble under the very icy breath of doom. . . . So, too, the peace that pervades many monastic dwellings — even though, long ago secularised, they have sunk to being hotels — may be due more to their structure and site than to the monks who laboured. Why, for example, had they chosen this position? — because it was, to their minds, blessed. What spirit inspired the humble, whitewashed yet aspiring beauty of the design, fitting as closely to the rock, and belonging to it as much as a barnacle to a ship's bottom, and why, before that, had a temple stood here? Similarly, think of the now domesticated temples near us in the Western Hills, with their sweet wistarias, their apple trees in flower, their pools and slanting eaves; the Buddhist priests had surely chosen them because the outlook from them influenced the mind towards peace and virtue?

Christopher Standish took on the argument in a different, more material vein, telling us, from his medical experience at Liverpool and in industrial Lancashire, how typhus can haunt the soil, so that the ground may never be cleared of infection. Thus a slum could be destroyed and a new palace erected instead; yet, however many times the buildings on this site were burnt or pulled down, the typhus would inevitably return. . . . But then, this disease is carried by vermin, and vermin can survive fire, and sword, and even sanitation: (think of the gaol-fever that used to make English prisons such haunted and horrible places of incarceration, attacking even at times the judges and the juries, so that it seemed as though this fever, born of criminals, were seeking to enact a revenge for them upon society!). . . . Such fevers are intelligible; nevertheless, it would perhaps be true, he thought, to say that typhus *haunted* the site of such a building. . . . Standish became silent, and again the cries and various metallic musical sounds of the night reached us. A fortune-teller was tapping his way down the lane outside, and one could hear the creaking wheels of the carts; (so, in England, centuries ago, must have sounded the plague-carts as they creaked through the streets of the city at midnight, their husky drivers crying, 'Bring out your dead!').

Now Angus Rockingham struck up for the first time. 'I suppose you will think that it is putting the cart before the horse,' he said, 'but somehow it seems to fit what you are saying. . . . You know that before I came out here, I was in Cyprus. I lived there for five years — in that outpost of empire where every day in the broiling heat the Briton takes off his topee, and eats roast beef and steak-and-kidney pudding, roly-poly, and then, as an offering to local colour, devours a viscous, melting square of Turkish Delight, to the accompaniment of sticky sweet wines. It is the only Greek island with no Greek statues, no Greek temples, no shape to its landscape; nothing except its one incomparable Bel Paese — a French Gothic building, flowering in a beautiful but inapposite position — and a few, as they seem, whitewashed English parish-churches masquerading as mosques. The natives, too — you must call them *natives* — are for the most part not Greek, but descended from the slave races of Roman times: dirty, stupid, cringing and for ever unfortunate. . . . However, you won't want to hear my views about Cyprus, for whenever an English paper reaches us, you always read that it is the Jewel of the Empire. Further, I lived, admittedly, in the most beautiful part of the island; in an ancient Turkish city some three miles from the sea. There, at least, as one walked by the tideless, deep-blue waters, something of Greece lingered. Although there were no temples, not even a pillar of them surviving, the shore was lined with fragments of marble wall and pavement, and with shells that seemed, equally, to be the work of some great, long-dead architect. Acanthus and asphodel grew from the broken, shapeless masonry, and anemones turned their fluttering eyes to the sun from any bank where there was soil: and any bank where there was soil indicated foundations lying buried beneath it. . . . On the surface there were neither ancient nor any modern buildings: at least, only one, a large, unused, melancholy looking low structure with the damp-stained plaster peeling from its walls. . . . It had been built as a smallpox hospital some twenty years before, I found out: and then, since smallpox here had been eradicated and extinguished — that much, at least, is to our credit — had, for some reason or other, never been adapted to any other purpose, but had remained virgin and desolate — though, as for that, had it been used, the desolation would, I thought, have been of the very same kind. In this climate — for so far as I could see, no attention had been paid to the fabric — it had remained marvellously whole. Flowering weeds grew on the roof, but the roof itself was still perfect.

'I have said that the building was desolate, but this does not mean that I want you to think that it was ugly: it was not ugly. On the contrary, it was spacious and well-constructed, standing upon an exquisite site; a poem, as it were, a *fleur du mal* in brick and plaster. The government official who had designed it must surely have been a genius, for, with the little money at his disposal, he had symbolised the idea of illness in general and smallpox in particular. Just as Vanbrugh piled up Blenheim Palace into a triumphal ode for the Great Captain's victories, so this obscure, perhaps unconscious, artist had made out of his rather pitiful materials an absolute expression, a personification, of smallpox, that horrible and disfiguring disease. . . . Not for a moment could you have mistaken it for a prison, nor even for an ordinary isolation hospital. No: smallpox was expressed in its every aspect. It seemed dedicated, in some way, to the development and flowering of this particular plague. Long before I knew its history, I had formed a correct conclusion — as it turned out — concerning its original purpose.

'After I had been there for a year or two, a retired merchant from Bombay came to settle in the town with his wife and children. It was cheap and warm, and after a long sojourn in the East he could not support the English climate. . . . But even here life was difficult; he was never well, he could not find a house, and he did not like the only hotel in the town. (Indeed this was not surprising, for the Cyprus hotel combines the worst points of the English inn and the Turkish caravanserai. . . .) The arrival of the Verskills was a great comfort to me, for I was growing more and more tired of the place, and the family afforded me pleasant companionship. I quickly formed a friendship with Clare, the daughter: a lovely girl and worthy of better things. Her charm, like that of her brothers, was obvious, and consisted in her vitality and health and good spirits. . . . But all the same she was charming, and charged with an energy delightful in this environment. I don't think any of them had much imagination, but they possessed the good-nature of all things that are young and healthy.

'Certainly the father was not imaginative, yet he allowed the town to get on his nerves. He could not bear the system of life he found in the hotel there, for he was used to being master of a house. . . . And then one day, walking among the deserted foundations of temples, down paths lined with asphodel and acanthus that had once been great roads, he saw this low building I have described, and in his dismal discontented fashion fell in love with it. He liked its air of space. Perhaps he even liked its air of loneliness — in any case, with his family about him, he could never be lonely. Servants were easy to secure in Cyprus, though difficult, perhaps, to drill; and he could run it. It would give him something to do. He, rather than his wife — that placid, silent woman — would assume the organisation of the house, inside and out; he would draw up charts for the servants, so that they should know when to get up, and what to do. As for the outside, he would decorate this terrace with geraniums (they grew here as easily as wild flowers), and there he would plant a grove of fruit trees, so that 'the missus' could make her jams again, as she had done, long years ago, in England. . . . I tried — I hardly know why, except that I liked Clare — to dissuade him, invented reasons for not taking the house, said it was damp, and that the provincial government would not sell it. It was silly of me, for after all there was nothing against it — there had never been a case of illness there. However, my arguments were of no avail; the authorities responded more quickly than usual, and, in spite of my pleading, Mr. Verskill acquired his bargain, and was delighted with it. . . . Here it is only fair to say that, to my surprise, he made his new dwelling in its own way charming and agreeable. It became much less depressing, seemed to have come into its own. The colours were cool and gay, the furniture quiet and very English. Even the fruit trees didn't look out of place, and I much enjoyed sitting out in the garden of an evening with the family. . . . I dined there, I remember, the last night before my leave.

. . . .

'When I returned', he continued, 'they were dead, all dead of smallpox; the first cases in the island for twenty years. . . . And do you know, such a massacre, a family of five, and eight servants, lacks the poignance of an individual tragedy; leaves little but horrified surprise behind it. . . . This is not to say that I did not miss them; I could never bear to pass that way. But sometimes I had to. . . . The house, I suppose, had been fumigated; the windows were shut and barred, the eyes closed again; no air ever blew in. Poor Clare!'

His voice trailed away, to be lost in the sounds of the Chinese night, drums and gongs and bells and wooden clappers, sounds that would continue until the morning; when the terrible anthem of the pigs being killed, thousands of them having their throats cut simultaneously, would complete the concert.

POMPEY AND SOME PEACHES

A Stereoscopic Story in Two Parts

(For Lorna Andrade)

I

OLD Mulready Maure had been at one time the leading English art critic. He had known every great figure of his period. But when he retired to the gaunt country house near York whence he had originally emerged, his neighbours complained that this lean, angular, quixotic man was a bore. Stories of Rossetti and Whistler, of Swinburne and Morris, meant nothing to these faces that looked permanently 'blooded', indelibly tainted with the smear from the fox's brush. Though my nature prompts me to dislike critics, seeing in them members of the opposite team in the game of Gentlemen *v.* Players or Foxes *v.* Birds of Paradise, I liked listening to the old man's talk, and it was he who first told me, one day when I went to see him, the story about the peaches.

'Even towards the end of Dubosque's life, you could have bought a picture of his, not for a song, but for the mere trouble of crying "Rags and Bones" out in the street. Whereas now that he's dead (where the dealers wanted to get him), only a millionaire can afford to *look* at his work, let alone buy it.

'And what an extraordinary man he was, what an extraordinary painter, more particularly for an Englishman!

'Some great artists construct, like Rubens or Titian or Tiepolo or Delacroix, their own gigantic and overwhelming lands of fantasy, new Indies of the imagination upon whose shores men have never yet set foot: others, like Rembrandt or Chardin or Cézanne, reveal a world equally new, whether dark or glittering with light, within the most familiar objects. And it was to this latter, perhaps almost rarer, division that Richard Dubosque belonged.

'In appearance, as well as in the way in which he approached the art of painting, he resembled much more a

Frenchman than an Englishman, and, as his name showed, he was of French blood; I believe, Huguenot. Even before he came to live up here, the life he led was extremely ascetic. By that, I don't mean that as a young man he had not had his fling, for he was full of temperament, but that his life was dedicated: his desire to paint ousted every other passion, and he would rather look at a glass of Margaux, let us say, and study it, than drink it. But the austerity of his life compared strangely with the greed — if you see what I mean — of his painting, in which I always felt a sense of consuming appetite. No French master, not even Cézanne, possessed a more complete understanding of material objects, a greater feeling for their texture, their volume and the unseeable — if I may phrase it like that — organisation of the interior as expressed by their contour and surface. With his painting of an apple, for instance, he seemed to tell us everything that was known, not only of this particular apple, but of every other apple in the world, and by the voluptuousness of its presentation it was plain that Eve had confided to him the secret hissed into her ear by the serpent. That is what gave him his unique place in English art; he painted objects, material objects, as only a lover could paint them.

'He did not really like seeing *people*, his life was too much occupied by his painting, and he had no wish for distraction. And so his cottage up here on the wolds suited him perfectly. It was a dear little rough, white-walled house, with a garden divided into four compartments by box hedges, and with a wall of loose stones enclosing it, an oasis in the vast prospect. This was his part of the country too, and he loved it and understood it, and the fact that the nearest village to his home was five or six miles away appealed to him as a positive advantage. Of course, various admirers — for he always had a little circle of fervent lovers of his art — used from time to time to stay in the district, so as to be near him. . . . Then, too, he and I were old friends, and now that I was living in the vicinity as well, I used to see a good deal of him. Indeed I believe my chief claim to renown after I have gone, will be that my articles on Dubosque's paintings helped to place him as a great modern master: but I don't think he liked me any more for that. He could have done without any of us. Even if he had made money in his lifetime it would have meant nothing to him — but, as you know, it is his widow who reaps the benefit of the vast sums his pictures fetch today.

'He had married this woman a few years before he settled in the neighbourhood. Perhaps he had not known much about her (for in matters of life, as opposed to those of painting, he always showed the vagueness of the disinterested) except that she had been his mistress, could cook and liked looking after men and things. She did not, of course, he must have realised, understand his pictures, or care for them: but after all, how few people did. And if they married, she could superintend the house, and so he could have more hours in which to paint. . . . There was always so little time, it seemed to him.

'Deborah was tall, large-framed, a handsome creature; about forty then, some fifteen years younger than her husband. And she could be pleasant, in a natural sort of way. But soon after their marriage she began to change. . . . Of course, in spite of the general neglect of him, he was always the centre of interest to a chosen — or rather, choosing — few, a prince of a territory composed of princes. And, now that she met his friends as equals, she became aware of it. . . . What it was all about she could not comprehend, but of one thing she was certain: he *could* make money if he wanted. But he did *not want* to, he was obstinate — pig-headed, she called it. And then, as he was poor — at any rate poor compared with many of his friends — he should not be so wasteful. Beautiful plates of apricots and peaches in the summer, just left to rot so that he could paint them! "Mustn't touch this" and "Mustn't touch that"! Never even asked if she'd like to eat one. And often he wouldn't even paint them, he would just sit there staring at the fruit in a way that irritated her beyond bearing, gazing at them as though he were consuming them in a sort of silent, mystic passion of the eyes. (I have often seen him do it.) Well, why didn't he eat them? He always seemed to keep the best fruit for painting, and when once in the morning, just before he woke, she had stolen into the studio and eaten two of the peaches on the plate, he had made a row; an awful, vulgar row, to her way of thinking.

'But she'd given him as good as she got: that was one good thing. He'd never had the rough side of her tongue before, she had always treated him different from other people.

But now he was her husband, and she meant to show him, just like she had shown Jack and Andy in the old days. . . . After all, if she stayed there, hour after hour, staring at the slops or the unmade bed instead of doing the chores, how would he get on, she would like to know! . . . Of course, she was fond of him, she admitted to herself (let anyone else venture to criticise him to her!), but he was silly, soft, let anyone treat him anyhow, so long as he could go on painting or staring. . . . And he hardly ever looked at *her*. She was just a fixture. If only she had been an old turnip or an apple or something, he would have sat gazing at her for hours with those love-sick eyes, she supposed. No, all he cared for was his painting; and what came of it? Never even a picture in the Academy: (they might think she knew nothing about Art, but she knew that painters ought to have pictures in the Academy). And no money. She was surprised his friends weren't ashamed of him, instead of crying and fawning round, with their "Yes, Dubosque" and "No, Dubosque" and "Do you really think so, Dubosque?"

'As for Dubosque himself, I imagine, from what I saw, that, as he grew ever more used to her, he became more steadily attached to her. . . . I don't know, but I think, all the same, that he hated her change of voice; for, as his wife, and so the equal of his friends, she had adopted a new voice, like theirs, she thought — a new "*accent*", as she would have said. The old rustic burr, that had been one of her chief attractions for him, had vanished, except when she was angry and momentarily reverted. I used to notice, when I was with them, how her new voice continually surprised him, in the same way as the new attitude of superiority she had developed in order to match it; the jump he gave, for instance, at her "Gharstley Creatchah!" . . . He had a pet tortoise in the garden, a wise tortoise that loved him, and, silently and slowly plodding, never interrupted him during his painting, though it entered the studio whenever it liked. "Pompey", he used to call it. "Pompey, armoured proudly as the greatest of Roman warriors." And in the autumn, Dubosque said, Pompey would go, just like a Roman General, into winter quarters, embedding himself till the spring in a mound of dry grass and sweet herbs specially prepared for him every year in the garden.

'Dubosque loved to paint Pompey. He would gaze at the

tortoise for hours, enraptured, unravelling the design of its armour, the marking and corrugation of its shell. . . . You would have thought, Deborah used to say to herself, that he was in love with it, ghastly creature! And, whenever Pompey was mentioned — and Dubosque's friends always made a point of inquiring after the tortoise —, she would scream out "Gharstley Creatchah!" in her new, affected voice. . . . Waste of time, she thought, looking after it; in the same way that it was waste of money to send her to buy those roses in York, in the middle of the winter, just because he "wanted to paint roses", and waste of good peaches, to leave them there, rotting on the dish!

'As her husband grew older, he seemed to her to grow more obstinate. She saw in him no longer that ardent, romantic youth of thirty years before, as she had first known him, and in whom she had in some dim, groping way divined the genius, but a tired elderly man whom it was her duty to look after, but who always tried to escape and to raise difficulties. . . . As a matter of fact, in a kind of way, perhaps she was right: as often occurs with a genius, with the passing years the fire had left him, and entered exclusively into his work. It flamed through his canvases, but no longer showed in word or look or action. He was gentle now, still without guile, and he did not want to talk much even to those who could understand what he said. He seemed to enjoy, chiefly, the company of my two daughters, who were then little girls; he loved the society of children. As for Deborah, he always treated her kindly, and with respect in front of his friends, however trying she might be. But he was determined not to encourage her to chatter in private about the high cost of housekeeping in this part of the country, or to complain about the tortoise, when he could be alone in his studio, either painting that old bottle he had found, and a glass and some oranges, or looking at them. . . . And why did she bother about money? — she had never enjoyed *any* before she married him, even if they did not have much now.

'His health gave way before such a collapse was due or could have been foretold. The fire had burnt him up. He cannot have been more than sixty. I know that, because we were about the same age, and that was eighteen years ago. . . . I suppose to you it sounds a great age: but I can assure you, as one gets on, it seems nothing at all. . . . But to continue. . . . It was that final winter on the wolds that finished him. In the autumn, when the last flowers, belated white roses and scarlet snapdragon, still nodded in the particular misty, golden sunshine of its early mornings and late evenings, we warned him. Already he had begun to cough. His friends, my wife and myself among them, implored him to go abroad, to Italy or the South of France, for the winter. But he would not listen to us. Though the hours during which he could paint at this season were so few and fitful, this was his chosen light, the light by which he saw, in which he lived and all objects lived for him.

'Just as the painters of Italy and the Netherlands have recorded for ever the quality and texture of the days in their countries, so it has been left, it seems to me, to two English painters alone — to Constable first, and then to Dubosque — to sum up and present the look and feeling of the light of their native land. This peach or this jug could have been painted nowhere else in the world: and an apple or an egg, which to the ordinary eye has so little individuality, was to him, in this clear, pure light, more beautiful, more worthy of being looked at, examined, searched, as it were, than were the most sumptuous objects elsewhere: the great mosaics of Constantinople or the jewelled enamels of medieval France.

'It was this light which "sang" to him. . . . But, alas, in the winter, his beloved light failed him. It was not that his eyesight had begun to go, but that the light itself suffered a change, for the snow, when it first fell, did not melt in a day or two, as usual, but rolled over the abrupt and breath-taking perspective of these parts its thick ugly carpet. It was impossible for him to indulge, even, in that laziest and most agreeable winter pastime of the painter, to look at the pictures he had painted in the summer and criticise them. He could not "see them", he complained. (Grumbling again, Deborah said to herself, as if no one had ever seen snow before! . . . Why couldn't he set to work, hard, and make money? . . . Portraits, for example. . . . Why, they'd easily be in time for the Academy, if he started them now. She saw it in her mind's eye, "Study in Scarlet and Silver: the Artist's Wife". . . . And everyone stopping before it in admiration.)

'Day after day the snow lay there, or it snowed again:

day after day, in consequence, lost interest for him. There was nothing to do. Wise Pompey slept in his mound: there was no fruit to look at, and even if there had been, it would have signified nothing. Every morning the same white light entered when he pulled the curtains, a hard, pitiless whiteness that glared up through the windows of the cottage from the ground, reached the white ceiling, to fall back with a redoubled white numbness on to the objects in the room or studio. He could see nothing, look at nothing. He wandered about continually, in and out of the house, wondering when the sky would alter, and the whole world with it. Surely it could not go on, day after day? Within himself, he asked which of his peers in painting would have derived inspiration from these scenes. Manet, perhaps, would have intoxicated his senses with this new light, and its effect on familiar things: the swooping lines of the wolds and the movement of the thick, foreshortened figures on the frozen mere below would have brought ecstasy to the heart and hand of Breughel the Elder; but to him, Dubosque, this world in which the ground in the distance was paler and more perceptible, and stretched further, than the sky above, held a terrible quality of sterilisation, as though the whole country had been transformed into a hospital ward.

'So he fidgeted, and grew to look more and more miserable. Deborah, who usually attacked him for working too hard, and thinking of nothing but his work, now reversed the engine, as it were, and, in the old language of her unregenerate days, "ticked him off proper" for being lazy. Why didn't he go to sleep for the winter, and bury himself in a heap of leaves, like Pompey, "Gharstley Creatchah"? But, even if *he* could, she couldn't afford to stand about talking all day: any more than she could afford to leave peaches about like his Lordship. (Oh no, she didn't forget those things!) *She* had work to do. She must, somehow or other, and it wasn't easy in this weather, get to the village for shopping—otherwise he'd have nothing to eat, and how would he like that? And also to see the new boy, who was coming in twice a week, as soon as the weather altered, to help keep the garden tidy. (She didn't like his friends to go away and say she didn't know how to keep the place decent for him, even if *he* didn't mind!) . . . But there it was, if he went on mooning about like that, he'd catch another cold, and then she'd have to nurse him, into the bargain, she supposed.

'And catch cold, sure enough, he did. . . . By then it was February, and the cold settled on his lungs. I saw him. In the morning, Deborah said, he had been quite clear in his mind, but in the afternoon he was both listless and feverish. Deborah did not seem to think much of it: it would pass. But I was disturbed about his condition. And though I didn't like the two children to see anyone seriously ill, for they were only about fifteen and sixteen then, I told them to ride over and call on him one day soon. I knew he was particularly attached to them — and they to him — and I thought their visit would cheer him up. When they went, they took with them — dear girls, it was their own idea — a basket of South African peaches, which they had bought specially for him in York out of their own money.

'It was, apparently, a lovely afternoon that they chose for their visit, mild and full of a serene light, for at last the weather had changed, and the snow had melted. Deborah took them in to see him. "Look, Rich, what lovely peaches they've brought you", she said, as they entered the room. . . . But he had seemed very odd, that afternoon, hardly noticed the children, they thought, and they returned home very distressed about him. From what they said, I don't believe he recognised them at all. He mumbled something when they came in, and then his eyes followed the basket of peaches, that swam that afternoon in a perfect painter's light. His eyes devoured them, he appeared to see nothing else. . . . And then suddenly, as he remained in this rapt staring at the fruit, large tears began to roll down his finely sculptured cheeks; rolled down them. But he did not speak. . . . The children thought it better to go home: it was too painful. As they left, they heard Deborah, behind them, reproving her patient for his manners. "That's a nice way to say 'Thank you' for a present. . . . Such lovely peaches, too. I shouldn't think they'd bring you anything another time."

'When the children told me, it sounded to me like his farewell to the visual world he had loved and served so faithfully. . . . After that, during the next three days I can only piece together what happened, from things Deborah and the doctor told me: I did not like to go over and interfere myself, and, indeed, now that pneumonia had set in, there was nothing one could do. I am sure Deborah looked after him well in her own way. But a year or two before, when they had the quarrel (about which I told you) over the peaches, he had said to me, laughing — for he told me about it at the time, making a joke of it — "If ever I see her eating another of my peaches, I'm afraid it will kill me!" And that, I believe, is, in a sense, exactly what occurred.

'He was only allowed orange juice, nothing to eat, the doctor said, when I telephoned to ask if there was any food I could send over for him. He had been told he could have a peach. But he would not; he just lay there, Deborah complained, staring at the basket, looking at the peaches with gooseberry eyes. Just the same he was, well or ill. She priced them up in her mind. They must have cost from 1s. 6d. to 1s. 9d. each, at least. And they'd been there three days, wouldn't last another twelve hours, and if there was one thing she hated, it was waste! . . . Now that it was growing too dark to go on staring at the peaches, he had shut his eyes. He must be asleep, she thought, so she snatched a peach. He wouldn't notice, was feverish all the time.

'Delicious, it was, but difficult to eat, there was so much juice in it. It ran down the corners of her chin, and she had to gobble it to prevent the juice from spoiling her dress. (There, that was better.) But just as she was finishing it, a glow shone in through the window. Something must be alight in the garden; a bonfire. It showed her face very clearly and outlined her figure against the darkness. The dying painter opened his eyes and saw her, huge and dominating to his sick brain, against the darkness, her face, very clear, as she munched, with the little rivulets of juice wetting her chin. For a moment he sat up and watched with intensity. "Richard, Richard!" she cried, but he had fallen back, and his panting for breath had ended.

'Outside in the garden, the bonfire began to die down. Near its still incandescent heart, Pompey, that "Gharstley Creatchah", "armoured proudly as the greatest of Roman warriors", had been sleeping. . . . The new garden boy had forgotten, had thought the mound in which Pompey passed his royal winter sleep was rubbish to be burned.

'Later, his gutted shell was found in the ruins of his funeral pyre. For a long time Deborah would not throw it away. After all, she said to herself, it was tortoise-shell now, and might be worth something to the right person, to someone who was looking for such a thing. I believe when she left, she took it up with her to London. . . . That was eighteen years ago, or so. But it was only two years ago that she parted, for eight thousand pounds, with the famous "Pompey and Some Peaches", which used to hang over the chimney-piece of her house in South Audley Street.'

POMPEY AND SOME PEACHES

II

'Everything is the same,' Miss Gertrude Stein says somewhere, 'and everything is different.' When the doctor told me the same story, it sounded different.

'If I were an artist feller, I wouldn't mind painting that view myself', he said to me one day, looking out of the window of the bedroom in which I lay ill. 'But I'm surprised *you* never have a shot at it! I should have thought painting was in your line. — Besides, a man ought to have hobbies. You'd find your health much better if you took to one.

'You're so artistic and all that, you ought some time when you're in London to go and call on Mrs. Dubosque. I've often wondered why you don't. She'd be pleased to see you, I know. And I'm sure the pictures would interest you: a wonderful collection. . . . Oh, my God, no! *Real* pictures; not by her husband. She got rid of most of those ages back. The last went two years ago — fetched eight thousand pounds, if you please!

'Never could make out how they brought those prices. Extraordinary thing. . . . Of course, I'm only a country doctor, so I know nothing about it. I don't pretend to be a judge. But to my mind they were just daubs, anybody could have done them. (The other day, the wife showed me a drawing in coloured chalks, what they call crayons, by Elise, our little girl, and I can tell you it was a masterpiece compared to many of his things.) He just didn't know how to put the paint on. I've never seen any other painter put it on like that. Never could understand how he got it across — and yet some of the critics thought the world of him. It's my belief you or I could hoodwink them, if we wanted to. . . . Anyhow, as I was telling you, with the money she made out of the sale of his pictures, she bought a house in South Audley Street and some magnificent paintings, new as well as old. After her husband died, she used to go round the Academy every year and pick out the best, didn't mind what she paid for 'em. Real high-class things, with no nonsense about them.

'Oh, Deborah's got taste! You can see it directly you enter the house. You'd be surprised at the dining-room, a huge great room, painted like that green stuff from Russia, with black marble pillars, and over the mantelpiece a magnificent portrait of her by Laszló. It's a stunner: real good style, in a silver dress with a tiara and white fox fur, and her pearls. (Lovely pearls, she's got.) It might be she herself—and opposite, another one, nearly as good, by Simon Elwes.

'Of course her hair is white now (by Jove, didn't Laszló know how to paint white hair well!), but she's still a fine-looking woman. You know, one of those figures, like that', and the doctor stuck out his chest, and drew Mrs. Dubosque for me on the empty air. 'Very striking, with wonderful eyes.

'I first came up to this mouldy part of the country just after I'd qualified. Knew nobody. Of course, I've got used to it, but it seemed funny then, after always living at the governor's tidy little place at Wimbledon. One was at the heart of things there, and could always run up to town for a show and supper afterwards, and get back easily. . . . So it seemed very cut-off and uncivilised here. No tennis. And I missed my people and the girls (three sisters, I had then). No one to talk to. . . . So I suppose I was rather taken by Deborah—Mrs. Dubosque—, and I often used to walk up there and talk to her. In time we became very good friends, for we "spoke the same language", as they say.

'People used to have it that she'd been a bit gay in her time, but I never saw a sign of it. She was handsome then, very handsome, but what I liked most about her was the way she spoke. A lovely voice: you know, *refined*. Quite different to all the people round here. And much too good for *him*, in my opinion. Always thought he was a fake, with nothing to him. And *funny*, too. Often I've seen him sit for hours without speaking, just staring at something. *She* was the real thing, worth a hundred of him. . . . And if, after his death, his pictures fetched those ridiculous prices, it must have been her doing. A clever woman, with her head screwed on the right way, and always very careful, keen on her money's worth and hating waste. . . . He was a lucky man, if only he'd had the brains to realise it. You don't find many women like that nowadays.

'It used to make my blood boil, the way he treated her. . . . Of course, looking back — I suppose one gets more tolerant as one gets older — I can see that, though different from other people, he wasn't *all* bad. But, by Jove, he *was* a queer chap. Couldn't paint at all — that was obvious — and yet you'd have thought that nothing but painting interested him. I wonder it didn't get more on her nerves, the way he behaved. . . . You know, all sorts of little things. . . . Often when I went to see them, he'd fasten his eyes on one particular thing, a basket of fruit it might be, or a bunch of flowers, or that beastly, smelly tortoise he always had about the place in the summer, and just stare and stare, as if hypnotised. When she spoke to him, he'd often make no reply, but just go on staring. And the same with me — would hardly speak to me, didn't seem to see me. (I tell you, I've attended cases no worse than his — dementia praecox, they call it — in the County Asylum before now.) Wouldn't answer when I tried to be polite: but then, I'm a man, and it didn't matter. But you can't treat a woman like that. (The governor was always pretty strong about that sort of thing with me, when I was a youngster, I can tell you. If any man had dared to treat the Mater in that way, he'd have knocked him down.) Yet, when some of his friends came to see him from London — their gross flattery of him used to make me feel sick —, he'd fairly talk his head off. All rot, of course, but still, it showed he *could* make himself pleasant, if he wanted. And his friends would repeat what he'd said, and even go on repeating things he'd said years before, as if they were wonderful.

'Dubosque was always painting that tortoise and making a fuss of it. I can understand a chap making a friend of a fox-terrier or an airedale — after all, they're very *like us* — much more intelligent, I often say, than any human I know. . . . You know my dog "Spot"? Well, often he'll bark at me for half an hour at a time, and I'll answer him. Each of us understands every word the other says. . . . But a tortoise! I wouldn't touch one with a pair of tongs. *A tortoise!* And I'm sure Deborah can't have liked the way he used to stroke it, and talk to it and stare at it, while paying no attention to her. But she never said much, not even to me. . . . Sometimes, she'd just look at it and say, in a voice that showed how much above that sort of thing she was, "Ghastly Creature!" Just like that, "Ghastly Creature!" Withering!

'And then he was so mean. I suppose he wasn't rich, but he didn't seem to *want* to make money. (It was as though it didn't interest him, extraordinary chap.) Still, he had a little put by: she'd seen to that. But he seemed to grudge her every single thing, even the fruit he was painting. Often I've seen him forbid her to eat a peach, or even an apple, just because he happened to be painting it. ("The poet of still life", indeed!) No, it had to be treated like something sacred, not dusted, not touched. Sometimes — there weren't any people up there for her to talk to — she'd confide in me. And I remember her telling me that once she'd taken two peaches off a plate in the studio, because she saw they'd be bad by the next day, and had eaten them herself, so as not to feel that they'd all been wasted. But, when he noticed, he made a fearful rumpus, went right off the deep end. . . . Well, you know, it's not nice, that sort of thing. It isn't playing the game with a woman. It wasn't straight. . . . And another thing. In those days — though you wouldn't think it to look at her now — she used to do most of the housework herself, and liked sometimes to sing as she worked. But he wouldn't let her. Said it distracted him from his painting! Imagine it! . . . At the same time, nothing was good enough for that beastly tortoise. "Pompey", as his friends used to call it, could have anything he damned well liked. Milk in saucers all over the place at all hours of the day, lettuces and fresh fruit and rose petals in the summer, and in the winter a special mound of grass and stuff for him to sleep in, piled up for him in the garden.

'As for Dubosque, summer or winter you could hardly get him out of the house. I'm surprised the muscles of his legs didn't atrophy! Never took any exercise, and I spoke to him about it — he was my patient (we doctors can't pick and choose our patients, unfortunately; have to place our scientific knowledge at the disposal of anyone who needs it), and it was my duty to look after him, whatever I thought of his "art". When I told him, straight out, that he must walk more and take more fresh air, what do you think he replied? . . . That he "hadn't time"! That'll show you the sort of feller he was. Lazy as they're made. And did nothing but paint — and paint badly at that, to my mind! . . . After all, it's not a matter of argument, but of fact. What would happen to me if I diagnosed measles, and it proved to be gallstones or appendicitis? In the same way, a peach is a delicate thing, no one can pretend it isn't, so it's obviously bad art to paint it with great, heavy clumsy strokes. All thumbs, as you might say. (Next time you come up to see me, when you're better, I'll show you a little gem of a water-colour of some peaches and a bit of mimosa that the wife did on our holiday at Cannes last spring. . . . I appreciate good work when I see it.) So it used to make me cross to hear his silly friends discussing his way of painting in their mincing, arty jargon: "Richard's brushwork is superb!" or "Just look at the broad treatment of those roses!" or "I feel I've never seen a tortoise before, till I looked at that picture!" Affected set of beggars, if ever there was one!

'He didn't show it much to me, but he had a *nasty* temper. Sulked about things that wouldn't affect you and me. So, one year, when the snow came down nearly every day for two months, it happened not to suit him, and he fell ill and developed "pneumo". After all, it's never exactly the Riviera touch in this neighbourhood during the winter; he ought to have known that, being born up here. Besides, you'd think that any real artist would have *liked* the snow. Lovely, it was. But I think he'd begun to go a bit balmy as well; and "pneumo" always attacks mentals. No resistance, you see. . . . Well, for weeks beforehand, he'd been skulking about the house and garden, sulking, and now, when he fell ill, he'd hardly speak; hardly even speak to me, though I was his medical adviser. Deborah behaved like an angel, the way she nursed her husband: and all the pipes bursting from the frost, all over the place; worked her fingers to the bone for him. He never so much as said "Thank you", just lay there, in bed, and even when the weather changed and became mild, he didn't get any better. Made no effort. And no doctor can cure a patient unless he tries to cure himself.

'Then one afternoon, some friends of his — the daughters of "Old Maure", as they call him here, affected old blighter — brought him a basket of peaches. Very kind of the children, really, don't you know. Had paid for them themselves. But when he saw the fruit, he paid no attention to anyone or anything else, but began to blubber, without even speaking to the little things who'd brought it; there he lay for hours, tears running down his face, and staring at the peaches — which, I must say, looked very good — in a way that made one's blood curdle. . . . Perhaps he knew he wouldn't see any fruit where he was going. But he should have been more considerate to his wife, and not shown his feelings. Besides, they'd been got for him to eat. (I allowed him fruit and things like that and orange juice: one day when we've got more time, I'll give you my views on orange juice.) But he wouldn't touch them. Just left them there in the basket, and stared and stared, perverse devil that he was.

'There the peaches stayed, on a table by his bed for two or three days. I went back to visit him one day in the evening; when I entered the room, it was difficult to see at first, it was dark, but there was a sort of glow coming through the window. The patient was lying back, asleep, — a good sign, for he'd been very restless — and Deborah was standing in the middle of the room. I'd walked up the stairs quietly, and she didn't see me, and, I don't know why, but I stood still in the doorway. There seemed something important — perhaps *dramatic* is the right word — about it. There she stood, you know, a great, big woman, outlined by that funny sort of light. "Eerie", I suppose, people would call it. I remember thinking how fine she looked, monumental. The windows were opposite, and this queer red glow wavered round her body, and shone full on her face. She was eating one of the peaches, because he wouldn't eat them, and they'd have gone bad by the next day. But what struck me was, I'd never seen anyone enjoy anything so much as she enjoyed that peach. It did one good to watch her (that's what I admired about her, the way she made you feel she'd enjoy things), and you could see it was a lovely, juicy peach. . . . At that very moment he sat up in bed, suddenly, without warning. And there was just enough light to see him staring and staring at Deborah, without saying a word. When she saw him, for at first she was intent on the peach, I could see it gave her a fright, and she uttered a cry. Then he fell back, still without saying a word.

'I had to sign the death certificate. I very nearly entered "Temper" as the cause of death: for that is what it was, in my humble opinion. Sheer rage, because she was eating one of his peaches. Real dog-in-the-manger: wouldn't eat it himself, and wouldn't let anyone else eat it. Much rather it went bad. . . . Now can you imagine a man's mind working like that? Extraordinary. Just Temper! . . . But, of course, he'd undermined his constitution, too, by never going out and by working at all sorts of hours.

'And, do you know, that tortoise died at the same time? A new garden lad mistook the creature's mound for a rubbish-heap, and had set a light to it. And that's what the glow came from, in the room. . . . Of course, Dubosque didn't know that, or he'd have died twice over from rage. . . . Funny thing,' he added, rising unexpectedly to a point of imagination, 'the way those two died together, like a witch and what they used to call . . . what was it? . . . a familiar spirit.

'Then, after he was dead, the dealers and critics set to at their games and, between them, rushed the prices up. . . . And Deborah, I must say, got out while the going was good, though — the most odd thing of all — the prices, I'm told, are higher than ever. . . . But I always say, it can't last. After all, it's people like you and me who are the final judges. . . . And I wouldn't pay a penny, not for one of them. . . . Any-how, she's made good; she's a rich woman. *And* charitable! Always doing her bit at those balls and supper parties and things you read about in the papers. . . . Sometimes I wish I'd had more time for painting, myself.'

TRIPLE FUGUE

FOREWORD

UNFORTUNATELY a story so far removed from the usual human experience demands some preliminary explanation of the scientific, political and social facts with which it is connected.

During the course of the last twenty years much has been written, in police-court news as well as in fiction, of the occurrence of triple or quadruple personality. Instances have emerged of an individual possessing three or four distinct egos, souls, personalities or whichever of the three terms is at the moment most in favour. Each of these entities, while unconscious of the proximity, the existence even, of the others, is yet liable, through we know not what operating cause, at any instant and without warning, to yield place to one of them. It is possible, therefore, that this rarer, more unusual narrative of three separate bodies with but one animating force between them, and each normally ignorant of the intimate tie which binds him to the other two, may be found to possess a certain psychological interest.

A theory has long been formulated as to the 'group-soul' belonging to various of the lower forms of life. Several eminent scientists and philosophers have suggested that, for example, blackbeetles — though each is physically an entity, a smaller or larger insect of dark colouring — exist spiritually (if the use of this adverb in such a connection is pardonable) solely as a group, or, perhaps, as a small number of groups. Each individual beetle forms a single link in the spiritual chain that binds them and is called the group-soul; each is a component part in a composite personality. And this supposition, too, may explain the phenomenon of enchantment. For these repulsive little insects can, like rats or snakes, be charmed, enticed, by one who has the gift or secret, out of the house. The professional usually claims to have inherited this faculty; it is difficult to get from him any explanation of it. But probably his secret is that he can practise a form of mass-hypnotism — he can hypnotise the group-soul of these creatures and lead them out into the wilderness. Thus is revealed to us the secret of the Pied Piper.

Similarly it should not surprise us to learn that one individuality is shared by several human beings; we have only to look round for it to be suggested to us that this form of economy is one that commended itself to the Creator. Indeed the possession by one person of more than one ego is increasingly, enviably rare. In genuine instances of this sort some method, surely, should be discovered of isolating the surplus ones; they should be treated as unearned increment, distributed among the many thousands in need of them — even if this filling of empty places should entail for their owners a fate like that which overwhelmed the Gadarene herd. Each individual, or perhaps one should say each unit or numeral, should possess under a democracy,* as adjunct to three acres and a cow, one personality — neither more nor less. But, alas, the influence of democracy, as we know it, appears to have been not so much to give each man a soul as to make the absence of one not so unusual as to be noticeable. Its trend has been, increasingly, to banish eccentricity and encourage its reverse; to make man alike in the possession of useless but pretentious knowledge, ill taught and ill digested, alike in their lack of simplicity, intelligence and personality. All that is now needed to make the tyrannical triumph of this system complete, is some form of eugenic control, which will finally banish both genius and imbecility, ill-health and unbounded vitality. And the reverse of eccentricity is, undoubtedly, that simian quality of mimicry which, inherent in man, now makes all men alike. Mimicry, indeed, is man's original sin, for when the first individualist monkey had decided to stand up for his rights and be a man (an eccentric monkey that, if ever there was one!) his fellows proceeded to mimic — or some say 'ape' — him, thus building on an insecure foundation, since, in the very act of declaring themselves to be men, they were in reality making a proclamation of essentially monkey characteristics.

The old dynastic and aristocratic systems of government encouraged, subsidised almost, eccentricity worthy and unworthy alike; and no eccentric, not even the least estimable,

* *N.B.*—When we refer in these pages to 'democracy' we are not considering it as an idea, but *practically*, as it has been known for the last fifty years in Europe and America.

would deign, except in the spirit of satire, to mimic his fellows. But with the coming of industrialised, commercialised and capitalised democracy, every man and woman too had, under pain of ostracism, to dress, talk and behave alike — or rather as they imagined their 'betters' would dress, talk and behave. Previously there had been no 'betters' — only richer or poorer, stupider or cleverer, only those better or less good-looking, less or more powerful; facts were acknowledged without envy; but now, with envy, came the assumption of 'betters'. A vicious circle was established. Everyone pretended feverishly to be something or someone he was not. The workman pretended to be a small shopkeeper, the small shopkeeper to be a large one, the large shopkeeper to be that mysterious thing a 'professional man', the professional man to be a country squire, the rich manufacturer to be a nobleman of long pedigree, dukes to be workmen, kings to be democrats and hereditary presidents. Each, by his own act, laid claim to some distinction which could never be his, and by this very claim admitted an inferiority. For if I shout in your face that I am as good as you are, at once I prove myself inferior in manners. Except for those whose struggle for life was so hard as to leave them no time or desire for self-deception, the world became a matter of acting and make-believe, giving such falsity to every value, such crooked perspective to every event, that when the greatest tragedy in human history came, every nation was equally surprised and unprepared, though each had, in reality, done nothing else except prepare for it, consciously or unconsciously, during the previous half-century. The war, certainly, was the final triumph of the system. Every man, the world over, was forced to fight to make the world Safe for Democracy, whether he believed in it or not — though the war itself was undoubtedly due to the very form of government for which he was now urged to fight, and one, in any case, peculiarly unsuited for the prosecution of a successful war. Emperors and kings, manufacturers of armaments, wealthy noblemen, humble profiteers, none of whom had previously shown much affection for his darling ideal, now advanced into the market-place to demand, to insist, that the world be made Safe for Democracy. And the Democrats of a lifetime were taken in once more. The people of every country allowed only the most brutalised or hypocritical of their countrymen to come to the top and rule them, thereby proving how much they had gained by education and the other blessings which they owed to the system they were now called upon to defend. The few democrats who really believed in the people, and saw how disastrous a war would be for them, were either hounded out of public life or thrown into jail.

Just as one man had for a century past been taught to regard himself as the equal of another, so had each nation been taught to consider itself the equal of its neighbour. Each country must have a bigger navy, bigger army, be a greater power, than those that bordered it. The result of this healthy competitive and democratic spirit was a war disastrous for all who entered it: and once the war started, since each man must be as his fellow, each country had to join in. It became 'the thing to do' — 'good form'. Every nation — except Spain, which had never been democratic, and the Scandinavian countries which were genuinely so — had to enter the arena on one side or the other. Even Oriental, lazy countries like Turkey lost their heads, or were driven into it. Each land must show that it was as great a power, that it could spend as many million pounds a day, as many million lives a year, as its neighbour. The general attitude towards a non-belligerent country was 'Yah-boo! You're not a great power. You can't afford a great war. Yah!'

The ultimate consequence for democracy of this orgy of killing and spending, was the utter revolt against it of Russia and Italy, two of the more intelligent European peoples, who seem to prefer, in the rage of the moment, any tyranny however awful as long as it is not the peculiarly smug one from which others are suffering. For years democracy had been talked of as if it were the ultimate aim of humanity, an end in itself; instead of being merely one more experiment in government, at the best one of many other methods of governing, and one obviously unsuited to certain races. But the war has broken down the tyranny of this idea in several lands.

In the meantime the same old system continues in most of Europe; for how long, no one can tell. Every man and every woman still insists on the acquisition of new rights and the abnegation of old ones. And in the middle of this whirlpool of aggressive action and abject renunciation, is still stranded, on a level surface of peaceful but quite pointless life, a society which insists on no rights and admits no duties except that of self-enjoyment — a worthy though humble aim, which it nevertheless seldom has the intelligence to maintain.

Even thirty years ago this world must have displayed character, a stupid, horsey, sporting character. But the bankruptcy of the aristocratic principle, the advent of industrialism and, above all, the arrival of rich Jews and Jewesses, entirely altered the scene. Mimicry became more general, for of all races the Semitic is most imitative, original as are many descendants of this remarkable stock. In order to mingle with the people among whom they must live, it has been necessary for them greatly to increase their natural gift for protective colouring. Even physically they alter their characteristics, becoming paler and fairer as they move north, darker as they move south, darker yet towards Africa, yellower and more almond-eyed as they move eastward once more. Theirs is essentially a cuckoo-civilisation. As artists they prove themselves executants more than originators. They excel in dramatic art, they play the tunes that others have written better than the composers themselves. They it is who have, perhaps, infused into the world of pleasure a new love of millionaire-art and respect for it, a love of the theatre, of dressing-up, and creature comforts. But there is a bad side to these activities; for the Jew who cannot pass as one of a crowd has to design a rôle for himself, and many of these are engaged in a febrile but fruitless attempt to be something other than they are — Irish patriots or Spanish gipsies, French barons and Austrian noblemen, viceroys or Pre-Raphaelite painters, Celtic mythologists and American citizens, Armenian poets and Persian princes. At the same time, without being eccentric, they are apt to run to extremes — to be poorer or richer than all others, greater capitalists or greater Bolsheviks, more 'modern' or more conventional in their taste for art.

The world they have influenced for the last quarter of a century is, then, perhaps a little more intelligent, but one with far less character, than before the corruption began; more cosmopolitan, more like the world of pleasure in every other capital — in New York and Paris, Berlin and Rome. But it has become the 'right thing' again to manifest a faint interest in music, poetry, portrait-painting, above all in house-decoration; and books, even if their pages are still uncut, lie about once more on the drawing-room tables.

In this world the prevailing and unexciting vice is that of mimicry. Each man has become the shadow of his neighbour, each woman the reflection of another. A few people, a very few who have personality, who are prominent for beauty, wit, impertinence or even for that attractive capacity for enjoyment which among these attenuated phantoms has become uncommon, are reflected a million times in their friends. A woman will see reflections of herself as many and varied as those contrived in the mirrors at a dressmaker's. Gesture, smile, colouring, clothing, even the tone of the voice, are aped by hundreds and passed on, like the sacred lamp, from one to another. In someone met casually a whole portrait gallery of friends can be discovered; while these, in their turn, will dissolve, to reveal the further, paler spectres of their ancestors. Depth after depth they stretch; a continual deepening of dimensions that becomes like the discovery and exploration of secret caverns, an exploration attended always by a quality of horror, for you may find the gigantic skeleton of an extinct animal, the remains of a dead friend; and places unlived in are apt to be haunted. To meet one of these shadows is not unlike pulling out section after section of a telescope — only, at each prolongation of it, to be greeted by a familiar yet unexpected and indistinct feature — which had previously escaped you — of the landscape. Another section is extended and focused, in order that you may concentrate on this new landmark and see it more clearly, but in the very act a further familiar object is disclosed to the eye, always slightly distorted by the lens, until the whole process becomes a nightmare.

For at each handing on of it, the imitation, though very recognisable, becomes a little different, as if the colourless soul of the person through whom it has passed had yet contrived to alter the image ever so minutely. One line is slightly firmer, coarser, in its drawing; another more blurred. Each image has behind it other ones, the family features, its portion of the group-soul. Each image is like one of those old-fashioned Christmas cards with a view on it, which, when a tag of paper is pulled, dissolves slowly into other landscapes; and at times the two melt into a muddled whole.

Apart, then, from the few genuine persons who move

among the shadows, each new arrival at party, theatre or restaurant exhibits a soul that is like one of those rooms of distorting mirrors that were to be met with formerly at Earl's Court, the White City, and Luna Park. Someone is reflected, reflected for ever in a thousand distorted variations, while the number of the reflections helps to disguise the emptiness and small dimensions of the place itself. In the relation of one mirroring to another, fresh designs are formed constantly, other shadows suggested, as in a kaleidoscope the same small pieces of coloured glass move ever towards fresh arrangements. Pondering every movement of these exquisitely lacquered but composite figures, new distant views are conjured up. At the end of one gesture you will see, as in a garden, a perspective of gracious but silent deities; and these again are reflected in the water that hurls them downward, head first, into the blue void of the sky. Each distant-sounding voice has an echo of other utterances; some even are echoes of voices, genuine voices, now for ever silent. The dead speak for a time as clearly as the living in these empty houses; yet are as bare and desolate, a vacuum into which no great wind will ever sweep.

It is, in fact, possible to unpack many people as if they were so many portmanteaux of stolen personal belongings; to take out of them a gesture, an expression, a tone, the palpable and familiar property of another. Let us illustrate this. Once we sat in a restaurant, at the next table to a polished and elegant lady, unknown to us, but whose every movement was recognisable; in whom, as she talked, a whole ancestry of shadows could be unravelled. That lifting of one finger like a shepherd's crook declared itself as a reflection of an early copy of Mme de Blank's rendering of a mannerism in her friend, Lady Carabas. To watch the wistful smile unfolding on those lips was equivalent to peeping through the keyhole of the garden of the Knights of Malta at Rome, where far away can be distinguished the solid, very personal dome of St. Peter's; for far away, behind this delicate echo, lies the caressing but bulky smile of Lady de Bludyer. The little dry laugh, too, lacquered as the west wind on a Chinese screen, is but a transposition in key of Mrs. Kinfoot's serving-up of Ethel Misborough's laughter; while that innocent, round-eyed sucking-of-the-thumb is merely an unauthorised version of

Lady Ethel Cressey's almost unconscious imitation of her cousin, Lady Septuagesima Goodley, a woman of genuine, if difficult, character, who, now in late middle age, employs this trick as proof of her lamb-like and misunderstood disposition — a proof which has finally convinced her easily gullible friends.

Thus in these varnished hollows could we isolate for the moment a hundred reflections of a few genuine personalities. Nor, altogether, do these mirrorings make the world unpleasant. The student of social life can play a detective game for his own amusement; while to the mirrors and mirrored, the constant vibration and echo, the innumerable variations on the same key, give a certain brilliancy and cold sparkle to gatherings, filling empty rooms with a scintillation of light thrown back as through crystal and deep waters. One or two colours are vibrated in every tone and shade; a note is struck out that is responded to by every shallow object, every translucent substance, in the room. Who knows but that if every shade became a person, every echo a genuine voice, there would be a riot of colour, a storm of sound too strong for us? . . .

. . . . .

In order to write it, the story that follows compelled us to advance along various tracks, already noticeable, until these converged, and we found ourselves in the year 1948. This future already looming over us is more difficult to grasp than any other, just as the equidistant past is the hardest to recall. Both are so little divided from the present, so fantastically alike, so grotesquely different.

If we take a compass and, fixing the leg that is to remain steady in the present year, begin to circumscribe, as it were, a circle, the diameter of which is twenty-five years, we shall notice that the people and background of the year 1898 through which it passes seem slightly contorted, are invested with a certain air of improbability which is termed 'quaintness' — rather ugly quaintness still, for it is too near to have become focused and 'picturesque'. Similarly, if we continue the circle into the future, the people and background near that circumference have the same quality — one which would be lacking in a more remote age, so strange would it seem.

Among a myriad possibilities the immediate future holds always two highly probable alternatives. One, ever the most likely and at this moment seeming almost a certainty, is of a complete break, a tremendous reaction against the immediate past and all that it represented; the other, an exaggeration of present tendencies. From these two it has been necessary to choose the latter, to make the future age like our own, so that as if comparing two similar profiles, we notice the likeness by the slight differences, and gain a more complete knowledge of one by gazing on the other.

We move, then, in the same world of rather hysterical shadows, the same state that somehow moves on by its own impetus. We are greeted with the familiar echoes and reflections that we have been discussing. Many of those prominent in the arts, in literature, in the State, are the same persons we know, only older and no wiser, while all are seen through the glass of time as men are seen through the medium of water. The water is unruffled and deep, so deep; and the bodies of the swimmers are near the surface; yet all are elongated and drawn out, or broadened and foreshortened, their colour subdued or accentuated by this seemingly transparent element.

PART I

The first scene of our strange drama unfolds itself in the respective bedrooms of Mr. Valentine Leviathan, Lord Richard Cressey, and Mr. Freddie Parkinson at the hour of 7.55 one Friday evening in the early May of 1948. In this way we are enabled to make the acquaintance of our three protagonists while they are still dressing for their parts.

Mr. Valentine Leviathan, impoverished but hopeful — from his own point of view — member of the great Anglo-American mercantile house of Leviathan, is discovered, hurried, harried and out of humour in front of a diminutive looking-glass in a hired flat off Belgrave Square. The apartment is fussily decorated, over-upholstered, yet uncomfortable in a hotel fashion. The softness and depth of the armchairs, the thick carpet and other properties would produce in one unused to them a feeling of asthma, hay-fever and croup. Too proud to work much, too poor to be idle, Valentine writes articles on French politics for *The Morning Star* — a newspaper, the venerable owner of which is a friend of the family. He knows no French and little politics, but by dint of a certain facility for skating over ice that no longer exists — which he was forced to acquire during several years at a large public school, where it was understood that though you need not learn anything you ought to pass the examinations — just manages to impress his readers with what he leaves unsaid.

'Clever chap, that! You can read a lot between the lines', the old gentlemen used to say, puffing whale-like in their club windows, which seem the glass walls of some gigantic aquarium. And, indeed, reading between the lines you could distinguish almost anything which suited your mood. Regarded strictly, however, as to what they said and how they said it, Valentine's articles were sympathetic yet impressive, having the character of essays written by a sick schoolgirl and subsequently corrected by a prim but kindly nursery-governess. They were full of suggestions, suppressed enough to be convincing, of being-very-much-in-the-know, and of what-fun-we-are-all-having. Occasionally these would be varied with distinguished compliments and authoritative warnings to our Allies. At other times this one of our three heroes turns a more honest, congenial, but secret penny by revealing the movements of friends, and interesting facts about them, to the readers of the illustrated daily papers.

While, with little corners of white lather still on his face from shaving, he hurries from one room to another looking for a towel, we are privileged to read the latest of these ramblings. 'Hats off to President Trotsky' we shall read tomorrow glancing through the pages, 'Salute Denmark', and then, sandwiched between these commands, come to Valentine's gossipy page, typical development of his time. At present these social jottings are lying in a scrawling handwriting on an untidy desk, while near to them is their envelope, ready, and addressed to the editor.

'A friend tells me', they run:

The Pecksniff Prize

'Pamela tells me that Lord Richard Cressey has been asked to present this year's Pecksniff Prize for English Literature; an event which will take place in late July at the Skimpole Hall. Lord Richard is, of course, the third son of the fourth Duke of Kirkcudbright and brother of the present Duke. He is also known as a promising diplomat (he is said to have been responsible for that *thrilling* Yugo-Slovak Jingo-Slav crisis last year) and is already quite a figure in literary and artistic circles. His novel of Balkan life, *In a Yashmak Garden*, created quite a stir, and, it is rumoured, was mentioned in private conversation by Professor Criscross to the venerable Earl of Chiswick, that last of the Great Victorians. He has also published latterly a slim volume of powerful nature-poems, under the title of *The Buzzard's Bastard*, in which he makes a strong plea for the feeding of young cuckoos. This, too, has been very favourably received by the critics, and has already gone into a fifth edition. Lord Richard's many friends hope that as well as being asked to present the prize, he will also be allowed to receive it.' . . .

A Notable Wedding

'Dearest, the Cressey wedding was quite the event of the 1946 season, wasn't it? How strange it seems that it is already two years ago! Both the bride and bridegroom, who are very artistic, were related to numerous important families, and such lovely clothes! The six bridesmaids were all dressed in sheath-gowns of ruby tinsel, and a note of originality was struck by the bride's wreath, which was made of silver paper and worn upside down. The orange flowers were made of mother-of-pearl, with gilded-tin stalks, and sewn on to the bandeau. So chic! Lady Richard — or Goo-Goo as she is known to her friends — is petite, piquante, and pimpante, and was, of course, niece to Baroness d'Arenheimer, the well-known French philanthropist, and daughter of Mrs. Silas B. Guggerty, a popular and charming transatlantic visitor who often has the honour of entertaining both Princess Marie-Antoinette of Metro-Schinkenberg and Princess Antoinette-Marie of Metroberg-Schinken in her fascinating London home. All six of them, Lord Richard, Lady Richard (Goo-Goo), Mrs. Guggerty, Baroness d'Arenheimer, Princess Marie-Antoinette and Princess Antoinette-Marie, are, of course, exceptionally artistic. I met Mrs. Guggerty in Bond Street yesterday and thought her looking quite a picture, with her mass of snow-white hair, in a short bolero of blue coney-skin, with a hussar-collar of Trotsky-lapin. Such a becoming toque, too, dark blue, trimmed at one side with little bunches of coque's feathers.'

An Original Hostess

'Dinky writes to me today that she immensely enjoyed the interesting party of artistic people that Lady Richard entertained last week at her country home, Little Titterham, Old Twits, near Cinderbury. Situated on the barest parts of the Sussex Downs, Little Titterham was just a small two-roomed cottage, with the dearest old barn, till Lady Richard — who, like her husband, is, of course, immensely artistic — turned out the family who lived there and converted it into an ideal country residence. It is unnecessary to say that she is extremely popular in the neighbourhood. Each guest is given a bathroom, swimming bath, tennis court and croquet lawn of his own, and a delightful note of simplicity is struck throughout. One of a number of charmingly modern touches that mark this unique home is the placing in each bedroom of a little homespun sack full of lavender, on which are depicted scenes from the Soviet-Art Cabaret; these are executed by Lady Richard herself, and are signed "Goo-Goo" in diminutive letters. These little touches, needless to say, are immensely appreciated by Lady Richard's friends.'

An Interesting House-Party

'The artistic party of interesting people at Little Titterham last week included Baroness d'Arenheimer and her two pretty debutante daughters, Angel and Desirée (doesn't she seem young, darling? to have grown-up daughters!); Sir Booster Babboon, the Picturesque Persian Philanthropist (who is taking such an *interest* in the bazaar that the Baroness is getting up in aid of the "Superannuated-Moneylenders'-Children-Benefit-Fund". He can always be depended on to help forward any worthy charity); Mrs. Guggerty; Mr. Matthew Dean; Mr. Valentine Leviathan, the clever and popular young writer on international topics; Mrs. Kinfoot, the well-known hostess, who has just returned from her first lion-hunt in Africa; Lady Selina Moonbury; Adèle Lady Fortcarrick (who is supposed to have gone round in four); Mr. Edward Tush; Mr. Charles Rotumjhy, the famous Hungarian portrait-painter; Mr. Freddie Parkinson, and others equally well known. Lady Richard, who, besides being *exceptionally* artistic, *adores* music, delighted her friends by a rendering of the "Jewel Song" from

Faust on the water-whistle and has now left for Aix-les-Bains. It is hoped that she will be back in Little Titterham, where she will be much missed, by the middle of next month.'

Valentine has re-entered the room, and is wildly opening and shutting various drawers, and ringing wireless-electric bells, which he knows quite well will not be answered : a form of neurasthenia resulting from a long period of underwork, for he does not really in the least mind how late he is for an engagement. As he moves about, very swiftly, half-dressed, it is difficult to grasp the salient features of his appearance. He is youngish, perhaps about twenty-seven, and taller than the average. Though still somewhat flushed from the bath, his skin is yet rather yellow and very smooth, his eye of that vacant blue which clearly demands a monocle ; but in this case the demand is unsatisfied. His toneless fair hair is brushed back, sleek and shining, and he boasts a moustache, short, fair, rather more bristling, drooping, and untidy than one would expect from the rest of his aspect ; for, as his dress grows more complete, a certain rather insect-like elegance evolves round him. Clothed, brushed, polished, he has a suave yet overblown quality, like the scent of syringa or the glossy, rounded and enamelled form of certain beetles. The rather shabby moustache, therefore, detracts from this, making it more bearable, like a flaw in a precious stone, though, at the same time, it imparts an air of premature age.

The rooms, usually noisy, are very quiet at this instant. Obviously, then as now, the taxicabs are in hiding, the drivers playing piquet in a thousand obscure shelters, happy in the knowledge that this should be their busiest hour. Hastily snatching coat, top-hat and cane, Valentine dashes out to retrieve one.

. . . . .

Half a mile away Lord Richard Cressey is presented to us in an upper bedroom of Kirkcudbright House, the family mansion in London. He has arrived back, rather late, from the Foreign Office, and is tired. The swelling waves of the treetops, now in their full green spray, stand frozen below, as if some wizard had thrown a spell over them just as they were about to flood the wide-open windows of this gaunt, severe mansion. Led by one of those small grey puffs of wind that are a feature of the London parks in summer, they advance once more ; this time, surely, they will invade the house, for the leaves are tilted up by the breeze, overturned for a moment with a flash of silver till they become the white-horses of this green sea, or the outriders of such an army as marched against Macbeth. Beyond the Park, above the droning, groaning clamour, broken by shuddering hoots, of the distant traffic, beneath the softer dragon-fly note of the hovering aeroplanes that pass every second, Lord Richard's wandering blue eye is rested by the stiff cubist arrangement of slate roofs, gables, spires, huge flat square warehouses, looking like magnified Roman tombs, and angular towers, that constitutes the London horizon. In among these, contrasting with the great width, heaviness and solidity of these buildings, rise the giant but slender wireless-masts, which, growing thus in clumps, look like cuttings of bamboo waiting for the spring to touch them into leaf. The prevailing colour of the outlook at this hour is soft grey, softer blue and a little gold, while over these pastel tones is superimposed the patine of light and shade that London has breathed on them, blurring and silvering them gently, as the breath of man lingers for a moment on a mirror or pane of glass. The three square windows that allow these tall buildings to lift their heads above the trees into the room are set in a large square chamber that has a steady air, like that of an old-fashioned butler. There is much solid mahogany furniture and a singularly respectable wallpaper. The air is pervaded with the familiar smell of ancient polished wood, and in this evening light the walls are enveloped in a rather thick golden glow, like the varnish on one of those screens composed of scraps, prints and Christmas cards, which, made in the early decades of the nineteenth century, still show boldly in the mess-rooms of old regiments, or lurk abashed in the lumber-rooms of decaying country-houses. No sign is here of Lord Richard's modern taste in decoration ; but then this is not his house, for Lady Richard is away at Aix : his house is shut up, and he is staying here for a few weeks with his brother.

Under the shadow of a large mahogany four-poster, placed on a thick white counterpane, white as a winding-sheet, lie the folded corpses that will soon be quickened ; black clothes that, as they lie there in the strong light, seem green, rather mouldy with age, but, when once more in contact with human vitality, will become fresh again, almost smart; for clothes are essentially vampiric, taking part of our life, though in return they give us something back. There lie, too, a white shirt, rigid and shiny, and a white collar like the section of a drain-pipe, stiff with death. On the dressing-table are a black tie, folded and looking like a large frayed moth, a square folded white handkerchief and a little mound of copper coins. These latter suggest, by their presence, that in due course a professional is coming in to lay out all these corpses in the proper manner, weighting down their empty eyes with these coins. And, indeed, the professional (Barnacle, Lord Richard's valet) is waiting outside even now for a summons.

Above the dressing-table, supported by two pillars, is balanced at an angle the reflection of what is apparently some sea-creature, some light-blue and deep-pink sea-monster, but is in reality merely a rare edition of Lord Richard — Lord Richard as he appears each day to his valet but not to the world, blue as to underclothes, coral-pink from his bath, while little sequins of steam glitter like sea-water on pink face, feet, arms and calves. This deepening of colour, accentuation of light and shadow, rather obscures the face, so that at one moment he looks in the later twenties, at another in the late forties, and is probably somewhere between the two. We notice a rather bristly downward moustache, fairish, rumpled hair and blue, blue eyes. The mirror reflects hurried movements: in it we see Lord Richard plunging head foremost into his white shirt. There is a rattle of white spray, and he comes up to the surface, his head showing again at the crest of this foaming, flashing wave, like the moustached countenance of a seal revealed from some breaker. As if he had really just returned from the salty depths rewarded with precious trophies of his skill in that other element, the reflection presents to us a pearl, round, fair and velvet-soft, being secured by red fingers, like crustacean pincers, in the centre of a flat surface of white foam.

Piece by piece the corpses assume vitality: the warm, magnetic flow of life courses through the fibre of shirt, collar, socks, trousers, waistcoat; and even the frayed moth takes the air again with a certain jauntiness. Lord Richard looks, on the whole, rather well dressed, but in contrast to our first hero, as if he did not care very much about such things. He glances anxiously at his watch, dashes with short, very quick steps downstairs, where he is helped into a large overcoat, his own quickness of movement being in such contrast to the leisurely actions of his valet that he is nearly strangled in the process. He runs into the waiting taxicab, shouting to the valet: 'Don't wait up for me, Barnacle. If anyone radios me, tell them to ring up 9234 Holborn, Mr. Dean's. And you might let them know at Mecklenburg Square that Her Ladyship won't be back until the middle of next month. Good night!' And, heralded by a startling series of rattling alarms, is borne out of the large sombre backwater into the choked streams of traffic beyond.

. . . . .

Westwards, Freddie Parkinson is nearly dressed, but in no great hurry. Valentine is sure to be late. The small, demure house always smells as if it had just been painted. The walls are nearly always grey, the carpets invariably green and self-coloured. There are, placed about in the rooms downstairs, several subtly ugly and completely undecorative little pieces of early Chinese pottery, which have either been snatched out of the sacred earth by tomb-plunderers and handed on through dealers at a price completely out of proportion to their value, or have, perhaps, just been made at that new factory outside Peking, where they will busy themselves with such things. Freddie is devoted to these 'pots'—pronounced 'pahts'—and is constantly caressing them with rather insensitive, blunt finger-tips, imagining that he can determine their age by the feel of their glaze, or get some esthetic pleasure out of the handling of them. These things are now everywhere inheriting the place of willow-pattern plates and long-ladies. Very few pictures hang on the walls, but there are a few etchings and woodcuts, simple and at the same time very fussy. It is curious that Freddie should collect both these 'pahts' and these etchings; it is a curious combination, for though he takes both seriously, one completely denies and cancels-out the artistic principles of the other. But above all Freddie collects the scandals of the day; on these he is a recognised authority, a connoisseur who is consulted upon scabrous discoveries, just as a great authority on early Italian pictures would be asked to pronounce his opinion upon some new and precious find.

Upstairs, on the second landing, the door is open, and

Freddie is fastening his collar. In appearance he is taller than either Lord Richard or Mr. Leviathan, and older, about ten years older. His face is more furrowed, and is becoming somewhat leathery. His hair — for he shows no trace of baldness — is more stubborn, his eye of a more faded, and therefore a more piercing, blue. Eyebrows and moustache are very definite and stubborn. He carries his head rather forward, peering a little, as if scenting some new scandal, and already well on its track. He comes out of his room to shout to the maidservant that he wants a taxicab; and it is noticeable that as she comes nearer, he shouts louder. Freddie looks rather tired; for, in this respect totally unlike Valentine, he works hard in an office all day for money that he does not need. He is well known in the social world — in fact everybody knows him because he knows someone else. Two gaunt sisters, tall as grenadiers, are his companions in the house, sisters who adore yet despise him. He is very fond of them, but is not attached to his numerous other relatives, of whom he is really rather ashamed, apt to avoid, however willing are they to see more of him. His voice getting ever louder as he goes downstairs, he bears off an old opera hat, which he opens with a snap, until, like himself, it is tubular in form. It elongates him, as if a snake had added to its stature — completes his appearance. He is seen sitting in an open taxicab, its wheels grinding slow, like the mills of God, until it has disappeared round the corner.

. . . .

At this moment Mr. Matthew Dean, R.D.O. (Royal Dodonian Order, 2nd Class, Grand Cross), is waiting rather agitatedly in his house near Queen Anne's Gate. There is little reason for agitation, but Mattie cannot bear being kept waiting; it is bad for his nerves. He walks from room to room, gazing vaguely, without seeing anything, at the pictures old and modern which are so numerous as almost to blot out the gaily painted panelling. The blinds are drawn, though a faint, cold light still penetrates them, and the rooms are lit by old-fashioned electric lamps, well shaded, that throw down rather ruddy circles of light (so much softer and prettier, his guests invariably say, than the hard false daylight of wireless lighting) on the tables where they stand. There are several of these tables in each room: on them, framed in tortoise-shell, stand signed photographs of many social and stage celebrities, reputed beauties, and a few popular, but not *too* popular, poets and writers. Lying about carefully arranged, but with an appearance of freedom, as if they had just been put down for a moment, are various books, political or literary, collections of rather rare modern first editions, novels or the last word in poetry or the drama. Among these, taken at random, we read such titles as *Down Sussex Way*, by Jacques Rosenheimer; *My Part in the Third Great War*, by the Rt. Hon. Winston Churchill; *Limpet, and Other Poems*, by Ego Aneurism Jones; *Scribblings*: a book of Literary Criticism, by H. Mollycod Moiré; Vol. II of the 'Bloomsbury Painters Series', *From Giotto to Gertler*; and several rare Squireana, consisting of *Baudelaire Flowers*, by Jack Collings Squire — suppressed by the author; a book of Early Essays by 'Solomon Eagle'; *Collected Parodies* (very rare), by Jack Squire; *Songs of the Slaughterhouse* (early and rare), by Jack C. Squire; *The Lily of Malud* (rare and curious), by J. C. Squire; *Australian Poems*, by J. Collings Squire; *The Soccer Match, and Other Poems*, by Sir Collings Squire; *Lesser Lyrics of the First Half of the Last Decade but One of the Seventeenth Century*, compiled by Ego Aneurism Jones, with a prefatory note by Lord Squire of Chiswick; *Simple Lyrics of the Countryside, with Glossary*, by Raoul Gelding, prefaced by a brief explanatory note by Lord Squire of Chiswick, O.M., and 'A Catalogue of a Portion of the Library of Viscount Squire of Chiswick, O.M., compiled by Professor James Criscross and Ernest Lympe, with a new portrait of His Lordship by Solomon Gluckstein, and an original poem by Mr. Edward Shanks'. On another table we see piled up, *From a Library Stool*, by James Criscross; *Drivellings*, by K. Mimicky Murrain; *Heather o' Moors*, a volume of Verse by Vincent O'Coddell; *How I won the Third World War*, by the Rt. Hon. David Lloyd George; *Myself and Trotsky*, uniform with *A History of my Fourth Campaign in the Dardanelles*, by the Rt. Hon. Winston Churchill; the last six volumes of Verse by Mr. Edward Shanks; the last dozen by Mr. W. J. Turner, and the last dozen and a half volumes of Collected Essays by Sir Robert Lynd. On a larger table are several bulky and fantastically bound scrap-books, in which during his leisure moments Mr. Dean, with one or two chosen allies, pastes photographs, and newspaper cuttings, or induces his numerous friends among present-day poets to write a favourite set of verses. There are also several vases of flowers.

It must be admitted from the first that Mr. Matthew Dean — or poor Mattie as he is to his friends — is essentially himself and, in spite of a rather feeble character, is reflected by many, while never reproducing the ways or tricks of others. Coming out of a solemn background at once scholarly and ecclesiastic, he has reacted away from it, towards, as he thinks, the worlds of fashion, gaiety and wit. These he has frequented for over thirty years; so, though his appearance does not suggest it, he must be between fifty and sixty years of age. But, since a man is judged by his friends, he must be counted as an honorary young man — young enough, in fact, to know better. His body, though not stunted, is punily, uneasily built; the shoulders are too broad, both for the head and body, more especially for the neck, giving from a distance an impression of strength that is immediately contradicted by the rest of his physique, and by the face. This latter is sallow in colour, nearly circular in shape except for a slight squaring of the forehead, and a dent, like a nick clipped out of a coin, that marks the chin. The black eyes are alive and kindly; the eyebrows, thick and dark, grow up at an angle, ending in a Mandarin-like tuft. These eyebrows, tilted up like the eaves of a Japanese temple, are really the natural feature of the face: but art has helped Nature, for beneath one of them is a round monocle that echoes in miniature the larger circle of the face, seeming to be a young one budding out of it. The hair follows the line of the eyebrow, turning up slightly at the temple, and is brownish-grey. The neck, as we noted, is peculiarly long, thin and out of proportion to the shoulders, so that when Mattie lifts up his head, with the nervous wriggling waggle that is his way, to talk, it is as if a ventriloquist's dummy is speaking — so thin is the wooden stalk of the neck moving in the too-wide socket of the collar-bone. The voice itself, when with great effort it sounds out, is extraordinarily high, lisping, innocent and irritating as the twittering of a fluffy young bird that lifts up head and gaping mouth from its nest, expecting to be fed. Like such a fledgeling, too, is the manner in which he raises his head, and moves his neck — or perhaps like a newly hatched chicken looking up out of its broken shell! — while the bright nervous eye, which seems to twitter also behind its glass section, has something of the bird-effect as well. On the other hand, when in a very good mood, his face and shoulders remind one a little of a smiling, purring cat. At this moment, however, he is more bird-like than cat-like; he is obviously waiting for someone, and as obviously dislikes the process. He is now dressed in a black dinner-jacket, black tie and white shirt: his clothes are always well made, almost too appropriate for the occasion, and must require an amount of attention.

Mattie, as we have noticed from the furnishing of his house, is a great patron of the arts, ancient and modern; a patron of advanced art even — as long as it has not advanced too far to make safe its retreat. In the social world he is one of the acknowledged arbiters of taste, especially of things new, and is being constantly implored in the drawing-rooms for help and advice on matters concerning art and literature, what pictures to invest in, what books to borrow. 'I'll ask Mattie; he'll tell me what to get', is to be heard on all sides. He is on every board and committee that exists for the acquisition of modern works-of-art, or for the reward of virtue in literature, and is one of the permanent judges who each year assign to some suitable neophyte the Pecksniff Prize. This consists of a cheque for £200, awarded to the writer of what is, in the opinion of the judges, the year's best piece of imaginative writing, whether in poetry or prose. Mattie therefore is essentially for Safety First in literature and the arts, for though he must startle his friends occasionally, and can afford to be a little daring every now and then, he does not want to risk the reputation for sound judgment which he has acquired among those friends who know less about such things than himself. His own personal inclination is toward an affected simplicity in art, just as the dyspeptic finds more enjoyment in plain food than in complicated dishes. But his own natural impulse has somewhat broken down. For, in spite of a genuine instinct and love for art and literature, he was originally a prig; an artistic prig, no doubt of it. But now success has made him a snob instead. He appears terrified that his past will be revealed, that his smart friends will know him for a prig! Thus he is battling always against an unspoken accusation, anxious to prove it false. This process has made his taste muddled and flaccid, for he has been forced to talk of musical comedies as if they were as important as the greatest operas, of music-hall comedians as if they were the greatest executants in the world; and in a voice so high that like a bat's note it is scarcely audible to the human ear, he is for ever singing inane little jigs and jingles to prove how up to date he is, and how much he enjoys these entertainments. And, as a matter of fact, he has really grown to like them. He attends every theatrical first night, of whatever kind, which gives him an opportunity to show his tact, for his clothes must ever be appropriate to the occasion, and yet he must differentiate according to the status of the theatre. A Lyceum melodrama demands from him quite a different turn-out from that which is necessary for a musical comedy, or Covent Garden. But if two first-performances at the theatres occur on the same evening, then his grief and perturbation know no bounds! He becomes a baby claimed by two mothers and awaiting the judgment of a wiser, more merciful, Solomon. Altogether, in order to prove that he is no prig, Mattie has had to cultivate that odious, authority-sapping theory of relativity in the arts that is so much in evidence. The chief symptom of this softening of the mental fibre is the series of tremendous attacks on such men as Dante, Shakespeare, Virgil and Titian, delivered by such 'high-brow' journalists as write every week for 'low-brow' readers. I am as good as you, Tchekhoff as great as Dante, Lord Squire as Shakespeare, McEvoy as Mantegna, Grock as Greco. This trait of Mattie, this equal devotion to God, Demigod and Beast, is the most modern thing about him, since, though he would never admit it, he actually belongs to the period of the first Great War — of Illustrated Society Papers and 'Jazz Bands'.

His position as a man behind the scenes in politics helps his prestige as a connoisseur of art, and is of use to him generally. He is of the type that, like certain Orientals, enjoys obscure power, loves power without the public appearance of it. Not for a moment does he wish for any more prominent position than that which he now occupies. Politically he has had much experience, has acquired much knowledge. His career had begun, as a matter of fact, many years before the violent disruption of the old Party System by the Press Barons, as they are called. Those of my readers who are old enough, remarked for themselves, doubtless, that steady increase of power which accrued to the Newspaper Proprietors over a period of some thirty years — a steady development only set back occasionally, or even tragically, by some such incident as that which befell Bottomley-The-Martyr. The first sure sign of the new power was the substitution of Newspaper, for National, Insurance. It was not until that momentous meeting in the spring of 1934 that the Press Barons openly claimed the right of the Journal with the Largest Daily (Net) Circulation to govern the country. They pointed out that the time had come for a more modern, more democratic, form of government, and that they were the fully developed heirs of the old system. For the old Party System had over a period of a century rightly attached supreme importance to universal education; it had taught every man and every woman to read — and what they read were these journals. Thus the power of the Press was proved to be the offspring of compulsory education.

And the politicians, or Elder Statesmen, as they are now officially designated, welcomed the change; before the *coup d'état* they had been the targets at which had been constantly fired the most poisonous darts of the Press. The latter would insist simultaneously on such things as Retrenchment and the most expensive Social Reforms, a great increase in armaments together with a reduction of 5s. in the £ on the Income Tax, Peace and a policy which would inevitably lead to War, thereby pleasing, by one proposal or another, every possible reader of their papers. As for the politicians, they had neither the strength nor the desire to struggle against these contradictory demands. At the same time, in order to keep up, or to increase, its circulation, the interest of every newspaper was really in the direction of greater excitements — more frequent and more brutal murders, vast explosions, huge conflagrations, gigantic battles on land and sea. Even Nature itself seemed anxious to please the omnipotent Barons, presenting them with tidal waves of unusual size, thrilling earthquakes, devastating eruptions.

Before the new system was declared, each succeeding Government was in turn exposed by the Press: Government succeeded Government with a bewildering rapidity — a rapidity made more bewildering, indeed, by the fact that, though differently labelled, the personnel of each Government was nearly identical with that of the one which it had replaced. The combinations of politician and politician were infinite and kaleidoscopic. At one moment they would be abusing each other like fish-wives in the market, at the next they would

'Achieve Unity' and embrace: within a month they would together form a new Government. This, in its turn, would fall within a few weeks, to be succeeded by a new arrangement of the dear old faces. Elderly ponderous peers would tread weightily from one party to the other and back again; but at each change the country would be put to the expense of a General Election.

Thus, when toward the end of the Third Great War (the Chinese one) the Barons seized the executive and proclaimed themselves the Trustees of the Nation, the politicians welcomed it, actually, as a release, for they were still to carry on the actual work of Government; but now the Press assumed openly the responsibility, and there would be no need for sudden changes of policy and, better still, no possibility of an election. The same old faces, under the Guy Fawkes-like masks of the Press Barons, still make our laws; and owing to the prolongation of human life made possible by the great advance in biological and surgical knowledge, it seems as if we shall be able to benefit indefinitely by the ever-increasing wisdom and experience of these Elder Statesmen.

The latter, it was arranged, were to be paid large salaries by the Press Barons, though liable to instant dismissal if they failed to please their masters; heavy penalties also were incurred by any attempt at insubordination. Till the new system was in proper working order, the two proprietors of the two journals with the Largest Daily (Net) Circulation formed a coalition in order to draw up the New Charter. We owe much to these two patriots, who sank their differences for a common purpose, Lord FitzBison and the old Duke of Badgery St. Lawrence. How typical it is of that admirable British spirit of compromise which has always influenced, for the good, our Rough Island Story, that these two men should have chosen to govern on their behalf those very same politicians for whose impeachment they had been clamouring but the night before!

The New Charter was drawn up with great moderation. No change was made — or even contemplated — in the Constitutional Monarchy, for, apart from any question of the relative merits and demerits of the monarchic and republican systems, the Sovereign grows, if possible, ever more popular as the years pass. Measures enacted have still, before they become the law, to receive the Royal Assent. But the Press Baron of the moment is, like the Sovereign, advised by his ministers, and can now do no wrong. Let it not be supposed for a moment, though, that by this I am suggesting the possibility of a newspaper peer doing wrong before his infallibility was thus legally established.

The old House of Commons was closed and converted into a Museum of Progress — showing the invention of the printing press, and its subsequent developments. The House of Lords, which had, some years before the *coup*, been reformed, was allowed to continue its deliberations and to a degree, to increase its power. Since 'the backwoodsmen', as they used to be termed, had been removed, no rancour was felt in the country at the influence of this august assembly, for the latter had taken care to make it obvious that not one among them could be accused of being a gentleman. It had become, in fact, under the final Labour Governments, a more democratic institution than the House of Commons.

Financially the Charter established important reforms. The National Debt now amounted to £1,000,000,000,000,000, 000,000,000,000,000,000,000,000,000,000,000,000,000, 000,000, 000,000: it was necessary, therefore, to increase the taxation on small incomes. Tax-payers with incomes of £50 per annum had, of course, to pay £25 a year in taxes. Though this at first seemed hard, the Press Barons felt it to be a necessary measure, and were not afraid to govern justly. Alleviations were made in other directions. The tax on incomes of over £100,000 was halved, the Super-Tax abolished, and taxation on incomes of over £200,000 done away with altogether, in order, as the Charter phrased it, 'to encourage thrift by a sane measure of economic democracy'. On the other hand, it was made compulsory for every citizen with an income of under £5000 per annum to buy a newspaper every morning and every evening (after this measure had been passed, it came as a surprise to find how many men there were in the country who admitted to an income of over £5000) and, on leaving his home for the day's work, to stand still in the street, at attention, and doff his hat three times to that foreign power to which, on this particular day, the governing newspaper had decreed the compliment. This — as we are all aware — one ascertains by opening the day's paper, which will have in large letters, at the top of its principal page, such captivating captions as

'Salute Denmark' or 'Hats off to Holland'. The enactment of these daily greetings, too, has done much to improve our relations with the Continent. Sometimes individuals are substituted for countries or the actual compliment is varied. A Two-Minutes' Silence may be proclaimed in honour of some more than usually public-spirited millionaire, Sir Booster Babboon for instance; while a silence of Ten Minutes is imposed each year in memory of Bottomley-The-Martyr. Indeed, one of the decrees to which the Coalition attached the greatest importance was the setting up of a statue of heroic size to Bottomley on Parliament Green. Of gilded bronze and nearly fifty feet in height, it was erected as a tribute to the memory of that pioneer who had first both divined the power of the Press and exploited its financial possibilities. Alas, since public opinion had been in his lifetime so backward and ill educated, Bottomley had suffered for the cause, had paid the price for his initiative, as had many a martyr before him! But there were many glad faces in London when the Bottomley Shrine was publicly unveiled four years ago, by the venerable Duke of Badgery St. Lawrence himself.

The three most important clauses in the new Constitution we have left to the last. Firstly, a ban was placed on the development of loud-speakers for news-giving, since it was thought that these might interfere with the legitimate power of the Press. The use of the radio was thus confined to purposes of business and communication, and was made, for political ends, dumb as the old telegraph wire. Secondly, it was made illegal for any British subject, or any foreigner domiciled in Britain, to start a new journal without the permission, signed and sealed, of the Governing Baron. Any infringement of this law was punishable with imprisonment for life — a more serious sentence now that the length of life has been so much increased. For though, as we shall see, the lengthening process has not been made compulsory outside the prison wall, yet it is felt that to allow a prisoner to die at his natural age would be to defeat the ends of justice — equivalent, indeed, to the encouragement of suicide.

Thirdly, it was decreed that no mention of public affairs was henceforward to be tolerated in the Press: these mentions, it was felt, would only serve to inflame public feeling, to stir up discontent, since, in order to conquer the Largest Circulation, and thereby the Government of Great Britain, the rival newspapers would have to make politics too thrilling to be truthful or healthy. This, the chief rivals agreed, was in the present circumstances undesirable. Royal speeches, accounts of the Royal Tours of the Empire, the epigrams of the various guests at the Mansion House Banquet — these can still be reported in full — will kindle the flame of loyalty, tend to keep public opinion patriotic. But such matters as Social Reform, National Finance, or Armaments, were, it was decreed, never again to be mentioned in the Public Press. This wise law has been of inestimable benefit to the nation in the increase of stability it has given, and could have been enacted under no other form of government. Yet, to those of us who are old-fashioned, and remember the reign of Queen Victoria, there is perhaps something a little dreadful in the thought that, since the Government of Britain goes to the journal with the Largest Daily (Net) Circulation and since no matters of public importance may be mentioned in the Press, the ruling and administration of the country actually fall to the owner of that paper which for the moment reports the most divorces, gives the fullest details of them, gets the first news of some really first-rate hold-up, enthralling murder, extraordinary villa-mystery, entrancing poison-case, curious suicide, or holds the most successful beauty competition of the year.

The Government, on behalf of the Barons, were still to speak and act as if they possessed the executive power. The old Civil Service, the Permanent Officials, still served the country as before; and Mattie, in his capacity of private secretary, still serves a minister; and being a kindly, timid little man, it has invariably been his fate to be the slave of the most filibustering, bellicose and braggadocio minister of whatever Government, or whatever form of government, was in power. These several swashbucklers he has served with the reverence and loyalty born of mingled love and fear, and with a surprising competence. They teased him, bullied him, made a butt of him, yet it was he, in every case, who composed their most fervent, characteristic and effective speeches (for though the Barons dictated policy, they encouraged the oratory of their ministers so long as it was understood that it must not be reported in the Home Press); his piping falsetto it was that first rehearsed and recited their most baying and leonine utterances. For example, that famous fanfaronade that once roused a weak-kneed Britain was, in reality, poor Mattie's: out of this sweetness came forth strength:

'Ladies and Gentlemen (thump), let me put it to you (crash and cheers): ARE WE to Meet the Menace of Armed Might (shame!), yes, Armed and Hostile Might, with a weak, and what seems to One here to-night (gesture) at any rate UNBRITISH, shrugging of the shoulders (long and painful silence)? . . . Or shall we look our foes Undaunted in the face, relying on the Strength of that Great Fleet whose ships crouch low (shudders) in the water, their iron prows curved like the Backs of Giants bent in prayer, ever on the Watch (frantic cheering and even more effective gesture)? Shall we, for fear of risking a few hundred thousand lives — a fear which I think, Ladies and Gentlemen, has never yet swayed a British Government Worthy of the Name — discard that National Honour which has been built up through so many centuries? Shall we, I say (I say it and I REPEAT it again), shall we lightly throw that away? England, look to your laurels! (Fine bull-dog grimace by watchful and expectant orator. Transcendental cheering, whistling, cat-calls and unfortunate cry of "Good Old Bottomley!" from rather muddled old gentleman in corner who remembers better days.)'

Yes, it was Mattie's! and this political connection gives the panelled rooms, in which we are waiting, a character and fame of their own. There would be, continually, little political, social and artistic parties, for it was Mr. Matthew Dean's pleasure to present the writers of nature-poems to politicians, to mix together several minor musicians, a duchess, musical-comedy heroines and young revue writers, to introduce obscure and penniless painters-with-a-future to prominent and penniless ladies-with-a-past. Little parties, not too big. There must always be a nucleus of young genius — pudding-basin hair, straight fringe and all the familiar apparatus of unprejudiced voice and vague, wide-open eye. Elegantly dressed shadows would engage in intellectual converse with rather untidy geniuses, would experience a thrill of excitement as if they had been talking to a bandit; though the bandit is of an origin as bourgeois and respectable as their own. Occasionally a real Whitechapeller would be called in, and oh! what flutterings would follow. *Such* an extraordinary-*looking* man, and what an interesting life! And the shadows would shudder and tremble with delight. People would come in after the theatre or opera; exotically dressed young men would be seen talking to tweed-clad, bearded critics; musical-comedy heroines would giggle artistically to earnest-eyed writers; our bull-dog politician would discuss Modern Art with Lady Carabas and Professor Criscross; Lord FitzBison, the reigning Baron, would ponder on the more obscure problems of literature with Bébé Milson, the leading lady in *Whatever Are We Coming To?* — while their host would sit there, smiling and feline, his eyeglass apparently budding from the outer circle of his face, his eyebrows uplifted as by a Chinese wind, wriggling his head and neck, laughing or talking in a twittering bat-like voice.

It was supposed that these gaieties were of use to the mop- or bobbed-haired, the earnest-eyed and tweed-clad; but their effect was more to benefit Mattie, bestowing upon him an importance in the eyes of both sides. The Ghibellines would welcome this whiff, as they thought, of the East End; for, while it made their flesh creep, and reminded them of the French and Russian revolutions, they yet experienced a feeling of pleasurable excitement. And really how clever Mattie was, so-modern-and-all-that, and such interesting people, always! The Blacks, for their part, would be overwhelmed with the lacquer and varnish of these elegant shadows and exquisite reflections, though sometimes surprised by a frankness of speech to which they were unaccustomed in their own almost Victorian homes; slightly intimidated, perhaps, but happy in the feeling that they were seeing life, and for this they would thank Mattie in their hearts. Then there was always a hope — always an unfulfilled hope — that one of the shadows would commission a portrait or buy a landscape, would give a concert for that new string-quartet, or buy the latest volume of verse. But the shadows preferred speech to action. They enjoyed talking about these things.

At this moment, however, the room is empty even of shadows, and Mattie is pacing irritably up and down, stopping every now and then to touch a book, to open and shut it swiftly. The lamp is brighter, or perhaps it is merely that the cold squares of light behind the blinds have faded out.

Suddenly, with no murmur leading up to it, sounds out the tinny rattling of several taxicabs, and, as if arriving down the three crowsfoot-alleys of the old conventional stage, three of these vehicles converge from three different directions on to the doorway below. They arrive there at the same moment, as though a careful stage-entrance had been contrived. Three taxi-doors are slammed simultaneously. Mr. Dean remarks to himself expressively, if not grammatically, 'This must be them', as an immense booming, roaring, and daft, cackling laughter floods the house. The sea, surely, must have burst in, and be whirling and swirling down in the basement. The flood mounts higher, sweeps relentlessly up the stairs, for a second dies down as the door is flung open, and a loud voice with no trace of comment in it, the voice of a machine, announces sonorously:

LORD RICHARD CRESSEY
MR. PARKINSON
MR. VALENTINE LEVIATHAN

When the three guests are in the room, the wave of sound leaps up into the air again, punctuated by little jets and spurts of talk from Mattie. In this confusion only a few sentences can be isolated. 'Mattie, I am so sorry, but it is this beastly Daylight Saving Bill. When it was one hour, I could manage it, but now that it's three—' '. . . They kept me so late at the F.O. One never gets away now till about eight.' . . . '. . . Had to write an account of the reception of President Trotsky at the Élysée for *The Morning Star*, and only got back at seven.' Mattie seems rather overwhelmed by the sheer volume of sound. His voice seems less now to spurt up, than to come down from above, as if a bat were bumping blindly against the ceiling, as if the invisible ventriloquist had just made up his mind to speak from an angle of the cornice.

The guests are still standing near together, side by side almost; and out of this juxtaposition gradually the fact of an extraordinary resemblance between them emerges. In opposition to the generality of persons encountered, among whom, as we have remarked, but one or two out of a large gathering are definite individuals while the remainder imitate them, copy others who are not present, or are even content to reflect these mimickings, we have here in front of us three persons who, though when apart from one another they present little personality, yet together, and in combination, seem to possess a collective character. Not so much that they are exactly alike, these three, as that out of their present proximity to each other it can be seen that through them runs a common denominator: three flowers from the same stalk or three separate stages of the same disease.

Here, then, in these three friends, we have what may be termed a 'short-circuiting' of reflections. Each member of this little group presents countless mirrorings of the other two, innumerable reflections of these two unconsciously mimicking each other; these are echoed on, *ad infinitum*, among the three, but going no further, not getting out of the group, are always thrown back upon themselves. Yet so used are we to the encountering of shadows, to the feeling that it is impolite to detect them as such, so accustomed to an endless repetition and reflection, that the similarity between them passed unnoticed until Fate itself drew attention to it: and even then, as we shall see, little was said about it, for fear that man should be undeceived about his soul, for fear of lowering him in his own eyes. At present the few who detected any resemblance were only pleasantly reminded of dear Valentine, dear Freddie or dear Richard.

Observed thus, seen together, they are somewhat like the various phases of development of some insect — caterpillar into chrysalis, chrysalis into butterfly: but the order of this evolution is reversed, as it would be if time were a mirror in which we could see these gradual changes reflected. Valentine is twenty-seven, Richard thirty-seven, Freddie forty-seven years old. Ten years separate Valentine from Richard, Richard from Freddie. But Valentine, not Freddie, is the most perfect expression of the slow transition from caterpillar to butterfly; his is the winged metamorphosis. With the overfull lines of his still-young body, with his rather full yellow skin, sleek yellow hair, small, fair moustache and general false air of prosperity, he yet has about him a certain overblown, insect-like elegance. But soon he, too, will have passed beyond this into that chrysalis stage in which we find Lord Richard. The latter is thinner, his body a little baggy, but sagging, his skin more lined, his moustache more stubbly, his hair less smooth, the aquiline tracing of his features more pronounced, his eye more vague, his clothes less elaborate; obviously his is the chrysalis, the torpid, stage. While Freddie, with heavier eyebrows and moustache, coarsened skin and a long thin body that wanders uneasily down the length of his shabby clothes, is plainly the caterpillar of this trio. Yet looking at them was like reading a palindrome — the same words, the same meaning, though perhaps not very much of it, manifested through them from whichever end you start. For all of them had the same dusty fair hair and eyebrows, the same dim, blue, vacant eye with an uneasy look, more often found in the eyes of older men. Each has, when talking, the same method of avoiding the eyes of others, without seeming to wish it, of behaving as if this was but a mannerism, the result of intense mental effort. The eye then assumes a sideways and upward glance, as if searching for something within, as if looking up and away from the drooping yet rather bristly moustache, which, in its turn, seems to be looking sideways and down, as it were, in the other direction. Each has the same loud yet hollow voice, as though perpetually engaged in an effort to communicate some item of news into the very impersonal black-frilled nautilus of an ear-trumpet, which, like a real shell, can never hold any sound with sense in it, but only a distant rushing of waters in buried caverns, an ominous roaring, a perpetual rolling-round of pebbles on the ocean-bed; and the latter is an accurate summary of their conversation — a continual grinding, rolling and polishing of pebbles — fashionable pebbles, though!

Yet each of them, as far as any one of them can be said to exist apart from his comrades, is a little more intelligent than the average — who, luckily for the rest of mankind, never exists at all! All the small stories that circulate in the London drawing-rooms, stories that revolve round and round until a feeling of nausea is induced, pass through them, are sifted, sorted, separated, boomed abroad, roared back again and distributed, finally, for general use, to be echoed, lisped and twittered-at in a thousand homes. In this respect they are like the sorting-machines in the Post Office, or the engines that beat out the chaff from the grain. They never originate a story, not even the most minute of this pygmy race, never initiate a thought; but, again, they never reject a thing of value to them as gossip, never choose anything unsuitable, and launch them, when tested, in the best possible manner. All three friends have the artistic and literary catchwords of the moment — which they are the first to jeer at when uncertain of their success, the first to grasp when successful, the first to discard when worn out — perpetually blowing off their tongues, lightly as bubbles. All three are absolutely saturated in the scandals of the moment. They are the possessors, too, of an endless curiosity, and will return to peck at the same subject day after day, pecking, mimicking and screaming like so many dull-plumaged parrots. Though they do not indulge in unconscious imitation, they have developed a fashionable talent for intentional mimicry which fits in well with their little stories: these imitations are not very realistic, but must pass as hieratic likenesses. With this mimicry, unlike yet recognisable, they usually invoke the memory of very distinguished persons. To those who are acquainted with the victims, and know whom the impersonations are intended to represent, the performance is a quite diverting one: while to those ignorant both of the victim and the intention it is a subtle tribute of flattery, suggesting, as it does, that the audience are themselves very important, very-much-in-the-know.

The actual volume of sound that they make, the sheer loud boisterous thunder of it, has helped to create for them a reputation for being 'so amusing'. And what courage they possess! Not one of them would hesitate to attack, when meeting a man or woman for the first time, the subject most dear and sacred to his or her heart; the topic most unapproachable, and by others the most feared. There are parrots in New Zealand which, though once vegetarian, and that not so long ago, have, since the introduction of sheep into their country, learnt to swoop down from a great height, tear open with their huge, hard beaks the woolly back of that animal, rip open the flesh, and remove the kidneys (their favourite food) all in a moment. The sheep has not time to resist. At one moment it is in a large green field, happy and stupid; the sky is blue and clear, the grass green and sweet; and the next it is doomed, writhing in mortal agony. This too, was their method. They would strike suddenly out of a clear sky; while even if detected in their preliminary swoop, surprise would paralyse their prey. And, though our three friends did not meet their victim again over a space of ten years, yet, when they did meet him, they would at once recall the position and nature of the wound and would proceed immediately to probe and deepen it. No matter how many thousands had fallen victims to them in the interval, they would remember. To watch the proficiency, adroitness, science, yet frank brutality with which they first attacked, veering down swiftly out of the void, was also, in a sense, like watching an operation performed, without the use of an anaesthetic, by some great surgeon. So violently, remorselessly, swiftly, was it done that the patient, overcome by shock, would at first feel nothing. But if ever one of them bungled an operation of this sort, his latest indiscretion, which he would attribute to a childlike innocence of disposition, would add to the volume of fashionable chattering and twittering. Without any respect for the feelings of others, themselves were somewhat pompous, easily offended, easily vulnerable.

By this time Mattie had managed to get his three guests anchored safely in front of their dinner. The dim golden light smoothed out the differences in age, distributed part of Valentine's over-glossiness among the two elder members of his spiritual family, making the likeness between all three of them more remarkable. It is obvious to a stranger, and probably to the host, that they appreciate to the full every peculiarity, physical, mental, and vocal, of Mattie's personal style, and are eagerly awaiting more material for little stories and little imitations. They respect, however, his position both as a source and object of gossip, as a man behind several scenes. The talk, though loud, was not without effort. 'Mattie,' boomed Freddie, as if trying to make his voice heard through a storm, from a vast distance, 'what has happened to that queer, interesting little man I met here last time? A poet, I think he was, or a painter or something?'

'Do you mean Jacques—Jacques Rosenheimer?' Mattie replied in a voice so high that it had an impact on the air like a diamond cutting glass. 'Wonderful little man . . . exceptional promise . . . such heavenly lyrics, full of real June . . . real English countryside.' . . . The sentences were thrown up into the air, staccato, abruptly, for only with effort could he make even these dying sounds! While to emphasise his feelings, he would let his monocle drop down on its string, clashing against his stiff shirt-front like a cymbal; and then he would go again through the ritual of fixing it in his eye, like a schoolboy trying to hold a penny there. '. . . Understands the birds and natural history.'

Lord Richard intervened. 'I believe he's going to be at

Old Septua's tomorrow. I've promised to take Valentine and Freddie down to Dodderingham tomorrow in my new plane. (Oh yes, I've got a new one: haven't you seen it?) I thought she'd amuse them. She's hardly ever in London now and has the most extraordinary people there.' (Mattie produced an angry spurt of sound. 'Well, you won't . . . find Jacques at all extraordinary . . . I'm afraid.' . . .) 'She goes in for farming. I think it's a great mistake. They neither of them understand it; the sheep have got something wrong with them this year, and walk about all over the place on their knees. One Sunday the Bishop came over and asked if he might hold an open-air service in the park — one prayer and a sermon; there wasn't a large congregation, but when he had prayed he looked round, and there were all the sheep on their knees! As he got up, they got up too. Septua was furious, and blamed poor Tootsie for it.'

'I can quite believe it!' Freddie roared, 'because I remember that in my grandmother's lifetime we used to have family prayers. When she said "Let us pray", all the servants got up from their chairs, arranged in line, and revolving silently, as if performing some well-practised exercise in Swedish Drill, went down on their knees; and an old parrot, standing in a cage in the corner, would invariably revolve through its hoop and then fold one claw over its eyes as if joining in the worship.'

'. . . Wonderful thing, birds' intelligence,' lisped Mattie; but his friends intended to escape romanticised natural history for the moment and essayed to trail a red herring. 'Isn't it true, Richard,' Valentine asked, 'that there has been a serious outbreak of Hand-to-Mouth disease at Dodderingham? I heard that Lady Septuagesima, wandering in the lanes, met a sow that was shortly going to suffer an accouchement. Being awfully kind and generous, she asked it to stay, and took it in at once. The bailiff warned her that the disease was very prevalent, and extremely infectious, but she wouldn't turn it away. Not, of course, that it mixed much with other people. She gave it a separate bedroom and all that sort of thing, but directly afterwards there was a fearful outbreak.'

'Poor Septua,' Richard murmured, 'I'm afraid she'll lose a lot. But she will do these things.'

'Talking about grandmothers,' Freddie prepared to embroider his theme, 'it appears that poor old Hetty Wardeburgh has developed a passion for death-beds — a regular complex! They say she positively breaks into the bedrooms of the dying. She got in . . .' But Mattie had got his voice under way and meant to be heard this time.

'. . . Wonderful thing, birds' intelligence,' he lisped again, 'and Jacques is the only man who understands them. In confidence, as you have promised to give the prize, Richard, I'll tell you, though I oughtn't to really, that we've decided to give the Pecksniff to Jacques. Don't forget, Richard, the 12th of July . . . I rely on you to whip people up for it . . . so important that the prize should be a success. Naturally Goo-Goo will be there, but we must make other people come. Goo-Goo must be made to bring all her friends. Can't you persuade Lady Septuagesima to come up for it? I don't mind even if she brings some of those people with her — though (and he winced) I must admit they are a little too advanced for me — but I suppose I'm getting an old fogy', and he tittered in expectation of a friendly denial. Since none came, he continued, 'And Jacques really deserves support, . . . such lovely poetry, . . . simply steeped in beauty . . . steeped in beauty; do you know that last poem, *Denial*? It decided us . . . lovely . . . I think . . . I'll try to remember it.'

The guests exchanged looks of self-compassion; and Mattie, throwing his head back and up, produced those high little jets of sound that bumped against the ceiling like a bat flying into a sudden light, and at other times was the cry of the bat, the fluffy twittering of young birds:

'I would not, if I could, be called a poet,
(Oh, tweet-tweet, feathered friends, how you do go it!)
But rather would I cricket in the sun,
Share in the genial crowd's warm-hearted bun
And ginger beer — go into politics and play
A man's stout part; let no man say me nay.
(Oh, dear, how does it go? Say nay, me nay, say me nay.
I've got it.) Let no man say me nay.
Build empires, or in some rough country place,
Throw silken flies, or tickle silver dace,
Watch happy pigs a-waffle in the weir,
The mornings come, the evenings disappear.
Like grains of sand!
Come, friend, your hand!'

PART II

No more perfect morning for a flight could be imagined — blue sky, with little cool bunches of white cloud knotted together above the horizon, waiting as if afraid to advance alone into the emptiness. They seemed, these white clouds, like ballerinas against an over-painted back-cloth of blues and violets, a cloth painted so brilliantly that the colours have split into refracting and scintillating fragments, a haze of diamond dust, while the dancers themselves are for once nervous, loath to respond to the music's invitation, fearing the huge empty stage in front of them, with its circle after circle of eyes, dull or mocking. Occasionally a grand cloud, a giant, flaunts across like an iceberg seen from under the transparent depths of water beneath it, so that its full thickness of ice-greens, ice-blues and faint rose colourings is visible to us, and it becomes a matter of wonder that the weight of this floating mountain does not overturn it. The air is warm, yet so coldly white is this giant that if it were only nearer, the polar animals, bears whiter than snow, and all the other creatures that have fashioned for themselves skins out of their native element, would show on it, horrified at its breaking away thus from their home in the frozen seas, looking down with wonder and resentment. The trees are very still. In the open space in Hyde Park where stretches the public landing-stage, the plane is waiting for them. The vast cement quay glares out, painted crudely with signs and symbols, placarded with gay if somewhat hideous advertisements. A great droning rises round it, as a thousand planes are launched on one side or come to anchor on the other, coming and going like a horde of dragon-flies, a swarm of bees, round some tropical plant. Lord Richard's machine was at the near end, looking in the morning light as if it were a swallow-tail that had fallen into a tub of liquid silver. The pilot, whom they were not taking with them, got out, and Lord Richard sat down at the wheel with Valentine and Freddie behind him. Suddenly the pilot, standing on the quay to see them off, grew smaller and smaller, as though performing the Indian vanishing-trick, but climbing down, instead of up, his long rope, and the earth swung away from them. The whole width of London swung beneath them, revolving round St. Paul's, the dome of which stood out as the hub of the wheeling city. A myriad grey ribbons, grey ribbon after grey ribbon fluttered and swerved beneath them, and over these crawled and hurried minute ant-like creatures, ever diminishing in size, fetching and carrying, dragging or propelling great loads. So much did the ribbons flutter and wave, that it seemed a miracle that those tiny creatures could keep their balance at all. Now the wheel of London trundles itself away into the distance, and they hang apparently motionless, over the open country, which slides beneath them, pushing them on, like a moving staircase. This prospect changes in the space of a few minutes from a landscape into a realistic but metallic-coloured map. Occasionally the atlas would be hidden from them, as they traversed white seas which, though floating in air, looked so solid that a man, willing to face the coldness of their breakers, would surely be able to wander among the hillocks of these waves, snapping off, here and there, a sprig of frozen spray, pure and flower-like: for the waves had been crystallised, seemingly, in the very rhythm, the very tilt of their life, the foam still leaping upward from their rush caught in attitudes as true yet conventional as the uplifted springing claw of a wave that leaps at you from a screen by Korin. And these seas were but what appeared from the city as timid little clouds! Now, again, the air below grew clear, and the ocean, the real ocean, revealed itself below; the whole line of east coast and Thames estuary showed there, as far as you could see, and the geography that had been to them as children so improbable, assumed for a space a reality of its own. Exhilaration seized Freddie and Valentine, and they roared and boomed loudly at each other, forgetting for a moment that no sound is audible up here, until each wondered at the other's mute grimaces.

Deep down under them grow tufts of grass that are really trees, spreading and noble, ant-heaps that are hills. The diminutive pediment, the prim dovetailing of grey slates would mark a Georgian mansion; and little figures would walk under the grass-blades or move over open spaces of green baize. And, as the plane passed over, it cast down on them a blue or mauve winged shadow, a small shadow that skimmed like a dragon-fly just brushing the still greenery with a breath of coolness. And within that flying speck, high up among the drifting white clouds, cheerfully roaring to themselves, Lord Richard Cressey, Mr. Freddie Parkinson and Mr. Valentine Leviathan are in the clutches of those Demons of the Upper Air, who, unappeased by any sacrifice, can still be heard howling, far away above us, on a dark winter night.

. . . .

Dodderingham Old Hall, their intended destination, lies beside the Cam : a simple Queen Anne house, like a pavilion of red velvet, with a long and wide staircase leading up to it, and down from it, on to stretching green lawns. It seems to have been improvised for some pageant that has passed long ago, lies embedded in all this intense verdure, sinking slowly into the flat country which is as rustic now as before the house was built. Only the avenue of wireless masts at intervals of five miles, rising to fifty times the height of the huge old trees, shows that the age of the Virgin Queen is over — for so Elizabethan is the countryside that Dodderingham Old Hall seems as much of an anachronism as the masts that join it to London. The present régime in the house appears to have something Gothic still lingering about it, strange and fantastic. For Lady Septuagesima patronises the advanced guard of art and literature. The large panels of the walls that had before shone dully, grey or brown, full of low lights and mouse-like colour, now blush under bedizenments of purple, scarlet and apricot, are blazoned with stripes, are chequered, or have gathered constellations of gold and silver. The pictures that liven, or sober, these walls are either frighteningly old or terrifyingly new ; illustrating the theory of the most modern painters that their wagon is hitched on to such stars as Giotto and Duccio. On the other hand, Raphael, who had enjoyed a temporary popularity with the vanguard, now bows the knee to Guido Reni and to Carlo Dolci, once again the last word in esthetic thrills. A small picture by Sassetta would hang side by side with the work of the youngest self-taught genius ; Guido would pair with Renoir ; a huge early Matisse faces a chiaroscuro altar-piece from Bologna ; yet all the pictures, all the furniture, are arranged with a dramatic sense that has enabled Lady Septuagesima to mount herself superbly.

This remarkable lady came, as can be deduced from her name, of a peculiarly religious family. Her father, the late Lord Fortcarrick, one of the richest land and mineral owners in Lancashire, had harnessed his portion of a notorious family eccentricity, and turned it into religious energy. This, though trying to his relatives, was in the end perhaps to their advantage. 'An odious bore,' old Lady Fortcarrick used to characterise it, 'but better than gamblin'.' To an extent she even encouraged this fervour, while, at the same time, keeping it in bounds. In her lifetime he was merely aggressively Low Church; but after his wife's death he became more imaginative. He would spend his time now, with enormous notebooks in front of him, reckoning out the precise date of the Second Coming; a calculation based, even more elaborately, upon such foundations as Joanna Southcott's unopened box, and statistics of the growing Catholicism in England, and inextricably intertwined with the fact that the Kaiser Wilhelm II of Germany was the Beast-in-the-Revelation. As time went on, as he became older (for this was before the prolongation of life had become such a simple affair), his mind became ever more original in its working. He would invariably invest his income (he was a very rich man) as it came in, and then, forgetting what he had done, would declare, would insist, that he had no money to live on unless he raided his capital. The necessary sums for his support he would borrow from his children. Finally, in a fit of prophecy verging on apoplexy, he identified poor Lady Septuagesima, to her face, with the Scarlet Woman of Babylon, and, shortly afterwards, passed peacefully away.

His daughter had started life by being as religious as her father. Devotion was bred in her; and many farmers and miners, who owe their conversion to her, would be surprised if they could see her now — which is improbable, since, whereas the late earl accused his daughter of being the Scarlet Woman, the present one, her brother, has proved her to his own satisfaction a Bolshevik; and the latter, however popular politically in London, is still a word of reproach in ancestral halls.

But in the early days of which we are writing, not even her brother could have brought against her such an accusation. She affected, then, an almost Salvationist simplicity of dress, demeanour, and speech. This continued until she was about thirty-five, and then a change came. The scene of her charitable activities had gradually shifted from the country village to the poorer districts of London. Another transformation, and she began to do her slumming in the studios of Fitzroy Street and Chelsea. It was a miracle. At once her religious zeal was converted into an artistic one, but equally Protestant, equally unyielding and fanatic in its new direction. At this time she would surely, without scruple, have started a crusade, a holy war, against the Royal Academy. To her they were now what the Church of Rome had been previously. Even the ever-present, farcical spectacle of these poor old men, in their greed for money, rushing out after Modern Art like a fat man after a passing omnibus, and always failing to catch it, could not soften her. Yet at the same moment that this miraculous conversion took place, herself became transfigured. The former possession of ordinary, simple good looks she now bartered for a grotesque yet actual beauty; while from her previous austerity of dress she blossomed into a garish glory of clothes, such as was never seen in this world before. Her language, her conversation, too, now threw off their swaddling clothes and came of age in a day.

Of impressive height — a height that was over life-size for a woman, so that without looking a giantess she might yet seem an animated public monument — Lady Septuagesima had an almost masculine face, deep-set flower-like eyes with a golden calyx, a long, definite nose and cut-out chin; strong, large animal-like teeth, which showed when she laughed, and a mass of red-brown hair, cut short but not cropped. Many of these features do not sound attractive, but it is certain that there was about her a quality of crazy, ludicrous, abstract beauty that few, happily, possess. Her voice, personal to herself as her looks, was equally absurd, and in it mingled the peaceful lowing of cattle and the barbed drone of wasp and hornet. As she moved (never afraid of attracting attention — indeed apparently oblivious of it) through the London streets in her gaudy clothes, large hooped skirt and vast hat loaded with feathers as that of any coster's wife, many who stopped to stare supposed that she was staggering by under the weight of odd-lots that, now past their use, had been bestowed upon her by a charitable theatrical costumier. Every year her appearance became more eccentric, more grim and yet more decorative, having the desolate yet rather extravagant beauty of a ruin-picture by Pannini; of severe classical remains decked out with bunting; of the Colosseum seen alternately under soft moonlight and by the fire and fizzling glitter of fireworks. In vain the crowd of dirty wide-eyed children, who would accompany her when she walked in London, raised their shrill anthem in the air:

'I see no reason
Why gunpowder treason
Should ever be forgot.'

For Lady Septuagesima these words contained no hidden implication. She liked children and, alas, had none of her own. She would merely remark, casually, on arriving home, that the children in London were so friendly and would walk with her all the way, singing.

At Dodderingham Old Hall the individual note in her clothes was accentuated still further. She would walk down the deeply hedged lanes, the flat roads, accompanied by her noble-looking, rather horse-like husband, and by a perfect menagerie of young artists and intellectuals. In winter or summer she would be supported, apparently, by the same court. But though identical in voice and look, those strolling companies were, with the exception of her husband, never the same in their composition for more than one quarter of the year: she quarrelled with them regularly every three months, and then no abuse was too bad for those for whom, only two months previously, no praise had been good enough. 'Never in my life have I been treated like that before', was invariably the burden of her song to the next assembly. The latter, this permanent though shifting circus, cultivated always the look of its part. One inevitable ingredient in it was a group of undergraduates from Cambridge, which, in its turn, could invariably be divided into two portions: one division consisting of youths painfully well-clothed, too precious in manner, with eyes too liquid; while the other was made up of callow young men, intolerably dirty, whose friendship was valued because of their simplicity. Then there were mop-haired, moist-handed individuals with greenish faces, grotesque and damply chilly as deep-sea monsters; art-critics, like sea anemones, with circular floating fringes of red hair, or with matted beards that seemed tentacular as the arms of an octopus; a superannuated bishop who believed in seeing life and making the best of things; one or two stray individuals from London, with no particular point; and several young women with golden hair and strawberry-and-cream complexions, who had, therefore, to insist on intellect by the cropping of their hair, by wearing breeches and by speaking about peculiar subjects in a peculiarly frank way, in voices whose even tones displayed no trace of emotion. Then there were oldish women with short grey hair, tweed skirts and green-leather football boots; middle-aged ones decked out with pince-nez and crowned with plumes — synthetic ones, though — of victory, like the goddess Bellona. This perambulating group was further augmented by a few stray 'studio-sweepings'. As they walked, one could see that some of them were tall . . . much too tall — others short . . . far too short: but all, as they marched through the rustic landscape beside their hostess, assumed an air of bourgeois respectability, of utter commonplaceness. And though in London the children followed her, here they were respectful and subdued. As she swept along, her clothes lent colour, an unusual quantity of colour indeed, to the insinuation of her enemies that in order to find such garments she must attend secret rummage-and-jumble-sales at the Local Asylum. But there was something splendid about her appearance; no snowball greeted her even on the coldest winter day, nor, as she sailed past, was any cry of 'Aunt Sally!' wafted to her ear by the spring breezes.

And the course of her previous progress through the countryside was afterwards easily to be traced by strangers; for, as she went, the most extraordinary, the most extravagant, objects fell from her and were lost. These, if left for future generations to discover, will greatly puzzle posterity. What strange race, it will wonder, what extinct civilisation had its centre, as testified by this accumulation of grotesque objects, in this flat, green, peaceful land? Even now the passing pedestrian is filled with awe and surprise. Tall trees rise up, covered with leaves from head to foot, every tiny twig of every branch flooded with leaves, the very trunks and arms green with moss, gold with lichen, as if they had just risen, dripping, cool and watery-green, from the ocean bed. Under them are whitewashed cottages, very white and crumbling, with windows, like wide-open eyes and thatched roofs that jut out over them, hair, brow and eyebrow combined in one slanting, moss-covered greenness. The whole area is calm, sleepy. Cottage gardens, raised above the road, are bulging with stocks and sweet-blowing flowers of many colours, are full as cornucopias. Even the windows of these cottages are full of flowers, whose faces, red and hot, are flattened against the windows, as ever tightly shut; the blossom in each pane seems the iris of an eye, alive and vibrant. Against this background, pasted on the boles of trees so ancient that they are antlered like king stags, or pendent in the boldly curving bow-windows of a village post office, among open boxes and glass jars of sweets like small overripe fruits, among barley-sugar gold as corn and twisted like the pillars of the Temple, among bundles of brown and black bootlaces hanging up like hairy scalps, among pyramids of snow-white sugar or mounds of honeyed Demerara, rods of coloured sealing-wax, rusty steel pens and all the other familiar properties of village life, he reads some such notice as this that follows:

LOST

LOST between here and Dodderingham Old Hall on the afternoon of May 2nd, 1948:

Seven herons' plumes set in brilliants.

A green ostrich-feather fan with tortoise-shell mount.

An Elizabethan whale-bone hoop.

One crimson shoe-heel with cairngorm inset.

A tartan shawl.

A Japanese embroidered bag, with panels of flying storks worked in salmon-pink and rose silks, containing:

A stick of orange-coloured lip-salve, with black onyx mounting and

A purse with platinum fastening, in which were:

A card of permanent invitation to the Trafalgar Gallery of Modern Art, London.

£3 12s. 6d. in silver, and

A paper bag full of bull's-eye peppermints.

ALSO

LOST between Skipton and Dodderingham Old Hall:

A blue-silk cushion of native workmanship.

A Congo Fetish in ivory.

A first edition of Milton's *Paradise Lost* (Simmons, in 10 books, 1667).

A volume of Jules Laforgue's poems.

The second volume of the Bloomsbury Painters Series — *From Giotto to Gertler*.

A photographic miniature of Cézanne, presented by the painters of the Black-Friday Group, set in half-pearls.
A green amber amulet.
A New Zealand Totem Pole, converted into a walking-stick, and
A wisdom tooth, mounted in turquoises, and inscribed 'To Septua from Tootsie, 1943'.

The Finder, on returning these items to their owner, Lady SEPTUAGESIMA GOODLEY, Dodderingham Old Hall, will be SUITABLY rewarded.

Tootsie, it must be confessed, was Thomas Goodley, her husband. Thus, in her progress round the countryside, would Lady Septuagesima distribute regal, if involuntary, largess.

On this fine Sunday morning, however, she indulged in no ambulatory adventures, preferring to stay in the garden surrounded by her court of the instant. Seen from a little distance, it was quite a spectacle. The entire assembly was broken up into knots of two or three persons; but all these groups were yet near together, as if each one feared to be out of earshot of any other; each listening to the conversation of the one farthest removed from it, while, at the same time, carrying on a conversation amongst itself. Some members of these various court factions were sitting on garden seats painted in sugar-stick stripes of red and white, some were lying curled up, or were crouching uncomfortably, hands clasped round knees in the manner of those rigid mummies of pre-dynastic Egypt, while others were sitting easily on the ground, as if never accustomed to any more comfortable posture. Under them were square rugs decorated with large square patterns, and over each knot spread a large striped umbrella. The light dripping through these, and cast up again by the rugs and flat stretches of green grass, spattered them with vivid patches of scarlet, purple, blue and sea-green, till they seemed hotly coloured insects nestling under the shade of a clump of iridescent, rather deleterious toadstools. A cloud floating overhead reduces the colouring, lowering it a tone or two for an instant as if a tinted glass had been interposed between the groups and the onlooker. The cloud would pass and the tones would jump up again to their normal violence. From under the fungi rose a continual droning, shrilling, hoarse cackling and shooting-out of the tongue, as the chameleon-coloured groups conversed. Little spirals of smoke rose, coloured, too, by their surroundings.

Nearly the whole day was spent here, and in this manner, for Lady Septuagesima was expecting three guests down from London. They should have been here by twelve o'clock or in time for luncheon at the latest; but there came no sign of their arrival. In the garden it was very restful; the lowing, whinnying laughter of the hostess fitted in with the prospect disclosed between the high green trees, pillars that framed-in the view, with its foreground of sun-baked, red-brick walls, seeming already to breathe out the honey-sweet scent of ripe fruit, though at present the flattened forms of espaliers, that clung to them like green cobwebs, bore only small constellations of delicate blossom, apple and peach, pear and plum.

The conversation was woven equally of high art and low scandal. An enormous man, with a blue shirt, an open coat, no waistcoat and a belt, a costume singularly courageous for so large a person, was, though he had an air of easy well-being combined with little intellectual effort, taking a severe line about esthetics. The cropped-haired young women were voluble too; their voices, calm and even, indicated clearly a conscious superiority which enraged the large gentleman; for as the Quakers are confident of the spiritual revelation within them, so were all these combatants sure of their essential rightness. The undergraduates were present as usual; the untidy spoke seldom but loudly, and when they spoke would not be silenced; the ones elaborately groomed and dreamy-eyed gazed on mutely, lost in some adolescent stupor. Jacques Rosenheimer interrupted occasionally, with abrupt, authoritative and rather snapping utterance; short, dark and thick-set, he was curly haired and curly nostrilled. Then, distributed among the groups, there were some cosmopolitans: a Danish dancer, a Spanish gipsy, a Russian artist, swelling out of his clothes, full of compliments, ever so gallant; and all the usual court, except the bishop, who was resting within. Tootsie, monumental, like one of the togaed statues outside the old House of Commons, remained immersed in his own nobility of mien and character.

All day the conversation wove its arabesque design, a design barely traceable, seldom leading to any very definite pattern; but the threads, drawn up above the several umbrellas by one hand, would have a certain vague significance.

The fat man's voice, loud and distinct, sounded out his

bass theme. 'Give me Giotto, give me Giotto,' he reiterated solemnly. 'I don't see how you can compare Guggenheimer with him. . . .'

'It isn't that' (and a feminine hand was waved descriptively), 'it's the solidity, the *pure* painting, if you know what I mean, the actual *pure* painting . . . like Defoe or Sterne,' and her voice drooped back into the general shrilling.

The threads are drawn closer, so that the fabric can be regarded.

'. . . Well, of course, if you're going to talk in that way, the argument simply can't be continued . . . must compare one painter with another. . . . But why? There is a likeness, don't you think, the same definite hardness, you know . . .' (Fresh theme announces itself.) 'Well, all I can tell you is, *he* told me so himself. I know she didn't. She didn't want it talked about, naturally . . . but he happened to tell me himself . . . After all, it had been going on for years, hadn't it, Septua? You know as well as I do . . . Oh! Breughel's not to be compared with Giotto . . . not in it simply. Besides, I don't like Ingres's drawings, I only like the *drawing* in his *paintings*. . . . Well, I'm glad he left her: came down here for two nights three years ago, stayed ten days; poor Tootsie was nearly driven off his head and played the electric organ for seven hours without stopping. So exhausted that the doctor . . . immensely improved . . . fine thing that, at the Black-Friday Club . . . Impressive design . . . I shall be out if she comes again — such a bore . . . She always was one, and quite crazy into the bargain, now. Why should one be lumbered up with people like that? . . . all I can tell you is this. Giotto and Tolstoy, they've made the difference to my life . . . don't see that Blake's a bit like Cézanne . . . and when she'd got into Italy, they had to come back again . . . very queer and interesting . . . and in Petrograd we (how you say it in English?) sledged down the Neva . . . what I wonder is will Mingler become a SUBJECTIVE or an OBJECTIVE writer? That is what I ask myself . . . judging by the last one, subjective and objectionable, I should say . . . that's merely silly. Of course, I like him, but he is pompous, isn't he? Goo-Goo is charming . . . pretty, and personally I like her accent. Of course no talent, either of them . . . Aix-les-Bains . . . no, I haven't seen the ones in Vienna, but in any case Breughel had no sense of form . . . Mattie . . . ridiculous but kindly. (Giotto and Tolstoy, Giotto and Tolstoy, Giotto and Tolstoy . . .) The minister had to disarm him. It simply wasn't safe to let him shoot. But he was allowed to carry a white sunshade; and the very next day he was charged by the only white rogue-elephant in Africa . . . never been the same . . . and the minister only laughed and said (Giotto and Tolstoy) that Mattie had got a white elephant in his sun helmet . . . well, you may not agree with me; but there it is, Giotto and . . . I can't bear that barn. It would drive me mad if I had to live in it (Giotto, and give me the Primitives). Doesn't look lived in somehow . . . for his children, but now they've had to abolish death-duties altogether . . . not quite so pleased . . . solidity, that's what I mean — pure painting . . . like Mozart. . . .'

But the fabric was torn suddenly by a maid, who hurried out of the house to tell her ladyship that she was wanted on the radiophone.

'The Superintendent, Cambridge, speaking . . . speaking . . . yes, yes. Is that you? Three miles away . . . like a lump of lead? Terrible . . . terrible! Yes, radio at once. Are you ready? Lady Richard Cressey, Hotel Splendide, Aix-les-Bains. Return at once Richard unwell will meet you Cambridge Septua. And one more, please; yes, Superintendent. Sir Vincent McNabb, 142 Wimpole Street, Inner London. Please engage Express Flyer Cambridge at once grafting operation Lord Richard Cressey most important on no account fail me. Stay night here Lady Septuagesima Goodley, Dodderingham Old Hall.'

. . . .

One of the most pleasing features of the progress of civilisation during the last quarter of a century has been the immense advance in the art of surgery, as well as in healing, mental and physical. If the dominating features of the nineteenth century were concerned with mechanics — with machines and mechanical inventions — this one surely will be remembered always as the Biological Century. Biology has disclosed to us miracle after miracle, and has not yet bestowed upon humanity the last of its gifts. To those who were children during the course of the First or Small 'Great War' (that one which, beginning in 1914, lasted until 1918) — still more to those born since that event — the extent to which the old pre-war world of 'statesmen', 'newspaper proprietors' (as they were then called), millionaires and philanthropists, was dominated by death, and by the idea of death, can hardly be credible. However accustomed the new generation may be to the prospect of that triple span which life holds for them, to us older men it must remain a continual cause for wonder, making us rub our eyes to see if we are awake. Nor are the full implications of the life-lengthening operation fully grasped even now. Because, since the first operations were performed barely twenty-five years ago, there are still with us but few men who have achieved over eleven decades, whereas in the future there will be many, mentally and physically in the prime of life, at the age of one hundred and eighty. To remind us that we are not dreaming (if one may still, without impropriety, mention that word . . .) there are, luckily, certain concrete facts constantly before us. When I first began to read the newspapers as a child of seven — for in those distant days the reading of newspapers, far from being compulsory for children, as it is now, was discouraged or actually forbidden — it was noticeable that hardly a day passed without the death of A Last Great Victorian having to be recorded. It was very depressing reading, that list of obituaries, which became like the accounts of the-positively-final-farewell-performance of some great stage favourite. Suddenly the torrent was checked, and, as we know, many of the last really great ones have been declared 'public monuments', and are with us yet.

Another proof that the miracle has actually been achieved is to be found in the abolition of death duties. Curiously enough, it was the iniquitous and vindictive incidence of this taxation — aimed solely at one small class rich enough to pay it — as much as any single fact, that in the end, perhaps, was responsible for the lengthening of life. An inevitable evolution it was, comparable to that neck which the giraffe has developed in its continual search for food at a considerable altitude. Each rich man was determined for the sake of his family, nay, of his country, to live as long as lay within his power. Each wealthy pioneer of longevity — for, as in so many other charitable causes, it was the millionaires who took the lead — made a public declaration that it was not the fear of death (on the contrary, such were his responsibilities that he would welcome a release from them) that made him wish to postpone the end, but the fact that if he surrendered to care, illness and old age, a disgraceful and punitive impost would fall upon his children. Nor, he would add, was this bad for the family alone, since the Family is but the Unit of the State! What, therefore, is injurious to the family, damages the State; what impoverishes the family, though it may at first appear to enrich, yet surely in the end impoverishes the Motherland. I remember what an effect a certain simile made on me in this connection: it has often been noticed that powerful and original minds work in much the same manner; and several of these grand old men said to me, oddly enough, the same thing in almost the same words. As they pronounced their faith, with a fervour that was convincing, there was about them something, perhaps a little ponderous, yet noble and statesmanlike. 'You cannot,' they would say, 'you cannot both have your cake and eat it!' And one felt, somehow, from the fact that they had thought out and pinned down the same phrase, that deeply, deeply, must these pioneers feel the truth of it. Great was their courage and resolution. No matter how their sons gave way to their own feelings, crying and imploring their fathers not to sacrifice themselves, not to pass this stern self-denying ordinance, urging them to release themselves from this bondage of family feeling which required such inverted immolation of father to son, the old gentlemen remained firm in their resolve. Patriotic, as well as family, scruples had entered into their decision; they could not, therefore, look back. Nor even did the threats of the Church intimidate for an instant these patriots. The Church, as ever behind the times, began by denouncing the surgical prolongation of life as a sin against God's ordering of the world, and one that would entail damnation eternal, the complete conquest by Satan of the soul of each man operated upon. A breath of humour was brought into this controversy by the declaration of old Lord Badgery St. Otter (as he then was), now the Duke of Badgery St. Lawrence, who, being eighty years of age, and about to submit to the operation, said: 'If the devil waants me, 'e can coome an' fetch me, an' a devilish touff job 'e'll 'ave!'

Such was the spirit of these men, willing to risk a presumable certainty of eternal happiness for the sake of another span of worldly care and sorrow in which to help their fellows.

Undaunted, these fine old Die-hards damned the consequences, flinging themselves down on the operating table in the same spirit in which Abraham had sought to sacrifice his dearly beloved son. And the sacrifice has not been made in vain, for the substitution by the Press Barons of the 'Re-marriage' — or, as they are popularly called, 'divorce duties' — for Death Duties, has been to many a great relief. The Death Duties had, as a matter of fact, long ceased to bring in much revenue; and the new ones are both less heavy and less easily avoided — for a man can, after all, avoid death more easily than marriage. But if the tax should become too heavy, it is not to be doubted that — ever at the call of patriotism and the family — the same grand old pioneers will no more hesitate to give up making a fresh start in their new life, than, on behalf of the same ideals, they feared to give up making a fresh start in death.

The Press Barons were among the first to undergo what was at the time a dangerous experiment; and while we owe our good government to them, and to the increasing wisdom and generosity with which the passing years have endowed them, it is right, surely, to admire that very British spirit of freedom which has actuated them throughout. Never, for an instant, have they sought to force these discoveries on others, to thrust them, for example, upon the poor! From the first they understood that the world was over-populated, and for the sake of those same ideals, for faith, family and Fatherland, the workers should be permitted to die at that age at which they had formed the habit of so doing — or, if they wish it, at one yet earlier. For, in effect, they are too old at forty. Thus it can never be said that the men with responsibilities sought to shift their burden on to the shoulders of those free of them; and it remains one of the consolations, the compensations, of poverty that a double — or even a full — span of life is not obligatory.

These political and social benefits are all due, in the first place, to the marvellous science of human grafting, the effect of which has been increasingly toward national stability. The workers must realise by now, one would imagine, that the holding of wealth, with its privileges and responsibilities, in the hands of a few permanent, indeed almost eternal, individuals, is a guarantee that while the former will not be abused, the latter will be respected. Apart from this self-obvious conclusion, it is one of the blessings of our present form of government that every day, in every way, in every paper, this thought is enunciated, this lesson taught. Again, it had long been noticed in every country where hereditary monarchy survived, that there was never a revolution against any king who had reigned for over fifty years — however good a ruler he may have been. And since 'O King, live for ever!' is now hardly an exaggerated expression of good-will, since reigns of two centuries will automatically become quite normal, the fear of revolution becomes continually more remote.

The first operation that proved the value, and advertised the miracle, of grafting was that performed upon Prince Absalom, son of the Emperor Dodon of Aquitania. It is not yet twenty years, though it may seem more, since that well-beloved prince, the darling rival of every cinema star, and scion of an ancient and august house, which had in an amazingly short period consolidated one of the greatest empires — and by making no use of it had managed for an amazingly long time to keep it — met with a terrible, an appalling, accident. Though possessed of immense charm, he was of a puny, frail physique, that contrasted forcibly with his marked mental powers and attainments. While seeking recreation one evening, in those few moments of leisure spared him from Empire's Call, by performing in what was then called a 'Jazz' band (a fashion that had spread to Aquitania from America via England), he fell into one of the noise-contrivances, his right leg being terribly lacerated. At the news, a thrill of horror passed, not only through his own people, but through the whole of the civilised world. At first the contraption refused to let go of his leg, but eventually its jaws were broken, and followed the tragic announcement that the surgeon had found it necessary to amputate the injured limb. Day after day enormous crowds, some of them sobbing or weeping hysterically, would gather outside the Emperor's palace in Atlantis to read the latest bulletins.

Then, one day, with a burst of joy, with such startling demonstrations of loyalty, such outbursts of shouting, dancing and singing as usually only mark the periodic declarations of a war to end war, it became known that one of the duskier players (or coons, as they were called) in the orchestra had come forward to give his leg in the Cause of Empire! And that operation, first of its kind, was successful.

In those inspiring days I happened to be in Aquitania, and through the generosity of Lord FitzBison, who had just at that moment appointed himself English Ambassador at the Emperor Dodon's court, was enabled to be present at the Solemn Service of National Thanksgiving at St. Andrew's which celebrated Prince Absalom's recovery. The discourse of the Archbishop of Atlantis was particularly impressive, full of original thinking, and I translated some portions of it.

'We are gathered together today, brethren,' he said, 'to celebrate the recovery of one beloved beyond all princes — by the people of this mighty League of Free Peoples, Nations and Commonwealths which we call Empire. And in him, for whose recovery we thank our God today — for whose recovery humble couples in their forest homes, in log-cabins and cottages, men gathered in the Service of Industry, and the darker peoples who kneel in their tents of grass and wattle, thank God too — we have more than ever, in his own person, what he has so long been called, "The Ambassador of Empire". In his own body blends he now the fair people of Atlantis and the northern states, with the dusty — dusky, I should say — dwellers in the jungle. One foot is set in Africa, the other in the Northern Isles. In his own body he binds together every class, every colour, nay, every creed; and the Thin Red Line of Empire cements the union. And, brethren,' and his voice sank dramatically, 'it is only right that' (crescendo), 'in this hour of triumph, our thoughts should go out to another son of Empire, to one of lowly condition and perhaps of but modest pretensions, yet one who, in his humble way, has done much to make possible this Union of Peoples. Hath a man greater love than this . . . that he lays down his foot for a friend? . . . can we not put it like that, brethren?' (Hissing slightly.) 'In that dusky and obscure player, too, was found the heart of Saint and hero; and there may be many of us amongst this great congregation who, though we have not appreciated the music of jazz bands in the past, will never be able to hear the sweet tones of the Swanee Whistle or the deep, melodious notes of the saxophone without heartfelt sympathy and emotion, roused by the memory of a great and gracious deed.'

But, though the happy recovery of the prince was everywhere acclaimed, yet from that moment, in spite of the Archbishop's prophecy, syncopated music began to lose its grip on the people of the world. Jazz it was that died.

This same accident was responsible for a curious fashion among royal princes, and one which is still prevalent, though it may seem strange to the Victorians who survive — that fashion of having the limbs variegated in accordance with the people of the dominions over which they rule. Thus they have now become, in their own bodies, walking examples of Representative Government.

In spite of the fact that the most important of these grafting operations is still known as the 'monkey gland', it ought now to be needless to point out that the use of these simian cells has long been abandoned. For the introduction of any element foreign to it into the human body, inevitably sets up an irritation, which is sure to develop into some serious, and possibly fatal, trouble. Whereas the same operation, with human material substituted, is without any possibility of danger. In view of this, special laws were passed, many years ago, to ensure an adequate supply of human material and a proper use of it.

As we know, every young man killed by chance, in street accident or sudden explosion in a factory, is sent at once to the Royal Analysing Institute, whence, if his remains are found to be satisfactory, they are passed on, for the necessary treatment, to the nearest Young Man's Dissecting and Cold Storage Association (Y.M.D.A.C.S.A.). Here, if his relatives so desire, a funeral service can be held by Royal Licence; and many relatives have found a funeral without any corpse — and with no actual expense, save that of the service — most comforting; preferable, indeed, to the ordinary arrangement. In the building of the association, each limb, each cell, waits till the time comes for it to serve its purpose with Elder Statesman, millionaire philanthropist, or famous general. Wars, even, have ceased to hold for the civilian population their former terror. For the essential horror of war was its utter waste and uselessness; but now, after each battle, there is a short armistice, and the slain are swiftly collected and laid by, that we may benefit — and our enemies as well — by the ever-increasing wisdom and ripe experience of those who have guided us through, and themselves survived, so many crusades to end war. Surgeons, as well as statesmen, may now declare:

'We will not lightly sheathe the sword. . . .'

In spite of these well-thought-out preparations, it has been found that freshly dissected limbs are more effective, safer to use, more swift in their results, than preserved ones. So, when Sir Vincent McNabb was warned of the accident that had befallen Lord Richard Cressey, he determined to patch the patient together — if it should prove possible — without the use of any but his own limbs, glands and other material. This might mean that the actual reconstruction would be a more lengthy affair, but in the end it would be of the greatest benefit to the patient, aiding his speedy recovery. In order, however, to be ready for any eventuality, the great surgeon brought down with him from London a complete regulation set of anatomical sections.

Within a half-hour of his urgent summons, Sir Vincent had arrived at Cambridge. There he was met by the Goodleys' agent; for Lady Septuagesima and her husband had been forced to stay at Dodderingham to make arrangements for the nursing of Lord Richard and the reception of his wife. The menagerie had been hurriedly dispersed, the striped umbrellas had been struck, the raggle-taggle gipsies were on the move once more. The wolves and jackals were already howling in the outer wilderness of London, the hyenas were laughing more hysterically than ever in their own homes, and the few lions that there had been were back in their dens, roaring sardonically. Everything had been tidied up, under the supervision of two trained nurses; and, as soon as the preparations were complete, Lady Septuagesima would join Sir Vincent. Meanwhile, the agent conducted him to where, among torn brambles, smashed hawthorn bushes, and earth thrown up as by a miniature volcano, lay the wrecked flyer, guarded by police. Several nurses were on the scene, in readiness. It was now getting dark; but with that rapidity and sureness of judgment which, in surgery as in other professions, is the very stamp of genius, Sir Vincent was soon able to decide that it was possible, as he had hoped it would be, to operate with the material on the spot. The mutilations and injuries were terrible: but a reconstruction was undoubtedly feasible, however formidable the difficulties. A theatre, fitted with the new wireless lighting, was hastily improvised. Everything, now, depended on swift, on determined, action.

During four hours the remains were under an anaesthetic, while the great surgeon grappled with the problem of their reconstitution. But, in the end, the problem was solved, and Lord Richard Cressey was given a chance of a remodelled but adequate survival.

So immersed had Sir Vincent been in the pathetic and perplexing work before him, that it was not until the long process of his art was completed that he observed, with considerable surprise, the presence among the wreckage of what were apparently, in his technical language, spare-parts. This astonished him ; for not even the most thoughtful — or morbid — of airmen would prepare for eventualities in this way. Superstition, alone, would forbid it ; nor, in any case, is flying sufficiently dangerous to warrant such an outlay. And, strangest thing of all, the texture of the skin, the tint of hair, the structure of bones, the composition of the flesh — all at once confirmed the first supposition of the trained eye that they, too, must belong to that body that was still lying, unconscious but reconstructed, upon the operating table. The great surgeon was puzzled . . . distinctly puzzled. In the whole course of a long professional career he had never . . . no never . . . met with a case like it ! Was he, then, to conclude, in the face of those very laws of nature by which he was permitted to practise his art, that Lord Richard, like some Hindu divinity, had been the possessor of six arms, had, like Diana of the Ephesians, boasted more than the normal pectoral development . . . or, like Janus, with his two faces, like Cerberus, with his three heads, had rejoiced in the distinction bestowed upon him by an unusual plurality ? Puzzled was Sir Vincent, distinctly puzzled. . . .

The timely arrival of Lady Septuagesima helped to clear up what was apparently inexplicable. Lowing and neighing at him, charmingly, she explained. It was so stupid of her, so careless, she whinnied — but in the sudden shock of evil tidings, in her sorrow for her cousin, her bewilderment as to how to break the bad news to Goo-Goo, she had completely overlooked the existence, and ignored the fate, of the unfortunate Messrs. Leviathan and Parkinson. The very fact of there being two such persons had left her. In the same manner in which she was accustomed to shed those fantastic articles we have described about the countryside, so, in that moment, had the lives of that ill-fated pair fallen from her, unnoticed — 'lost between here and Dodderingham Old Hall'. . . . Oh, how tiresome and unfortunate! And really too bad of Tootsie, who had never reminded her! He was getting so very careless and remiss. He knew quite well how forgetful she was! And now it was too late, was it, Sir Vincent, for anything to be done? She lowed entreatingly at him. Alas! it was now no longer possible for him to treat the other two passengers. The police had better warn the relatives by radio. Sir Vincent came forward heavily, and informed the police that, in any case, the fragments were so much injured as to defeat any attempt at reconstruction.

Lady Septuagesima, in order to pacify the two families, who might think she had been careless or inhospitable toward her guests, undertook to use her influence with the old Duke of Badgery St. Lawrence, and the Home Office, to secure for the two victims a special Burial-Permit under Clause 2 of the 'Only Children to Widows Relief from Compulsory Anatomical Service Act of 1936'. She obtained the further favour for them of interment. They were laid to rest in one grave in the cemetery of the Parish Church at Cambridge — in which latter place, too, the funeral service was held — though usually in such cases it had to be celebrated on the premises of the local Y.M.D.A.C.S.A.

. . . . .

The return to consciousness of Lord Richard took a more than average time. For ten days he lay in the darkened room at Dodderingham, not speaking, hardly breathing. Goo-Goo watched by his side. His pale face, with its closed eyes, seemed to her, in the twilight of that sick-room, to be remote and strange. Some indefinable alteration had, surely, taken place in him? . . . Did he look older or younger — ten years older, or ten years younger? Yet though he remained lying there senseless all these long days, Sir Vincent appeared pleased with the patient's progress. There were no signs of a relapse; the grafting had been completely successful, a triumph such as could only have been achieved by the skilful use of the patient's own limbs and material, the surgeon said. The scars were healing, were disappearing. But Goo-Goo was puzzled by the presence of two birth-marks, one on the neck, and one on the right wrist, which, though they were familiar to her, had been absent, she was certain, in her husband formerly. At any rate, compared with his recovery, the presence of these two blemishes was unimportant.

In the house reigned a great stillness: no rolling-round of tongues sounded from the lawn, and a ban had been placed on the electric organ. Day after day Goo-Goo sat there, dressed as a nurse; for even in her blackest hour she could never resist the lure of an appropriate costume. However admirably a widow's weeds would have suited her — and it must be confessed that in idle and impersonal hours the image of herself floating ethereally in a cloud of black chiffon with those large eyes and a small black cap, had visited her — yet she was willing to forgo them for her husband's sake. But who knows (her mind took wings, without her wishing it) that she might not marry again? White chiffon suited her better than black; and another image would float through her imagination; large black eyes looking through a white veil, a cloud of white — rather as a mosquito tries to get through a mosquito-net. But the latter comparison did not suggest itself, and in any case she was willing to forgo all these things for her husband's sake. Yet as she sat there, waiting, waiting, everything seemed unreal, and she could not help wondering . . . was that really Richard, lying there, white and drawn, upon the bed?

Then one day, about four o'clock in the afternoon, he began to speak a little; he looked round, recognising pieces of furniture and pictures — but ones that were not in the room! Indeed, as far as Goo-Goo could remember, the things her husband saw and described had never been in any room he had occupied; in his talk, rather broken and rambling talk, he recalled incidents from the past — but was it the past of Lord Richard Cressey? As he grew stronger, he would tell the nurses of things that had happened to him at school . . . but when they told Goo-Goo of them, she was surprised to hear the name of the school, which was not the one at which he had been educated! Then, one day, the truth (or at any rate a very agitating inkling of it) began to dawn on her mind: for he asked her to fetch his mother and sister (the Duchess had been for many years in her coffin, and Lady Ethel was in South Africa), and added, as if each man was born into the world with several mothers and a variety of species of sisters, 'You know, either Mrs. Leviathan or Miss Isabel Parkinson'. Then, again, his mood would alter, and he would talk to Goo-Goo about herself, himself and their home, very rationally, very sensibly. When she mentioned these inconsistencies to Sir Vincent, the great doctor pronounced that they were nothing, and would pass away with the patient's gaining strength. — 'Growing pains, dear lady, growing pains! That's all. Don't worry yourself. Leave it all in my hands!'

But the periods of insensibility continued, and when he roused himself from them, it took a little time, apparently, for him to focus his mind. He looked up at his wife one morning and said, 'Goo-Goo, when is your husband coming to see us? . . . It's very kind of you looking after us, but I can't say that I think *he* behaved very well!' and then once more lapsed into oblivion, as his voice trailed off. What could it mean? In any case there could be little doubt that, as Barnacle put it, 'His Lordship didn't seem quite-himself-like'.

Convalescence was, to those by his side, an eternity. The fortnight was magnified into a hundred years. As the invalid's strength increased, his mind grew more logical; but, at the same time, his aberrations, though they occurred less often, were more concrete and tended to last over a longer period. For days he would be perfectly sure of himself, would talk to Goo-Goo about Little Titterham and how he longed to get back there. He seemed, even, to want to get back to his work at the Foreign Office. Then his wife would leave him, hoping he would sleep a little; but, when she returned, would find him quite different, wild-eyed, as if possessed, his bed littered with papers. His counterpane was so completely covered with these white drifts, that at the slightest movement there was a rattling and crinkling and falling as of autumn leaves. He had, evidently, got up (which he was forbidden to do), and had found these sheets, and a pencil as well! These various papers, none of them completed, were all addressed to the editor of *The Morning Echo*, and contained such matter as this that follows:

Lord Richard — Cuckoo writes to-day from Dodderingham Old Hall — is making a splendid recovery after his recent serious accident. Lady Richard — or Goo-Goo as she is to her friends — has borne the tragic events of the past three weeks with stoical fortitude, and looks sweetly pretty and piquante in the nurse's uniform which she has adopted for the occasion. With it she wears no jewellery except a large ruby and diamond swastika, once the property of the ill-fated Czarina of Russia, which was given her by her mother, Mrs. Guggerty — which reminds me, darlingest, how beautiful we all looked in nurses' uniforms in the last Great War! I sometimes wonder . . .

But the documents differed. One, at least, had an almost sinister tone:

From Dodderingham Old Hall, where she is the guest of Lady Septuagesima Goodley, or 'Mad Septua' as she is known universally to her friends — Grannie writes to me by today's post. Apparently Lady Richard — or Goo-Goo as she was to those who were her friends before she took to the water-whistle — has been pretending to nurse her unfortunate husband. It is to be supposed that she likes dressing-up, or perhaps she thinks that a nurse's uniform suits her. One can never tell these things oneself, can one, dearest? Her husband, naturally, is not progressing very fast; and his action in absorbing the two friends who were with him at the time of that fatal flight has, of course, created considerable and rather hostile comment. Lady Richard's common old mother . . .

And here, again, the manuscript, which did not even appear to be in her husband's writing, broke off. But poor Goo-Goo, on reading this brutal reference to herself, and still more, to her mother, fainted away.

Another document was yet harder to explain; it ran:

The funeral took place last Friday fortnight, at the Old Parish Church, Cambridge, of the mortal remains — or rather of such as had not been appropriated by Lord Richard Cressey — of Mr. Valentine Leviathan and Mr. Frederick Parkinson. These two brilliant men — now, alas! no more — were deservedly popular wherever they went, but among . . .

The queer thing was that, though Richard must have written this, he had never been informed either of the fate of his two friends, or the date and place of their burial!

Then there were also lying about several importantly written disquisitions, of unmistakable style, on the subject of the Détente Cordiale between France and England, and several letters to dim dwellers in the country, people of whom Goo-Goo had never heard. The letters appeared to be in two different hands, while the persons to whom these strange communications were directed were addressed in them as relatives: 'Dear Cousin Toto', 'Dear Uncle Harry' or 'Dearest Aunt Violet'. The signature on most of them was 'Your affectionate nephew' (or cousin) 'Freddie', though some were signed 'Valentine'.

As his vitality grew day by day, the patient's voice became more resonant. And in the middle hours of the night, when so fragile is the dark crystal bowl of silence that any vibration, scratching it ever so faintly, smashes it utterly, making an overwhelming din and clatter, the nurses would sometimes be woken by a roaring of empty, vacuous laughter. They would find Lord Richard sitting up in bed, telling himself fashionable little jokes or stories, or performing one of those hieratic mimickings which we have mentioned. There were questions and answering voices; it was as if a conversation were being carried on between two or three people. But the next morning he would remember nothing about it, and the doctor thought it better not to disturb the patient's equilibrium by asking him about it, or recalling it to his mind in any way.

Ignorant of his night's doings, he would be charming to Goo-Goo when she went in to see him, talking to her affectionately, discussing with her the many subjects that had interested them before his accident. Yet within a few seconds of her leaving him he would begin to act strangely again. He would examine his own looks and character with the nurses, acknowledging things about himself quite needlessly, things which it had not previously been his habit to confess — in fact, he would say such things about himself as were, in his world, usually a privilege confined to intimate friends. He would criticise and laugh at his personal appearance, he would deride his manner very frankly, and neutrally. And, more embarrassing still, he would make remarks about his wife that were as unnecessary as they were untrue.

Poor Goo-Goo, her mind almost unhinged by suffering, had retired to seek a temporary consolation by indulging her artistic and musical gifts (the latter ever so quietly), while upstairs, unbeknown to her, Lord Richard was denying her water-colours and anathematising the water-whistle.

On another night the nurses, hearing a sound coming from His Lordship's room, peeped through the door, having opened it soundlessly, and caught him examining the bedroom china, fingering the glaze, and murmuring soft 'Sung's, 'Ming's, 'Han's or 'Pu's to himself — almost, had they known it, in the manner of the late Mr. Frederick Parkinson.

The serious thing about these outbreaks was the fact that they were gradually beginning to impinge upon Lord Richard's consciousness. From being unconscious impulses, they were becoming conscious; and the effort to repress them was a constant strain upon the patient. He underwent, now, trials such as he had never known; he experienced the uncanny sensation that while being one ego, he was yet three people, the three separate branches of the same tree; worse than this, he was often affected with harassing doubts as to his own physical identity, or with even more puzzling convictions of it. In fact our three poor heroes, now surviving in one body, were soon unable to make up their minds which they were — or rather which he was. Richard, though he never openly confessed these uncertainties, became painfully, tragically depressed, or unnaturally hilarious. One day Goo-Goo caught him before a mirror, gazing into its watery depths. 'Funny thing,' he said, pointing to the birth-mark that she had noticed when he had been lying unconscious, 'curious, but I've got a birth-mark here! I'm sure it wasn't there before the accident, but I remember that Valentine had one like it!'

This was the nearest approach to the subject that he ever made. Nor did his realisation of these outbreaks, and of the need to repress them, prevent their recurrence, though he tried to control himself.

A very unfortunate incident took place on the occasion of Lady Septuagesima's first visit to him since his accident. She had been goodness itself; the whole house had been turned upside down on his behalf, and he was always telling Goo-Goo how grateful he was to his hostess, how he felt that such kindness could never be repaid. She swept into the room, neighing sweetly, a very tall and gracious presence, her red-gold mane floating, her large yellow skirt, like a crinoline, swaying a little, as she walked. Lord Richard at first thanked his cousin in the most heartfelt manner for saving his life, and talked to her rationally and intimately — for he was one of the few relatives with whom she had never quarrelled, had always been on terms of affection. Then, suddenly, she noticed an alteration in the expression of his eye, which seemed to become vaguer, bluer, yet more faded: the voice lost its warm tone and became, though the same voice, that of a stranger; he burst into rude, shuddering hoots of laughter, and said, talking obviously to himself, yet as if to a second person: 'Richard always liked her, I know. He used to say to me, "Poor old Septua's not a bad old thing really; she'd amuse you and she's very picturesque to look at!" But she looks to me just like a mad chestnut mare that's got entangled in one of Queen Elizabeth's old dresses!'

In a moment he was again transformed into himself, and Lady Septuagesima — though Tootsie remarked that she seemed rather 'upset' for the remainder of the day — maintained a discreet silence.

Soon Richard asked if he might be allowed to see other visitors. The doctor thought it would be a valuable discipline for him — as well as for his friends! Goo-Goo decided that Mattie was the best subject for a first experiment — bright but sympathetic, dependable and even-tempered. It was, therefore, arranged that he should come down. But he was only granted a half-hour's interview with the invalid, since it was still most important that the latter should not be fatigued. Richard remembered quite well dining with Mattie the night before his accident. He was full of questions about — and seemed to look forward to — the Pecksniff Prize, which would be the occasion of his first public appearance. They discussed books for a while: Mattie brought him down several new ones — a novel by Edward Shanks — the first that writer had published for six months — and a reprint of the earlier poems by the Earl of Chiswick. Richard was delighted with them. Then they reverted again to the dinner-party at Mattie's, and, this time with no change of expression, the invalid observed: 'I thought Richard so very pompous that evening. Of course I'm devoted to them both — though I know they're pretentious — but I think Goo-Goo's the better of the two as long as she doesn't let herself go on that sanguinary water-whistle. But what a pity it is that they neither of them know anything!' Poor Mattie wriggled, winced, wavered and twittered, and by the time he had managed to produce his voice, Richard had gone back to the more usual incarnation of himself, appearing, luckily for Mattie's peace of mind, to be quite unaware of his words a few seconds before. As Mattie left the room Richard was leaning back; his vague eyes were looking upward and away from his moustache, which was drooping down and under. It was curious how alike those three had been, but till now Mattie had never noticed it!

Goo-Goo talked to her guest, and to a certain extent confided in him. As far as she knew, Richard had not displayed any symptoms of aberration for a fortnight; while Mattie, for his part, was still far too taken aback to recount his recent experience. He urged her, nevertheless, to let Richard fulfil his engagement at the Skimpole Hall in a month's time. It would dispose of rumours. He need not be on the platform long enough to tire himself. The others could make the speeches, while he could just give the prize away. And what a wonderful reception he'd get! Incidentally, from the prize-winner's point of view, it would be an excellent thing; Richard's first appearance since his accident would lend an added interest to the proceedings and ensure a full hall, since, besides all his friends who would wish to be there to welcome him, many people who would not otherwise go to such a function would come to this one out of curiosity — for a man who has met with an accident will always receive both more attention and more sympathy than a poet! One has only to notice the relative density of the crowd that collects round an overturned hand-barrow, and the one that surrounds a poet declaiming his verse in public, to observe that! Besides, Richard was much looking forward to giving away the prize, while both Sir Vincent McNabb and his own doctor admitted that there could be no harm in it.

As Mattie went back to Cambridge he reflected how strange it was that he had never remarked the likeness before . . . Valentine . . . Richard . . . Freddie . . . He supposed that there had always, yes, he was sure that there had always, been a look . . .

PART III

The hall seemed to be filling quite satisfactorily. Not that there was as yet anyone in it, but peeping out from a little punch-and-judy window at the far side of the darkened stage, Mattie could distinguish, beyond the open doors, the shifting white lights (for outside it was a fine summer day) that fell between the flower-like shadows of the assembling audience.

These shadows on the floor were agitated as if by some wind, while an insect-like chirping, chattering and chirruping was borne into the sombre hall, as though this were a Southern night, where the cicadas were so insistent in their crinkling, castanetted music that the lolling stalk of every sun-weary flower, the cool glazed leaves of every cone-shaped magnolia-tree, rattled and sang together. Out of this general seething and murmur it would be difficult to disentangle a particular tune; yet occasionally an individual insect voice shrilled loud enough to be heard above its comrades. Thus, too, out of the voices beyond the door, from this distance alike as grains of sand rolled round by an eddy of wind, a particular tone, however infrequently, was sometimes recognisable. For instance Mattie was able to identify that plaintive yet playful neighing as Septua's property.

A few single figures were now making their appearance in the hall — men, nearly all of them, and each obviously a lonely, mocking genius, betraying the stigmata of the consciously inspired and persecuted — overcoats on this hot day, mop, bobbed or pudding-basin hair, pince-nez that made the eyes prominent as those of prawns, or owl-like tortoise-shell circles, open collars and vague distinguished looks, a few beards and solitary misunderstood voices. In fact they were all remarkably alike — more especially in the persistence with which each protested his dissimilarity from his neighbour. After glowering furiously, but wonderingly, at each other, they sat down in a very determined manner, as if once more publishing their resolution to Make No Compromise with the Public Taste. Then opening their eyes rounder and wider, they gazed through, right through, poor Mattie, as if, by reason of some inner revelation, they were able to use him as a telescopic lens through which to examine some bewilderingly interesting object beyond.

Poor Mattie was already beginning to feel very ill at ease, when the timely arrival of his Chairman, Professor James Criscross, completed his discomfiture. The Professor's face was feline — more feline than Mattie's — but his heavy, greying, downtrodden-looking moustache showed, as well, a certain canine sympathy. A very old dog, he seemed, with a cat's soul, and a cat's stealthy gait and claws. His smile of exquisite malevolence, as he came forward, was an index of his intention, which was, now as always, to throw down, by a form of mental and verbal ju-jitsu of which he alone held the secret, anybody with whom he shook hands. In this drawing-room-sport he displayed an ingenuity and agility completely out of keeping with his years. Mattie went down at his first clutch.

As the beloved author of *From a Library Stool* and a million critical articles advanced across the stage, he looked round constantly, as if both expecting a welcome and fearing an ambush. Next, he allowed the smile to fade out of his face, as though the hall were a large railway station at which he had just arrived, where he was to have been met by some dear friends, but, on looking round, had this moment discovered the long draughty platform to be bare and desolate, with only a plaintive clanging of milk-tins for his comfort. Finally, he arrived in front of Mattie, looked at him fixedly for some seconds, without the faintest glint of recognition in his cat-green eye, then gave an almost too realistic jump, and treated him to an affectionate pat on the shoulder.

These paraphernalia were but the stage-properties which the Professor had, through a long course of years, constructed for himself, without which he never ventured out of his own house — stage-properties at once the disguise and weapon, the cloak and sword, of a curious and intricate terrorism. The method of it was very personal. Certainly he was old, aged indeed, but not so old as he pretended. His vagueness, and the senility which excused it, were in reality part of that armour he had evolved for himself, while from under its protective shelter he aimed his cruellest and most deadly shafts. Thus he made it his rule at first not to recognise his friends, and then, when recognised, to call them by some unfamiliar and unwelcome variant or, if possible, variants of their name. This subdued their spirits at the start; and he would follow up his preliminary advantage by inquiring, in a voice that was painfully sympathetic, after some ailment which was altogether confined to his imagination, some illness from which they had never suffered or even claimed to suffer, talking about it as if it were a permanent disability with which they were well known to be afflicted. This should, if the victim were an instrument sufficiently sensitive, worthy of the Professor's virtuosity, crush resistance and make the rest easy. For example, Mattie was called Mattie. Anyone who knew him well enough to call him by name at all, called him Mattie — and nothing else. Further, he was very timid; while the only peculiarity about him, of which naturally any mention would make him additionally nervous, was that high, jumpy little voice. Professor Criscross began, therefore, by saying to him:

'I'm so sorry, Mark, that I did not at first recognize you; but being so short-sighted and old (too old, too old, my dear Matt*hew*) I mistook you, until I saw your face more clearly, for one of your own geniuses — not one of whom, I may say, is familiar to *me*!' And then, beaming over his gold spectacles, added, before Mattie had time to answer: 'And, poor Mat, how is that tiresome sore throat of yours that gives you so much trouble?'

It was hopeless for Mattie to attempt battle. The only gap in the Professor's armour was an intense snobbery; but, at the moment, there was no title available with which to hit him over the head and temporarily stun him.

The gloomy geniuses, in their seats apart from one another, had watched the encounter with intense relish, and it was all very annoying. The Professor was just about to start a new skirmish, when the other chief speaker of the afternoon, Mr. Ernest Lympe, the well-known critic and man-of-letters, arrived on the stage. The long thin body, shaped like a capital S reflected in a mirror, was surmounted by a small head and a face that was brave, and consciously noble in the extreme. A grey kiss-curl floated down over the upright forehead; and he had a smile, grave yet excruciatingly sweet, that at the same time understood and pardoned everything. In fact he looked like a missionary who had taken the wrong turning and become a writer — which is exactly what had happened. His father was a little-known but decorative clergyman of the Church of England, and enemies cite the son's continually appearing volumes of bright leading-articles — which on their appearance in book-form are immediately converted by the other critic of the very paper in which they had been served up daily into 'Mr. Lympe's brilliant book of essays' (a miracle as great as that other transmutation of water into wine) — as the final, undeniable argument in favour of priestly celibacy. Poor Mr. Lympe was terrified of only one man in the world — and that man was Professor Criscross! He dared not try to oust him for, in this era of grafting, the Professor would have a century in which to revenge himself — which, noticing what he could do in this way during a few seconds, was a formidable thought. Besides, Mr. Lympe's façade of knowledge was an eighteenth-century library door on which are presented in counterfeit the bindings of many rare books. And the Professor, who had at any rate read very many more books than he could understand, had detected, but not yet published, this fraud. Hence poor Mr. Lympe's abject terror.

Leaving the latter gentleman with no straw to catch at, Mattie walked away to meet Lord Richard Cressey, who looked quite well now, in spite of that air of distinction so often bestowed by the winnowing fire of a long illness. On seeing him, the Professor stopped his little games, and became, this time genuinely, solicitous about his health. Mattie thought — and the other two agreed with him — that it would be better for Lord Richard to wait in the small room at the back of the stage until it was time for him to make the presentation. It wouldn't fatigue him to the same extent; while, too, it would be a very dramatic appearance, just giving that necessary touch to the whole proceedings. As they came on to the stage, Lady Richard's voice could be heard outside the door, coming nearer; and then the insect-like chirruping and drone invaded the room all at once, pouring in at the door, giving the room a life of its own, till the lifeless void that it had been began to throb and stir. The light, giving a radiance to the hall without being visible, was turned on, and the drone increased its volume, as if the sun had risen and drawn out the winged creatures from their hiding-places. After infinite hoverings, whisperings, and rustlings, the audience settled; only a few remained standing. Heads would nod together and sigh in rippling waves, as if the wind were breathing down a cornfield, tossing the golden heads together. There would be a silence, and then a sudden movement in one patch of the audience, as though some animal, that had been sleeping among the golden stalks, had stirred and woken. There was, for such a gathering, an unusual air of excitement. These things are hard to explain, and the reason may have been merely that the fine day of early summer outside was sufficient to stir the blood, however wooden, of any audience. Mattie could recognise a great many of his friends, but from where he was seated it was difficult to see 'who everybody was'. Whether it was the light, or this year's fashions, he couldn't make out; but somehow or other from this distance everybody looked the same, shadowy and indistinct. It was very good of so many of his friends to support him, for Mattie could not help regarding it — except when he caught the gold-rimmed eye of Professor Criscross — as rather 'his show'. Over in one corner he observed the familiar grimace, bull-dog and triumphant, of one of his favourite bellicose filibusterers and 'Shall We, I say, yield to the Menace of Armed Might?' rang in his head like the latest successful musical-comedy number. Beyond, in an almost royal seclusion, sat those two rival Trustees of the Nation — Lord FitzBison and the Duke of Badgery St. Lawrence. Wonderful old man, that! So small, and yet so dignified with his aquiline, rather curling profile, and little bunches of yellowy-white ringlets beneath each ear. Poor Goo-Goo, he thought, looked rather worried. She must have spent a very trying two months: still, *he* looked much better today. With her was Baroness d'Arenheimer, with Angel and Desirée, looking very Spanish, he thought — gipsy-like, almost! Sir Booster's voice was also to be heard in the land: how odd it was, that habit of his of speaking so loudly; but then, like many other remarkable men, he was completely unself-conscious! As he spoke you could almost hear the rolling 'r's' gathering moss as they rolled; the guttural, agglutinous sound of his voice, like the speech of the ghost for ever imprisoned within an American soda-fountain, could be heard all over the hall; and his genial smile was spotted on everyone in turn, like a limelight, with an orange-slide over it, at a theatre. Able and philanthropic, as he was, Nature, Mattie reflected, had yet hardly treated him as he deserved; and surely it was a mistake on the part of the Press Barons always to put up Sir Booster to lead the attack on Socialism, the defence of Capitalism, when, to anyone ignorant of the sterling qualities of this Persian Philanthropist, his personal appearance must seem ultimately the complete refutation of the very arguments he was advancing. Lady Babboon was with him, looking very young, rather wan and blanched — a little bleached, even, Mattie thought. The strabismal glance of her eyes, when she smiled, was so attractive — a slight cast often helps a face. Behind her he noticed Eddy Tush with Selly Moonbury, and

Ned, looking rather like a seal out of water, with a large party of overfed, under-bred friends, youthful revue-writers and elderly stage beauties; the latter looking, under this artificial light, very young and exactly like both each other and everyone else. Many of the shadows were so animated that Mattie could not see who they were. And all those mirrors at the back of the hall helped to muddle one, making a stage-army, reflecting the same people, giving the reflections a certain life. Rustlings and whisperings still ran through the audience as the shadows of leaves move on the ground when a slight wind plays above. Meanwhile Mattie, up on the platform, was communicating with his friends in his own way, shaping sentences at them with his mouth, letting his eye-glass fall or loop-the-loop on its black string, or making daft little beckonings and esoteric signals. Twined in among his gaily coloured friends, like a dead branch in a rosebush, he noticed two strings of black. One in the fourth row, one at the back of the hall. Gazing intently through his monocle, he recognised the nearest string. It was the Leviathan family! He jumped down at once to speak to Mrs. Pulborough, Valentine's aunt. Yes, she said, they had come to welcome poor Lord Richard, who had been in that terrible accident with her nephew. Oh, yes, a dreadful affair! Besides, though she had little time for it, she had always been very much interested in poetry — it was that lovely line . . . for the instant she couldn't remember who'd written it, 'A thing of thingamajig is a what-d'you-call-it for ever' — lovely. Oh, yes, Keats, wasn't it? And then, what she really liked was originality; and she was told that Mr. Rosenheimer was so original, wasn't he? Perhaps dear Mr. Dean would bring him up to her afterwards, and introduce him . . . but Mattie had at this moment to get back on to the platform, as the Professor was beginning to get restive. Gripping his monocle with Chinese eyebrow, Mattie peered over the heads of his friends at the other black line. That tall ebony regiment of women seemed familiar . . . of whom did they remind him? Richard? . . . there was a look, too, of Valentine. . . . No, no, of course, it was Freddie Parkinson! They must be poor Freddie's relatives, but how many there were of them, and how few of them had he ever mentioned! Obviously, then, they had come up to London for the same reason as Mrs. Pulborough and the others. It was really very nice of them.

The ceremony began. It was Mattie's duty to make a small preliminary speech of introduction. Coming forward, Mattie spurted his jets of sound up into the air in such a manner that only a few truncated sentences were audible. '. . . and gentlemen . . . not going to speak . . . only to tell you . . . that Professor Criscross (hear, hear) . . . in the chair, I need say no more to introduce . . . so deservedly beloved . . . in literary circles . . . Lympe . . . later.' . . . Then, following a few remarks, quite impossible to hear, about literature in general, Mr. Dean sat down.

The Professor, with a really intimidating glance of dislike and disgust toward the audience — a glance much enhanced by an evidently false look of nervousness — then formally took the chair. The audience, quite unafraid, fluttered and preened itself to silence, like a bird alighting on a branch. This stillness, gradually making itself felt, welling up from them, was only broken by the voice of a gloomy genius at the front of the gallery, who was blowing his sentiments up into the air, like a whale spouting water. After rising some distance in the air, they fell back on the audience and the platform. 'Simply doesn't count, you know', he was saying in a painfully level voice. 'Afraid Leonardo doesn't interest me at all: just l'Art Pompier: has nothing to tell me . . .' The Professor looked up over his gold rims, as if ready to spring at this intrepid sparrow — and the consequential voice died suddenly in a violent spasm.

This afternoon the cat had the upper hand of the dog. The Professor looked the sublimation of smiling felinity — as much at home in the Chair as the Cheshire Cat in his tree, purring already, as if stroked by the public applause. Mattie had twisted into the seat on his left, and was trying to look as if he wasn't on a platform at all. Mr. Lympe had, like a serpent, coiled himself into the seat on the right. The prize-winner, looking prosperous and curly, sat at the corner of the gangway below, ready to scramble up the side and receive his cheque. If he climbed up, instead of walking round, it would look more boyish and unconventional. Besides, they must all know that he was an athlete. Still, Jacques Rosenheimer could not help feeling that he was not quite the hero he had expected to be on this occasion. The Professor looked down at him for a moment, as if intimating that he would settle him after he had finished with the rest of them. As the speeches proceeded poor Jacques felt, indeed, less and less as if he were there at all. For whereas the prize-giver, the judges, the speakers, the person who presented the prize, were all made much of, the name of the prize-winner scarcely occurred. Mattie had lisped the learning of Professor Criscross, and piped the virtues of Mr. Lympe. The Professor, after his own fashion, paid a few cat-and-mouse compliments to Mattie, dealt a few more to Mr. Lympe, spoke of the prize, the history of it, dwelt a little on his own life, and wound up with a warm tribute to Lord Richard Cressey. The amiable and brave Mr. Lympe, next, sang loudly the attainments, virtues and popularity of Professor Criscross, presented a verbal bouquet to poor Mattie, a verbal palm-leaf to Lord Richard. He then very nobly denied his own merits. But not one of the speakers appeared to be aware of the existence, even, of the prize-winner, Mr. Jacques Rosenheimer.

'Ladies and Gentlemen,' the Chairman began with a literary clearing of the throat, 'I had come here with a few suitable platitudes prepared; but, sure enough, Mr. Dean has already delivered most of them to you, and the rest of them I shall leave for Mr. Lympe. I must, therefore, confine myself to a few historical remarks. It is but thirty years since the first award of the Pecksniff Prize took place at this hall. And I think that, if we examine the Roll of Winners, we shall feel that it is one that reflects credit on the judges, and on the late Sir Champion Pecksniff, who instituted this annual award. We do not, perhaps, find on it any names famous in poetry; yet we do undoubtedly find the names of many distinguished critics and men of letters. Mr. Lympe (with a bow) was one of the earliest prize-winners, with that charming if slender little volume of poetry which first established him in the hearts of all book-lovers, and endeared him to all those whose soul is with the birds, out in the fields — I refer to *Crowsfeet*.' (Applause.) The Professor's expression had relaxed, for his intention was to charm and captivate. But now his face assumed a more stern expression as he said: 'The Pecksniff has never, I think, stood for mere eccentricity or contortion. It has never — and I think you will agree with me, Ladies and Gentlemen, that it has *rightly* never — been associated with the names of those young men and, I regret to say, young women as well, who believe that to stand on their heads is the only duty of the modern poet. On the contrary, from its inception it has been connected with those poets of good heart and upright living, who sing, dulcetly as ever, of English countryside and of those wild creatures that move through it — those poets, modern in the best sense, who are inspired by the sweet English sentiment so well summed up by a predecessor in that exquisite line, 'Llewdly sing Cuccu'. (Rustlings, cheers and cries of 'Oh, how sweet!' 'Oh, how pretty!' and 'Isn't it like him?' from those admirers in the audience who are under the impression that the Professor himself has written the line.)

'It is, perhaps, not yet the moment for me to disclose the name of the winner of the prize, for we are concerned' (with a look of mingled hatred and contempt at poor Jacques Rosenheimer) 'not with the man, but with those principles which, *however unworthily*, he represents. Nor need we discuss my two fellow-judges — or should I say *conspirators*?' (mischievous glance through gold rims, and delighted cooings from audience) '— Mr. Dean and Mr. Lympe! — they are too well known to you for any word of mine to help them — but we shall, I am sure, all of us, be particularly delighted to welcome in a few minutes' time on this platform, the Prize-Giver — Lord Richard Cressey!' (Here the Professor's too genuine, sincere and perhaps not un-English affections — one for a title, the other for an amateur — the force of which is quadrupled by the combination of the two — nearly overcame him. He sips the names, turning them on his tongue as if he were going to pronounce upon the merits of some rare vintage wine — 'generous, fruity, full-bodied'. Tears appear about to spout from his eyes, as from the eyes of those lachrymose loyalists who, when a military band passes, rush from bar-parlour into the street. 'Not only shall we greet him warmly this afternoon because it is his first public appearance since the terrible and painful ordeal through which he has passed; we shall welcome him, also, as one who has already made for himself a name in those worlds of diplomacy and literature to which it has pleased God to call him.' (The Professor's voice took on the lyric note.) 'We owe to Lord Richard — I say it with no fear of contradiction — the solution of that recent crisis between the Yugo-Slovaks and the Jingo-Slavs, which, because Englishmen still believe that right is stronger than might, he had himself done so much to create and foment. But the strong know when to give way; and by a graceful diplomatic gesture, which consisted in losing all the papers concerned with the matter, he was able to solve the very difficulties which he had himself designed. But we have in him also an author and poet of considerable distinction. Those of us, and I hope we are many, who had enjoyed reading *The Buzzard's Bastard*, have found in it an unaffected simplicity, moral purpose and genuine strength, for which we have to search in vain through the pages of even the strongest lady-novelist — while to many of us, and to me amongst others, *From a Yashmak Garden* brought a new revelation of beauty.' . . . After this the speech trailed off into a series of compliments, interspersed with a great many pin-pricks, for Mattie and Mr. Lympe. As each bouquet was handed to them, a pin, hidden among the stalks of the flowers, drew blood.

The Chairman sat down, amid considerable applause, and soprano but muffled cries of '*Isn't* Mr. Criscross wonderful?' then stood up again, and, as if looking for something he had lost, called on Mr. Ernest Lympe to address the gathering.

The latter gentleman uncoiled himself from his chair, and, tossing the careless kiss-curl back from his forehead, proceeded to say a few words about Professor Criscross, who watched him as if willing to play cat-and-mouse again for a minute or two. But, at the lightest sound of insubordination! . . . Mr. Lympe, however, was far too frightened to make any attempt at retaliation.

'It is a great pleasure to mey', he said, 'to be on the same platform this afternoon with one who may well be termed the Grand Old Man of Literature. Eminent as is our friend in the Chair, busy as he is, he yet still finds time to come down here among us and encourage the young. Ai will not speak to you about the praize-winner; but Ai should like to be allowed to speak a few words about Professor Criscross. A famous poet, distinguished as a Munofletters even above his contemporaries, one whose learning and whose delicate malice has long endeared him to us' (Professor looks pleased, loud applause and stifled cries of 'Isn't he delicious?') 'in the pages . . .' And the speech rambled on for another five minutes.

The Chairman stood up again and gazed, almost benignantly

for him, at the audience, now thoroughly settled in their stalls, and with a tone of rapture in his voice, called on *Lord* . . . Richard Cressey . . . to come forward and present the prize.

Little eddies of curiosity and interest passed through the audience, rustlings of heads like branches swept by the wind, as the tall, spare form of Lord Richard stepped forward across the stage. Applause started with an unexpectedly loud smacking rattle of hands clapped together — surprisingly loud; yet, while continually increasing in volume, the character of the welcome appeared gradually to change. It seemed as if little sighs, sobs, cries and exclamations were mixed up with, and covered by, the volume of sound. The Chairman looked startled and, standing up, gazed toward the back of the hall. Perhaps someone was unwell. The noise was swelling, rising crescendo like the solemn roar of an organ when first its spray breaks against the stone walls. The noise was swelling, increasing in volume; a clamour, as when some sudden hit at a cricket match, sudden goal at a cup-tie, or sudden dagger at a bull-fight, rips open the chests of those watching and lays bare their pulsing hearts. The Chairman looked taken aback, this time really old and vague. The applause, ever louder, had yet altered its kind. The change was gradual in a sense, yet very swift. The cries were rising, coming to the top. People stood up on their chairs to see they knew not what, and the very action of standing, peering, increased the expectation and excitement. The cries were rising in it, but feet as well as cries sounded in the tumult and there was movement. The clamorous confusion increased: like a cuttle-fish it seemed both to discharge a cloud of blackness under which it could hide, and then, octopus-like, to stretch long tentacles toward the stage. A tall black line, noticeable among the colourful, fluttering audience, surged from the back of the hall, and rushed up the gangway, waving hands and black parasols, shouting 'Freddie! . . . Freddie! . . . it is Freddie!' . . . Louder and indescribable grew the commotion, fiercer the excitement. The audience were all standing, moving, waving, watching. The Professor's dog-like reproofs could scarce be heard through the uproar, though occasionally an angry barking sound would be audible through the other noises from the platform. Goo-Goo's convulsive calf-sobbing sounded in the air like the gurgling of a fountain. But little attention was paid to these minor manifestations, for another, nearer, black line advanced, waving and shouting, 'Valentine! . . . Valentine! . . . It is Valentine!' . . . and closed round the platform which was attacked, stormed, lost in a dark, dancing, whirling cloud of revolving black arms and parasols. Out of it came the far-carrying suctional clucking of kisses, as a hundred unknown relatives embraced Lord Richard and claimed him as their own. Excitement had spread to the gallery, where could be heard, winging up above, the tired, fluttering, bumping cries — like a bird bumping against the ceiling — of poor Mattie lost and bewildered; cries like those of a bird that is trying to escape from a room into which it has flown blindly. Lord Richard's head could still be seen, as he stood encircled by his smaller relatives, the point of the swarming, the centre round which the whirlwind spun its course, distracted, almost hypnotised by the sudden roarings; distracted, pulled, tugged; his clothes hanging in shreds and blown up, as if by winds, with all this fury of sound and movement. A machine working on three gears, slipping back from one to another continually . . . Richard . . . Freddie . . . Valentine . . . Freddie . . . Richard . . . Valentine . . . Valentine . . . Freddie . . . Richard . . . Three tunes that were continually being broken and resumed . . . forty-seven . . . thirty-seven . . . twenty-seven . . . thirty-seven . . . forty-seven . . . twenty-seven . . . ten years older . . . ten years younger . . . Yes, he was Valentine . . . he was Freddie . . . he was Richard. Yes, yes, he was, he confessed. He was. Rival parties of relatives were appealing to the audience to bear witness to this birth-mark and to that, through the gaps torn in his clothing . . . Yes. He was. . . . The audience began to take sides; and, at the same time, the hysteria was mounting. The confession of his triple yet single identity completed the work. Everyone in the hall was laughing, crying and sobbing. No one remembered why he was there, why she was there, or what had happened — for the great truth had dawned on them! The hysteria passed in waves through the assembled shadows. A few minutes before they had been quiet and peaceful, cultivating this smile, that gesture, this voice, that look of the eyes, forming fresh reflections of the same thing, revealing endless vistas and avenues of repetition. But the truth had now dawned on them, and was animating them with a false vitality; like a current of electricity it made these corpses twitch and caper, shudder and jig. With this scene of riotous confusion can only be compared one of those outbreaks of epidemic dancing-mania that seized on Greece and southern Italy in the Middle Ages, when those infected danced on, whirling and shrieking, in the market-place, till they died. Everyone was shouting, waving, gesticulating, dancing, even. Some saw the tall ghost of Freddie, others the spectre of Valentine, standing, like the angels of Mons, beside their spiritual brother on the stage. The mob surged round the platform, hats lay like trampled flowers, crushed under the triumphant progress of a Bacchanalian rout. Veils were torn, clothes were ripped and dragged, faces were like large poppies, red and angry, or excited and pleased. A few held out, a few isolated towers, like the towers of the nobles in the Middle Ages. Lady Septuagesima could be heard telling the wife of a bishop that she was not her, and never had been. What is more, she did not intend to be! For the confession of identity was spreading, as the figure on the platform confessed he was Freddie, he was Freddie . . . he was Richard . . . he was Valentine. Yes, he was. He was Valentine. He was Freddie. He was Richard. As if the atom had been exploded, and all the atoms had broken with it, confessions were hurled up into the air, shouted and boasted. The whole miniature world of the hall confessed too. He confessed, and the world with him. At last they realised that they belonged, one to another. The tumult was now indescribable. Handkerchiefs and hands were waving through the air of the hall with one movement, as at an arena during a bull-fight. This one was the same as that; I am as the same as you: only shadows are real in this world of shadows.

. . . . .

The starched exterior of Bond Street quieted them. What had happened? It had been enjoyable, very enjoyable, but what had taken place?

'All the same,' said the venerable Duke of Badgery St. Lawrence, as he tried to bang out with his fist a dent acquired somehow in his top-hat, 'all the same' — this to Lord FitzBison, his powerful and formidable political rival — 'I don't believe there's much difference between us!'

IDYLL THROUGH THE LOOKING-GLASS

'THE service in this hotel is shocking, very bad indeed', the Count pronounced. . . . At this point, as though the remark were in some way connected with what he was doing or, further, had served to evoke his action, he rose from his chair to regard his image in the mirror opposite, first examining minutely eyes and mouth and nose, the innumerable connecting lines incised by laughter or anxiety, and then, sprucing himself, fingered his tie and touched the grey hair on his temples.

Startled at such an irrational outburst — as it appeared — of personal vanity, I, too, considered the features and the rather small figure reflected in the tall glass. . . . At any rate, he should be easy to recognise, I decided; except, of course, that he must have presented a very different aspect as a young man.

But then, somehow or other I had never thought of Count Dragone di Dragora as a young man. . . . Ever since I could remember him — and that was now for some thirty and more years — he had looked the same, as though he had triumphantly defeated time by outliving it. . . . Not that he was old, any more than that — so it had seemed to us as children — he could ever have been young: he must have been born thus, found inside a cabbage, dressed in a frock-coat and high collar, and top-hat. And in my mind this diplomat, with, despite a rather tropical air, his Edwardian suavity and gloss, had been posed, always, against the contemporary London background of Grosvenor Square, hansom cabs — those equipages as frail and delicately balanced as the shell of Venus — and rooms full of palm trees and royal photographs in silver frames; so that it was with difficulty that I had accustomed myself to the idea that his proper setting had been one of prickly pears striking their attitudes from tufa rocks, or orange trees and lemon groves, and the smoke-tufted summit of a volcano. (Indeed, it must have been inside a cactus, rather than a cabbage, that he would have been found as a baby, according to the innocent deceptions of his period.)

All this had naturally lain beyond my vision, as a child of seven, but, nevertheless, in his English surroundings he had been able to exercise upon my mind a very special fascination, an exotic charm such as would have attached to a Zulu chieftain or Red Indian brave; and, since Italians are invariably fond of children, we soon became most intimate friends. . . . How clearly I can see him, as he was then, when he came to stay with my parents in the country; moving among the croquet hoops in the summer, in white flannels with a thin black stripe, and a panama hat; in the winter, for shooting parties, dressed in the most elaborate check creations — English 'sporting' clothes dramatised by a rich southern imagination, so that, on him, these garments were in no way ostentatious, matched his style, in the same manner that the mandolin-like twang of his accent in French and English — both of which languages he talked fluently and well — suited his speech. However, to one of my years he had seemed vastly, immensely old, and, because we were such good friends, I have little doubt that I must often have told him so.

Of course, as I now rather covertly considered his reflection, I could see that he did look, after all, a little older; the lines were still more numerous than I remembered, and the frizzled hair, grown grey, made his skin of an even darker tint than formerly. . . . His whole appearance proved his descent as plainly as did his choice of clothes and personal adjuncts: for he was head of a famous Neapolitan family and possessed his share of Spanish and Sicilian, and so of Arab or Saracen, blood. The whites of his eyes betrayed a curious dark, shadowy glitter, and his skin was very thick and yellow, like that of tough-hided, tropical fruit. Moreover, a southern love of jewellery showed itself in rings and tie-pins which would have pleased the Gabriele D'Annunzio of pre-1914 days. . . . Never before had I tried to picture him as a young man, and it had been a surprise to me to be told, a year or so previously, when the conversation had turned on the Dragon, as we affectionately called him, that, as a boy, he had been very good-looking, in the flowery, volcanic fashion of his neighbourhood. Nor had I realised, until I learnt it at the same time — for he always seemed, when I knew him, to have been destined for a bachelor existence, and the love-affairs in which he had been engaged (and to which, as I grew older, he made frequent allusion), had been those, plainly, of a very matter-of-fact, Edwardian order — that as a young man he had been of an intensely passionate and romantic nature, suffering deeply, continually threatening to emigrate, or to shoot or drown himself. It was as though, in his soul, the tender and amorous airs of the Italian seventeenth- and eighteenth-century composers had yielded to the rather sodden harmonies and tunes of Puccini, as though the scents of bath salts and pomade had replaced the odours of jasmine and orange blossoms in which he had spent his youth. Of his sufferings and passions, nothing was left but an immense tolerance for the weaknesses of others, and an intelligence which was intuitive rather than intellectual. But intelligent he certainly was, well read in several languages, and with a fine taste in many directions: but all this he subordinated to life; his sole aim, perhaps, being to curb his sensitiveness, and so his powers of suffering, and only to make use of it sufficiently to enable him to obtain the most enjoyment out of existence.

Even after the Count had left the Embassy, he had always spent part of the year in London, as well as a month or two in Paris, Vienna and Rome. Friends welcomed him in every capital, for he was cosmopolitan in the mode of the day; European, more than purely Italian. And the reason for this, it may be, was principally that as a young man he had developed (if we may suppose a thing, so common today, to have, equally, existed then) an 'inferiority complex'; because, if in those times an Italian hailed from any part of the country south of Rome, he experienced certain disadvantages, even apart from the main one, that, in addition, he would certainly be poorer than someone from the north of similar origin and situation. Moreover Count Dragone could remember better times, could just recall the old kingdom of the Two Sicilies and its decaying court, the disintegrating splendours of Caserta and of the capital itself: for he had been six or seven years of age when the insurgent troops had invaded Naples, and had finally driven the King and Queen to Gaeta, where they had endured a long siege, and then to exile; an exile which the Count's father, as Chamberlain of the Court, had shared until his death a year or so later.

A fate similar to that which overtook the rich families of the Southern States of America after the Civil War had now fallen to the lot of many of the noble houses of Naples, and specially of Sicily. Some became destitute and disappeared entirely, while the palaces, even of those who survived, lay empty. The long vistas of rooms, with their pillared, marble-panelled walls and mirrored ceilings, their periwigged busts of ancestors, the gardens, with their parterres and gesticulating statues, stood deserted through the long, burning summer days; while the cactuses and circles of prickly pears grew more thickly and violently round them, as though to hide their present void of humanity with an African pullulation of green life. . . . But the Dragone family had been more fortunate than many of their friends and relatives, and the Count seemed rich in a modest fashion, though — or, perhaps, because — he had never yet inhabited, since he came of age, any of his ten palaces that, now largely unfurnished, were scattered over the country from Naples to Syracuse, far across the Straits.

As a boy, he had lived with his mother, the old Contessa, in the smallest of his houses, situated at Sorrento: a little rococo pavilion, very elegant and old-fashioned, full of mirrors and tortoise-shell cabinets, with twisted tortoise-shell pillars crowned by little golden capitals, and of gilded chairs and Neapolitan pictures of the same epoch, displaying chiaroscuro processions of camels and turbaned drivers winding under palm trees, and many Madonnas melting into clouds. But, since I had known him, he had never until now visited any of his ancestral estates, had never ventured farther south than Rome, as though, indeed, he had feared that, were he to do so, the past would steal back upon him to his disadvantage. . . . When the 1914 war had come, however, he had returned to Italy, to make it his home. We heard that he had been working in some capacity for the Italian Government, and had settled in the capital, but otherwise we had, during that period, lost touch with him completely; as, indeed, with all our other Continental friends.

It was not, then, until a year or two after the war that I saw our dear 'Dragon' again, meeting him thus by chance one afternoon at Sorrento. . . . I supposed he was about sixty: the mirror did not really, to my mind, register much change in him, apart from the details I have noted. He had seemed pleased to see me, if only, it may be, because of many visits, many years spent in England in younger and happier days, and overwhelmed me with questions concerning his friends. In return, he told me that he had been living here, in this hotel, for a whole year; during which time (for he was a sybarite by nature — as, indeed, he should be, since the site of Sybaris itself was in his possession and had for centuries belonged to his family) his own little palace was being prepared for him. Bathrooms and heating and electric light were being installed, carpets were being introduced upon the bare *terrazza* floors, and the furniture was being thinned out, and rearranged in a more modern mode. (I thought these last improvements sounded a mistake, but I was careful not to say so.) The workmen had taken six months longer than they had estimated already, and the alterations, apparently, were by no means as yet completed. . . . But he loved his house, he said, and would be quite happy there, would never want to go abroad again, even if he had been able to afford it . . . but think of the exchange!

'I never thought to return to Sorrento,' the Count explained (how often have I wished that I could reproduce his voice, how much I long now to be able to treat his Italian accent phonetically, but these are tasks too complicated and beyond my powers), 'but I am getting an old man — yes, I am, my dear boy, you know I am: I saw you examining me just now in the mirror. . . . Don't make excuses: it's quite natural when we haven't met for years — and in the end something drew me home. Do you know, it was over forty years since I had been here? I was nineteen when I left, and very different from what I now am. . . . Sorrento, too, how different it was! a joy to visit, for there was nothing like it in all Italy. You should have seen the lovely English carriages driving down the little Corso here, every bit as good as Naples itself, with smart English coachmen in capes and with cockades in their top-hats, and horses and equipages all shining and varnished. . . . And even this hotel, in which we are talking (though I seem to be doing most of it!), was, though smaller, infinitely more agreeable, always full — and full of people the like of whom you do not see here now; people from England and France and Austria and Russia — and from America. . . . For those were the days when American girls were beginning to take Europe by storm, and they were lovely, *lovely*, with their beautiful neat hands and wrists and feet, and their odd little voices and use of words. . . . There was something very strange about them to us Europeans: they showed such an unusual combination of boldness and prudery, of sophistication and naïveté. And such beautiful clothes; for they bought them in Paris, when English and Russian and Italian girls had to be content to buy them from the nearest town in their own countries. . . . (Ah, you young men laugh at such antiquated fashions, but then, you can have no idea of the *allure* of the dress of those times, the bustle, the small waist, no bigger than my neck, the fringe, the bonnet, trimmed with flowers or cherries, all full of style: and the rustle of the skirts as they walked.) . . . And life here was such fun (I love that English word, for which there is no translation): for many of us Neapolitans then still lived in our villas, and, you know, we are not the Tuscans or Venetians, who will seldom ask a friend, if he is a foreigner, inside their homes: but we, even when we are poor, give dinner-parties and dances and enjoy ourselves. So, though my mother, being a widow, entertained little, there was my cousin, Leo Casteleone, who received a lot, and Giuseppe di Bandanera and the Nestore di Noceras. Then there were the Ouraveffskys, who had a villa here and were very generous and hospitable, like all their countrymen, and the Mellins, an American family, who lived up there on the hill, and three English families, all cousins, the Cleghornes, who were the great wine people and owned the whole valley and mountain side towards Positano; there was always a great deal going on. All this, perhaps, may bore you, but just the same, I must tell you, even the climate seemed better. It was never like today, with a cold wind — hotter, though not too hot (but we none of us ever felt the need of central heating, as we do now) — and the flowers sweeter. In the evenings, from the terrace, which then only reached as far as that black rock down there — you could watch the little feather of a cloud, which always lay on the very summit of the volcano's cone, glow with an inner radiance shot with flame: (whereas now Vesuvius, like Europe itself, seems always either dead or in eruption). A thousand boats would gleam, in front here, on the softly rippling water, each with a bright lantern (such as our ancestors used to say the mermaids carried) to attract their prey, and every now and then the fishermen would beat the boards of the ship with their oars, for that sound, too, entices those poor silly fish. The lights would seem a thousand glowing stars reflected in the water, the sea broke in the lightest foam upon the pebbles, as though in accompaniment to the serenade of the nightingales (how they sang then, day and night!), and over every wall was carried the heavy scent of orange blossom when a sudden little warm breeze played among the glossy leaves. . . . Whereas now, when you stand out there in the evening, all you can smell is petrol!

'And the hotel, though there were only two bathrooms in it (quite enough, people considered: think of it!), was so well managed. Never, as now, did a guest have to ask for anything twice. . . . Of course, I lived in our little *palazzo* with my mother, but I often came here to lunch and dine, though my mother — she was very old-fashioned and thought I should only know the people she knew — kept a strict watch on me; as strict a watch as she was able. I suppose "our misfortunes", as she always called them, the loss of her King and Queen, and the whole system of life — to which she had belonged — that had revolved round them, had made her proud: she was not what you would call a "snob", but she did not like the rich and the modern. According to her code, and to that of her ancestors, I must marry a girl whose parents she had always known, and whose grandparents had, equally, known mine throughout their lifetimes: that was the least upon which she must insist. . . . And so, in the end, I never married at all.

'It was here that I fell in love (and though you never tell me your love-affairs, I tell you mine, for I am from the south), fell in love, you cannot imagine how deeply, how violently, with an American girl, Ethel Burkefield-Stoddard; to me, this was a beautiful name then, making my heart beat, my eyes flash. She was rich, an only child, and so beautiful: but we were never allowed to marry, for I was only nineteen, and my mother became very angry (she brought in those wretched priests to talk to me by the hour, and I, though my heart was breaking with love, had to listen to them with respect and attention). Nor did Ethel's father like the idea, for I was too young, he said, and he would not let the millions he had made be wasted. I told him I did not want any money from him, but I think he disliked and distrusted all foreigners, especially if they possessed an old name. . . . But at any rate my darling loved me, though I say it myself, and though she was a little older than I was, would have married me, if only her parents had consented. Nor did she have any distrust of me — but then, she was not *like* an American girl, for she had a romantic and passionate nature, similar to my own in those days. . . . And, of course, I did not look then as I look now: by no means. . . . I would bring her every day enormous bouquets of flowers, and I believe her people laughed at me, saying they were taller than I was — for to present flowers was a southern custom, not Anglo-Saxon: many hours, too, I spent under her window, for the whole world seemed full of music, and I could not sleep. Or sometimes I would hire bands of Neapolitan singers (and in those days, again, they were not merely hoarse beggars, trying to earn money by blackmailing our ears, but had lovely voices, soft and full) to serenade her. . . . And though to me, thinking over it all, thinking back, the whole thing is sad, it was at the time beautiful and wonderful and, besides, as I have said, "fun". . . . And then came a great quarrel between our parents; her father took her away. . . . And though we had so often pledged our faith, our love, for all eternity, yet, as a matter of fact, I never heard from her, never heard of her, again. . . . Nor ever, after that, did I fall in love in the same way. . . .

'As you see, then, from what I have been telling you, I often came here. The entire place spells my youth to me. I know every inch of every path up the mountains, of every rock in the bay, where I so often used to swim. . . . But now, I never bathe: the water is too chilly . . . or perhaps it is my blood . . . I do not know. In youth, blood is hot, and one is strong.' And the Count, after this typically Italian generalisation, threw out and squared his shoulders, as if about to box.

'No, everything is different,' he continued. 'In those days you asked for something, and it was brought before you had time to say — who is it, I forget, Jack Robinson? But now, as I started to tell you, the service is very bad. You are left to ring the bell for ever; no one answers it. I have talked to you, *car' amico*, already far too long: but let me tell you, at least, about that.

'When I returned to Sorrento a year ago, I came straight to this hotel, and, though it seemed different and is, of course, double the size, at first there did not seem to have been such a big change — except that today everyone is so independent.

. . . But it was just the same weather as it had been when I left, over forty years before, and at times I had almost the illusion that I had never gone away. (Such weather now is rare, but I did not know this.) As I walked in the town, many of the shopkeepers, and of the peasants, standing in groups by the market, recognised me and saluted me, and my tenants hurried to kiss my hand, so that I became proud, and thought, after all, it seems a very little time ago, and it may be I have not changed so much. . . . The hotel was rather empty: and, though the waiters seemed more numerous than the guests, none of them ever answered a bell: but they would rush about, in opposite directions, with napkins in their hands, looking eager and occupied. . . . Well, one day I saw an old lady, very fat and lame, get up with difficulty from her chair, and waddle over to the mantelpiece to ring the bell. . . . No one answered. . . . So then I rang the bell for her, a second time. It was, as I have said, a very hot day, and she wanted a glass of iced water. But even when she had ordered it, no one brought it. So at last I became very angry, and I rang the bell again, and said: "Unless that glass of water is brought immediately, I shall leave the hotel. It is a scandal!" And then, since they knew me, they were frightened, and brought it at once. . . . Well, that started an acquaintance with this poor old lady, for whom I felt so sorry, because she was so lame and looked so ill: and I think she was grateful to me, and liked me. . . . And I wondered, once or twice, how she had appeared when she was young, for if you stripped the fat from her face, and imagined a different colouring, she might have been handsome in her way. I asked her name of the concierge (she was a Mrs. Clacton-Biddle). Every day at luncheon she would bow and smile, and perhaps, afterwards, we would exchange a few words in the hall, about the weather, or politics. . . . Then, one day, I said to her: "So this is your first visit to our beautiful Sorrento?"

'"No," she answered, "I stayed here once before, long ago. . . . I should hardly like to tell you how long. Twenty-five years; a quarter of a century. . . . Just such days as these."

'This interested me, and I said: "Did you know any of the people in the villas here?'

'And she replied: "Yes, I knew many of them: but they

are all gone now, Nestore di Nocera, and the Cleghornes and the Mellins."

'"They were all friends of mine too," I said. "Though you must excuse me for saying so, it is a longer time than you think, for it is over forty years since Nestore was drowned in this very bay. . . . I wonder if we ever met, for I lived here too then?"

'But she was thinking to herself, and paid no heed to my remarks. There was a smile of reminiscence on her face, which lit it and made it momentarily assume a certain familiar beauty, and yet one which I could not identify in my own mind: though now I saw that she must, indeed, have been beautiful in days gone by.

'"They were all friends of mine," I repeated.

'"And then," she continued, "there were the Ouraveffskys and the Bandaneras; so many friends: and my particular friend, Count Dragone di Dragora: but he is dead, too, they tell me."

'"Madame," I cried, "everything you tell me is true except that. Count Dragone di Dragora is not dead: he stands before you!" . . . And then I saw who she was, this fat, lame old lady. . . . It was Ethel Burkefield-Stoddard: and, as her eyes rested on mine, just for that one instant I heard all the nightingales singing again in the glossy darkness of the orange trees. . . .'

. . . . .

'But do you know, the queerest part of it: afterwards, now that she knew who I was, it seemed as though she wanted to put a barrier between us. . . . She became more distant in her manner, grew unwelcoming, and spoke to me little. . . . I do not know why. . . . Perhaps — who knows? — she regretted our intimacy; perhaps — indeed, surely — I disappointed her, and she bore me a grudge for it; perhaps she felt a different person herself, and thought I knew too much about her; or, again, she may have wished that, as she now was, I had never recognised her, and thus been forced inevitably to match against her present appearance the image of her which I must retain from past years. . . . Or perhaps it was merely that she had been married — and widowed — in the interval . . . I do not know. . . . But, after a time — shorter, I believe, than she had intended — she left, and sailed home from Naples. . . . And, since then, I have received only two letters from her:

the first to ask me to obtain for her one of those red lacquer boxes — you know, the kind that they make here — in which to keep her handkerchiefs: and the other, remote and bleak and impersonal, to thank me for having sent it. . . . It was all such a long time ago, I suppose.'

The Count stopped talking, and looked in the glass again. And for a moment I, too, caught a glimpse of a person lost long ago; a different dragon, warm and with a soft shell. And then again, it hardened into everyday armour.

CHAMPAGNE FOR THE OLD LADY

ONE of the most peculiar qualities of gambling is the power it possesses to make even the laziest man work hard, if only for a limited period; the period being, of course, limited by the money he has — or can borrow — to lose. Any gambler will toil through long, exhausting hours until daylight creeps cruelly through the curtains to reveal columns and shafts of cigarette-smoke and a suffocating atmosphere in which only germs could thrive; toil, at that, only in order to squander as much money as he could gain elsewhere by honest work in an infinitely shorter time. . . . Certainly I laboured far harder in the Casino — or 'the Studio', as, for that reason, I preferred to call it — than I do now in writing this story.

Roulette was the game. We were both of us far too poor to afford to gamble, and we both liked to lose our money in different ways. John Treguze had invented a real system for it, and whenever he had lost at the tables the whole of the money he had taken in with him, would comfort himself with the same vague sentiment: 'It's no good breaking off now. I ought to give my system a fair trial'. As for myself, I relied for my efforts upon intuition — a gift which can prove quite as expensive as any more intellectual method, for he who is endowed with it just scatters the counters over all the numbers that catch his eye or take his fancy. On the other hand, should he win, the laurels that crown prophecy are added to those of triumph.

We often argued the faults of our various ways of play. To begin with, I would point out to John, his methods were too complicated: for, if you were determined to experiment with a system, this necessitated taking with you to the table an immense quantity of counters of every sort, from ten-thousand and five-thousand francs down to hundreds and tens — far more than you could afford to lose; but the possibilities of a system, a thing so high above mere chance, justified in your mind the slight risk, as you saw it, of losing them. Indeed, it became a duty. (If you had lost heavily before, it was not because your system had betrayed you, but because you had not played it long enough.) And then, always just as the end to which you had so long been progressing was at last beginning to come in sight, human frailty entered too; either you forgot for a single throw to back one of the essential numbers, or the ball might be started over-soon (so that you were not given the time in which to complete your usual lay-out of counters), or you found that you had already, without noticing it, lost all the money you had brought in, and so were obliged to miss the very spin that would have made your fortune. Whereas my lack of system — which, in itself, almost amounted to one — was simplicity itself, easy to manage: you took as many counters as you wanted, placed them where you liked, and when you had forfeited them all, you either left the building or obtained some more — and lost them in addition. No fuss or brain-fag. . . . Nevertheless, at times when I scanned John's face, looked at his dark, luxuriant hair, his regular and determined features, his eyes that, though short-sighted, were so far-seeing, or regarded his large frame, his system seemed to me so well to match and express his physique that I wondered whether he might not win with it after all.

That night at dinner, on the terrace in front of the hotel, we discussed these problems again. Dinner lightened the sense of our losses: it was a warm night of early summer, and the grass, of so vivid a green, and growing singly from the soil like the tenderly nurtured hairs on the head of a bald man, the flowers and palm trees and kiosks and cupolas of this holy city of chance, presented the enchanting vistas of a mid-Victorian stage-setting. And all this beauty had been created out of the money lost by gamblers! We began to feel that we, too, had 'done our bit' towards it, for this evening we had been victims. . . . But soon, over our brandy, we began to talk of other things, until it was nearly time to go, to start again. . . . John chose a cigar — to smoke later, he said, when he was winning, for it helped him to keep his head cool; and then we spoke of cigars, how expensive in France and England, how cheap and good they were in Holland and Germany — and in Austria; where, he informed me — for he had at one time lived there — even women, and especially those of the former, aristocratic régime, smoked them in preference to cigarettes. . . . I wondered if I had ever seen a woman smoke a cigar in England. . . . But I was sure I had not, for it would have looked so odd that one would remember it.

We walked across to the Casino and found its marbled saloons, smelling so strongly of post-offices and old scent, unusually crowded, airless to the point of suffocation. A pleasure-cruise had touched here this afternoon, and the pleasure-crusaders were standing round the tables in staring groups, ox-eyed with Swiss or Scandinavian wonder, and getting very much in the way of the habitual, as it were resident, gamblers : those old ladies with delicate complexions enamelled over thousands of cobweb-like wrinkles, with many veils and bags, and a slight, harassing twitch, who, harmless old flotsam of Edwardian days, compose the steady population of such places. Little processions of black-clothed croupiers, with down-turned eyes, like the mutes at a funeral, marched through the rooms, guarding a coffinful of counters.

The public rooms were too thronged tonight for John to be able to obtain the share of the croupier's attention which his system demanded; besides, it was far too hot and one felt penned-in at the table, as though one were waiting to be sheared, so we entered the *Salle Privée*, usually to a certain degree free of tourists. It was now about a quarter to eleven, and the gambling was in full swing; it seemed much cooler, though we found that the cruising parties had even penetrated here in their urge to gape. In addition, there was, of course, the usual *Salle Privée* circle of old witches, with tousled white hair, sitting round the table, staring at the wheel, mumbling spells and curses through nut-cracker jaws. They themselves never played now, all their losses were in the past, but they paid money still to enter, in order to inconvenience as much as they could the real players by taking all the chairs so that the others had to stand up, thus too far from the table to be able properly to place their stakes.

John, however, found a good seat, next the croupier, and began sorting out and arranging his columns of counters as a preliminary. I stood for a moment to watch. The old lady who had at the same time taken the empty chair next him attracted — and held — my attention. She differed so greatly from those all round her who so plainly lived in the town and made this their headquarters. Unused as she must obviously be to the Casino, she appeared too good — too *morally* good, I mean — for her environment. Well over seventy, I should say, she was slight in figure, her complexion was that of a girl of seventeen, and her eyes still had a youthful, meaningless caress in them when she looked at you. She was dressed quietly in black velvet. A sort of black lace mantilla framed her head and flowed over her soft white hair, being tied in a wimple under the chin, thus emphasising a profile that was, even now, of a du Maurier-like calm and purity; and she carried, as her only impedimenta, two fans, one painted, the other of black lace: these she put down on the table by her. Regarding her, one saw that she was, in fact, one of those rare creatures, an old lady who, besides retaining her beauty, had retained her prettiness — a far more difficult achievement.

I reflected how lucky John was to find her as a neighbour instead of one of the usual clawing harpies of the Casino, and then left him, in order to have a drink in the bar. There people were swallowing coffee and cocktails and brandy and every sort of drink for every hour. For a while I listened to their desultory fragments of talk. An elderly, voguish American gigolo with very smooth black hair, and hands flapping like a seal's flippers, was heard remarking to a much older American woman, dressed in a low evening dress of white lace sprinkled with pink roses, 'My dear, it's *chic*, and it's *soignée* (swánee), but it gets you nowhere!'

When I returned to the table John was immersed in his system and had lit his large cigar. Smoking was, of course, allowed, but I noticed (as he did not, for he was too busily occupied) that the pretty old lady next him, with her soft white hair and large soft blue eyes, had begun to show symptoms of distress, to cough and fan herself gently. John's great frame, posed next to hers, served to make her look still smaller and more shrinking. The coven of Casino witches round the table, with their gnarled, veined, grabbing hands that might have been carved from the root of a box tree, their hard faces and circular parrot's eyes, seemed by no means impressed by this display of sensitiveness, and glared cynically at the victim (this, no doubt, would have been their attitude to any show of natural feeling), but the strangers near by, and the barricade behind her of Scandinavian and Swiss tourists, soon became interested and sympathetic, solicitous on her behalf. What a shame for a great big man to smoke a huge cigar like that, next to her, their plain faces said plainly! Probably in the old French *manoir* whence she must have sprung, she had never even seen a cigar, far less smelt it. (How curious, indeed, to see a lady of that kind in the Casino: she was not at all of the type they had expected to discover; must, somehow, have wandered in here by mistake.) But that was the rich all over, trampling on the feelings of the poor and refined. Why, though she was sitting down, if you looked, she was not even playing! Too poor to afford it, that must be the explanation. *There* was self-restraint for you! But you did not see people of that stamp nowadays; too gentle and good for this gas-mask, weakest-against-the-wall world.

The old lady was by this time fanning herself vigorously, first with one fan, then with the other. She would take one up, use it, and then lay it down again on the table, near John's counters. Her manipulation of these instruments was wonderfully expressive. Like that of a geisha, or a great Chinese actor, every movement bore its burden of significance. She turned her exquisite profile away from her neighbour, and his vile habits, as though to obtain air. By now both the cigar and the system were well under way, and I do not think that, until this minute, John had been at all aware of the growing interest and disturbance round him. But suddenly the old lady became vocal, began to complain audibly, partly to herself, partly to the crowd, in beautiful old-world French; and the crowd started to take her side, to murmur in their various doric tongues. (As she spoke, I wondered was there not, after all, a hint of foreign intonation in that telling, vibrating voice; was not the use of idiom a little too perfect for a woman speaking her own language?) The croupiers alone remained unmoved, their eyes glazed with fatigue and boredom, or with a slight furtive and reminiscent smile hovering round their colourless lips, according to their types. Now she fanned herself, almost truculently for one of so gracious a personality, grimaced, showed her distaste in many evident ways, and finally made an open protest to the croupiers and the world in general. The croupiers remained silent, indifferent, but the world in general responded. Once more she appealed to the nearest croupier, who, waking himself from a despondent trance, in which, obviously, he despaired of humanity and its greed, declared that he could do nothing; smoking was allowed.

She demanded to see the *chef du parti*, and plied the fans incessantly, taking them up, putting them down, holding them at angles, in order to protect herself, and using them to attract the crowd's attention and to point out to them the delinquent. Meanwhile, John had grown conscious of the tension in the air, and had become thoroughly annoyed, for his neighbour had created and worked up this scene without ever addressing a single request to him personally: so he continued to smoke, and endeavoured, against increasing odds, to maintain outward calm and to concentrate successfully on his complicated system of gambling. Eventually, however, the muttering, and the general carefully cultivated feeling of antipathy towards him, affected his nerves, and, accosting the pretty old lady, he offered to put out his cigar, adding that he would have been delighted to do so at any previous moment, had she seen fit to ask him. She did not even reply. It was too late: she was offended beyond repair. Elegantly, with conspicuous grace of carriage and dignity, she collected her fans, rose from the table, and glided out of the room in a rustle of resentful black velvet. The onlookers glared furiously at John, who, in return, blew out defiantly a small cloud of smoke. Poor old lady, they said, to treat her like that! What a shame! A great big brute, with no respect for age or delicacy. But how truly she had shown her breeding! How beautifully she had walked out, without a word! Why, she could not have done it better if she had practised it for years! There was a *real* lady for you! You didn't see that sort nowadays.

John certainly felt uncomfortable at her ostentatiously quiet departure (moreover, he had been losing again for some time, though he had begun well this evening, when he first arrived. Because gambling has an element of exhibitionism in it: the player, to win, must compel the wonder and admiration, even the envy, of the spectators; but their disapproval and dislike will ruin his game). The whole affair had depressed him and spoilt his evening — but it was not until ten minutes or so after she had left that he realised that all his high counters had gone with her. The better system had won.

The pretty old lady, I was told afterwards, was an Austrian, in spite of the elegant and lovely French she spoke. And it was her custom always to select an evening when the rooms were crowded with Swiss and Scandinavian naïfs for the testing of her system. The smoke-screen was a regular trick, and one that usually worked well, since large cigars and quantities of counters seemed to go together in the Casino: like the chatter of a conjurer at the moment of counterfeiting his magic, her protests were designed to distract the attention, both of her audience and of her chosen dupe, from the sleight-of-hand which was in progress before them. The opaque film from the cigar resembled, too, the cracking of the magician's pistol, while the smoke itself afforded some disguise, comparable to the cloud of ink thrown off by an octopus when engaged in combat, in order to mask its manœuvres—except that, in this instance, it was the octopus, still more wily, who compelled her prey to emit the concealing veil. But, had she been ejected by the authorities, doubtless aware of her game, a riot would most surely have ensued, so firmly did she always establish herself in the hearts of the onlookers.

I did not stay in the Casino long enough that evening to see the end of John's system. (We were leaving the next day.) The rooms were far too hot, and I strolled out towards my hotel. The night was delicious. The feathery palm leaves lay motionless on the air, laden with the scent of orange blossom and strong-smelling night flowers. On my way back I passed a large café, like an illuminated conservatory, with a uniformed Tsigane band stationed near the entrance, playing waltzes. The chairs set outside looked so inviting that I took one and ordered a drink. In the opposite corner sat the pretty old lady, nodding her head in time to the waltz the band was playing; she had evidently just finished her supper; an empty half-bottle of champagne stood in a silver pail of ice by her side. And, as I got up to go, I noticed that in the manner of many compatriots of her sex in the old days, she was just lighting a cigar.

LOVERS' MEETING

It was the ideal afternoon of a May day. Down below, ants moved along their tracks, and we flew over a model of Petworth, over miniature bare slopes, over towns and then across a marbled sea. The plane was crowded. A few 'good-timers' were still there, faithful to an ideal that grew increasingly difficult to follow, loyal to their favourite beat: Paris for Whitsun.

'I may as well have a holiday,' my neighbour remarked, a smooth-faced, rather handsome Jew of the Stock Exchanges. 'I shall never have another. I join up next month.'

In the enormous omnibus, dashing up from Le Bourget, several fat women, rolling luxuriously at each turn of the road against their neighbours, made friends with them in this way. The men rolled back at them, hip to hip, with a *can-can*-like audacity: (the local atmosphere must have affected them). Though so near, the noise forced them to shout to one another.

'I always say there's no place like Paris!' they yelled. 'You feel different directly you get here. . . . Especially now, with all the chestnuts in flower. It ought to be lovely. . . . And Josephine Baker is back at the old Casino! I *love* her, don't you?'

'*Shan't* we look silly if the Germans invade Holland and Belgium, and we can't get back? . . . But they won't: they can't: of course they won't, or our people wouldn't have let us come. . . . Yes, it was quite easy. I was surprised. But I felt I wanted a change; growing stale in Brighton all those months. . . . Look, there's *Le Lapin Vert*! It's still open then? Someone said it was shut.'

The next morning, Friday, I was woken at five by wailing sirens, and again at eight by the voice of the speaker on the French Radio, his calm and politeness exaggerated a thousand-fold by the impersonality of the instrument. Moreover, the very loudness of its amplification made it sound as though the announcer were glad and the news were good. No one would dare to give bad tidings in such a tone. . . . The German armies had invaded Holland, Belgium and Luxembourg during the night, and had launched their great attack on the West.

It was difficult for me to know whether to continue my journey to Italy. I had been told not to go 'if the situation deteriorated'. At moments I thought that the dissolution of three further independent states marked such a stage. Besides, I knew that Italy was planning to enter the war, was convinced of it. Accordingly I cabled to the authorities, 'Shall I still proceed Italy'. . . . After three days of suspense, and of mingling with crowds walking up and down in the holiday sunshine, the reply came, on the very afternoon on which my train was due to leave.

'Think you had better continue but must be on your own responsibility.'

I cabled back, 'Proceeding Italy this afternoon but consider Tennysons celebrated lines theirs not to reason why theirs but to do or die would have lost in vigour had poet added further line on their own responsibility Sitwell', and drove to the Gare de Lyon.

The train happened to be the last permitted to reach Italy by the Simplon route. When we left, there was still some doubt as to whether the Swiss Government would allow it to enter Switzerland. But the conductors, who, looking in their hats and uniforms like overgrown telegraph-boys, stood poising pencils above charts, remained sanguine. It was impossible to divine their race, they belonged to the blue-chinned international tribes of the European *wagons-lits*, super-gipsies with a languid *chic* all their own. They showed no animus. Nothing would happen: why should it? The Italians would not enter the war. . . . But Sanctions, those Sanctions!

As usual I reached the station too early; so, having secured my compartment, I walked up and down the platform, watching fellow-passengers arrive: Balkan diplomats, with sleeked hair and high, giggling voices, returning home, French business men, Americans *en route* for their ships at Naples; and an enlarged — you could not have said *fat* — middle-aged Frenchwoman, much painted, with very golden hair and dark eyebrows and with several extensions of personality outside herself; jingling bangles provided, for example, music for every gesture, and there were cigarette cases and holders, bags in which to lose things and, finally, a minute, high-stepping griffon which, with a collar of bells, also contributed its own music for each step it took. A coat was strapped to its middle to keep it warm. (It was so small, the creature, that it made me think of Jean Cocteau's story of the woman who bought from a Paris dealer a little angel of a dog, in a coat, with little shoes even, on its feet. Naturally she was obliged to give a large sum for such a treasure, but none the less delighted with her purchase, brought it home. Once safely there, she left it for a few minutes alone in the drawing-room while she found it some food. . . . When she returned the little creature had run up the curtain ; it was a rat, disguised.)

The owner of bangles and griffon was certainly very conspicuous. . . . Nevertheless the least conspicuous person on the platform was at the same time the most noticeable to myself, as she walked slowly up and down it. She was a woman of between sixty and seventy, bulky, dressed in black, with a puffy, emotional face, its flush emphasised, as is so often the case, by the whiteness of her hair. It was a kindly, silly face, and of a type often encountered. She was, no doubt, a person who obeyed the conventions and who, while good in the sense of being generous and amiable, was also greedy and, to some mild extent, pleasure-loving, indulgent to herself as to others. She might have been the original of Frances Cornford's

> O why do you walk in the fields in gloves,
> Missing so much and so much ?
> O fat white woman whom nobody loves . . .

Yes, somewhat self-indulgent. And she had the air of one who was used invariably to kindness, had always been protected. Yet her face held the attention, for there was more in it than that ; something mad and tragic, the dignity of Lear in his appalling abnegation and abandonment. Her blue-grey eyes, unimaginative and rather protruding, were strained, and straining, full of emotion, did not see, but nevertheless saw, surely, beyond the objects at which she looked. Her mouth, which many years ago must have been so pretty — though its pouting had now, at her age, grown ridiculous — worked the whole time as if she were talking. . . . One could not help wondering about her, because of the contrast between her appearance of being so ordinary, her mobile, puffy face, and the attitude and the mask of classic grief which her pose and countenance sometimes assumed. . . . But the passengers were getting in, the train was starting.

. . . . .

Next morning I sat in my *wagon-lit*, watching the touchingly beautiful Italian landscape roll by, under the tender early light. This country of mountain and lake pulled at the heart-strings, even if this were the first time you saw it; still more if you were familiar with trees and flowers, and loved the people as I did. But under the lightness and sweetness of the air could be detected the stench of the treachery infecting it. Now we were passing Baveno, and Stresa, and Isola Bella with its marble decks and pinnacles, and old trees in shrillest green leaf, lay like a full-rigged ship above the calm, mirror-like water. . . . How often had I seen it, how often had I done this journey! It seemed just the same. . . . Suddenly I heard a voice, hesitating and sad, speaking behind me, from the doorway, in broken English.

There stood the old woman in black, her eyes seeming fuller and more brimming as the light from the windows fell direct on her puffy, discoloured face. Her whole attitude, even through the jolting of the train, seemed inspired by some unbearable dignity, forced upon her in rigid, unwelcome mould, as if a great sculptor had chosen for once to shape a conception out of a medium so unsuitable as to make the effect of it all the more astonishing.

'Do you speak English?' she asked. 'Forgive me, but I must talk to someone. I cannot stop talking. I am a bit crazy, I know. But I do not know what to do or what I should have done. I come from Belgium; you cannot believe what I have seen; my only child, my son, home on leave, seized out of my own house before my eyes by German soldiers, before I knew we were at war. I could not follow him. I do not know whether he is alive or dead. Perhaps I should have stayed there, but I did not know what to do, and all my friends were leaving. . . . And the roads, the refugees, the poor refugees; two days to go a few miles that in peace-time would take an hour. No pity, no pity anywhere. I saw Louvain burning for the second time. . . . I do not know; what could I do? Oh, what could I have done? I could not follow my son, they would not let me. My friends made me go to Paris, and from there, from the Embassy, I telephoned to my husband in Venice, where I am joining him — he is our Consul-General. All my life I have loved him, but now he is old, and when, at last, we were able to get him on the telephone, he could not hear well. He could not understand about our son. He thought I should not have left him — but what could I do? They caught him and took him away. And I never stop thinking of him, saying to myself, what could I do or have done? . . . The poor refugees, struggling, running down the roads, all of them the colour of dust, and some lying where they fell in the ditch, not troubling to get up. . . . You don't mind my talking. I must talk to someone, or I shall go mad. (But I am a little mad already, I know.) . . . I could not have believed what I have seen. All my life I have been *dévote*, but now I ask *le bon Dieu* how He could have permitted it. The fires, the people, the poor people, running. . . .'

There was a pause. The sweet, calm Italian country sped past the windows. In the corridor, just outside, the fussy, spindle-legged, *petit-maître* griffon danced and pranced and sneezed and thrilled with pleasure, his bells jingling at each movement and curvet, while his mistress sounded her bangles, giggled in the manner she had for more than a generation found successfully attractive, and shouted, slapping the front of her thigh with a fat hand, '*Ninon, Ninon chéri, viens voir Maman*'. The dog danced more than ever, its eyes bulging with pleasure.

The monologue in the doorway started again. 'All in three days! The roads choked, and I saw the faces of the German airmen as they dived and machine-gunned us, saw them laughing. . . . No pity anywhere in the world. . . . And my son! . . . What am I to say to my husband? He will be at the station. He is perhaps angry and I do not know how to explain, do not know what to say . . .'

THE WOMAN WHO HATED FLOWERS

My parents had sent me into a nursing-home. The hours were of the usual grey monotony, and the day-nurses seemed to spend their periods of duty in whisking flowers in and out of the room, pouring more water into the vases or spilling a little out of them, in offering me glasses of a thick, viscous barley-water, very tainted in its taste, and in talking interminably — it was spring — about 'daffies'.

The night-nurse, though, in spite of her plainness, was not ordinary; in her quietness she was unusual. Her voice was a human voice, containing no special inflections for the 'cheering up' of patients. She brought into the room a certain air of humanity, a quality of comfort. Reserved, placid, her lashless eyes — the irises, not the whites — shone sometimes with a glow of their own, as she sat gazing absorbedly into the embers, while her tall, spare body rocked a little, and by this movement rescued itself from the immobility of sculptured stone.

One night, I believe she told me her story. . . . But I could never be quite sure, for every evening I became feverish, and she never referred to the incident afterwards.

When she came in, the day-nurse had only just left me and had omitted to turn down the lights. I saw the new-comer breathe heavily as she entered, her nostrils dilating. Then, their scent attracting her attention, she noticed a vase of flowers — wallflowers, they were — which her predecessor had forgotten to remove, and at once carried it away into the passage.

This action I thought out of keeping with her usual dignity and slow-moving restraint, just like that of any other nurse. . . . On her return, she stood watching me for several minutes without speaking, then said, suddenly, with great force, 'I *hate* flowers!', switched off the lights and went out.

I woke up later, and could distinguish her figure by the fire. She was rocking a little, as though her body were still seeking that marvellous balance which her soul at such cost, and with so little reason, had long found. Sleepily I asked her, speaking partly to myself, 'Why do you hate flowers?' And perhaps the fact that I was then very young, or perhaps merely the anonymity of darkness, made her tell me. But alas, from this distance I can no longer offer you her precise words; can only tell you what I remember. And some of the details will be inaccurate, for it is long ago; but I can give you the general impression of what I believe she told me.

Aurelia Graybourne had come out of a comfortable home in the suburbs of Dublin, but it nevertheless contained a spiritual suffering that outweighed material circumstances. Her father had long been dead, her three sisters were married, and her mother drank with ardour and endurance, devoting her life to this almost touching appetite. For its sake, she would brook any discomfort, mental, physical or of the soul. Even the priests proved unable to restrain her in her pursuit of it.

The outward respectability of Aurelia's middle-class home, the chintzes, the bureaux, the fringed cushions, the calendars, the 'easy-chairs', the 'occasional tables', the Victorian knick-knacks in silver, all threw into a greater relief the grotesque horror of life within its walls. Hogarth's 'Gin Lane' would have supplied a far more apposite background for the squalor of dozens of empty whisky bottles, ingeniously but often inadequately concealed, and for the snoring torpor or crazy gaiety that resulted from them. The working-up of scenes, the horrid, dull satisfaction of the drunkard in the pain which her inspired words could give, and the subsequent maudlin scenes of reconciliation, poisoned equally the whole existence of this young girl.

Even when drunk, Mrs. Graybourne, as the daughter of one officer and the widow of another, felt obliged to keep up appearances, so she sought no convivial cronies but vented all the technique of her recurring bouts upon her youngest daughter. In the morning, when well enough, she went out shopping alone, a sort of martyred, mystical sweetness, together with a very red nose, being the only visible tokens of those hectic afternoons and evenings which she spent in the torture, conscious and unconscious, of the being most dear to her in the world.

Eventually, after a very bad outbreak, the doctors and priests intervened and insisted on the eldest daughter, now a widow herself, coming to look after Mrs. Graybourne. They said she needed someone of experience with her. . . . During this interlude, Aurelia declared her intention of entering a convent. Ada, her sister, who, though perfectly aware of what had been going on, had, until the priests sent for her, never offered to help in any manner, now took sides openly against her. But Aurelia was just of age, and could do what she liked: she possessed a hundred and fifty pounds a year of her own. No one could move her, hitherto so gentle.

Mrs. Graybourne, too ill to argue, wept a great deal, but could not succeed in persuading Aurelia to remain at home. At last, though, she relented sufficiently to promise that for the first two or three years she would work as a lay sister, thus giving herself time to see whether she was fitted for the novitiate. But this affectation of lowliness, as she chose to consider it, yet further embittered the convalescent.

When Aurelia left, Mrs. Graybourne was still confined to her bed. Sweetness and resignation, with a dash of menace and a hint of prophecy, were her specialities at the moment.

'To think that you should leave a loving mother and a comfortable home, all because of your own unnatural selfishness,' she had begun, when the cab was at the door. But sobs choked her at this point, and she had been obliged to pause. 'I've nothing to say against convents,' she had continued, in her wily brogue. 'I'm a religious woman, I hope. But I warned Father Clement . . . "That girl will bring disgrace on St. Ursula's, just as she has on her poor mother".'

. . . . .

Aurelia had driven up to the convent in an old cab, through pouring rain, but in spite of the clouds that lay low upon the mountains, her heart was at rest. From the first moment when the Abbess received her, she felt she had done the only thing that could give her peace. The rain, the calm, the routine, soothed her nerves and made her happy. Through serving so humbly, she regarded herself already as dedicated to God's service. Perhaps Mrs. Graybourne's reproaches had touched her, and underneath her extreme devoutness may have existed the apprehension that only by an entire surrender of herself could she atone for abandoning the earthly ties of duty, however degrading and destructive. Henceforth no task could be too menial for her.

The severity of the life suited her. Her eyes took on reflections of sea and lake and cloud and mountain, and her skin attained the delicate suffusions of colour that tinge Irish cheeks alone, nourished by generations of soft, continual rain. Notwithstanding her desire for self-suppression, a sort of animal radiance, derived from a new contentment with her surroundings, became manifest in her, showed through the movements of her limbs, encumbered by their heavy, medieval garment, and, with the conviction it carried of youth and innocence, appealed to every heart.

The seasons were quickened in their passing by the regular tenor of her existence. Twice she had seen the winter disappear. Soon she would become a novice, and sever the last tie with her old self. Meanwhile a thousand tasks employed her time, cleaning the rooms and passages, gentle gardening, picking fruit. Since she had soon won the trust and affection of the nuns, she would often be left alone at such pursuits. Or it would be her duty to sweep out and adorn the chapel; that Irish-Gothic edifice of the nineteenth century, vast and ill-proportioned, every pillar and arch too narrow and too poor, but built, nevertheless, with a sense of the theatre, full of bright light and deep shadow and incense through which the realistically painted saints trailed flaring and tawdry dresses, their shrines decorated with arrangements of tinsel and imitation flowers.

Outside now, the days of spring were thick and heavy with a pagan, impermanent joy. The sunlight issued in spears and shafts from behind fat, lolling clouds. It lay like cream upon clustered blossom of apple and pear tree, and gilded with a warm effulgence the grass at their roots, throwing into vivid individual relief the flowers among it. The wallflowers, with their turrets of crumpled tawny velvet, growing by the base of the chapel walls, hummed with drowsy insect life, and their sweetness, which appeared to be less a scent than the very perfume of the golden day itself, hung above the paths and entered a little way into the chapel, there to be defeated by the Christian smell of incense. Often, the glittering lances of the showers in their sudden charges similarly dispersed it for a time in the garden itself. . . . But directly the sun came through, those sweet odours mounted once more into the air. Vague, luxurious longings of the flesh assailed her, and she would return to the chapel for the seeming permanence of its meagre arch and pillar, cold stone and hard benches, to allay them.

These by now familiar objects offered their own assurance; here things were as they always were, had been, would be, unaltered and inalterable as the love of God. The life in the garden, though temporarily disturbing to the senses, was fitful, seasonal. . . . But how sinful, she reflected, that the flesh of men and women should be subject to these earthy and godless permutations.

Nevertheless, as she swept clear of dust the ugly ecclesiastical patterns of the tessellated floor with her medieval broom — composed, like a gardener's, of twigs bound together — she was conscious that the joy from outside had invaded the most sacred places. The welling up of life in her body, as much as in every tree and flower, now tinctured for her every inanimate object, so that the paper flowers appeared to blossom more bravely, the patterned floor to assume harder, brighter colours, the incense, even, to become less spiritual in its appeal.

One day, when she was sweeping the chapel, she thought she would look into the street, and, just as she opened the door, it happened that a man she had known in Dublin passed by. About ten years older than herself, he was a musician (indeed, many thought that he possessed great talent as a composer), and her mother disapproved of him, which had added to his already considerable charm. In spite of the change in her attire, he recognised her at once. (She supposed, afterwards, that when he called her name she ought not to have answered. But how could she have refused? It would have been rude and unkind.) She stood there in the warm shadow, and he in full sunlight, so that it beat down on his dark, handsome face and bold jutting features, and showed her a flattering admiration, surprise and pleasure in his large, dark eyes, usually nonchalant and melancholy. As he spoke to her, her whole body came to life beneath the heavy, stone-like folds of her dress, as though a statue were starting to breathe.

After that, she did not so clearly remember the course of events. Some intoxication of the senses appeared to have affected her, leaving behind it a state bordering on oblivion. For about two months, however, she struggled for her beliefs; then she began to meet Terence Marlowe by appointment on many occasions. After all, she would argue with herself, she was free, she had as yet taken no vows.

Chance favoured their love for each other; almost miraculously, they were never seen together. The months passed. But though gay and happy when in his company, at other times a consciousness of the wickedness of what he had asked her — and what she intended — to do, weighed her down. For he pleaded with her continually to abandon the idea of the cloister and run away to London ; where, later, he would come to marry her. . . . Not at once, or the Abbess and the nuns would talk, and would no doubt find a way of injuring him in the eyes of members of his family. And that neither he nor Aurelia could afford, because by copying out parts and by playing the organ, he was earning little enough money : but he possessed expectations of a moderate sort from his relatives.

Many were the nights when desolation of the spirit kept her awake, and by day in the garden, as she swept the paths and inhaled the perfume of the wallflowers, her face often burned with shame. But at other moments, when she recalled that Terence loved her, just as she loved him, a certain feeling of joy and pride comforted her. . . . It was indeed fortunate, she would then reflect, that she had allowed her family to persuade her to wait, before making any irrevocable decision. She could still escape. The life of the convent would soon be behind her, just as was the life of her old home. . . . Almost she had forgotten the existence of her mother and sister, the protests and uproar that would arise when they heard that she was taking their advice. . . . Meanwhile, she could not bring herself to tell the Abbess or consult the nuns, though, but for her fear, there was nothing to prevent her. No obstacles would have been placed in her way, whatever she had decided to do. . . . But in her own mind she still regarded herself as dedicated to the service of God, not of man. . . . She loved the sisters, so she must run away without saying good-bye to them.

When she ran away, leaving behind her a letter to the Abbess, worded in a business-like, brisk manner, she hardly experienced the remorse she had anticipated. It seemed no more than the changing of her old-fashioned livery for the dress of the times. In the same style, her old life was folded up, hidden out of sight. She stood on deck now — so she felt — a modern figure, finished with restraints, welcoming the life of the day. And though numbered among those in whose hearts, however much they may transgress its teachings, religion had taken root, and would never die, of this she was unconscious, and she rejoiced as the sea and air sang the word 'freedom' in her ears.

She was to wait a month in London for her lover. At first time sped by, but, as day followed day and six weeks and more had elapsed, it began to drag. His early letters, long and affectionate, had been frequent as even she could wish, but they were now few. And, although she was living cheaply in a boarding-house in Bloomsbury, her money showed signs of becoming exhausted. She began to lose interest in this city, so new to her. . . . And still he did not arrive to claim her. . . . Not even now, however, not for a moment, did she doubt him. If she did, the world would fall in ruins round her.

Letters started to arrive from her mother and sisters, who had succeeded at last in tracing her. These contained dull reproaches, coarse taunts and much talk of the suffering she had brought upon them. 'You have', Mrs. Graybourne wrote, 'cast a slur upon your own father's good name.' . . . *Who* was the *man*? the chorus demanded and reiterated. . . . Aurelia did not answer. . . . Then Ada came to see her, and talked of their mother as a martyr, never even allowed herself to admit that Mrs. Graybourne drank. *Who was the man?*

All right, if she would not say, they would find out. But, whoever he might be, he was after her fortune. (To many men, it might seem a lot.) Of that, both Ada and Mrs. Graybourne were sure.

. . . . .

At last a letter arrived. It could not have been an easy letter to write. . . . She opened it in her room. He was afraid, he said, that she might think he had been silly, but he was sure that if they had gone on, they would only have regretted it. He had just married; an old friend of his. He hoped Aurelia would be sensible and would not write to him, as Naomi might see the letter and it would upset her, since she knew nothing about their friendship. . . .

So they were wrong! He was not after her money; nor after herself. It had been merely a matter of play. . . . He had waited two months — until the spring had come again — and then had married this woman of whom she had never heard.

'Nothing', that was the word that haunted Aurelia.

Nothing. It had meant nothing; nothing. She was not even to be given the crown of a great betrayal. It was all paltry, insignificant. She felt sick, suddenly, as though she were going to die. (She could not bear that scent of wallflowers: on her dressing-table stood a small bunch she had bought yesterday. She got up, took it from the vase, went to the window, and threw it out into the yard.) Nothing. . . . For days she stayed in her room, shunning the light, sitting dully in her chair in her sordid, damp-stained attic, for she feared the repercussion, even from a distance in a great city, of the humming ecstasy of apple trees in blossom and the indefinable, pervading sweetness of wallflowers. She feared the air itself.

. . . .

At any rate this intolerable misery had been real. Soon — after the passage of these first few days, and then of a month or two — she was real no longer, even to herself; nothing. Now she could go out again, buy newspapers, walk in parks, reply to letters; reply to them, moreover, hit by hit, kick below the belt by answering kick. But she was nothing.

Her religion, dormant in her, proved of no avail, for she had betrayed it, as Terence had betrayed her. She could not face a confessor. . . . To what could she turn, so as to escape the misery of the senses, to avoid trees and music, sunlight and moonlight and, above all, flowers?

She found the answer. Hospitals resembled convents in their routine; only the religious core was absent. She was intelligent and soon learnt her profession. And in this world of order, devoted to healing the body, she found an anodyne for her wounded soul. Its matter-of-factness, its strict rules, its divisions of light and darkness, were helpful to her, and the antiseptic smell of ward and corridor drove out the scent of the day and season, triumphed over the perfume of the flowers in the wards, sterilised them.

It was, she thought, as though her heart had been cauterised. She altered in her aspect, became part of the hospital and its routine. Her body now seemed rhythmless and without purpose, except for giving medicines and smoothing pillows. Her efficiency transcended kindness, a loveless, sublimated love. And, if she felt no pleasure, she felt no pain. . . . Night-duty she enjoyed, for then she saw no daylight, slept through it, and the flowers had been put away by the time she arrived in the evening.

For many years (endless years, they appeared to her) this kind of existence continued; until you would have thought that Fate had forgotten her, had thrown her life aside, intending to make no pattern out of it. . . . And then, one night, a case was brought into her ward, a drunken man who had been knocked down and crushed by a motor-car. . . . She recognised him at once. He had become poor and old, his talent for music had come to nothing. His wife had left him. He had no children. . . . There was no one to look after him except Nurse Aurelia.

She used to sit with him in the day-time, as well as nurse him at night. The great bare windows were flooded with the golden light of unforgettable spring days, and the scent of the flowers that had been brought to the patients by relatives and friends, apple blossom and cherry, tulips, narcissus and wallflower, was often overpowering under the strong sun. . . . Day by day the old man grew worse, and after ten days he died. He had never been fully conscious, so she was not sure how much he knew or whether he recognised her. . . . But somehow or other, through looking after him, she had regained her faith.

After it was all over, she had left the hospital and taken a post in a nursing-home. She had felt she needed a change, she said.

. . . . .

Nurse Aurelia was silent for a while, staring into the embers, and then she turned to me, the irises of her eyes glowing with that strange fire of the animal world, and added, 'But I still hate flowers'.

LOW TIDE

It was an entrance that, however unconscious, never failed of its effect, and one to which the eye could never become accustomed. The two little figures at the top of the steps, though put-in on a large and crowded canvas, inevitably and entirely dominated the scene at this precise moment of the day. Behind them under the pale blue canopy of the sky rose the intricate perspective of steep cliffs, trim but wind-cut trees, and dells of a cultivated wildness; while the sharp cries of the children, as they raced round these, falling down, laughing, and dropping wooden spade or metallic pail, gave a certain poignancy to the otherwise flat blur of the band wafted up from below. The staircase was the culmination of the garden. On to it led every dell, dingle, and asphalt path. With heavy stone balustrades, crushed down beneath rows of weighty, clumsily carved, stone vases overflowing with purple petunias and a new, very municipal variety of dwarf sweet-pea — salmon-pink in tone — it held its own with any other feature of the town. It competed successfully for the attention with funicular-trams, which by their movement continually caught the eye as they performed their geometrical operations up and down the cliff with the precision of a drill-sergeant; it outshone the flashing eyes of the bandstand, encased in panes of glass, and even outvied in interest the lion-coloured sands flecked with moving, gaily dressed people, and spotted with trestles, centres of little groups, on which white-clad figures gesticulated, or opened and shut soundless mouths. On each side of this imposing structure, set in wide sloping surfaces of grass, smooth and green as baize, two enormous five-pointed stars — frilled out at the edges with variegated leaves of iodine-brown, ochre, green-white and lemon-yellow, lined again within by lobelias of a copper-sulphate blue that in their turn enclosed a round pupil of coral-pink begonias and red and purple fuchsias — glowered out to sea like two bloodshot eyes; one Cyclops guarding each side of the steps.

When the first terrace, overlooked by all this glory, was

reached, the blur of the music sharpened into focus, settling into so many familiar and machine-made moulds, for its broad platform was level with the gilt knob of the circular cage from which rose all this sound. Under cover of that cage — or glass case — alternately scorched on warm days and frozen on cool ones, the band discoursed the whiskered, military joviality of Waldteufel or in a sudden frenzied modernity hurled itself with ineffable vigour into the country dances of Edward German. Then, though the majority of residents were content with such a programme, the orchestra must also propitiate that select few who took pride in knowing 'what was going on' in London almost before Londoners themselves had found out. This section of Newborough was, apparently, satisfied that the only important happening in the capital was the advent, and subsequent failure or success, of the latest musical comedy. Nothing else counted. For the Winter Garden band to be a fortnight late in their first reproduction of the strains which accompanied it — if it had proved a 'hit' in London — would be, one understood, a local disaster of the first magnitude. Thus, for the benefit and edification of the select, the orchestra must rehearse feverishly, and perform quite soon, such forgotten favourites as *The Belle of New York*, *The Geisha*, *San Toy*, *The Country Girl*, *The Messenger Boy*, and innumerable other and equally popular variants of these masterpieces.

Distributed round the centre of music was a mathematical arrangement of seats; while beyond, on the deaf side of the bandstand — for it was glazed toward the sea — stretched a long terrace, its farther wall dropping, according to the tides, straight down on to sand or sea, rising out of them, shaded toward the bottom with dark, tough seaweed and well plastered with limpets and barnacles. This final and most important promenade, from the whole length of which the steps above are visible, was crowded with young women of a provincial smartness, wearing dresses in such a height of fashion that they would have been unrecognised in Paris or London; light-coloured young women from Leeds or Halifax, with turquoise or false-pearl ear-rings jangling down hardly on diminutive gold chains or screwed tight into the unpierced ear. With them would stroll laughing young men in white-flannel trousers, crowned with straw hats, or, more imposingly, with panamas. The latter were a sign of grace and distinction but recently come into favour, entering hand in hand with ping-pong and the Boer War on a short but strenuous conquest of England. Cecil Rhodes had patronised them; and a good one, it was murmured, cost £100! Then there were the residents. Old military gentlemen, rather red and puffing, with long white mustachios, and heavy walking-sticks, are pacing up and down, their elbows out-turned, the two joints of the arm forming a right angle; they are continually pulling at their cuffs — stiff, white cuffs with coloured lines on them — as if on the point of conjuring, the verge of exhibiting, an alive but miraculous white rabbit. All the summer days they spend here, in-the-open-air-damn-it, and all the winter on the cliff above, with eyes fixed to the end of a gigantic telescope, pointed like a gun at the sea, in the bow-window of the commodious Gentlemen's Club, the exterior of which is painted a thick but appropriate magenta. Then, but sitting down more often than walking, there are groups of two or three old ladies, grey-haired, broad-based, who, if they move, sway a little from side to side like ducks on their way to the pond. There are always a few curates, thin, eager, and raven-coated, who have come down from the Ecclesiastical Rest Home on the West Cliff; while several bath-chairs are wheeled up and down or remain stationary — bath-chairs that, so near the sea, look like the gigantic shells of ocean snails, deposited and overturned by some fierce wave, their tenacious inhabitants, sadly out-of-element, stretching out wandering tentacles and adhesive surfaces. Finally, Newborough being a health resort, there is spread among the rest a whole cohort of infirm, elfin, and imbecile. As if in some nightmare drama, these men, women and children loll and lollop about, with curious uncouth gait, blind or deaf or dumb, hunchbacked or idiot, or armless from birth. But none of these, as they move among the throng, attract much attention. It must, therefore, be taken as a tribute to the personality of the Misses Cantrell-Cooksey that they should invariably claim such a measure of public notice on their arrival.

Perhaps the best place from which to witness their triumph was from one of the seats on the upper terrace, though the spectacle was visible, actually, from nearly every chair in the gardens. The flight of steps, like all monuments of its period both mean and magnificent, looked theatrical as well, as if set for some very material but ridiculous ballet of the Second Empire, some startling and quite pointless convolution of blue muslin, yellow hair, and arms and legs of full muscular development. In place, though, of this ordered and golden whirlwind came down the steps, treading very gingerly, yet unable in their good-natured weakness to resist keeping time to the domineering rhythm of the Waldteufel that greeted them, these two little elderly ladies of the same height and dressed alike. Sisters obviously; indeed, such was the resemblance between them that they might have been taken for twins. Mild and timid in bearing, they yet boasted a singular bravery of apparel, in which, though the nineteen-hundred note was dominant, there were many recollections of past fashions. They were bedizened and a-jingle with little crinkling ornaments, ruby bars, gold bangles, slave bracelets, small watches set with half-pearls hanging from enamelled brooches shaped like true-lovers' knots; they were decked out with little pieces of lace, numerous ribbons and a thousand other joyous trifles. Regarded more as objects of virtu than as the covering or decoration of human beings, their dress had a certain beauty, a very intricate quality of design — design that, while outwardly unconnected, had in it a strange rhythm and logic of its own. It was as full of *motifs* as Burmese art, and as complicated. If the band stopped playing, if every voice in the garden sank down for an instant, the dress of the Misses Cantrell-Cooksey would, one felt, play its own accompaniment, announce the entrance of its wearers. All these small, shining ornaments, apparently meaningless, would tinkle, trill, and jingle sweetly, giving out a sound peaceful and silly as any cow-bell heard in the Alps. But, alas! Waldteufel offered no such opportunity.

If their dresses were individual, so were their faces; for though the Age of Cosmetics had not yet returned to us, the cheeks of the two sisters, both of whom had surely seen sixty summers, were a blaze of Babylonish colour. The lips were of a cherry richness, and the hair, showing under the fashionable toque, was not so much golden or primrose as succulent scarlet. All this flaunting splendour was in rather quaint contrast to the gingerly tripping walk, the hair and cheek in direct contradiction to the pale but kindly timidity of their eyes — and, indeed, in the latter difference lay hidden the clue to their entire appearance. Determined to look young, they refused to wear glasses: and to insist on youth after it has passed requires sound eyesight as well as sound judgment. Resultantly, they looked like a pair of music-hall sisters, some popular variety turn of the late 'seventies, left over from that age but defiant of time — looked as though they had made up for their entertainment by the green, value-changing gaslight of mid-Victorian times, and after a Rip Van Winkle slumber, had woken to find themselves here, alone on the staircase, under the sunshine of the East Coast, in the hard dawn of a new, rather sinister, century.

Their appearance, in fact, as they descended the steps, was distinctly open to ridicule, yet so painfully lonely that it was with a feeling of relief that one saw them gain the upper terrace in safety, for the descent of these *opéra-bouffe* steps had taken a considerable time.

The numerous youths who were always to be found loitering on this platform, staring down at the people below, now turned round slowly, drew the knobs of their walking-sticks out of their mouths with a loud pop, as if a cork were being drawn, planted their backs firmly against the railings, and thus outlined against the sea, transferred the extreme vacancy of their gaze upon the two sisters, staring at them fixedly, and, after a time, smiling. The small boy selling programmes, and frilly-edged carnations of an ice-cream pink, made a ribald joke. But then, as the Misses Cantrell-Cooksey rounded the farther corner on to the steps that led below, the sensation on the first terrace began to die down. The youths once more pivoted round listlessly, their eyes following the bands of giggling young girls who strolled beneath them, staring in awe at the smartly dressed visitors, or resting quietly beyond on the similar blue vacancy of the sea.

When the two sisters arrived on the lower terrace, where the band played, there was again a distinct sensation. As they progressed down the middle of the audience, glancing from side to side in the hope of securing adjacent chairs, with a loftiness of manner that was the disguise both for bad eyesight and an intense shyness, a small, rustling, tittering wind moved the heads of the flower-bright rows of people, and even the groups walking up and down the promenade beyond stopped to watch. On the other hand, a few elder members of the feminine section of the audience — residents, probably — far from being amused, appeared to disapprove, quite definitely to disapprove.

Pretty Mrs. Sibmarsh, the wife of Dr. Sibmarsh, was sitting with her back to the sea talking to her friend, Mrs. Merryweather. As the two sisters went by, her face was contracted with a spasm of absolute fury. 'I don't know how they dare come down like that; I don't really!' she said in hard, even tones. 'Perfect sights I call them! Twenty-eight, indeed! more like sixty-eight! If you'd seen them, Mabel, at the Hospital Ball at the Royal the other night, dressed like débutantes, with white feathers in their hair. I'm surprised they were let in. They've been here about fifteen years now, and know no one; and I always say that if people have no friends, it is their own fault. And odd, odd to a degree! I can't bear people who aren't like anybody else . . . a little too odd for my taste!' And Mrs. Sibmarsh looked severely at the band and tiers of greenery above, for it was before she had become artistic and psychic, before she had begun to cultivate originality, before the coralline stethoscope of Dr. Sibmarsh, which, like a conjurer, he produced out of his top-hat, had reaped its asthmatic harvest, and her house had become, as her friends said, 'a perfect museum'— a wilderness of old oak and Staffordshire pottery. No, that story belongs to the subsequent development of Newborough, which one day we hope to relate. At present, then, oddity offended Mrs. Sibmarsh, and looking at them once more with an intense disgust she completed her verdict: 'Odd to a degree — and rich — very rich; and mean into the bargain! And to look at them, it wouldn't surprise me if they drugged! They've got a very queer look in their eyes.' And she sent up a shrill spiral of hard laughter into the blue air.

Owing to a fortunate concatenation of circumstances, it was some time before the Misses Cantrell-Cooksey discovered the disfavour with which they were regarded in the town. Indeed, at this period they were happy — more happy than they had ever been in their lives. Even their loneliness was not felt by them, so devoted was Miss Frederica to Miss Fanny, so devoted Miss Fanny to Miss Frederica. If they were both rather 'odd', as Mrs. Sibmarsh stated, yet the accusation of being unlike everybody else was unjust. On the contrary, they were all too human. Nor did they drug, as was suggested, but found their release from a reality which at any rate was not too hard upon them in material matters, in the roseate view of life inherent in those gifted with the Romantic Temperament. In fact they still believed in the Age of Miracles. They felt young, to each other looked young, and when, however seldom, a doubt assailed them as to whether they appeared as youthful to others as to themselves, they found a refuge in cosmetics. The rouge and dye-pot they affected were only the methods through which a laudable, very respectable desire to keep up appearances found its vent. But, while growing ever more devoted, while hardly noticing their lack of friends, themselves accentuated their isolation by the extreme vividness of their exterior. Otherwise, loneliness was no such uncommon thing in Newborough as to have attracted all this attention. Through their own fault, alas! they had made themselves targets for ridicule; and the vision of the town, a vision sharp and narrow, could not pierce through this extraordinary outward aspect to the essential goodness and kindness within.

Apart from the childish vanity that prompted the extravagance of their appearance, and the simplicity which led them to believe that Newborough would accept their own conservative estimate of their age, not much oddity was evident in them. These facts would lead one to suppose that they had always led rather secluded lives. This, then, would account for their being unaware of their loneliness, for their rather painful gaiety, and the resolution with which they participated in every local function. Thus were they making up for a youth that had lacked diversions by extreme merry-making in their latter years.

The daughters of a country clergyman, whom they had worshipped, and on whose behalf both of them in their young days had made certain sacrifices — suffered certain disappointments, one understood — they had found themselves, some fifteen years before the time of which we are speaking, possessed of a considerable fortune and alone in the world. For, unlike most of his calling, old Mr. Cantrell-Cooksey had been a rich man. Furthermore, the sisters were undoubtedly 'well-connected' — a fact which, owing to their disposition, afforded them a more constant and considerable pleasure than the inheritance of wealth, since, in its milder forms, snobbery is but a symptom of the Romantic Temperament.

They had been pretty, with a surface prettiness of skin and eye, golden hair and round, pale blue eye. The Rector would never, of course, for a moment have condoned the use of cosmetics, so that it was only when at his death they emerged from some forty-five years of seclusion, that they adopted such methods of beautifying themselves — methods not meant so much to attract others as to calm themselves. And one consequence of the pavonine glory into which they then blossomed was to make those valuable connections of theirs seem rather frigid in manner. The more rosy grew their skins, the more golden their hair, to that extent the less friendly grew their relatives. One season, the second summer after their father's death, they spent in London, but the neglect of their numerous cousins, the barren coldness of a great city in which they had no friends, were more than their sensitive hearts could bear for long: and sensitive their hearts undoubtedly were! It was a curious trait in their characters, pointing to some latent eccentricity in them, that while thus responsive, they should have still done nothing to tone down the intensity of their clothes and colouring. Surely they must have felt that there was some little connection between these and the coldness with which they were treated. Either their weak eyes must have prevented them from realising the full oddity of their appearance, or else their romantic disposition must have already and for ever warped their judgment.

They were well pleased to settle in the large red-brick house overhanging the cliffs at Newborough. Their dear father had been fond of the town, and though they had not visited it for many years, they had often been taken there as children and, as a place to live in, it suited them exactly. The Red House, appropriately named, was large, and besides what was described by the agents who disposed of it as its 'unique situation' — which consisted in the dangerous angle of the cliffs beneath — had the additional advantage of raking, enfilading indeed, the Promenade with its east-facing windows. In this new house the sisters began a life of peaceful happiness, and at the same time, contrasted with their former existence at the Rectory, of feverish excitement. They loved the house, and each one of the fifteen years they had spent in it had made it more dear to them. They liked the town — like is but a moderate term for the affection they felt for it — and were superbly unconscious of unfriendly eyes or cruel laughter. 'We like Newborough', Misses Frederica and Fanny would say together, as if with one voice, 'because there's always something going on — and then it's so pretty! We can never look out of our windows without being reminded of the Bay of Naples. In the summer there is always the band; and London is so *noisy* nowadays.' And they loved the house. Yes, they *loved* it. It wasn't quite like anyone else's. Oh, no! Not, of course, that it was 'queer' in any way — for the sisters, curiously enough, shared Mrs. Sibmarsh's horror of oddity. It was such a comfortable house, and had such a 'nice' garden, too, on the other side — quite like being in the country. It was difficult to imagine, when one was in it, that one was in a town. The garden, edged with split-oak palings, was full of speckled laurel bushes and dirty evergreens, graced in the spring by the spidery, thin mauve flowers of a few Indian lilacs, the dying fireworks of a laburnum tree with a hollow in its centre which had at some time been filled with cement, and later by a few perfectly correct but rather scentless roses. And in the autumn, chrysanthemums ('they do so well here') — beds and beds of chrysanthemums! The garden acted as clock for the seasons. Laburnum pointed to full spring, roses to full summer, chrysanthemums to rich autumn. Though Newborough was situated so far to the north, the climate seemed to them so mild — but very bracing, of course. The east winds were, perhaps, a little trying. Then everything had its disadvantages, hadn't it? And it was a source of the greatest pride to them that in the depths of winter, between Christmas and the New Year, it was usually possible to find one unfolded and frost-bitten rosebud, brown as if it had passed through the ordeal by fire, dank and dark as a drowned man — but a rose none the less — lurking in the garden. In fact this square space was a continual delight, so admirably suited for garden party or church bazaar, just big enough but not too big, and so convenient! But no function of any sort ever took place there.

Nevertheless, the sisters were always remarking to each other that it was 'so nice for entertaining one's friends'.

In anything they did or proposed to do, this phrase was for ever on their tongues. Whatever they contemplated was considered only in the light of aid or hindrance to the entertainment of this imaginary horde; an evidence of a need for friendship and of a hospitable disposition.

Beyond the garden, as far as the eye could see, rolled what in our childhood we were taught to regard as the 'German Ocean', displaying its various shrill and strident moods, lapping, singing, shouting, roaring or moaning. And this music, so romantic and strange, was always the pleasantest of sounds to the two sisters.

In the summer, as we have seen, Miss Frederica and Miss Fanny Cantrell-Cooksey would, on each fine day, walk down by the carefully preserved cliffs, through the trim woods, on to the terrace by the sea where the band played. They were due to arrive there between 11.15 and 11.30. In the afternoon — after lunch (at 1.15) — they would walk a little or sit in the garden. There were, of course, frequent rests, for one got so tired doing all these things, and lying-down freshens one up so. Tea at 4.30 with a large silver kettle, with a flame under it, silver teapot and silver sugar-basin. Ceylon, *not* Indian tea. The milk must, naturally, be poured *first* into the teacup. So many people fail to do this. And one must make the tea *oneself*: servants never learn to do it properly, do they? Emily, for instance, though she had been there many years, had never learnt to use boiling water. It must be *boiling* water. Miss Fanny, in person, would pour the water from the kettle into the teapot; and, in due time, Miss Frederica, the elder sister, would pour out the tea.

Tea, regarded not as a beverage but as a social function, was one of their extravagances — for though few people came, unless Archdeacon Haddocriss looked in to tell them about one of his new funds, it was always prepared for ten people. Lots of little cakes; and scones, supported on a bowl filled with hot water. There were certain days, however, when, if the ladies felt the need for some unusual excitement, they would inform Emily that they would be out for tea, and would walk to one of those artistic and half-timbered cafés which were becoming such a feature of the town, where, beneath Gothic canopies of fumed German oak, and by simple dressers of peasant and cottage crockery, in a stifling atmosphere of English coffee and strong tea, they would partake of a cup of chocolate — very dainty — with the white of an egg frothed on top of it to represent cream. This would appeal to their feelings, reminding them, as it did, of that visit to Germany, in company with their Dear Old Father, some fifteen — or was it fourteen? — years before he passed away. Thus stimulated, they would return home.

Dinner, the crown of the day for every respectable inhabitant of Newborough, was at 7.30 P.M. The Misses Cantrell-Cooksey had always been used to dinner at this hour, so for them it was nothing unusual. But for most of the well-to-do in the town, dinner was a shibboleth, its hour dividing mankind — not so much a meal as a Declaration of the Rights of Man. A whole revolution was fixed between those who enjoyed their dinner at midday, and those who dined in the evening. Between those addicted to late dinner and those who still revelled in the primitive simplicity of high-tea was fixed such a gap in the social ranks as could never be bridged. And for the former, two things were of the utmost importance. One of these was never, in any evil hour or by any unfortunate accident, to refer to the midday meal under any other title than 'luncheon' — or perhaps the more familiar, more vulgar, 'lunch'. Dr. Sibmarsh had, for instance, once referred to it in public as 'dinner' — and it took him long to live down. The other, and even more vital, thing to keep in mind, was the absolute necessity of 'dressing' for dinner. Invariably, inevitably, one must 'dress' for dinner — otherwise the nature of the meal might be mistaken! Once 'dressed' one was secure, since no man 'dresses' for high tea.

Thus in every red-brick villa in Newborough at 7.30 on a summer evening the dining-room would be illuminated; the electric light would show splendidly in its mounting of chased or wrought copper through shades, bell-like shades, of opalescent glass; and, though it was still daylight without, if one were lucky enough to walk down Prince of Wales's Avenue or Albemarle Road at this hour, one would see row after row of these glowing interiors, the very pageant of late Victorian and early Edwardian prosperity. Beneath the golden lustre of four lights that hung from the ceiling, seated before a white table, in the centre of which was usually a large doily composed of lace over a ground of dead-orange silk, upon which would stand four little trumpet-shaped silver vases, with frilled edges like sharks' teeth, each displaying at this season three or four yellow poppies, four or five sweet-peas, and misty bunches of that nameless though universal white blossom that is more like white muslin than a flower, the diners would be sitting, carefully dressed. The hostess, in a pretty gown of pink satin, low at the bosom and with puffy sleeves, wearing an amethyst or aquamarine brooch, would be talking amiably and sweetly — wearing that charming smile that made such a difference to her face, 'lit it up', as the phrase was — to the gentleman on her right, while at the same time directing a glance of such flaming contempt at her maid-servant for falling into those very mistakes of service about which she had warned her all day — and as for that, just a moment before dinner — striking her dead with a look of such awful, such diabolical hatred that any other mortal, except this girl accustomed to it, would on the spot have perished and sunk down. The earth itself might well open beneath such vehement passion — so well disguised.

The rules-of-the-game, too, were very strict. It was not, even, an easy affair to get into the dining-room; for again in this it was necessary to disprove the possible if unspoken allegation of transcendentalised high tea. If there were more than four or five guests, a regular and courtly procession would walk across the small space from drawing-room to dining-room: arm-in-arm: lady on right, gentleman on left: polite, but easy, conversation. If, however, there were but a few people, three or four, the same effect could be produced by saying in a careless Bohemian way: 'Oh, don't let's bother. Can't we go in as we are?'

Fortunately Emily was seldom forgetful, and unfortunately, it was seldom that Miss Frederica or Miss Fanny Cantrell-Cooksey was able to sweep in to dinner on the arm of a cavalier. If, though, one was alone for dinner — and had not got a headache — one could go down to hear the band again. When the evenings were cool, the orchestra, escaped from their glass case, were sure to be playing 'inside'. 'Inside' indicated an enormous hall near the bandstand, built to look as if it were part of the Louvre — Newborough architecture was both informed and cosmopolitan — and tastefully decorated within, in a Second Empire scheme of chocolate, turquoise-blue and gold — all by now very faded and dry-looking, like an old sugared biscuit. Round the frieze, high up, were inscribed on scrolls the names of composers at the height of their fame when this hall was constructed. A queer medley it was, and one that would be an interesting footnote to that *History of Taste* which is now waiting to be written — for these names, considered then of equal value, represented the judgment of a generation . . . MENDELSSOHN . . . HANDEL . . . SPOHR . . . BEETHOVEN . . . GOUNOD . . . VERDI . . . SCHUMANN . . . WEBER . . . DONIZETTI . . . BERLIOZ . . . LISZT.

The hall had been specially built for music, but unfortunately the acoustic properties were such that not a note could be heard properly, except from the roof, where the sound was as nearly perfect as possible, but there were no chairs! The concerts were nevertheless much appreciated. Every evening the bandsmen became suddenly transformed into individuals, escaping from a sober uniform into evening dress; became definitely recognisable as persons. This, again, affected their playing, making it more individual, less a composite whole. The two ladies had in some mysterious way conceived a great passion for the music of Wagner; and since in the evening performances the conductor, who prided himself on being catholic and modern, was allowed more to please himself than in the mornings, they were often able to gratify this passion. Perhaps this Wagner-worship was one of the oddities to which Mrs. Sibmarsh had alluded: it was a curious phenomenon certainly, for otherwise they were devoid of any musical appreciation. But there is no doubt that, as much as anything in Newborough, they enjoyed sitting here in the evenings, and wallowing in the sensual melodies of that master, as in a hot bath.

In addition to these concerts there were, in the season, other entertainments. Touring companies would come down for six nights to the two theatres, the 'Royal' and the 'Ghoolingham'. Our two heroines did not often visit these, except during the annual appearance of the D'Oyly Carte Gilbert and Sullivan Opera Company. For this event, to which all the year they looked forward, it was their habit to book a box on the opening night and a stall for each subsequent performance. Such pretty music, and oh! how witty and amusing. And nothing in bad taste, nothing that anybody need be offended at! Even the Rector, who had not much cared for festivities, had thoroughly enjoyed *The Gondoliers*. Otherwise they did not go much to the theatre unless it was something special. Then, out of curiosity, they would book seats. Once, for instance, they had been to hear Sousa's Band, which paid a flying visit to the Ghoolingham. What an extraordinary man! how extraordinary it all was, so noisy and vulgar! Still, the marches were most inspiring, one must say, and so patriotic! He had, had he not, a true gift of melody?

Then there were the occasional appearances at a special performance of famous but ageing actresses — Lady Bancroft and Mrs. Kendal — or of indomitable but ageless beauties such as Mrs. Langtry. It would be a pity to miss such a treat. Thus there was always something going on.

This continual round of diversion was broken every seventh day by church-going, the event of the week. Now that the Rector was no longer with them they went to church only *once* on a Sunday (churches are so badly ventilated); in the morning. After church ensued church-parade. This took place on the promenade overlooked by the Red House, and lasted until the luncheon hour.

Clasping a black-bound Prayer Book, divided by a vivid blue or purple watered-silk marker, in a well-gloved hand, and gorgeous as the Queen of Sheba, Miss Frederica and Miss Fanny Cantrell-Cooksey would walk — though 'walk' hardly describes such stately progress . . . march . . . saunter . . . up and down, as would all the other respectable inhabitants and worthy visitors. It was, consciously, one of the 'prettiest' sights of the town, and, what was of more importance, an observance that helped to keep up appearances.

Innumerable people walked up and down, up and down — individuals for a moment, then dovetailing into the crowd. Most of them were elderly — though there were a few children — and looked incongruous in clothes of such elaboration, as must all people of over middle-age who adopt a minutely decorated style. For a surfeit of decoration is no more suitable to the elderly than a surfeit of food. Up and down they paced, under the hard northern sunlight, anthropoids that having massacred a diverse regiment of beasts-of-the-field now masquerade in their pitiable skins; to the latter they have added the feathers raped from the osprey, and now look as though decorated for some primitive, some awful, rite. Up and down they progress, past cream-painted houses, roofed with damp-blue slates; on each sill is a box of red geraniums, before each house a stretch of green, prim grass. Far below, constant companion to their march, rolls the steely northern sea: the prospect on the other side varies. The cream-painted houses give way to golden lawns, the colour of which is enhanced by an artistic green-painted cab-shelter covered in by red tiles, a recent inspiration of the municipal architect: then, again, follow Gothic stone drinking troughs for beasts, and portentous stone houses for men. Not all the people walk. A few drive in large open cabs, that rumble slowly; while others, ladies of fabulous age, with trembling blue lips and palely purple faces, with hairy growths on the chin, and black bonnets nodding on the top of their helpless heads, are being drawn along in bath-chairs that are so many black insects. As they are rolled past, in a flutter of bugles, heliotrope-velvet ribbons and black kid gloves, there is a trilling of jet-like petrified laughter. Each venerable image, thus trundled, would be accompanied by a niece or daughter, pale, flat-looking women with vague but crucified expressions, like the female saints whose tortures are depicted by German Primitives. The aunts and mothers in their bath-chairs look happy though grim ('poor old things', the Misses Cantrell-Cooksey would say, rather nervously) as they clasp a Prayer Book tightly in their gloved hands, as if it were a passport for that equally tedious Heaven which they had prepared for themselves. Already there sounded from them the characteristic music of their Heaven, asthmatic and wheezy; so old were they that when through blue lips they murmured, their voices sounded like harmoniums played at a distance; and when their faces were in repose, the bones would show under the sagging parchment, for the skull was already asserting its lordship over the flesh.

In this setting our heroines showed almost to advantage. Yet as they went by, while other promenaders would be continually stopped by friends, and would stand talking together in little groups, they would never be greeted. The old ladies would stretch out tentacles from their shells in welcome to others; but our two friends would never be hailed by them. Indeed, the old ladies would be galvanised into life by the sight of them, looking at them as sourly as any younger members of the community. The burden of their complaint was the same as that uttered by Mrs. Sibmarsh. 'Perfect sights! How they can get themselves up like that I can't think! And they were properly brought up too. Twenty-eight, indeed! they'll never see sixty-eight again, I should say! Real Aunt Sallies!' And after some such declamatory effort their voices would ooze back to a whisper.

In among the promenaders and listening groups Mrs. Sibmarsh herself was continually imparting information. 'Have you heard the latest, Mrs. Spirechurch? What do you think those two old bundles have done now?' And many a macabre march was halted for an instant in order to hear a recital of the latest Cantrell-Cooksey folly. About three years before, the two ladies had undoubtedly given their age in the census return as twenty-eight and twenty-six respectively. By 7.30 the next night every dining-room in the town was discussing this lamentably absurd lapse from verity. It became, this topic, another thing that divided dinner from high tea. It lightened the life of Newborough; and, ever since, each movement or saying of the sisters had become an object of mingled interest and contempt.

On wet Sundays — which were almost as enjoyable as fine ones — Miss Frederica and Miss Fanny would drive to and from church in their heraldic 'Lonsdale Wagonette'. This vehicle, of which they were intensely proud, was regarded by others almost as the symbol of original sin. It was, in truth, an odd conveyance: a large, long, polished, black, roomy affair, lined with railway-carriage-blue material; indeed the interior was not unlike a railway carriage, except that the windows were above the seats, one narrow end turned toward the horses. Whichever seat one occupied, one's back shut out the view, while the view opposite was likewise obscured by some person. When the door shut, the step shut with it; when the door opened, the step precipitated one upon the pavement. How either of the two ladies ever got in or out of their conveyance, with their weak eyes and faltering footsteps, remains one of the mysteries of the past! The coachman, smartly dressed in a buff coat, sat — immense — on the box, while the door had emblazoned on it the very rampant arms of Cantrell-Cooksey. The wagonette was, really, an extraordinary creation; one of the last, most imbecile inventions of equine traffic, originally intended to aid the more rapid and complete incarceration of guests in various country houses. Its owners, however, were very content, regarding it as the supreme achievement of civilisation. It was neater and more unusual-looking than a brougham or victoria; not so 'fast' — in any sense — as a tandem; and how much nicer than those horrible, snorting motor-cars that were coming in! Not that they would ever be seen in one of those things; so trippery. And then the 'Lonsdale', most important quality, was so hospitable. There was room in it for one's friends. It would hold at least eight people, where a brougham would hold three, and it would be so useful for picnics in the Sherbourn Woods. In fact this lumbering conveyance made a special appeal to the Romantic Temperament.

Sunday afternoons in the season were also very pleasant, for there were concerts in the Winter Gardens at 3.30. The band, discarding its uniform, would adopt frock-coats, while the conductor would walk round the corner into his glass case, curling a waxed military moustache and sporting a top-hat. When securely within the shelter, the bandsmen would stand up to greet him; he would take off his hat, turn round, and bow. *God Save the King* — for it was Sunday — would then be played. Usually a *vocalist* would come down from London for these concerts (a vocalist is a very different thing from a singer — more sabbatical). The vocalist, running to extremes, was generally a very young girl or very old man. The programmes of these concerts were, of course, composed of sacred music, and were regarded by the town as being 'very classical'. Some, even, took objection to them on this score, for not all Newborough enjoyed 'classical' music. The adjective had a special significance. For the town divided all sounds made by piano, orchestra, or human voice into two categories: 'classical' music and — just music! Music meant *The Country Girl*, *The Belle of New York*, Offenbach, Waldteufel and, generally, anything that had 'a tune in it'; Sullivan — except for *The Lost Chord*, acknowledged as sacred — was an exception, belonging to both worlds, pagan and 'classical', but universally popular. Then came the 'classical' division, comprising any composers who had comprehended and used the rules of counterpoint, the laws of harmony, and at the same time any mid-Victorian composer, who, neglecting both, had written anthems or oratorios. For sacred music was the inner and spiritual core of 'classical' music. Furthermore, it was understood that any music played on an organ became transmuted in some mysterious fashion into sacred music. And, by virtue of this, Wagner had crept into the Sunday Afternoon Concerts, as a sort of Honorary Sacred Composer; for it was well known that the organist at Holy Trinity — the best organist in all Newborough — played Wagner at his recitals. Thus our two ladies were privileged to bathe in those luscious strains each Sunday.

After music came tea again, at five o'clock, half an hour later than usual. It was always nice to have a cup of tea.

This routine continued through their fifteen years of prosperity, from about May 24th till September 27th. About this latter date, every year, it would occur simultaneously to many that the evenings were drawing in. Chrysanthemums would strike a rich note of gloom and warning in many gardens, and through the windows of the Red House, especially, would be borne-in their peculiarly muffled and musty smell, mildewed and damp as the air of the tomb. Poor old Miss Waddington — whom they saw from time to time — would inaugurate the winter season with one of those cyclone colds that were her unique gift. Bath-chairs would disappear from the Promenade and Winter Gardens. The band would be dispersed, its members drifting away to London or to various theatre-orchestras elsewhere, and soon the whole town would be echoing with the more wintry music of howling gale, roaring sea, and their domestic equivalents, wheezing, sneezing, snoring and coughing. Blinds would be drawn down for tea. There would be comfortable fires; the yellow wallpaper of the drawing-room would take on a warmer tone, the large oil-picture of 'Sunset, Egypt' of which old Mr. Cantrell-Cooksey had been so fond, a richer glow; and all would burn more brightly again in the various items of the silver equipment on the tea-table. Christmas, it would be felt — in the Red House, and universally — will soon be here again. Already the shops would be getting ready for it, with an ever-increasing number of imbecile 'novelties' and a great display of red flannel and cotton-wool snow.

The winter festivities would start in mid-November. Every five weeks there would be a hospital ball, a hunt ball even — so picturesque with all the red coats and bits of foxes and things — or perhaps a concert in aid of the local lifeboat, or the performance of the Newborough Philharmonic Society which took place every six months; these concerts were also very picturesque — quite a sight indeed — with all the girls in white dresses and all the men in black and white evening clothes. In every one of these gaieties Miss Frederica and Miss Fanny Cantrell-Cooksey would, for a varying payment, participate. Yet at the most spirited and exhilarating of these functions it may be surmised that though clad in a low-cut glory unequalled by any other ladies present, though boasting diamond constellations fixed in their hair like those stars that twinkle so brightly above the head of the Queen of the Fairies in a pantomime, the two ladies were more lonely even than in their unfrequented house. Not, one imagines, that they realised quite what it was they felt; for as the only form of human companionship to which they were accustomed was to be together but otherwise alone, or else to be together in a crowd but equally alone, since few spoke to them or acknowledged their presence, they were not so much aware of the separation from their kind as to let it altogether spoil their pleasure. In order fully to appreciate the honour of being sent to Coventry, it is necessary to have experience of other countrysides and towns. Such had never been the lot of our heroines. Nevertheless, as they left concert or ball, as wrapped in filmy, feathery cloaks they waited outside on the doorstep for the arrival of their Lonsdale — which, in spite of their constant generosity to the commissionaire, was always the last to be ushered up to the door — an inexplicable and terrible feeling of depression would assail them. Perhaps, they thought, it was only the reaction that follows on intense enjoyment. It was curious, though, for in the Rectory they had experienced no such feelings. But then life at the Rectory had not been so full of pleasure and excitement, had it, dear?

When the Carnival Ball (Costumes Voluntary) took place in February, in aid of the Children's Convalescent Home, a riot was very nearly provoked in fashionable circles by the two sisters. Few people wore fancy dress. The arrival, therefore, of Miss Frederica as a Dresden Shepherdess and Miss Fanny as Carmen was all the more noticeable. Miss Frederica wore a white-powdered wig, a sprigged-muslin dress, carried a crook, and had one very captivating black patch near the chin; while Miss Fanny, particularly alluring in a bright red gown in which sequins glittered like a rainbow, and with an orange Spanish shawl flung jauntily round her shoulders, cast sparkling glances over her fan from those weak, pale eyes. It was rather an appalling spectacle, this *danse macabre*, though they enjoyed it thoroughly, quite unaware of the sensation caused. They stood among the waiting groups of young girls at the ballroom door, or sat together by one of the walls. But Newborough never forgot: it ranked as an event, as a topic, with that census return.

In the winter, too, there were countless bazaars in aid of various charities — not so important as the ones that took place in the summer, but more of them, and, in a sense, more exciting, more personal. The great lady of the district, Lady Ghoolingham, let it be understood that though willing to open an infinity of bazaars and sales of work in July or August, nothing and no one would, or ever should, induce her to face the harsh winter winds of Newborough, the cold of the railway carriage that would take her there from London, or the overheated atmosphere of the restaurant car, full of that mysterious and emetic scent of cabbage that haunts it always in the winter. It became necessary, then, for the organisers of good works to find continual substitutes for Lady Ghoolingham. And the Misses Cantrell-Cooksey would often remark to each other that they could not — no, they could not — think what they would do if Archdeacon Haddocriss should ask them to perform some such ceremony on his behalf. You see, it must be quite twenty years since Miss Frederica had opened that one for her father at Hubbard Stanton, and that was only a jumble sale! But Miss Fanny had seen the Archdeacon out that morning, and thought he had looked rather as if he wanted to ask something. No, she wouldn't be at all surprised; and if Frederica was asked, it would hardly be graceful to refuse. . . . Alas! the venerable gentleman knew that if out of respect for their wealth and generosity he invited one of 'those two gaudy old scarecrows' — as he had heard them termed in his presence — to open any function, or even so much as to appear on the platform, the parish would be rent in twain. There would be civil war. If he wanted trouble of that sort, he might just as well introduce ritualism at once.

We have noticed, in passing, some of the minor eccentricities of the two sisters, which might possibly justify the charge brought against them of 'oddness', but now we come to other, more marked, peculiarities. Every fine morning or afternoon in the winter they would, like most other respectable inhabitants of the town, call at the lending library to exchange their novels. There was nothing very unusual in this, except that little Mr. Garrett, behind the counter, founder of the establishment, had become almost a friend. He was more friendly to them than were most of the townsfolk. Like other habituals of the library, they would demand a new novel every day — something 'amusing' and 'light' — an E. F. Benson, for example — and, unlike them, would actually get it. Mr. Garrett was such a nice polite little man. A pity he was so untidy! They would then leave the library, exchanging its warm smell of cloves, sealing-wax and thumbed volumes, for the salt air outside. Coming out into the air was, indeed, like being hit in the face, at this time of year. And now they would turn their steps towards the sea-front! This was considered an extraordinary thing to do. Of all the wealthier members of the community, they were the only two who did not conspire to regard the sea as non-existent except in the summer months. All the rest of them forgot the ocean till the first spring day, and preferred to walk in the streets, among the shops, away from the fierce white wings of spray that fluttered and flapped up over the stout stone walls below. Every day in the winter, when it was not actually raining, our heroines, with that love of extremes — great light and great shadow, sun and black cloud — which is the portion of those afflicted with the Romantic Temperament, would walk by the cold, tumbling brown cliffs along the tawny sands, away, even, from the humanised sea-front. Especially after a storm would they enjoy walking along the lonely white sands. Their scarlet hair, their faces so badly made-up that the expression of each side would vary as if one half of the mask were tragic, the other comic, their absurd and complicated dresses, looked all the more fantastic for this submarine setting; and such it seemed after a storm, some strange undersea view. The sloping, pebbly border of sand and sea would be littered with a wild disarray of broken glass, worn down to round gleaming jewels by the constant fret and foaming of the breakers, of starfish, sea-urchins and queer-shaped monstrosities, heaped up with seaweed like small brown palm-trees or the long black matted hair of mermaids. There were so few people about, and the few there were would haunt the sands each day. There was always a tramp, keeping in to the shelter of the rocks, a little bent man with a thin red beard, a battered bowler hat and a torn frock-coat, a queer parody of prosperity. Then there were the gatherers of limpets and winkles, who would pile up their salt harvest in scaly baskets. One of these men, especially, they noticed — a broad bacchanalian character, with huge northern physique, who ought to have found work harder and more remunerative than this. Him they would see bent nearly double over the flat rocks that were covered by the sea at high tide, as with a knife he removed the molluscs and threw them into the deep basket at his side.

And, most interesting of all, after a storm there would gather together those men who make a living by combing the golden sands. What profession they followed in between the gales, or where they came from, it was impossible to find out. The bacchanalian character would join them, deserting his limpets and winkles for this more profitable and entertaining employment. They would rake over the slope of pebbles and the sands beneath, just at the point where the high tide deposited its hostages. It was a gentle but fascinating exercise, and one requiring very competent eyesight and a certain agility of mind. The sisters would stand there for many minutes watching the alternately romantic and prosaic treasury which the storm had precipitated on these bleak sands. As the men combed, they would find silver pennies of the Plantagenets, old biscuit tins full of sea-biscuits, gold coins from Spain, a piece of rusty armour that had been gnawed by the waves for centuries, coppers that had been thrown to the pierrots in the summer, a glass bottle with a faded message in it — the family to which this agonised scrawl was addressed had been dead these ten years! — a bit of a weighing-machine that had stood on the sands in the summer, a Dutch cheese still round and fresh and cherry-coloured, a long clasp-knife with a curious tortoise-shell handle — all the trifles that time and the cruel tides had left over. Really Miss Frederica and Miss Fanny felt that they could stand here for hours watching, if it was not for the cold. Even when they had walked away a little, they would return for a last glimpse. Gradually a bond grew up between them and these strange diggers for treasure. To the latter there was such a break in the surface of the world between themselves and the dwellers on the West Cliff, that these two queerly caparisoned elderly women, with their dyed hair and painted faces, seemed no further removed from everyday experience than any others of their class. They were a funny lot, ladies and gentlemen! But these two, though they asked constantly to which parish the treasure-seekers belonged, also distributed shillings. Suspicion was allayed. 'It was meant kindly', the men thought, and in the presence of Miss Fanny and Miss Frederica the very living language of the fish-market was stifled by unexpected better feelings.

In short, to watch these men at their work was, to the two sisters, like looking-on at gambling. And here we have the second secret. This was the spark of passion that burned in them. In spite of the quiet orderliness of home and upbringing, these two ladies were, by nature, born gamblers. But for many years timidity, not of the possible consequences — for these held no terrors for them — but of the means and methods by which gambling could respectably be effected, had deterred them from rash action. They must not do anything 'fast'. Horse-racing was out of the question, since their father would never have countenanced the smallest bet. It must be very absorbing, though, they thought. Monte Carlo, too, was a dreadful place, full of *queer* people: never a morning went by — the Rector had told them — except a revolver shot rang out a life. One did not always see these tragedies reported in the Press, because the Casino authorities hushed them up. It was disgraceful — a blot on Europe; but then, of course, queer people *would* do queer things. And foreigners were so queer, what with Monte Carlo and bull-fighting and things like that!

Their own method of gambling would not be gambling, so much as speculation; quite a different matter. And for them an unfortunate sequel to their actions was incredible. Security had ever stood by them. Their world was not subject to these chances, these accidents, but was a solid affair of Law-and-Order, Church-and-State, governed for sixty years by Queen Victoria and now inherited by her worthy and popular son ('God Save the Queen' . . . somehow they felt they would never get used to 'God Save the King' . . . it sounded so funny, didn't it? . . .). Investments were not like gambling at Monte Carlo, but part of an ordered and stately society. 'The very life-blood of commerce' they had read in a *Times* leading article, not long ago. No ill would befall them, for they, too, were part of an ordering of the world. It had pleased God to call them to their position. And things were going on as well as could be expected, considering that the Queen was dead. The Income Tax, though deprecated by all Newborough, was negligible; and the pale spectres of disaster and revolution were still stalking the outer confines of the world, to which they had been banished by the general prosperity, unable as yet to make a sufficiently imposing reappearance on the modern stage after such long exile. The Boer War was dreadful, but apart from the revelation of human brutality and degradation offered by the obstinate desire to fight on behalf of their country shown by those brutal, bearded farmers, there had never been really much reason for worry. After all, we were an island, and brute force had never won yet! And we had the Navy, and our generals too. Of course it was true that there were 'cranks' at large in London, 'Fabians' who wished to overturn the whole system of civilised society. But one did not hear much of them now at Newborough. And since the ordering of the world had been ordained by God, it could hardly be upset except by the Devil himself; and even he would not prevail for long.

If they gambled, being part of the ordering of this world, they would win. Of course they would win! Their temperament assured them of success, and urged them to find the means. Ever since the death of their father they had been able to gratify every desire within a limited circle — that wagonette, for example! If they could find some method of gambling which — since success was inevitable — meant that they could double or treble their income, two birds would be killed with one stone. For, while it would satisfy their need for excitement, the extra wealth accruing to them would thus enable them to buy more 'Lonsdales' — taking 'Lonsdales' as the symbol of worldly ambition. It never occurred to them that there was a penalty attached to possible failure. They had not the nervousness of the very rich. Yet the absence to them of danger did not make the game any less exciting.

Some years before the time of which we are writing, Miss

Frederica had, after a period of study, found the way. Her conclusion was that herself and her sister should sell out of Consols, which now only brought in 2½ per cent, part with their other gilt-edged securities, and invest in one of her own discoveries. Miss Fanny, implicit believer in Frederica's genius, at once concurred.

The elder lady, like many of her generation, had been greatly impressed by the towering genius of Cecil Rhodes — a millionaire was then regarded as a being of high romance, a Napoleon of Finance, a Caesar of Commerce — and by his roseate views of the future in store for South Africa. With utter faith in his views and in the solidity of wealth, Miss Frederica invested most of their joint fortunes in South African Mines and other speculative concerns. Their trustees, in this case powerless to forbid, implored them not to alter their old investments. But Miss Frederica knew better. She knew — for the newspapers had told her — that one must Think Imperially. What were those lines of Kipling's?

She wrote a severe, identical letter to trustees and lawyer, in which she pointed out that one must cease 'thinking in a *narrow* little way', adjured them to put away notions inherited from the past, and to realise that we were, all of us, treading (and how true were her words) on the path that would lead us to an Imperial Tomorrow.

Not one single word of these unusual developments reached Newborough, and for some time the ladies prospered almost as much as they had anticipated. Soon, though, the first cracks appeared in the ice upon which they were skating; but warnings held no meaning for them, and were not heeded. Another year passed. Nothing exceptional transpired. The summer passed, and they were a little behindhand with their accounts. The winter began, and the storms raged.

One afternoon they had been down to the sands, as was their custom, to watch the disentangling of that irrelevant treasure accumulated by the northern waves. As they walked along the Promenade they noticed that the storm was dying down. The lamp-lighter was pursuing his magic calling, and as he touched the lamps with his tall wand there was no flicker of wind and light. The blinds were already down at home. But a rich glow showed through them. It looked so comfortable. The postman had been, too. And a letter was waiting for them. Their tomorrow had come, and they were ruined.

. . . . .

So rooted were they in material prosperity, so protected had been every thought in all their lives from any frosty breath of reality, that at first they were not so much worried as excited. But then, suddenly, the world began to take on the most unexpected and unpleasant contours. Action, for the first time, came into touch with them. Their loss unlocked the gate, and all the aversion and contempt in which they were held came pouring out, overwhelming them in a filthy, muddy torrent. Little pity showed in any face. Even those who had greatly prospered by the worldly possessions of the Misses Cantrell-Cooksey, tradesmen and their like, could not now see any further reason to disguise their feelings, however carefully they had concealed them before. People became offhand, and so rude. Some had always disliked them for their 'oddness' (they had never been like other ladies), while the rest were jealous, feeling that to be ruined was a luxury of the rich. Miss Frederica and Miss Fanny felt that they could stand anything but rudeness, for even yet our two heroines could not envisage the full consequences. Their instinct was to keep up appearances; and this was their courage. Not one word of reproach passed between them, not by one syllable would either admit that the world had changed. Everything now depended on keeping up appearances, on seeming not to mind. The fear was there, buried and smothered, but the material pinch was as yet absent.

They were perhaps a little more excitable now in their manner — on the verge of a breakdown, I thought. Miss Fanny, the injured one, had nothing but soothing and heartfelt compassion for her sister, who, though she would not discuss their calamities, would sit alone, silent, and trembling. Before Miss Fanny she was different, more talkative, more uneasy, for in truth she felt too ashamed and remorseful in front of her handiwork to utter, but she must keep up appearances.

In every shuttered red-brick villa, in every avenue and terrace in the town, the Cantrell-Cooksey affair was discussed at 7.30 each night. Folly of this sort was felt, generally, to be equal to villainy. It was, Mrs. Sibmarsh opined, more than a personal disgrace on the two painted old hags; it was a blot on the fair name of the town. What would tradesmen think that Newborough was coming to? Running up bills with no intention of paying them. An absolute disgrace! But then one only had to look at their eyes . . .

Other people were kind but rather inquisitive. Old Miss Waddington, who happened to be laid up with a bronchial cold that was bad enough to prevent her leaving the house, even on such a visit of commiseration as this one would be, sent her niece across to them at once. The latter returned to her aunt in a marvellously short time with a full budget of information, and Miss Waddington seemed really to be 'more herself' that evening, and had a glass of port after dinner, which she seldom did — invalid port, of course. The Archdeacon, too, was kind, very kind. Directly he heard of the affair he came round to the Red House (the sisters were still in it) and offered to say a prayer with them. Afterwards he addressed a few solemn words to them on secret vices, and, arising out of this, on the particular iniquity of avarice and gambling. But his words served no purpose, because, even if the Misses Cantrell-Cooksey had wished to continue such a career, they had now nothing with which to feed their passion. Avarice would be henceforth a difficult vice for them to practise.

The house was sold. The horses were sold. Everything went, and was lost to them beneath the ghastly sound of the hammer. The Lonsdale fetched but seven pounds. Even the silver teapot, kettle and equipment were taken from them. Nothing remained except a few of their old clothes — which did not prove very attractive items at the sale — and some photographs. The servants had left, two by two, as if leaving the ark on an excursion, laughing, happy and without leave-taking, a few days before the Public Examination.

This event was the wonder of all Newborough, and the charge of 'oddnesss', so often brought against the sisters, was fully borne out by their demeanour in court. The suggestion that they drugged — for drink was too trite an explanation of such behaviour — was widely accepted by that more temporal section of the community which, although it existed in a seaside town, was alive to all that was going on in London, knew every musical-comedy success, had visited all the large hotels there for dinner on Sunday night, and had thus acquired a thorough knowledge of the greater and more wicked world. No secret vice could for long be hidden from them.

Rouged, dyed and a-rattle with little ornaments, Miss Frederica and Miss Fanny arrived in court. Their answers were mostly inaudible, except that when Miss Frederica was asked where she was born, she replied that she did not know, and, in answer to the next question, gave her age as twenty-eight; and then broke down.

The total outcome of the affair was that the Misses Cantrell-Cooksey of the Red House were now left homeless, with twenty-six pounds a year between them. With unexpected generosity a few distant but notable relatives, to whom the Archdeacon sent a written appeal, came forward and made up the sum to fifty-two pounds a year — on the condition that the extra twenty-six pounds per annum should be divided into a fortnightly allowance of one pound, and given to them personally, every other Saturday, by a responsible individual. For the relatives were determined that there should be no more extravagance, no more gambling. Finally, dear old Miss Waddington, in spite of growing infirmity and advancing age, volunteered for the office of bursar. She was fond of good works.

The relatives considered that the two sisters should now find some work to do, and perhaps in time relinquish their allowance. They ought to make an EFFORT, they ought to DO SOMETHING. People must learn to support themselves. However, even Archdeacon Haddocriss, sensible man as he was, had to admit to himself that it was difficult to know for what exact profession the two ladies were fitted.

Now, indeed, the pinch had come and the excitement had gone. But the two sisters kept up appearances to each other — for no one else was taken in! 'The worst of it is', they would say, 'that we shall never be able to entertain our friends again.' Though the physical deprivations, to which they were condemned from this time forward, became gradually manifest, and must, after such a comfortable life, have seemed more cruel, neither of them ever mentioned these. Even less than mental torture can cold and hunger be acknowledged by respectable members of society. Once their presence was admitted, even tacitly admitted, self-respect would go out of the window.

. . . . .

At any rate it looked very clean. That was a comfort! Their room was right at the top.

The tall boarding-house, fronted with that particular white brick which is only to be encountered at seaside resorts, rose like a tower of ice, with blue shadows, from beside a suspension-bridge. The Gothic doorway, carved with cast-iron ivy leaves, had a crooked notice, 'Apartments', stuck against the glass above the door, like a rakish patch over a very Wesleyan eye. The white side of the house, fronting the street which was a continuation of the bridge, was only five storeys high; but the back of the house went down another two storeys: here the brown brick of which it was built showed undisguised, and rising among tall green trees and slopes of grass — for the back looked out on the Dale — a public pleasure-ground — it lost some of its horror, becoming merely a high brown tower. The Misses Cantrell-Cookseys' room was the top one on the street side, under the tall gable covered with rain-blue slates. The window, from the street, looked like a sinister eye. Inside, the bottom of the window was on a level with the floor, while the top of it was so low down that it was necessary to bend in order to get the view from it. The vista it disclosed was made up of a large asphalt playground flanked by a red school-building, with lines of cinder-coloured brick inset in the façade. Away on the right rose the stone clock-tower of the railway station, modelled on eighteenth-century Dresden architecture, for the architect of the railway company had been a man of wide knowledge and appreciation. On the left was the bridge, with a few tree-tops showing above it. In the day-time, especially in the summer, it was quite lively. The sound of traffic, the vibration of the bridge, the clanging of trams, cawing of rooks, and cries of the children as they tumbled round their playground, came in at the high window. For some reason or other Miss Frederica and Miss Fanny found the noise made by the children very irritating — upsetting indeed. In the winter the days were quieter; but the evenings were so long — and the nights!

It had been March when they had moved in: very cold, but the warmer weather would come soon. At first the change was so abrupt, the contrast to their past life so fantastic, as to be equally unreal. It was like playing a game, a childish game of house-keeping or Red Indians. It must, surely, be only make-believe, and at any moment they would find themselves back in the Red House, able to resume their old life. The last few days there had been — though they would never admit it — very bitter. Everyone on the West Cliff knew them; and if they moved out of their home, people stared so. Here they had not been so well known in the days of their prosperity.

They missed their bedroom more than anything else. In this house they occupied just one room, sleeping in one hard bed. There were a few rickety pieces of yellow furniture, an empty fireplace, a tin basin to wash in. Of course, in the summer, the house was full of visitors, and it was not dark till nine. But the winter evenings were very long. They had no novels to read, and it was very cold — no fire, and nothing to do except go to bed — not even a hot-water bottle. They thought they could not be very well — so chilly and stiff, with a funny sinking feeling inside. It might, Miss Fanny thought, it might be the food. It was not quite what they were used to. Meat, for instance, only twice a week. Still, some people thought meat-eating bad for one, and in the end one might feel all the better for the absence of it . . . when one had got used to it. And no dinner at all seemed strange, didn't it? And then, that horrid Indian tea. She was sure she would never get to like that!

Yes, the nights were long, especially the winter nights, and so cold, but they had never before moved in a real world; and if now it had become painfully real, it should yet be kept at a distance! Never would they admit to each other their fear of the winter. They might complain themselves of small things — of the tea, for instance — but they must never voice to each other any mortal dread. Yet though they never mentioned it, each knew that the other did not sleep for long through those interminable winter nights. It was too cold, so near the roof. Outside the bare branches would be swaying and creaking in the wind. The bridge would surely be blown away one night. At about ten a cab would rumble over it in a leisurely manner. And then for hours there would be no sound except that of the striking clocks — it would be too quiet, except for that icy sound. The sound was so cold, it was like touching iron rails in a frost. It almost froze the ears, and the brain within. Certainly it gave them a headache. The station clock would start first: the four quarters, and then the hour; but a fairly cheerful, business-like sound. Then would toll out the others in a sequence, each following at an interval of a few seconds. Each one would strike the four quarters and then the hour; and for all the clocks audible in the town to strike midnight took up a full quarter of an hour. St. Catherine's would knell eastward with its deep bell; Christchurch would sound near by, scolding and shrewish. St. Thomas would be angry and foreboding, Holy Trinity surprised. The hour was tolled out as if in sorrow: perhaps a worse one was coming in. Sleep was at an infinite distance, beyond the sound of bells and the touch of cold iron bars. Their minds were waking. They were living, and it was cold.

Then the winter days, though actually so short, seemed both long and cold; and the landlady was not at all a nice woman, very impolite. In time they grew to avoid Mrs. Snaggs whenever it was possible. When they passed by they would hear her laughing and giggling. She was not respectful. 'Goodness, what sights!' they would hear her say.

No longer could they go to concerts or bazaars, nor were they ever asked to knit anything for the Christchurch sale-of-work. It was too tiring to go out for a long walk, and too cold to stay in. They had been forced to give up the lending-library: thus that stroll, which would have given them something to do, was barred to them; and if they stayed at home, they had no books to read. Except that Mrs. Snaggs had once lent them a copy of *The Family Herald*. And Mr. Garrett was very kind and had offered to continue their subscription until better times came. But they could not accept his offer; it would not be the right thing to do. And then Mr. Garrett was altering; his waxed moustache was very untidy, his hair dishevelled, he had a vacant eye. Things were going badly with him, too. Newborough was altering. The new big chemist's at the corner had started a lending-library; and things were not prospering with the smaller shops. Drink was a dreadful thing, but they could understand it. Poor little man! He had always been so kind and respectful. No, it was no good staying in unless the weather forced them to do so. A little walk in the streets, but not in the main streets. People stared so.

Alas! there was some excuse for the staring. Now that

there was no one to look after their clothes, hats and boots, the two sisters presented a more than ever extraordinary spectacle. The dresses, getting daily more antiquated in their design, were yet as gorgeous in colour, and were still fluttering with torn ribbons and cobweb-like lace, but draggled, torn and untidy. Their hats had acquired shapes that could only be described as grotesque; their bronze buttoned-boots were dirty and worn down; but cheek and hair still burnt with an unnatural and unsteady flame.

One day two little boys followed them right up to Miss Waddington's door, making fun of them. It was too bad! Every fortnight they paid this, their only visit in the town, to old Miss Waddington. They would arrive in time for tea. At first, going so near their old house was very painful to them. They would ring the bell, and the maid, Elsie, would open the door, leave them waiting in the small hall between the two doors for some little time, and then usher them into the drawing-room. In the winter, when the blinds were drawn, it reminded them so much of the drawing-room at the Red House. A fire burnt brightly under a solid white-marble mantelpiece, on which were several photographs in rococo silver frames and a solid white-marble clock. On each side of this were a Dresden shepherd and shepherdess. But the old lady was 'artistic', and there were several ferns, especially little ones, in art pots, green merging into yellow-ochre. There was usually, in the winter, a silver vase, shaped like a small trumpet with a crinkled edge, full of jonquils, so pretty and bright, like the spring; nice comfortable armchairs, and a sofa, full of dark green silk cushions, with large frills.

Sometimes Miss Waddington would not be well enough to come down herself, and her niece would give them tea instead — such good Ceylon tea. The niece was not exactly pretty, but bright-looking: yes, that was the word, bright-looking: people said she was 'clever'. 'Aunt Hester is not so well today', she would say as she came in, 'and has asked me to entertain you for her'; and then, before they answered, as if entering a preliminary defence, she would add quickly: 'How well you both look. I am sure they must make you very comfortable in your lodgings. I saw Mrs. Snaggs the other day, such a clean, sensible, respectable-looking woman!' Tea would be brought in, many small cakes and scones. And finally, after a visit lasting from half an hour to three-quarters, they would get up to go, and would be handed an envelope containing a cheque for one pound. No other visitors ever disturbed these tea-parties.

As a rule, though, Miss Waddington would make a special effort to be there herself to talk to them. She thought that she really must be getting quite fond of the two Misses Cantrell-Cooksey; at any rate she enjoyed their visits. Perhaps they were nicer since their misfortunes — but they were certainly rather odd. She was, therefore, not 'at-home' to other friends. No, Elsie.

There would be a preliminary coughing and wheezing upstairs and in the hall. The door would open, and the dear old lady, with a white shawl round her shoulders, would totter in, shivering as if it were very cold. Miss Frederica and Miss Fanny found it rather difficult to talk to her. Indeed, the former lady seldom spoke now, even to her younger sister. Besides, what was there to talk about? They had seen so little and done so little. There remained in the summer the weather and the visitors, in the winter the weather. Or Miss Waddington would try to impart a little religious consolation to them, endeavour to make them go to church again, for latterly they had given up going to Christchurch. Certainly, Miss Waddington reflected, as they left the house with their envelope, they were getting very odd, very odd indeed. But after they left she felt better than she had done all day. Kindly and charitable; and at the same time the room had grown brighter, the fire warmer. It was a terrible thing, to gamble!

And the two Misses Cantrell-Cooksey would be walking, under cover of the winter darkness, back across the suspension-bridge to their high back window in the tall white house.

Apart from their fortnightly call, the chief thing they looked forward to in the winter was their walk on the sands, away from the town. They grew to look forward to this event of the day with more and more pleasure. Even when the north-east wind blew straight from the top of Norway, they would sit on a rock, impervious to any chill, and converse with their friends, who would, if there had not been a storm, be gathering their winkles and limpets. If there had been a gale, on the other hand, they would be engaged in the more exciting task of combing the gold sands. Excitement would flare up again in the eyes of the two old ladies as they watched the sea-hoard being uncovered. And, though they were now no longer able to distribute shillings, the men who lived by this strange employment were, even when a little the worse for drink, so kind and respectful. They treated these two poor old bundles of bones, decked out in their torn fine feathers, as if they still lived on the West Cliff. They even appeared to regard them as human beings. And, to the men's great credit, they never allowed their pity to obtrude itself.

The summer was not so difficult. The town was full of visitors and cheerful sounds; while, at low tide, they could walk under the wall of the terrace where the band played, and hear it quite well. And if they kept close to the wall they could not be recognised from above by people leaning over — though once Mrs. Sibmarsh caught a glimpse of them from one of the gaps — like the intervals between battlements — in the wall. It gave her quite a turn. Still pretending to be young — and to be rich, she supposed — dressed up like that. They didn't behave like poor people; so stuck up; and one ought to cut one's coat . . . oughtn't one? Their eyes were worse than ever. There could be no doubt about it. They must drug . . . morphia . . . cocaine . . . though how they could get it without money, she didn't know. It was positively disgraceful.

The sands themselves were so crowded with mothers and children, nurses and children, donkeys and pierrots and ice-cream carts, so vibrating under the reflected lights of sea and pool and sky, that the presence of the two sisters attracted but little attention there, except once; when, advancing near a group waiting round an empty platform, they were asked what time the performance began. After that they began to avoid the sands, until the winter brought loneliness back to them. Yet, curiously enough, they made no effort to quieten their clothes, or to subdue the colouring of hair and cheek. Though cosmetics were costly, they clung to them. For, once they let these pretences die, with them would perish the last vestige of self-respect. Their eccentricity had turned into this extreme patience, and into the final agonising pretence that all was as it should be.

They had almost lost count of time. How many years was it? The most definite fact in their lives was a continual dread of the coming winter, the cold, the cold! The long winter nights closed round them. And there was nothing to do but lie awake, for they had no books, and they must save the cost of lighting.

And this November Miss Fanny began, suddenly, to notice a change in Frederica, something vague in her manner. All one night she muttered to herself, and the next day, coming up from downstairs, Miss Fanny found her crying. She did not feel very well, that was all. Appearances were a heavy burden, a difficult load. How was she to keep it up?

It was an extravagance, she knew, but would Fanny mind fetching her a small bottle of sal volatile from the chemist? Yes, it was only a headache, but a rather severe one. It would be gone by dinner. Miss Fanny walked out with the money to Hoare & Blunt, the chemists. Mrs. Snaggs, downstairs in the empty house — for in the winter there were no guests — heard Miss Frederica calling her. It was really too bad! One might be a slave, running up and down stairs with nothing to do except look after those two. Miss Fanny, indeed! For Miss Cantrell-Cooksey had asked Mrs. Snaggs to tell Miss Fanny, when she returned, not to worry. She was just going out for a walk, and might not be back for a little time. She was fully decorated, a-jingle with ribbons and ornaments, while a hat, gorgeous but flattened and out of shape, crowned it all. Under her arm was a brown-paper parcel. Mrs. Snaggs looked at her in amazement, and then went back to the kitchen. She did not actually hear her go out, but, though angry, gave Miss Fanny the message when the latter came in, muttering and making the most of the two flights of stairs she had been forced to come up by panting in a hollow, owl-like way. Miss Fanny stood with her back to the door, talking to Mrs. Snaggs for a few seconds. Just then there was the sound of a gathering crowd outside on the bridge, and looking back out of the door Miss Fanny saw a murmuring circle of black-coated men and a few women backing away toward the other side of the road, with white, mask-like faces. Within the circle Miss Frederica's clothes were lying in a heap. She had gone out for her last walk. She had stepped, fully-dressed, with a brown-paper parcel under her arm, straight out of that high window on to the stone pavement below. She must have had to bend down to get out of it. In the parcel were a black-bound Prayer Book and the few old photographs that belonged to her. But she had kept up appearances.

Miss Fanny did not really feel it much. There was the inquest, and then the funeral; a great deal of activity! Mrs. Snaggs had given her the message. And she often sits up quite late expecting Frederica to return, till the light in her eyes equals the flame of cheek and hair.

I last saw her at low tide, one winter morning, dressed in a white-flannel costume (a new departure for her) and very much made-up. She must really be old by now. There had been a storm, and she was sitting on a rock talking to the men who were raking over the pebbly edges of the sands and watching them capture their strange treasure. They found that morning a William-and-Mary gold piece; a small chest covered with rusty iron nails and green with age, with nothing in it; a small box, hermetically sealed, of China tea; a straw ship in a glass bottle, and two George IV four-shilling pieces.

THE MAN WHO DROVE STRINDBERG MAD

SITTING in this large old house, in this freezing winter, in this winter of the world, with icicles clustering their stalactites round every old lead pipe, transforming the implements of utility into shapes of glittering fantasy, much as the mind of the poet changes all that he sees, or the magic of time touches the forest in which lies buried the palace of the Sleeping Beauty, transforming every dull material object into something brilliant and crystal-clear, I thought of lands across the grey and swirling waters where every year these processes take place. I thought of the north — but my mind recoiled from the horrors of Finland and Russia. Sweden, whatever the immediate future may hold in store for it, is still (as I write) itself, and so I thought of the snowy slopes and bare trees of Uppsala, so like a Hoxton print in their clear blue-and-white tinsel precision, and of the life, on skate and sleigh and ski, so suited to its conditions, which prevailed there. . . . Here the snow drifted in long, upward curves towards the tall eighteenth-century windows, and we watched for the thaw: but all the pipes were solid, and even the telephone wires had in some fashion given way to the spite of winter. . . . And now, as I thought of Sweden and Uppsala, of Uppsala always more than of Stockholm, all the electric bells in the house began to ring without stopping — the frost and snow working on them in some manner unknown to me, I suppose: but I do not understand the ways of machines or of currents, can form no conception of the tricks by which inanimate objects pursue their careers.

. . . . .

For an hour or more the bells continued, and, thinking of Sweden, my mind reverted to Strindberg, the greatest artist Sweden ever produced, and I wondered how he would have treated this incident, from what cocoon of fiery and unbalanced poetry the episode would have emerged. Because, as you, Gentle Reader, will remember, he was ever assailed by the spite of inanimate objects, trying to plague him, trying to drive him mad. In many books, but especially in *The Inferno*, he tells us of their dull but deadly machinations, the sponge that threw itself into his bath from the wrong and ominous corner, the picture-frame that fell as he passed, and, above all, the bells, the bell. The front-door bell, especially, was rung at intervals, day by day, and only stopped when he went to answer it and found no human being waiting there . . . above all, the bells; and as I thought of him, pursued by these innumerable inanimate materialisations of fate, suddenly I recalled an incident which I had forgotten, and longed to record it. Not only did it in itself appeal to my way of thinking, but, in addition, it carried me to a distant equatorial land where the heat broods all the year over mirror-like lagoons and where, at dawn and dusk, the thousand little winged inhabitants of the jungle open and close their day with such a shriek of pride and possession as can only be imagined by those who have heard it; so loud and victorious a paean that listening to it throbbing through the ground, through ear and throat and limb, one was obliged to doubt its very existence, it was too loud and insistent to *be*, just as the heat was too hot to appear genuine.

. . . . .

I suppose it was because I have so great a reverence for Strindberg and understand so well how his mind worked, and why in its particular directions, and because I think, although I usually do not care to admit it, that his theory of life contains more truth than would seem possible to the dull disciples of everyday (indeed this war is the culmination of his theories, the fulfilment of them upon the *world*, instead of upon the *individual*), that this incident occurred to me. But however that may be, when I was seventeen or eighteen and attached to a cavalry regiment, I discovered two stars for myself, the dire radiance of Strindberg — a light, indeed, from another planet — and the middle-class comforting doctrines of that lesser luminary, Samuel Butler. With Strindberg, I, too, watched the conspiracies of little objects, the way they precipitate the imaginative into disaster, and it seemed to me then — as it seems to me still — that in his work was a beauty that, also, lay beyond the world of reason. His heroines could live for years in cupboards, then half-way through the play turn into parrots, and yet they existed in their own burning world of unreason, quite as surely as you or I in ours. . . . In any case I have a special and personal feeling for this sad and tortured author; even though I suppose — I do not know — that I have little in common with him, for fun comes easily to me and I was — I hope the reader will excuse my boasting — born with wit in the tips of my fingers as much as on the tip of my tongue. I have a natural vitality, born of centuries of riding and not-thinking (as opposed to not being able to think); a vitality which it has taken two world wars to destroy. . . . But all the same, in spite of my own innate attitude toward life, I reverence Strindberg as a great writer with, for me, a personal illumination.

. . . . .

The rains were coming in San Salvador: the bootblacks kneeled listlessly at their work and the dark-skinned singers were silent. All day long, grey clouds drifted over the top of the palm trees and a hot wind ruffled and scurried their plumes. An emanation of former massacres seemed to invest the city, the fires of the Inquisition seemed still to smoulder just below the ground, and the rain of bullets that, only a few months before, had been responsible for the deaths of ten thousand Communists, shot *à la russe* in droves of fifty by machine-guns, seemed hardly to have spent itself in the air. At the windows, relentless parrots clacked their iron tongues like castanets and gave way to bouts of Delphic prophecy in Spanish. Old gentlemen were eating enormous ices in the windows of the clubs, and marimbas sounded their haunting, icy music down the lost alleys of the city. . . . The world was waiting — it, for the rains, and I, for a boat — and so I, too, sat in the club, reading the newly arrived European papers and hearing in them the six-weeks-old rumble of impending tragedy. . . . Every day, as it came, seemed to contain a number of siestas, but of such a kind as to be free of peace, invaded by poisonous thoughts; every night brought the glamour of southern nights, their sounds and scents and relaxations; and to these last I added my private gambler's joy.

At ten-thirty every night I would sit, in that tremendous heat, in a large over-illuminated room, helping, for once, the dull spite of inanimate objects as an ally, or being, in turn, its victim. I love even the sound of the roulette wheel, and often it has seemed to me that some special link connects its spirit temporarily with those of some of its devotees. For hours at a stretch, without a hint of boredom, I could play this game in which only good — or usually bad — fortune exists, where there is no such thing as skill or intellect: only swift action and luck, and an ability to be for an instant in league with the spirit of the inanimate, the blind, the thing without thought — yet as you watch its revolutions, it seems very surely to possess an individuality, to have its own inexplicable preferences.

Sometimes I can win — though even then the quickness and alertness which, in order to gain, must accompany good fortune, soon desert me, rapidly worn down, like every other gambler, by worry, excitement, fatigue and heat: generally, like all gamblers, I lost. Even then, in this climate, I would find it impossible to go to bed. The heat was too great, the excitement too recent. . . . I would stand for a time on the balcony, watching how the very fireflies in their curves were trying to outline the numbers that lie between zero and thirty-six, watching their scintillating implications, trying to gather their meaning. Then, for a moment, forgetting that I had lost all my money, I would return to the table; only to find myself obliged to assume a passive rôle. Fortunately I had exhausted every shilling that was on me and so I would sit in a sullen sweat and observe the intricate design in numbers woven by the wheel spinning.

Every night the man of whom I am going to tell you came in very late and by himself, with a pile of chips, and played with an enviable — and yet in a sense, it seemed to me, unenviable — good fortune. At first I thought he was English. He was still young-looking, and rather handsome. He was certainly well dressed and dressed with a touch of vanity, but his appearance exhibited also a touch of over-sleekness, while his eyes, hard and yet pleading, seemed to belong to some other body than his own. Their blue and rather cruel, if cringing, inconsistency did not seem to match the physique of the athlete, the rhythmic body, the fair hair and fair skin. For the eyes were cold, very cold for all their strange and inconjecturable pleading. He played with courage, conviction and an almost diabolic luck. I had never seen a man who, at certain times, seemed more sure of what was coming. His long, well-shaped fingers — one, with a sapphire and platinum ring on it — knew exactly where to place his stakes: never, for a moment, did he show indecision, although his system was founded, so far as I could see, on nothing but a belief in his own good fortune. There was about him, as he played, something immensely attractive and repellent, an air of mystery. He never spoke: but I could see now that he was not English: nor German, I was sure, he was too like an Englishman for that, so he must belong to Denmark or Sweden or Norway. . . . Yet he seemed at home here. He suited, for all his northerliness, the tropics, as a snake suits the burning ground over which it darts. He seemed very much at home, too, without speaking; and to be on good terms with the world, with people and with things; above all, with *things* — hence his diabolic fortune at roulette. . . . But there was nothing mysterious about him. I made inquiries, and was told that he was a prosperous Swedish merchant. He possessed an interest in the railways here, and he also exported coffee and spices to Sweden. . . . It was true that he won great sums. He would not bring his wife to the Casino, for people distracted him: hence, too, he always entered late, when the majority of gamblers had met their destiny, and his icy judgment came fresh to a community of soiled and broken players and of tired, despising croupiers. In this disruptive world he could hold his own. If he lost, he left: if he began to win, he seized with a cold imaginative power upon his good fortune, and left as soon as it began to desert him. . . . But in the phrase of the gamblers there, 'the table liked him'. He was its favourite. The dull, inanimate creation beamed upon him as upon one of its own.

Then I met him at luncheon in a pavilion under a tree. The vultures alighted ponderously on their observation posts and watched us with the heavy, hooded eyes of armament kings. Occasionally they staggered, as though from sleep, and turned reflective profiles to the sky. In the darkness of the scrub beyond, many other birds yelled out. The clouds, day by day, hour by hour, were drifting down. There were only present my host and hostess — American friends — myself, and the gambler and his wife. After luncheon our hostess, together with that other plain and resonant-voiced woman, left the table and I sat next to him and we talked. He spoke excellent English, but with a typical northern inflexion. I told him with how great an interest I watched his play, and we discussed many things and places; drifting towards Sweden and then to

Strindberg. He did not seem to be proud of the greatest poet his country had produced, though he had lived for a long while in the same small town in which Strindberg had lived while he was writing, among other books, *The Inferno*. I told him how deeply I admired the great writer, but he did not seem interested in such a subject, and wanted to talk of other things or, perhaps, not to talk at all. And then presently, as I insisted, as I continued to dwell on Strindberg (for I felt he must know something of him), I noticed for the first time a light, other than that cold light I had observed in the Casino, illumine his eyes; they flickered with the memory, you would have said, of some past joy, became alive, animated in a pleasurable way. Presently he said in his soft, low voice: 'As a boy I used to make fun of him. . . . Often I would run into his garden, ring the front-door bell, and then hide until he had opened the door and had gone away again, finding no one there. . . . And then, ever so many times, I would creep out, dart up the stairs and ring again. . . . And how puzzled he would look! . . . One never has fun like that nowadays; too sophisticated, I suppose.' But I was silent, overcome by horror at this being in league with the inanimate in its dull, cold vendetta against a man of genius. . . . 'Childish pleasures are the greatest of all,' he continued in his mechanical, meaningless, sing-song voice.

DEATH OF A GOD

(For Alice)

THE chief difficulty under which, at the moment of writing this story, the creative artist, more especially the novelist, labours is this: that the violent agitation, from end to end, and from top to bottom, of the background against which his figures are placed, renders the movements of these characters meaningless and unimportant. As well try to concentrate upon a game of chess in an earthquake! The act of writing (if you think of it — which fortunately the born writer seldom does) is comparable to the action of the band which played a hymn as the great ship *Titanic* was sinking. . . . Well, the loss of the *Titanic*, 'the luxury liner on her maiden voyage', as the papers of that day loved to describe her, was symbolic of things to come, but not more than the disappearance from this earthly scene of Mr. Snowberry. . . . With him, for many others as well as for me, went the whole of the nineteenth-century panorama, and especially the works of Henry James and George Meredith. Even more than the novelists of convention, Mr. Snowberry belonged to a dying age.

Ever since I could remember, my life — and long before that, the lives of my parents and their neighbours — had been regulated and set in motion every week by Mr. Snowberry. Without him we should have been lost. He was our god, controlling the life of each week. Lacking his aid, the vague, Meredithian life of childhood in a country house would have come to nothing. Dressed in a faded livery of dark suit, bowler hat, heavy gold chain, which divided his little body into two halves, his face adorned with moustache and whiskers, he drove over the moors to us every eighth day from Bakewell to wind the clocks. The chain I have mentioned supported a heavy gold hunter watch: and by this watch he set the clocks.

These machines were numerous in all the houses he visited. At home there was the stable clock (the pendulum of which subsequently proved, appropriately enough, to be the seventeenth-century sundial from the old formal garden, removed to make way for a landscape in the mode of Capability Brown); the lacquered Queen Anne clock, on the stairs, with flamboyant flamingoes blown in gold upon the surface of its case; the Louis Quatorze *buhl* clock in the Cocked Hat Room; the tall walnut clock with a silver dial, surrounded by patterns of fruit, in the Ballroom; in the Boudoir, the *Directoire* clock, which played a minuet by Mozart at the end of every hour; the tortoise-shell clock, with a gold figure of Father Time and his Scythe, in the Great Parlour; and the inlaid and domed clock which my father had brought back some years before from Sicily. This stood in the dining-room, and with an extreme display of individuality, indulged at odd hours in almost any form of dissonance that it chose. . . . (And all these instruments of time were still ticking, perhaps, in the age appropriate to them, controlling on some other plane of vision the movement of their coeval puppets: Dutch figures with periwigs and large feathered hats were walking hand in hand in a tulip garden to the ticking of the walnut clock, and, already coming up the other side of the Revolution, the *Merveilleuses* were conducting their exaggerated lives to the beating heart of the little gold clock; while my parents and their friends, in the bowler hats, tight trousers and coats, the tailor-made skirts and leg-of-mutton-sleeved coats of the 'nineties, were still playing croquet to the rhythm of that little clock in a leather case which my mother told me had been given to her as a wedding present.) Thus everything we did or said, our every function and thought and dream, was instigated by Mr. Snowberry. We could hardly have eaten without him.

Moreover, the same thing was true of daily life in all the country houses round; that existence which has now so completely disappeared. On Monday he drove, let us say, to Chatsworth — a full day's work there! — on Tuesday to Hardwick; on Wednesday — I remember it was always Wednesday — to Barlborough and Renishaw; on Thursday to Clumber; on Friday to Welbeck; on Saturday, perhaps, to Wentworth Woodhouse. On Sunday I imagine he must have wound his own clock (but of that I have something to say later). He was the local god of time: albeit sometimes a breakdown in it caused him to be summoned earlier, so that he became the healer of time, as well as its overlord. At his nod innumerable clocks sounded their silver tinkling, or echoing, rhythmic or cracked notes over the little corner where the counties of Derbyshire, Nottinghamshire, Yorkshire and Lincolnshire meet. Week after week for nearly fifty years this amiable, good little deity had progressed from temple to temple — this prince, from palace to palace.

Round Mr. Snowberry, then, the whole invisible mechanism of many great estates revolved. The woodman in the shrill green light of summer mornings, when the call to action from the ground seemed to sound clear as a hunting-horn on a frosty morning, rose to his chimes. Later, when the sun had rolled above the horizon, and its rays glowed among the feathery tree-tops of the avenue, the horses would begin to neigh in the stables, but the grooms did not get up until Mr. Snowberry's clock sounded the correct hour. In the spring, when, after the hard winter of the north, the bulbs could almost be seen growing, whole russet choirs of birds sang uninterruptedly from the earliest dawn, but even they seemed to cease from their carolling when one of Mr. Snowberry's clocks struck the hour. In the brittle, icy winter, when trees as tall as a ship's masts were roped with frost, and every blade of grass became a crackling spire, it was Mr. Snowberry who roused the sullen housemaids from warm slumber.

On the other hand, while Mr. Snowberry made time advance for others, it seemed, equally, to stand still for him. I had grown from childhood to man's estate without being able to observe the slightest change in him — none at all; not by the greying of a hair, nor by any variation or loss of strength in his voice (which so often betrays the ageing of those who do not show it in other ways), had he altered.

What life did the god of time lead at home, I wondered, between these ceremonial visits to great and lesser houses; between the greetings of grooms and footmen: 'Good morning, Mr. Snowberry!' 'Good morning, John!' 'Pony going well, Mr. Snowberry?' 'Yes, thank you, John. . . .' 'Lovely morning for the time of year, Mr. Kembley.' 'Yes, Mr. Snowberry, what we want is three munths o' this, and then tak' oop.' How did he spend the crisp October evenings, or the lazy summer twilight up there on the moor near the site of the Roman camp, so close under the sky, where heather and bilberries supplied the only vegetation? Just as an emperor is always said to live so simply, to lie on a camp-bed in preference to a state four-poster, and to prefer a glass of fresh milk and a rusk to meals prepared by a most skilled French chef, so, too, doubtless this Mexican Prince-Priest, this Maya Time-God preferred, when he considered the riches and extent of his kingdom, to live on goat's cheese, and on bilberries which stain the inside of the mouth to the blue-black of a chow's tongue.

As a child his trade fascinated me and I used to conjecture what his own clock, by which he set his gold watch, could be like; the clock that governed this god, though equally governed by him; the central clock, as it were, of the whole universe. . . . And, finally, I found out, when I went to tea with him and was thus able, on the same Saturday afternoon, to satisfy my curiosity concerning his house. It was a very small house, not a cottage, with mullion windows, and the stone between them quilted with little pink roses. In the porch stood an enormous very clean-looking wooden spade, which showed very distinctly its grain, and which was for shovelling away the snow, so it should not even in the winter prevent him from reaching the various temples so dependent upon him. The sitting-room was full of feathers, feather-flowers and stuffed birds and patchwork cushions. . . . But when he showed me his bedroom, I was dismayed to find that the all-important clock upon which he, and, in consequence, our whole world, depended was an alarm clock, a common machine of base metal, the tintinnabulations of which awoke him every morning. . . . I must have shown my surprise and disappointment, for he added, 'Well, my dear young man, you see I'm alone here now. Mrs. Snowberry and Esther have been dead these last ten years.'

Somehow, I had not previously connected him, so highly did he stand above mortals in my regard, with earthly ties, and it was only then that I realised that the monster over which he reigned had dared to devour those dearest to him; so that his own life was an insecure tenure, his seat on the throne shaky in the extreme. But even when I grew up, I still continued to feel that he should be immune from time's laws. . . . It did not surprise me, therefore, that he showed no signs of growing old. And, in consequence, I was in no way prepared either for his own final disappearance, or that of the system of which he seemed the mainspring.

Right up to that moment the machine was ticking away without a sign of any internal corrosion. There had been changes, of course: one or two mansions had passed to newer and richer owners (Mr. Snowberry disapproved of such usurpers): no grooms now saluted him, but though the chauffeurs were more independent and wished him 'Good morning' in colder, less rural and rather condescending voices, nevertheless, the fact that the motor had replaced the horse seemed only to emphasise the beneficent influence of Mr. Snowberry's activities.

The whole world seemed to be working up, like a magnificent and ingenious clock, to strike, under Mr. Snowberry's governing, its comfortable, full, rich, traditional chimes. . . . Towards the end of June, however, something went wrong. An Austrian Archduke, who had often been entertained in one of Mr. Snowberry's palaces, now, while driving in an open motor-car through a distant Mohammedan town, fell victim to a bullet from the hand of Gavril Princip. . . . I was with my regiment in Wellington Barracks at the time, and my sister wrote to me from my home to tell me how upset Mr. Snowberry had been at this regrettable occurrence. Just as if a person under his protection had been injured, some sense of responsibility seemed to haunt him, she said.

In July I came home on leave for a month or two, and in the peculiarly golden summer of that year, under the old trees or in the cool interior of the darkened rooms, rumours from the outside world drifted in sleepily. It seemed as if the whole earth were waiting, waiting for bells to sound or a clock to strike. . . . And, being of a superstitious turn of mind, I was unhappy when on the 1st of August (for by then the outside world had already invaded us with clouds of flying, scurrying reports) I counted the lacquered clock on the stairs outside my bedroom strike thirteen at midnight. . . . It had never done this before, so it must have been my reckoning, I supposed, that was at fault. . . . All the same, two veins of uneasiness now ran through the substance of my mind: one concerning Mr. Snowberry, and the other for the whole world: (and as it happens, I have never in my life, so far, heard a clock strike thirteen again).

I went to London on the night of the 2nd. On the night of the 3rd, I was among those who saw the Lord Mayor's gilded coach roll trundling up the Mall, moving, unless my memory misleads me, along the narrower side-path strewn with peat moss for riders, to Buckingham Palace; a sure sign of the imminence of the catastrophe that was coming. On the 4th, war was declared, and on the morning of the same day Mr. Snowberry met with his accident. . . . Pan and Mars had broken loose together and had set out to conquer the newer god, Mr. Snowberry.

In spite of the general progress, himself had never approved of motor-cars, and he was driving his pony-cart in the neighbourhood of Renishaw when this event occurred. I know the place well. The cinder pyramid of a small mine heaped an ugly screen against a wide expanse in which huge chimneys, plumed with smoke, and stout furnaces raised their bulk. Behind the slag-heap crouched an Elizabethan house, lost and desolate, and then came a rustic prospect in which industrialism did not exist. First, there was a lane between deep hedges, and the other side of it stood a small stone farm, while beyond, an abrupt perspective of stone walls and meadows that leapt and fell at improbable levels stretched towards the moors and the far horizon.

Mr. Snowberry was coming down this lane. For all that the coal-mines were so close, it was a lovely place in summer, the old stone farm, the near meadows with two spoilt donkeys stretching their furry muzzles across loose stone walls in hope of sugar, the pigs grunting from their sties, or hurrying with their clumsy, fairy-story bodies inflated above short, thin legs, across the green grass — the mountain grass, like the green hair of mermaids, of the high places in this district. Bracken grew tall along the sides of the lane, making intricate, lacy patterns. The air coming from the moors smelt pure and mossy, and you could hear the trout-stream purling below. The whole of this vista exhaled a primitive, Noah's-ark charm and offered a feeling of comfort; the green meadow and stone wall, pigs and chickens, donkeys and orchards and stone trough, had always been there and, even in spite of changes for the worse elsewhere, would prevail, and with them a certain rough kindliness. It was this impression of comfort and kindliness that perhaps made the shock which Mr. Snowberry was to receive all the worse.

He was driving quietly along, when suddenly he saw before

him a white billy-goat tethered tight, but wildly running round a post, rearing up in pain and then jumping down again on its four cloven feet; a pure white goat that was like a flame in its proud, white maleness against the dark green of trees and grass. In front of the animal were two girls, fourteen or fifteen, with the flaxen and tow-coloured hair of the countryside, rolling with lewd, brutish laughter, and aiming as hard as they could at the most vital part of the goat's body. Something in the masculinity of the goat maddened them beyond bearing, for they were at that queer stage of adolescence when young girls are no longer themselves, no longer individuals, their consciousness joining that of all young female things, so that they are able, as we see from time to time in the cases of haunting by poltergeists, to produce psychic phenomena mysteriously and with an inexplicable ease. They were laughing under the influence of some horrible kind of intoxication or control — perhaps at other moments they were good children, perhaps they would grow up to be reasonable human beings, but now they were possessed. The god Pan was loose in them, and they were in reality crucifying that which was within themselves.

Mr. Snowberry, a lover of animals, who was filled with a loving-kindness towards all the created world, made no allowance in his mind for such fury. Anger beat up in him at the sight of this cruelty; he pulled up, shouted, and was just going to jump out of the pony-cart to stop them torturing the poor beast, when all at once they saw him and, in their fright, hurled a stone at him, which hit the pony. The pony ran away, and Mr. Snowberry was thrown out and killed instantly. The watch he carried with him stopped at the hour of his death.

Beyond the sea, as here, the primeval, brutish world was breaking out, and it was several days before the little universe of which he was god discovered what had happened to Mr. Snowberry. Everywhere in Elizabethan long-galleries, with their stucco figures in green and pink hose hunting through dark forests, in panelled drawing-rooms, Palladian stables and Adam dining-rooms, the machinery of the clocks ran down and no chimes sounded the hour. It seemed, my sister wrote to me, as if the figures, too, had run down with the being that regulated their lives. No one now knew what was going on in the world beyond: no one in these houses knew the correct time to take a walk, to eat, or to sleep. Everything was running down. And in that priest's cell high up on the moors, the metal, clacking tongue of the alarm clock, the central clock of the universe as it were, set by Greenwich, itself remained silent and unwound.

LONG JOURNEY

In the Tuscan towns the sound of trams creaking, their bells ringing, and of the open exhausts of motors blares through the narrow streets at sundown; streets, tawny as a lion, but in which it is nevertheless impossible to observe the full drama of the autumn, so intense on the outskirts and in the country behind, where it drags a hem of purple over the dusty hills and into the woods of ilex, the leaves of which glisten like the glossy night forests in the canvases of Uccello. Through the middle of each town flows desultorily a dwindled yellow river. The palaces, balanced and proportioned as a mathematical formula or a problem in Euclid, hang above streets too narrow, again, for the passer-by to be able to judge of their pure, incredible beauty, now for the most part remote and dead as that of the Parthenon or of the clustered, broken towers of San Gimignano. The streets, for all their bustle, are similarly dead; it is the activity of the devouring worm more than of life itself. The palaces, except for the cobblers and fruit shops on the ground floor, are dead too; but the cobbler hammers all day long at his last, and the old women, who gossip or haggle over *soldi*, peering from behind their autumnal mounds of green figs and purple figs, of grapes and of orange persimmons, fit into these elegant, slightly rusticated arches so well that they seem as much part of them as a snail of its shell. . . . Up above on the *piano nobile*, either a dressmaker, as if engaged in black magic, stabs a silken bust with pins, her mouth still full of them, or a lawyer interviews his sullen peasant client, so unable to explain himself, or an American is giving a cocktail party. For the most part, the former owners, the renown of whose ancestors has echoed down the centuries from the time of Dante — just as a footstep now echoes through the mirror-like view of door after door, ceiling after ceiling, room after room —, have disappeared, have sunk like stones to the bottom of these clear pools, leaving only the enlarging circles of their proud names to float upon the darkening surface.

The Palazzo Corineo, however, is an exception. Built by

Alberti, it lingers with reproachful perfection in a crowded by-street: where its fragile arcaded façade, one of the surviving wonders of the world, hangs almost out of sight, so that the lover of beauty who wishes to examine it will very soon be hooted out of his survey by a motor-car or belled out of it by a cycle. Herein, however, the descendants of those who caused it to be built still live, far down their endless pillared vistas; there are footmen in livery, and a vague air of the eighteenth century still attends upon the public goings and comings of the old Prince and Princess. Yet even for them the view here is one that diminishes year by year, uncertain to the point of certainty; for they are childless and have few relatives. The last palace will soon be uninhabited.

The Prince, a quiet, bearded scholar of the mandarin type, sadly floating above the life of the day, possesses manners as formal and beautiful as the rooms in which he lives: but the Princess, on the contrary, opposes to them a different and ebullient system of life, a different upbringing, a different set of manners. A Russian Princess in her own right, a Cossack by blood and inclination, she was born during a Court Ball in the Winter Palace in St. Petersburg, and was, so she says, baptised in a golden ice-bucket filled with the pink champagne reserved for the use of the Imperial Family. This indomitable old lady remains unaware that she appears as much a stranger to the present day as would a Princess of Byzantium. The double-headed eagle still flutters its wings about her: her hoarse, interminable chuckle fills the dead rooms with life. Many of them she has reduced to the level of an Oriental bazaar; Russian silver and ikons, jewelled watches and boxes, tinsel brocades, swinging censers and the endless junk of that lost civilisation, litter and clutter-up the delicate, finely counter-pointed perspectives. . . .

The Princess's day is a full one. Every morning she rolls for half an hour on the floor, to keep her back straight and preserve her suppleness. Then she skips. Then she has to dress, a complicated process, arrange her wig and eyebrows, and colour her complexion. Her morning is divided between prayer and the samovar. About twelve, the ravages of time repaired as far as she can repair them, she comes downstairs in full splendour. But by this time the Prince is working, disentangling the pedigrees of noblemen long perished, restoring order down these other perspectives of time — arches which have collapsed beneath their own weight and have become overgrown. (Italian culture resides in these finely balanced vistas which it has invented, vistas of rooms, vistas of music — each note echoing under a vault —, vistas of the theatre, fading and illusory.)

Luncheon is at twelve-thirty, and they eat often alone, one at each end of an immense table. All through the day the table-cloth, very large and very white and clean, is left on the table and is thickly encrusted with glittering, bulbous Russian silver, with silver roses and silver flowers (the dowry of the Princess); even Nanina, her fringed and fussy dog, eats off a silver plate in its own corner.

For the Princess, the day begins with the afternoon, when she goes out driving with Nanina and Count Ranucci, her *cicisbeo* (for she is one of the last to preserve this Italian habit). Barricaded against the wind behind a cockaded and cloaked coachman and footman, wearing Russian capes of fur, they drive interminably through the public gardens, round and round that delta between the two yellow rivers, arguing, laughing, quarrelling at the top of their voices, while Nanina snarls and motors whizz and hoot past them. Then come interludes of tea-parties and cocktail-parties, or else the Princess receives until seven — when, unless there is a ball, which happens very rarely, the day ends for her and the night swallows her up. She dines alone with Nanina and the Prince, or with Count Ranucci. When the Count is there, the Prince goes to bed, where he dreams of climbing family trees and swinging from heraldic branches. With the Count, her loved Pepino, the Princess plays bezique in her boudoir until two or three in the morning.

Even in warm weather the room is very hot from a porcelain stove, and the chuckles and laughter, and the angry interludes, are wheezy as the asthmatic breathing of Nanina in her tight-laced coat; that odious, corseted dog, with her false voice continually rapping out commands and saying things which she does not mean. And Nanina is always hiding, always having to be called, replying with a horrible yapping, the direction of which she yet contrives to disguise, so that both her mistress and her friend have perpetually to rise from their game and hunt all through the long, dark vistas. Ever, with one exception, since the Princess married and came to live here nearly sixty years ago, there has been a Nanina: and it has always looked like this, twelve years old, with a pointed, dancing-master nose and a corseted bust, an air of busy, fussy command, wheezy but inconsequent.

I could never make out to what breed Nanina and her four or five predecessors belonged, but it appertained obviously to the sixties of the last century; a breed imported into the cushioned, silken boudoirs of Russia from the Paris of the French Second Empire, a living symbol of western culture and emancipation. When she was not carried, the feet of this dog seemed to rap out, like a step-dance, the mid-nineteenth-century French airs of Delibes or Offenbach upon the hard, polished *terrazza* floors of these unending vistas. . . . Sometimes I thought that Nanina, the apparently eternal, was, despite her western origin and affinities, — in this comparable with the mounds of Russian silver and jewelled dolls —, but another symptom of the emphatic opposition the Princess offers to the classical and orderly life under the arches and coffered ceilings of her palace: for the Princess's blood must ache at moments for the gipsy wailings and the songs from barges, for the immoderate and unmodulated landscape of Russia — so large as to have no perspectives —, for the glitter and illusion of the Old Régime, for the bulbs and spires and crowns of the Kremlin and the amethyst-quartz grottoes in the frozen gardens of Tsarskoe Selo.

One evening I sat with her, drinking honey-tasting tea and eating complicated sandwiches (for the Princess loved people to be with her, was especially kind to those younger than herself and liked to examine them about their love-affairs). But for my presence, indeed, she would have been alone this evening, for there were no parties in the town and she had indulged earlier in the afternoon in one of her violent, recurrent quarrels with Pepino, that large, big-featured punchinello. Through the door of her little sitting-room, crowded with ill-assorted objects (a room which in its essence — though not, perhaps, in its profusion — so much resembled the dressing-room of a great theatrical star), I could perceive the darkening vista of the grand halls, room after room, *sala* after *sala*, empty, sad and echoing, yet full of beauty and courage and vision. Usually their extraordinary quality vanquished the human interest of the people who had lived in them: you did not wonder concerning them, did not muse about the men and women of succeeding generations — in armour, in striped hose and doublets, in wigs and velvet, in crinolines and panniers —, who through a lifetime had walked down these perspectives until finally they reached the past: you did not try to catch the dying sound of their voices, their accents echoing down through their descendants, in the same way that, in their own day, they had echoed up into nothingness under these high ceilings.

It was a warm evening as we drank our tea. Our room alone blazed with light, and from those beyond were wafted darkness, coolness, and, it seemed, a feeling of expectancy. . . . Someone out there, one might have imagined, was waiting for us — or were we waiting for someone? There was a crackling outside, and Nanina creaked her bones about her and barked. . . . A ghost, I wondered: and I recalled that the palace bore the reputation of being haunted. . . . So few Italian palaces possess ghosts that you would have thought the story easy to remember. As I talked, I tried to recollect what it was, and to what age the haunter belonged. . . . Not later than the time of Napoleon; because this whole system of life had died with him and Stendhal. Now the owners possessed no souls to leave behind them, were only animated shells, for all the Princess's energy. And certainly upon this evening the past seemed nearer than the present.

After a time I gave it up, and asked the Princess openly about the ghost, and if she had ever seen it. . . .

It had belonged, apparently, to the age of Romeo and Juliet, a fifteenth-century apparition, a girl who had died for love of a man whom circumstances forbade her ever to see, for he was a Guelph and she was a Ghibelline, or vice versa (indeed, I *ought* to have remembered, for she had been famous for her beauty, and her name was a household word here). It had been a romantic love, of swords and flowers and cloaks and serenades; a fifteen-year-old girl, with golden hair braided round her forehead, and with the dark, golden skin, slanting blue eyes and softly moulded aquiline nose of the Tuscans. There had been a portrait of her in the palace, but it had been sold and carried off to America more than thirty years ago. . . . Only the house itself remained, and its shadows, living and dead.

Even as we talked, it seemed to me, at any rate for the moment, that the air began to alter, to inspissate, to become colder; every teaspoon taken up or put down redoubled its tinkle; every plate was moved with a thud. The house seemed, more than ever, to be waiting. It was that hour of silence before the innumerable sounds of the Italian evening begin.

'No, I have never seen the ghost, the poor thing,' said the Princess, 'but once, long ago, I heard her voice. It must have been soon after I married, and long before we sold the Botticelli portrait of her in order to install the electric light. (Now, you see how comfortable it is!) It was an evening like this, and in those days, after Petersburg, it seemed quiet here, and I was restless. I remember what a beautiful disturbing day it had been, like this one; I could not sit still as I do now; I suppose it was my nomad, Tartar blood. The Prince had gone out, and my dog, my first dog, who was named Tita (though my husband didn't like my calling her that, because it had been the name of his ancestress, the ghost, the famous Tita), had disappeared, just as Nanina does — Nanina, darling, where are you? — and I could not find her anywhere. (She is always so naughty, my beautiful angel! Although my Tita has long been dead, she was just the same to look at, though not so lovely — no, darling, not so lovely!) The sun had not long hidden itself behind Santa Croce opposite, but it became very dark in this house and I walked through room after room calling "Tita! Tita! Tita!"; but there was no sound of my dog, not a bark from that angelic, furry throat. My voice echoed strangely under those high ceilings that were now so black, and little breaths of cold air swept over the bare floors. Even my footsteps echoed, and if I had not already come to know the rooms so well, and how they were disposed in a square round the court, I would have been afraid of losing my way. . . . Still I went on calling, calling, until the whole air seemed full of the cries: "Tita! Tita! Tita!" . . . You know, I am a Cossack, and I am not nervous. At the age of seven I saw the peasants riot and try to burn our house and did not flinch when they were beaten and mown down. I have — how do you say it? — no *fancies*. . . . And yet the number and size of the rooms, room after room, their coldness and darkness, began to weary me. In the furthest *sala* one window was open, and the blue dusk came in at it. I wondered for a moment, as I entered, if I saw a figure standing by the balcony. . . . There was nothing . . . I called again, "Tita! Tita! Tita!" . . . And, suddenly, a voice — a lovely, golden, warm Italian voice, sounding, though, as if, in spite of being in the room, it came from a great distance, down a vista of centuries — answered me: "Here I am, here I am! *Eccomi!*" and then seemed to diminish — *diminuendo* — and die away back into those endless years down which it had travelled. After that, the silence gathered round again, with no sound except the thudding of my heart. It had seemed cold, very cold, during those moments, the cold of the tomb or of an infinite distance. It was a lovely voice, though — poor thing, poor thing! But I never saw her, saw nothing, only the blackness which gathers to itself all shadows. . . . And I never again named a dog Tita: my husband had been right for once. Now, if Nanina is lost, I can turn on the electric light and call boldly — I never miss that picture. . . . Later, I found the dog in the street outside.'

Beyond the windows the animation of the evening was beginning. I heard the trams clanking and ringing, and the resonant strong voices of workmen returning home; and in the room, too, the sounds had regained their proportions. Nanina began to bark comfortably. No one was waiting: the story had expelled all shadows.

TRUE LOVERS' KNOT

EVEN when I first knew him — and it must be many years ago — Carey Totnell appeared to be an old man, with the bearded face of Socrates, only in appearance a more elegant philosopher, tinged, in the passage of time, by the epicurean. He seemed to survive as a type, the perfect bachelor of the eighties of the last century, suave in manner, cultivated in mind, leading a life both ordered and orderly. He might — except that his mind was more emancipated — have stepped straight out of the first act of one of Pinero's plays, set in Albany. Well read, in a fashion now almost extinct, a lover of the classics, so that he would often read Greek and Latin poetry for his own enjoyment, he displayed in his choice a natural taste for all good things, and he showed, too, a great respect for food and wine. I much appreciated his taste and intelligence and culture, his tired wisdom and kindliness; but sometimes I wondered at the garnished emptiness of his existence.

Only once, I think, did I hear him enunciate, in a deliberate, very individual voice which gave point to every word he said, sentiments that sounded as though in some way bound up with his life. And the theory that he had then propounded, fantastic as it seemed that evening, returned to my mind later when I heard of his death.

I had been dining with him — in Albany, of course — and he was talking to Robert Hovingford — then a young poet — and to myself in a corner of the library, while the others played bridge. Both Robert and I were in our twenties at the time, and he was rallying us on a supposed desire to avoid family responsibilities and ties. 'My dear boys,' I remember his concluding, 'it's no use your ever trying to escape. You are provided with only a few people among whom to play during your life. Some enter at birth, others drift in later. You can hate or love them as the threads that are their lives touch and knot yours, inextricably or loosely, as it may prove: but that doesn't matter; there they will be at every turn in your life, whereas others, whom you may like better, appear only once, for a month or two, and it will be no use your trying ever to see them again. . . . Better at once to accept defeat and try to like those with whom Destiny has thrown you. It saves trouble; for there they'll be, sure enough, at the end! And so it is, too, with places. In normal times — not, of course, during wars or revolutions — only a few scenes are provided as background to the action of your whole life: to these you seem chained throughout your career on earth, and even when Death himself arrives for you.'

. . . .

All those who had ever stayed in Miss Pomfret's house liked to return at least once a week to see her, because it was easy to look in at St. James's Place and they were sure of welcome and amusement. Moreover, she could boast that strange gift, given to so few, of making all her friends their friends. Originally, I had found my way thither by chance, her lodgings having been recommended by the porter of my club. But I had soon — in company, indeed, with all her guests — taken a great liking to her. She was a personage altogether uncommon, surviving from the age of Shakespeare, audacious and robust as Juliet's nurse, and with a natural gift for original observation and trenchant phrase. By nature Elizabethan, it had been her earthly lot to live through more than half of the Victorian reign, and so she had learned that people could now be shocked, and that a great many of them deserved the sensation.

However, to tow this warm-blooded, vigorously reacting human being, built on so magnificent a scale, both morally and physically, with her keen, peasant understanding of men and women (rare, because reached entirely through her individual eyes, in an age when the whole population has been taught to read and write), to attempt to tow her, then, and anchor her within the limited space of a short story, is a little like trying to introduce a whale within the confines of a swimming-pool. We will only, therefore, take a single glance at her large frame, its many rotund contours encased in black silk, on which were disposed several gold ornaments, and at the high black collar round her neck, surmounted by a little white ruff, which imparted to her smiling and rather creased face the shining geniality of a Frans Hals; so that, most of all, her visitors liked to see her — as sometimes, but not often, they did — holding up a wine-glass under the light, drinking to the health of a friend.

One evening, I found, as usual, a good many people in her sitting-room on the ground floor; and among others, Carey. . . . I had not realised before that Miss Pomfret and he were friends. I remember the occasion well, because she gave us a lively description of her new lodger, above, in the best suite. She had taken a great fancy to him — though he was a spiritualist, a faith of which she could not altogether approve — for he sent her enormous bunches of flowers from time to time, and she admired, too, the way in which he had done up his sitting-room, with, as she said, 'Hindian 'angings and Hegyptian bronzes on marble pedestrians', cats, bulls and hawks. 'Five thousand years old, some of 'em are,' she said confidently. But now came the sound of a bump overhead, followed by intoning, and Miss Pomfret broke off to remark, 'That's 'im. Pr'ying to that blooming 'awk agine, I suppouse.'

She liked to stay up talking as late as she could, till two or three in the morning if possible — perhaps because this to her was a symbol of being her own mistress at last, with no need to get up early. So, to gratify her propensity in this matter, I stayed behind after the others had gone, and it was then that she told me she had been nurse and personal maid to old Mrs. Totnell, Carey's mother, from about 1882 till her death in 1900, and had known intimately her numerous — there were seven sons and daughters — offspring. Their father, a famous counsel, had long been dead, and Carey was the eldest son, the cleverest, the pride and despair of his family. . . . I obtained from her, little by little, a picture of my old friend as a young man; a full-length portrait in the pointillist manner, acquired by placing a blob of paint here, a blob there.

In spite of those same responsibilities, about which he liked continually to harangue me, the inhabitant of that elegant, empty shell of today had been, it appeared, fierce, wild and untrammelled, a source of anxiety, instead — as now — of quiet comfort to his relatives. And in any particular difficulty that arose — or, more generally, that himself had created — it had been his very sensible habit to consult Miss Pomfret, since she could understand anything, however unglossed, that belonged to human nature, to ask her advice, and to request her to act as intermediary between himself and his family. Moreover, whatever he did, or whatever she may have pretended to the contrary, she was, in reality, fonder of the gay, exquisite, audacious 'Mr. Carey' than of all his brothers and sisters, with their better regulated lives — of everyone, indeed, except his mother, to whom she was devoted.

I gathered that by far the greatest imbroglio (one could not say *scandal*, but difficulty is altogether too mild a word for it) in which Carey had been involved, was a tremendous love-affair with an Italian *prima donna* of international fame. For two years he had lived with Forelli in a house in Welbeck Street, and during that comparatively brief period there had arisen a succession of tempests and hurricanes, born of the hot suns of her native Neapolitan country, and often culminating in episodes of intense strangeness and absurdity.

Always bounded by the conventions of the Italian operatic form, limited to weeping, storming and threats of suicide, even to the pretence of madness, they were followed by scenes excruciatingly sweet, for all that their airs were yet unformulated, but nevertheless peculiarly unsuited to the social life of the English capital and the quiet of the London clubs. (I mention clubs advisedly because on several occasions Forelli invaded the upholstered seclusion of the Mausoleum in quest of Carey, and had to be barred from a search of its cloistral apartments by an unspeakably shocked, if comprehending, hall-porter.)

The effect of this upon his relatives can be imagined. They had accused him of bringing scandal on the family, and of neglecting his affairs in the City. Accordingly, Miss Pomfret had often been designated to approach him with suggestions of reform. But, as it happened, Miss Pomfret was, rather surprisingly, a devotee of grand opera; which, together with racing, constituted the twin lights of her life. Moreover, Forelli had taken a great liking to her, and this flattered such an amateur. . . . Indeed, in only two matters had Miss Pomfret stood against the lovers: she blamed him for causing continual worry to his mother, and she did not want them to marry. ('It wouldn't do.') But in any case, nothing would have persuaded Forelli to marry him, and this had been, in fact — though his relatives were too proud to believe it — the most frequent cause of the quarrels between them.

Opera has fallen low in man's esteem, and no one now, I am aware, ever falls in love with a *prima donna*, but in those halcyon days of waists and bustles and bonnets, of hansom cabs and top-hats and frock-coats, when life was serene and unruffled except for the disturbances that you, as an individual, chose to make for your own diversion, nightingales were lovely of feather, as of voice. Into the brief space of their singing lives they crammed whole careers of artistic and amorous experience. When, for an immense fee, paid in gold sovereigns, such a diva consented to sing at a private house, at the mere opening of her lips talk would die away as though the archangel of music himself had entered the room and clapped his wings for silence. And the crowds that applauded her singing would be interested, equally, in the events of her private existence, would be in possession of a great many true, as well as false details, and would discuss them eagerly. Every night elegant, ardent young amateurs waited outside the stage door to see Forelli emerge and drive off with Carey in his private hansom, and nearly every day, too, he could be seen attending her in the Park or escorting her through a restaurant with something of the pride of a drumming peacock. Bouquets and messages, lyres and harps and wreaths of roses and carnations, arrived for her at all hours. And these tributes helped to charge the atmosphere suitably for scenes of passion in real life.

In spite of their reasonless and perpetual differences, in spite of incongruity, in spite of her willingness to live with, and yet steadfast refusal to marry him, each had been in reality devoted to the other. Carey was in love with her voice as much as her person, and for him she would sing as for no one else. Notwithstanding frequent ludicrous and painful situations, there had existed in their relationship a quality not only genuine, but tragic and unforgettable, and this Miss Pomfret had seen for herself and somehow managed to convey to me, even after the passing of many years. Here, then, in the drawing-room of his house in Welbeck Street, the turmoil of both their lives had spent itself (for, being a born *prima donna*, Forelli preferred scenes set in the drawing-room to, as it were, bedroom scenes), and they had loved and quarrelled with a vehemence and ebullition unsuited to this city and its surroundings, had often parted for ever, only to return, dove-like, within a few hours. Here, with her back to the huge piano smothered up in a Chinese shawl, with many objects standing upon it, she had practised her parts, and trilled her joys and griefs in coloratura.

Miss Pomfret described the room well, could even remember the identity of some of the silver-framed, enthusiastically autographed portraits of tenors with whom Forelli had sung; for she had often been sent there with messages from anxious relatives, or had been summoned by one or other of the lovers themselves. Evidently Carey had furnished it for his mistress with an ostentation born of the recent romances of Ouida and of the influence of Sarah Bernhardt; had filled it with arabesque hangings, with Persian rugs and flowers and palm-trees, with bronzes and fine pictures, ancient and modern; and Forelli, for her part, had added operatic trophies, crowns and sheaves of flowers, photographs of elephantine tenors in armour, or with lace collars and hats crowned with flowing feathers. Certainly for him the place had been charged with vital vibrations such as he was never to give out, or receive, again. The battery, the dynamo of his soul, had been, for those two short years, working at its highest pressure. After that, he became the shell I knew.

Eventually the lovers had quarrelled and really parted for good, much to the satisfaction of all concerned, except themselves. And not long after, Forelli had died in Paris, still in the height of her powers and her celebrity, so that only the echo of that golden voice lingered in the minds of men.

. . .

It was Miss Pomfret who told me first of Carey's death. He had been nearly seventy — a good span, I suppose: but somehow, all his qualities, physical and mental, had appeared to be specifically calculated to support him into extreme old age, so that the news came as a shock to his friends. Though, as I perceived, she deeply felt his loss, and his sufferings, yet, reverting again to her Elizabethan character, she could not help manifesting something of Webster's fascinated delight in death. She showed herself determined, in spite — or, perhaps, because — of my affection for him, to spare me no detail of Carey's final distress and dissolution. One could almost hear in her voice, as she talked, the rhythm of the poet's lines:

Of what is't fools make such vain keeping?
Sin their conception, their birth weeping,
Their life a general mist of error,
Their death a hideous storm of terror.

When he sent for her, she had found him in a typically fashionable nursing-home, made up of several old houses, superficially altered. The lift, she had noticed, was hardly wide enough to hold her, but possessed a curious, long rectangular shape, just able to receive a coffin when it came down. 'Oh yes, he's getting on nicely,' the sister had said in a 'pleasant' voice, cool and clear, 'and much more "comfy" than he would be at home. . . . There's always a nurse with him, even at night, to cheer him up. And he's less grumpy: quite affable to everyone now.'

Carey Totnell lay, propped up on pillows, in a large front room on the first floor; rather dark, and to Miss Pomfret's way of thinking, 'too cold-looking', with its sanitary surfaces and enamelling. It contained, also, a litter of pseudo-scientific apparatus, lamps and cylinders and bed-tables, and of spindly fittings in aluminium and steel, the uses of which remain fortunately unknown to the lay mind. 'Why, the very bed 'e l'y hin 'ad more the look to me of a dentist's chair than a Christian bed,' Miss Pomfret remarked to me. . . . Nevertheless, she had rather liked the room; it had seemed in some way familiar and, in consequence, comfortable and not to be feared.

But she was shocked at the change she saw in the invalid, for he had paid her one of his usual visits, apparently in his normal health, only a few evenings previously. Carey had betrayed from the first, it seems, 'that nasty blue look', his voice had come from far away when he spoke, his nails ''ad no life in them', and his hands kept plucking at the sheets; all these symptoms being well-known harbingers of death in the system of divining which she had projected for herself. ' "You'll never come hout of 'ere, except a corpse, laid hout flat in that lift, my man," Hi said to myself,' she added, 'but, of course, I didn't let 'im see anything. Hi couldn't 'elp crying a little, and jest said, "Oh, Mr. Carey, dear, to think of seeing you *like this*!" '

The sister had first turned the nurse out of the room, then, after indulging in a miniature power-dive, patting and tugging at the pillows which he had managed at last to make comfortable for himself, and pulling cords for windows and ventilators, she had squared her chin, saying, 'Now I'll go. I know I can trust you not to tire the patient or stay too long', and had left them.

At once Carey had turned his face to Miss Pomfret and said (he seemed to have to make an effort, she had thought, even to speak), 'Mary, my old friend, I'm a dying man. I know. It is only a matter of hours, not of days. . . . So I wanted to see you once again, to thank you for everything you've done for me, always . . . and to ask you one question. . . . You've seen so much of the course of my life: do you recognise this room?' . . . And then, as she looked round, she had understood; the enamelled cornices and doors, the distempered walls, the metal furniture, had taken on other colours, other lines. A gold-lacquered paper flowered again over the walls, a Chinese screen stood in front of the door, a Symphony in White, by Whistler, hung over the mantel. (The fireplace was now filled in, to hold an electric heater.) In the far corner, on the muffled piano, stood rows of silver-framed photographs of Forelli in the rôles of Carmen, La Sonnambula, Lucia and a hundred other operatic heroines, or of mellifluous male singers decked for their parts, and on the tables the vases of sick-room flowers had been ousted for the instant by vast, formal trophies of roses, orchids and lilies. . . . He lay now dying in the very room of the very house in which his life had been crowned and consumed.

. . .

He told her that he had fought — as she had been certain he would — against the idea of leaving Albany at all. But the doctor had ordered him to be taken at once in a motor-ambulance to his favourite nursing-home. Carey had not even known where it was situated, and had felt too ill to ask questions. On arrival, when the old atmosphere had begun to distil itself round him in the room, he had felt sure that this was the result of his fever: but during the night, as he lay awake there, he had become convinced, on the contrary, of its reality. And a curious mingled sense of comfort and inquietude had assailed him. . . . However, the slight effort of describing his feelings evidently tired him out, and as he seemed to be growing sleepy, Miss Pomfret had soon left him.

Next morning she had returned again to see him. But this time he did not know her. . . . He was apparently talking Italian to someone on the other side of the bed. She tried to make out what he was saying, but it was no use: she only knew a few words of Italian. Then he fell silent again, intent, as though listening. . . . And was it her imagination, she wondered, or did she really distinguish, just for a moment, a coloratura trill, high up and far away, almost out of hearing? . . . She wished her ears had been sharper, for it sounded, oh, beautiful; heavenly, you might say.

Probably it was a gramophone or radio somewhere near by. You couldn't get away from them nowadays. But she was never sure.

THE MESSENGER

It was in the afternoon, for there were no evening performances. We had both of us seen *Les Sylphides* a hundred times, and much better danced, so we left the theatre and waited in the empty *foyer* until the next ballet began.

Painters are apt to talk well, writers badly; for by the end of the day they are tired of words. (The members of no other profession are obliged to express themselves solely by means of their wares.) Robert Hovingford, though an excellent writer — no less original and celebrated as an author than his wife is as a painter —, stands out, an exception to this rule. I love to listen to him, however preposterous may be the theories which he continually expounds, for underneath the queer brand of decorative nonsense in which invariably he indulges, gleams a vein of truth; a vein strange and at first unconvincing, because so unlike the truth of other people.

A man passed, without seeing us, and Robert smiled and called out to him, 'Good luck!'

'That's my mascot,' he remarked to me. 'And he knows it. I feel elated, for whenever good fortune is in the wind for me, I see him — though I have never got to know him very well. But he understands that, too. It's part of his contract, so to speak.'

'If you both like the Ballet, it's inevitable that you should see him,' I began to argue. 'I don't think much of your reasoning, Robert.'

'"Inevitable", *inevitable*,' he repeated, 'don't use that word, *please*. . . . Did I tell you about The Messenger? . . . No? Then I must tell you now. . . . "Inevitable" is the word I dread. All my life I have been able to hear the Juggernaut creaking down the immutable course of its steel rails towards its destiny. I cannot explain the reason *why* things happen as they do; I can only humbly note fragments of the design, the vast scale of its conception, here and there the minute working-out of the details attached to it. . . . You know that I have long held that, if you are frightened of something happening, that event is brought so much the nearer to you by your fear: or you may even be treated to a counterfeit semblance of it, or a rehearsal for it, in order further to terrify you. The sort of thing I mean is that, if you have a peculiar dread of, shall we say, smallpox, and think you have been exposed to infection, then, the very day on which you expect to develop the disease, your body will come out in a rash: but, instead of smallpox, it will prove to be some lesser, children's illness. . . . But I mustn't wander away from the question of inevitability.

'Do you remember old Carey Totnell and his theories?* I used to make fun of them, but events have since converted me to them. I believe, too, now, that we are born into the world with certain people for our companions; these alone we may see, play with, quarrel with: we cannot avoid them. We are confined with them, as it were, in a compartment of eternity of which the walls are invisible, so as to give us the illusion of the whole earth at our choice. It is futile to try to escape the reiterant impacts of these people on our lives. They may bore us, they may enchant us, but there, sure enough, they will stand at our life's end as at our life's beginning. . . . And this story — an episode more than a story — which I want to tell you, shows at least how superb is the timing of Destiny, and proves that it is of no use attempting to delay the effects she wishes to obtain.

'First of all, let us for a moment examine the nature of the playmates provided for us. I hope I am not over-superstitious, but I observe coincidences. . . . There is the man who passed by just now, for instance: my mascot. Obversely, there are those whose presence darkens the air for me, the harbingers of evil. This whole genus, an important one, can be divided, I think, into two species: the first, harmless chatterers who, as the whole world reels for you though you must not show it, rush up to worry you about things that do not matter. They seem to emerge suddenly, from nowhere, with a certainty of technique that belongs only to the virtuoso — for their mere appearance discloses whole avenues leading back into the past, down which Disaster stalks towards you. They like to ask questions: "How is your dear Aunt Emily; have you heard from her lately?" or "Did you ever get the address of that shop I

* See 'True Lovers' Knot' (p. 373).

wanted you to go to? You never let me know", or "I thought of going down to Dorset in April to stay with your cousins; will you be there?" or "Have you seen Dicky lately?" (a man you have been avoiding for years). Indeed, this branch of the tribe never fails to collect the friends you have shed in the course of a lifetime. (And, let us be frank, the friends we possessed at eighteen are not, if we develop normally, those we should choose, or choose to see, at forty.) They are like retrievers, producing corpses for you, with an air of pride, just at the moment you least expect it. They specialise also in knowing, never the celebrated man himself, but always his duller connections; had they then been alive, they would have concentrated their attention upon Leonardo da Vinci's maiden aunt or Michelangelo's cousin ("So much more original, yet simple", they would have, no doubt, explained), though occasionally, of course, they would have materialised in some moment of agony, to ask the Master after the tedious relatives whom he had for so long striven to forget.

'The second species, however, is more incisive in action. Retrievers, too, to a man, they are also essentially the bearers of tidings. If there is something it would be better for you *not* to know at a particular moment, they spring out of the earth, like a *jinnee* out of his bottle, to tell you, with a grisly savouring of their pleasure, rolling the words round in their mouths in the same way that a connoisseur allows the flavour of good wine to linger upon the palate. They belong to a race apart, the witless avengers of forgotten injuries; their whole bearing, inspired by their subconscious minds, testifies to it. The countless indignities inflicted unaware upon the dwarf by the man of ordinary stature, upon the ugly by the beautiful, the stupid by the clever, boil up suddenly within their brooding blood.

'You may think I exaggerate; but let me tell you. . . . Do you know Ralph Mudey-Mulhall? Well, he has the attributes of both the species I have described. Please don't mistake me. He is kind — more than kind, tender-hearted. He possesses many invaluable qualities that in someone else we should all of us estimate at their true worth. He works hard, supports several idle relatives, is a faithful friend, and does good in many directions. I could never dislike him, never be rude to him. I wish him well, infinitely well, but from a distance — it must be from a distance. . . . To begin with, when I meet him he always talks to me, immediately, of those friends of my parents whom I most dislike. They speak of me, he tells me, continually, and he repeats some of "the nice things they say". Thus his conversation, always bringing with it the memory of distant but unhappy days, lowers the temperature of mind and heart and body. "You cannot escape us", the voices of the Gorgon sisters moan in your ear.

'Both Frida and I have known Ralph since we were children — before we had ever met each other. He had attended all the same children's parties to which we went. And then, when we had grown up and frequented ballrooms, there, too, he would be; now a very tall, stooping, lanky figure, dark, with a bumpy forehead, a small, clipped moustache, and brown eyes, intent but curiously empty, and a voice, deep and deliberate, summoned up like the voice of a ventriloquist rather than seeming a natural mode of expression. On these occasions he would appear always to be rather lonely, would dance seldom, so that one wondered why he came. But to us he was very friendly, and, at the time that Frida and I became engaged, just before and just after, he would invariably suggest joining us for supper. It was difficult to refuse, but you know, when you are in love, you want to be alone and don't relish extraneous company; so that, though we still liked him, we tended to try and escape his presence, but that only added, you would have thought from the result, to the fascination we exercised upon him. He was willing — and able — to ferret us out anywhere.

'The years went by then, and we saw less of him, because, as he grew older, his utter contentment, the fact that he was so happy with the collection of old silver and of our old-style-calendar friends that he was forming — for this, too, had become really a *collection* — irked us. He was quite rich; so, feeling the necessity of perpetuating his likeness, he sat, of course, to Laszló, and it was very trying to be invited to see that painter's flashy misrepresentation of him as a dashing Magyar magnate rather than a mild English business man. We grew tired of hearing of his garden, the new kind of sweet peas he was growing, and the perfection altogether of his way of life. In fact, he was so enchanted with himself — in a lesser degree, often a delightful characteristic —that it became a bore, as did his quirks and quips, his little jokes and sallies and imitations. Much more full of talk than formerly, he liked to tell you all about himself, what he ate every day, what he felt, at what time he was called and when he went to bed: these things were all of intense concern to him and so he thought they would equally interest his listeners. And he would give us, too, the opinions of his friends on many matters; he seemed to live in a perpetual house-party of those who had been dead to us since we had reached years of discretion. While, therefore, he has no spite in his whole composition, not a grain of it, he is himself its blind and unavowed instrument, the Mercury of the forces that govern the lower regions.

'You can understand how bad things have been for us lately, because you know the circumstances; cruel for Frida and bad enough for me. John is our only child, and it would have been dreadful to see any child, even if he had not been our own, suffering like that, so ill and helpless and unable to understand what was the matter or tell us what he felt. And, in order to be near the right doctors, we had to stay in London through the bombing, exposing him to dangers of that kind as well.

'As a mother, Frida is sometimes a bit vague. She has always adored John, but, all the same, her whole life goes usually into her painting. (And, what's curious, I believe the little chap comprehends it and isn't jealous.) But, when he fell ill, the full strength and resilience of her character came out. She gave up her work entirely, and nursed the boy night and day. I don't know how she did it, for she wasn't used to that kind of fatigue: but I think that was what pulled him round; because it's a rare illness, and the doctors cannot help much as yet, though they do their best. For a whole fourteen days, she never had a thought for anyone but John. I was completely forgotten. She would hardly even allow her sister, Isabelle, to help her. The strain must have been — and anybody could see it was — immense. . . . At last, one morning, about a fortnight ago, the specialist pronounced, "If the child gets through the next twenty-four hours, his temperature will drop. He will live, and the illness will leave no mark on him. . . . It is a terrible thing to have to say to his father and mother, but I must warn you; it all depends on the next twenty-four hours."

'Isabelle had been splendid. Her kindness and tirelessness, her support of Frida, and the consideration she showed for her in everything, great or small, won my affection more than ever. (And I've always said that I would have married her, if I hadn't married Frida.) On the morning that the crisis of John's illness began, she came to me and said:

'"Robert, what are we to do? . . . Natasha Danbury is dead. She has died of pneumonia following on influenza. We *can't* tell Frida at a time like this. And if we don't, she is sure to find out."

'Natasha — I don't believe you ever met her — had been an old neighbour of Frida's parents in the country, and Frida and she had soon become great friends. As her Christian name tells you, she was Russian by origin, and she had married a delightful old man, much older than herself, Bill Danbury. He was rather an extraordinary character in his way, a squire, devoted to country pursuits, but loving books and music as much as hunting. Really, very exceptional. Natasha was beautiful, like a greyhound, and, while Bill was alive, passed for an intelligent woman. Alas, when she became a widow, the full extent of the influence her husband had exercised upon her became apparent. She had absorbed his taste. But now she showed that she had no opinions of her own, though she produced every *cliché* with an impressive manner. She needed someone like Bill to grow round, and to take her out of herself. Now that he was no longer there, she brooded in a mystical way upon the intricacies of her own uninteresting nature, and expatiated upon them incessantly to her friends, in a special voice she reserved for this subject, slow and emphatic. The high points she marked, sometimes by affected spirals of laughter, sometimes by a trick she thought attractive, of putting out her tongue at right angles, and in the opposite direction from that in which she rolled her eyes. (A very difficult feat of facial acrobatics; you try it in front of the mirror when you get home!) . . . Poor Natasha! She expected her friends to give the whole of their time up to her. In the end, a year or two ago, Frida, who has all the hardness, as well as all the softness, of the artist, came to me and said:

'"Robert, I've got to choose between Natasha and my painting. I've chosen my painting. I am fond of her, but she's inflated herself into a whole-time job, and I can't take it on. . . . Besides, she has plenty of other more suitable friends. I know she'll *pretend* to mind my neglect of her. I feel a brute, myself. But she won't *really* mind, though she will enjoy being huffy and mysterious when my name is mentioned. She won't *really* mind, because she knows how interesting her character is, how important to the world, and she knows, too, that we don't know it."

'I don't blame Frida. Her first duty was to her painting. All the same, since she is genuinely kind, I thought I saw, from time to time, signs that Natasha weighed on her conscience. And so now the news of this sudden death — Natasha who was so healthy and had never been known to be ill for a day — was bound, especially in the circumstances in which we found ourselves, to upset Frida beyond reason.

'Her sister and I talked it over. We settled to keep *The Times* away from her — Natasha's death wasn't in the other papers —, at least until our own crisis was over. If the boy took a turn for the better, she would be more fitted to hear the news; if he grew worse, nothing would matter any more. . . . The hours dragged on, the strain increasing all the time. How we got through that day and night I shall never know. They seemed interminable. . . . Then, all at once, about eleven o'clock the next morning, the danger was over, — John's temperature had fallen, and he breathed without difficulty and slept, for the first time for a fortnight, the easy, unstirring sleep of childhood. . . . The change was incredible at first.

'It was only, though, in this moment of utter relief, that the full fatigue of what we had been through settled upon Frida, Isabelle and myself. You can't imagine how tired we felt.

'None of us had left the house for many days, none of us had eaten a proper meal, or felt that we could eat one, and now, in spite of our exhaustion, there suddenly welled up in us a sense of gaiety, a need for relaxation. It was as though we had been on a long and very rough ocean voyage and had at last reached land. There was no reason to stay at home any longer; John could be safely left to the nurse's care. So we decided to dine out, tired or not; but, since we did not feel inclined as yet to face people who had not shared our experience, we selected Le Perroquet Vert; because it's amusing, the food is excellent and you never see anyone you know there. . . .

And since Frida still had not looked at the paper, and was in this mood, we determined again to put off telling her about Natasha, to leave it till the next day; otherwise, it would only spoil her evening.

'We had ordered a table, but when we arrived we found the *maître d'hôtel* had made a mistake, and that it had been set for four persons; a nice table with a wall-sofa and two chairs. . . . It really was enjoyable to be out of the house again, to be able to order a dinner, to be able to eat it. And there were no sirens tonight, none of those wailings which are the signature-tune of the twentieth century. . . . We might as well have a cocktail, we thought; it was an occasion.

'Indeed, we were feeling care-free in spite of the war — and I believe both Isabelle and I had, for the time being, completely forgotten about the death of Natasha, which had been haunting us all day, because of its possible effect upon Frida.

'"How lovely," Isabelle said, "to be by ourselves, but to have the whole evening before us without anything on our minds . . . I long to hear you talk again about other things than medicines."

'Almost as she said the words, we saw Ralph Mudey-Mulhall, sitting there, alone, in the middle of the restaurant, reading a book.

'"It's all right, he doesn't see us," Frida reassured us. "And it's a good thing. I'm happy, but I'm too tired to deal with people — especially Ralph. I only want to see you two."

'"Oh, he sees us; never you fear," I replied. "He is preparing something, an eclectic joke of some kind or other, I should say." I could deduce it from the manner in which his head never moved from behind his book.

'Isabelle urged, "Have the fourth place removed at once! Or he'll come and sit through dinner, this heavenly sense of being at peace will be broken and we shall none of us be able to talk at all. . . . And I have masses to say; I don't know if you have? *Please* call the waiter and have it taken away."

'"We can't," I said. "It will take too long and look too rude."

'Now a waiter hurried up to us, with a note written in pencil: "Herr Hitler would like to look at you". The waiter pointed out the table (we pretended not to know it), and we gazed across. Suddenly Ralph dropped his book. Then he pulled — for imitations of Hitler were fashionable at the moment, and Charlie Chaplin's "Great Dictator" was the popular film of the hour — a lock of hair over his bumpy forehead and treated us to an impersonation of the Nazi Leader. I must say, with the hair and his little moustache, he succeeded in looking — though one would never have expected it — terrifyingly like him, or, at any rate, like other imitations of him one had seen. . . . We smiled and laughed, in what we hoped was a convincing manner, although the astonished expression on the faces of the people sitting at tables between us and him made us feel a little self-conscious.

'Ralph then reassembled his features, laughed a good deal at the joke, as he considered it, that he had played on us, and got up and stalked towards us, rather like, I thought, a walking lighthouse, with his lanky form and projecting eyes, shallow but burning. He still laughed and chuckled as he approached us. Once near enough to speak, however, his expression changed to one of sympathy and commiseration. . . . For an instant, I thought he had heard, somehow or other, about John's illness. Then I realised.

'"Frida, dear Frida," he was saying. "I was *so* grieved to hear of Natasha Danbury's death. I know what friends you two were. Though I never knew her very well, I had seen more of her lately, and had grown to appreciate her, and her wonderful powers of introspection and self-analysis. Introspective people *are* so interesting, don't you think? I can quite see why you two got on so well."

'Two spots of colour leapt suddenly into Frida's pale, tired face, and she said:

'"*Natasha? Natasha dead?* . . . Surely not? We should have heard," and she gazed at her sister and myself with a sort of shocked inquiry and reproach in her eyes.

'There was no help for it. We had to explain.

'"Isabelle and I decided it was better not to tell you, darling, at present: you've had so much worry lately. We were going to break it to you tomorrow. . . . She died two days ago." And to Ralph I said, "You see, Ralph, I didn't let her know, because she has been nursing our little boy — and it's been a great strain. He has been very ill for the last fortnight. But the crisis is over now. . . . This is the first time we've been out since his illness began: and I didn't think we should see anyone who would be likely to tell her."

. . . Meanwhile, Frida was mastering her surprise and shock.

'Ralph is kind, really very kind. An agonised look came over his face. "Oh, how dreadful! I am so sorry. You *didn't know*? How stupid of me! I wouldn't have done such a thing for the world."

'Then he stopped apologising. I saw the thought go through his head, "I must help them", and he said, in his ordinary, deliberate way:

'"Well, as it's your first evening out, you'll want cheering up, so let *me* sit down here and talk to you."

'All through our dinner — for he had finished his — he sat in the fourth place at the table, thereby in his own mind atoning for his lapse by charity — I never saw a man work so hard, either, to be kind. . . . At first, to distract Frida's attention, he talked of friends, old friends, friends of her parents, all of them longing to see us, he said, and often wondering how it was they never ran across either of us. Of course, they didn't approve of my wife's painting, he added, or of her marrying a man who wrote for his living: but they were fond of her, oh, so fond, and anxious to *help*. And they liked me, too, it appeared, would like to get to know me better; they thought there was probably a lot of good in me, *when* they got to know me. Similarly, he said, he had seen many old friends of *my* parents, and they were eager to get to know Frida better, were sure they would perceive things in her that they had not hitherto noticed, if only they saw more of her. And they were quite sensible, and stated openly that they did not expect even to understand — or like — her paintings. It was so much better to be frank, like that, and not to pretend, wasn't it?

'I am afraid he saw this line was not proving a success, so he imitated Hitler again, in order to give himself time to think. We all three laughed a lot. Then he told us about the last few bits of silver he had bought before the war, and where he had sent them for safety. From that subject he passed on to his life in the country, to his evacuees, and how it had turned out — you'd never guess, he said! — that my old tutor and Frida's governess were among them. They were always talking of us, telling stories of our childhood, and of what *absurd* children we had been. "Mind you," he said, "they're fond of you; don't think they're not." Now he veered towards more congenial subjects.

'He confided in us what he ate, and what he drank. Sometimes, owing to the organising genius of his cook, he had meat three times a week, sometimes four. Good meat, too. The cooking was good *bourgeois* cooking, and there was nothing better! On the whole, perhaps, he ate less than in peace-time, but he felt none the worse for it — if anything, better. (He had got into his stride by now, and at times stopped the flow, copious but deliberate, to regard us, most severely, to make sure we were paying attention. The slightest failure in this respect, the flicker of a single eyelash in another direction, he seemed in almost psychic fashion immediately to divine.) Often he drank cider now, he avowed, or ginger-beer, even. After all, it was war-time. And coffee, lots of coffee. He was called at 7.30, or, it might be, on one or two days a week, at 8. . . . We seemed almost to be watching the hours going round.

'We did not speak: there was no necessity, he did not expect it. We did not dare, even, to catch one another's eye. We gave — had to give — our whole attention, concentrated on the vast vista he was unfolding. . . . Suddenly he broke off, looked at his watch, and said:

'"*What* a time you've kept me here! . . . Why, it's ten, long past ten, and I see the waiters are trying to clear away. We mustn't delay them. I always say it's unfair on them to sit on and on. So I shall leave you now. I ought to have gone an hour ago, for I'd promised to go in, Robert, and see your Aunt Muriel for a few minutes on my way home. We often talk of you, she seems so lonely and loves to talk of past days. . . . Now you've made me late."

'He went to get his coat and hat and then, just as we thought him gone, returned to say, "I forgot to tell you, Frida, how I stuck up for you the other day. . . . No, I won't tell you who they were, or what they said, but I always stick up for you with everyone. You can depend on that."

'*He* had forgotten all about Natasha Danbury, I think, and went home quite happy.'

Robert stopped speaking, and we got up to go into the theatre, for the next ballet, *Petrouchka*, had already begun, and the puppets were moving their feet and arms within the open booths, while the old magician watched them.

ALIVE — ALIVE OH!

It has long been apparent to the discerning that in this country to be a poet — or, at any rate, a good one — is a rash, a hazardous, activity. It may be that there are critics who will object to this doctrine, who will urge that, for example, Byron, Keats and Shelley were not driven from their native land, but quitted it of their own accord, gladly even. Nevertheless it cannot be disputed that these three most remarkable Englishmen of their day preferred to spend their last years, or months, in a foreign country. Whether hounded out to die or themselves eager to go, they went: that is sufficient. Nor will it be disputed, one imagines, that since their passing weak health has come to be demanded as first token, an early death as final guarantee, of poetic genius.

Historically, the death of the three poets I have mentioned was divided by no very great interval of years from that of Nelson, who had first framed in burning words the national conception: 'England expects that every man will do his duty'. Once this doctrine had been formulated, the part of the poet in the community immediately became defined and acknowledged: it was to die young. Surely, too, he must be, not only willing, but anxious to aid those critics who spend so much of their time in helping him? A post-mortem is always more certain than diagnosis (vivisection, though it would be a more complete solving of the difficulty, is at present forbidden on human beings, even on artists), and it is inevitably easier to spot a dead poet than one alive and kicking. Moreover, once the man is removed, the critics, like so many calamaries, can surround the body of his work with such a cloud of ink that it soon becomes impossible to distinguish its essential features. Thus it must be admitted that more has been written about Shakespeare since his death than ever in his lifetime, albeit his plays are more seldom performed: and that the mass of critical footnotes that, much as parasites cling to an animal, encrust the text of every classic does not make it any the easier to read.

Yet when all these arguments have been stated, there are still to be found those willing — or, if not willing, obliged — to pay the penalty of genius. Perhaps, just as the great whales have, during the last century, transformed their tactics with the object of making the hunting of them the more perilous, so the poet may have become better, if more difficult, sport. I know not. But surely some facts of this kind can be deduced from the story of Joseph Bundle, the Georgian poet, and of his untimely death; that true though tragic narrative, which, never before told in full, I now propose to relate.

There must, of course, be others who have survived these long years: there must be others who recall, as I do, the aureole of fame which once emanated from those four inspiring syllables — Joseph Bundle. It was some fifty years ago, toward the end of the First European War, and in the lustrum following its conclusion, that they reached their fullest effulgence. Yet even before that splendid culmination to diplomacy — one, of course, to which no Englishman can ever look back without experiencing a physical tingle of pride at the magnitude of the national effort and its resultant losses — had been reached, the name Bundle was one of a growing celebrity, a sound seldom off the lisping lips of the more cultured. Nor was it difficult to comprehend why such a coruscation issued from the very music of these syllables. Everything about Bundle, everything that concerned him, was romantic, mysterious. Apart from his altogether exceptional knowledge of bird-life (the only other qualification, besides ill-health and its latent promise of an early decease, that is demanded by the public as essential in an English poet), it was understood from the very beginning that in some peculiar, almost mystic, way he was not only connected, but positively identified with the soil of Sussex, whether chalk or clay: that, like Venus arising from her shell, borne in by the racing, foam-flecked horses of the tides, so had Bundle been discovered by Mattie Dean* and other *literati* — though, of course, fully dressed and more conventionally educated — cradled in some half-hidden juniper-bush on the Downs.

And this impression of secret contact with Mother Earth that he induced was not misleading, for he was in reality —

* For a full description of Mattie, though when he is some years older, see 'Triple Fugue', p. 224.

and he kept it skilfully concealed — the son of a prosperous doctor in Shoreham, and though he had been, as it were, born with a silver thermometer in his mouth, this was indeed due to the united action of the Sussex soil, and its faithful ally, Winter, upon the tubes, livers and lungs of wealthy old ladies in the neighbourhood. This same rich hibernal harvest it was that had supported the expense of his excellent education, and that had finally enabled him to study for a year at that Dramatic Academy where he had acquired the pleasant, rustic burr of his speech — a burr which never deserted him and much enhanced his popularity with those crowds of nature-lovers immured in cities — though I have heard a cavilling native purist denounce it as more Somerset than Sussex.

His appearance, too, fitted him admirably for the part he had so judiciously chosen. Its chief attribute, and that most responsible for his early success, was a perhaps deceptive effect of extreme physical delicacy. And then, hollow-cheeked and hollow-chested though he was, yet with the deep-set brightness of his eyes, the curve of nose and chin, the long body and rather anomalous legs, he suggested — and what could be more appropriate? — a bird — the Bird of Wisdom, the Athenian Owl. At this period the old-fashioned poetic preciosity he exhibited was comparatively little. He to a greater degree cultivated, on the other hand, a you-don't-mind-if-I-slap-you-on-the-back-though-I've-just-been-cleaning-my-Ford-car heartiness of manner that must have been somewhat disconcerting at first to those esthetes accustomed to a more lilied artificiality. But this soon earned him a reputation for being simple, and unaffected. He encouraged his intimates, too, to call him 'Joe' rather than Joseph, Joe Bundle, so that his name might link up with those of Will Shakespeare, Ben Jonson and Kit Marlowe, and was wont to drink ale in almost too Mermaidenly a manner. In all he said or did there was a smack of the soil — a smack so pronounced as almost to constitute a 'knock-out'. Yet though at the beginning of his career he valiantly upheld what he conceived to be the Elizabethan ideals of beer, sweet and rich, full-mouthed, full-blooded, English — a girl, for example, was always to him a wench — yet he was capable of modifying his affectation to his environment. Thus, were one to inquire of those who remember him, one would be given many varying and apparently contradictory accounts of him. For the Mermaid Tavern rôle was only the chief of the several he could play: indeed, his appearance of ill-health tugged in an exactly contrary direction, never allowed him entirely to forget Keats, or Shelley either as for that: and often even in those days, working as it might be on a sort of spiritual second gear, he would open his collar romantically for a day or two and dart liquid fire out of his eyes: while in after years, when clamorous critics had so obviously given him his cue, and when he had at last come to realise the full significance of his destiny, he was seldom seen except in this other part.

Bundle's first volume of verse, which was published some time in the year preceding the war, had won for him a swift and gratifying recognition, for the poems combined many familiar and therefore delightful ingredients: a sound bottom of Cowper and Wordsworth (Clare was to come later), a little Marlowe, a hint of Shelley, a dash of Marvell, with Keats's beaded bubbles winking at the brim, all shaken together by the local village idiot and served up very cold with a plate of bird-seed to accompany it. The slight foaming which resulted was Bundle's own contribution. Yet in all this there was nothing to startle or affright, everything was soothing and of the kind to which one was accustomed. Indeed, the most sensational feature of the first book was its success. 'The critics', quoted the publishers, 'are unanimous in hailing an English poet not unworthy of his forebears.' And Mattie Dean, who, since he did their reading for them by some process of substituted service, had long been the arbiter of things poetic in a thousand drawing-rooms, became so excited and overwrought by the book that he read two poems from it aloud after dinner to three Cabinet Ministers (two of whom had never heard a poem before); their wives, whose quarrelling was so suddenly stilled by this shrill, sweet piping that they even forgot, for a moment, how the score of the evening stood; a young priest singular for his journalistic wit — one, that is to say, the existence of which only journalists could perceive; an old lady who in her young days had been painted by Burne-Jones and had never since allowed anyone to forget it; a middle-aged woman who had sat to Sargent for her portrait thirteen times and had since been able to remember nothing else; two celebrated, serious-minded but dreadfully bad actresses of musical comedy, who said 'sweet-sweet' and 'I call that clever' throughout the recitation; an esthetic general with very white antennae; a mad, canary-coloured hostess from Paris, the only possible explanation of whose appearance must have been that she had, by some obvious mistake, been interned in a home for lunatic children and had escaped with one of their dresses as her only wear; the literary editor of a literary weekly, very mousy, with the furtive eyes of the school-sneak and hair which had just greyed in time to impart an almost distinguished expression to his rather mean features; the actual editor, who more resembled another public-school type, the fat-boy-bully; two young artists, naïve and surprised; and the Burne-Jones lady's athletic grand-daughter, rather large and 'out-of-it-all', and whose only interest was in breeding dachshunds. 'Eckthquithite,' pronounced Mattie, 'thuch marvellouth underthtanding of birdth.' And, indeed, his delicious twittering of the two poems had been so soft and feeling that it had sounded like a flight of young starlings. Everyone was glad to accept Mattie's judgment.

The heralds went forth, and Bundle's name was securely established in nature-loving Mayfair. For Mattie, as we have had occasion to point out before, when genuinely enthusiastic would spare himself — and others — no pains.

. . . . .

Then the War came, and to the recipe which he had already invented, Bundle now added a very personal brand of pseudo-maternity — as if there were not in the world at that moment already enough suffering mothers. He seemed to have appointed himself as a sort of literary *Marraine*, a synthetic Mother, not only to the men under him (he was a lieutenant now) but to all the troops everywhere. Oh, the hidden, the haunting, sob of Motherhood which convulses every line in these new poems! A few simple onomatopoeic devices were introduced, in addition, to produce an impression of the 'real thing'. The old gentlemen of literature — and all the old ladies too — went wild about his work. He became the Head Boy of the Younger School. Old women read his poems aloud to one another at sock-knitting parties, young ladies edited anthologies solely so as to have an excuse for writing to him, in various schools the masters made their pupils learn them by heart, and all of them were set to music, and sung whenever possible at every charity concert. And each time they were read, sung or recited there was a glow at the heart. For Bundle was at the front. There was something glorious, wasn't there, in giving of our best?

It can be imagined, then, that it was not without apprehension that the elders received tidings that their new favourite had been invalided back to England. There was almost a slump — but soon a firmer tone established itself. For he was in a bad way, it was said, a really bad way. Not only was he suffering from shell-shock, but he had broken his leg for the cause. Well — well — well! It was an inspiring example. 'Always knew the boy would do us credit.' But there was a certain vagueness as to the particulars of the valiant act responsible for this physical and mental damage.

Quite by chance, however, I was to learn the details. And here I should like to confess that from the very beginning I always felt about everything connected with the poet a singular curiosity, as though his career was in some way very specially my own affair. It was as if some prophetic instinct had warned me that alone of his contemporaries I should see this life, and see it whole. And as though he in his turn felt some responding chord he would, when I was present, often address to myself his remarks on life and literature.

One day, then, I was standing up at the bar, drinking a cocktail, when I noticed next to me an officer leaning with an air of negligent elegance across it, occasionally emitting a loud laugh, and jerking back his out-turned, angular arms with a marked effect of dalliance, as he flashed his eye-glass over the polished wood barrier that divided them at the rotund and purple lady, much powdered so that she seemed built in layers of white and purple Turkish delight, who served the drinks. She, in her turn, was heliographing back her pleasure at his sallies with a flashing, golden tooth. In spite of the no doubt numerous years she had spent behind the bar, heavy curls of farmyard laughter hung about her in the smoke-stained air, and struck answering notes out of the thousand bottles (each one stuck with an Allied flag) behind her, while from above the fat golden cupids of the 'nineties peered curiously down. 'Well, you are a one,' she was pronouncing, 'but still I always say that all you boys are like that naow. It's the war 'as done it.' Watching them, as he began to speak I recognised in the jaunty figure at my side an officer whom I had known slightly in France, and who had belonged to that very unit to which Bundle had been attached as artillery-observer. Thus it was very resolutely that I broke in on this gallant conversation, and after a few preliminary greetings, inquired about the poet. Those were heroic days, in which men had forged for themselves a language in keeping with their deeds. I therefore transcribe in his own words this eye-witness's narrative, otherwise it may seem as though a certain savour had been allowed to evaporate from it. Moreover, though, looked back on, it seems a queer, stern, concentrated tongue, it yet gives the atmosphere of reality more than can any words of mine. 'I hear Bundle's got shell-shock,' I said. 'I'm so sorry.' 'Doncher believe it, old bean,' my friend replied. 'If he ever had, it must have been before the war — must have brought it with him. But I don't mind telling you how he broke that damned lower-limb of his. We were billeted in an old farmhouse, a mile or two behind the lines. It was just before luncheon on Christmas Eve, about one pip-emma; Bundle was on the roof observing. All the rest of us were having sherry inside. The Colonel, not a bad old bird, had been having one or two lately: but that day he was quite cheery. He was just saying: "Well, boys, there'll be no Father Christmas down the chimney this year to fill our stockings," when there was a blasted crash down the bloody chimney, and out of a blinking cloud of soot came that mingy blighter Bundle. My word, the Old Man was upset! Thought he'd got 'em again, he did. Knocked the blooming glass straight out of his funny old hand. My word, that was Tootaloo for Bundle — a fair tinkety-tonk, I assure you. What had happened was that the poor boy had seen one of those ruddy birds he pretends to be so fond of, and had stepped back suddenly and down the chimney without looking. We did have a Christmas-and-a-half, I can tell you. Well, chin-chin, cheerio, so long, old boy' — and delicately selecting a clove, he continued his interrupted conversation across the bar.

After this adventure, Bundle's war-poems became more tenderly bloodthirsty than ever. A new volume soon made its appearance, for which it was claimed by the publishers in their advertisements — and rightly: 'This little book of poems has swept the critics clean off their critical feet'. Nor were eye and brain for a moment allowed to enter in. They had been eagerly scanning the bloodshot horizon for a Great War Poet (only he must be after a certain model) and now they had found him. Just as, though Generals are always prepared for war, it is never the next, but always, alas! the last, one for which they are ready, so are critics invariably prepared for the reception of a great poet. In the days of Keats they had looked earnestly out from their high watch-towers, anxious to acclaim another Dryden: similarly, in 1917, they were determined not to allow Keats or Shelley to escape them. And now they had captured him. The sensitive feet grew weaker and weaker from enthusiasm. A week before they had proclaimed Bundle only as an embryonic Milton: today he was a full-fledged Keats.

Yet even now the young poet was as far as ever from seeing whither the path he trod, so blithely yet yearningly, would lead him. Milton, it is true, had lived out his span before the rule that immortal singers must die young had been established. Blindness was all that had been required of him. But when, amid the universal acclamations, Joe Bundle was compared to Keats, he ought to have searched diligently for the cause of such exceptional popularity: he ought, then, surely, to have understood the fate immanent in it. Had he read *The Golden Bough* all would have been plain to him. For in those pages we read much of a custom, a common custom more usual among the primitive races, but which was to be studied in its most extravagant development in the ancient civilisation of Mexico. In that world of remote and fantastic beauty, where the great cities stood on lakes in the craters of the high mountains, and the white-clothed walkers in the streets, instead of leading dogs behind them on a chain, are said to have been accompanied by brilliantly plumaged song-birds that fluttered and leapt and sang above, attached to the outstretched hand by a coloured ribbon; where the flowering was so intense that one blossom when it opened exploded with such violence that it even shattered the houses that gave it shelter; in that civilisation so strange yet so pronounced, there were many features which strike us as revoltingly barbaric because we cannot at first find for them any parallel. Thus it is with a feeling of horror that we discover that one man, picked for his type of looks and for his talent, was chosen by the priests and elders each year for the purpose of human sacrifice: but first, for twelve long, golden months, he was Emperor and Dictator, was invested with powers of life and death, not merely over the nobles and the people, but also over the priests, those very persons who had appointed him to his fate. Unimaginable wealth, countless wives, were at his disposal, every whim of his must be obeyed, every wish gratified. But always underlying the beauty and power was the ineluctable condition — Death. Every morning that he rode out with falcons and a retinue to the chase, while the snowy summits of the mountain towered above to temper for him with their ice the heat of the crystal-clear days, every night that, wearing a golden or jade crown from which whirled the dyed plumes of Mexico, he feasted among the flowers, brought his terrible end so many hours the nearer. The gods were inexorable: and soon his young red blood would spout into the blue air, stain the vast and garlanded stone altar, and drip down to the terraces below, while the crowds who now cheered his progress, would shout their joy to the heaven and struggle to dip a corner of their garments in his blood. So, too, it was to be for Joseph Bundle.

The priests of literature had selected him and now with varying degrees of patience awaited the end. Yet not for a moment did he feel the thorns clasping his brow under the very mutable roses with which he appeared to be crowned. He sometimes, it is true, had a queer lurking impression that something was expected of him: but what was it? He reached no conclusion. Meanwhile he still existed in the full glory of his brief reign, the full tide of his temporary infallibility.

Yet it would not be correct to think that the priests were entirely displeased at his return. Theirs was a far, far higher standard of culture and kindliness than that of their prototypes in ancient Mexico. From their point of view an early death from tuberculosis ranked higher than a mere name in the Roll of Honour (for that was a very common fate just then): while, if peace were not too long delayed, a peace-time death would be more effective, and much more creditable to those who had sponsored him. Certainly if he could not die then he should have sought his end at the War. But luck favoured him: his appearance of frailty had accentuated itself, and now won for him a job in the Ministry of Propaganda. And here, too, the results were very satisfactory. As a casualty, he could, after all, only have been one in a million: but now his name was worked-up into that mysterious thing, a 'clarion-call', and through his hysterical advocacy thousands of boys of eighteen were induced to look on a war as a virtue and thus to meet their deaths happily.

His most famous poem (which was not only recited on every possible occasion in England, but was even read aloud to neutrals, whenever they could be induced to listen, in Sweden, Holland and Denmark, as propaganda to impress them with our genius, to show them 'what England is doing') was that one — is it forgotten now? — in which a fortunately imaginary mother carries on a quiet, imaginary conversation with her dying son.

MOTHER:
Even such gentle things as birds and mice
Must pay the fair, the final sacrifice,
And, though the way be hard, you'll see it through
Remembering that Mother follows you.

SON:
But did I love you, Mother, had I love
Ever but that for brothers now above?
I have forgotten — ooh — ah — It is done.
(Rat-tat-tat of rifles — A bullet spun.
Rattery-tat-rattety-tat-tat of machine gun.)
Oh, Captain Donkyns — good-bye, Sir — the sun
Declines . . . I must away — is that a swallow
That blithely (chirrup) leaps and I must follow?

Such poems further endeared him to the great-big-baby-heart of the public. They sold by the thousand. He, though still ambitious, was content: while the literary hierarchs had what seemed the certainty of his death to look forward to at no very distant date. (Then, what junketings beside the tomb, what jubilant trumpetings through the Press, what perfumed bouquets to those who had discovered him!)

. . . . .

The War ended, and it was now that Bundle really proved his cleverness. Within a month or two of its conclusion, he had converted the large munition works over which his Muse had so long presided to peace-time service. He succeeded, as it were, in beating his literary sword back into a rusty ploughshare. Sussex came into its own again. He offered a special line in birds, fresh-water fish, and saying good-bye to bull-dogs. Now that he was by circumstance compelled to abandon that maternal note towards the troops which he had adopted, his innate humanity directed itself instead towards the old people in alehouse and workhouse. In fact, he skipped a generation, and became a spiritual and synthetic grandmother. At times, too, the *vox humana* of sexual frenzy dying down to a deep roll of Byronic disappointment was allowed to make itself heard, but never *too* often or *too* obtrusively. The factory must have been working all hands and twenty-four hours a day. It issued continually new books of poems, received everywhere with the usual ecstasy. Then was announced the news that Mr. Joseph Bundle was at work on his FIRST PROSE BOOK. 'For that England which cares for literature', the paragraph added, 'it is an event for which to wait with bated breath.' Critical feet must have been in a state of presumably almost painful suspended animation. The day came, the book appeared and was, just as I had expected, extremely, beautifully simple, though full of whimsy and rising, indeed, at the end to a climax of tragedy.

The story concerned Shelley. In it he was represented not, as in reality, drowning at sea (that was merely a ruse of his to escape from the world), but, instead, as going home to Sussex to become a shepherd on the downs. He lived, it appeared, to a ripe old age, but eventually was made to lose his teeth. Anxious to preserve his looks, and not altogether to lose his power of conversation (he was always talking with the other shepherds, and had, as time passed, instinctively adopted the Sussex dialect), yet nervous, naturally enough, at having to face a local dentist after shunning the world for so long, he decided to contrive a false set for himself: thus, after killing a sheep, he took its jaws and adapted them to his own. But since sheep have some forty odd teeth to the human thirty-two, they were an ugly failure. Here the book ended.

As to the merits of this novel, the priests of literature were divided. Some critics were so enraged at the nasty idea of Shelley evading his fate — it was really tactless of Bundle — that, quite unmoved by poetic fantasy, they hinted that, judging by his conversations with his fellow-shepherds, the mind of the great poet had scarcely been improved by the new, free, open-air life of the downs. Some, again, accused him of plagiarising a story by Miss Sheila Kaye-Smith, while others found the discussions entrancing, and voted the book 'a classic and a gem'. Yet it certainly did not achieve the success, measured by sales, that had been expected of it.

The hierarchs in private were much more disquieted at his behaviour, though they could not afford to let him down yet a while. . . . It was nearly a year after the War — but, if anything, he looked stronger. But Bundle, though he noticed in their eyes an increased brightness of querying expectancy, still had no notion of what it was they awaited from him. Not for a moment did he notice the earnest examination of his features to which the literary elders subjected him, nor the quiet prods, even, with which they sought to gauge the date of his impending doom. He had blundered through instinct, and with none of that intention of revolt which they imputed to him.

Fortunately, and again without intention, he followed up *Nameless Shepherd* with a book entitled *Dialogues on Parnassus*, which consisted of a series of discussions on life and literature between himself and the soul of Keats. In it the spirit continually dwells on the beauty and advantages of an early death for a poet. And in a moment Bundle had recovered his lost prestige and was once more Head Boy.

'It is', wrote one of the high priests, 'a singularly happy coincidence which has inspired Bundle to write a book of conversation with one with whom he has so much in common, both in mind, and, as many think — and have not been afraid to say —, in outward appearance. A book crammed with insight and teeming with beauty, it is a book for which we have long been waiting.' *

* This passage, subsequently quoted on the jacket of the second edition by the publisher, earned for poor Bundle his only bad review. So quickly had the first edition been sold out that this sentence caught the eye of Mr. Shins (another Georgian poet) before that gentle young man had finished his review of the book for a leading morning paper. For some years Mr. Shins had made a practice of sitting directly under the portrait of Keats — at the Poetry Bookshop, in his own room, or in any other place where he could find one — with his profile at a similar angle to emphasise what he believed to be a quite extraordinary resemblance: when, therefore, he saw the pretensions of his rival so boldly stated, he tore up his favourable review on which he had been at work, and made of it the full, furious use which the opportunity afforded him.

It was soon after the publication of his dialogues, when the halo of success blazed once again, and more radiantly, round his pale features, that I met Bundle for the first time since the War. The occasion was one of those artistic yet 'chic' little parties given by Mr. and Mrs. St. Maur Murry in their charming small house in Chelsea. Anne Murry particularly cultivated those artists, poets and musicians who were very advanced — so advanced, indeed, as to be out of sight altogether. By certain painters of this school she was much admired, and often served as their model: and, indeed, with her little whitened face, smoothed-back hair, lashless green eyes peering out from above her trim figure, rather as a snail from its shell, she had something essentially of the age about her. With these friends she would giggle feverishly at the dull ordinary lives of those other artists who occasionally do a little work: 'Too queer and absurd', she would titter attractively, and the loose, grey lip and chin, the batik kerchief that half-strangled a stringy neck, would ripple with delicious laughter. Yet the tracks were there for one to examine, and if her inclination appeared to be toward advanced artists, she yet could never resist the famous ones. But this must not for a moment be known, so when successful in kidnapping them to her parties, it was always to be assumed by her intimates that she had no idea of the identity of such guests (how like Anne, so unworldly, so artistic), but had taken a fancy to them for some obscure, capricious reason — a mole near the eye or a way of walking.

Meanwhile her method worked in smoothly with that of her husband: for St. Maur Murry, a wizened little man, always convulsed with a boisterous laughter which in itself passed for wit, aimed at fashion. Thus a party organised by his wife had all the mystery and attraction of a first-rate circus for *his* friends — who were, therefore, for the evening, civil to *hers* — while *her* friends in their turn regarded the 'beau monde', as Anne called it, with a charming affectation of eighteenth-century *cliché*, in precisely the same light. 'Simply too extraordinary', they would murmur in corners to one another. Meanwhile each menagerie, completely unconscious of its own tricks and mannerisms, stared with that blinking which is born of intelligence, or with the perfect assurance that lurks under plucked eyebrows, at the other, while the two trainers bravely cracked their whips.

This gave to the parties an atmosphere, at once stilted and over-familiar, that was all their own. As we have said, Bundle's celebrity was at this time at its height, and it was now that Anne, who had known him for many years, of a sudden took a fancy to his 'funny little smile'. She had contrived, withal, to make him feel that his own and her notion of his importance coincided.

She led me up to him. Bundle, I soon decided, had somewhat modified his style. The eighteen-twenties had gained at the expense of the Mermaid Tavern. He was in the highest degree affable, but his voice had taken on that bitter, broken cackle so widely recognised as one of the stigmata of greatness, while each time he looked at you, he now slightly opened his eyes, thereby just for a second revealing a flashing white under and above the iris, as though attempting some subtle species of hypnotism or one of the snake-with-rabbit tricks developed by Rasputin.

This new grimace served with most people to enhance the original impression of genius. He also limped a good deal. Yet the distant, almost tragic look of the eyes, when not thus in action, made me wonder afterwards whether he was not already beginning to guess that which lay ahead of him. In any case it must be admitted that he made full use of the plenary powers which the irrevocability of his fate for so short a time bestowed on him. For the party was 'going' beautifully, the preliminary surprised snigger of introduction had swelled into successful fits of tittering and giggling, when, without any invitation, Joe Bundle suddenly advanced into the centre of the room, and announced that he would read his poems aloud.

This, first heralding it with a little address on the principles of true poetry and what the War had taught him, he proceeded to do with immense effect until two o'clock. The two circuses, even the two trainers, were disgusted, resenting this rival one-man-show that had usurped their place; but nothing could be done, and no one even dared move, such was the compelling force of that poetic eye.

The only diversions were a maid, who obtained a sudden but violent popularity by upsetting a tray of plates outside just at the most effective passage in a poem, and an old lady who woke up with a start and began crying like a baby.

. . . . .

If the months that ensued were the greatest in his career, it is true that tragedy now ever mingled with his triumph.

Even if Keats and Shelley found themselves every day more and more attached to the name of Bundle, on platforms, at prize-givings, in every literary column and above all in the woolly pages of the *London Hermes*, bound captive, as it were, to the progress of his chariot; even if I heard, as I did, Professor Criscross say, as Bundle left the room, to Mr. Lympe: 'There, Lympe, goes, perhaps, the most remarkable and gifted young man since the death of Keats', yet into the volume of this praise had crept so general, so unmistakable a note of macabresque but pretended apprehension, that Bundle could no longer misunderstand, pretend to misunderstand, or in any way resist the decrees of those who had made him. At last he comprehended fully the brutal determination that lay buried everywhere under the sweetness of the bedside manner, at long last he perceived the empty, the waiting coffin, under the piles of laurels, bays and roses. And since he had delayed, sales were falling. Now he understood the anxious looks with which the elder *literati* scanned his face — not, as he had thought, to reassure themselves as to his health — but eagerly, to welcome the first sign of ailing lung or heart. (Sales were falling.)

The priests were impatient for their sacrifice, began to feel that his fame had been obtained on false pretences. Even Mattie, dear, mild Mattie Dean — he noticed — allowed his bird-like eye, incubated behind its monocle, to wander over him cruelly in search of symptoms. (Would he never be able to publish all those letters? Mattie was thinking.) Nor was it a happy time for the priests. After all, they reflected, he was nearly twenty-eight. But, and herein it seemed to the hierarchs lay the essential unfairness of their situation, it was difficult for them now to rend him. The trumps of praise must blare on, though the hollow, owl-like hooting of expectancy might be more emphasised.

Yet they possessed one mighty ally on whom they had not enough counted. Sales were falling, falling: and Joe Bundle knew it. For if the English public is thwarted of its rightful poetic prey by a strong constitution it soon turns nasty, demands its pound of flesh, endeavours to starve him in a garret. Nevertheless this great-big-baby-hearted public is a treacherous one, for if too long disappointed and kept waiting, it will turn even on those who feed it, the priests themselves, and devour them, just because they have misled it as to its feeding-time.

The elders were in danger, and therefore would soon be dangerous. Bundle saw it (and sales were falling, falling!).

It was true that he still had the good luck to look fairly delicate (this a little appeased them). But it was all very well for the high priests to say continually within his hearing that he was too good, too clever, too sensitive, to live. Himself was not so sure of it. The nature of his quandary, enough to crush a lesser man, was only too clear to him now. Something must be done, he knew. But to die is not necessarily an easy matter. Suicide was, as it were, a breach of rules. It made winning too easy. Even the death of Shelley, for example, was hardly playing fair (Keats's end was, from the critical point of view, the perfect score). Moreover, Bundle was young: possessed, despite his appearance, of much natural health. What was he to do? (Sales were falling.) And as he pondered, fretted and worried, fortune favoured him again; for so intense was his genuine love of life, that the prospect of the early death demanded of him nearly brought it about. Visibly he began to wilt and wither. No sooner had this process become noticeable than a glad shout arose from the watching priests. Every day the trumpets trumpeted more bravely, and jubilant whispers puffed out the grey moustaches of the hierarchs in their literary clubs. Bundle was all right; Bundle was 'doing his bit'. Once more they had backed a winner for the Parnassus Stakes. Always put your money on 'Skull and Crossbones'. In the smoking-room of the Lumley Club, old Sir Wardle Diddlum, Joe's publisher, dispensed a veritable fountain of port wine. A winner again. (Sales were mounting, mounting!)

Alas, Bundle could not bring himself to it. Again he held on a little too long. (Sales were falling, falling!) Through the notices of his last book of poems crept a horrid, malicious, menacing note. A chill wind enwrapped him, who so long had been tenderly treated in the literary nursery. When he showed himself at 'the Lumley', where of old he had been eagerly welcomed, the hierarchs would hide behind their newspapers, or even put on a pair of black spectacles, presumably as a hint of that mourning which it was now their due to wear. This they would follow up by coughing in a death-like way, in intimation of what England expected from him. 'How is your health, Bundle? We hear very favourable reports of it', they would say in the most mordacious manner. (Sales were falling.) One or two early turncoats began openly to announce in paragraphs that Mr. Bundle's later works had disappointed his many admirers, and poor old Sir Wardle, who was made to feel that the whole thing was his fault, had to adopt, by doctor's orders, a special diet to reduce his blood-pressure.

But now Bundle executed a really amazing piece of strategy, not unworthy of Fabius Cunctator, and by it succeeded in delaying his enemy. He realised undoubtedly, I think, at this point, that which was expected of him. He was aware, too, that the conditions of his past success were irrevocable, that he could not repudiate his bargain without bringing disaster on himself. But for a little while longer he was able, by his own cleverness, to remain dallying in the world he loved, his fame and repute ever increasing. For, all this time, he had been preparing in secret a new book of poems. This was the moment to publish it. It was called *Farewell to Poesy*; each line was permeated with a wistful note of unmistakable self-elegy. The sob had deepened into a death-rattle. Pegasus had donned bat-like wings and was flying through these pages, decked out in considerable funereal pomp, for the last time. In this book Bundle boldly proclaimed who were his equals, for at this solemn moment who was to say him nay?

And how warmly Bundle was now taken back to the fold! Songs of sad, glad rapture echoed and re-echoed through the Press. The undertakers of literature dusted their top-hats, cleared their throats, allowed a tear to fall on their black-bordered handkerchiefs, while they measured the body with a practised eye and prepared for it their articles of obsequy. In the offices of every newspaper the obituarists nonchalantly whetted their nibs. (Sales were soaring, soaring!) It was the climax of Bundle's career. The chorus of praise never faltered, except that the mousy little literary-editor described in an earlier page wrote, probably with unintentional ambiguity: 'This book is one which you will want to give away', a phrase rather unfortunately quoted at once in every advertisement by Diddlum & Co. Nevertheless it obtained the greatest sale that any book of poems had achieved since the early days of Alfred Austin.

Yet, he realised it only too well, either himself or his sales must sink — they could no longer, soaring together, keep company, and herein, as Bundle must have reflected, lay the most cruel part of the poet's lot. For, should he die, his triumph would be more than ever broadcast through the Press: those who had first detected his talent would see to that. Money would, consequently, pour in — but he would not be there to receive it; indeed in this instance, unless he made a will, old Dr. Bundle, who had never for years been anything but unpleasant to him, who was already rich and whose very existence he had managed to disguise, would reap the benefit.

It was after the publication of *Farewell to Poesy*, after his ill-health had become more accentuated, that I met Bundle for the last time *before* his death. The occasion was a memorable one. And it seems to me that, for my young readers apparently eager to collect anecdotes that belong to the period as much as its paintings and furniture, a description of this party may convey a sense of the advanced scene of those days as vividly as would any picture of the old *London Group*, or the finding of a forgotten poem by some such author as Mr. Conrad Aiken or Mr. Maxwell Bodenheim delved for in the pages of a now dusty but then very up-to-date American journal; but to appreciate it, it must be remembered that at the time of which I write the great religious revival of the early thirties was as yet undreamed of, and that, for the intelligentsia, psycho-analysis had usurped the place of religion, and was treated with an awe and deference accorded to nothing else in this world or any other.

The setting was for Bundle in any case a new one, and, as a habitat, rather unsuitable. Spiritually, it was many thousands of miles removed from Sussex; in its style nearer to the jungles of Africa, with their zebra-striped flashes of light and darkness; nearer to the hot, moist, scented and voluptuous airs of the Brazilian forests, resonant with the xylophone-tongued cries of tropical birds — forests where even the sleek, snarling pumas that glide and sway stealthily through the undergrowth are too languorous to be of very much danger to mankind — than to his beloved downs, for ever swept by the steel-billed breezes of the northern seas.

But then this constant, though always unexpected, mingling of sects that proceeded in the London of my youth must be regarded as one of the chief delights the age afforded, for it imparted to life a great variety. Just as it was the first epoch in which it was possible to be comfortably nomadic, ever in luxurious flight from Cairo to Rio, from Rio to New York, from New York to Morocco, from Morocco to London, each journey taking up the space of but a few days, so in any great city was it possible mentally to traverse whole continents and centuries, to move from this to that civilisation in as many seconds.

But in this perpetual migration Bundle took little part: he was one the boundaries of whose temporary kingdom were so defined by the tastes of his subjects that it made his appearance here a singularly gracious act. It is true that he would have told you — as would every other person in the room — that his predilections in art were all for the primitive: but lovers of the primitive, since they are apt to pride themselves on their sincerity, are thus wont to quarrel among themselves more than any other tribe, and between the rival lovers of the African kraal and of the Sussex cottage (however alike in their simplicity these may seem to outsiders) is fixed a deep chasm over which no rope-bridge may be thrown. In art it was not so much that Bundle knew what he liked, as that he liked what he knew. After the manner of all English-village-life-enthusiasts, he was as ignorant of everything outside his own county as he was misinformed about the village itself. Every architectural system devised seemed to him a decadence from the high art of thatching a cottage — of which he had read, though he had never seen it. Oast-houses, like comfortable red brewers sporting an incongruous witch's hat, and the flinty tower of any local village church, were also agreeable to him. In painting there were Cotman and Crome, but even these were a little beyond his taste in their range; in music, an old folk-tune, scratched out on what he would be careful to term a 'fiddle', to which accompaniment a few whiskered and toothless octogenarian gaffers, first carefully excavated and coached in their steps by horn-rimmed-spectacled young Jews from Oxford and Cambridge, would gaily foot a measure.

One did not, therefore, expect to encounter him among people who worshipped strange gods: gods among whom he was not numbered. The party was given by an acquaintance of mine, in conjunction with three or four other men, in a large room up in Hampstead. I had never been to the house before, and found it crammed with guests, their arms pinned to their sides, unable, perhaps fortunately, even to reach the little cup of dark green, searing coffee that was so hospitably provided for each of them. Gazing over the sea of heads, a whole new world was exhibited to me. Alas! myself in evening clothes, I felt rather uncomfortable, for most of the men present were dressed in the loose, floppy esthetic manner of the time, corduroys and bandanas, tweeds and pipes, while the only people attired in the conventional men's evening clothes of the period, black coat and starched white shirt, were a few heavily shod, self-conscious but determined-looking middle-aged women, most of them with an eyeglass clinking against the buttons of their white waistcoats. It was obvious that, except for them, anyone in evening dress was regarded as an unpleasant anachronism. Luckily, the packing of our bodies was so close that what I now began to regard as my shameful nudity might pass almost unnoticed. Wedged in as I was, my face only a few inches from other and unknown faces, I began to feel lonely, except that from time to time a shaggy head would drift up and — with some difficulty, for it was like trying to maintain one's place and balance in the middle of a football scrum — inquire, politely yet intimidatingly, if I had visited Dash's or Blank's last exhibition. Rather priding myself on my acquaintance with modern art, I could not but be profoundly chagrined at my ignorance in being unaware of the names they mentioned — or, rather, for the noise was great, roared — with such reverence. After confessing, then, one was left to stare this close-up of curious heads directly in the eye, always a rather confusing experience. My gaze wandered in search of rescue, over the jostling waves of faces. Who was there? Not far from me, rising up out of them like a jaunty if rather angular boulder, I observed a well-known lady novelist, the ends of her long ear-rings swinging down in the crowd. Who else was there? Did I see a glossy white shirt flashing its kindred signal to mine? Was it — it was — Bundle!

At first, then, I was astonished to find him in a room painted with yellow, scarlet and purple stripes, and further embellished with such innocent, unsophisticated ornaments as totem-poles from New Zealand, fetishes from Dahomey and the Congo, blood-bowls from the South Seas, and two or three wizened, black and dried human heads, hung up on the wall and swinging above us from their nails by a few remaining locks of coarse, lank hair. The explanation of his presence in these surroundings was to be found, I take it, more in the fact that he realised only too acutely how numbered were the weeks that now stretched in front of him, in which to play his kingly part, than it lay rooted in the essential eclecticism of the age. It was bold of him, too, one reflected, to venture thus far afield, for the immunity and infallibility bestowed upon him by his approaching fate was not, as a rule, recognised here among the grinning ogre-masks and phallic symbols of a different and alien superstition. Doubtless, though, he had been inducted hither by Mrs. St. Maur Murry, whom I now saw smiling subtly in a corner to a few very civilised devotees. The subtle smile was intensified soon into a shrill, frenetic giggle. He could here have found no more influential sponsor.

At this moment and as I thus studied the scene, a sudden, a very positive and ominous silence — all the more menacing in this tropical room — fell down upon it. It resembled that instant of dreadful calm that precedes an equatorial hurricane. The only person who did not immediately respond to this magic and infectious cessation of effort was the lady novelist, whose barking, busy, inquisitive voice hung dramatically in the air. Resolutely she finished her sentence to the little group of heads clustered round her shoulders. 'I know it's *true*,' she was saying, 'for *he* told me *in confidence*.' After this little effort, she, too, became mute. And now the threat inherent in this silence materialised itself. The floor was cleared. 'Something must be going to happen', everyone said as they scurried away to the sides of the room, where those who could find them sprawled on cushions. Some went out, while others leant upon the mantelpiece, draped themselves limply round the doorway, or sat, even, in a bowl from the South Seas. Chatter subsided again. Somebody, wisely hidden behind it, struck up on a piano, and into the centre of the floor minced a very young but tousled and dishevelled zany of a young girl, with a tangled mop of flaxen hair hanging over a freckled, earnest, though at the minute smiling and rather damp, face. Her feet were bare, and she was dressed in a classical, night-gown-like toga. Obviously, if only on account of her pretended timidity, she must be a favourite, one felt. Sure enough, after a preliminary rattle of starched cuffs, as the women in men's evening dress adjusted their monocles to see and applaud, there was a regular burst of enthusiasm. Now the piano broke into a regular rhythm, and the dancer began to caper, peer and prance round the room to the immense, if solemn and scientific, appreciation of the audience. Rather puzzled by the significance of some of her gestures, I turned to my shaggy, long-haired-terrier type of neighbour, and asked: 'Could you tell me exactly what she is dancing?' and he replied lightly: 'Oh, just two rather jolly little things out of Krafft-Ebing.'* From these she passed on to interpret one of Freud's instances of the 'Œdipus Complex', which was generally held to be her finest achievement, both in conception and execution.

These dances were much encored. The artiste slunk out deprecatingly amid cheers and calls. Then, again, there seeped into the room the silence of expectation. One of our hosts came in with a reading-desk and announced that Mr. Joseph Bundle had kindly consented (alas! a euphemism, I fancied, for 'insisted') to read some of his new poems, if his health would permit him to do so, from *Farewell to Poesy*. The guests at once began talking and looking angrily round. However, Bundle was not to be thwarted. He began by asking his audience to forgive and understand, should he be forced to break off during a poem. He was not, he said, very strong (as they might have heard) just now. And after this he put up such a good act of coughing, finding the place, and clearing his throat, that even this gathering of modernists was in spite of itself impressed. Anne Murry could be heard in a corner, saying hopefully: 'Now, didn't I tell you? — there is something in his odd little smile — it's like Blake.'

He read on. It was the first time I had heard these poems, and one detected the invention of several new and poignant devices. In several of the verses Keats and Shelley are addressed personally, directly by name, as though they were boys in the sixth form and Bundle was the popular master in charge ('an awfully decent chap, and talks to the Pater about Footer'). The tone was one of 'Smith Major, it's your turn now. What do you say?' I remember a couplet or two:

Shelley and Keats! By your example borne
I quaff the potion from the bitter horn.

My heaven will be where the sheep still bleats
Of Sussex: there I'll meet you, Shelley, Keats!

* Author of *Psychopathia Sexualis*.

In others he would direct the boys, knowing his influence over them. This sentiment, for example, was beautifully contained in the little poem he wrote to his friend, and contemporary poet, Mr. Edward Shanks. It ran:

> And when you go to brighten Heaven, Shanks,
> Shelley and Keats will offer you their thanks.

However, to return to our party, his health permitted him to read to the end, though the lilt and dying fall, alternating with the bitter, broken cackle, of his voice took on a note that was a little wearied.

In spite of the original prejudice of his audience, Bundle achieved almost a triumph. At the end there was loud applause, and my neighbour said to me: 'I must own I'm agreeably surprised. There's something positively Polynesian in their starkness.'

After he had finished, Bundle came up to me, bringing a friend with him, and suggested that he should take us in his car to 'the Lumley' for a drink. Much flattered, I consented. We sat in a large, empty room, red, with vast chandeliers. I examined the poet carefully. Though still sure of himself, he was certainly much changed. There were distressing signs of the internal conflict through which he must have been passing. In his eye there shone, too, the light of an heroic resolution. Looking back upon that night, I can see now that to him we were posterity. Much time he spent, almost as though he wished us to hand on his banner, in telling of his work and its aims, of early life on the downs and of the message, of which he was, all too unworthily, as he said, the medium. Birds, birds, and again birds, he conveyed to us authoritatively, was the Message of Life. And after them, bulldogs, and again bulldogs. And, of course, sheep. He spoke to us, too, of the names of poets: of how the very sound of them 'smacked of the earth'. 'Let the words loll on the tongue, so that you get the full flavour of them', he advised us. 'Drinkwater, Keats, Shanks, Noyes (pronounced, I then discovered for the first time, in no equivocal, facing-both-ways manner, but, boldly, to rhyme with "cloys") and a hundred more.' . . . '(Think, too, on the names of the great double-barrelled women of fiction . . . Sackville-West . . . Kaye-Smith . . . Kean-Seymour.)' . . . 'Even my own name, Joe Bundle,' he said, 'has something, perhaps, of Sussex in it.' Now, again, the talk veered in its direction, and the Christian names of famous figures — though sometimes in an unusual and abbreviated style, which served both to cause you to ask whom it was he meant and to prove his intimacy with them — would trip easily off his lips. We were made the repository, perhaps owing to our appearance of health, of many little stories of the great, of which, years afterward, we were doubtless to inform the young: 'I remember Bundle telling me in '23'. A sigh of wonder, a new light in young eyes, and an awed voice, trembling out: 'Do you mean to say that *you* knew Bundle?'

Now we had to leave him. He accompanied us to the door of the Club. Love, he confided on the way, had treated him as it always treats a poet. 'It's the penalty we poets pay', he announced with amiable condescension. He coughed once or twice, a hollow, dramatic cough, put out his hand and shook mine in a marked and morbid fashion, looked into my eyes, blinked his eyelids several times very widely, as though this was the last occasion on which the snake would fascinate the rabbit. The door swung to, and he was swallowed up in its blaze of light.

· · ·

Rumour spread, evil rumour, that Bundle was ill, very ill indeed. The literary world was intent, waiting. Then came the news. Bundle was a dying man. He had been ordered to Italy under the care of a nurse — gone thither, like those with whom he had so often been compared — gone there to die. The eyes of the elders glistened fondly as they thought of that other corpse so soon to rest under the wistaria in the little English Cemetery at Rome — stretched out there by the side of his peers. The obituarists even went so far as to get ready their captions and to turn down the corner of the page of Rupert Brooke's 'There's some corner of a foreign field', for they must not be behindhand with appropriate quotation.

The dark horses could be heard taking a preliminary canter through the Press. The mutes chattered shrilly while they might.

'Lovers of English poetry', we read in *Gleanings*, 'will hear with regret mingled with anxiety that Mr. Joseph Bundle, perhaps better known as "Bundle of Sussex", and assuredly the leader of that striving young England that found itself in the War, has suffered a complete breakdown in health. Always of a rather frail physique that was the counterpart of a fiery spirit and a rare poetic intelligence, he never spared himself in Beauty's cause. It has long been an open secret that our leading critics and literary men, who had hailed him as heir and successor to Keats, were fearful of the strain that his genius — for such they deem it — might place upon his health, which must, indeed, in these days be regarded as a national asset.' Or, again, the paragraph might be couched in language yet more grave: 'There is always something singularly tragic', it would run, 'in the delicacy of men of genius, and were it to force Bundle to relinquish his work at an early age, our literature would undergo a loss only comparable to that it sustained by the deaths of Marlowe, Keats, Shelley, Byron, and Rupert Brooke. . . . Bundle comes, of course, of Sussex stock, and is peculiarly identified in the minds of all lovers of poetry with the soil of London's favourite county. Nor is he the only Bundle to have attained national fame — for many will be interested to discover that he is a cousin of P. T. Bundle — "P. T. B." as he is affectionately known to thousands in the football world — England's foremost dribbler. Some readers may infer that the relationship between poet and athlete is no casual one. Both of them stand rooted in English earth. The famous poet is now far from the country he loves, for the doctors have ordered him to Italy — where in earlier days other English poets have sought solace — and many will be the good wishes he will take on his way with him.' The paragraph ended 'God speed!' though it did not enter into details of what, exactly, the writer wished sped.

These little notices — who knows but that perhaps they may have been breathed into the ears of the paragraphists by a confiding publisher? — ran round the Press, and inspired, indeed, one regrettable error. The literary editor of the *Sunday Depress* had latterly been very much overworked. The owner of the paper had told him to praise, the editor to abuse, the same book. In addition, while reviewing a novel, he had mistaken a rather unfortunate passage quoted in it from the Bible for the work of the writer before him, and had called loudly on the Home Secretary for its suppression, and for the prosecution of the author. The Home Secretary had eagerly responded, but had inadvertently omitted to read the book:

the publishers had kept their secret; and consequently, when it leaked out in court that the author of the passage in question was no less or younger a person than Moses, the prosecution had broken down. After it was over, the proprietor, himself a particular authority on the Holy Book, had sent for the literary editor and had reprimanded him. This had much shaken his nerve, and, soon after, since things never go wrong singly, he, owing to some slight confusion, published an article on Bundle, in which he treated Bundle as though he were already dead. After the inevitable comparison to Keats and Shelley, and congratulations to him on what was captioned as his 'Sane Sex Viewpoint', he had hailed him as 'Lord of Lyric Verse', and had proceeded to demand his interment in Westminster Abbey, 'the National Valhalla'. Moreover, he insisted violently that the Peers and Peeresses should be made to attend the service in their robes, for, he added, with one of his most picturesque touches, 'only with passionate purple and screaming ermine can they do justice to the immortal singer now no more'. This article had induced his chief to purchase a story by Bundle, to be run as a serial, under the idea that, now he was dead, people would stand it, however good it might be. It can be imagined, therefore, what were the feelings of proprietor and editor, when they discovered that Bundle still survived. They relapsed once more into insurance talk, their trump card. But meanwhile the rival journals were immensely enjoying themselves with talk of 'a lamentable error of taste', and 'ill-informed and wicked gossip'.

Yet the impression was rife that the end could not be long delayed. All the old gentlemen of literature joined in the death-bed revels. The consequent rush on Bundle was immense. First editions soared to a price which only ghouls could afford to pay. So it was with the familiar waving of flags, beating of drums and blare of trumpets that Bundle faded out into the azure horizon of Italy.

. . . .

What was the precise nature of the drama enacted there, I know not. But it was a year or more before the awaited obituary notice actually materialised. Few details of the end were given. It ran, as he would have liked it, simply: 'On October 27th, 1924, in Italy, Joseph Bundle, of Sussex, Poet, in his twenty-ninth year. Nursed through a long illness by his devoted wife.' It was obvious, then, that Bundle had married his nurse; and this was all that could be deduced until the next day, when the more fully inspired, appreciatory notices began to appear.

Now even the most august papers thundered England's loss. We were treated to charming little stories of the death-bed ceremony, when Bundle was married to his nurse. Not one romantic detail was spared us. The literary editor of the *Sunday Depress*, spying an opportunity for rehabilitation, repeated his former obituary, clamoured for a burial in the Abbey, so that All should Take a Part. Other critics even went so far in their enthusiasm, and perhaps in the need they felt for a day's outing in good country air, as to demand that Bundle's ashes should be brought home and scattered over the Sussex Downs by the Prime Minister. But the inconsolable widow intimated that such junketings were not at all what her husband would have desired for himself. She communicated to one or two papers an intimate, but no doubt highly paid, account of his wishes. One day, she had left him for a few minutes it appeared, and when she returned he sat up suddenly in bed, and with the utmost clarity of diction, so that there could be no mistake of his meaning or of his being fully conscious at the time, had said: 'I remembered England in Her Need. She will remember me. Let no one meddle with my bones. Let me be laid down by the Man Keats. I shall be content. Where I am, there shall a smaller Sussex be.' And though he had never reverted to the topic again in the few days which he had still to live, it was generally felt that in this touching idea there was much that was appropriate.

. . . . .

Many critics have pointed out how in *Frankenstein* it seems as if Shelley had been able to transfer some of his sombre genius to his wife's pen. It is as though, while he was with her, he had been able to infuse into her at least a little of his overwhelming power: yet even he had not been able to bestow enough genius for her to continue writing at this level after his death. But with Mrs. Bundle it was otherwise: it was as though some portion of her husband's magic mantle had descended on to the shoulders of his forlorn widow. In the numerous articles about him which she now contributed to every paper, there were whole phrases and turns of speech that, it seemed to me, bore his imprint. Yet though the stories of him, the diminutive tales and touches, were typical of the man, the mystery which had ever surrounded all he did still attended on him, even in death: for little was told us of its actual circumstances. Yet that description of him in his last moments, how true it rang, and how the actual writing of it reminded me of the deep, compassionate instinct of motherhood manifested, for example, in his war-poems!

'There he lay,' Mrs. Bundle wrote, 'ashen and listless under the ilexes, with the rich Italian sunlight drifting down to him through the branches and a wistful smile ever touching the pallor of his features. How poignant was the sight of that white bed upon the burnt-up grass! But never for a moment did he repine: never, never for an instant, did he allow himself in his suffering to forget or upbraid Nature. Always, racked and tormented though he might be, did he gladly suffer little birds to come unto him.

'There are some moments in life so peculiarly tender, so mystical, that they cannot be revealed. It may be, even, that there are those who will consider that it is not strictly the duty of a wife to reveal them. But Bundle belonged to England, and I shall tell, for only England (and, of course, the United States of America) could appreciate such a memory. Right up to the last, then, right up to the final, bitter hours, he would commune with the birds. It was pretty to see them together, for they, too, seemed to understand. Well, one day I heard a sound of twittering, and stealing up on tiptoe, so as not to disturb Joseph, found that he had, without telling me, sprinkled his moustache with hemp-seed, and that the tiny feathered things were chirping and tweet-tweeting at his mouth. It was a sacred moment: one of such a kind that nobody who has experienced it would ever be able to forget.

'After this, it became a regular practice with him. And, one day, as thus he fed them, the end approached. Came a time when he was delirious, racing again over those downs from which he had sprung, his boots, his clothes, all covered with the good earth of Sussex. He called the birds that still fluttered round him, addressed them by name, under the impression that they were his favourites of fifteen years before. His speech became once more the musical speech of the countryside. Again, again he was running merrily over the downs, or climbing a juniper bush to help some little bird in travail. Now came the great events of his life: once more he was performing that valiant deed that won him honour in the War; once more he was batting for the *London Hermes* Eleven; and then, turning over on his side like a child in bed, gently sighing, he was at rest. . . .'

Bundle, I reflected on reading this account of him, had been very fortunate in finding birds in Italy, where they are more often to be found on a plate in front of you than singing in the bushes. The only bird one ever sees there is, in the mountains, an occasional eagle, and that, from the angle of the English bird-lover, scarcely counts as a bird at all.

Mrs. Bundle, of course, inherited all the dead poet's property and effects, and was also found to be his sole literary executor. In most ways she was, however, very easy to deal with. She appointed Mattie Dean to edit his letters and write his biography, only retaining a final veto as to what was or was not to be included. The letters had a great sale. The reviews transcended even expectation. The only critical exception came from Lady Richard Cressey, who in a letter to one paper stated that Mattie had cut out, in the letters from Bundle she had lent him for publication, several passages in which her poems had been warmly approved and commended and had substituted for them instead paragraphs, presumably written by himself, in praise of his own critical insight. In one of these, indeed, Bundle was made to hail him as first patron and discoverer. This allegation on the part of Lady Richard was never definitely either proved or disproved. But a certain amount of unpleasant bickering broke out in the Press from the hierarchy, each of whom was now publicly claiming to have singled out Bundle originally. All this, however, only served to heighten interest in all that pertained to him.

Mrs. Bundle continued to live in Italy. She was, it appeared, so overcome by the tragedy, of which she had been so close and intimate a witness, that only once after the death of her husband was she able to summon up the courage necessary to meet his friends. (Memories of him were both too dear and too painful.) It was for the opening of the 'Bundle Bird Fountain', erected in Kensington Gardens to the memory of the dead poet some eighteen months or two years after his decease, that she made her sole, brief, public appearance in England. Even then she was, it seemed, nervous and ill at ease, anxious to return, to be alone, to bear the burden of her recollections by herself: a phenomenon very sad in one still young.

The ceremony of inauguration was singularly simple, and gained much in interest from the presence of the widow. The elders had thought it advisable to capture a lay-figure for the chair, and had successfully contrived to entice old General Sir Blundell Bullough-Bloodworthy to occupy it for the occasion. As a speaker, he was effective and thoroughly in keeping with the proceedings, while he possessed in addition an undoubted talent for anecdote. First of all he blew out his red cheeks and white moustache as though inflating an invisible air-balloon, and then suddenly addressed his audience of bishops, old ladies, venerable critics, publishers and esthetes, as though he had them before him on the parade-ground. 'Not much of a poet-chap myself,' he roared at us, 'but I do know a bit about birds. Love 'em, I do. Know more about birds than poets. Positively love 'em. Never so happy as when shootin' 'em. (Birds, I mean, doncherno, what, what!) Shot thousands of 'em myself in my time. But getting old now, ha-ha' (and here he was convulsed with laughter for a minute or two). 'Spent a great part of my life in India. Not many birds there — Vultures, of course, and plenty of 'em. After one of my victories, battlefield used to be a perfect sight. Bird-lovers would come for miles to see it, so my aide-de-camp told me. Tell you an extraordinary thing. Forget if I tolger: Lady Bloodworthy, doncherno, decided to give a tea-party at Government House. I was always against it — ha-ha! Well, there we were, all sitting in the garden in our topees — might have been in an English garden. Tea with silver kettles and scones and all that, when (would you believe it?) crash in the middle of it all fell a human leg and arm, ha-ha! What it was was a vulture was flying over from where a Tower of Silence was, doncherno, where a poor devil of a Parsee was, donchersee. Devilish clever bird, what! Wonderful thing, birds' intelligence. Extraordinary, I said at the time, extraordinary, quite extraordinary it was. But nothing in India except vultures — and parrots: and minahs, cunning little devils they are, too, I tell you! Had a minah that imitated the Missus so as you simply couldn't tell. Used to answer it myself. Why, that minah can make a fool of *me*, I used to say to my aide-de-camp: remember it quite well, doncherno. Still, nothing comes up, in my opinion, to a good English bird. And I'll tell you another thing about birds. Some of 'em sing beautifully, by gad, what, what! Wouldn't have believed it till I heard 'em, ha-ha! Well, what I mean to say is, doncher-see, is that poor fellow — Mumble — Trumble — Stumble (Thankee, Sir, thankee) — Bundle, knew about birds, too, I should say.' And the General sat down amid prolonged cheering. After strength came sweetness. Mr. Mattie Dean was called upon, rose, adjusted his monocle, inquiringly, and, mildly beaming, said: 'All thothe, I think, who love Thuthekth, all thothe who love poemth, will realithe only too thurely, that in Jotheph Bundle — "Joe", ath thome of uth were privileged to call him — we have lotht a mathter. The thoughtth of thome, it may be, will, like my own, turn to Keatth and Thelley: two other gentle poetth lotht to uth.' The speech continued for some time. The old lady who had been painted by Burne-Jones fainted from excitement and had to be helped out of the crowd; while her rival with the vacant eyes, who had sat thirteen times to Sargent, could be heard saying in a loud voice: 'How true — So true! Just what Mr. Sargent used to tell me.' At the end of it, an old gentleman like a foolish verger stood up and said: 'La—dies and Gentle—men, I have now a lee—tle treat for you — Mrs. Bundle.'

Amid tremendous applause the widow of the great man stood up. She was nice-looking, dressed in very fashionable black, but to my mind, rather inappropriately covered with every possible assortment of dried fin, dead fur and dyed feather. She was a perfect riot of shark-skin bags and shagreen purses, sealskin coats and ermine trimmings, osprey feathers, tortoise-shell umbrella handles and animal-skin gloves. Owing to nervousness, her speech was quite inaudible, but the gestures with her hands, her playing with a rope of false pearls, were all that could be desired. The silent opening and shutting of her mouth, as by a goldfish, the whole galaxy of tricks she displayed, was singularly moving: so much so, indeed, that at the close of the proceedings, the Committee of the Pecksniff Prize for English Literature, anxious not to omit so novel a turn from their platform, waited on her to inquire whether she would not present it for them at the Æolian Hall in a few days' time. It was always difficult to find something new, they said: though whether they referred to the book which would incur their prize, or to the stage début of Mrs. Bundle, remained uncertain. But she refused, and left for Italy the next morning.

A few days later it was announced that Mrs. Bundle had been awarded, on account of the services of her dead husband to literature, a Civil List Pension of three times the customary amount. This served to mark definitely the apotheosis of Bundle. The Prime Minister of the day referred to him at a Guildhall banquet as one of the Future Glories of the English Heritage. Sir Wardle Diddlum was advanced from a knighthood to a baronetcy. Mattie was given a 'K.C.B.' It was rumoured that a Great Personage had bought 2000 copies of *Farewell to Poesy* (Sir Wardle said that he had made a wonderful bargain, too) for distribution to his friends next winter in place of a Christmas card. The Archbishop quoted two touching lines about a robin in one of his sermons. A Bundle Society was formed, the members of which were to dine together twice a year — and once every summer must meet for a picnic luncheon on the downs. Now the boom spread to America: a branch of the Bundle Society was formed there, and it was arranged that the American section should entertain the English one the following year. Yet there now entered into the cult that touch of exaggeration which many of our fellow-countrymen are apt to associate with the States: for example, several enterprising journalists started a 'story' that the great poet was not dead at all, had been seen walking, apparently under the spell of some unbearable sorrow, by lonely stretches of the Italian coast. Soon, the English papers retorted, the American Press would announce that Bundle's poems had been written by Bacon! Such discussions, however, served but further to increase the enormous sales of his works: for the dead man's books now sold by their tens of thousands. Money poured in, and he no longer there to receive it! Such always is the way of the world. Still, it was a comfort to think that poor Mrs. Bundle would not now be entirely dependent on her pension. But gradually, very gradually, the interest died down. Even his widow's essays and articles on his work became less frequent, and then ceased altogether. As a topic at lunch or dinner Bundle was dead.

. . . . .

Little, I think, has been heard of Bundle for the past forty years. Yet during a recent visit — alas! it will probably prove to have been my last — to Rome, my thoughts wandered back to early days. I thought of Bundle as an old man thinks of those he has met in his youth. It seemed to me sad and pitiful that one who had been so sure of immortality, and indeed so famous in his day, should now be held, even by students of poetry, in so little esteem, and be by the world forgotten. Would it not be kind, I wondered, to visit his tomb in the English Cemetery? There, hemmed in by the dark blades of the cypresses, under those small bushes of pagan roses — not the big-headed darlings of the horticulturist, but loose-petalled pink roses with that faint and ancient smell which no visitor to Rome in May can ever forget — under the mauve rain of the wistaria (the only rain which, it seemed that spring, ever fell to cool the dry earth), while high up above them the bare branches of the paulovnias held their mauve torches toward the blue sky — lay those whom he had definitely adjudged his august compeers. But where, I wondered, was the grave of poor Joe Bundle? The sacristan disclaimed all knowledge. I could not find a tablet. To me this seemed to make his fate all the more tragic. A man famous in his generation; and now no stone, even, to mark his grave. And was Mrs. Bundle still alive? I could not remember.

. . . .

Some weeks later I visited a little town on the southern coast of Calabria. Even now its exceptional beauty attracts no tourists. In these days of flying, people like, I suppose, to go farther away, to India, China, Africa; and though the great aeroplanes continually hum like a horde of wasps over this walled rock, clustered with white houses and set in so transparent a sea, not one stops here for its passengers to admire such miniature and intimate loveliness. It seemed to have been overlooked by the world since the time that, a thriving fortified town, it had defied first the enemies of the Hohenstaufens, and then the Turkish slave-raiders, or even since, many centuries before, it had been one of the great cities of Magna Graecia.

I had been here as a boy, and really it seemed to have changed not at all. The crumbling walls were yet as they had been in my youth, further guarded by an outer fortification of Indian fig-trees, some of the stalks thick as an olive-trunk, such as one might see growing round an African kraal. The golden, slender towers still rose like minarets above a town of dazzling whiteness — so white that the sun glowing down on it threw up dancing lights like those given back by a mirror to play on the walls opposite. The kilted giant of a Roman Emperor still smiled cynically in the piazza, which rested heavily above the Roman theatre, while the harbour had yet lingering in its shelter one or two large sailing-boats. Out of the enormous cellars, natural caves deep in the rock, issued the heavy, acrid smell of southern wine. Over the cliffs still fell in formal swags the trailing, fleshy, green leaves of the mesembryanthemum (that flower the name of which has the sound of an extinct animal), sprinkled with magenta tinsel stars. The olive groves seemed no older — some of the trees were, it was said, above a thousand years of age — and the drifts of spring flowers still surged over the edges of the roads. Only one new feature did I notice in the landscape, a very large, white villa: modern, though it had been probably built within ten years of my previous visit. It looked well-kept, comfortable and incongruous. Though created in a muddled southern style (Spanish-Italian-American), it lacked the flimsiness and squalor of modern construction in this neighbourhood. All round the garden, a large one, was a very high, solidly built wall. It seemed, I thought, an odd place to choose for building. Though the town was enchanting enough to make anyone wish to live in it, the country outside was flat, and, in spite of the beauty of its groves, dull to live in, one would have supposed. There was, I reflected, a great deal to be said, after all, for English landscape (think of the Hog's Back, or the rolling Sussex Downs, with their delicious air). Probably, though, it was some emigrant to South America, at last returned to his native place, to which he was devoted as only an Italian can be, who had built this rather palatial dwelling, thereby also ridding himself of the inferiority complex which early poverty begets. However, the whole matter intrigued me, challenged my curiosity to a degree that is rare when concerned with a matter so essentially unimportant and unconnected with oneself. It was very singular how interested I felt in it.

I decided, therefore, to make inquiries from the *padrone* of the inn in which I was staying. In spite of his numerous activities, talking, cooking, taking orders, bustling from one room to another with a plate of succulent soup in which little octopuses floated all too realistically, waving the napkin held in his other hand imperiously at the knock-kneed waiter who assisted him, and moving his vast bulk about with surprising ease considering the limited space, he had yet found time to pile up an amazing store of knowledge relating to local life.

Yes, he said, the villa had been built some thirty or forty years ago. The man who lived in it was a great English milord. Enormously rich. Lived in great style, with clean sheets every week, they said, and everything he wanted to eat. A great English milord, in disgrace, it was supposed. People knew very little about him — he was just known as 'Il Milord Inglese', though his letters were addressed 'Smithson'. But there were very few of them. Nobody ever came to stay with him, and he never went outside the grounds. What the scandal could be, he did not know. Milord was respectably married. His wife was a very nice lady, and sometimes came into the town. But neither of them ever stayed a night away. He was, of course, eccentric, like all Englishmen. Not a soul was admitted into the house, and the servants were forbidden to answer any questions. (Still they must like him, or they would not have stayed so long.) Very eccentric. For example, he had a curious dislike, more than dislike, a horror, of birds. And while all round in the countryside they were now trying to preserve them, prevent their extermination, any bird on his property was shot at sight — and he employed several men specially to guard him from them. And it was not that he liked to eat them. Never a thrush was put on his table, not one. No, it must be connected with this story — with the scandal. They reminded him of something he wished to forget, or else it was his wife, perhaps, who thought them bad companions for him. What it was, the *padrone* had never been able to make out.

How odd it was, I thought, this continual tradition of the eccentric Englishman living in some small Italian town, and how well justified one always found it to be. (I remembered the English hermit I had once seen living in a cave near Ancona.) But what kind of sad story was it which had been responsible for making these two people, now old, and obviously, by their surroundings, very prosperous, stay here all these long thirty summers or more, never to go away, never to see anyone of their own kind? Even in that comfortable villa, the summer heats must have been very severe and trying to the health (think of this flat countryside under the blazing sun of July or August). Perhaps they had lived a long time in India. But, surely, then they would have been more frightened of snakes than of birds! Indeed, the bird-phobia was the most unusual, the most individual, feature of the entire story. How, I wondered, did it link up with the reasons which had forced them to come here to live? The whole thing was inexplicable, and the only answer possible to the queries one framed to oneself was to be found in the simple reply that he was just an 'eccentric Englishman'. That was probably all there was in it.

However, my interest did not in the least fade during the few remaining days I stayed there. Involuntarily, my mind would play about the facts, and try to find some solution. Several times, many times even, my feet led me past the smartly painted and handsome iron gates, with their high spikes, past the stout, tall walls, their tops glittering with the varying angles of the broken glass that crowned them. And one evening, the last evening, my curiosity was rewarded. As I walked, screened from view by the shelter of the walls, towards the gates, I heard voices — English voices — speaking. Somehow, I knew the tone (unconnected as I was with the whole affair, my heart was yet beating with excitement). — Surely I knew it — a hollow, rather impressive, but now very irate voice. I heard it ejaculate: 'There, there! another beastly bullfinch! Why hasn't it been shot? What can the men be thinking of?' And the answering female cry: 'Don't worry yourself, dear. Don't let it upset you. After all, the poor little thing can't do you any harm now.' Carefully, soundlessly approaching, I looked round the corner at the gate. There, pressed close up against the bars, stood an old lady, with white hair, an old man, very carefully dressed, with a trim beard trained to mask rather cavernous cheeks. He saw me. A terrified glance of recognition darted out at me from his rather inspired eyes, that, as they gazed into mine, mechanically opened wider, and then narrowed, to give an effect of radiance. Hurriedly he turned away and shuffled behind the wall; but not before I had, in my turn, been able to identify the body of the dead poet, Joseph Bundle.

A PLACE OF ONE'S OWN

(For Sybil Cholmondeley)

Note.—The ghosts in this story are purely fictitious, and any of them attempting to materialise outside it will be prosecuted for fraud.

The facts which follow have long been known to me and I have always intended to put them together; but, remember, I do not pretend to offer any explanation, can only record them as they were told to me.

The Dale, a green, residential valley enclosed between steep hills, leads down to the sea and forms, as it were, the backbone of Newborough, dividing the body of the town into two parts. Behind the tall trees which line the broad grey road that flows through it, taking the place, surely, of a stream now buried, stand houses and gardens and, just as the trees have been drawn up from the darkness of the valley, so, too, these houses seem, long ago, while they were being constructed — 'long ago', I say, but they are ageless — to have outgrown their strength. Built of brick, either in a dark colourless red, with, over it, an insect-like blue sheen, or the dirty grey-white, intensely spectral yet matter-of-fact, in which seaside resorts love to indulge, they had upper windows level with the rooks' nests that sway all the year through with the northern winter's bellow or on the thin, restless wind of summer. From above, from the lofty iron bridge, which in a gale shudders also a little, you look down on a maze of tree-tops and slate gables, the very colour of rain; and a perpetual cawing, mingled with the striking of innumerable clocks and, very often, with peals from bells of countless frosty, mock-gothic churches, serves as an orchestration for all the happenings there below; where, in the centre, a long pool with an island and, on it, a summer-house of thatch and contorted woodwork, to which fragments of the original sheath still adhere, lend interest to a wilderness of asphalt paths, spotted with black and white after the fashion of a Dalmatian dog.

Down these, steep and slippery, in the long-eyed months when dawn and dusk were almost one, droves of trippers used always to stamp happily from the station towards a day of freedom on the beach, where the roar of the summer sea and the summer crowds, the cries of hokey-pokey men and of the sellers of bananas — an exotic novelty — and of chocolates, nougat and Newborough Rock, the clamour of several packs of stray dogs, manœuvring over the sands to the waves' edge for a piece of wood, about to be thrown for them by a bark-lover, and the singing of rival pierrot-shows, nigger minstrels and German bands, blended into an unforgettable and intolerable whole.

With these gay months, then, during the golden Edwardian reign, and not with today or with those dark hours of winter when the town rocks with the northern blast or wears a shroud spun of its own spume, my story deals. For, so far as I can recollect, it must have been in 1902 or 1903 that Mr. and Mrs. Smedhurst, after four decades of successful shopkeeping in Leeds, and anxious now to pass some lotus-eating, if declining, years in an agreeable neighbourhood, came to Newborough to find a house, a place of their own in which to settle. And, though admittedly they had been in a good way of business and had always lived well in a frugal Yorkshire fashion, their acquaintances were a little surprised at their purchase of Bellingham House, one of the largest, though outwardly most plain and yet imposing, of these mid-Victorian mansions in The Dale.

Solidity and respectability were Mr. Smedhurst's outstanding physical qualities. A stranger seeing him for the first time felt immediately that the cloth he wore and the leather of his boots might not be the most splendid or attractive, but were the most substantial and enduring, the least pretentious in their composition. Even his white moustache and the wart at the side of his rosy nose would, it was obvious, stand as long as flesh and blood could bear it. Further, everything was his own, and its very lack of compromise with any standard of beauty proclaimed it to be so. And, in consequence, for a man of between sixty and seventy years of age, he remained unusually well preserved. Mrs. Smedhurst, however, was of a lighter and more impermanent mould and, with her clear skin, soft brown eyes and a 'transformation', made of her own hair, was still pretty. Resolution, kindness and a certain natural gaiety were the qualities which showed most in her regular-featured face, but, in a conventional way, she was not unimaginative.

Husband and wife were mutually devoted, and Newborough had been connected always with the story of their lives. They had, for example, they often used to remind each other, spent their honeymoon here (in those days, Mr. Smedhurst had been a shop-assistant; think of it!), and since that time, with one or two unfortunate exceptions, had passed all their holidays in the same place. In addition, Mr. Smedhurst had always tried to attend the Newborough Cricket Festivals, early in September, if only for one match, because, after the manner of so many people of his sort, this game constituted the sole link he possessed with the open air and with the careless life of boyhood, and, in consequence, it infatuated him and he read the cricket averages and scores in the papers every day during the summer months. Moreover, it reinforced his other love, already great; they had, both of them, long loved Newborough and had long determined hither to retire when the moment came; *loved* it.

Any house, therefore, here, where they had enjoyed so many happy times, would have pleased them, but in Bellingham House they had plainly secured a bargain. . . . Of course, they acknowledged, their new home was too big for them, not *quite* what they had intended; for, being a childless couple, they had, with their northern sense of thrift, made up their minds, even though they could well afford it, not to keep more than one servant. On the other hand, it was situated in the most aristocratic part of the town, where all the best people in Newborough lived, and the air, siphoning through the valley from the sea, seemed always at its freshest, most invigorating. And, though it had stood empty for several years, it was so well fitted up; *you know*, really *good* fittings.

The house must have been almost the first in Newborough to be equipped with electric light. The converted gas-brackets and chandeliers of former days displayed a chiselled, decorative richness which later objects, created solely for their own purpose, would have lacked. If they were a *little* 'old-fashioned', still, as Mrs. Smedhurst said, they were handsome, undeniably handsome; all their friends would marvel at them. And, what was most uncommon, nearly every room, certainly every principal room, was provided with a *speaking-tube*, rearing its head up at the side of a heavy, white-marble chimney-piece. (Except in the best bedroom on the second floor. There it was fixed to the wall, by the door — near the place, evidently, where the bed had stood.) First of all, to use this contrivance, now nearly extinct, you seized it by the supple, undulating neck, unhooked it from its brass support, removed its crest-like stopper, and lifting the vulcanite cup to your lips, receiving in the process a suffocating mouthful of dust, blew down the tube to make it give a vibrant whistle in the room to which you wanted to speak. You then gave your instructions.

Actually, neither Mr. nor Mrs. Smedhurst had noticed the speaking-tubes at first — no doubt because they had not been expecting them. (They were not mentioned in the printed description.) . . . This is how it was. Mr. Tidcroft, the young house agent, who bore the reputation of being the most enterprising in the whole town, himself conducted them to Bellingham House; partly because he was most anxious to dispose of the property, which had been on his books for a long time, and partly because he believed that what counted most in business deals was 'the personal touch'. He had made himself most affable, talking all the way there; such a well-spoken gentleman. When they had arrived, he said to them:

'It's better for you to look round the place by yourselves, Mrs. Smedhurst; you can talk so much more freely. I'll stay down here in the hall.'

It was a lovely October morning, and Bellingham House wore none of the forlorn aspect that most houses untenanted for a long period manifest. Of course, as Mr. Smedhurst said, it was a little dusty, but that would soon clean up. And, as the crisp autumn sunshine poured in at the windows, it seemed, though empty of furniture, to have quite a 'lived-in' look. That was what most attracted Mrs. Smedhurst about it, a kind of living brightness. . . . But both husband and wife had taken a fancy to the place from the very opening of the front door. The dining-room was splendid — too good, really, for what they wanted, and a very nice room behind it. Then they went up to the former drawing-room, on the first floor (a lovely room, too, though less original, and oddly cold today, colder than the other rooms — because of the large windows, no doubt), and it was there that a sudden piercing whistle drew Mr. and Mrs. Smedhurst's attention to the existence of the speaking-tube. For a moment, since she had not been expecting it, it had given Mrs. Smedhurst quite a turn. . . . She answered, but there came no reply. . . . And then she guessed the explanation: it must be that nice young Mr. Tidcroft, afraid that she might overlook these instruments because he had omitted to point them out.

Well, it showed how useful they were in a house, even without talking down them — and must have cost a lot of money. Though the place appeared to be so large, communication would be easy — especially convenient for a small number of people — and would save the servant so much trouble. You could just whistle, and then inform her of your wishes. Thus you would avoid all bells and stairs; so Mrs. Smedhurst, urging him on to the purchase of the house, explained to her husband as, after a satisfactory tour of the whole premises, they descended to rejoin Mr. Tidcroft.

'You gave me quite a fright, Mr. Tidcroft, I declare,' she said to the young man, 'whistling down the speaking-tube like that. I wasn't expecting it. Old people like us don't have the nerves of you youngsters!'

'Oh, you weren't expecting it, weren't you?' he had replied, giving her rather a queer sort of look, and laughing nervously.

From his manner, Mrs. Smedhurst deduced that he must have felt that she was accusing him of being over-familiar, so she tried to convey in return that she entertained no grudge. But she did not make progress. He continued to be unlike himself, diffident and absent-minded.

The work at Bellingham House had been finely executed all through; no expense had been spared, you could see that. The one monumental bath, which was on the second floor, had mahogany casing and high brass taps, really magnificent. Even the wallpapers were still in good condition; rather dark papers with incised patterns, they looked costly and impressive, the sort of thing you could not obtain now that the Queen was dead and everything was cheaply made. Though the nails, from which some former owner's pictures had been hung, remained in certain instances, this did not seem to matter. . . . Better not to remove them and so leave the surface of the wall pitted with little holes. After all, they were scarcely noticeable, and the papers had hardly faded at all, showed no darker oblongs and squares where the frames had been.

There was no need, as Mrs. Smedhurst pointed out, to go to a lot of expense where it was not necessary. Their own pictures and ornaments would, admittedly, look very small here, but the rooms were beautiful, that was the main thing. Every house had its drawbacks, and, though a lot of dusting would be needed — oh no, she did not attempt to disguise that — well, Ellen, you could see, was a strong girl. In her last place, they had said she was good at her work and took a pride in it. Elbow-grease could do a lot. . . . Besides, where was the necessity to fuss with all the bedrooms? Just shut them up, and only worry with the rooms they were using — for they had not left many friends behind them in Leeds who would want to come and stay with them here. On the contrary, they had settled here in order to make nice new friends.

In fact, the size and grandeur of the interior appealed to a streak of romanticism present, albeit they were unaware of its existence, in both their natures. . . . And it was true : Bellingham House *was* unlike the ordinary house, exhaled a character of its own ; further, it had been *remarkably* cheap — perhaps because the place had stood vacant for so long. And, as things happened, no one related to them the history attaching to it, for they were newly arrived, and, up to the present, had been too fully occupied in house-hunting to have had the time to meet many people, and such new acquaintances as they had made were so far mostly recruited from the same stratum as themselves, rich, retired tradesmen and their wives, hailing from the industrial cities and not long settled in Newborough. A few said, 'Oh, you've taken *that* house, have you?' in a rather ominous tone of voice, but this reference to it was made from jealousy and not because they knew the story.

. . . . .

It was something about a rich old lady — no doubt the house had been so well fitted up for her use. . . . Let me try and recollect. . . . Yes, an old Miss Bezyre, an uncommon name. I say 'old', because she was old when as a child I first remember her, but she had come to live here some time in the sixties. Newborough, in addition to being in the two following decades a centre of northern fashion, was, as it still is, the very metropolis of the halt and maimed, yet you could not say that she was mad, or that those people, Mr. and Mrs. Pont, whom I recall as looking after her latterly, were her keepers. Nor could it be alleged against her, as against that blessed band of glandular idiots (creatures so permanent in their type as to seem both eternal and eternally youthful, who, in charge of a serenely smiling grey-haired woman of determined mien, continually paraded the newly washed expanse of gleaming sands, straining at their leashes, picking up, as it appeared, after the manner of a pack, some invisible trail, understanding nothing, intent only on the scent, their little eyes peeping in brutish fashion from highly coloured cherubic folds of flesh, their foreheads and cheeks and chins distorted and ill-proportioned as though seen through the wrong end of a telescope) that she was 'odd-looking' or 'a little dull'. With her slim, tall figure, fresh colouring and finely shaped oval face, Miss Bezyre remained, in spite of her grey hair, extremely young for her age. Perhaps one physical trait alone afforded a clue to her inner lack of balance, and that was her voice, which seemed not to tally with the rest of her; a curious, childish, half-strangled voice rather like that of a male impersonator or as though another voice, not her own, spoke from her body. Otherwise, she was all of a piece, well bred, even her hands and feet showing a natural distinction.

Sometimes for months together she would appear to be quite ordinary, only rather delicate, sensitive, full of an elusive charm and an indefinable personal dignity; a little singular, whimsical, perhaps; that was all. . . . And then suddenly her condition would change and, for a few days at a time, she would become a lunatic of an exceptional, peculiar kind, a being composed entirely, not necessarily of malice, but of mischief, exulting in pranks and tricks, supernormally active and strong, able to plan surprises and delighting in outbreaks of meaningless temper, breakings and grabbings like those of an ungovernable child, or, still more, it may be, of a pet monkey, and demonstrating in these expressions of her new and temporary self a curiously sub-human cunning, very irritating to those who looked after her. She would, for example, now find pleasure in smashing to fragments her own fine china vases, generally so prized by her, and, giving the prolonged and high-pitched cackle of laughter that was a habitual warning and symptom of this state of mind, would sweep them off the mantelpiece or throw them down into the road. Or she would barricade herself in one of the rooms in which there was a speaking-tube, and blow down it until Mr. and Mrs. Pont's ears nearly split their drums, and, when they came up to try to persuade her to stop and to open the door, she would laugh again or say something stupid and incomprehensible, until, in the end, her behaviour would oblige them to force the lock and enter. Or at other times, she might hide behind a curtain and jump out at you, shrieking, or contrive any of a whole repertory of sad, zany devices, thereto impelled at these moments by the inexhaustible ingenuity of her ailing brain. It was very difficult to defeat such surprises.

These manifestations — of which, after they were over and she had relapsed into her usual dignified self, she remembered nothing — ill suited the appearance I have tried to describe, which, indeed, prepossessed strangers in her favour. If they did not see her 'in one of her moods', as the Ponts euphemistically termed it, everyone liked her and was charmed by her; for there was something very lovable about her, a kind of unexpected, gay elegance that infused her whole being. Moreover, the whole town gloried in her as an exhibit; the last of a family that had gathered distinction in many fields, though always its members had tended toward eccentricity; had, in addition to their attainments, been 'beaux' and 'macaronis' and 'dandies', fashionable, self-willed and vicious, their actions not to be conjectured by ordinary laws. She was rich, too, and, it was said, 'could have married the Prince of Wales himself in her time'. But she had refused to look at any of the men in love with her, because she had been so proud, so erratic — or perhaps because she had been aware of the doom lurking in her own blood. . . . And so, at the age of forty, she had fallen a victim to it, and had come here to live in retirement, to escape unnoticed. For she was not certifiable — or, if at moments she were, people of her position, it was felt, should not suffer such an indignity. In any case, she was not certified.

At the time of which I write, Miss Bezyre had resided here thirty years and more — indeed, though I cannot vouch for it, Bellingham House may have been built for her and thus from the beginning have owed its individuality to this strange woman. The old lady's-maid, who had looked after her for so long, had died and Mr. and Mrs. Pont now served her, or guarded her, and had been here, already, eleven years. Apparently, she now possessed no relations, only trustees, who seldom troubled themselves to come down from London to visit her. When they did, however, they invariably found everything in perfect order, the house well run. Indeed, Mr. and Mrs. Pont bore all the semblance of an exemplary couple, perfect custodians for an old lady of this type, very calm and respectful, very fond of her, even if she did on occasion give them trouble and oblige them to be firm with her. . . . It might be that, having been constrained through her own wilful behaviour to use force, to break open the doors of the rooms in which she had barricaded herself, they had found that a little violence paid in their dealings with her and that, as, when she returned to her right mind, she remembered so little of what had occurred, they resorted to its use more frequently as time went by. . . . But the winter months in Newborough made people turn in upon themselves for news, and they were therefore wont to exaggerate. It was wiser to believe nothing.

Certainly in the town, though, the legend grew, — no doubt from servants' talk, for a great many were employed at Bellingham House and they were always either new servants or just on the point of leaving and, further, the supremacy of the Ponts in the house would be sure to render them unpopular with jealous subordinates. It was even said, then, that during her periodic outbursts Mr. and Mrs. Pont ill-treated old Miss Bezyre, tied her up and gagged her to keep her quiet, beat her without mercy and inflicted many cruel little tortures upon her in the tradition of the eighteenth-century code for the treatment of lunatics. Occasionally, late at night, issuing from her bedroom on the second floor, at one place level with the road that ran zigzagging up the hill behind it to the Promenade, passers-by affirmed that they had heard a curious, loud, childish voice, sometimes laughing, but not seldom whining, or was it moaning? — and that this whimpering had risen now and again to a high scream.

Probably, others maintained, it was all talk, and if there were sounds at all, it was only the perpetual wind whistling and howling round the corners of the tall, angular house. And there was the roar of the sea; always, the roar of the sea. Her old doctor was dead, it was true, but that nice, dapper young

Dr. Favelle attended her — though he seldom had to be called in except during one of her bouts, for her physical health was excellent. All his patients loved him. He would never allow such a thing. Further, when she returned to her normal state Miss Bezyre never complained of the Ponts' conduct towards her, nor did she at any time appear to be timid of them. And if, during 'her moods', she indulged in wild assertions and injurious allegations against them, why, it could only be a symptom of her malady. . . . Besides, she must have liked and trusted the Ponts, as much as she did Dr. Favelle, because, when her old trustees had died, she nominated, first the doctor, in place of one, and then Mr. Pont, in place of the other.

Nevertheless, the legion of invalid old ladies in the squares and crescents above, with servants, nieces and companions subdued for a lifetime to their tyrannical powers of will, of one kind or another, liked to believe these rumours and, in consequence, ignoring the total lack of evidence, continued to do so. . . . And, one winter day, faith enjoyed its reward.

'Have you heard', the watchers at the bedsides would inquire of the indomitable mummies, embalmed in shawls and propped upon pillows, 'Have you heard' — and then would pause again, conscious of being about to spring a pleasant surprise and, also, of being obliged to speak even more loudly and distinctly than usual, for the north-east wind, which had roared all the night through, was still blowing a gale, — 'did the doctor tell you, when he called, that old Miss Bezyre has *gone*? Committed suicide, so they say.'

And the aunts and mistresses, melted by the news to an unusual geniality, would reply either, 'Stuff and nonsense. Suicide, indeed! It's stiff, stark, cold-blooded murder! I've been waiting to hear it for a long while'; or, 'I don't call *that* old; she ought to have been good for another twenty years'; or else, 'I've no patience with that sort of thing; if one suffers, one must learn to bear — "grin and bear it", as my poor old aunt used to say'. . . . But each, whatever her view, added in the end, 'But tell me about it, all the same, my dear'.

It appeared that the old woman had been found hanging, and, to execute this design, must have jumped off the chair. . . . At the inquest, a few days later, it transpired that her body was covered with bruises. But though various statements and questions in court, concerning Miss Bezyre's testamentary dispositions, caused a certain amount of prejudice in the minds of those present, the evidence of Mr. and Mrs. Pont, and of Dr. Favelle, served to dispel it to a considerable extent. (There are, of course, some people who persist in believing evil report.) The old lady, having no relations, had bequeathed a large part of her substantial fortune to charity (that, dissentients maintained to be the cleverest touch in the whole affair!) and small legacies to servants still in her employ: for the rest, Dr. Favelle came into thirty thousand pounds, the London solicitor into five thousand, while the bulk, some eighty-five thousand pounds, together with Bellingham House and its contents, went, in the phrase of the testator, 'to my friends Jeremiah and Mary Pont, in some slight token of my gratitude to them for their devoted service to me for so many years'. . . . Incidentally, the document was in perfect order, had been drawn up a year or two previously and had been witnessed by two servants who were still with her at the time of her death.

Mrs. Pont, a rosy-faced woman of middle age, with frankness written upon her round, voluminous pink cheeks, with dragged-back hair, deep-set brown eyes, blinking honestly behind very powerful spectacles, slightly protruding teeth and a very pronounced dint in her resolute cloven chin, had been especially good in the part. Her grating matter-of-fact voice carried conviction. Miss Bezyre, she told the Coroner, had seemed perfectly all right that evening. There was no question of her being 'in one of her moods', and, that being so, and knowing that when normal she was safely to be trusted and liked to be left alone, Mrs. Pont had not slept in her room, as was her wont when Miss Bezyre was 'bad'. If the old lady wanted her during the night, she had only to use the speaking-tube — a great convenience in sick-rooms — which was beside the bed. . . . Well, Mrs. Pont had gone in, at about ten o'clock, to see that she was comfortable and to say good-night to her. Yes. That was the last time she had seen her alive. Everything had been in order, and she had seemed happy and sleepy, really 'comfy'. The night had passed without event, she had heard nothing . . . but, in the morning, entering, she had found (here Mrs. Pont took off her spectacles, with their strong, distorting lenses that, by magnifying her eyes and, as it were, floating them to the surface, so greatly emphasised their appearance of ox-like frankness and good-humour, and applied a handkerchief. The Coroner ordered an attendant to give her a chair and smelling-salts. 'Thank you, sir, I'm very sorry to have broken down. I'm all right now again'), had found her dead in this dreadful fashion. . . . Naturally, it had been a great shock after eleven — no, nearly twelve — years of waiting upon the dear old lady, anticipating her every wish and guarding her against her own erratic impulses.

Then Dr. Favelle took his stand and certified that death had taken place at about 2.30 on the morning of the twenty-first, and that the bruises and abrasions on the body of the deceased had been due to a fall she had suffered a few days previously. Next, the servants — the Ponts thought them the *nicest* staff of servants they had ever had, so willing and obliging — came forward and declared on oath that there had been no call from the speaking-tube in any of the upstairs bedrooms, and that they had heard no sound at all during the night. It was true, they added, that the clamour of the sea had been very great, and the wind had howled round the house so loudly that other noises were more difficult to catch than usual, but they had heard nothing; no, nothing but the screaming of the wind — there was always the wind — round the corners of the house. . . . It must have been the wind.

The jury brought in a unanimous verdict, approved by the Coroner, of '*Suicide while temporarily of unsound mind*'. Nevertheless the Ponts soon decided, after all that had occurred, to leave Newborough. They felt they needed a change. They missed the dear old lady so greatly, they explained to their friends, and they were reminded of her nearly every day in the dear old house. Besides, it was too large for their simple requirements; what would they want with all those servants? And Newborough itself had changed so much, was not half so *refined* as it had been when they had first come here. . . . And the Doctor, too, chose to retire, though comparatively young, and went to reside in Sussex. (I never heard what happened to him after that, but it was a long time ago, and he can hardly still be living.) As a matter of fact, however, Mr. and Mrs. Pont did not continue to enjoy good fortune. It had been some time before they had seemed able to settle down — after a wrench like that, it was not to be wondered at! And they were discovered one morning, about two years after Miss Bezyre's death, gassed, in the charming small house they had recently bought in Bournemouth. They had not lived in it for more than two months. They appeared to have had no worries to account for their suicide — unless, of course, it had been an accident.

Meanwhile, after the passing of a few months in Newborough, the talk there had subsided. The behaviour of rich strangers or of poor trippers offered other and equally appetising subjects for conversation. The strange death of Miss Bezyre was forgotten. Someone, I forget who, had bought Bellingham House. But the new-comers did not stay, and the same autumn let it to a rich draper and his wife. Certainly there was no idea of there being anything *wrong* with the place until *after* the death of the Ponts. No doubt, the report of their suicide in the newspapers started it off. At any rate, the occupants now declared that they were always being disturbed at night, and gave notice. Since then, no one had seemed to remain in the house for longer than a few months, or even weeks. Indeed, it let more easily at first than later on, for, after six or seven brief leases, it stood vacant for as many years — until, in fact, Mr. and Mrs. Smedhurst bought it.

. . . . .

The new owners moved into Bellingham House at the end of November, so as to avoid spending another winter in Leeds. Of course, it had been a sad moving, leaving the old house at Leeds; such a comfortable, roomy home, even if it were rather black. But the excitement of their new dwelling had quickly put it out of their minds, and the past few weeks had been a turmoil of measuring, choosing and matching with the aid of their friends — or, rather, of fellow-guests from the Eglantine Hydro, who seemed almost as interested in the new house, and proud of it, as the principals themselves. (Really, they were very kind, if scarcely 'the sort' that Mr. and Mrs. Smedhurst had migrated to Newborough to make friends with.) But then, after all, as Mrs. Smedhurst recognised when at night she communed with her own soul, it *was* interesting, because it formed a culmination to all the worldly strivings of two lives. On the day itself, she tried to take the matter calmly, not to show anything as she said good-bye. It was bad to get over-excited, especially for Mr. Smedhurst. All the same, as she paid off the cab at the door of their new home, where Ellen stood in her new uniform to greet them, she was surprised to find that, in spite of the many happy holidays spent there, it was a relief to have left the Eglantine and to be in a place of one's own again.

Soon, after their own fashion, they had made themselves very comfortable. The rooms had, of course, been thoroughly washed, every inch of them, and it was wonderful how they had cleaned up; really wonderful. And since Mr. and Mrs. Smedhurst had not been obliged to spend anything upon re-decorating, they could afford to lay out a little bit extra upon the furnishing. 'You know, nice "homey" things', as Mrs. Smedhurst explained, chintz covers and plenty of those new, round cushions in bright-hued, pleated and embroidered covers. She had draped the massive, white-marble chimney-pieces, square and uncompromising, with pretty fringed materials, with loops and borders and tassels, very stylish, and had filled the sitting-room and Mr. Smedhurst's 'den' with that delicate-looking wicker furniture in cream and pale green, that had just come in as the fashion, and with wicker stands, too, for plants, so that the rooms should not look 'cold' or 'stiff'.

The dining-room, done up in the Moorish style (it must have cost hundreds to make!), they preserved as it was, and bought for it a Spanish suite of ebony and ivory — they had been lucky enough to find it at a sale; the very thing. . . . Perhaps the room, with its horse-shoe arched recesses and high, honeycombed ceiling, was a little dark, but it was a wonderful room really, just the sort of room, Mrs. Smedhurst thought, that an Italian Cardinal might have built in order to give dinner-parties (a dinner-party, with little silver trays of almonds, and of chocolates, wearing glittering crystallised rose and violet petals like tiaras, was something she had hitherto seldom glimpsed; as opposed to high tea, it still constituted both an ideal and a symbol. . . . And it would mean hiring a waiter and, too, that Mr. Smedhurst could not slop about in his slippers). They made their sitting-room next the dining-room, and there was, behind it, another small room; the perfect den for Mr. Smedhurst, in which to smoke his pipe, read his papers and keep his letters. They took the whole of the first floor for themselves; the back part for Mr. Smedhurst's dressing-room, and the large apartment in front — the former drawing-room — as their joint bedroom. (Perhaps it was rather *too* big, after their bedroom at Holmdene, Mrs. Smedhurst admitted this to herself, but they would soon grow accustomed to it.) And so Ellen was particularly fortunate and got that lovely big room on the second floor — it had been the best bedroom — for her use. It was bigger even than their own, for it went right from the front to the back, and had windows both sides!

'You ought to think yourself a lucky girl, Ellen,' Mrs. Smedhurst said kindly. 'I don't know another maid who has such a lovely airy room.'

'Yismoom.'

'Any girl ought to be pleased to be in service in Newborough. . . . Look at that view! Why, you can see the ducks on the mere, and, if you lean out, like this, there's the sea with all the fishing smacks on it!'

By this time, intoxicated with her own generosity, Mrs. Smedhurst had given the girl the whole of the North Sea and the herring fleet; but alas, as in life so often, bounty met with little response.

'Yismoom.'

'Look at those tints, too! . . . It's just like the country! Listen to the rooks and all the dogs barking down there. . . . I only hope you'll show your gratitude to Mr. Smedhurst and myself by working hard and being pleasant-spoken. . . . But all you girls are the same today; all spoilt.'

Ellen made no reply this time. . . . Still, Mrs. Smedhurst was pleased with her, a new acquisition, about twenty-six or twenty-seven years of age; a good, healthy, pleasant girl from the wolds, reliable and well disposed, who plainly understood, and enjoyed, her work, even if she was somewhat solid, heavy of foot and hand; but that was better than being hysterical, like most of the creatures you were recommended nowadays. One did not want a maid to chatter and behave in a fast way.

. . . .

The winter months passed quietly and agreeably, and it was not until one Sunday morning at the beginning of April that the trouble started. It was a lovely morning and Mr. Smedhurst and Ellen had gone to church — not together, of course. (Indeed Mr. Smedhurst felt much annoyed with her; she had done a very stupid thing that morning. Perhaps church would cheer him up.) Mrs. Smedhurst had a cold and was obliged to remain in the house, reading her chapter. It was a pity, because she had been looking forward all the week to the austere elegance of Church Parade, and people said that the tulips in the beds at the side of the Promenade had never been so gorgeous as they were this year, nor the lilac, that lay like mauve rain-clouds poised on the terrace gardens which rose, tier upon tier, from the gull-winged sea. . . . Still, it could not be helped.

Nevertheless, though the chapter, the twenty-eighth of the first book of Samuel, usually interested her, she found it hard to concentrate this morning, was always coming back to the printed page with the realisation that for several minutes it had meant little to her, albeit her lips had shaped the sounds. She did not know what it could be, but she felt, well, 'fidgety', as though waiting for something. She must make an effort. . . . Her eyes returned to the book, and she had just reached the words 'Then said Saul unto his servants, Seek me a woman that hath a familiar spirit . . .', when suddenly a prolonged whistle issued from the speaking-tube.

'So the girl can't have gone out after all! How queer; something must have happened!' Mrs. Smedhurst exclaimed to herself. . . . What could it be? Well-trained servant that she was, Ellen would normally never dare to use the speaking-tube to her mistress unless — as occasionally during the past few weeks — to announce visitors. But nobody would be calling at this hour.

In the instant before she answered, while getting up from her chair and proceeding to cross in front of the fireplace, Mrs. Smedhurst felt, somehow, uneasy; the room appeared to have increased in size, to be very large, lonely and cold; curiously cold, as though an instantaneous but marked drop in the temperature had occurred. (The whistle sounded again. Surely it was not necessary, whoever it was, to *go on* whistling in that way!) She looked at the 'daffies' (she had lately caught the habit of calling daffodils 'daffies' from Mrs. Beazley-Boggarde, the wife of the Canon) that were standing near by in a little three-lipped vase of iridescent glass — five or six blossoms only — in order to reassure herself. (How silly to get into this condition because of an ordinary, material thing such as a whistle on a speaking-tube!) They looked so yellow and transparent in the bright spring sunshine; very comforting. . . . And then, while she looked, a single flower suddenly broke into a violent oscillation, as sometimes you may see one leaf quiver upon a tree, its leaves otherwise without motion, upon a still summer evening. But the flower stopped this warning as swiftly as it had begun. . . . Well, it *could* only be due to a draught — no wonder the room was cold, though all the windows and doors seemed to fit so well. . . . Oh, that noise!

By this time, she had reached the speaking-tube. She unhooked the instrument, and held it close to her ear, listening. . . . But nobody spoke. She replaced it on the hook. At once the strident insistence of the whistle began again. The process was twice repeated. The third time she took it down, however, a high childish voice, with a sort of insane and querulous gaiety in it, cried, 'Come and find me! I'm hiding!' . . . Mrs. Smedhurst of course saw the explanation at once. With Mr. Smedhurst and Ellen both out, one of those naughty children from next door must have crept in, unobserved, and be hiding somewhere in the rooms above. (Mrs. Smedhurst, though she had none of her own, loved children, encouraged them to come and see her, and spoilt them with barley sugar and chocolate — the delicious new 'Swiss Milk Chocolate' that had just made its appearance.)

'Is that you, Hilary?' she demanded loudly; but she received no reply. So she went upstairs. . . . In her own room, she had the impression — it was difficult to define — that somebody was there, quite near her, and in the passage outside she could have sworn for a moment that she had been touched, softly, on the face. But she could find no one, though she made a thorough search, everywhere, including in Ellen's room. (The upper rooms were locked, so she did not bother about them.) Directly, however, she had shut the door, and was going downstairs, she heard the shrilling of the whistle in the room behind her. Patiently she climbed up again, although she was a woman of spirit who disliked to be made to look foolish: some instinct warned her that she must not get angry or in any direction let go of herself. She took up the tube. The same voice as before (it must have been Hilary's, but in spite of its childish timbre it did not altogether resemble hers — no doubt the tube distorted it a little) said:

'You've been hot, very hot. . . . Once I touched you, but you couldn't see me!'

Full of mischief, the child sounded, Mrs. Smedhurst said to

herself, glossing over, for her own solace, the alien quality she had noted. (It must be Hilary!) At that moment, a door slammed. . . . Of course, Hilary escaping! . . . But though Mrs. Smedhurst walked as fast as she could to the window, she could see no one passing through the garden.

She decided not to tell her husband. He disliked children — or said so —, and it would only make him worse if he knew that she had been treated with such a lack of consideration. Instead, to relieve her feelings, she wrote a pleasant little note to Hilary's mother, telling her what had taken place and confessing that she was growing old and did not like to have tricks played upon her, though she always looked forward to visits from the dear child.

She tried to show nothing of her feelings at dinner, but that same afternoon she received an answer from Mrs. Thatcher, in which the injured mother protested that both she and Hilary had been in church at the time mentioned. . . . Mrs. Smedhurst now almost wished that she had told Mr. Smedhurst, since, what with her cold, the strange episode of the morning, and then this letter, she felt quite 'queer'. She decided to rest. It *must* be her imagination. If she could be quiet for a little, she would soon forget all about it.

Everything was very still, for it was Ellen's afternoon off, and Mr. Smedhurst had gone out for his Sunday walk. (She had explained that her cold was still very heavy and prevented her from accompanying him.) Certainly she was tired. She lay down on the sofa in her bedroom; such a nice comfortable sofa that she had bought at a sale. It was curious how cold it was in the house today; Mr. Smedhurst had said it was quite hot out. Perhaps she only *felt* cold because she was not well. . . . So she pulled a blanket over herself and was asleep before many minutes had passed. . . . But she was woken, about a quarter of an hour later, by that whistle — at least she thought so, but she could not be sure, as there was no answer this time. . . . Perhaps she had dreamt it. All the same, she said to herself, she hoped her imagination would calm down, or she would begin to feel uncomfortable in the house. (She shivered suddenly. At the back of her mind, I believe, were two ideas: that unconventional things should not happen to people who led conventional lives, and — though this was still more undefined — that a man-made convenience, planned for the use of human beings, such as a speaking-tube, rendered the opportunity it here offered as a medium for haunting all the more horrible, in somewhat the same manner as, to some minds, the application of electricity to the old, barbarous habit of putting a criminal to death, always invests that kind of execution with a greater sense of horror, even, than attaches to hanging, which itself is primitive and savage as the sentence it consummates. But these thoughts nevertheless remained very much in the background, unformulated, for she dismissed such reflections from the surface of her mind as 'morbid'. Nor would she allow herself to use, even to herself, the word 'haunted' in connection with Bellingham House, of which she was so proud. . . . Once that word were admitted, it would be irremediable.)

Somehow or other, she could not settle down again for two or three days, and the persistent cawing of the rooks, as they flew backwards and forwards, laden with huge twigs, much too big for them, in their spring fever of house-building and house-warming, for the first time annoyed her. . . . And Mr. Smedhurst seemed so irritable.

As a matter of fact, if only she had realised it, Mr. Smedhurst had been given cause for irritation, though he had said little about it. . . . Things had begun to go wrong on Saturday night, when he had been reading in his den. He had tried to concentrate: but it had been impossible, he found. First, the two wicker armchairs had begun to creak, for all the world as if two people were sitting in them or had just got up, and then, at that very moment when his book was beginning to grip him — and it was a book everyone was reading, *The Garden of Allah* —, the light had been snapped off at the door; snapped itself off, he supposed, as he blundered through the darkness to turn it on. . . . Well, that was enough for one evening. . . . The next day, when he had gone up from his bedroom to the floor above for his hot Sunday morning bath, something still more annoying had occurred; he had unsuspectingly swung right into it, unable to stop himself, only to find it was stone cold! (And he had been feeling oddly cold before that, so that in consequence he felt chilly all the morning, even in church: but the walk home had put him right.) Yet Ellen, who had prepared it a quarter of an hour before, maintained that she had, according to her custom, felt it with her finger, and that it had been the temperature he liked. If she was telling the truth, there had not been time for it to grow cold. A bit of a mystery there! All the same, though she did not usually lie, it *must* have been her fault; these modern girls were so careless. And the next day — or was it the day after? — she must have begun to talk to herself, for he had distinctly heard voices; low voices; a man and a woman, he would have said, if he had not been aware that Ellen was the only person upstairs. . . . And he wished, too, that she would not giggle in that funny, high voice: it did not seem to 'go' with her. But he had heard it on several occasions lately in the passage downstairs. He would have to speak to her about it.

Then, all at once, everything became quiet again for a spell. Mrs. Smedhurst immediately sensed the change in the atmosphere. In spite of the delicious spring weather and the fires that had been kept in, past April the fifteenth, the house had been cold for a full fortnight; frigid, with a leaden quality of cavernous chill. But now, though the days were colder and overcast outside, the rooms were warmer. Her cough, too, was better, and she soon expelled a faint, lingering sense of uneasiness, that lurked somewhere among the shadows of an infancy long past. Indeed, only for a moment did it revive; when she came to look through the list of things, to see what had been broken during the last fortnight, and discovered that, instead of the single plate or saucer which she would have expected, Ellen had smashed more than a dozen of each! When Mrs. Smedhurst had drawn her attention to it, the girl had burst out crying, insisting that she had not done it, but that, a few evenings before, she had heard, just behind her, a singular, cackling laugh (she imitated it — and for a dreadful instant Mrs. Smedhurst recognised it); when she had turned round to see who was there, all the china on the third shelf of the dresser had been suddenly swept off it, as though by an invisible hand, for there was nobody there. . . . Of course, it was an impossible tale; it must be an excuse. . . . Yet it was not *like* Ellen, Mrs. Smedhurst recognised, to invent a story, nor did she seem to be lying now. Nor was it like her to cry in that way; *hysterical*, that must be it.

However, since she was a useful, willing girl and a good cook, all Mrs. Smedhurst said to her was:

'I'm surprised at you, Ellen! You must be careful another time. . . . *Now*, I don't want to hear any more.'

. . . . .

With the approach of midsummer, the days were lengthening rapidly to their climax. In spite of the noisy trippers — who, as Mrs. Smedhurst said, appeared to think they had bought the whole town for the price of an excursion ticket (there was no such thing as Respect nowadays), life was exceedingly pleasant. Peonies and flags offered their large faces to the sun in the gardens of square and crescent, and the bushes of syringa were starred with blossom, too fragrant and languorous for northern air. And joys, other than those of Nature tamed for residential consumption, were also at their height. Church Parade, for example, had become really exciting.

For many years past, Mrs. Smedhurst had been looking forward to being able to study it every Sunday instead of for only a few hours torn from a normally humdrum existence. Between morning and dusk it was — except at mealtimes — full of beautifully dressed men and women; just like Paris, she conjectured, but without the horrid foreign flavour. Nor was it in the least 'spoilt'. The trippers, for all their vulgar audacity, just did not *dare*, she supposed, to frequent it, but confined themselves to the roar and clamour of the moth-coloured sands below. Of a Sunday, the battalions of old gentlemen with a nearing eternity on their hands, so smart, in an almost military manner, with their curled white moustaches, blue chins and nicely flushed faces — Mrs. Smedhurst liked a man to have colour in his face — exchanged their brown or grey billycocks for brown or grey top-hats. (Mr. Smedhurst himself now sometimes wore a grey tail-coat and a brown bowler, though he had taken much persuasion; he had rather the air of a major, she thought, if only he would brush the ends of his moustache *up* a little more.) Fashionable family parties, with low-waisted women in toques and feather-boas, and elaborate gowns of lace and embroidery, holding their moon-faced children to them, drove in carriages or smart open cabs along the road at the side, against a background of pillared, primly painted Regency houses, with stout, round bow-windows, or delicate balconies of iron trellis supporting Chinese canopies.

The Winter Garden running down between the Promenade

and the sea, stood also at its zenith. The flower-beds were beautiful, in their intricate, involved designs, and the groves of stunted trees were carrying their fullest summer sail in the cool, refreshing wind, laden with salt. All the shops were now open along the stone deck that, strongly fortified, rose from the sea itself when the tide swept in; sweet-shops and leather-shops and shops full of attractive new 'transformations' and — for fancy-dress balls, of course — of white Pompadour wigs displayed above waxy faces frozen into dimpled smiles. And, right in the middle of the terrace, there was a pavilion of elaborate and gaily painted iron-work, filled with trim button-holes, roses with a florist's false dew lying upon them and picotees striped like summer dresses, all mounted on a shield of green plush. (Even the holy band of cretins and mentally defectives, those hopping, lolloping, loose-eyed cherubs, now paraded here to lend an undeniable interest to the scene, were brought to the kiosk in twos and threes, so that a woman, with her mouth bristling with pins, could select one from her lips in order to fasten a neat flower on to each of these distended coats in turn. It made the wearers look 'jollier', their grey-haired guardians proclaimed.) And, on week-days, the celebrated Winter Garden Orchestra played selections from Waldteufel and Johann Strauss or, better still, from *modern* pieces like *Florodora* or *San Toy*; three programmes a day, morning, afternoon and, most enjoyable of all, in the long gloaming when the lights shone yellow against the prevailing blue, dark but luminous, and the glow of their cigars replaced the colour that dusk removed from the faces of the old gentlemen.

With this atmosphere prevailing throughout Newborough, there were other things to do besides sit moping at home and wait for mysterious incidents! Nerves, all nerves! How silly it seemed, Mrs. Smedhurst said, when you looked back on it! In this delicious sunny weather, not too hot and not too cold, even The Dale, formal and sober as it was, had grown animated. The idle, summer repartee of tennis-balls here and there replaced the prevalent cawing, the gardens were full of roses — rather chlorotic and drawn up, it is true, because of the tall trees overhead — and flotillas of ducks proudly sailed on the waters of the pool that seemed to catch all the more light because of the surrounding shade, and fussily trimmed their chequered and streaked wings or waddled up on to the island, where now the rustic summer-house was embowered in pink cushions of Dorothy Perkins roses.

How enchanting Newborough could be, and Bellingham House, too! Mrs. Smedhurst once more congratulated Mr. Smedhurst and herself on their joint choice of a residence, and of the town in which to find it. There was no doubt of it, in spite of its size, Bellingham House was comfortable; though that, of course, was largely their own doing. And they were making such nice new friends, *very refined*. A whole world of social activity had opened itself to them and they were thoroughly enjoying themselves, though sometimes things became a little difficult, sometimes conversation was not easy, because Mr. and Mrs. Smedhurst had, as it were, been born, elderly and fully dressed, on the arrival platform of Newborough Station. The commercial past it would be bad form to mention or admit, for it would taint their new friends as much as themselves. Nothing had existed before they had arrived here; nothing. . . . Among their acquaintances now were a few Army people, and though they undoubtedly gave tone to any gathering, at Bellingham House or elsewhere, they were over-given to inquisitiveness: both men and women shot questions at you, as though they were bullets from a quick-firing machine-gun: 'Where did you live before you came here?', 'Do you know Lord Ghoolingham?', 'Have you ever been to India?', and many other such inquiries. Yet they certainly lent an air, and added an excitement of their own. But life here was full of pleasure and excitement. . . . And then, abruptly, after weeks of peace, about the middle of July, everything changed again.

This time they were both present, sitting in the 'drawing-room' (Mrs. Manning-Tutthorne, the wife of the Major, and almost the nicest of their new friends, had gently but firmly insinuated the *drawing-room*) after dinner — or *luncheon*, as they were now obliged, with a certain lack of sureness and continuity, to call their midday meal —, when a strident whistle announced a summons to the speaking-tube. (Somehow, though it was so convenient, Mr. and Mrs. Smedhurst had not used it much for the last month or two.) Mrs. Smedhurst was nearest to the instrument, and waited a moment, until the shrill, childish voice she had heard before said:

'You weren't expecting me today: I can see that. I know when I'm not wanted.'

Then there was a laugh, and nothing else — except that, though it seemed a quiet enough summer afternoon outside, the French windows rattled with a singular hammering tremor, and finally, with a crash, blew wide open. And a lovely little vase, to which Mrs. Smedhurst was much attached — she had bought it at the Wedgwood factory while on a holiday in the Potteries many years before — fell off the mantelpiece and was smashed. (It could be riveted, she decided, examining the damage.) Mr. Smedhurst said nothing, he did not ask who was speaking. . . . For the first time she understood why earlier in the year her husband had been so irritable; they shared an unspoken secret.

Practically every day for a week or more — and such lovely weather, which made this inner fear seem so much worse — one odd incident or another had occurred. Mr. Smedhurst now usually answered the whistle and, every time, heard a voice; it must be the same that she heard. But neither of them showed by a flicker of a muscle in their faces that anything might be amiss with their house. After all, it might suddenly stop. . . . So, by a serviceable compromise, each pretended to the other to think it was Hilary. 'Really, Hilary is very naughty today,' one of them would remark. 'I must speak to her mother.' But this brave simulation deceived neither of them. It was only a shield, a small, pasteboard shield contrived against the immensity of the universe.

In general, but not invariably, events were heralded by the speaking-tube. Once, for example, without any warning, Mr. Smedhurst, while going into supper, received a blow on the temple. He supposed he must have bumped himself — after all it could not be the voice, could it? . . . But it was strange: he could not remember how he had done it, and he did not feel inclined to go back and look, for it had made him quite giddy and cold — so cold. He could not get warm again the whole night, not even with the help of the cup of hot Van Houten cocoa he always drank last thing. . . . Then, another time, Mrs. Smedhurst had been watching Hilary's younger sister, Marbelle, who was five years old, laughing and playing by herself in the garden — she was allowed to come into the garden of Bellingham House and play, for Mrs. Thatcher knew she could come to no harm there. But really, when you came to think of it, the child was behaving in a very odd sort of way, talking and laughing as though there were someone else there! Mrs. Smedhurst called to her rather sharply, 'Marbelle! What are you doing? Don't be silly, child!' But Marbelle only looked at her, surprised, and answered, 'I'm not being silly. I'm playing with funny lady who lives with you.' . . . It had been disconcerting.

. . . .

At the end of ten days or so, Ellen asked leave to speak to them, and said she must give notice, could not stand it any longer. At first she would state no reason, except that she was frightened in her room and could not sleep; she would rather say no more. . . . When pressed, she pleaded the difficulty of describing her experiences; she did not know how to put it, but lately she had begun to wake at one or two in the morning, disturbed by the sound of voices, and though it had been dark, it had seemed as though she could see shadows struggling in the darkness, could feel the movement of these figures in the air by her. Several times after long, violent dreams in which she had been struggling and fighting, she had woken up to find herself standing in the dark, close against one of the walls of her bedroom; the same place, always, because she could tell it by a nail on the wall. And one night she had been attacked. She had been woken up — she was sure she had not still been dreaming — by violent blows, a rain of them, on her body from each side of the bed. Besides, she still bore the marks, and she lifted up the sleeve of her dress to show a bruise on her arm. Nor even did these happenings stop by day, for the other morning, when she had got up, tired out by not sleeping, somebody had been hiding behind the door of the housemaid's pantry and had sprung out at her with a horrid screech of laughter; only Ellen had seen no one, had merely felt an ice-cold wind sweep past her.

'The place must be 'aunted, moom, it mus',' she ended up stoutly.

Haunted: the two syllables fell on the air with an astonishing impact, as though Mr. and Mrs. Smedhurst had been waiting for it. Neither of them looked at the other, but they knew that, now that the word had been mentioned, Bellingham House would never be the same to them. (In her own mind,

Mrs. Smedhurst admitted it; yes, *haunted*. . . . But it seemed so silly, such a lovely house, and so cheap too. In her imagination she saw Ellen's room. There was *something* she did not like about it; she knew she would never have felt comfortable in it herself. . . . Perhaps it was only just the size, much bigger than her own room.)

'You mustn't imagine things, Ellen,' Mr. Smedhurst said. 'Ghosts don't exist — if they do, it's our own wicked consciences.'

Mrs. Smedhurst added, kindly, 'You're a little overdone, Ellen, that is all. Your room is bigger than you are used to, and it's the strong sea air. . . . But we don't want to lose your services, so you had better take a month's holiday.'

A month was a long time. . . . Ellen was so pleased at the idea of immediate release from the house, as well as of a holiday, that she at once withdrew her notice and started that very evening for the wolds, returning to her native existence of placid farmhouse life, of processions of geese to a pool, waddling unsteadily on their clumsy webbed feet, of chickens and ducks and pigs and cows in chorus at feeding-time, and fritillary-speckled guinea-fowls, of loose stone walls and of tufts of mountain grass like the flowing hair of the Nereids, and of apricots and peaches ripening upon their lichened trees through the long golden silence of the long afternoons.

. . . . .

During her absence they managed without a regular servant, going for their meals to one of those nice half-timbered cafés that had lately sprung up in the town, or eating cold things at home. But Mrs. Kimber, the widow of Kimber, the former captain of the Lifeboat, came in every day 'to do the rooms': for Mrs. Smedhurst had retired, as it were, at the same time as her husband and, whatever might happen, did not intend to demean herself or to bring discredit upon her new friends by making the beds or dusting in person. Things went round the town so quickly, even without a servant in the house! People seemed to know exactly what was going on.

For about a fortnight after Ellen had gone home, everything appeared to be normal again. But this improvement was not long maintained. Though Mr. and Mrs. Smedhurst still continued to share their secret, heavy and interminable as it seemed, in silence, never, even now that their maid had brought it into the open, mentioning it to one another, yet both of them had obviously grown more nervous and, on days when the atmosphere was serene and plainly there was nothing to fear, would sit waiting, listening in a strained sort of way. Mr. Smedhurst, indeed, now gave a jump at any little thing that occurred. (His wife decided that soon she must take him away for a little holiday — only they could not very well leave Ellen alone in the house directly she came back. . . . The best thing they could do at present, in this lovely weather, was to go out a lot, benefit by the Newborough air.)

It was true : Mr. Smedhurst's nerves were very bad indeed. For so steady a man, he had become full of fancies. . . . For instance, though he could never prove it, he was sure that someone was moving his things and hiding his letters. Every single object on his desk seemed to be in a different place, or would vanish for a whole day and then turn up again as unexpectedly. On the lowest plane, if Mrs. Kimber were responsible — and it was wiser *not* to ask her —, this proved extremely annoying. Then, in the last few days, the creaking of the wicker chairs in his den had grown beyond bearing. Sometimes he could have sworn that he had not only heard, but almost *seen* people getting up out of them ; the hazy, blurred outline, filled in, as it were, clumsily, with tobacco smoke, of two squat and dumpy figures. . . . Of course, though it had seldom troubled him before, it must be his imagination. It *must* be, because there were no such things as ghosts. They did not exist. . . . And yet, uncomfortable ideas shaped themselves in his head ; for example, if chairs could for so long hold the impression of the living body that had sat in them — his own wicker chair was still creaking from the release of his weight — why should not a room, or a whole house, hold something of its former occupants, long after they had gone ? (Who had they been ? he wondered ; though he would rather not have known, would never ask for fear of hearing.) But all that whispering — the summer wind among the leaves, Mrs. Smedhurst had assured him —, all that stealthy coming and going, would make any man nervous ; even without the whistling.

For the whistling had begun once more, and had, further, grown so frequent that Mrs. Smedhurst, who had fallen a victim to the great Bridge epidemic which was sweeping the leisured classes of the country, scarcely dared to ask her friends in to make a four. (And she would lose ground if she failed to do so. . . . After all, what was the use of having a place of one's own — 'one's own', a mocking, high voice seemed to echo — if you could not entertain your friends in it?) And what she had feared would happen had now happened on several occasions. People *must* notice that something was wrong. They knew Ellen to be away, and of course they observed the trembling of Mr. Smedhurst's hand as he unhooked the mouth-piece, and the sort of false cheery manner he adopted when he replied — such non-committal answers, too, — though his face lost temporarily its accustomed colour. (He *had* to answer, he realised, *had* to pretend to reply, even to carry on a conversation, or it would look odder still.) Sometimes, when outsiders were present, the voice would not talk at all, there was just the whistle, and then only that high, meaningless laugh. It was very difficult, when that occurred, to make the conversation sound natural.

Or, again, the voice might be quite loquacious in an inconsequential way. Once, for instance, it had said a lot about people called *Pont*. ('The Ponts can't get *me* now,' it had remarked distinctly, and another time, 'Turn them out of your room; the Ponts are sitting in your room. Tell them to go.') More than once Mrs. Manning-Tutthorne had asked, point-blank, who was at the other end, speaking to Mr. Smedhurst, and Mrs. Smedhurst had found herself obliged to invent a lie, so as to disguise the disreputable truth.

'It's a friend of ours upstairs, dear,' she had said; 'she's an invalid. You've never met her. She's spending a little time with us, so as to get the Newborough air.' Another time, when the Major had demanded who it might be, she had pretended it was a temporary servant asking for instructions.

'By Gad, madam,' he had replied, 'I wouldn't let a servant of mine, temporary or not, whistle for Mrs. Manning-Tutthorne in that way! Downright impudence, I call it!'

The Catterwicks, too, were observant. One really hot day Mrs. Catterwick shivered in the drawing-room and had said how singular it was that this house should be so cold in hot weather. She had harped on it with curious insistence, as if she suspected something. . . . But what could you do? Mrs. Smedhurst asked herself. You could not sit by yourself all day — or be out the whole time, for that made you nervous of returning. You began to dread the moment of arriving at the gate.

The fact was that they had come to hate the tubes which had once — and how long ago it seemed ! — appeared to them as such a delightful convenience. When alone in the house, they would no longer answer — at least, they would try not to answer — the instrument. But it exercised upon them a kind of fascination. Moreover, often if they failed to reply, a little vase, or some object they valued, would fall down and be smashed, or Mrs. Smedhurst's thimble, even, be swept off the table by her side, as she sat mending, or embroidering the centre for a cushion cover. . . . Perhaps it was best to give way to the thing, to humour it —, and yet this method was not always successful either, since if they did not respond the very moment that the instrument sounded, it would often refuse to speak and just go on whistling whenever it was replaced.

Then the manifestations began to alter their character. Mrs. Smedhurst, though she had not been conscious of it before, grew to dislike sitting in the drawing-room, because of the incessant creaking of those wicker chairs of which she had been so proud. Probably, she said to herself for her own comfort, they had always done it, or it might be due to the weather ; a fall in the temperature, perhaps. But her own arguments did not convince her. Often, too, she heard whisperings outside in the large, cold passage, and when at last, in desperation, she would tiptoe to the door and fling it open, nobody would be there. The hall was empty, as she had known it would be, though the whispers had only stopped at the very moment she had opened the door and had started again as soon as she had shut it. . . . What could they be saying so secretively ? what could they be plotting, or have been plotting in the past ? was it something fresh or something that had taken place long ago ? . . . Her heart told her they were plotting.

So far, her husband and she had slept well, but now, two nights running, they were woken up by the sound of thuds and moans, as if someone were being attacked upstairs in Ellen's room, and then by a loud screaming. . . . Nothing there, either, for Mr. Smedhurst went up to look. . . . It must be rats — though Mrs. Smedhurst had never seen a sign of them —, they told each other ; rats made such strange scuffling sounds. It must be the wind howling. It *must* be. (But how suddenly the wind had swept down on this soundless summer night.)

After that, the darkness of the long, long nights became less active, more stealthy. It was silly to be nervous like that, but sleep was impossible, there was an inexplicable sense of expectation and tautness in the air ; no blows or moans, only all night the padding of too quiet feet, the clink or crack of little objects that had been moved, often in the room itself, the restrained, unbearable stir of voices hushed for some purpose, the feeling that something — something appalling — was in preparation behind the velvety unfathomable silence. And if you turned on the light, it was as though you had stopped a play that was in progress by blundering on to the stage.

Then, just as the misery of this life at Bellingham House had overwhelmed them altogether, and they had made up their minds, each of them, that they must face the mystery, discuss it together, and take the decision to leave and find another home, the disturbances stopped. The atmosphere in the house cleared, became ordinary, so that it could no longer be recognised as the same place. During the hours of August sunshine, when a honey-coloured haze lay on sea and land, the whole of the experiences through which they had passed appeared to be remote, silly, impossible, though on certain nights their fears returned, for a short while and in a diminished form. But they were able once more to sleep, and thus, in comparative peace, the days passed quickly.

. . . . .

Mrs. Kimber had been so careless, letting things slip out of her hand, that Mr. and Mrs. Smedhurst were quite glad she was leaving the next day. You could say what you liked about Ellen, but she was a well-trained servant. It would be a treat to see her about the place again. . . . Mrs. Smedhurst felt so tired herself that she was sure that she and Mr. Smedhurst ought to go away soon. In spite of her thriftiness, she decided to try and find another good servant temporarily to keep Ellen company, and then Mr. Smedhurst and herself could take a holiday. You see, it was important to get their nerves right, for if it leaked out that they could not sleep there and had become 'nervy', people might guess there was something wrong with the house and, if they were even obliged to sell it, they might then lose on the transaction; a shame it would be, such a fine, well-built residence; (that was the word, *residence*). Or their friends might even think them mad. 'Ghosts, indeed!' she could imagine, could almost hear, how Major Manning-Tutthorne would pronounce the words. The very curl of his white moustache by itself would announce that, to his way of thinking, well-bred people did not behave in such a manner, running away like little children from a dark corner! It was not done.

On the other hand, going away for a holiday was, most emphatically, 'done'. She might not know much of fashionable ways, but she knew that. Indeed 'a change of air' would add to, rather than diminish, local prestige; say, first ten days at Hindhead, with walks over the moors and excursions to that extraordinary 'Devil's Punch-Bowl' — she would never forget it —, and then a few good shows in London. . . . The train service from Newborough was wonderful; one ought to make more use of it. A change, that was what they needed to put an end to such fancies. But they had better not go away before the Newborough Cricket Festival, which was due to open now in a few days. Mr. Smedhurst always looked forward to it so much and, besides, there was going to be a great Cricket Ball in the Hotel Superb. They said it would be a lovely sight and she had persuaded her husband, in spite of the expense, to take tickets, so that they could watch it for an hour or two and have supper. (One must have a little amusement; it took one out of oneself.) Meanwhile, it was necessary to make the best of things, go out a great deal and enjoy the air, and the sense, too, of mounting excitement which always accompanied the coming of the Cricket Festival. In this perfect weather, with a healthy crispness in the air and the golden clouds of sunshine lying over the world, altering every distance and every prospect, lengthening or foreshortening it, there was a charm which Mrs. Smedhurst could not define. And the town was 'filling up', not with those horrid trippers — their August orgy was nearly over, and on the sands a certain flaccidity, a failure of the communal effort to enjoy, already manifested itself — but with nice, substantial persons in flannel suits and panamas and the esoteric striped ties of the cricket world, and with women neatly dressed in tweeds, who sat all day long waiting for the approaching carnival round the canopied doorways of the chief hotels. And Major Manning-Tutthorne said it was difficult to recognise the Club as the same place, full as full now, and always at least one member with his eye clapped to the telescope in the bow window.

So, husband and wife clung to the exterior world, hoping that its glare would blind them to other vibrations. Yet they were not cowardly. Moreover, Mr. Smedhurst, in spite of his ordinary and unimaginative outlook, and Mrs. Smedhurst, in spite of her respect for public opinion, were, both of them, by nature kind and conscientious. When, therefore, her husband announced that he proposed to pass the night in Ellen's room upstairs, in order to be able, if necessary, to assure her, when she returned the next day, that he had slept there and found nothing wrong with it, Mrs. Smedhurst made no objection, though she did not much relish the idea of being alone in their big room for the whole night. . . . Still, things had been quiet for the last ten days or so, the house seemed all right at present. And in fact, nothing occurred to disturb her and she slept better than of late.

Mr. Smedhurst's night began well too. He went upstairs about eleven, said good-night to Mrs. Smedhurst, undressed, and fell asleep almost immediately. He remembered nothing more until he woke to find himself upon his feet, standing somewhere in the uncharted darkness of a strange room. . . . For a moment he could not, try as he might, recollect where he was. . . . Then it came back to him. So unusual was the experience that, though startled and alarmed, too, by the curious atmosphere prevailing around him, he did not have much time for fear. Consciousness of danger — which, afterwards, he could not explain to himself — overwhelmed every other sensation. He must reach the switch at once and turn on the light. Groping, he stretched out his arm, and discovered that he was quite near, almost touching, a wall. Moving his hand along, he scraped the edge of a finger against something. He felt it; a large nail, he perceived. But it was no helping guide to him through the blackness, for he could not remember ever having seen it in the day-time, though it seemed now — as everything does in the darkness — large enough to have attracted anyone's attention. Presently, however, he touched the edge of a frame, and since there was only one picture hanging in the room, he now knew where he was and — albeit the process appeared, in the suspense he was enduring, to occupy a full hour or more — soon attained the door and turned on the light.

Yet at first the flooding illumination from the naked bulb did not help him, afforded no greater sense of security. He recoiled from the brilliance of it as much as formerly he had wanted to escape from the darkness. It exposed him, he felt, like an animal out of its burrow, to eyes he could not see. He hated this room; something was wrong with it, something mad and something cruel. Nevertheless, it was empty, superficially in order. He could not tell the right time, for his watch, he now noticed, had stopped just before two o'clock — though he was sure he had wound it up before going to bed. (It could not, he thought, have stopped long, however.) But, notwithstanding that everything was so normal outwardly, the more he looked back on what had occurred, the more uneasy Mr. Smedhurst became. After all, he had never been a sleepwalker. And at the back of his mind, something remained; he tried to summon it up, to drag it up forward from the troubled recession of his dreams — a dim, confused memory of being hauled out of his bed and propelled towards the wall.

Howbeit, as the minutes drew out, and the sleep he had left in so peculiar a manner became further away, his fears began to be allayed. Now that his eyes had grown accustomed to the light, everything was ordinary again with no undercurrent to it. Almost, he was ashamed of himself. It just showed what nerves would do, for he supposed he must have been — well, nervous, all the previous evening, and his effort not to show it had only made matters worse. (He went back to examine the nail on which he had caught his hand; a nail stouter than usual and driven well into the wall, about a foot above his head. . . . It was strange that he had not noticed it before, it was so prominent.) No, he did not feel nervous any longer, only relieved for some reason or other to be awake, to be alive. He smoked a cigarette — how delightful to be *able* to smoke a cigarette! —, then returned to bed and read a magazine and dozed, with the light on, until dawn; when he fell into a profound and delicious sleep until Mrs. Kimber called him.

The next morning his emotions of the night before and its incidents seemed merely foolish. Why spoil such a lovely day

— it was the first of September and one of the best days he ever remembered — by thinking about things; why spoil it for Mrs. Smedhurst by confiding in her the long rigmarole of his adventures? After all, they amounted to nothing. So let Mrs. Smedhurst and himself enjoy, instead, the sparkle of the golden air, the indescribable cleanliness of air and light which this northern town manifested on such days as this — though, indeed, a day such as this was rare, even here, in dear old Newborough. Mr. Smedhurst's heart warmed to the place. He loved it, and was looking forward with the utmost eagerness to the Cricket Festival, which would open the day after to-morrow. Already, in his mind's ear, he could perceive the dull wooden response of the bat to the ball, the eager hum of interest from the deck-chairs, the roars and cries of delight or rage from the crowded tiers of seats at the back; could see, in his mind's eye, the enormous tents of the President and of the various cricketing clubs, the confetti-like gaiety of the onlookers, and the shifting score on the blackboards, let, like eyes, into the contorted scarlet pavilion. In the face of real things, such as cricket, how fantastic the events of last night seemed! Besides, reaction had set in; now being at peace with the world, he could not bear to upset anyone. He could see that Mrs. Smedhurst had been worrying lately, so why disturb her further? How could he, for instance, tell her of anything so ridiculous as the incident of the nail? He could not; he resolved, therefore, not to say anything. And, having made this decision, he saw it was impossible, when he had not told his own wife, to say anything about it to Ellen either.

Thus when, after Mr. and Mrs. Smedhurst returned from an excellent dinner — no, luncheon — at a café on the West Cliff to find that Ellen had made her appearance, Mr. Smedhurst felt still more sure of the correctness of the line he was taking, and contented himself with telling Ellen, in front of Mrs. Smedhurst, that he had slept the previous night in her room and had found it quite all right. (Subsequently, he blamed himself bitterly for this 'deception'; he ought to have told his wife and sought her advice; he ought, further, to have possessed the courage of his own instincts, and to have ordered Ellen not to sleep in that particular room again.)

For her part, Ellen had been restored by her holiday and was glad to be back in Bellingham House. The pay, nineteen shillings a week, was good, and she liked Mr. and Mrs. Smedhurst. In rather a shamefaced manner she admitted that she had quite overcome her silly fancies. She must have been tired, she supposed, what with getting the house ready, and one thing and another. But it should not happen again, she promised them that. . . .

'And you look tired, too, moom,' she added. 'It must be the air, like what you said.' (Mrs. Smedhurst was glad the girl had proved so sensible; that was just it. Mr. Smedhurst and herself would be all the better, too, for a change of air.)

. . . . .

That night, as she foretold, Ellen was not in the least nervous. She got out of bed to turn out the light, and returned through the darkness to its shelter without qualm. . . . And Mr. and Mrs. Smedhurst also felt the safer because she was in the house.

All the same, Mrs. Smedhurst did not like the 'feel' of the place that evening, and was glad Mr. Smedhurst was sleeping in her room. There was something odd about it. For example, though it was so late in the summer, and the air, in spite of its Newborough freshness, was warm, warmed through by an uncommonly hot season, she found it so chilly in her bedroom that she was obliged to ask Mr. Smedhurst to take an extra blanket out of the cupboard and put it on the bed. . . . She must not 'let herself go', she reflected, as she lay there waiting for Mr. Smedhurst to rejoin her. It would never do. So, in order to avoid this process of disintegration, she concentrated upon pleasant things, thought how glad she was that Mr. Smedhurst was looking forward so enthusiastically to the Newborough Cricket Festival — it would keep him occupied — and meditated upon the perfection of Church Parade two mornings before. . . . It had been lovely. . . . Then she dwelt on how comfortable they would be, now that they had seen the last of Mrs. Kimber. . . . It was a blessing, too, to have a third person in the house again.

But that took her back; why, she asked herself, should it be such a relief? In itself that was an admission that something was wrong, must be *wrong*. . . . The lurking sense of uneasiness returned; she fixed her attention, therefore, upon the details, so satisfactory in their outer aspect, of her big bedroom. (Material objects, she must have felt, were of help in tethering her to the ordinary world of which she was an inhabitant.) She appraised the comfort, beauty, solidity of the various fixtures and pieces of furniture. . . . And then, how bright the room was, how airy! (A little *too* airy, perhaps, too large; in front of the windows the curtains stirred in a cold strange breeze that they alone caught in this stillness. . . . How quiet Mr. Smedhurst was, next door!) Such a fine, bright room. The brass bedstead looked splendid, she said to herself, desperately clinging to the supports she knew. (She must keep a hold on herself.) It presented such a dainty appearance with its cover — over the central rails — of quilted, tinned-salmon pink, embroidered with mauve chrysanthemums, and with the brass knobs catching the light. (There was no need to be frightened: Mr. Smedhurst would be here in a moment.) And the big, ivory-painted, crescent-shaped dressing-table, with the glass top and electricity attached to the mirror, was just what she had always longed for. It was so — well, so convenient, like much else in the house; 'Like those speaking-tubes, for instance', another voice, it seemed almost, said to her. (Why *must* her mind revert to such things? How stupid of her to think of them! Would Mr. Smedhurst *never* come in? She called him but he did not hear.) Yes, that dressing-table was ideal! How she had longed for one, nearly every day during the last ten years. . . . What happy years those last, just before Mr. Smedhurst's retirement, had been, with the vision gradually turning into reality before their eyes.

As she drew further back into those days, things became better, more reassuring. And now, at last, Mr. Smedhurst entered, in a pair of new pyjamas (he had always worn a night-shirt until he came to live in Newborough).

'I thought you'd never finish undressing, Ernest,' she reproached him.

'Why, it's only just eleven,' he said. 'I wasn't more than ten minutes.'

Mr. Smedhurst turned out the light, and before long they were both snoring in quiet, contented counterpoint.

. . . . .

Suddenly — it was difficult to tell how long they had been asleep — something woke them. . . . What was it? . . A heavy silence ensued of a few seconds' duration, and then a whistle. The speaking-tube!

Mr. Smedhurst lumbered out of bed and switched on the light as quickly as possible. They looked at each other. . . . This was new. Hitherto, the whistle had not been blown during the night. Neither spoke, but both of them understood that it would be better to answer, to try and find out what was wanted or what was amiss. Mr. Smedhurst approached the coiled instrument carefully, as though it were a serpent, unhooked it. . . . The loud and prolonged scream that reached him down it was almost a word; it seemed to be trying to form the word 'Help!' An exclamation, at any rate, with an immense urgency implicit in it. So loud was it, that it jarred the air of the whole room, and Mrs. Smedhurst, still in bed, plainly heard it. . . . Then nothing more . . . nothing.

'What is it, what is it?' Mr. Smedhurst demanded, but there was nothing now except this seemingly interminable and agonising silence. . . . 'What is it, what is it?' he implored.

Then, at last, a voice spoke a few words; that high-pitched and childish voice he had come so much to dread. But its bitter, senseless tones had now acquired a curious and despairing quietness.

'. . . Mad . . . mad and useless . . . unwanted. . . . But now it's someone else. Come up! Come up!'

'I think I'd better go upstairs, dear,' Mr. Smedhurst said timidly.

'Not without me, Ernest,' Mrs. Smedhurst answered, putting on her dressing-gown. And he did not try to dissuade her.

He looked at his watch. It was just two o'clock. . . . Then, seizing the poker — though everything seemed very quiet in the house, not a sound overhead — they advanced into the passage, Mr. Smedhurst going first, and crept upstairs by the light from their bedroom door, which they left open behind them. They did not turn on the switch at the top of the stairs, outside Ellen's room, because they could tell by the golden chinks between the door and its frame that the light was on in her room. . . . Still not a sound. . . . Mr. Smedhurst turned the handle softly. . . . The bed was empty; that was the first thing they noticed, no sign of anyone. . . . Then by the brilliant illumination of the one naked bulb, they saw Ellen, looking very lonely in this enormous room. She was sitting upon the floor, against the wall by the door, and with her back to it, in a curiously listless attitude. Her legs were stretched in front of her, her arms lay limp at her side. Her round, bucolic eyes were wide open in a fixed and glassy stare, and her neck was creased into bulges of flesh by the cord of her dressing-gown, wound about it and secured tightly to a nail on the wall.

. . . . .

Medical evidence at the inquest proved, however, that the cause of death was not suffocation, due to hanging, but heart-failure from shock. The noose was not tight enough to have killed her. If, as was plain, she had just been about to hang herself, death had intervened in another manner, and she must have collapsed in the posture in which Mr. and Mrs. Smedhurst had found her. There was no indication of the nature of the shock she had received, but her body showed bruises on it, inflicted apparently very shortly before her death. . . . The Coroner, commenting on the facts, found them rather difficult to reconcile, but said two things stood out: that Ellen Pycroft was a very highly strung, nervous girl, and that death had been due to natural causes, as the jury had found. No blame, he added, attached to Mr. and Mrs. Smedhurst.

Soon Bellingham House stood empty again, to be let or sold — and perhaps stands empty to this day —, the windows dead, like the eyes of a corpse, even though it may be that a mysterious life, or reflection of life, still proceeded behind them. And sometimes, when I was a boy and obliged to go through The Dale on a winter day, when the grey clouds scudded only just over the house-tops and the rooks' nests swayed wildly in the north wind, which whistled at every angle of every building, I would notice how the passers-by seemed to hurry on the faster in the wind's teeth for the sight of its cold and derelict desolation. And at night, it was said, the wind howled and screamed and whistled round the corners of the house with a particular vehemence. There always seemed to be wind there, even on fine days. . . . There was always the wind.

FRIENDSHIP'S DUE

(To Muriel Draper)

Some have for wits, and then for poets passed,
Turned critics next, and proved plain fools at last.
—Alexander Pope

It was on a particularly crystalline morning in the early spring, after street and square had been cleansed for a while of their flowing smoke-draperies by the splashing and tintinnabulation of a hundred country-scented showers, that I was first enabled — compelled even — to observe the hero of this story. The omnibus, empty save for myself, glided smoothly on its way, and from the level of the middle branches flung out by the fine old trees that still linger in the lower part of King's Road, Chelsea — old trees, though edged now with fresh green lacings, on which the distilled moisture glistened like so many fragments of crystal, echoing back the various hard lights refracted by the wall-topping of broken glass — I could watch the antics of my kind.

Suddenly there sounded a muddled hurricane of hurrying, rather clumsy, feet; but to my surprise only one person, to whom, as to Jove, these thunderbolts must have belonged, was precipitated on to the seat opposite as the omnibus sailed, red and proud as a turkey-cock, round the corner. Thus were we isolated on our noisy moving trestle, set half-way between the tree-tops and the ant-like world below. My fellow-passenger enjoyed the fresh air, obviously; yet it seemed somehow as if he regretted the absence of the larger, more appreciative audience which, at this time of the morning, he had the right to expect. Was he, then, with his obvious love of public notice, an actor? In any case he did not look like a prosperous one, but undoubtedly there lurked in his eyes the expectation that he would be recognised. In a sense he resembled an old-fashioned player. He possessed, superlatively, that air of dominion by which it is possible to single out the stage favourite — and even more, perhaps, the stage failure.

Yet though his appearance was highly accentuated, it was hardly sufficiently so for an actor; he was like an old 'But-me-no-buts' ranter, seen through the minimising glass of a *Punch* drawing. Still, if he belonged to the stage, he was a ranter, and not a naturalistic-whimsical-charm-schooler.

His face was heavy; not fat, but heavily boned. Yellowish in colour, it seemed to be supported on the two sharp points of a high white collar — higher in front than at the back — round which was twice wound a large black tie. This apparatus helped to define the prominent nose and protuberant mouth which, when open, displayed strong bony teeth that suggested a Scottish origin. His hair, black and lank, flowed a little over the back of his worn fur collar, while in the buttonhole of the stylised but anciently cut blue-cloth coat he affected sprouted that small bunch of faded violets that was, in truth, the freshest thing about him. A dandified cane was held in one hand, and with the ochreous black-tipped fingers of the other he was continually rattling and scratching the dull-gilt interior of a large silver cigarette-case, which lay open on his knees, taking out a cigarette, lighting it, and then throwing it away. These convolutions, obviously, were intended either to draw attention to himself, or by their familiarity to secure his recognition from others better informed than myself as to the genius of the day. Could it be, he hoped I was thinking, could it be the famous man-of-letters — the poet? . . . But, unfortunately, my mind had wandered along the wrong track, and I was busily scanning my memory for the faces of actors in the old Lyceum dramas.

How, in any case, could he have expected me to think of him, in these days and without a knowledge of his identity, as a poet? It would have been a survival almost too interesting and absorbing . . . for though I have known many poets (and already wish that such had not been my privilege) I have never encountered one by whose face could be distinguished his calling. Well-shaven, clean, and short-haired, the poet of today resembles a prosperous business man; but, and I ought to have recognised it, here was that unique Victorian survival, 'the poet's brow'! Under the grey felt hat, black-banded, bony ridges and angular wrinkles dwindled down from beneath the greasy locks to an almost horse-like nose. Perhaps, if my mind had not been otherwise occupied, I might, on the strength of nose, teeth and hair, have diagnosed a critic — but never should I have dared to hope for a poet — for I have seen many decorative critics with curly hair, pince-nez and an earnest look. But, as I afterwards discovered, this was Ferdinand H. McCulloch, a former writer of verse, and a critic who is still allowed to thunder denunciations of modern poetry in various twopenny-weekly or halfpenny-daily papers.

Now because the hero of this tragi-comedy is a critic (but remember that he is a poet as well), and even though I have been so old-fashioned as to head my sermon with a text (an instinct dormant in the right hand of every author of our Puritan race), it must not be concluded that I am so antiquated as to indulge in any attempt at throwing the slightest shadow of ridicule upon the critical calling. That I leave to the poets who have gone before me; for such an attempt at it on my part would be ungenteel, unnecessary and injudicious, insomuch as I am here on my trial, and to throw a boot at the jury, however unbiased they may wish to appear, would be an act little calculated to prejudice them in my favour. Nor, perhaps, is the quotation that precedes this story altogether apposite, for in this serious age of co-ordination and psychoanalysis no wit would ever be taken for a poet, while the link between humour and criticism appears to be even more frail — only to be found, in fact, in the eye of the watching poet. For, as our text shows, and this is my excuse for embroidering such a theme, it has long been the custom of poets to watch with interest the critical hoop-revolving of their span — a span which this hoop-revolving has so often helped to shorten.

When an epigram becomes a platitude (the Hell to which all epigrams are eventually condemned) the truth is no longer in it; and that critics are but disappointed poets has long been a platitude. In these days, on the contrary, they are the only satisfied ones, able both to confer the cake and then, subsequently, eat it themselves. Curiously enough, too, though the critic is popularly supposed to have a more logical mind, to wield a more consistent pen than the poet's, it is a fact that while critical opinion is still divided as to the comparative merits of our more famous English bards, the judgment of the latter as to the critical opinion of their day appears to have been nearly identical. Could a written testimonial be obtained from the shades of, let us say, Dryden, Pope, Coleridge, Gray,

Keats, Wordsworth, Shelley, Byron, Swinburne, and from their heirs, the worst-sellers of today, it is probable that though the words would differ with the individual, the purport which this varying language would serve to illumine, or perhaps for the sake of decency to obscure, would be found on examination to be remarkably alike in every case. Some poets have even gone so far as to pretend that there must be more than a casual connection between the decay of poetry, which criticism has from its birth detected, and that rise of the professional critic which was apparently coincident with this disintegration. But, for myself, I prefer to think that this gradual falling-away of the English Muse is due to the fact that the better, nobler, more serious minds among us are tempted from the profession of poetry alone towards the higher, more lucrative one of journalism; for, as many critics have themselves informed us lately and in print, their contribution to literature is, in reality, one of more importance than that of the creative mind, whether poet's or prose-writer's — the shadow more lasting than the substance, the parasite more interesting and enduring than the victim on which it thrives! Then, too, one has to live. . . . Reviewing, compared with the profession of poetry, is a well-paid one; and, as for that, the wielding of a critical pen need not prevent an occasional 'banging of the tins' (i.e. TREES — BREEZE; WOOD — GOOD — GOD; LARK — HARK; WIND — SPIN'D — BLIND), provided that it is a simple one, and may, indeed, procure for that music a more favourable reception than it would otherwise be awarded.

No one then, it is established, has a greater respect for the professional critic than the writer of this homily — because for a man to surrender the unravelling of his own mind and soul (unless these be tedious ones) in order to tear off the draperies concealing those of other people must be an act of noble altruism and Christian abnegation. And, to make a personal confession, let it be recorded that it is impossible to admire more than I do the weekly pursuit of Dostoieffsky and Tchekhoff through the Fourth Dimension conducted by the Ariel-like mind of Mr. Muddleton Moral; while after Mr. Jack Daw's revelation of the dormant beauties in the verse of Mrs. Hemans, I, too, can only cry 'Excelsior!' and am the more prepared for the perception of these same qualities in his own — at first sight — strangely different subject-poems, *Soccer* and *The Slaughter-*

House. Excelsior, indeed! For when these distinguished critics, very busy men, find time to use the antiquated medium of verse, yet never fail in a twice-weekly-and-once-on-Sunday donative of buns and ginger-beer to their protégés, or even an occasional laurel for the fallen (from whom no rivalry need be feared), my admiration knows no bounds.

If, then, this story is headed with a text, it is because that unpleasant and needlessly spiteful couplet, though no doubt useless as a generalisation, helps to explain something in this particular instance. For though the suicide of a minor poet would, as being an example of cause-and-effect, excite little interest, to poets the suicide of a critic — even his attempted self-destruction — would be a matter for wonder. The critic, in the exercise of his calling, commits a thousand attempts, successful or unsuccessful, at literary murder, and goes unpunished; yet if he were to attempt his own death — and fail — he would be tried, and possibly punished, for endeavouring to take his own life. And how curious is the law's accusation of a man for attempting suicide, when obviously his crime (except in cases of incurable disease) must be, not his failure to die but the confession of his failure to live, which is what attempted suicide amounts to! But of this a man is never accused, for this never punished.

. . . . .

Even as late as the year 1907 the name of Ferdinand H. McCulloch was one to conjure with in the more serious salons of West Hampstead. His reign had then lasted about ten years. For it was in the late nineties, only a few years before the armed might of the Great Transvaal Republic threw down its gauntlet to the people of these little islands, that our hero, already and always his own impresario, made his bow to the London public. He was then about thirty years of age, and but recently escaped from — though this was a secret hidden even from his appointed biographer — Ulster! There he had received a very Orange upbringing at the hands of three gaunt, rigorous maiden aunts, for his father, a clergyman, had died before Ferdinand could remember him, and his mother had married again. For this sin against the Victorian moral code the Misses McCulloch had never forgiven her; and devoted to the memory of their late brother, they succeeded in wresting the infant from her (she did not, in reality, seem very unwilling to part with him), and then brought him up in the same stern family tradition that had made themselves and their brother what they were. But Ferdinand, and this was in his favour, proved a difficult child. Nothing could be done with him. The Church, even, was out of the question. But he must earn his own living; so, as a very young man, a boy even, he scraped together a few pounds by writing what, we believe, are technically known as 'fashionable pars' for the Belfast papers. It cannot be said that the Misses McCulloch approved of this; but it brought in a little money and kept him out of mischief. Ferdinand, for his part, was thoroughly frightened of his aunts, and would have welcomed anything that took him out of their clutches. Soon the glamour of London and of the escape it meant cast its spell on him, and he began to dream of the city he had never seen. Latterly he had been reading the lives of great men — an interesting study, no doubt, but one perilous for youth, and still more fraught with danger for the elders of the house. The life of Michelangelo, for example, is responsible for more trouble between budding artist and — if such a person still exists — art patron than is imaginable. In that school it is that the Slade student learns with surprising ease the importance, not of being an artist, which is, after all, the fact that really matters about Michelangelo, but of being disagreeable, grasping and rude. Similarly, lives of Napoleon and Lord Byron have unforeseen and deplorable consequences; while we are told that every dirty and uncouth versifier at the universities, should he occasionally get a little drunk, excuses it by announcing that he is the reincarnation of Verlaine — or (even at this date!) of Dowson! Luckily Ferdinand had got no further than the Borgias, Michelangelo, Napoleon and Byron. Still, he was determined to be a great man, perhaps more of a Byron than a Bonaparte; and for the accomplishment of this design he must be daring and a little wicked. How, then, was he to do it? For though it is easy to be unpleasant anywhere, it is difficult to be a Borgia in Belfast. What is more, the gaunt and triple-headed spectre of the Misses McCulloch guarded, like Cerberus, the mouth of any possible Hell, ferociously barking. There was, of course, only one thing to be done — to escape to London as soon as he found a chance of doing so. After that it would be easy. Only one obstacle would then interpose between Ferdinand and Lord Byron — the writing of verse, and this was an impediment he was determined to overcome.

It must be five years before we meet Ferdinand again; five years must elapse between his escape and his transfiguration.

In those days two traditions strove and clashed together in the drawing-rooms of artistic ladies, for the shadow of the Celtic twilight, destined later to attain the density of a London fog, already lay heavy on the suburbs, and the Voice of Cuchulain was uplifted in Liberty's Drapery Department, or wailed through Soho; while older, but competing with it, although perhaps already a little losing ground, was the influence of Ernest Dowson. In many gatherings of 'modern young people' the mist wafted from the Land of Heart's Desire would be rent in twain, as an even then slightly old-fashioned 'advanced' young woman would rise to thunder 'Cynara', or a romantic-looking young undergraduate from Oxford would proclaim, and reiterate, that he had been faithful to the lady in his own fashion. Alas! these things are altered: the daughter of the 'advanced' young woman, her hair cut short like a pony's mane, now plays the more intricate game of complex-and-inhibition with the romantic young man's son (who, like all the young men of today, has a post on the League of Nations), and the leaden weight of *The London Mercury* now rests on those slender tables upon which had once been laid the grotesque beauty of Beardsley's drawings.

In this mingled atmosphere of a wet-Sunday-afternoon on the Irish Lakes and Greek Passion, which we have attempted to outline, out of the harder, more material light that beats upon the city-ways of Belfast, stepped Mr. Ferdinand McCulloch. But it was a Ferdinand transfigured, for like a chameleon he had absorbed both the colour and tone of his new surroundings — and had already composed numerous sets of verses! The clean, callow, tweed-clad, large-boned, Ulster-mouthed boy had flowered into what in those days was known as a 'Real Bohemian', a dashing yet dreamy-eyed figure, full of psychic qualities and the charm of the Southern-Irish people. He sported now, for the first time, that bunch of violets to which he still clings; his black hair became lank and matted, his finger-nails were allowed to grow longer, while his formerly harsh voice became almost too soft and dove-like, for he had developed what he yet considers to be a very attractive brogue. Ulster, with its business habits, worldly outlook, and stern Puritanism, he placed behind him, becoming — or rather pretending that he had always been — Catholic, Celtic, and sometimes, we regret to say, a little Twilight. For in the very advanced taverns, like caves, which he frequented, it was necessary occasionally, for the sake of his reputation, to plunge through the purple mists of wine. After midnight he could sometimes be seen stumbling out of his cave, like Caliban, his hair tousled, his feet a little uncertain. Once too (and it made him a memorable figure) McCulloch met Dowson in a cab-shelter. It is true that the latter poet did not pay much attention to him, hardly, indeed, appeared to see him; but it gave our hero an aura, created a legend that clung, so that years afterwards, as with head held up, and a winsome smile hung across the protuberant cavity of his mouth, he entered a room, there would be a rustling whisper, 'You know . . . the friend of Dowson's!'

Though McCulloch was not a clever man — in the sense that few ideas visited him — yet his hold on one, when once he had grasped it, was singularly tenacious. Quite early in his career he managed to pin down one principle of success — that lesson about which we heard so much, twenty years later, from the weekly preachers in Sunday papers — the VALUE of CO-OPERATION and UNITY. It will be remembered by those who succeeded in living through the 'Great War', that our Best Minds, in the course of 'giving one furiously to think', founding bond-clubs, or 'exploring avenues', announced constantly that the war had not been fought in vain if we learnt the 'Value of Co-operation' — a lesson, it appeared, well worth the losing of a few hundred thousand lives. There would be no more strikes or disturbances; the workman, in the sacred cause of unity, would always give way; and a maypole and morris dance would flourish once more in the congenial atmosphere of Sheffield, Birmingham, and Manchester. Well, McCulloch realised the value of co-operation and unity at an early date; and it was his own discovery. In fact, he formed what would now be known — according to whether you liked or disliked its members — as 'an interesting little group of thinkers', or a 'clique'. There is, by the way, I believe, supposed to be something peculiarly disgraceful about a 'clique' — and if a book by someone you dislike happens to be well received, you should invariably describe its success as being the work of a 'little clique'. Ferdinand's 'clique' was a small one, consisting, as it did, of three members. For the other two he chose, wisely, Arthur Savage Beardsall, an amiable minor poet, of rather bad health, a little real talent, and a certain slapdash facility combined with an admirable aptitude for posing, and T. W. Frendly, a poor but intensely energetic little Cockney journalist. In appearance Beardsall was slight, short and bearded — the dark beard disguising his want of chin and look of ill-health — and Frendly, with his beady little eyes, was dapper, small and sharp as a sparrow, while his voice would trail off unexpectedly into a high Cockney accent. His simple mind was intensely impressed with the genius of his two companions, and he reserved all his energy for the preaching of their gospel. In this association of three friends his was the humble part; he would listen admiringly, collect their epigrams and sayings, repeat them on every occasion, learn their poems by heart, recite them, and generally do an immense amount of clique and claque work. He might be described, indeed, as their boom-companion.

Beardsall, McCulloch and Frendly became inseparable; they would lunch together, dine together, and toward the end of an evening get a little drunk together. They would write, even when seeing each other every day, 'Posterity-letters'* to the other members of their clique — or rather Beardsall or McCulloch would write them to Frendly, whom they had tacitly appointed as their biographer.

Each of the three would quote, praise, imitate, caricature the two others, and finally write articles about their work, though to get either the former or the latter writings printed, it was first necessary for a review — expensive but short-lived — to be started by the richer members of their as yet limited circle of admirers. For gradually there formed round this nucleus an outer circle of Admirers of the Misunderstood. The

* Letters written by minor poets for posthumous publication to friends whom they can trust to print them. For this purpose should be chosen a rather old, distinguished critic, who will at once understand what is wanted and whose position guarantees that after his death (which, with any luck, cannot be far distant) all the letters he has put away will be published by a literary executor, or a still younger minor poet, who can be depended upon to treasure the letters, and publish them subsequently for the sake of his own importance.

leaders of it, who lent a little feminine grace to the gatherings, were Mrs. Stilpepper and Miss Ellen Durban. Juliet Stilpepper, small, dark and rather pretty, known among her friends for the charm of her speaking voice and laughter, was the wife of that well-known artist whose problem picture at the Academy in 1897, depicting a woman in leg-of-mutton sleeves and a straw hat, kneeling down on a sandy beach, her face wet with tears, with one hand pointing to an enormous orang-outang, the other to a whale spouting water — the whole composition entitled *The Mother of the Gracchi* — caused such a sensation. Her *salon* was famous throughout Hampstead. Within the hospitable red-brick house one would meet prominent exponents of Woman's Rights (not yet become notorious as Suffragettes), a few Fabians, many Irish and neo-Greek poets, a few lesser stage celebrities, and, later on, numerous hysterical admirers of Mr. Stephen Phillips. Between the latter and McCulloch's group there was an incessant, deadly warfare. But in these battles their hostess always gave her valuable aid to the three friends; for if they prospered, how much the greater would be her credit for discovering them. It was a gamble — an outside chance; but she meant to win. This, then, was the chief platform upon which our three characters disported themselves before an appreciative audience of young ladies shod in sandals, and crowned with dusty golden hair, whose curving necks still showed a trace of the gradually disappearing Pre-Raphaelite goitre. To this latter class belonged their other chief supporter, Ellen Durban, whose sandals betrayed her as one of the first, last — and, alas, least successful — of classical dancers.

Juliet Stilpepper and Ellen Durban, the earliest and most fervent disciples of the three friends, soon began to feel that their faith had been justified; for the clique began to arrive at a certain importance. Beardsall's small, easy, meretricious talent was winning him a wider recognition — shedding even on the other two a certain lustre, which at the time could not be distinguished as a borrowed radiance, but appeared to emanate from themselves. This recognition was just enough to make the clique a matter of wonder, but not sufficient to deprive its members of their prerogative of feeling ill-used, neglected and misunderstood; while it seldom occurred to them that, had they really been good poets, they would be objects, not of interest, but of ridicule. Their lives, and carefully prepared little eccentricities, helped them, too, with their special public. From the taverns and clubs where they spent their evenings the rumour of their Tiberian but really very innocent orgies would spread excitement through Hampstead, or flicker like marsh-fire through Chelsea. By this time they had all bought brown velvet jackets, with a sash round the waist, and large romantic black hats. Beardsall had in his room a skull out of which he pretended to drink (this must have been a recollection of some life of Byron which he, too, had read as a boy), while McCulloch had, hung round one of the brass knobs of his bed, a long necklace, made of vertebrae torn from the skeleton of a man, stained purple and looking in reality rather like the chain of a bicycle after an accident. Much of their time, when not occupied in praising one another or laughing in a hollow Homeric manner, was spent in contemplation of suicide. Only after death — they felt — would their genius be fully recognised, while the more sudden and violent their end, the more effective for their posthumous glory. Cups of poison, a fall to the crowd below from the Nelson Monument, the lily-green death-look of Chatterton, the decline of Keats, a cloaked figure found floating on the Thames, a revolver shot in Piccadilly followed by a dramatic collapse, or the quieter, less sensational, but sudden 'Strange Death of a Literary Recluse' — all these passed through their minds, were mentioned in low tones or lay hidden, for all to read, in the intentionally gloomy fire of their eyes. But the chorus of sandal-footed and golden-crowned young ladies implored them constantly to remember their families — not to do anything rash — though perhaps these same young women found that the thought of it gave them, too, no less than the three protagonists, a little tremor of wonder, excitement and importance. In their less exalted moments, however, the chance of getting this thrill in real life seemed ever so remote — merely a dream of fair women.

But, to return to our hero, Ferdinand was by now turning out stanza after stanza, poem after poem, and in these masterpieces very cleverly backed both popular favourites at the same time, for while in feeling they were fervently pagan, full of wine and roses, full of the free life of the Greeks as seen through the dusty spectacles of the nineties, they were yet addressed to a dreamy deity, implored by the poet as 'Dark Rosaleen' — or when it became necessary to find a rhyme for 'Thee', as 'Rosalee'; later, he was even clever enough to mingle with these other ingredients, neo-classic or Irish, a little of the epic touch conveyed by Mr. Stephen Phillips. Very poignant were these odes, and the Belfast accent made manifest in them was audible only to Hibernian ears. 'Oh, Mr. McCulloch,' they would importune in the *salons* set on the hills, 'do recite that one . . . you know . . .' At first he would refuse, gracefully refuse, offering instead to read them a short lyric by Beardsall, but in the end he would always yield and recite to them his favourite poems, which, as with many other poets, luckily happened to be his own. Sometimes he would refuse to declaim without a harp accompaniment from Mrs. Stilpepper. 'It reminds me of Erin', he would say, and while Juliet's slender fingers would draw out the syrupy music from the strings, he would wail scarcely recognisable words in a gloomy, pathetic, almost frightening way, or sing on one note in a winsome, tenderly caressing manner. 'Doesn't it make you understand *them*?' the earnest, enthusiastic band of young women would remark rather vaguely.

As he stood in the centre of the room, with eyes half closed, his face, framed in by its dark hair, and balanced over the two points of his high white — still white — collar, seemed to have little connection with the short, thick-set body below. Hanging there, among faded green velvet curtains and the spreading host of little pieces of pseudo-Oriental china, that surged in blue-and-white foam over the walls, tables and piano, it seemed but a large mask for his voice. Through the mouth, with its too prominent lips and teeth, came the warm high tones and winning pronunciation — tricks which, as he intended them to do, prejudiced many women in his favour, and secured him a few lifelong friends: friends who would have remained faithful to the end — if only there had been one! Thus Ferdinand, his boots planted uneasily in the Celtic twilight, his head bathed in the sunshine of the growing garden cities, spent many pleasurable years, passing through the long level plateau of early manhood with his two friends beside him.

. . . . .

When the suicide of one of these three did occur, it came with the greatest shock of all, the shock of the long-discussed and half-expected; for when something long talked-about, and even long prepared, happens — as was the case with the European War — then surprise overwhelms one. Beardsall, on a short holiday from his journalistic duties, and possibly from his friends, was found shot dead in the bedroom of a small, shabby hotel in Paris. Ferdinand, Frendly and his group of admirers were overwhelmed with sorrowing astonishment. His death was, perhaps, a greater tragedy than any of them imagined, since the end of this poor, tired, ill, little man may have been due, not so much to poverty, weariness or ill-health, *or* to the feeling that he was an unappreciated genius, as to his recognition of the fact that he possessed very little real talent, and that his reputation was already out of proportion to it. For a long time he must have felt the strain of being forced to carry more than he could bear. It was in August that his death took place, and one hardly likes to think of him wandering about in the city with its holiday air. To the English, accustomed to London, there must be always something heartless and too logical about Paris, a quality that must make even death more hard to bear. The streets, set out for the pageant of a vulgar imperialism that has long been swept away, are like a plutocratic feast prepared years ago for some swindling financier, a feast that still remains dusty and untouched. The architecture, always hard, logical and equal, is nowhere as good as London's best, nowhere as bad as London's worst. The large stony gardens, set with hundreds of statues that lack the wistful, unconscious humour of our togaed senators, or Achilles Monument, are emptier than usual, and the sun beats fiercely down upon them, while the idyllic, rich tranquillity and falling green shadows of the Bois only mock the lives of the needy, reminding them of the hateful contrast between farmhouse and city slum, garden and tenement, rich and poor. In this smooth-faced, very luxurious city, the sad little poet's fate overcame him; he was in his room for some two hours before he died. We know nothing of his thoughts during those two long hours that preceded him into eternity, as he walked about in that small, hot, gloomy bedroom.

After the first shock had passed for the two survivors of the clique and their friends, a period of intense activity set in. First of all there were obituary notices to be penned, articles on Beardsall's life, accounts of his death to be written, then his literary remains to be edited and many poems and letters to be published. How well, and with what kindness, the dead man had played his part, for in all the letters, and even in most of the poems, were affectionate references or glorious tributes to Ferdinand and Frendly. Finally came the great work, *The Life and Letters of Arthur Savage Beardsall*, by T. W. Frendly and Ferdinand H. McCulloch, profusely illustrated, and issued by a famous publishing house at a guinea net.

This book was a masterpiece of judicious booming. Frendly did the hard work, McCulloch embellished it; and as far as the latter was concerned it was a truer form of autobiography than many to which we have lately been treated. Affectionate references to him appeared in nearly every letter, while not only did our hero-editor include in the volume poems, letters, jokes, epigrams and denunciations of his own, but there were almost as many photographs of him as of Beardsall, and whenever the latter appeared in group or caricature, there, at his side, was the very easily recognisable face of Ferdinand! After the publication of this *Life*, the dead poet's work received a wider recognition than he had ever hoped or deserved, so that in country-houses, when conversation had ebbed, the artistic member of the house-party would say, 'I suppose you knew Arthur Beardsall?' and point to a book lying uncut on the table. But, oddly enough, Ferdinand McCulloch's fame did not appear to grow similarly, or to the extent expected of it.

During the two or three years taken up by this juggling of life, letters and poems, there were, of course, many meetings between the two survivors of the group and their old friends. At first our hero was seen — if anything more often than formerly — in Juliet Stilpepper's drawing-room, or in the *salons* of the other artistic ladies; though, whereas at one time he had always been asked to recite his own poems, he was now invariably requested, instead, to declaim those of his dead friend. Even Ellen Durban, formerly the most fervent admirer of his Muse, now only asked him to recite Beardsall's work. The truth of the matter was that their friendship with a temporarily rather famous poet — and still more with one who had perished by his own hand — shed an unearthly radiance not only on Ferdinand (which halo cancelled out his own) but on all the friends, and especially on Mrs. Stilpepper and Miss Durban.

This was not at all what our hero had expected. Gradually he began to shun these parties, and would more frequently meet the ladies at some club or restaurant, pleading as excuse a growing absorption in literary criticism and journalism. But the truth is that he did not care much for gatherings at which he was no longer the chief personage, ousted always by the spectre of his dead friend. Frendly, or 'T. W.' as he called him, was still in constant attendance, doing as much propaganda as ever. Ferdinand's verses were yet to be met with in the pages of journals, but his signature seemed an omen of little prosperity, insomuch as his name printed — if only in the list of possible contributors — was a sure indication that this new review would live for one number only. By this time the world of the late nineties had passed with the Boer War, and we soon find ourselves in Mid-Edwardian days. The neo-classic form of verse, though still surviving — like everything else — at the universities, was dead elsewhere; the Irish twilight was beginning to deepen into night; and signs began to appear of a modern movement in English poetry, similar to that which had blossomed in France through the last few decades of the old century. And this new poetry attracted to itself all those who liked — or liked to like — things modern, so that many of our hero's former admirers forsook him, and even neglected to read Beardsall. Ferdinand's verses appeared less and less often, and, instead, he wrote critical articles devoted to the iniquity of the new verse, and signed, impressively, 'Ferdinand H. McCulloch'. And what thunder of the Gods against modern decadence was contained in these prophetic messages, though he always attacked the less well-received, and therefore probably better, poets. For he would never attack popular idols, hoping always to obtain their favour. His abuse of those he dared to abuse only equalled his fulsome praise of those he dared not attack, whom he would describe as 'Standard-bearers' or 'Knights-of-the-Grail'! But what roused his ire especially was that quality described as 'obscurity' (the latter being anything he could not understand), and one could only conclude that to be an 'obscure' poet was somehow worse than to be an obscure journalist.

It must be admitted that, with the passage of time, Ferdinand's manner lost none of its jauntiness. On the contrary, he developed more and more that air of dominion we have noted, remaining faithful to all the developments of his personality. His long finger-nails, the fingers stained orange with nicotine, still feverishly scratched the inside of his cigarette-case as he drew out a cigarette, lit it, threw it away. His long hair, bunch of violets, Irish brogue, high collar and serpent-like tie were all in their pristine splendour. Constant he remained, as well, to his *lares* and *penates*; however often he changed his apartments, there you would find that necklace of purple-stained vertebrae, which had been hung round the end of how many lodging-house beds, and the skull-loving-cup which he had inherited from Arthur Beardsall. Only two alterations, apart from those which Time made for him, could be detected in his appearance. The collar was less white — had now more the tone and texture of vellum — while the velvet jacket and large black hat had been discarded for more sober garments, better befitting a critic and solid man-of-letters! The rest of his detail sufficiently proclaimed him a poet. Whatever the development of his personality or circumstances, our hero could be trusted to dramatise them for his friends.

Lately Frendly appeared to have been doing more propaganda for himself than for Ferdinand, and was in consequence prospering, for he was a sharp, active little man. This unexpected turn of events — or of the worm — annoyed McCulloch considerably, and, consequently, he saw less and less of 'T. W.' Other admirers, such as Juliet Stilpepper and Ellen Durban, clung to him; for now that the boom in Beardsall was beginning to decline, they remembered the second string to their bow. They cherished him, still expected something of him. . . . But what was it? — what could it be?

Ferdinand would never enter the *salon* now. He was determined never more to risk being asked to recite the poetry of another, and Mrs. Stilpepper's harp lay there dim and golden as Ellen Durban's hair, its strings silent and untouched. Instead, then, of his going to these gatherings, the two ladies would meet him each week for luncheon in a little restaurant at the side of a narrow alley off Fleet Street. The meal was fixed, always, for the unusual, almost exciting, hour of 2.15. Ferdinand's office was round the corner, and though he occupied a rather subordinate position there, at each step away from it his importance grew visibly.

In the midsummer of which we are writing the sunlight falling through the leaves of the few scraggy trees in the court outside made a pattern of wavering golden disks, flat and round, on floor and pavement. It played, too, with rather terrifying effect on the faces of those eating, bringing out again the more dusty, less golden, tone of Ellen's hair, exaggerating her high cheek-bones, revealing her large bony feet shod in sandals, and contrived a whole set of tricks for poor Mrs. Stilpepper's too sweet countenance. It magnified the pores and wrinkles, intensified the romantic lines, of Ferdinand's head, till one was reminded of Gulliver's horror when, lifted up to the level of the Brobdingnagian faces, he observed the pits, hollows and furrows that graced them. In the room, too, the sunlight seemed to draw out the smell of stale food, to unmuffle the incessant noise. But not one of those present talked louder or more often than Ferdinand, though it was, in reality, quite unnecessary, as this little table of three people was in any case very noticeable ; even Juliet, the most ordinary of the group, won public attention by her speaking voice, which, noted among her friends for its dulcet tones, was now almost too musical in its utterance. As for Ellen, her appearance could be trusted to gain attention anywhere, since with her large sandalled feet, big bones, general untidiness and that cloudy crown of golden hair which had been — and still was — her pride, she now more resembled an animated haystack than a human being.

At the end of luncheon, when our hero leant back to light a cigarette, taking one with difficulty from that voluminous and dented silver case, drinking a cup of coffee — which, like the coffee in most English establishments, tasted alternately of meat-extract and iron dumb-bells — it was an experience to see his manner, as of a conqueror, at whose slightest word the journalistic world, here assembled, would quake. The ingratiating brogue slid on its oiled passage round the room, winging its easy way from table to table, so that all could hear ; while invariably, at the end of the meal, would come the familiar menace of suicide. Year by year, month by month, these threats increased. But it almost seemed, as he continued to talk in this way, as if the expression on the faces of the two ladies brightened a little, for an instant became animated, as though instead of threatening them he had promised them something . . . Ferdinand was too immersed in his own grievances, in the perpetual recitation of his troubles and ill-treatment, to notice any of these subtle, very slight, changes of expression. Perhaps it may have been due to some alteration in the falling lights and shadows dripping through the small branches of the trees outside. Yes, he was sick of it! he said . . . absolutely sick of it! . . . (and he would laugh in that hollow way) . . . sick of it! Ellen and Juliet were, naturally, very upset. It would be too, too dreadful — appalling — after all that had happened . . . Still, of course, he was right in a way, in what he said, and they agreed with him that he would probably never be properly appreciated in his lifetime. After his death, undoubtedly, his reputation would stand higher, much higher. One couldn't doubt it. Look, for instance, at the posthumous appreciation of Beardsall, a friend of all of us, a good poet, certainly, Ferdinand, but no better than you are! But McCulloch, though looking rather pleased at this declaration of faith, would point out that such was the deterioration of the public taste that even Beardsall's fame stood less high than it did ten years ago, just after his death. 'I'm sick of it!' he would reiterate; 'I've nearly made up my mind to do it — sick of it all.' . . .

But, 'Oh, no,' they cried, he couldn't, he mustn't do it! He must think, not only of himself, but of his friends . . . think how they would miss him, reminded at every turn by letters, poems, photographs . . . might even be blamed. . . . (As they talked the colour came back a little to their faces.) After all, they might say it, mightn't they? Wasn't there something . . . something due to friendship? Something? And as they continued to plead they experienced again that little thrill of wonder, expectation and importance which had visited them after Beardsall's death. 'But promise us, swear to us, that you will never DO IT!' they cried.

'I won't promise now,' Ferdinand answered, 'but I will give you m' definite decision on Monday at this table, after luncheon. But in your turn y' must promise NOT to mention the subject to me till after the meal is over, for if it must be m' last, at least let it be a jolly one'; and soon after this the two ladies fluttered out into the open air, while Ferdinand, a grim look on his face, his chin upheld by the apparatus of tie and collar, slowly swaggered out after them.

Now it happened that on the Monday I witnessed the final scene of the drama; but, alas! the final scene was laid not at the end but in the middle of the tragedy, which may continue for another three decades after it should have finished.

Rather later than the usual luncheon-hour I went to the restaurant to meet a friend. The room was very full and noisy; there, at a table set for three persons, were seated two rather queer-looking middle-aged women. They were very quiet, hardly speaking to each other at all, but on their faces could be detected a slight flush of expectation, while in their eyes gleamed a fire which I had seen before in other eyes, but when? Then I recalled the faces of the older women-gamblers at Monte Carlo.

Presently there was borne in on us the sound of important footsteps outside, and a little man entered, with a large bony face and a high, not necessarily white, collar, round which was coiled twice a large black tie, like the Delphic serpent. In the buttonhole of his coat was a bunch of violets — or rather violas, for the former could not be obtained at this season; and I remembered, suddenly, my earlier meeting with him on the top of a motor-bus a year or two previously.

He wished his two friends, whose excitement had, in the meantime, obviously increased, a good-morning in his succulent Irish voice, ordered luncheon, and sat down with the air of a monarch, who sits down so that others need not stand. But, in spite of his importance, he seemed depressed. His two companions said little and ate less, but fever shone in eye and cheek. It was a rather gloomy affair, the luncheon, though it lasted long. The conversation was confined to politics and a certain amount of heartfelt condemnation of modern poetry. Only once, too, sounded out that hollow laugh. But it seemed to me, watching, that the excitement of his two companions was steadily increasing.

And, after the coffee, the little dark woman said, in a voice musical as a xylophone or a set of musical glasses: 'Well, have you decided . . . Ferdinand? Tell us as quickly as you can; remember Our Suspense.' And, with a solemn expression, came the answer, in that rich tone, 'I have' (and after a long pause) 'I have decided . . . NOT TO . . . ! I give you m' word.'

The light faded out of their faces as they thanked him;

and for the first time in all these long years of association they found they had to hurry away quickly, after paying the bill. Ellen Durban had to take her class in classical dancing earlier than usual that afternoon; Mrs. Stilpepper had her family (and all that) to look after. . . . So he wasn't going to, after all . . . and the two women stepped into the bright sunshine outside and quickly parted.

In the dining-room I was asking my friend, 'Who is that little man just going out?' and he replied: 'Oh! that's an Irish journalist; McCulloch. I believe he used to write verse; he's always here with those two women . . . he was a great friend of that poet, the fellow who committed suicide . . . what was his name?'

Many times in the years that followed we saw him there lunching alone, for the other actors in the small drama would no longer play their parts.

TOUCHING WOOD

I DO not yet know how this story ends: for what I am going to tell you happened only yesterday morning, before I left the boat at Suez.

With a pile of books and an empty soup-cup beside me, I sat in a deck-chair, staring out into mist-edged nothingness, where not even a dolphin or a flying-fish leapt for the diversion of the passengers. Everything seemed to be warm and damp, very damp. The edge of the sky was hung with ragged banners of cloud, and the edge of the sea melted into it. My neighbour, also with several books by his side, and one lying open upon his knee, stared, with a similar fixity, into the watery, empty perspective. The vast melancholy of the sea — only supportable because of the laziness it engenders, and of the manner in which it causes one day to telescope into another, inducing in many persons the subsequent conviction that they must have enjoyed the voyage for the time to have passed so quickly — hung over both of us: that much was clear. Tall, thin and with rather fine hands, my neighbour displayed in his physique an unusual sensitiveness, and I wondered, idly, who he was. . . . The books afforded no clue, for they were of several sorts; a translation of the Greek Anthology, a novel by P. G. Wodehouse, Dunne's *Experiment with Time*, a new biography of some dead diplomat by Mr. Harold Nicolson, a volume of short stories by the late D. H. Lawrence, and — I noticed now — one of my own books, *The Man Who Lost Himself*. Suddenly he turned his eyes from the water and addressed me.

'Do you *like* the sea?' he asked.

'Yes, I love it, in a way,' I answered, 'in spite of the boredom — and, with me, alas, of the terror. For I'm quite a good sailor: but when other people are lying in their bunks, wishing they could drown, I'm lying, fully dressed, on mine, praying that I shan't, and thinking of the wastes of water on which a man's head would be almost imperceptible. That's why I prefer the Mediterranean, where you can usually see land. . . .

But it seems to have disappeared altogether today. . . . Or, better still, give me the Suez Canal; I look forward to an enjoyable afternoon.'

'Oh, I know: I'm a bit like that myself,' he said. 'In fact, as you're a writer, I'll tell you a story about it. But I hope you're not superstitious?

'Perhaps you can hardly call it a story, really,' he added; 'it's an illustration, more than a story, or the proof of a theory. . . . And in this instance the theory or the moral is the old, obvious one, which D. H. Lawrence was so fond of emphasising, that what you *feel* is — and must always be — more true than what you merely think: judge by touch, as it were, rather than sight. But people don't have the courage nowadays to act on what they feel: they act by reason, and then try to invent rational explanations afterwards, of the singular things that happen to them. But it's no use: no use at all.

'The ship, bound for South America, left Tilbury on a wet December afternoon: but the next day and for two days afterwards the sea, even when we crossed the Bay of Biscay, resembled a blue summer lake. In spite of the calm, though, we were late in arriving at Lisbon, while, once there, the interminable arguments of the harbour authorities seemed specially calculated to make us later still in leaving it. I stood watching the departing passengers, and listening to a fierce Portuguese quarrel that spluttered like a damp firework, between the ship's agent and an official of the custom-house. . . . There were only two new arrivals of whom to take notice, an Englishwoman and her husband. She was certainly beautiful in a curious way, like one of the Fates. Her eyes, wide open, had the blue depths of an oracle, in which many meanings, one true and many false, could be read. There was something classical, or pre-classical, about that startled and stony visage, something of Cassandra, something of the doom of the House of Atreus. . . . Something, too, I thought — or should I say, I felt? — at the time, of a mermaid: for her eyes belonged to the sea. . . . And yet it was at Mycenae, in the broken palace above the deep ravine; on that hill which seems to be alone for ever with the sea and the sky, as though they were washing it free of that doom, and the taint that caused it, that she would have been, I think, most at home. . . . Beside her, her husband looked pleasantly matter-of-fact: but it was only her appearance which was unusual; her clothes seemed specially designed to destroy the particular kind of beauty she possessed, to degrade it and make it ordinary.

'The following morning, sitting on deck, as we are now, I found myself next to them, and, after playing for a while with our books in the listless manner which the movement and vibration of all ships — for there is a very strong link between sea-sickness and print — enforce, we began to talk a little. . . . They gave an ordinary enough impression, too, when they spoke, and her voice — quiet, busy, comfortable, though rather empty — had no element in it of either prophecy or tragedy. . . . And yet I knew, I felt, I was *aware* — informed, I suppose, by the exploring of those antennae which so much excel the faculties of the mind — that, somehow or other, she was inextricably associated with these qualities. . . . We talked in a desultory manner for two hours or more, and during the whole of that time the sea, which had been up till now so unruffled — even in those latitudes where you would have expected it to be at its most swelling and boisterous — began indubitably to show increasing symptoms of a change of mood. It felt as though it were trying out its powers, though only, as yet, with some future occasion in view. Little winds whistled in the corners, and there was a roll on the boat that caused the usual jokes and laughter among the younger passengers, tramping noisily round the deck, and instilled in the players of quoits and other games a desire to be more hearty and jolly than ever, in order to cover up a certain incipient queasiness. . . . You ask what we'd been talking about? . . . Well, I forget, but all sorts of things, politics and books — safe, dull books — and travel.

'With every minute, though, conversation became more difficult, for there were sounds of things crashing from time to time, and the wind howled ever more loudly, though ours was a comparatively sheltered corner. . . . They were going, she told me, to Buenos Aires — or "B-A", as she called it, with her affectation of ordinariness — for the voyage; weren't even going on shore for a day or two at Rio. No, a week at "B-A", and then straight back home; "that's the place for us", she said. Mr. Ruevinny — for that was their name — had been ill, it appeared, and had been ordered this voyage by the doctor. "I tried to persuade my wife not to come," he explained, "but she insisted. I didn't persuade you to come, did I, darling?" he added, turning to her. "I did everything I could to stop you."

'No, I don't recall the whole conversation with any distinctness: only one or two things like that. I remember Mrs. Ruevinny saying, in her practical, putting-up-with-no-nonsense and yet singularly empty voice — a voice which said things as though it did not mean them — "Well, I'm a fatalist: you can't escape what's coming to you — so there you are! You must make the best of it. No fox can escape for long, if the pack is out after him." . . . I recollect that very well, for at the moment this remark — so ordinary, and of a kind to which we have all had to listen against our wills so often — irritated me almost beyond endurance. It accorded so ill, I thought, with that curious beauty, with that face which seemed waiting for one of the great emotions — and it was *fear*, I felt sure — to make it a supreme vehicle of expression. . . . But in that way, people so often disappoint one by enunciating sentiments which do not suit them. . . . Then she went on to talk of bazaars in the home counties, and gave way to little bursts of self-importance, equally inappropriate.

'And yet were they, I wondered at the time, in reality bursts of self-importance? She brought them into the conversation, I felt, not so much to impress a stranger as to comfort herself. Because such functions belonged to everyday life, as a rule lacking in both heroism and disaster, just as the opinions she voiced were the opinions of everyday life: and she clung hard to them because she was desperately anxious to impress upon herself that life was really of this pattern for her, and that some dim, huge existence of antique catastrophe, to which she belonged, and from which she had once fled, possessed no actuality. Every opinion she uttered, every occasion to which she referred, was as though she pinched herself to be sure that she was awake, and that the nightmare had passed. . . . So, I felt, might one of the Atridae, Clytemnestra or Elektra, in the intervals of those catastrophic events to which their names are, for us, indissolubly attached, have told acquaintances of the Sale of Work she was getting up in order to aid the honest poor of Mycenae.

'Rougher and rougher it grew; and I did not see them again that day. Certainly it had grown too stormy now for one to take any sort of pleasure in the voyage. It was not even possible to sleep: though storms, as a rule, make me feel sleepy; and at night, if for a single moment you dozed off, you were sure to be woken at once by the flying open, flapping and slamming of cupboard doors, or by the sensation that the soul itself, the *psyche* round which the body is built up, had slightly shifted its habitation. . . . "Why," all the passengers, as so often during a voyage, were asking themselves, "*why* did I do it?" . . . But my own chief emotion, and one that I nearly always experience on the Atlantic, though it has been my lot to travel a good deal upon it, was of fright: I did not feel sick, I felt frightened of those cold valleys beneath, endless and undulating, as deep, we are told, as the island mountains are high. . . . Incidentally (forgive me for interrupting my own story), hasn't it grown much rougher since we began talking, or is it my imagination?'

I had to admit that the weather had changed. The boat had begun to pitch about in an unexpected way.

'I thought so,' he said, and paused a moment. 'Still, it will at least be smooth in the Canal. . . . But let me proceed,' he continued. 'Fortunately I was leaving the boat at Madeira, and that was only two days ahead. But how sincerely during those hours I longed for it, that nest of purple bougainvillea and peroxide blondes, poised in mid-ocean under its cosy of Atlantic cloud.

'The next day was of too unpleasant a character for one to be able to take an interest in anything, in food or drink or sleep or passengers: but I noticed, all the same, that Mr. Ruevinny was alone at luncheon. . . . The following morning the storm appeared to have abated a little, though not much, and, while walking up and down the deck, I met him.

'"Good morning!" I cried, with false sea-heartiness. "And how are *you* this morning? . . . I'm sorry to see you're alone."

'"Yes, it's a nuisance," he replied. "I had so much hoped it would be fine. . . . After all, we're getting near Madeira now, and it ought *not* to be like this. . . . I tell you, it worries me. . . . You see, it isn't so much that my wife's a bad sailor — she doesn't really feel ill now; the truth is, she's frightened in a ship!"

'"That's nothing to be ashamed of," I said. "I am, too.

. . . I believe a good many people are, if only they'd allow themselves to admit it."

'"I dare say. . . . But you see, it's different for her: the last time she was on a proper voyage was in the *Titanic*: her twin brother went down with it, and she was only rescued herself by a miracle. . . . Why, for years she wouldn't go abroad at all, even refused to take on the hour's journey across the Channel; though, before that, she used to love Paris. . . . And I'll tell you a peculiar thing: the sea can be as smooth as anything, and the moment she sets her foot on board, sure enough, it begins to get stormy. I've seen it happen in the Channel, scores of times, so that often I wished I hadn't persuaded her to change her mind and come with me, even for that short distance. . . . I ought never to have let her come on this journey; never; I ought to have forbidden it absolutely, from the start. . . . But she had been worrying about me — I'd been ill a long time, and those damned medicos said a long sea voyage was the only thing to put me right — and she insisted. I couldn't stop her: it seemed as though she *must* come, although she dreaded it, if you can get my meaning." . . . So that was it! . . . no wonder she was frightened, even at the surface level. I thought of the magnificent ship on her maiden voyage, of the two bands playing, and of that sudden ice-cold crash, and silence, as the breath of destruction reached it; and then of the watery confusion, of the strange, voiceless last meetings in green, deep alleys between the waves, where those who could swim bobbed up and down; or were knocked together like corks, but, their voices being lost already beneath the sound of the ocean, could not communicate in any way, and thus, it must have seemed, had become hostile to each other. . . . So that was it! . . . That was the meaning in those wide-open eyes, like the eyes of a statue in bright sunlight: that was the meaning, perhaps subconscious, under her casual, silly yet intent words, "No fox can escape for long, if the pack is out after him". . . . No, nor a human being, if the whole pack of Furies attend his coming and his going.

'That afternoon we arrived at Madeira, and I said goodbye. The Ruevinnys — beset though they were on deck by the islanders, who were trying to sell them embroideries, flowers, sandals, boxes of palm-wood, models of bullock-carts, native dresses and budgerigars — waved to me as I left for the shore in a motor-boat: and I noticed, again, the singular lack of expression in her face, which yet showed, when once you comprehended, so much more terror than terror itself. She gave a look, too, I thought, of longing towards the land: but I was too far away to see clearly. . . . At any rate, they should be all right now. The rest of the journey, especially at this time of year, should be one of tropical calm, of deep, blue phosphorescent gardens beneath the waters, and of flying-fishes leaping over them as birds skim a lawn.

'It was not until a fortnight later, not until a fortnight after it had happened, that I saw the newspaper: "*Hurricane in South Atlantic Seas. Coastline Towns Swept by Tidal Wave*", I read. "*British Liner Sinks Off Rio. All Lives Lost.*" I thought at once of Mrs. Ruevinny. . . . So it was over now. . . . She belonged in some way to the sea, and it must reclaim her: she had always known that, I reflected; even though she could not always rationally believe it. At any rate, it was over, whatever it might mean: the end of some long pursuit, of which one could not tell the beginning; or perhaps — who knows? — it was only the middle act of a drama laid over several centuries, or epochs. . . . I wondered how that lovely face had looked at the end, and, knowing what was in store for her, how much more matter-of-fact she had contrived to make her voice, when she talked to her husband for the last time. . . . And yet, as so often happens, actuality and its foretelling had been a little at odds. . . . I turned over to the stop-press news. "*Survivor Rescued*", I read. "*Strange Coincidence*. . . . Mrs. Ruevinny, who was rescued yesterday afternoon in a state of exhaustion, proves to be one of the survivors of the *Titanic*: her twin brother perished with that ship. It is feared that Mr. Ruevinny, well known in the sporting world, and all the other passengers and hands are lost." . . . So it had not got her after all: the fox was free once more. The last act, poor woman, had not been played.

'. . . I suppose you'd call it superstitious of me to feel like that? But life sometimes seems easier to understand, if one is superstitious. . . . Well, that was thirteen years ago. . . . And, touching wood, she's on this ship, bound for Ceylon to see her son. (I spoke to her this morning: doesn't look a day older.) But what ought one to do, act on superstitious belief or defy it? . . . Somehow I lack the courage to do anything so silly as leave the boat at Suez.'

He stopped talking, and became silent, pondering — while I, though obliged to hold on to every object I saw in order to preserve my balance, managed to get downstairs to send a cable.

DEAD HEAT

LOOKING back, the story of the friendship between the old Duchess of Martenburg and Princess Mouratinzky, the actual length of it, and the opposing points of view upon which it thrived, seems to me to possess all the fascination of a nursery rhyme, such as 'Jack Sprat', or of a fairy-tale similar to the 'Three Bears', exhaling in its essence a numerical, repetitive beauty implicit and continuous throughout its unfolding. . . . And for this reason I want to tell it to you.

I knew them both for what to me was a very lengthy period, but no doubt to them, out of their great age, merely represented the time occupied by the flashing of an angel's wings. . . . When I was a child, I first knew the Duchess of Martenburg. By birth a Princess of Southern Germany she had, with her wrinkled skin and brown eyes, rather bulbous now, albeit full of fire, all the charm of a well-educated and cultured toad, but a toad that was talkative, warm-blooded and loved dancing. (Indeed, she danced well, when I first remember her, though even then she was much over sixty.) With all the good-humour and high spirits of the Southern Germany of former uncontaminated days, she was witty in a straightforward way, and courageous: very downright and sure of her own mind: further, she was religious, intensely devoted to her Church — rather unexpectedly, the Protestant Church of the North. According to the ritual of the seasons, she moved with considerable pomp from one palace to another, from one set of Italian rooms decked out with plaster cupids, red brocade and pillared cabinets showing false perspectives of tortoise-shell, coral and lapis, from one grouping of plumed fountains and cut trees, to another. . . . And every autumn, for a fortnight — the equivalent perhaps of a Catholic retreat — she came to England to stay with a bearded bishop, with whom, to the pride and pleasure of his wife and eleven moustached daughters, she was carrying on one of those mild flirtations so often manifested among the devout. . . . How well I remember her then, the Parma-violet-coloured velvet toque and dress which she always at that time affected, and the way she had of wrinkling her already wrinkled nose when she laughed.

But the 1914 war — still more perhaps the coming of Nazidom — had obliged her to alter completely her manner of life. . . . So that when I saw her again, after a lapse of twenty years, she had become a dignified refugee, banished from Germany because of her too great love for her Church, and because of her alleged consequent anti-Nazi activities. In the interval she had grown (and one could have expected nothing else) immensely old and very poor — for her, very poor. Nevertheless, she could still indulge in a certain style of living, for she dwelt now in a small *pension* on the very shore of the Lake of Geneva, and against this economical background, could still afford a maid (who, in any case, after fifty years would have refused to leave her), a footman and a sitting-room. But though her exile was easy, she resented her place of refuge. After the pleasant Bavarian Alps, these mountains seemed to her exaggerated and melodramatic. Despite her Lutheran affinities, she missed the graces of old Catholic Germany, the Madonnas at the corners of buildings high above the junctions of streets, the bunches of flowers upon the ledges of rustic shrines, the deep purple petunias hanging from the window-box of every window; things for which not all the blue and yellow tinsel stars of the Swiss spring sweeping over meadows and dark, damp earth, spread with scented pine-needles, could compensate her. . . . She was old, far too old for exile, she would say (indeed, she was over ninety), and what harm could a poor old woman like herself have accomplished, she asked, even if she had been wicked enough to wish to injure her own country?

Still, one must make the best of it. The fish was good (those nice pink trout); that was one thing. . . . And there were — yes, there were — a few nice people here. She admitted it; that was why she was at-home every evening from four until seven. For at that early hour she retired for the night, being called at six the next day and breakfasting on fine mornings at seven under a glossy-leaved magnolia by the side of the Lake.

Indeed, she possessed a fanatical love of fresh air, lived in it the whole spring, summer and autumn. Even during the winter in this climate, her windows were always wide open. Sometimes I used to try to soften her feelings concerning her place of exile, by saying to her how good the air was. 'Look at the way you can sit out here under the magnolia all day long!' I used to urge, but nothing would mollify her. 'I know,' she would reply; 'that is why I chose it — that, and to be near my dear old friend Princess Mouratinzky (I fear she is getting *very* old and infirm now, though she makes out that she is a few years younger than I am). But I do not like it: no, I do not.'

A different hurricane had blown hither the Princess. In her youth a great and famous beauty, still, at her present vast age (for she was a contemporary of the Duchess, though, as we shall see, the vanity of former years prohibited her from boasting of this), she retained the manner and bearing of one; even a certain worldly wit, which sometimes goes with this kind of appearance and renown. Coquettish, alluring, full of *brio*, she talked continually, laughing and fanning herself the while — she was always opening and shutting a fan. And into the quality of her attraction yet entered a great deal of feminine hard work, none the less arduous because it was unconscious. Apart from her animation, apart from her beauty, she might have seemed at first sight a more usual character than the Duchess; just a very pretty old lady with round blue eyes, beautiful and undimmed. But such a conclusion would have been false. . . . So far as her history was concerned, this fascinating old woman had become an orphan at an early age. Brought up at the Smolny Institute, she had, through the influence of the Tzarina of the day, been married on her seventeenth birthday to a great Russian nobleman and landowner, and had become one of the leaders of fashionable life in Petersburg. Subsequently for thirty years she had been lady-in-waiting to the Grand Duchess Vladimir Constantine, and had been driving with her mistress in the second carriage at the moment when that clever, gigantic monster, the Grand Duke, with his courage, his immense stature, his brutality and fatalistic wit, had been blown up by Nihilists as he was returning from a review of the Imperial troops. For a further twenty-five years, until the Revolution, it had been her lot to comfort the beautiful and saintly Grand Duchess in her widowhood.

But the assassination of Russian royalties had now ceased

to be an individual martyrdom, and had become degraded to mass-murder, a holocaust: (a dead man may trail a shadow behind him as a memory, but a dead army has none; wars and revolutions leave no ghosts). The Grand Duchess herself, who had formerly been so beloved and respected, had now been murdered these many years, her body robbed and thrown into the Black Sea. . . . But fortunately her lady-in-waiting, the Princess, had been staying with a married daughter in the south of France when the war had broken out in 1914. Unable to return to Russia, she had so escaped sharing this fate, though the death of her mistress in such a manner was something from which she could never recover. It had been, in fact, more of a grief to her than the loss of her own fortune — for now she was penniless, living here, in the middle of a little Swiss town, in a boarding-house.

This establishment, however, was less unfriendly and impersonal than it sounds. Her daughter and son-in-law managed it, and they looked after her as well as they could. Her room, at the top of the house, was excessively small, and (though I think the Princess herself remained unaware of this) it had been in this same attic in which she was now dwelling, then cold and bare, that Lenin, a bitter fugitive, had existed for two years, working all day and all night, turning letters into cypher to send to Russia, writing endless pamphlets and books, eating nothing except when forced to do so by Kroupskaya, talking seldom — though when he talked a faint line of foam flickered from his sneering lips. Now, however, it was no longer a Swiss garret, for the Princess belonged so completely to her dead world of sleighs and furs and jewels and musical-boxes, that everything round her still proclaimed her adherence to it. No trace of Lenin here now, only endless photographs, signed, of murdered Russian royalties: the Tzar and Tzarina; the unfortunate young Tzarevitch and his four lovely sisters; Grand Dukes and Grand Duchesses and their children; photographs of their palaces and the gardens; photographs of them sleighing and skating and, for the rest, many brightly coloured ikons and bits of fur and lace — all that was left! But there was also a large stove, out of all proportion to the size of the room, and some small vases of flowers. . . . And these, for the momentary comfort they gave her (and all through that long life, after the manner of most Russians, she had lived from moment to moment), enabled her to bear her age and misfortunes more lightly.

For seventy years she had been the Duchess of Martenburg's most intimate friend. Neither of them had allowed so big a thing as being on different sides in the bitterest, so far, of all wars to make a difference to their friendship. There existed, nevertheless, *little* hindrances. Though they lived so near to each other — in order, they said, to be together — it was not easy for them to meet at all, and, further, proved still more difficult for them, despite their mutual affection, to meet without quarrelling; because the Princess for her part rose at five every evening and retired to rest at five every morning. (You may ask how, in a neighbourhood not famed for the gaiety of its night life, she spent the small hours. . . . Well, there was always tea and cigarettes; and often there were parties, for the boarding-house was full of Russian relatives and connections, all engaged in trades which apparently obliged them to come in, from time to time, during the night — and, of course, to reach their work late. And so they clustered round the tall china stove, in the communal sitting-room, talking to the old lady; otherwise she would have died of ennui long ago. . . .)

It was only, then, during that single hour between 6 and 7 P.M. — before dinner for the Duchess, and after breakfast for the Princess — that the two old ladies could meet. Nor was this the sole obstacle to their companionship even during that short space of time, all too brief, one would have said. For in the summer the Princess would not sit out in the garden with her friend; it was too draughty, very treacherous, she would protest. Still less would she remain out of doors in the yet hot but shortening evenings of the early autumn when the mist rose from the Lake, like the wraiths of the murdered (certainly the Duchess's mind would never have entertained such fancies), and filled her bones with a chill depression. Sometimes at this season the Duchess would insist on remaining out of doors, and so reaching a compromise they would face each other angrily across the window-sill for nearly the full hour, handing cakes and tea sullenly across this bar which divided the Teuton from the Slav. In the winter, the Princess, fitted out in the remnants of a fur coat which, though tattered, still possessed a certain air, could only bear to sit in a room with the windows fast shut, and an enormous stove burning in it; while the Duchess, dressed as though for a heat-wave, felt it essential for her health to have all the windows wide open. It was an especial offence to her, as well, that the Princess should live in an attic in the town, in the very heart of noise and heat and dust, when she might dwell in this glorious, cool air by the side of the Lake.

It was not easy, then, this friendship. To each of them, their years had now become a source of pride. They had grown — though originally the contrast between their natures and outward appearance had been the foundation of the feeling between them — into rivals, competitors for the palm of old age, and, in consequence, the two old friends allowed themselves in this hour of frost for one, and fire for the other, to quarrel a good deal. . . . For, years ago, many long years ago, when the Princess had been forty, the, as it seemed now, needless fear of growing old, combined with a certain vanity, had driven her to underestimate her age, so that even today, when she was in reality over ninety, her former deceit debarred her from any hope of ever catching up in the race. The Duchess, of course, knew her friend's age quite well, for it was the same as her own, but she intended to see that the Princess never staked a full claim, or that if she did, she would be convicted in no uncertain terms, and possibly before other people, of lying and self-pride. So she must remain a poor eighty-seven to the Duchess's self-avowed ninety-two; a sad eighty-eight to her ninety-three. Of course, even the eighty-eight to which she could admit was creditable, but ninety-three, ninety-three, ninety-three! . . . How deeply, how frequently, the Princess regretted that now so distant moment of coquetry! . . . Moreover, though she knew that the Duchess was well aware of her real age, she must never allude to it. On the other hand, the Duchess could, when it suited her, taunt her with it in a veiled way. . . . Sometimes their conversation would be in English, a neutral tongue, for the Princess refused to talk German and the Duchess to talk French.

'Anastasie, I can't believe you are cold in that fur coat, and with such a fire! . . . But if you are so, why fan yourself continually? Even *I* should feel cold if I fanned myself the whole time! I'm sure that house of yours is unhealthy. . . . Perhaps you have a fever like one gets in one's youth.'

'No, I can't help it, Rita, I always fan myself. It's like you, how you do all that embroidery, so pretty, with your good German taste! . . . Besides, if you suddenly feel hot, *you* can ask your maid to open the window for you; but I can't. . . . I have to do everything myself.'

'But work is useful, Anastasie: fanning oneself is *not*. . . . Why, you fan yourself enough to turn a windmill: and at your age, it is not good! . . . But I forget, I was back in years long ago. You are younger, much younger than I am now, are you not? . . . You must look after your old friend. . . . How I wish you would come to live here in this glorious air, where you can hear the birds!'

'But I do not wish to hear the birds, Rita. I ha-a-te them! They are so cruel, with their beaks! . . .'

Nor were these the sole seeds of discord. The Duchess thoroughly disapproved of the Orthodox Church and all its ways, and though a service was only held in the minute Russian Church here, with its mad, painted domes and bulbs, once a month, and though, even then, the Princess did not attend it, since she was in bed and asleep in the mornings, the Duchess would often make pointed references to 'mummery' and to 'gingerbread places of worship', while the Princess would in turn feel herself called upon to defend the cause, and to attack in return the undecorative Lutheranism of Germany. Further, the Duchess would very seldom visit the Princess, would always insist on her coming to the *pension* to see her. This was because she pretended not to like Anastasie's daughter; it was a fiction, long kept up. . . . Really, I think, they had long grown fond of each other; but pride prevented them from publicly admitting by a reconciliation that their misfortunes had to this extent softened their natures. Nevertheless, on the rare occasions of their meeting, they got on well, seemed pleased to see each other. When the Princess was unwell, however, the Duchess would continue always to say 'That stupid girl of hers' (she was sixty-seven), 'she does not look after her mother properly'.

Then, too, though originally the Duchess and the Princess had thought — or should one write, felt? — alike, of late years the direction of politics in their countries had tended to separate them. . . . The Duchess possessed a radio, with which, from time to time, she fiddled, producing the sounds of whole covens of witches riding through the air on broomsticks over snow-covered peaks, shrieking, singing, screaming; she seemed, even, to like these noises. But, occasionally, she would during that hour, and always by mistake for some concert or entertainment, tune in to one of the speeches of the dictators, and the Princess could, in those days (for it was before the Hitler-Stalin pact), no more help applauding the words of Hitler, who then saw 'the Bolshevik demon' as the chief opponent of civilisation, than the Duchess could prevent herself from showing enthusiasm at the utterances of the Paladin of Bolshevism when he so piously acclaimed democracy and denounced Hitler and persecution. Thus from six o'clock to seven would often grow poignant enough.

In spite of their differences of view, in spite of their disagreements, however, if either of them ailed or was unhappy, the other felt it as though it had happened to herself. Through the long days spent without her, though she was so near by, the Duchess would continually refer to Anastasie, her friend, just as during those long nights round the stove, drinking tea and smoking cigarettes through long paper holders, the Princess would talk of Rita, her energetic and lively compeer. In addition to the warm feeling that existed between them, it became clear to those round them that the continued existence of one supported that of the other; they resembled the balanced scales of a machine finding an equilibrium, the equilibrium of truth. If one fell, the other would rise unduly.

Both, on the contrary, continued to prosper. The sensibilities of those who have lost profoundly become hardened except in small things, and the perpetual tragic developments of the thirties seemed now to worry them but little. They lost no faculties. The Duchess, in her charming way — in, even, her beautiful way — with her skin infinitely wrinkled and yet soft, her glowing brown eyes and uptilted nose, humorous and contemptuous and proud, grew still more ugly, her manners more typical, more imperative and abrupt: the Princess more vivacious, her blue eyes, still so large and full of light, more rounded, her white hair, that had formerly been golden, now still more white and soft — she seemed to smoke yet more cigarettes, as she sat in the corner by the stove, fanning herself, while through her head ran the nostalgic, circular melodies of Tchaikowsky, so that once more there came back to her the swinging movement of the Court Balls, the uniforms and crinolines and scents and sloping shoulders, the pink champagne, the whiskers, and the dying hum of talk at the rattle and drumming of the tall golden maces on the floor when the Imperial Family entered the room. As though the exile which cut them off from the circumstances and places that had formed their characters had yet still further defined their respective traits, made each of them more typical, the Princess could now detect a draught at one hundred yards, the Duchess feel faint in the frostiest winter room if a jonquil scented it. The Princess would sit almost at the side of the stove, like a cat warming itself, while the Duchess would complain, even, of the heat of her unheated church. They altered little, very little : though the Princess would, from time to time, shuddering in her furs, allow herself the indulgence of a cold, while eau-de-cologne and smelling-salts would aid the Duchess's headache, caused — after one of her rare visits to the boarding-house — by Anastasie's stove. . . . For the rest the two old ladies were sound in wind, hair, eye, ear and tooth.

And so they lived on through the changing seasons by the side of the Lake, watching the glacial shadows of green deepen to summer blue, watching the magnolias extend white cups that later turned to tawny vellum on the glossy trees, the mauve chalices of the autumn crocus starring the lawns, until even the Princess could admit to ninety-two and the Duchess was undeniably within sight of her century. Both ladies grew more and more revered each year ; for death is the chief — if last — dishonour to the living (and one which most of us will go a long distance out of our way to avoid), and so, in consequence, great age is everywhere honoured, because the overdue survival of any individual proves that in the long run humanity in the mass can lengthen, albeit only by ever so little, the normal span of its days.

Nevertheless the end was, naturally enough, drawing near. . . . This particular year had been, as usual, an unusual one. In March, it had been August ; in May all the flowers of the vines had been destroyed by a hail-storm ; in July there had been such a drought that the Lake had evaporated far enough down to show the lake-dwellings of paleolithic times, still fixed in primeval mud ; September had exhibited the borders of the Lake again with all its luxuriant gardens flooded and drowned; and now, at Christmas (admittedly for once at the right season), came the Great Frost. The whole Lake was frozen over, a thing that had not occurred for a century, and people accepted the event with joy.

For a full week the entire population skated day and night, with a strangely anti-Calvinistic fervour. Flares could be seen after dark, in every direction, gilding the flanks of the mountains, and bandsmen, with faces and hands blue from cold, blared out Waldteufel waltzes, leaving a dragon's-tail of breath behind them on the air, while dumpy, Breughel-like figures, in their warm, padded clothes, danced and glided in ecstatic time to them. Huge fires were lighted on the ice, and oxen were roasted whole.

Frigid as was the air, the Princess could not resist this gaiety. And so, when it was at its height, she persuaded the Duchess to walk down with her to the edge of the Lake to watch the carnival. The Princess moved a little tremblingly with the aid of a very delicate, tortoise-shell-topped cane; the Duchess walked boldly, supporting herself with a stout country stick. The Princess wore her fur coat; the Duchess, a thick woollen outfit of some sort. It had not been long dusk; the fires were blazing, the torches flickering in a light breeze flecked with particles of ice. Both of them stood there in their snow-shoes in this icy world on the border of the Lake — on, as it were, the very edge of eternity — watching and listening. What a delightful scene!

'Do you remember the first time you came to stay with us in Petersburg, Rita, and all the bells ringing as we tore through the night on sleighs . . . and how we thought those times would never end?' . . .

'And that winter in Munich, Anastasie, the skating and the supper-party in the Pavilion?' . . .

The Duchess looked at her watch. 'But that was all long ago — and now it is my bed-time.' . . . Indeed it was ten minutes past seven, very late for her, and they both returned to their homes, one plodding her way along, the other swaying a little on her feet.

It proved to be their last appearance together. The next day the Duchess developed a fever which she attributed to the heat of the fires, that had flamed, waving their golden wings, high above the ice; whilst the Princess was attacked by ague, due, she said, to the intense cold of the previous evening. Within forty-eight hours they were both dead.

Their illnesses were not painful, and merely seemed the ailments of two children. . . . It was nothing, the Duchess said, and would soon yield to fresh air. Through wide-open windows she had listened to the music on the ice and had enjoyed it. When darkness came, she would not have the curtains drawn, but watched the fires — which she considered responsible for her present state — being rekindled. At seven in the evening, the hour, originally, of her retirement, she sat up in bed and with great vigour asked her maid to push up the windows still further. Elsa, the woman who had for so long attended the Duchess, did as she was bidden, and to her surprise, heard the old lady croak a few notes, harsh but gay: then the voice stopped. And, when she turned round, it was to find that her mistress was dead.

The Princess had not slept. All day long in her room, so high up, with panes of glass misty from the heat, she had bent across the vases of anemones and narcissus to peer at the flying figures on the ice. From time to time she would retire to bed again, but always the distant sound of the music drew her back tremblingly to the window. The curtains were drawn as soon as it was dusk; the music only reached her faintly and she lay still. When she looked at her watch it was about six o'clock — she was late! It was past the time for her to begin getting up, she said. . . . But she was tired. She shivered, and fumbled with the things by her side, boxes, bottles, ikons. She pressed a button, and up out of a box sprang a little enamelled nightingale, moving from side to side with fluttering wings, and for a moment sang. She smiled and listened, and then, as it fell back into the darkness of its box, her heart, too, fell suddenly, and all her memories went with it. . . . Even from the neighbouring houses her relations could be heard crying the whole night long, and the whole of the next day.

‘YOU CAN CARRY IT, MRS. PARKIN’

OR

MONOLOGUE WITH A CLOTHES-BRUSH

(From *A Century of the Common Man*)

‘You can carry it, Mrs. Parkin. . . .’ She could see Madame Rosalie — now as she had knelt on the floor, and then suddenly looked up and said, so nicely, with a smile full of pins, ‘You can carry it, Mrs. Parkin’.

Mrs. Parkin gave the coat a despairing, angry shake, and then a hit, and disconsolate threads, hairs and pieces of mud and fluff floated down from it. Her face must for many years have been that of such a pretty baby, but now it was only a round disc with a stubby nose thrown upon it — fortunately in the centre. When she grew angry it puckered and pouted, the lines hardened beneath the surface of fat, the lips became two violin strings, parallel, in a hot mould of anger.

Six weeks the coat had been used, if not seven! . . . She gave it another shake and a large piece of trimming fell from the sleeve — fur trimming. ‘Never be fit to put on again, never . . . must have been wearing it day and night, by the look of it, and it isn't even as if it *could* have suited her. It wanted a woman, not just a girl, flat all over, someone with what you call *presence*.’ And, oh, it had been a fine thing, a lovely thing. . . . Mr. Parkin always believed in getting the best. ‘Best in the beginning is best in the end,’ he used to say, ‘and then it lasts.’ So Mrs. Parkin had ordered the coat to be made for her specially. . . . Arthur was doing nicely now and she could afford it, could easily have a car and two maids, dressed differently in mauve and brown, with caps to match — if only there were cars and maids to find. As it was, just as she had been expecting to sit back and have a little comfort at her age, here she was, obliged to work harder than ever. And that was what made it so much worse about the coat. ‘I wouldn't have minded,’ she said to herself, ‘if the girl couldn't have afforded it. Neither I nor Mr. Parkin are the sort to be mean and miserly — but after all I've known Doreen — to me she'll *never* be *Dolores* — since a child, and Mrs. Ridder, her mother, had always been a friend of mine. In all the twenty years — or is it twenty-one? — I think it's twenty, but I won't be sure — we've never had a wrong word, except once, nor has Mr. Parkin with Mr. Ridder — and then to return the coat in that condition! Not that I'm saying anything against *Mrs. Ridder*. I speak as I find.'

Mrs. Parkin could see the scene now, as if it had been yesterday, how the coat had been chosen, how she had worn it. . . . It must have been three years before the war, when things were already going better, that she had decided on it. 'But just look at it now! The buttons gone as well — and you can't find buttons!' she said aloud in a tone of anguish. 'Can't get 'em — at any rate to match. . . . All the airs and all the graces, and to look at it you wouldn't think she kept good company. . . . *Ugh! It smells awful, too!*' she said, holding part of the coat close against her nose, 'awful. I can't think where she has been, all creased and greasy, worn here and there. You might think she'd been sleeping on the Embankment. You wouldn't know it for the same thing.'

Mirrors, dusty and fly-blown mirrors, black-framed mirrors that seemed freckled and wrinkled with time, had stared each other in the eye, with Mrs. Parkin pressed between them, when she had tried it on. Oh, Madame Rosalie knew how to make a good thing and was not expensive. 'Not that I'm saying,' Mrs. Parkin would say, 'that it is cheap. It *isn't* cheap, but that you can't expect, and Mr. Parkin wouldn't wish it. He often says to me, "Mother, I am not a rich man," he says, "I've had my ups and downs, as one might say, but you must have the best, always the best. The best is only good enough for Mrs. Parkin."'

Madame Rosalie had crouched there like a black dwarf. Sometimes she knelt and sometimes stood on tiptoe. She could not speak, except in a muffled voice, because of the pins — and even that required concentration. Every now and then she took a pin, miraculously saliva-free, from rouged lips, looked at Mrs. Parkin attentively, and stabbed the bust, drew in the cloth, just where it was needed. It was extraordinary the way she *built* that coat — that is where the art comes in.

'And I should have the fur edge a little lower here,' she had said, 'or it might be a little higher there. It wants what I call a sweep. Anything smaller would look skimpy on you. It isn't that you're stout. Of course you're not. But you've a figure, and it's a pity not to show it, only we must be careful — a little carelessness, a little negligence, and we lose the whole effect.' . . . The dressmaker now revolved the image of Mrs. Parkin in the fly-blown mirror, as if her customer had been a bit of meat — hung not in good cloth, but in muslin to protect her, in a cool and stony larder, the mirrors being the gratings for the air. 'It wouldn't do. It's no good pinching, pulling in and lacing you, Mrs. Parkin. *You* don't want lots of fussy little ornaments, *you* want something bold and with a line. . . . You see what I mean, a sweep towards the hip, and just a simple pleat below the bust. The stripe *is* broad. I admit it. The fur *is* highly coloured, I confess. It would not suit everyone. But you can take it, madam; *you* can carry it, Mrs. Parkin.'

When finished, it did not cling to her, the coat; it swept round her like a battleship pursuing its own course upon the sea; a rich sepia brown with a suggestion of every sort of varnish chequered by a musty, botulistic stripe of purple, and edged with lilac fur that looked the *real* thing. . . . The first time she had worn it was at Newborough and, as she had advanced down the steps from the Italian Pergola into the Rosarium, as they called it, the coat had caused a sensation; that she could feel; *where* had she got it, the shouting crowd of holiday-makers was asking, where had she got it, the musing crowd of rose-lovers demanded. And yet it was not that the people looked at it because it had a bit of this and a bit of that, it was the *line* and the *colour*. ('You can carry it, Mrs. Parkin.') She had worn a hat to match, a fur-trimmed hat with a purple flower, but of course, coming down the flight of steps, with the blue peace-time sea below and sands lying, where the sea had receded, like acres of washed-out linen, and the bands playing swing, and Sandy Macpherson sounding out from the cafeteria at the corner, she could see it *would* look its best, wouldn't it? . . . She felt she walked differently, too, when she was wearing it, sailed as you might say, for though it swept quite low towards the skirt's hem, it was loose, fell as though draped, and in no way impeded movement.

People admired it equally at home when she got back. She did not put it on every Sunday, not by any means, and more in spangled summer than in spring. It seemed to suit that time of year when all the flower-beds groaned with bees and bluebottles. If she went to church with Mr. Parkin and Sonia, she would wear it sometimes, and everybody liked it, and she'd worn it at the Confirmation. 'Three years ago, already. . . . Dreadful how time flies! It seems it was only yesterday that Sonia was christened!' . . . She remembered well the first time she had worn the coat at church and Mr. Pilcher, by the lych-gate, had stopped her, and stood there talking, and had said, 'It's a lovely coat, Mrs. Parkin, the sort of thing you would expect a Bride's Mother to wear at a fashionable wedding, with lots of big people there. And who knows, Mrs. Parkin,' he had added, 'that you won't soon be a Bride's Mother, Sonia as pretty as she is, and like her mother?' And then Mr. Pilcher had pinched the child in a way that Mr. Parkin had not liked at all. (You never could tell, Mr. Parkin used to say. 'Stranger things have happened, mother. You don't read the Sunday papers like I do. *Pretty as she is!* . . .') 'And who knows,' Mrs. Parkin asked herself in a fury, 'that Mr. Pilcher mayn't be right? After all, there *are* coupons now, and things *are* difficult, and if Sonia and Basil do get on together — I know it sounds silly when they're so young — but *if* they *do*, then where, I ask you, can I get another coat like this? I might well have chosen to wear it. . . . Look at it now — and all, as usual, because of kindness.' Her face set firmer. 'But I must say one thing, Mr. Parkin always warned me. Time after time, he said, "Mother," he said, "you're too kind. That's what it is. You let them all make a fool of you, but I see through them! You may *think* they like you. They don't mean a nice word they say. *It's all put on.* You're too kind, far too kind. You *ought* to give them the rough side of your tongue, Mother, like I do. I wish you'd heard how I ticked off Mr. Pilcher afterwards, Mother." (There's something mean and sly, I don't know what, about him. . . . Sonia! Sonia! Where is Sonia? Her father thinks the world of that girl: I don't know what he'd do if anything went wrong.) "And I ticked him off like that, too, when he asked me to lend him the ladder again. 'Ladder,' I said, 'ladder? Not on your soul,' I said, 'and if you ask me again, you won't want anything any more, you dirty, sneaking hound, always coming round for this, that and the other. I'd be ashamed in your place,' I said, 'I'd be ashamed.' But you are too kind, Mother. No, I won't say kind; I call it soft. You *won't* give them the ticking off they need. You let your name be dirt, you do. Don't stand for it. Don't let them ride rough-shod over your body, Mother." And he was right. . . . Look at the coat now!'

Last summer the girl had come down to see Mr. Ridder. And since Doreen — I can't and won't call her Dolores — has been on the films, Sonia had sort of taken a fancy to her (and I don't like the child to see no one. I'm not that kind. To my mind, it was what led to Pamela going odd like that. Her mother never let her see boys and girls of her own age.) . . . Well, Mr. Parkin and me are not like that. Live and let live, we say — of course, if we like them — and Sonia *is* a funny girl: very artistic, they said, at the school, sings now quite a lot as well as plays, for I was determined to have her taught the piano. "She must have a chance," I said. "*I* never had it." "Chance of what?" Mr. Parkin asked. "I think you're silly, Mother, spoiling her and wanting to buy a fumed-oak-harpsichord-piano for all that money, and things what things are now." But I had made up my mind, because my cousin Betty — the one that married Mr. Barber — could play anything she heard by heart, straight out of her head, and only with two fingers, though it sounded so natural that strangers often thought she must be using ten. So it's in the family, you see, and I want her to have a chance. *I* never had it, and if she don't take her chance, then she doesn't deserve it, and I'll sell the piano. It's always worth the money. . . . But everyone now says that I was right. Sometimes she'll play with all the wireless going, and still you'll hear her. . . . Well, she took a sort of fancy to Doreen. I said to her, "Sonia, you *are* silly. Don't cheapen yourself. People will say you are running after her, just because she has made a hit, and *I* think she gives herself airs. If I were you I'd tell her off. I'd tick her off, I'd tell her straight, I would; I wouldn't put up with it, and you know what your father says, 'As it is, you're too easy, Mother.'" . . . Well, Doreen came down, and I'm not saying that she wasn't nice spoken. It was June and hot, and she had a swanky fur rug and no coat. Of course she had been accepted, and passed the tests, and *had* walked on in the films, that one can't deny, and she was nice to Sonia and made her play the piano to her. "I think you are too wonderful, you little darling," she said to her, very old-like, "and it's just what the Public adores." Well, after that, when it turned cold and I found she hadn't got a coat, I said to her, "Doreen — you won't mind *me* calling you *Doreen*, I know — *I* could lend you a coat to go home in, but send it back to me directly — not that it's the only coat I've got, but I value it because Mr. Parkin likes it, so you will return it, won't you? You'll be sure to send it back to me tomorrow or Tuesday at the latest? Send it back to me, won't you, Doreen?" And she said, "Of course, darling Mrs. Parkin. How angelic of you!" — like that. And seven weeks, nearly eight, passed by — and then returned to me — just look at it — with a note I wouldn't have written to a chimney-sweep!

'DEAR ALL,

Thanks awfully. Here goes to return the coat in case you still need it.

All the best. DOLORES

'Eight weeks, it was, and nearly nine, and I'll tell her straight, I will, I'll tick her off if ever I see her, and so will Mr. Parkin. "So will your dad, Sonia," I said. "And it isn't even as if she'd looked well in it. She's got a skimpy, niggling figure."' . . . Then Mrs. Parkin fell silent and hit the coat again with the brush, and was quiet, for high in the air, sweet but melancholy angel voices sang for her, 'You can take it, madam. You can carry it, Mrs. Parkin.'

THE GREETING

From outside the long, large windows fires could be seen flickering in many wide grates, while the comforting sense, more than smell, of warm food oozed out of the whole house, subduing the sharper scent of frosty air. The dining-room table, she noticed as she passed by, was laid for three persons, and decorated with four small silver vases, from which a few very rigid flowers drew themselves up into the light of the windows. The sideboard showed beyond, bearing various drab meats and some pieces of plate, its cold glitter tempered by the flames with patches of warm orange.

As soon as Nurse Gooch was shown into the drawing-room, almost, indeed, before she had shaken hands or remarked how nice it was to see a fire, they went in to luncheon. But seated before this white expanse, these three people could not succeed in materialising any conversation that, as talk should, drawing its strength from the group but stronger than any individual member of it, would continue almost automatically, reproducing itself or taking on a fresh form from time to time. In the same way in which spiritualists claim that the presence of one sceptic at a séance is sufficient to prevent any manifestation, however hoped for and credited by the majority, here it was difficult for the talk to glow or prosper, when one of this small party was continually exerting her will to the utmost in order to produce a lasting and uncomfortable silence. The stagnant quiet of the room was seldom broken, then, except by the rather horse-like stepping of the footmen, or by the thin, stringy voice of the invalid projected through the mute air in querulous inquiry. And, in the very act of speaking herself, both by the purpose and calculated tone of her question, she enforced a silence on the others. Colonel Tonge tried to make conversation to the new-comer, placed between him and his sick wife, but his abrupt, pompous little sentences soon withered, frozen on the air by his wife's disapproval. Mrs. Tonge, however, as we have said, permitted herself to ask a question occasionally — a question which, though it appeared innocent, was designed to convey to her new nurse the impression that she was an injured, ill-used woman. 'When, Humphrey,' she would ask, 'do you intend to put electric light into the house? I have asked you to do it for so many years now. I am sure I should sleep better, and should not be such a worry to you or to Nurse', or 'What about that summer-house, Humphrey? Will it be ready for me in the spring? If I am still with you, I intend going there every day when the weather is warmer. Perhaps I shall find a little peace there in the woods. But I fear it hasn't been touched yet.' To these questions the Colonel returned smooth, soothing answers, but ones which did not commit him in any way; but these, rather than conciliating the invalid, seemed only to vex her the more. But at this early period, before she understood her nurse, before she knew that anything she said would soon be pardoned, she did not actually as yet accuse her husband of doing all in his power to make and to keep her ill, but was content to let this accusation remain implicit in her questions, and in the sound of her voice. Still, Nurse Gooch felt instinctively that Mrs. Tonge did not want to hurt her, that she was not in reality ill-natured, but that this calculated putting-out of the social fire was the outcome of a thousand little injuries inflicted by an imagination warped by constant illness and want of sleep. But whether it was due to the atmosphere created by this friction between husband and wife, or to something in the surroundings — in the house itself — she did most certainly, at this first moment of her arrival, experience an uneasy feeling, a slight repulsion from the Grove, which passed as soon as she became better acquainted with it.

Tonge's Grove, a square house, lies like a box thrown down among hanging woods and open commons — a charming residence in many ways. Like a doll's house it seems, each room giving the correct proportion to the rather under-life-size figures it displays. A curiously inappropriate setting, certainly, for any drama, the protagonists of which must find themselves cramped in their action by the wealth of detail imposed. The very comfort and well-being of the place would give a grotesque air to any but an accustomed or trivial event. For here, long habit appears so much more important than the occasion or fact it originally enshrined, inanimate objects so much more actual, more active, than human beings, that it is upon the house, and not upon its owners, that our attention is first focused. It is this superfluity of things, combined with a rigorous pruning of reality, that gives a certain significance to any fact of life should it be strong enough to enter these gates, yet remain quick. For reality, which is usually unpleasant, seldom touches lives such as these except at birth, of which, fortunately, we are all ignorant, or at death, a latent, lurking fear (an ogre at the end of every passage), but one which it is our very human convention to ignore.

The Grove is not really a small house; the rooms in it are large and numerous; but, like a square toy thrown in among garden beds and stables, crinoline-shaped lime-trees and red-walled angular orchards, among, in fact, all the long-settled paraphernalia annexed to a prosperous, well-ordered way-of-life, it was endowed with a perfection such as at first to make it seem miniature, like some exquisite model seen through a glass case.

Certainly there is beauty about an estate of this kind: that tamed country sentiment, so English in quality, clings to it, till even the bird-song that trickles down through the dripping blue shadows thrown by tall trees seems arranged, punctual, and correct as the mechanical chirping of one of those clockwork birds that lift enamelled wings out of a square black box; and even the cuckoo, who makes so ominous a sound from the cool green fortifications of wood or hedgerow, here changes his note till it rings hollow and pure as a church bell. No sense of mystery broods in the green and open spaces bathed in yellow summer sunlight; here are no caves, grottoes, tumbling torrents: everything is neat, shallow as the clear, slightly running streams that border the wood; yet surely such beauty is, in a way, more fantastic than any of Leonardo's piled-up rocks or those worlds of ogres and giants to which we are carried off by some of the primitive painters.

In the winter it is that all these country places are seen in their best, their most typical, phase. Stout built for cold weather, these houses take on a new quality, upstanding among hoar-frost, glowing warmly through the crisp, grey air. The first impression of the Grove would be, we think, a childlike memory of potting-shed smells, full of the scents of hidden growth; an odour of bulbs, stoves, rich fibrous mould and bass, mingles with the sharp aromatic smell of the bonfire that crackles outside. On the walls of the shed the bass is hung up like so many beards of old men — ritual beards, like those of Pharaoh or Egyptian priest, which, perhaps, the gardener will don for the great occasions of his year. This one he would put on for the opening of the first spring flower, coming up glazed and shrill, its petals folded as if in prayer, out of the cold brown earth, beneath the laced shadows woven by the bare branches of the trees; this he will wear for the brazen trumpet-like blowing of the tulip-tree; while that one he reserves for the virginal unfolding of the magnolia, or the gathering-up of petals let drop by the last rose. But the gardener himself soon dispels these tender imaginings, as you see his burly form bent over various cruel tasks — the trapping of the soft mole, or in aiming at the fawn-coloured fluffy arcs of the rabbits, as they crouch in their green cradles, their ears well back, nibbling the tender white shoots that he has so carefully nurtured.

Outside the shed in many glass frames large violets, ranging in tone from a deep purple through magenta to an almost brick-red, their petals scintillating damply, glisten like crystallised fruit seen through a glass window, sweet but unapproachable. The ground of the kitchen garden is hard and shiny, starched with frost; trees, shrubs, and the very grass are stiff and brittle, sweeping down under the slight wind with a shrill, steely sound. But the orchard walls still glow as if stained with the juice of the ripe fruits that press against them in summer and autumn, red, purple and bloomy, while the house beyond shows warmly through the tree whose topmost twigs pattern themselves about it, like cobwebs against the sky; soft it is, as if cut from red velvet. Out of its doors and windows sounds the monotonous, dry-throated rattle of pet dogs setting up a comfortable yet irritating competition with the noises of stable and farmyard, where rosy-faced men bustle about, lumbering in heavy boots; or, leaning to one side, the right arm lifted and at an angle, blow loudly and whistle, as they polish still more the varnished horses, their breathing lingering on after them in the sharp air like dragon's-breath. Through the windows of the house each fireplace shows up, while the red flowers blaze in it, or die down to a yellow flicker, fighting ineffectually against the thin silver rapiers of the winter sun.

But more than all these things would you notice here the bitter cackle of a green parrot, falling through the drawn-out air with a horrid clatter, tumbling all lesser sounds down like a pack of cards. Certainly that menacing silly sound of a parrot's laughter would be your most abiding memory.

On such a noon as this it was that Nurse Gooch had first driven up to the Grove; so that, even if her first impression was a rather uneasy one, she had at any rate seen it wearing its most pleasant, most comfortable, aspect; for at night the character of every house changes — and this one alters more than most. The smiling comfort of the surroundings is lost, fades out into utter blackness, and a curious sub-flavour, unnoticed in the day, manifests itself. There are places and moments when the assumptions, the lean conventions on which our lives are based, become transparent, while, for an instant, the world we have made rocks with them. It is, for example, usually assumed that there are no such creatures as sea-serpents, yet there are certain places in Europe, on our own placid coasts even, of such marvellous formation that we feel, suddenly, that the existence of these monsters is a certainty — that it would surprise us less to see a vast beast, such as those painted by Piero di Cosimo, with flame-forked tongue, gigantic head and long writhing body, coming up out of the fathomless green depths, than to see a passing country cart, a clergyman or anything to which our experience has accustomed us. There are moments, too, when death, which, as we have said, it is usually our custom to hide away in a dusty corner of our minds, peeps round at us, grimacing — and we realise it as one of the universal and most awful conditions upon which we are permitted to take up life. So it was with the Grove, when darkness coffined it round. The dwarf perfection, which we have attempted to describe, would gradually disappear; for the very dimensions of the house seemed to alter as the rooms became swollen with darkness, full of inexplicable sound. Dead people walk here with more certain step than the living, their existence seems more substantial, their breathing more audible. The boarding of the floor yields under an invisible step, as if some strange memory stirs in it, and the panelling of the walls, the very furniture, make themselves heard with a hard, wooden creaking, which is magnified in these rooms now grown to the new proportions with which night endows them. And, in the darkness outside, everything moves, stirs, rustles.

It was therefore not to be wondered at that the Grove should have acquired the reputation of being haunted, though, really, the unhappy restless air that pervaded it at night may have been due more to its long association with a family of sad, unfortunate temperament — amounting in certain cases to something worse — than to the actual walking presence of any ghost. For ever since the present house was built, late in the seventeenth century, it had been in the possession of the Tonges and, until recently, until in fact the present owner had inherited the estate, there had been a long history connected with it of brooding melancholy, that must have been nearly allied to madness.

But Colonel Tonge, as we have seen, presented an ordinary enough character, with nerves unaffected, betraying no sign of hereditary disorder. Among the properties we have described — house, lawn, garden, farm and stable — this not altogether unattractive figure emerges, strutting like a bantam. A proud little man, with a fairly distinguished military career, fond of hunting and shooting, he was much engaged in the business of an estate, the extent and importance of which he was apt to magnify in his own mind. In addition to these interests, he was involved in the affairs of every district committee, and, as became him in his dual capacity of squire and military man, was much to the fore in all those local philanthropic schemes which had for their object the welfare of the ex-soldier, or the helping of widow and children.

Yet in spite of this inherited make-up of country gentleman and the acquired one of soldier, there was about the Colonel on closer acquaintance some quality that removed him ever so little from the usual specimen of his class, just as there was something about the Grove that differentiated it from the run of English country-houses. In what, then, did this difference consist? Partly, perhaps, in the stress that he laid upon the importance of his belongings, and therefore of himself; but more, surely, in the extraordinary calm that marked his demeanour — a quiet unruffled calm, not quite in accord with his bristling appearance and apparent character. One never saw him lose his temper, never even about trivialities, such as is the way of most military commanders; yet his restraint did not seem to arise so much from good nature as from the fear of losing his self-control even for a moment — suggesting that he was suppressing some instinct or emotion which must be very strong within him, if it was necessary continually to exert such an iron self-discipline. This contrast between nature and manner showed itself, too, in the difference between his uneasy, wandering eyes and the tightly drawn mouth. But if Nurse Gooch had, with more than her normal sensitiveness, felt at first that there was a rather queer atmosphere about the house, she had at any rate detected nothing unusual in the look or manner of this amiable, rather pompous, little man, and, indeed, the only person who appreciated thoroughly these various subtle distinctions was Mrs. Tonge. This poor lady had married her first cousin, and appeared to have inherited or acquired his, as well as her own, share of the peculiarly nervous temperament of this family. Thin, tall, and of that ash-grey colour which betokens constant sleeplessness, her rather sweet expression, while it was in direct contradiction to her restless, irritable soul, was the only remnant of a former prettiness. For, when first she married, she had been a good-looking, high-spirited girl, but had suddenly, swiftly, sunk into this state of perpetual and somewhat nagging melancholy. She was in reality a stupid woman, but her frayed nerves bestowed upon her an understanding of, and insight into, the unpleasant side of life that were alarming in the sureness of their judgment, and must have made of her a trying companion. She added to these heightened perceptions a sense of grievance aggravated by an absolute lack of any interest or occupation, and by the fact that she was childless. She complained constantly, her chief lament being that there were only three creatures in the world that cared for her, two dogs — a Pomeranian and a Pekinese — and her beloved green parrot! Often she would add a remark to the effect that her husband would like — was, in fact, only waiting for — Polly to die. His triumph would then, apparently, be complete. And it must truthfully be said that the only thing which ever seemed to disturb the Colonel's calm was the idiot-laughter which the parrot would let fall through the darkened air of the sick woman's room. But though the slightest noise at any other time would strain Mrs. Tonge's taut nerves almost to breaking-point, she appeared actually to enjoy her bird's head-splitting mirth; while the parrot, in return, seemed to acknowledge some bond of affection between his mistress and himself, for, were she more than usually ill, he would be ever so quiet, not venturing to exercise his marked mimetic gifts, even repressing his habitual laughter.

This love for her parrot and her pet dogs, together with a certain trust in, more than affection for, her young nurse — a trust which developed as the months passed — were all the assets of which Mrs. Tonge was conscious in this life. For the rest she was lonely and frightened . . . very frightened. Her whole existence was spent in a continual state of fear — one of the worst symptoms, though quite a common one, of neurasthenia; she was afraid of her neighbours, her husband, her house, terrified by everything and everybody alike. But, while frightened of everything, she was as consistently opposed to any plan for the alleviation of these imagined terrors.

Afraid, though seemingly without reason, of her husband, she was yet never able to refrain from making the fullest use of any opportunity to irritate, hurt or annoy him. But he was very patient with her. She would taunt him with things big and little; she would attack him about his self-importance, or goad him before the nurse about his fondness for giving good advice to others, in a manner that must have made him feel the sting of truth. She would even accuse him of wishing to be rid of her — a poor invalid and one who was in his way — an accusation which, however, she could never really have believed for a moment. She would tell him that he had a cruel soul, and in her sick mind seemed to have fashioned a grotesque, caricatured little image of her husband, which, to her, had at last come to be the reality — an image, unlike yet in a way recognisable, of a queer, patient, cruel, rather wolf-like creature, hiding his true self beneath the usual qualities attached to the various very ordinary interests and pursuits in which his life was spent.

In spite of this extraordinary conception of him, Mrs. Tonge was always calling for her husband. Her plaintive voice echoing through the square, lofty rooms would be answered by his gruff, military tones so often that one of the parrot's most ingenious tricks was a perfect rendering of 'Humphrey, come here a minute!' and the answering call

'Yes, Mary, I'm coming', followed by the sound of hurrying footsteps. Thus, though frightened of him, though almost hating him, the invalid would hardly allow her husband to leave her, if only for a day.

Still more was Mrs. Tonge frightened of her house — that home which she knew so intimately. But, in the same perverse manner, she would never quit it, even for a night. While suffering terribly from insomnia, and from that fear of darkness which, though it usually leaves us when our childhood is past, had never wholly left her, she was steadfast in her refusal to allow Nurse Gooch to sleep in the same room, thus lessening these nocturnal terrors by human companionship. On the contrary, the sick woman not only insisted on being alone, but was resolute in locking both the doors of her room, one of which led into her husband's bedroom, the other into the passage outside, so that had she been seized with sudden illness, which was not altogether unlikely, no help could have reached her. Thus, bolted securely within those four walls, she would indulge her broken spirit in an orgy of sleepless terror. The dogs slept downstairs: her only companion was Polly, noiseless now, but faithful as ever, sitting hunched up on his perch, his dome-like cage enveloped in a pall of grey felt; and, even had he sounded his bitter, head-splitting laughter, it would have seemed more sweet than the music of any southern nightingales to the poor invalid, tossing about on her bed. For the parrot, alone of the animal world, could give his mistress some feeling of momentary security.

Day would come at last, to bring with it an hour or two of grey, unrefreshing sleep. The afternoon she would spend knitting, seated in a large arm-chair in front of the fire, in her overheated boudoir, crowded with strong-smelling flowers. Photographs of friends — friends whom she had not seen for years and had perhaps never really cared for — littered all the furniture, and clambered up the walls, over the fireplace, in an endless formation, imbuing the room with that peculiar morbid tone of old photographs, yellow and glazed as death itself. Bustles, bonnets, then straw hats and leg-of-mutton sleeves, showed grotesquely in these little squares of faded, polished cardboard, set off by a palm-tree in an art-pot, a balustraded terrace, a mountainous yet flat background, or one of those other queer properties of the old photographic world. The wistful smiles on these pretty faces were now gone like her own, the smoothness of the skin was now replaced by hundreds of ever so small wrinkles, the fruit of care, sorrow or some seed of ill-nature or bad temper that, undreamt-of then, had now blossomed. The rest of open space on table, piano or writing-desk was taken up by diminutive unconnected vases of violets, freesias or jonquils, their heavy breath weighing on the air like a cloud, seeming among these photographs so many floral tributes to dead friendship, each one marking the grave of some pretended or genuine affection. The room was overloaded with these vases; the flowers lent no grace to the room, no sweetness to the over-burdened air. The Pomeranian yapped at Mrs. Tonge's feet, the Pekinese lay curled up in a basket, while at her elbow the parrot picked at a large white grape, the stale odour of the bird's cage mingling with the already stifling atmosphere of the room, till it became almost intolerable. Here the invalid would sit for hours enjoying one of the thousand little grievances from which she was able to choose, turning it over and pecking at it like the parrot at his grape; or, perhaps, she would be gripped by one of the manifold terrors of her life. Then that supreme horror, the fear of death (which, as she grew older, claimed an ever greater part of her attention), grimaced at her from the scented shadows, till it seemed to her as if she sat there knitting endlessly her own shroud, and the vases of flowers transformed their shapes, rearranging themselves till they became wreaths and crosses, and the hot smell they exhaled became the very odour of death. Then she would ring again, calling for Nurse Gooch, but even that familiar footfall would make her shudder for an instant.

Her only pleasure now consisted in the tormenting of her even-tempered husband, or, in a lesser degree, of the poor young nurse — to whom she had now become attached in the same sense that a dog is attached to any object, such as a doll or an indiarubber ball, which it can worry. But Gooch, good and amiable, clean-looking rather than pretty, her face fully expressing that patience and kindness which were her two great qualities, won the affections not only of the invalid but of Colonel Tonge, and even of the servants — this latter no mean conquest when it is remembered that there is a traditional feud between servants and trained nurse, almost rivalling the other hereditary vendetta between nursery and schoolroom. Nurse Gooch was really fond of her patient, in spite of the maddening irritation of her ways: nor had she been unhappy during these eighteen months that had followed her luncheon at the Grove on that first winter day. For after the hardships of her own childhood, she appreciated this solid, very comfortable, home, while it presented to her a full scope for the exercise of those protective instincts which were particularly deep-rooted in her nature. Often, in a way, she envied Mrs. Tonge her kind husband and charming house, thinking how happy the invalid might have been had only her disposition been a different one. For in Colonel Tonge the young nurse could see nothing but consideration for his ill wife, and kindness indeed to everyone, till, slowly, she formed in her own mind an image of him very different from that fashioned by his wife. To Nurse Gooch he was a model of suffering chivalry; to her his stature and heart seemed great, his importance equal to his own estimate of it. In fact, he became that very appealing combination — one which always fascinates the English people — a hero in public, a martyr in private life. And it was a source of great comfort for her to reflect that by keeping Mrs. Tonge in as good a mood as possible, or, to borrow a military phrase, by intentionally drawing the fire on to herself, she was able to some small extent to alleviate the trials of the husband. Then she could feel, too, in some mysterious manner, that he was grateful for it, that he began to take a pleasure in her society, in the knowledge that she understood his difficulties, applauded his moderation. Often they used to sit together, consulting with Dr. Maynard, a clever doctor, but one who lacked courage, and was in the habit of giving way to his patients. Gradually, therefore, if any new symptom showed itself, if any new problem arose regarding the invalid, it was with the nurse and not with the doctor that Colonel Tonge would first come to talk it over.

Existence at the Grove, though each day appeared to her encompassed in the span of an hour, so that she was continually finding herself landed, as if by some magic carpet of the fourth dimension, at the corresponding time of the next day, yet seemed eternal; even the state of the sick woman, though her nerves became ever more affected, appeared to be stationary. Outside there was the fat, placid life of the countryside to be watched, the punctual revolution of the seasons. First came the ice-green glitter of the snowdrops, frosting the grass of the park with their crystal constellations; then these faded, withered, turned yellow, deepened to the butter-colour of the daffodils that ousted them, flowers swaying their large heads under the spring winds, transparent, full of the very colour of the sun; and, almost before you had time to observe it, they would flush to a deep purple, would be transformed into anemones, the centre of their dusky blossoms powdered with pollen, black like charcoal dust, or would adopt the velvet softness of texture which distinguishes the rose from other flowers: and summer would be in its full flame. Then, inside the Grove, you found good food, punctual hours, a calm routine broken only by the outbursts of Mrs. Tonge, or by the bitter cackle of the parrot, its feathers green with the depth of a tropical forest, its eyes wary and knowing. It looked cunning, as if in possession of some queer secret — some secret such as that of the parrot encountered in Mexico by the traveller Humboldt — a bird which alone in all the world possessed a tongue of its own, since it spoke a language now extinct. For the tribe who talked it had been killed to a man in the course of America becoming a Christian continent, while the bird had lived on for a century.

The summer was a particularly hot one, and as it burnt to its climax, Mrs. Tonge's irritable nerves inflicted an increasing punishment on those around her. The Colonel, who was drawn away on various long-promised visits to old friends and taken to London several times on the business of his estate, left the Grove more than usual this July, so that the full brunt of any trouble in the house fell upon Nurse Gooch, who would often have to shut herself up in her room, and, strong-minded, well-trained woman though she was, cry like a hurt child, so intolerable was the strain imposed upon her by the invalid. The latter soon realised when she had made the tactical error of being too disagreeable — or, perhaps, one should say of concentrating a day's temper in one short hour, instead of spreading it thinly, evenly, over the whole of the sun's passage, so that, looked back upon, it should tinge the day with some unpleasant colour in the minds of her companions or servants. And being possessed of a certain charm or a false kindliness, which she could exert whenever it was necessary to her, she was soon able again to engage the nurse's pity and affection.

'Poor thing', Gooch would think to herself. 'One can't blame her for it. Look how she suffers.' But however true was this reflection, it was the sick woman who was still the chief opponent of any plan for the mitigation of her sufferings. Though her sleeplessness became worse, though the prospect of those long, dark hours threw a shadow blacker than the night itself over each day, yet she still refused to allow Nurse Gooch to rest in the room with her; while Dr. Maynard, who should have insisted on it, was, as usual, completely overborne by his patient.

It is difficult to describe, though, how much Mrs. Tonge suffered, locked in her room during those sultry nights, for their darkness appeared to cover a period easily surpassing the length of any winter night. As she lay there, her limbs twitching, memories dormant in her mind for forty years would rise up to torment her. Her parents, her old nurse (all dead how many summers past!) would return to her here in the silence. All the disappointments of her life would revive their former aching. Once more she would see the gas-lit ballrooms in which she had danced as a girl, and the faces of men she had forgotten half a lifetime ago. Then, again, she would see her wedding. All these memories would link up, and coalesce in feverish waking dreams of but a moment's duration, but which would yet seem to hold all eternity in their contorted perspectives. Wide awake now, she would recall her longing for children, or ponder upon one of her thousand little grievances, which took on new and greater dimensions in these hours. Here she was . . . with a parrot as her only friend . . . in this everlasting blackness. The thought of death would return to her, death that was at the end of each turning, making every life into a blind hopeless cul-de-sac. Long and hard she would fight this spectre of finality, against which no religion had the power to fortify her spirit. Then, after midnight, new terrors began, as the Grove woke up to its strange nocturnal life. Footsteps would sound outside, treading stealthily, stealthily on the black, hollow air; the furniture in the room, cumbersome old cupboards and chests of drawers, would suddenly tattoo a series of little but very definite hard sounds upon the silence, as if rapping out some unknown code. But when everything was swathed in quiet once more, this new absence of noise would be worse, more frightening than were the sounds themselves. It would smother everything with its blackness; everything would be still . . . waiting . . . listening! The silence, from having been merely a form of muffled sound, or perhaps a negation of it, became itself positive, active — could be felt and tested by the senses. There it was again, that creaking — as if someone was listening . . . someone certainly . . . someone standing on a loose board, crouching down in the darkness outside, afraid to tread for fear of waking one. Then would follow a distraction. A new code would be rapped out as something tapped on the window-pane . . . tap — tap — tap, like a mad thing. Only the wind with that branch of ivy, she supposed. There it was again . . . tap — tap . . . like a mad thing trying to get into her room . . . tap — tap . . . into her very head, it seemed! Outside the house a dog would bark once, menacingly, and then its rough voice would die suddenly, as if silenced. Footsteps would tread again down the long passages, footsteps more distinct than ever this time. And once or twice they lingered stealthily at the bolted door; the handle would creak, grasped very carefully, turned by an invisible hand; and was there not the sound of a smothered, animal-like breathing? The wolf-at-the-door, the wolf-at-the-door, she says to herself in that fevered mind, where it seems as if two people, two strangers, were carrying on a whispered conversation of interminable length. Then silence comes once more; an unequalled stillness pours into the room, and into the corridors outside, so that the tapping, when it returns, takes on a new quality, rippling this quiet blackness with enlarging circles of sound, as when a stone is cast into a small pool. Tap — tap — tap . . . again tap. Perhaps she is only dead, being fastened into her coffin. Tap — tap . . . they are nailing it down, tap — tap; and she lies dead in the silence for ever. Then far away the taps sound again and the coffin is unnailed. But this time it is the parrot rapping upon the bars of his dome-like cage with his hard beak; and she is reassured. Grey light clutches again at the swathed windows, and the furniture of the room grows slowly into its accustomed shape; the things round her fall back again into their familiar contours, and are recognisable as themselves, for in the night they had assumed new positions, new shapes, strange attitudes . . . and the poor nervous creature lying on the rumpled bed falls asleep for an hour or two.

But as the light drips stealthily in, filling the black hollows of room and corridor, the housemaids, warned by Nurse Gooch to be more than usually quiet, scratch gently in the passage outside like so many mice, scratch with a gentle feeble sound that must inevitably rouse anyone — even a person who sleeps well by habit and is at that moment deep-rooted in slumber. For this timid, rodent-like noise is more irritating to the strongest nerves, will awaken more surely, than any of that loud, sudden music to which we are accustomed — that music of blows rained accidentally but with great force upon the fragile legs and corners of old furniture or brittle carving of ancient gilded frames — blows delivered with the back of an ever so light feathery brush. Thus Mrs. Tonge would open her eyes upon one more hot and calm morning.

As she lay there, in the semi-darkness, she could hear faint voices sounding in the passage. Soon after she has rung her bell, Nurse Gooch comes in with the letters, as clean and kind as is possible for a human being to be, bright as are all trained nurses in the early morning; too bright, perhaps, too wide awake, and already making the best of it. Her hair has a dark golden colour in it under the light, and gleams very brightly under the cap she is wearing, while she talks in an even, soothing voice. As she goes down the corridor toward the invalid's room the housemaids take her passing presence for a signal that they may resume that noisy bustle of cleanliness with which they salute each day. Suddenly motes of dust whirl up into the air beneath their brushes, turning under the already searching rays of the sun to columns and twisted pillars of sparkling glass that support this heavy firmament, pillars prism-like in the radiant array of their colour. As the housemaids, bent nearly double in their long white print dresses, move slowly over the carpet, brush in one hand, dust-pan in the other, their movements break up these columns, so that the atoms that compose them fall through the air like so many sequins, and are violently agitated; then these take on new shapes, and from pillars are converted into obelisks, pyramids, rectangles and all the variety of glittering forms that, bound by the angles of straight lines, can be imposed upon this dull air and earth by the lance-like rays of the morning sun.

In the room she still lies in bed, turning over the unopened envelopes of her letters. Gooch goes to the window and talks to the parrot. As she uncovers the cage the bird breaks into its metallic laughter, that rattles down through the open window into the shrubbery, like so many brassy rings thrown down by a juggler, for they curve in again at the pantry-window, where John the footman is standing in an apron, cleaning the silver with a dirty-looking piece of old yellow leather and some gritty rose-pink paste. As he polishes the convex mirror formed by the flanks of the silver bowl, while his face reflected in one side assumes a grotesque appearance, the contorted trees and twisted perspective of lawn and garden show in the other. The second housemaid peeps in. 'Oh, you do look a sight!' she cries, bridling with laughter, pointing to the bowl in his hand. 'I may be a sight,' he says, 'or I may not, but I'm not a blarsted slave, am I?' 'Well, you needn't answer so nasty', she said. 'It's not that, it's that parrot — 'ark at it now. I shall be glad when 'e comes back; one can't do no right in this place. Everything is wrong. First it's one damn thing, then another. Nurse sticks it like a soldier,' he says, 'but I stand up for my rights! I'm not a slave, I'm not, that I should stand there letting that blarsted parrot screech at me like a sergeant-major on a parade ground, and her talking a lot of nonsense. I'd like to wring its bloody neck, I would — they're a pair of them, they are!'

And certainly — Nurse Gooch herself had to admit it — the invalid was this summer more than ever exacting. For many months past she had worried her husband about a summer-house, for which she had formed one of those queer, urgent longings that sick people consider themselves free to indulge. The hut had stood there in the woods, year after year, unnoticed, falling to damp decay, when, as if given new eyes, Mrs. Tonge saw it for the first time, and determined to make it her own. Here, she felt, it would be possible to sit quietly, rest peacefully, in an atmosphere different from that of the Grove, and perhaps find that sleep denied her in any other place. As the summer-house was in a very dilapidated condition, she asked her husband to have it repaired for her, but met with a very unexpected opposition. The Colonel, used as he was to furthering every plan of his sick wife, absolutely ignored this new entreaty. Which fact, unfortunately, only strengthened her determination, and made her persist in her caprice.

There was, in reality, some danger in letting Mrs. Tonge remain alone for a long period in a spot so remote from the house — she refused, again, to allow anyone to wait with her in this solitude — for though, as is the habit of permanent invalids, she might live for many years, yet she was a nervous, delicate woman, very liable to a sudden attack of illness, and here no help could reach her. But Dr. Maynard, with his customary inability to say 'No' to a patient — or, perhaps, because he felt that the rest she hoped to obtain here would be more valuable to her than any unexpected attack of illness would be dangerous — gave his sanction to the new scheme. Colonel Tonge, however, still urged the doctor to forbid it, making a strong protest against what he considered this folly, and himself steadfastly refused to have the place touched up in any way, or even swept out. The invalid changed her tactics: from anger she passed to a mood of plaintive injury. 'I know, Humphrey,' she moaned at him, 'that you only go on like that because you hate to think that I am having a peaceful moment. What harm *can* there be in going to the summer-house? It doesn't hurt you, does it?'

The Colonel, patient as ever, would show no sign of ill-temper, putting the case as reasonably as he could. 'Mary, my dear, it is really very unwise and foolish of you. I know how much unemployment there is, how unsettled is the countryside. You should see some of the tramps that are brought up before me on the Bench. That summer-house may seem deep in the woods, but it is very near the high-road. You can never tell who will come into the park. Anyone can get in. There's no lodge near that gate. I tell you, my dear, it isn't safe. I can't think how you can be so silly. It's folly, sheer folly!'

Mrs. Tonge cried a little: 'I'm not afraid of tramps or motor-cars, or of anything on a road. But I know you'd do anything to prevent my getting any rest, Humphrey. I believe you'd like me to go without any sleep at all, as long as it didn't worry you. I know you're only waiting for me to die.' . . . And the poor little man, discomfited, walked away. He was always so patient . . . like that . . . and kind, it made Nurse Gooch feel a great pity for him. But she thought he was wrong in this particular instance — wrong ever to oppose the invalid's wishes, however seldom he did so ; and knowing her influence with him, she persuaded the Colonel to say no more about it, though he still seemed a little uneasy. Yet so great had become his reliance on the young nurse's judgment, that she easily induced him to pretend to his wife that he now thought his opposition had been mistaken.

But Mrs. Tonge could not be deceived. She knew perfectly well that he did not really approve, and it therefore gave her an increased pleasure to rest in the summer-house. Getting up later than ever in these hot months of the year, she would go there every afternoon. She forbade her two pets to be with her, so that a piteous, plaintive yapping filled the Grove each day after luncheon ; only Polly, devoted Polly, was privileged to share this new solitude. Curiously enough, she did not feel frightened here. The rather ominous silence of the woods held no menace for her ; she was happier among these dank shadows than in her own bedroom or placid flowering garden ; and, whether from perversity or from some form of auto-suggestion, it was a fact that when the nurse walked out to the hut to bring the sick woman back to the house for tea, she often found her in a slumber more peaceful than any she had enjoyed for years.

Between two and three o'clock each fine afternoon a queer procession could be seen walking over the lawn between the beds of flowers that lay like embossed embroidery among the sleek grass. First of all came Mrs. Tonge, never glancing aside at flower or tree, her upright carriage and slow-moving walk bestowing an almost ritual air on the proceedings ; then followed the uniform-clad figure of the nurse, holding newspapers and a small cluster of three or four grapes for the parrot in one hand, while from the other dangled the sacred dome. The grapes, transparent, jewel-like, catching the prevailing colour, which was that of the penetrating glow of sunlight through green leaves, focused the eye as they moved along, till they seemed like some mystic regalia, even drawing the eye away from the more metallic colouring of the parrot, who, as he was borne along, shrieked continually, taking an obvious pleasure in scaring the poor timid birds of the English countryside by a display of flaming plumage and alien, rather acrid, laughter. Slowly they passed over the shrill, water-smooth lawns, where single high trees stood up fleecy against the sky, or, over-burdened by the full weight of summer, trailed their branches right down upon the fragrant ground, into the dark woods cloudy with foliage and rank with the smell of tall nettles, elder-trees, bracken, and all those things that grow in unkept places. No bird-song sounded now in this ultimate unfolding of the seasons, and the little path that led winding through this wilderness lay like a curling green ribbon, of a brighter hue than the surrounding shrubs and velvety with moss, from which weeds sprouted up at the corners like small tufts of feathers. This untidy ribbon, lying without purpose across the woodland ground, led to the rustic hut which the caprice of some former mistress of the Grove had caused to be built here, rather pointlessly, some ninety years ago. Under a round roof, sloping down from its centre, and covered with the rough bark of trees, it lay mouldering beneath the structure of branches which hung motionless, as if cut from cardboard, on the heavy air. Sponge-like, it seemed, in its dampness, like some fungus lying about at the foot of a tree. Great knots of ivy clung to the upper part of the door, while, where the peeling bark had fallen away, were revealed arrangements of rusty nails, geometrical, but growing like thorns out of the wood. No view was framed in the pointed spaces of the two windows, except the light which trellised itself with the shadow of green leaves along the ground, or, flooding a stretch of bracken, played first on one leaf, then on another, bringing out unexpected patterns, making each bent-back leaf, as it was touched, the centre of some shifting arabesque design such as is woven in Eastern carpets.

The parrot would be placed on the dingy, bark-covered table; a grape would be half-peeled, and pressed, like a melting jewel, between the bars of the cage. The wire dome would then be draped ceremoniously with grey felt; the invalid would lie back in her long chair, a rug over her knees, the countless newspapers which it was her habit to read placed at her side; and Nurse Gooch would walk back briskly through the dark stillness of the wood out again into the droning odorous languor of the garden.

As Mrs. Tonge rested in her long chair, she found, certainly, a peace otherwise denied to her in the grim world of a sick woman's fancy. No argument, she determined, should ever persuade her to give up this siesta. Day followed day, each warm and bright-coloured as the other; only the leaves became a little ranker in their scent, the woods yet more silent. But sometimes, as she was on the border of sleep, already seeing the queer avenues of that land which she could so seldom reach, while through its landscape she could still distinguish the more rational, familiar features of her real surroundings, a sound like a rushing wind or as if gigantic wings were beating on the taut drum-like fabric of the air, would startle her for a moment, and, looking round, she would see the tall stiff trees lift up their canvas branches, caught by a false breeze, as a motor-car passed between the two high hedges that concealed the road. Above this hidden white scar a high whirling column of dust would dance for a few seconds, as if it were some jinnee of the air made visible for the moment; or, again, she would be lulled by the kindly, cooing voices of the country people, which floated over to her, for, as her husband had pointed out, the road was in reality very near the summer-house. But these things did not appear unpleasant to her; and, in any case, how much better were these explicable sounds than that state of suspended animation, alternating with a sudden show of life, which she had grown to dread so much at night in her own room!

The hot weather continued, and with it the life of the Grove. Colonel Tonge, as we have remarked, was away this summer more than was his wont, but the routine of the invalid, the nurse, and the servants repeated itself almost automatically. Every afternoon Nurse Gooch would walk out with the patient to the hut and would leave her there, only returning in time to fetch her back to the house for tea. One afternoon, when the Colonel was expected home from a short visit to Major Morley, an old friend and brother-officer whom, though a near neighbour, he saw very seldom, Mrs. Tonge suddenly made up her mind to stay out in the summer-house for tea, telling the nurse to bring it out to her at five o'clock. Now, though there was nothing very original or startling in this idea, Gooch, who in matters relating to an invalid did not lack a certain subtlety, at once expostulated — not, indeed, from any feeling of disapproval, but because she well knew that the sick woman would in reality be deeply disappointed if her nurse seemed pleased, or even satisfied, with this new break away from the normal programme. The nurse, therefore, succeeded in putting up a show of anxiety, saying such things as that the patient ought not to be too long alone, or that the Colonel would be hurt and annoyed at finding his wife absent on his return. Finally, pretending to be persuaded against her better judgment, she agreed to bring tea out to the summer-house at five o'clock; then, placing the parrot's cage on the table, she covered it up, completed her ritual, and walked back to the house through the hot, strangely sultry, afternoon.

Mrs. Tonge felt an unaccustomed luxurious ease steal over her as she lay stretched out on her couch reading her papers, though perhaps perusing them less carefully today than was her custom. As a rule, she read them from cover to cover — births, deaths, marriages, sales, advertisements of all kinds; and, while these journals represented every shade of political opinion, she was quite unmoved by their varying propaganda. She regarded them, in fact, as her one form of relaxation. This afternoon, however, she could not fix her attention on them. She peeled an amber, honey-scented grape for Polly, who mumbled back lovingly but softly. What a difference even an hour's sleep makes! She wondered when Humphrey was coming back, feeling that she had been rather hard with him lately — in fact, for some time past. With a sudden impulse of affection the image she had formed of him in her own mind was broken, and he became to her again the young man whom she had loved. She determined that she would be nicer to him; and certainly she felt a little better today. The afternoon in the summer-house seemed just warm enough . . . and quiet . . . nicely quiet, she thought. Slowly, almost contentedly, and for the first time for many years without any fear, any nervous feeling, she stretched her limbs until every nerve in her body became quiet, and sighing gently, let sleep wash over her tired limbs, her worn-out mind, in soft delicious little waves.

But, though the dampness of the hut may have tempered that afternoon heat for Mrs. Tonge, it seemed very breathless outside. Even Nurse Gooch, as she sat sewing in her usually cool room, felt rather overcome. Oh, how hot it was! And the house was very still. As a rule you heard the servants chattering, moving through the passages; the jingling of silver or the rattling of plates would reach you from pantry or kitchen. But today there was no noise — not a sound, except the hot insect-like droning of the sewing-machine, as she bent over it, running the needle along the white edge of the new linen, which filled the room with a rather stifling scent. But directly she stopped, even for an instant, silence flooded the room. Well, one can't look after a case like this for eighteen months without feeling odd oneself sometimes, she supposed! Yet there was something queer about the stillness. There must be going to be a storm, she thought.

No sound came in from farm or stable at this high-up, open window, on a level with the motionless green cradles of the birds; but down below on the lawn a single leaf would suddenly burst out into a mad fluttering, as if trying to indicate the secret of this general alarm, and then be still, too still, as if it feared to be caught in an act of rebellion. . . . In the flower-beds, then, a single violent-coloured blossom would wave out wildly, flicker for an instant like a tongue of flame, then float once more stiffly upon the glazed heat. She was quite glad to finish her sewing, get the tea ready and leave the house. But the air outside was even hotter than within — suffocating — so that one could not breathe, and as she passed out into the furtive silence of the woods she seemed separated from the world she knew. If I go on like this, she said to herself, I shall soon be the next invalid! Yet the walk seemed longer than it ought to be, so that she was continually being confronted with little twistings in it which she did not remember, though she had trodden this path at least four times a day for several months past. Still she knew, of course, that it must be the right one. But somehow or other, she was startled this afternoon by things that usually she would not notice — the ordinary, rather inexplicable rustlings of the woodlands, for instance. Doubtless these were audible yesterday as today, but as a rule she did not heed them; and once or twice, certainly, it seemed to her that she heard a peculiar scampering, as of a hurrying through thickets, or the dragging crackle of twigs and brambles as they released their clinging hold on invisible garments. It was with a distinct feeling of relief, then, that after what seemed quite a long walk, she caught sight of the summer-house round the next turning. It had a very human, friendly look to her this afternoon ; yet it belonged so much to these woods, this soil, that it was like a large mushroom growing out of a taller green tangle. The invalid did not call out to her, even the parrot was silent — an indication, usually, that its mistress was asleep. (How queer it is the way she can sleep here, and nowhere else !) Nurse Gooch cried out cheerfully, 'Wake up, wake up ! I've brought you your tea !' Still there was no answer, and, skirting the blind corner of the hut, carrying the tray in front of her, she was already standing in the low doorway before she had even cast a glance at its dark interior. Thrown suddenly into the quiet smallness of the summer-house, where she was at such close quarters with everything, almost within an arm's span of each wall, she was unable to breathe for a moment. An overwhelming sensation of nausea took possession of her, so that she felt that she, too, would fall upon that terrible floor. Yet, though the whole universe swung round, her trained eye observed the slaughter-house details. There lay the murdered woman, her head on one side, her skull crushed by some ferocious blow, her face twisted to a mask of terror — that queer unreasoning terror which had never left her. Dumb, blinking in its overturned cage, the parrot was hunched up, its feathers clotted together with blood. Clutching the bird's cage as if to save it from some fresh disaster, Nurse Gooch rushed wildly out of the summer-house into the motionless woods.

. . . . .

As she approached the Grove, her own sense of discipline asserted itself, forcing her to slow down her pace, to set her mind a little more in order. But now it was, actually, that the full shock came to her, for in that sudden blind moment of fear, when her limbs had melted one into the other, when her heart had bounded to her very lips, she had been unable to think, had experienced no feeling except an endless surprise, pity, and disgust. Afterwards curiosity, as well, intervened, and she began to wonder who had done this thing, and why such a brutal fate had engulfed the poor, timid, elderly woman. And then she was forced to steel her soul for the next ordeal : she would have need of every particle of strength in mind and body, since it devolved upon her to break the news. Through the library window she could see Colonel Tonge standing by the empty fireplace, and even while she was still labouring under the blow that had befallen her, she dreaded telling him of it as the not least awful incident in this terrible adventure — nearly as overwhelming, indeed, as had been the actual moment of discovery. Her respect, and fondness, even, for him, her knowledge that his had not been a happy marriage, only made the task a more difficult one to face and endure.

With an unexpected nervous susceptibility the Colonel seemed to feel the burning, panting breath of tragedy almost before she had spoken. Perhaps something out of her control manifested itself in her face, in her air; but as she entered, he looked at her with eyes as fearful as her own, and it seemed as if he, too, were mastering his emotions to confront something that he dreaded. 'Go on, go on,' he said, 'what is it?'

. . . . .

Month followed month, and he still shut himself up in his room, till he became so changed in looks, in manner, as hardly to appear the same man. All pride, all self-importance had left him. The spring had gone out of his walk, the jauntiness out of dress and carriage. Every hour of the day he loaded himself with reproaches — for not having been firmer, for not having absolutely refused to allow his wife to stay out there alone — for having been away at the time of the tragedy. Gooch would hear him, unable to sleep at night, walking about the passages, pacing up and down, up and down, till the first grey light crept in at the corners of blind and curtain. It was as if the spirit of sleepless terror that had haunted his wife had now transferred its temple to his body. Incapable of attending to the business of his estate, to which formerly he had devoted so much consideration, he now seldom left the house in the day-time, and, if he did, in whatever direction he might set out, his feet always led him sooner or later to the same place, and he would be startled, aghast, to find himself in the woods again.

Anything that reminded him of his dead wife had to be hidden away. The two poor little dogs were removed by his married sister when she went home, after a quite unsuccessful attempt to cheer her brother and give him comfort. The parrot, now never laughing, never speaking, languished in an attic, attended only by Emily, the housemaid. The other servants, too, were kind to the bird, since it had for them a fatal attraction: not only was it connected with death, having about it the very odour of the cemetery, but it was in itself the witness and only relic of a brutal crime, so that it possessed the charm popularly associated with a portion of hangman's rope, and, in addition, was a living thing possessed of a dreadful secret. But the parrot would never utter, and downstairs — where the conversation, however wide the circle of its origin, always in the end drew in on to one topic — they had to admit that Polly had never been the-same-like-since. Occasionally Emily would leave the door of the cage open, hoping that he would walk out or fly round as he used to do. But nothing could tempt him out of his battered dome. As for Colonel Tonge, he had never liked the bird, hating its harsh laughter, and this solitary, now silent, witness of his wife's end filled him at present with an unconquerable aversion.

Great sympathy was evinced everywhere for the poor widower, crushed under a catastrophe so unexpected and mysterious. But the public sympathy could do little to help him; and though some solution of the mystery might temporarily have distracted his mind, even if it could not have rallied his spirits, none was forthcoming. He went through all the sordid business associated with murder — inquest and interview; the crime remained odd as ever in its total absence of warning, intention or clue. Who, indeed, could have plotted to murder this invalid lady, possessed of few friends and no enemies? And what purpose was served by this intolerable brutality? It is true that, after a time, the police found a stained, blunt-headed club, obviously the weapon with which the fatal wound had been inflicted, buried deep in the bracken; but, in a sense, this discovery only removed the murder further from the public experience, in that the possible motive of theft was at the same time disposed of — for with this weapon were found the few rings, the gold watch and small amount of money that the dead woman had about her, as she had lain asleep in the summer-house on that sultry August afternoon. The police, thinking it possible that these articles had been hidden from an impulse of fear, that the original motive had indeed been the ordinary one, arrested a tramp found wandering in the district, hiding himself at night under hedges and in the shelter of empty barns; but though he could not give a very detailed or convincing account of his doings on the day of the 'Hut Murder' — as it was called —

the evidence that connected him with the crime was not enough to secure his conviction. It remained, however, the impression of many people, among them of both Dr. Maynard and Nurse Gooch, that he was in reality guilty of the foul act of which he had been suspected. Colonel Tonge, though he followed every detail of the trial with a painful interest, could never be induced to discuss the possible guilt of the tramp, but it was noticeable that after the man's release his nervous condition became more than ever marked, which led them to conclude that, in his opinion too, the person accused should never have been acquitted.

The bereaved husband's insomnia troubled him sorely; he had no peace, no rest by day or night. The only person able to bring him relief, to lighten his burden even for a moment, was Nurse Gooch; so that Dr. Maynard felt it his duty, for once, to insist on her remaining at the Grove until the Colonel should display some sign of returning health and a reviving spirit. The nurse, for her part, had always liked, pitied, and admired him, while, by one of those curious human instincts, all the compassion, all the affection even, which she had given so freely to the dead woman, was now made over to her new patient. And then she, too, felt remorse; had things on her mind with which to reproach herself. How well she could understand and sympathise with his self-accusation! Why, conscious as she had been of her influence over him, had she not supported the Colonel's wise protest against his wife's use of the summer-house, instead of urging, as she had done, that it was a reasonable plan, and finally persuading him to withdraw his objection to it? Terribly she felt now the responsibility so foolishly incurred, that perhaps she was in part to blame for the tragedy, even in the matter of allowing the invalid to wait out in the summer-house for tea on that dreadful afternoon; and in the months that followed the murder it was one of the few pleasant things in her life to reflect that she could, by her presence and sympathetic understanding, lessen his misery ever so little, giving him for a little while a passing sense of comfort.

When, after many long, lonely months, he made her an offer of marriage, saying that life without her support would be to him an intolerable burden, she accepted his proposal, realising that the interest she felt in him, the overwhelming pity that sometimes clutched at her heart, was but a disguise for love. Regardless of any difference in age or outlook, she hoped, by becoming his wife, to help and ease the remainder of a life, the unhappy tenor of which had now deepened into a more dreadful tone.

. . . . .

The honeymoon was spent in France, in order to make for them both a complete break from the background of their lives. But even among the lush meadows and rich trees of Normandy, away from any sting of association, Humphrey did not recover at once, as she had hoped, his old buoyancy. Listless, uneasy, restless, he would for hours be silent, wrapped in a melancholy that did not ordinarily belong to his temperament, while, in his broken slumber and sudden awakenings, his wife could detect the existence of a great well of sorrow that even her anxious affection could not plumb, a grief her love could not solace. The discovery of the extent of his affliction caused her further worry, made her dread their return to the scene of his past life. But as time passed it was obvious that his spirits were returning; and when he told her that during their absence the Grove had been entirely repainted and redecorated, she began to feel happier, hoping that it would seem to him like the beginning of a new life.

Almost two years to a day after the crime, they returned from their honeymoon, but Colonel Tonge did not seem conscious of any sense of anniversary, while she, naturally, would not mention it to him. But it made her feel a little uneasy.

As they drove back from the station, the new chauffeur quite by chance, by one of those dreadful inspirations which are only given to stupid people, drove the newly married couple down the concealed road near the summer-house, instead of taking them in by the near lodge. Colonel Tonge obviously experienced no emotion, but his wife felt for the moment as if she would be stifled between these two high hedges. How like was this afternoon to that other one! No leaf moved on any tree, no bird let its song trickle through the cloudy, too-dark leafage; the air was hot, motionless and still, though through it ran those same secret tremors, inexplicable tremblings. For the new Mrs. Tonge the whole atmosphere was stained with memories.

Yet she soon forgot the uneasy promptings of her heart and mind in the pleasure she felt at the reception which awaited them. She had always been a favourite with the servants, and the latter could never forget the poor Colonel's sufferings, so that they had taken an especial care to give the newly wedded pair an inspiriting welcome. The Colonel stopped to talk to them, while Mrs. Tonge, eager to see what alterations had been made, stepped into the house alone. It looked charming, she thought, with the new smooth paint on the old walls; and, unable to repress a slight thrill of pleasure, which she felt to be wrong, though she could not quite exorcise it, at being for the first time mistress of a house — and such a lovely house — she walked on through the empty, gleaming rooms that led one into the other. The last room was the boudoir. She entered it softly, closing the door behind her, wishing to explore its impression to the full, for she wondered whether it would make her feel a usurper, a stranger in someone else's place. But no! it was a new room to her: gone was the feverish atmosphere of the sick-room, with its dead air, over-heated and scented with innumerable flowers: gone was that dead look imparted by the yellow glaze of countless old photographs and by the spreading litter of trivial little objects. And while she bore towards the dead woman no feelings but those of pity and affection, yet, being of a practical nature, she was glad that nothing remained of the old mistress — nothing that could call up painful memories. The room was quiet and restful; the long windows stood wide open on to the pleasant water-cool spaces of the lawn, that unfolded up to the borders of the wood where stood tall fleecy green trees, while under their blue shadows ran the murmur of shallow streams. The healthy scents of tree and grass, the peaceful watery sounds, and honey-gathering, contented drone of the bees as they hung over the flowers, drifted into the house, diffusing an air of ease and comfort. This was *her* house, *her* garden, *her* home, and she now had a husband to whom she was devoted. Why, then, should she ever allow her mind to dwell on the tragedies of the past? Was it not better to forget utterly, to obliterate the memory in her husband, by offering him all her love, till gradually these possessions to which he had been so attached became dear to him again? . . . but just then, behind her, she heard the thin voice of the dead woman crying out — a voice grey with fear and breaking. 'Humphrey,' it sighed, 'what is it? Oh, my God!' . . . And then the sound of a heavy dumb blow and low moaning, followed by burst after burst of idiot laughter, as with a fluttering whirl of flaming green feathers the parrot flew up again to its empty attic.

THE END

PRINTED BY R. & R. CLARK, LTD., EDINBURGH